P9-CRI-774

PRAISE FOR
THE END OF WAR

"Robbins is an accomplished storyteller."
—*The Denver Post*

"Robbins is now the novelist of choice for
authentic World War II fiction."
—*Richmond Times Dispatch*

"Sweeping in scope . . . gripping . . . war buffs
should find this an entertaining perspective on
the end days of WWII."
—*Publishers Weekly*

"Start reading *The End of War* . . . and you'll wish you
were on vacation so you could read on right through to
the end without a break. . . . Authentic . . . keeps the
reader compulsively turning page after page. . . . Robbins
takes his place among the ranks of today's first-rate
American novelists."
—*Style Weekly*

"In this sweeping war novel, Robbins puts a very human
face, indeed, on the horrors of modern war."
—*Abilene Reporter-News*

"A first-rate tale of war. Thoughtful, gritty, and compulsively
readable, this work is enthusiastically recommended."
—*Library Journal*

"A pitch-perfect blend of fiction and history . . . in the
tradition of Irwin Shaw's *The Young Lions,* Herman Wouk's
The Winds of War, and James Webb's *The Emperor's General,*
both the fictional and historical characters are excitingly real
in their sheer psychological depth."
—*The Plain Dealer*

RAVES FOR DAVID L. ROBBINS'
WAR OF THE RATS

"Compelling and graphic . . . A good candidate for the thriller of the summer."
—*The New York Times*

"Brilliant . . . Riveting."
—*Publishers Weekly*

"Engrossing . . . Robbins can snatch a time and place out of history and make it come alive."
—*Kirkus Reviews*

"A great novel of one of the epic battles of all time."
—W.E.B. Griffin

"White-knuckle tension . . . Immensely exciting and terribly authentic."
—Frederick Forsyth

"This credible action thriller should hit home with buffs of military historical fiction."
—*Booklist*

ALSO BY DAVID L. ROBBINS

Souls to Keep

War of the Rats

*Only the dead have seen
the end of war.*

PLATO

This book is dedicated to
Jim Bacon, Jim and Rey Banks, Mike Benson,
Chris DeWilde, Tom Dykers, Alan and Wendy Gayle,
Asa Graves, the Kennedy & Green family, Dan Kohler,
James Laws, Mark Lazenby, John Lowe,
Daniel and Sarah McMurtrie, Gene Pendleton,
Bo Poats, Melissa and Roger Price,
Jim and Sarah Redington,
Betsy Woolfolk, and John Young.

To loyalty.

T HE FALL OF BERLIN TO THE SOVIET ARMY IN THE spring of 1945 determined much of the political future for the remainder of the twentieth century. Historians agree that the entry of the Red Army into the capital of the Reich, preceded by the American decision to halt the West's armies at the Elbe, was a turning point in Soviet prestige and authority, as well as the fortunes of communism. If historians haggle at all, it is only over orders of magnitude. But there is no question the Soviet Union launched emboldened from the conquest of Berlin into an era of global rivalry with the West. To this day we feel the concussions of Russian bullets scarring the Reichstag, and hear the crunch of bootsteps of Red soldiers past the pillars of the blackened Brandenburg Gate.

Like any novelist, I ask the reader to enjoy my presentation of the story. However, on equal footing, I beg the reader's trust that what you will read in *The End of War* stems not from my imagination but from the annals of fact. The basis for the book has been gleaned from personal interviews with survivors of the battles described herein, and from many respected histories, documentaries, biographies, and analyses (see Bibliography).

In this novel I have drawn no conclusions, leaving that to

more accomplished historians than myself, and, of course, to the reader. The story is built around several extraordinarily well-known historic figures and events. Each of my characters has a clear viewpoint, and you may choose sides as you see fit in the long-held debate over whether or not Anglo-American forces should have halted on the Elbe River and allowed Stalin to take Berlin.

The End of War is constructed along the lines of a Greek tragedy: the gods discuss the affairs of man, then their Olympian intents are played out at human level. In this novel, the gods are Winston Churchill, Josef Stalin, and Franklin Roosevelt. Lesser deities include General Dwight Eisenhower and Field Marshal Bernard Montgomery. The book's corresponding mortals are three fictional characters—one Russian soldier, one German civilian, and one American photojournalist.

It was seductive to follow the historic figures far afield, as their lives and times are fascinating and well chronicled. But *The End of War* carefully restricts itself to episodes that deal with the natures of these men and others only in the context of the race and battle for Berlin in the final months of World War II.

I have taken as few liberties of fiction with true characters' conversations, correspondences, actions, and motivations as I could. Likewise, with my fictional people, I hope the reader will mark an authenticity of insight and deed.

To do otherwise would have been to supplant my creativity for history, and there is no way I could have made up a more tragic tale.

DAVID L. ROBBINS
Richmond, Virginia

— GREATER BERLIN —

— CENTRAL BERLIN, 1945 —

NORTH EUROPEAN
Theatre of Operations

BALTIC
SEA

EAST PRUSSIA
• Königsberg

Danzig •

POLAND

SACHSENHAUSEN

Oranienburg □

ROKOSSOVSKI–
2ND RUSSIAN

ZHUKOV–
1ST BYELORUSSIAN
FRONT

8GA

Berlin

Seelow

Küstrin

1GTA

THE ODER MARSHES

Oder

Poznań •

Warta

• Warsaw

Vistula

CHUIKOV
8TH GUARDS ARMY

Magnuszew

1ST GUARDS
TANK ARMY

KONIEV–
1ST UKRAINIAN

Torgau

Elbe

Neisse

Dresden •

Breslau •

Oder

Vistula

ZHUROV–
1ST BYELORUSSIAN
FRONT

□ MAJDANEK

Sandomierz

KONIEV–
1ST UKRANIAN
FRONT

YEREMENKO–
4TH UKRANIAN

Prague •

Kracow •

CZECHOSLOVAKIA

Danube

Vienna •

Bratislava
•

T R I A

HUNGARY

Danube

	Troop Movements
	Siegfried Line
	Allied Group Boundary
	Allied Army Boundary
	Allied Armies
	Russian Armies

The End of War

Instruction in geography can be restricted to a single sentence: The Capital of the Reich is Berlin.

ADOLF HITLER,
from a discussion in July 1942,
when asked how the conquered
peoples in the East should
be educated

JANUARY

———

*I*n the intoxication to fall upon the enemy at the charge, who cares then about bullets and men falling? To hurl ourselves, with eyes a few moments shut, into the chill face of death, uncertain whether we or others shall escape him, and all this close on the golden goal of victory, close to the refreshing fruit for which ambition thirsts—can this be difficult?

CARL VON CLAUSEWITZ
On War

O N E

A BOVE HIS HEAD, IN THE COLD, DARK, WIND-
creaked rafters of the tobacco barn, Charley Bandy
sees withered souls.

Clustered five stalks to a stick, stepped several rows deep,
they are hung upside down as though in punishment. The
ten thousand leaves fill this lower reach of heaven. The air
reeks of tar, thick, like the times Bandy has smelled blood.

Brown and drying, crowded and alike, these are not the
souls of soldiers, Bandy thinks. No. The spirits of the battle-
torn shine and are upright in a much higher neighborhood.
There's room among war heroes where they are; what they
earned for eternity with their courage and their deaths is
space, distinction. Bandy is having a melancholy moment, he
knows; he's being drawn back. He shakes his noggin to rattle
the pull away. But the tobacco leaves drip their sticky scent
and the odor is so much like gun smoke and gauze and the
morning mists of Europe.

He lowers his gaze to the dirt floor of the barn. Several
empty tobacco baskets lie about, waiting for another moist
day to put the tobacco in case, that condition where the hu-
midity is high to make the leaves supple enough to be handled. But this has been a dry winter, and the burley tobacco
leaves, though sufficiently air-cured now dangling on their

sticks overhead, can't be touched without breaking like ancient parchment. This Christmas came and went with little
gift money. The family is edgy, waiting for the weather to
cooperate and put the tobacco in case long enough to bundle it into hands, arrange the hands into the big woven baskets, then truck it all to the auction hall down in Marshall.
The family needs to make some money, get school clothes,
fix some machinery, buy next season's seed. Only a third of
the leaves have been stripped and separated. The lowest
leaves, called "lugs," and the paltry tips at the top all get
tossed on a pile outside the barn to be used as ground cover
and fertilizer. The broad middle leaves, the "smokers," get
sold for bulk tobacco. The best leaves make it as far as cigar
wrappers. A good, heavy harvest of smokers pays some bills.

Inside the house, Bandy's mom and dad, wife, sister and
brother-in-law, dozen or so uncles and aunts and cousins and
their kin wait for 1945 to arrive in another ten minutes.
Every one of them lives nearby, a dog wouldn't get tired jogging between all their houses, either in Big Laurel, Little
Laurel, Shelton Laurel, or on a rural road associated with no
town. They are tobacco farmers up here in the Appalachian
hollers. The clefts between the high slopes are narrow, and
arable land comes only in slim patches, always beside the
roads. Nothing makes a buck better on so little land as tobacco. The Bandys, the Ketchums, the Wallins are woven
together by marriages and births like the tobacco baskets,
broad and firm and white, hundred-year-old clans of soil
and nicotine, pocketknives, and Saturday nights at the Ma-
sonic dance hall.

The clamor of his family's revelry—generational, those
kids still awake squeal, the adults clink glasses and toast what
they're going to do next year, the old folks cackle, the oldest
ones cough—skim like sounds over a lake, tinkling and clear
to Charles Bandy through the crisp, frostless mountain night.
The mountain doesn't know it's New Year's Eve. The war
doesn't know it's New Year's Eve.

Bandy opens his palms to the kerosene lantern he
brought to the barn. He washes his hands in the little heat

above the vent and thinks of the GIs freezing right now in foxholes and slit trenches in France, Belgium, Holland, Luxembourg, and Germany. Pall Malls and Lucky Strikes are dangling from beard-shrouded soldiers' lips right now. Surely some Tennessee tobacco is glowing over there.

The barn door slides open. Leaves in the rafters rustle their wrinkles; the barn takes on the feel of a cave coated in restless bats. This eerie sense disappears in just a moment, because it is her and no room she enters is a cave. She shuts the door. She has another lantern with her.

"Charley."

"Hey."

"What're you doing out here? Everyone's inside. It's almost time."

Bandy hears the piney woods in his wife's voice. Her accent is sugary, with rounded corners, not the serrated Appalachian tongue, not the mountain laurel. She comes from the flatlands, from Hendersonville, North Carolina. Her people farm tobacco down there too. Flue cured, where they keep a fire stoked in the barns day and night. They've got big plots of land, not the sloped slivers Bandy's tribe makes pay. The two met at Vanderbilt when he was a senior and she was a freshman. He graduated in journalism, then she got her teaching degree. They married and stayed in Nashville five more years. She taught third grade, he took photos for any rag that would buy them. Then eleven years ago he carried her up here to the mountains and everyone, kids, parents, family, farmers, fell over themselves for her. She could be mayor if there was a mayor; they have a postmaster and a sheriff, that's the extent of the government in these hills.

"You all right?" she asks.

"I'm fine, Vic."

"Well, come inside. Everyone's missing you. Your mama asked me to come get you."

"I'll be along directly."

"Charley, I'm not going to celebrate the new year with you out here in the barn. I have spent enough time without you already." He thinks Victoria is referring to their war-time, years gouged out of the last decade, years of fear for her, and that she wants to make him sorry for it right now, again. But she steps up close and says something different, sweetly.

"You have been working way too hard since you got back. Your daddy's roof. Alvin's fence. Jane and Edgar's trac-tor. What about our house?"

She sets the lantern on the dirt floor. She slips her arms around his waist. "What about me?"

Bandy takes in her brown hair nestled under his nose. She's only five feet five, he's a good six-footer. She's got that teacher scent, squeaky clean, a role model for the kids, for sixteen years of marriage now. She's still cute, the cheer-leader she used to be in college keeps dancing and doing splits in her eyes and smiles. Except for the difference in height, they look very much alike. Both have mousy hair, both are lean-faced with brown eyes. Perhaps that's why they took to each other with such speed when they met six-teen years ago, they recognized they were cut from the same tobacco-stained cloth. Bandy breathes her in. For a moment he can't smell the leaves in their firmament, or the war in its new year.

"Victoria?"

"Yes, doll?"

"I love you."

His wife squeezes him. She is happy right now, and that makes this the moment to tell her, because he must yank the happiness away from her. It's the only fair way to do it.

"I'm going back."

She does not release him, nor even flinch. Her head rests on his chest, her ear gentle against his heart. This saddens him; she knew it was coming. He hadn't ever fooled her, hadn't once in the two weeks he'd been home given her a single moment to believe he might stay.

"Haven't they gotten enough out of you?"

The "they" is *Life* magazine, Bandy's employer for the past eight years, since the magazine's inception in 1936. He is a staff photographer. His name is known nationwide for his byline, Charles Bandy, LIFE SPECIAL CORRESPONDENT, for the remarkable black-and-white images he has captured of war and warriors, of both friend and foe. His exposed negatives go via military courier from the battlefield to London censors, then by wire to New York, then onto the glossy pages of *Life*. Just days after the pictures are taken, the hopeful and weary eyes of the home front stare into the magazine as though into a crystal ball, for it is there that they witness their sons and fathers and enemies far across the ocean, they peer through haze and exploding earth and risk. America wonders and weeps through Bandy's camera.

Bandy makes no reply to his wife's charge. She has not lessened her grip about his waist. Nor has she taken her ear from his chest, as though to make certain that he indeed has a heart, to be leaving her again.

She speaks into the wool of his sweater. There is no sadness in her voice. She is not appealing to him, not beseeching, but prosecuting a point. She thinks he is wrong to go back and will try to prove it.

"Nineteen thirty-six, the Spanish Civil War. Nineteen thirty-seven, the Sino-Japanese War. Nineteen forty, the Battle of Britain. Nineteen forty-one, Manila, Tobruk. Nineteen forty-two, Libya and Egypt. Guadalcanal."

Victoria now lifts her head from his breast. She sniffles. She has lost the struggle to stay calm in the list of his assignments and the misery of his absences. She grabs at his eyes with hers, which are unblinking and damp. The yellow lantern light creates small suns in the wet trails down her cheeks.

"Nineteen forty-three, Sicily, Messina, Salerno, Naples. Nineteen forty-four, D-Day, for God's sake, you were in the first wave. Normandy. Holland. Belgium."

Bandy weakly smiles down at her. "You've been following my career."

She is not amused and answers in a quiet voice. "I've been praying for your life, Charley."

Inside the house, only a hundred feet away, someone calls

out, "All right, y'all! One minute! One minute!" Someone else squawks a noisemaker and a child shouts, "Not yet!"

At this Victoria releases her arms from around him and steps back.

"I want children. Your children. I'm not getting any younger. You get killed, what am I going to do? You think about that?"

"Always."

"And? It doesn't seem to make you want to stay home."

But this time he'd come home from the war really wanting to stay. Two weeks ago the Germans were beaten. France had been liberated. Italy switched sides. The Russians were gathering along the Vistula River in eastern Poland for their final thrust to Berlin. *Wehrmacht* soldiers were surrendering by the tens of thousands to Eisenhower's and Montgomery's troops. The war was expected to end by Christmas, January at the latest. Odds were that Hitler would sue for peace once the end was in sight. So Bandy had figured that was it. He notified the magazine, said his goodbyes to those men and officers around him—the soldiers always changed: the instinct of the war photographer to sense where the action will happen next is his greatest asset, more vital than any facility with a camera, because a bad shot of action is better than a great shot of nothing—and boarded a plane west. He traveled for three days to get home. Then the morning he arrived, December 16, even while he set down his duffel and held his wife, the Germans launched a massive winter counteroffensive, with two hundred fifty thousand men, thousands of tanks and artillery pieces. The assault was staged opposed to all logic. It was a last roll of the dice against the American and British forces in Belgium and Luxembourg, launched through the thick Ardennes forests, the biggest battle yet on the Western Front. Hitler attempted to drive a wedge into the Allied forces, recapture the port of Antwerp and reclaim the initiative. In the first few days he succeeded, stabbing west to a point just shy of the Meuse River on the French border, forging a pocket that became the name of the battle, the Bulge. Eisenhower responded to the German attack by mobilizing six hundred thousand men. The American airborne commander of the surrounded town of Bastogne, when asked to surrender, replied to the Germans, "Nuts." The Battle of the Bulge will be won in the next few weeks, Hitler turned back. But the war has been prolonged by who knows how long. Now it looks like it won't end until somebody—either the Reds or the Western Allies—assaults and takes Berlin. Hitler has screwed Bandy's plans.

Bandy says to his wife, motionless in his arms, "I'll be back."

Victoria takes this like a slap. She even starts to bring up her hands to fend off the words. She bites her lip and turns away.

"In a box, Charley?"

Inside the house, Bandy's dad calls out, "All right! Here comes 1945, the best damn year of 'em all! Right?"

Answering shouts agree, the best damn year of 'em all.

The family counts down from ten, nine, eight, seven . . . Noisemakers start to blow seconds early.

Bandy stands four feet from his wife. One of her tears dots the dirt floor. They stand apart, separated by an ocean.

January 1, 1945, midnight
Kuntsevo dacha
Moscow suburbs

ALL THE BELLS ARE RINGING.

Even this far outside Moscow, twenty kilometers, the Marshal can hear them. He leans his nose close to a chilly windowpane. He has pushed aside the thick blackout curtain to gaze into a moonless, overcast dark. The glow of Moscow is missing from the horizon, shrouded for safety's sake. All the other structures nearby in his compound are likewise extinguished. The night has total victory outside, save for the lanterns of his security guards strolling the crunchy ground around the dacha. The distant din of the bells is incongruous, joy and hope playing against such blackness. This is the Russian way, he thinks. Beauty meshed in tragedy, never one without the other for us.

Along the same wall where the Marshal stands, one of his generals thrusts aside the curtain of another window. This general turns to the others in the giant banquet room— Politburo members, military men and their wives, all pomaded and powdered, brass and lace. The general calls out to them, "Hear the bells!"

The Marshal does not swivel around but keeps his back to their cheers for the new year, the kisses of men given first to their comrades on both cheeks, then to the women on lips, the bear hugs and handshakes. He turns only to the general near him looking out into the same inky Russia.

He says, "Close the curtain, Comrade General."

The general hesitates only for a moment, in surprise. He lets go the curtain and it falls into place.

"Yes, Comrade Stalin," he says, inclining his forehead. "My apologies, Comrade."

The general makes his escape back to the arms of his fellows and women. Stalin continues to stare through the glass at nothing.

He looks west, toward Poland. There he has his two generals, Zhukov and Koniev, his two studded fists, poised on the Vistula with a million men and ten thousand artillery pieces and twenty thousand tanks. Before the month is out, he will brandish those fists and pound the Germans first out of Poland, then into pulp in their own homeland. He will not unfurl those fists, will not wipe the blood off them, until he wipes them on Hitler's shirt in Berlin.

That's the lair of the beast. That's the trophy the world wants. Whoever captures Berlin wins the war.

The English and the Americans long for the prestige of it. They've turned back a nasty winter offensive from Hitler. Their noses have been bloodied one more time. Plus, Hitler has stepped up his rocket bombings of London. All this will make them push back even harder, move even faster into

Germany. Now they will believe even more that Berlin can be theirs.

But Berlin belongs to Russia. By might. By sacrifice.

He trusts none of his generals. The taking of Berlin is too vital to delegate control to anyone but himself. Stalin has taken control of the coordination of all three fronts involved in the assault on the German capital, First and Second Byelorussian and First Ukrainian.

Nor does he trust that English bulldog Churchill or the cripple Roosevelt. No matter Churchill's lengthy toasts or Roosevelt's slavering courtship. They will do anything to take Berlin from Stalin.

That is why anything is warranted to take it first.

He holds back the curtain for a minute, breaking his own hard rule, staying apart from the revelers behind him. When he hears the party fade at his back, he lets the curtain relax, and turns. His boot heels click, he comes to attention at the window. With the report, all eyes are on him. Even the chattiest of them shuts up. Stalin stands like a rock, a chipped boulder, really. He knows how squat and ugly he is, with a face pock-marked by childhood smallpox, short forehead, squinty hazel eyes, only five feet four inches tall. Do any of these leaders and ladies rapt now before him know that the second and third toes on his left foot have grown together? He's a grotesque little gnome, chiseled from a poor quarry. No, he thinks, they don't anymore see Iosif Vissarionovich Dzhugashvili, the little Georgian bandit. They see only Stalin.

Rightly so, he thinks. Rightly so.

The Marshal casts his eyes over the pack, forty or so of them invited here to his dacha to celebrate the new year. They stand ramrod straight out of fear or respect, he's not concerned which. Who are these suit fillers and dress curvers? All of them, even the women, are his creations. What power they wield they possess only in his name. The shoulder boards, the stiff shirts, boots and handbags, flesh and bone would end up crackling on a bonfire with a wave of his hand, and within hours some forty others would stand here gaping. Who are these newcomers to the new year of the Red victory? What have they done to stand here before Stalin and not be swept away? Nothing. There's not one left who knows Stalin as less than a god, who has any claim at all to pity should his god turn on him. Not one of them with the bells ringing far away, full glass in hand, woman in tow, eyes stuck on Stalin, would hesitate to put a knife in Stalin's back if he could get away with it. They want power. These are the ones Stalin is wary of. The ones who do not desire power, Stalin despises.

But the power is Stalin's alone, his right. None of these celebrants were there half a century ago to study with the boy Iosif, the seminary student of ten years. Who among them ran and hid with Koba, the revolutionary? Or shivered in exile with the hard young Stalin who never once left Russia, while others waited in Paris for the revolt to begin in St. Petersburg? Or as a political prisoner who made five escapes? Which of them sat at the right hand of Lenin himself, or battled the Whites at Tsaritsyn so fiercely that the city was named after him, Stalingrad? What man alive has branded his own name on the Revolution more than Stalin?

These frippish fools know only Stalin, "man of steel." They knew Lenin, but did they know the young fire-breather Vladimir Ulyanov, who took his *nom de guerre* from the river Lena in Siberia, where he was exiled? And you can bet they remember that bastard Trotsky, but do they recall him when he was that bastard Leon Bronshtein, the wire-haired Jew who adopted the name of one of his jailers? Trotsky died abroad, fearing for his life. And that loudmouth Lev Rozenfeld, who would have us call him Kamenev, "man of stone." Where is he now? Under a granite marker where Stalin put him years ago, after arrest and a very public trial and an admission of guilt. Stalin killed a few other birds with the stone Kamenev, flung him to fell Bukharin, Zinoviev, Rykov, Tomsky, and the rest who would deny Russia the leadership of Stalin.

Those men knew both Lenin and Stalin in the early days. They too were coauthors of the Bolshevik uprising. They held power of their own making. But they spoke of things regarding Stalin that history has proven to be lies. They dared consider that they and not Stalin might be the true interpreters of Lenin, that they were the brightest lamps for Russia's path. History has proven them wrong. Look around now. They are gone, all of them, with their families and everything they touched. Steel proved stronger than the river, the stone, the prison keeper. History is Stalin's courtyard, while their names are dust on the bricks. How many? Dozens, hundreds, thousands, Stalin does not keep tabs like some Arbat merchant of the goods that have gone through his hands, no one calls Stalin to account.

He notes the Moscow bells have stopped.

He does not know how long he has stood like this, rigid, staring over the crowd's head, hating ghosts in the air. A minute, perhaps a second. When did the bells stop? It seems to him that even time does his bidding. He relaxes his eyes, widening the sockets. He takes a breath and runs two fingers over his moustache.

The young ambassador to the United States, Andrei Gromyko, lifts his glass.

"Comrade Marshal," he says. "It would be an honor to have you make the first toast to the new year."

Stalin thinks he will do so and that he will watch a bit more closely this upstart politico who lifts his glass first.

Stalin steps forward from the window. "Bring me a glass."

When his hand is full, he raises the drink in toast. Stalin is a teetotaler. But for the beginning of this year of victory, he will drink vodka. His hand in the air is still below the chins of many in the room. The rest of the glasses go up, and just for a flash Stalin fights his claustrophobia; his eyes are so far below all the crystal hoisted and packed above his head, he senses he is beneath a shining and crowding weight, like the surface of a sunlit lake.

He takes a step backward. This relieves him; he speaks.

"In a matter of days, the mighty Red forces gathered on

the Vistula River will strike the first blow toward the heart of the German beast. In 1945 we will put an end to this senseless and horrible war to defeat fascism. In the years we have fought the Hitlerites, we have lost over twenty-five million soldiers and civilians. That is more than ten Russians for every meter of land between Moscow and Berlin."

Stalin watches the faces grow somber. A few of the glasses waver in the air. He lets the moment hang; some boots shuffle. He has invited the millions of war ghosts into the room where everyone can see them. These legions of Russian dead join the spirits which only he sees, overwhelming them into anonymity. Now Stalin feels comfortable.

"There is not a single Soviet citizen who has gone untouched by this war. Every man and woman in the ranks, every factory worker, every farmer, has a score to settle. Our soldiers will fight from what they have suffered. They will fight from what they have witnessed and from what they have lost. Atrocities scar every village and city the Germans have touched. Have no fear that we are about to win. Have no fear of Hitler. I give you my word we will wipe our asses in Berlin soon in the new year."

Men in the crowd smile at Stalin's coarseness. The women titter behind gloved hands.

"To the victorious Red Army! *Na zdrovya!*"

Glasses are turned bottoms to the ceiling, all of them. Stalin watches elbows and swallows and satisfied gasps. When they are done, his own glass still full, he makes a private toast.

I will take Berlin. The cost is of no concern. Whatever it is, we've already paid most of it.

He drinks. The gathering applauds.

"Budenny!" Stalin yawps. "Did you bring your damned accordion?"

A spry old marshal of the Red Army puts up his hands. "Yes, Comrade Stalin, of course. You know I can't come to a party without it. I always get sent home to bring it back."

"Then play us a polka. Let's dance to some German music!"

The military man hurries to a corner and returns, strapping on his weathered accordion. He stamps his boot four times to set the tempo, and launches into a rousing Prussian tune. Couples set down their glasses and partner up. In moments the room is swirling, stamping with gaiety. Budenny, the former cavalry officer, is quite the catalyst. Stalin sidles out of the way.

The accordion renders waltzes, folk songs, ballads. Stalin fetches his English Dunhill pipe from his place at the head table. From a pouch he pours another bowlful of shredded Herzegovina Flor cigarettes and lights up. He paces the room through clouds of blue smoke, enjoying the dancers, savoring his pipe and his separateness. He has reduced his need for human relationships to almost nothing. He has seen two wives die. First, beloved Kato in their youth, from disease. Then the traitorous Nadezhda, who committed suicide in 1932 after arguing with him over politics. Yakov, son of his first marriage, an artillery commander who surrendered to the Germans—a coward, only cowards surrender. Vasili, a sniveler. Daughter Svetlana, acid-tongued like her mother, estranged. Stalin, the *vozhd,* the supremo, cannot afford the normal human luxuries of emotion or values. He must have steel cords where others have nerves. How can he dote on one, or two, or twenty, when he must envision and guard the future for hundreds of millions? He cannot want for himself when an entire nation is told every day, "Stalin is thinking of us."

He wonders, What could be lonelier?

Stalin watches his guests grow drunker with the dancing. Marshal Budenny has made himself quite popular tonight.

"Semyon," he calls to the musical marshal. "Rest your hands for a moment. I want to see your feet in action."

Budenny halts his playing. Sweat breaks on his brow from an hour of the accordion's buttons and keys. The dancers freeze like figurines.

Stalin walks to the gramophone. No one else in the room moves. He picks out a disk and slides it beneath the needle. The dancers lower their arms, no longer porcelain dolls but uneasy humans. Out of the gramophone bell emerges a scratchy ditty, a balalaika plucks a fast-paced folk melody along with a clarinet, drums, and a wailing violin.

Stalin approaches Budenny. He puts his arms out to relieve the old man of the accordion.

"Dance for me, Semyon. The Gopak. I have seen you do it, you're magnificent."

"Comrade"—the marshal raises his palms in defense—"not in many years."

Stalin sets the accordion on the ground.

"And many years from now, you will say that you did it tonight. Dance, Semyon. To victory."

Stalin steps back. He claps his hands to the music. The crowd joins him now and they form a rousing circle around Semyon Budenny, a seventy-three-year-old marshal of the Red Army. The gray warrior squats on his haunches, crosses his arms, and kicks out his heels in the classic Cossack dance.

Budenny dances with fervor. He begins rickety but soon limbers and is impressive for his age. The others shout "Ur-rah!" and clap in time to the music. Stalin studies Budenny's face. The dancing marshal keeps a pleasant smile. Stalin knows that Budenny is in great pain.

January 1, 1945, 0115 hours
Magnuszew bridgehead
West bank of the Vistula River
Poland

THE SOLDIER BEHIND ILYA TUMBLES INTO A HOLE.

Ilya, on his stomach and elbows in the freezing dirt, hangs his chin to his chest while the little private he brought with him tries to clamber out without making more noise than he made going in.

When they are again side by side on their bellies in the dark, Ilya sighs.

He whispers, "Misha. You move like a blind cow."

"That wasn't my fault."

Ilya sighs again. He resumes his crawl forward. Misha follows, mumbling.

"You pushed me in."

"I did not. The ground gave way under you."

"You did too shove me. You're twice my size. You don't realize sometimes. You didn't leave me enough room to get by the lip of that crater."

"Well, then, move me out of the way. It'll make less of a racket."

Misha huffs. "Sure. Move Ilya Shokhin. Me and who else?"

Ilya grins. He is proud of his size, the attention it draws from the others. Two meters tall, two hundred and forty pounds, he has shoulders square and wide, an expansive chest, and arms white and big as birch trees. His thighs are the girth of bomb casings. He knows he has a merry face where blue eyes preside over a kind, upturned mouth. For a fierce countenance he shaves his head clean.

"Almost there, I think."

Ilya halts their slither to get his bearings. Winter-naked trees rise all around. Between every trunk there is a tank, a T-34; there must be a hundred silhouettes he can make out from where he and Misha lie in the starless gloom. The tanks are silent, turrets elevated like saluting troops, all pointing west toward the German lines. Behind these tanks there are a thousand more, and behind them rows of artillery pieces by the ten thousands arranged backward by caliber. Men and machines, everywhere—two full armies, half of another—crammed into this fourteen-mile-wide bridgehead which Zhukov captured on the west bank of the Vistula in August. Another two tank armies are lined up behind them on the east bank of the river. South of Zhukov's force, there is another, larger bridgehead on the river, where there is massed another battle group just as big under Koniev.

In days or weeks, Ilya thinks, the signal will come. This

gigantic, pent-up hammer will strike west into Poland, then pulverize all the way to Berlin. Nothing will stop us.

Once this battle starts, I will get it all back. More. There are a million men around me. But I will be noticed.

I will be cleansed.

Through the trees Ilya catches a glimmer of lantern light dimmed by the thick canvas of a tent. It is a strange sallow glow, a mushroom of light on a forest floor covered by sleeping metal beasts. Officers, Ilya thinks. Only they will have a lantern lit this time of the morning. Only officers will be up this late gathered around a bottle and a deck of cards and letters scribbled for home. Ilya knows. The regular foot soldiers aren't drinking right now; they're resting, if they can find the comfort under a tarpaulin or in a hole to do so. When the cold sun is overhead the lowly Ivans have too many artillery pieces to camouflage, roads to grade, tons and tons of food, ammo, and fuel to lug forward, privies to empty, garbage to bury. Fortifications must be built and trenches dug in case the enemy in the dark decides to go on the offensive first. The railway tracks through eastern Poland are the wrong gauge, they have to be widened for Russian supply trains. Wreckage from the frequent German artillery barrages must be repaired or hauled away. Field trips are taken to the fetid death camp in Majdanek, liberated by the Red Army last July, where political commissars drive home even harder the point that the Germans are monsters. No, those men inside the warm tent have their feet up. Ilya begins to crawl toward them. Officers. He knows this because four months ago he was one of them.

Ilya is powerful stealing over the frozen ground, in and out among the barely visible tanks. The only breathing he hears is from skinny Misha behind him. He turns to see billows of vapor heaving out of the man's drooping mouth. To keep his comrade from giving them away to the guards who must be posted near the command tent one hundred meters away, Ilya pauses at the treads of a tank.

He sits up to ease his back against the tank. He leans against a painted wooden crate.

Ilya suppresses a laugh. This is one of the hundreds of false tanks, part of the massive *Maskirovka* campaign Zhukov has put in place to fool German reconnaissance, artillery, and bombers into wasting their barrages in the wrong places. The weapon at his back is made of sacking, wire, and a pipe for the gun barrel. Very convincing. Ilya wonders how many he and Misha crept past tonight. He wagers that all the tanks he sees around him are *Maskirovka*. Clever. He decides he likes these tank officers in the tent ahead of him.

Misha slips next to him. He runs a slender hand around the rim of a wooden cask that suffices for a wheel.

"Nicely done," Misha murmurs with a wheeze. "I never saw better."

Ilya nods. He waits while his companion's breathing slows to normal. After two minutes, Misha seems ready. Ilya rolls onto his stomach. Misha makes no move to follow.

"Misha. Now. Let's do it like we discussed."

The other private wags his head. "No, Ilyushka. I'm thinking no. You go the last bit without me. I'm not really designed for this sort of thing."

Ilya shifts forward to sit again next to his companion. "I've got you this far. You can come the rest of the way."

"I'll make a mistake. We'll get caught."

"Maybe. Maybe not. We have to go on to find out."

"Why do you want me with you, Ilya? We just met. What do you know about me? I'm the last person in the company I'd take."

"That's why you're the one I picked."

Ilya looks into the man's eyes. He does not tell his comrade the complete truth: that he wants the others to see that if Ilya Shokhin can get puny, scared Misha to do this, he must still be a very good leader of men.

He looks into Misha's eyes. This little sissy will finish the job.

"Michail Stepanovich. Let me ask. Do you like being in the Eighth Guards penal battalion?"

Misha makes no answer. None is needed.

"You've been stuck in it since, what, July? Do you like

knowing you'll be in the first rank of every attack from now on, just a target so the men behind you can find out how strong the enemy is and where they're shooting from? Hmmm? Do you take pride in being an infantry private, surrounded by cowards, bandits, brawlers, and madmen, instead of an intelligence captain carrying General Chuikov's coffee? Do you like your shame as much as you used to like your medals and your cot? What do you hear from home, is your family proud of your accomplishment?"

Misha tenses at this mention of his family.

"I didn't run," he says. Ilya raises a finger. Misha lowers to a hiss. "I didn't run. I evacuated headquarters before the Germans surrounded us. I had battle maps all over the place. I couldn't let them be captured."

Ilya eases his tone. "The commissar tells me you were screaming, Misha."

"I grabbed the plans and I evacuated. That's all I did."

"You ran to the rear without your rifle."

"I forgot it. The commissar was wrong. I forgot my gun. There were Germans everywhere."

"And General Chuikov, if I'm not mistaken, informed you that's when you need your gun most, Misha."

There is not much light but there is enough for Ilya to note a gleam rimming Misha's eyes.

"Ilya," the man says, "please."

"Yes"—Ilya pauses and chews on the word—"please."

Please nothing, he thinks. There is no please in this life, no being granted a favor for the asking. Does Misha believe there is justice, that you get what you deserve, or that you can keep what you earn? No. Ilya will never make that mistake again. Anything can be taken away, whether or not it's fair, or if it even makes no sense. Do or do not say "please"; no one hears you.

Misha has dried his eyes. He looks firmly into Ilya's face. He wants to ask a question of his own now. This must be what Misha's training is: queries, not battle.

"You were a major?"

"Yes, Misha. A major."

"How long have you been in Eighth Guards?"

"Before Stalingrad. When we were still the Sixty-second."

Misha's eyebrows go up. Anyone who fought at Stalingrad has an aura for those who did not see it, the greatest single battle in the history of mankind. One medium-sized Soviet city on the Volga in the winter of 1942 became the dead end of the German advance into Russia. There the Red Army killed or captured 1.2 million Germans, Italians, Romanians, and Hungarians. Russian losses were titanic as well. But from Stalingrad on, the Germans have not taken a step farther east into the *Rodina*. They did not cross the Volga. The tide turned. Chuikov's men fought so well, they have become known as the Defenders of Stalingrad, and were awarded the honorific "Guards Army." Once the signal is given here on the Vistula, the offensive across Poland will scorch a path to the Oder River, the German border. Then the Nazis' retreat back into their own homeland will be complete, and the battle will rage around their villages and cities, not Russia's.

Misha swallows before continuing. "How . . . ?"

"Don't ask"—Ilya cuts him off. "It was bad and it was two years ago. Let it rest. I'll tell you some other time." Ilya lays a big hand on Misha's lap. "We'll talk about it in Berlin, all right?"

"What did you do?

"Misha, no."

"That's my deal, Ilya. If you want to show off that, after only a week in the penal battalion, you can drag someone like me all the way out here in the middle of the night to steal another division's banner, then you have to answer me one more question. Tell me, and I'll go with you."

Misha. A cunning and quick little devil.

"What did you do?"

"Nothing."

"Ilya Borisovich. No one gets busted from Stalingrad major to penal private for nothing."

"Nothing is the truth. But it seems I am related to the wrong uncle."

Misha prods not with his voice but by knitting his fingers, to say, I'm listening.

Ilya puffs his cheeks once, then speaks.

"My uncle Pavel was a general on the STAVKA staff in Moscow. Last October, when the Polish Home Guard rose against the Germans in Warsaw, he was in favor of helping them. He said this at a meeting attended by Stalin."

Ilya looks into the curtain of the Polish night, northward where fifty kilometers away the city of Warsaw lies in ruins along the banks of the Vistula. The Germans put down the brave revolt by the Poles with brutality while the Red Army, the strongest gathered force on the planet, sat on the opposite shore of the river and let the Nazis obliterate one of Europe's oldest cities, butcher its citizens, and stamp out the last of the resistance. Poland, an ally of Russia, cried for help which had only to come from ten kilometers away. Stalin sat on his hands for months while the Germans did his bidding, exterminating those Poles who might feel they had liberated their own country.

Ilya's uncle said this openly. He first wrote it to Ilya in a letter, whose reply, a prayer for Pavel to keep quiet, was either not received in time or not heeded.

Within weeks of the meeting, Pavel was removed from his post. He was forced to retire from the army, then put in the basement of the Lubyanka Prison across Red Square from the Kremlin. His wife was evicted from her home. His three children, Ilya's cousins, were taken from their schools, separated, and placed with foster parents outside Moscow. Pavel's older brother Boris—Ilya's father—had early in the war met a hero's end starving to death during the three-year siege of Leningrad, Ilya's birth city. Ilya's mother and sister, both nurses, were left untouched by the long fangs of the *vozhd*. But Pavel's nephew, Major Ilya Borisovich Shokhin of the Eighth Guards Army, thirty-year-old commander of the proud Second Rifle Battalion, three times wounded, who had killed Germans with every weapon put in his hands, and even without weapons a dozen times with his huge bare fists, was tracked down by the minions of Stalin's wrath. Last week he was stripped of his office, his awards and command, and dropped into hell. Company A of the Eighth Guards penal battalion. Stalin is thinking of us, indeed.

Now, on another chilled and dreary night of waiting for the order to attack, Ilya will steal the divisional banner from the First Guards Tank Army, their battle partner rammed in close at the rear of Eighth Guards. Tomorrow morning, First Tank's orange-and-black flag will fly over General Chuikov's headquarters tent. It is an act of boldness, insolence, and revenge. First Tank stole Chuikov's jeep two days ago and painted it orange and black. Their prank must be topped. When word gets out that someone from Eighth Guards penal did this, First Tank will be humiliated. Ilya and Misha might not be punished; if so, only with light sentences. Eyebrows and open hands will be raised at their backs. Misha will have done his first brave act for all to see. Ilya will prove again what he has proven many times under lethal conditions, that he is a born leader of men.

Explaining his history to Misha in whispers takes five minutes. When he is done, Ilya is surprised that he was so open with this man he knows nothing about except that he is a coward and a fellow officer. But it feels good to have spoken to Misha's intelligent eyes. There is no one else to talk with. The company and battalion officers are martinets, themselves trying to remove some smirch on their records. The rest of the men are the dregs.

Misha continues to nod even after Ilya has grown silent.

"Stop that," Ilya says.

"Sorry. Old habit."

"Can we go now?"

"I'm sorry, Ilya. It's not right what was done to you."

"This is war, Misha."

"Perhaps." Misha rocks forward from the wooden tank. "All right, Comrade Major. I will follow."

Ilya joins him flat on the ground. The cold seeps through his coat into his chest.

"We'll get to within twenty meters, then stop and see what we see. Move quietly, Misha. Go only when and where I go."

Ilya slides over the ground at a pace he believes the smaller man can keep up with. He thinks back to Stalingrad now that Misha has brought it forth. From September of 1942 until February of '43, you moved like this in the rubble, with stealth and strength and patience, or you drew a bullet from a sniper. There were no alternatives.

The eighty-meter creep seems to take a long time, waiting for Misha to catch up, but Ilya knows it is less than ten minutes. When they come to rest behind a log pile, Ilya notes that Misha's breathing is not labored but under control. The little man has done well.

The lantern inside the tent has stayed on. Now Ilya hears voices fluttering into the bare branches overhead, a card game among the officers. And vodka, surely.

A single guard strolls a wide circle around the tent stakes. He has no lantern. At the front of the big tent no more than ten meters from the flaps, a skinned tree has been driven into the ground for a flagpole. At the top of the pole, attached to a tether, is the First Tank's pennant, limp in the breezeless night. Ilya counts under his breath while the guard makes two revolutions around the tent. The man walks without hurry. One lap takes him about a full minute.

"Misha."

"What's the plan?"

"When the guard is at the far corner of the tent, he'll have about thirty seconds until he comes out there on the other side. When I say go, you run out and take down the banner."

"Me?"

"Quiet."

"You want me . . . ? What kind of a plan is that? I thought you came out here to do it."

"No. I came out here to make you do it."

Misha drops his face on his hands. Ilya grabs the back of his coat and lifts his head for him.

"Get ready."

"Ilya, please."

"Don't ever say that to me again. Now, get ready. Are you ready?"

"What if I don't go?"

"You'll have to face me later. And if you do go, I'm on your side later. You choose."

"Why me?"

"Because I'm too recognizable. If I'm seen running off with the flag, I'm easy to pick out of a crowd. You, no one will remember."

Misha rattles his head.

"Besides," Ilya whispers, "I want you to get the glory."

"You want me to get the stockade. All right. I can't believe I'm doing this. When?"

"Get up to your knees. Quiet. Wait . . . wait . . . and . . . now. Go."

With startling nimbleness, Misha leaps to his feet. Bent low, he hurries to the flagpole. He grabs the rope and tugs to lower the pennant. But the line is tied around a peg, and Misha's chilled fingers struggle with the knot. Ilya counts to ten, fifteen.

Misha looks back to the log pile, the lantern glow from inside the tent illumines the whites of his frightened eyes. Ilya rises to his knees and swirls his finger in fast circles, hurry!

The guard emerges from the far corner of the tent. He does not yet see Misha, who picks at the knot, but in five more seconds he will.

At that moment, Misha untangles the knot. With fast hands, he lowers the banner just as the guard rounds the corner.

The guard lifts his rifle from his shoulder and walks over.

"What are you doing?" His challenge is not loud nor violent. He doesn't want to disturb the officers and their drinking game. He can handle one little unarmed interloper.

Misha freezes, but only for a second. He begins to fold the standard.

"Do you know this banner has to be taken down at night?" Misha asks in a resolute voice. "It's disrespectful to have it up after the sun goes down."

Sharp, Ilya thinks. Very sharp.

The guard shoulders his rifle, any threat seemingly absent. Misha continues to fold.

"All right," the guard agrees, "leave it with me and I'll have it put up at sunrise."

Misha wags his head.

"No, I'm afraid I'll have to take this with me. This is a violation. I'll have to show it to my superiors."

The guard reaches for the flag. Misha holds it back. The guard asks to see Misha's papers. "What unit are you with?"

Inside the tent, a voice calls out, "What's going on out there?"

"Something about the flag, sir," the guard responds, beginning to tug at it with Misha.

Misha calls into the tent, "There's no problem, men. Go about your business."

But there is a problem. Ilya hears chairs scraping. The lantern light moves, shadows on the tent walls shift.

Ilya has slipped without sound two meters behind the arguing guard. With one blow of his fist to the middle of the guard's back, he fells him facedown at Misha's feet.

Ilya grabs Misha and hauls him and the flag away at top speed, dodging the dark trees and fake tanks.

January 1, 1945, 2:00 A.M.
Pariser Strasse shelter
Wilmersdorf, Berlin

LOTTIE IS EXHAUSTED. HER FINGERS ACHE. SHE HAS played her cello without break for two hours.

She completes the final passage and lowers her bow hand. Enough, she thinks, I've done enough tonight.

The thirty-five people in the air raid shelter pause before they clap, the way they've been trained to do. In Berlin, classical music is loved as nowhere else except perhaps in Vienna. When Lottie indicates she is finished, they clap fingertips to palms, not to resound too much ruckus off the cold dirt walls. Besides, they are still moved by Lottie's playing, she can tell, especially the last piece, a soaring solo from Strauss's *Don Juan*. Gentle applause is appropriate. The appreciative faces flicker, are made angular by candlelight and shadows.

"I'm going to put it away now," Lottie tells her mother, Freya, seated next to her. An older man, saying nothing, rises to help with the large cello case. When the instrument is stored, the man sits. Lottie slides again next to her mother. In the absence of the music, silence detonates among those gathered on the benches and plank floor. The quiet is a crater, as though a bomb has found them after all in their hole beneath the small church and they are every one of them dead but still sitting upright.

No one moves. Eyes lock straight ahead or dart like spooked minnows. Freya knits her hands in her lap and closes her eyelids.

There is a stranger among them tonight.

Lottie sighs. She has already played all afternoon with her string quartet at one of the few undamaged homes on the Kurfürstendamm. Why did he have to come tonight?

In every shelter, Lottie knows, there are taboos and good luck charms. There are regulars with preferred seats who bustle down the steps with the sirens blaring. There are special concerns: some residents fear fire most and have buckets of sand handy; others are preoccupied with the possible collapse of the building above and keep shovels and picks near their seats. There is also trust and sharing of meager foodstuffs with the faces one sees every day in the neighborhood, the gray heads and the children.

And in this shelter beneath the Ludwig Church on Pariser Strasse, as in every other corner of Berlin, there lurks a palpable mistrust of anyone unfamiliar, and certainly any unknown men of military age. The unasked question: why is he in Berlin and not at the front? He must be Gestapo, a Nazi functionary, an informer, maybe a deserter. Whatever he is, he spells mischief and bad luck for your shelter.

On those few occasions when there is in their midst an unknown for whom no one vouches, not one person in the shelter speaks. Even normal conversation, about potatoes, clothes, the Opera, is struck dumb, all words are vipers that can bite their handler in the presence of an unfamiliar face. The *Berliner Blick,* the quick, furtive glance over the shoulder to see who is listening, fills the hours of waiting, making them even more racking. Now that the Russian army is surely coming, Goebbels has made it a crime punishable by death to speak of anything that smacks of defeatism. The official term is *Zweifel am Sieg,* Doubt about Victory. Stories are rampant of innocent remarks that have led Berliners into unwitting oblivion. The man who joked that the Reds won't attack Berlin, why would they come here when all the bigwigs will have taken off by then? He was shot in the street by the SS. A woman who hoarded bread and cheese for her family was punished for spreading lies that there was not enough food for Berlin under Goebbels' leadership. She was stripped naked and forced to wear a placard reading I DO NOT BELIEVE IN HITLER. Those elder folk who complain about the deaths of their sons, or housewives grumbling about the unavailability of shoes, at best are made to scrub police station floors. At worst, they're beheaded. Last year, the Berlin People's Court passed fifty-one death sentences against some who did no more than listen to a foreign radio broadcast and were denounced for it by a relative or neighbor. Children are encouraged to inform on their parents. A teacher, who likely is a Nazi, might ask, "What did your family have for Sunday dinner?" If the response is roast and sauerkraut and applesauce, not the economical casserole *Eintopf* ordained by the government, the mother could find herself reported.

Tonight, when the air raid sirens wailed at 11:30, thousands of New Year's Eve parties were ruined. Lottie was at one near her flat on Regensburger Strasse, with her mother. She ran home first to gather up her cello, as she always does when there is a raid and she is anywhere near her flat in Wilmersdorf. Freya met her at the church. Lottie was disappointed, the party was fun and there had been real coffee, not the lousy chicory *ersatz*. Still, a raid was not unexpected tonight. The English, whose Mosquito bombers handle the nighttime chores over Berlin, have a black sense of humor. Many of the Anglo attacks are calculated to aggravate as well as kill: bombs on Hitler's birthday and German holidays, raids following notable Allied victories, and the like. The English relish civilian targets. That's only tit for tat. Hitler tried to make a pyre of London. By comparison, the American B-17 morning raids are punctual and careful; they're always at work in the skies by 9 A.M. and are aimed at factory districts, often in Spandau and the northern reaches of the city. The message from the Americans has no black hidden laughter, it is simply: "Berlin, stop the war."

This evening the church shelter filled in minutes. By law, Berliners in every part of the city are to be off the streets until the all-clear signal; anyone other than diplomats caught aboveground can be shot as a looter or spy. The raids have been a part of Berlin life for more than four years now, since September of 1940, when the first British bombs rained on Reinickendorf, Pankow, and Lichtenberg districts. In the intervening years, Eisenhower and "Bomber" Harris have teamed up to destroy forty percent of the city's buildings, over half a million flats, displacing millions of Berliners, killing fifty thousand. But on nights like tonight, after enduring years of destruction and close escapes, when the neighborhood people of Pariser Strasse see a new face crowding on their bench, they are less afraid of bombs than they are of speaking to one another.

At times like this, when there is a stranger in their shelter, when a single offhand comment, a grouse, even idle speculation about the war, can be lethal, Lottie plays the cello. With

Lottie here, no one will forget themselves, grumble, and go missing tomorrow. Her music enforces silence.

Lottie resents the new man's presence. She takes his measure, crammed between two big-reared women who will not look at him. He has not spoken either, all night. He is balding, dark-haired, and fair-skinned, with a long neck and sunken cheeks stippled by a day's growth of black beard. The man is bug-eyed, though that may be his distaste at being treated like a pariah. He seems to be between thirty-five and fifty. In Berlin nowadays, hunger makes everyone look older. His gray suit has some shine at the knees and sleeves, his brown tie is pulled up tight, the knot shows chafe, as does his white shirt collar. Lottie thinks he has worn this outfit for some time. There is a keenness to his glance, and something feral, as though he knows important and wild things the rest in the shelter do not.

Of course, he does know one thing they do not: who he is.

Lottie sees her mother lift her lids and make eye contact with him. Freya smiles. The man blinks.

Freya clears her throat. Lottie's chest squeezes.

Her mother says to the man, "Did you enjoy my daughter's playing?"

Lottie licks her lips. The others in the shelter glare at Freya. One does not speak with a stranger.

Lottie scoops her mother's hand into her own. "Mutti, stop fishing for compliments for me." Lottie flashes the man a quick and cheap smile.

Freya pats Lottie's wrist. "She plays beautifully. Doesn't she?"

The man's face is graven. His eyes seem to look far past Freya and Lottie, even into the cold earthen walls. Lottie wants to look away from him there on the bench, the way all the others in the shelter have, but she cannot, the way one cannot look away from a ghost.

Lottie tightens her grip on her mother's hand. She mumbles, "Mutti."

The man's lips part. Nothing of him moves, not his teeth, his lids, only his lips and tongue when he breathes, "Yes."

Freya nods. She has moved the stranger to speak, and smiles at him. Lottie glances between the two, sees that some business of Freya's has been concluded, and lowers her head. Her blond hair curtains her eyes. She stares into her lap at her mother's hand in hers. The hand is not old, still smooth. A man might still want Mutti—she's only fifty-two—though Lottie is uncomfortable with the thought. Freya was Lottie's age, twenty-six, when she gave birth to her only child, the musical daughter. Her father, Frederick, was killed in the final days of World War I. Freya says Lottie was conceived on her parents' last night together. The daughter was named Charlotta after the Berlin district Charlottenburg, where her well-to-do mother and father grew up and met as children playing in the forested groves of the Tiergarten, where Freya still lives.

Mutti is not flirting, Lottie thinks. She is not making eyes at this specter of a man in our shelter. She's being nice, by her own lights. Mutti is often too nice; she can be led, even gullible. Lottie cannot imagine her mother with any man but her father, the handsome, winsome fellow in the old photographs, forever young and brave. Growing up, Lottie sent her mother on make-believe vacations with Frederick to beautiful places. Frederick became her pretend playmate, her guardian and inner voice. He was Papa, wise and strong, and never was he absent. Mutti had male friends through the years, and Lottie always made it known that she was watching, and through her so was Papa, and the two of them did not approve of anything beyond innocent companionship with men. Why should Mutti need men? Lottie was a wonderful daughter, pretty and proper, wasn't she? At age five she played her first cello concerto. By the time she was nine she could tune the family piano by herself. Wasn't Mutti proud enough of her daughter? Papa was, certainly.

The arguments began when Lottie became a teenager and Freya did not need to stay home with her every night. Freya began to go out, to dances and social functions. Lottie stayed in to practice. Other nights, Freya's female friends dropped by, they smoked cigarettes and sometimes smelled of drink. Mutti never brought men home to visit, but Lottie did not have to see with her eyes what she knew to be true. Lottie and Papa watched. Often they spoke out. In short time, Lottie's talent with the cello grew to local renown. She joined a German national youth orchestra. She played first chair, and was taken from home more and more by performances and traveling concerts. While on the road, in Switzerland and Austria, Hungary and Italy, Lottie worried about Mutti. Who might be misguiding her while Lottie was away? The more her head was filled with notes and troubles and suspicion, the less clearly she heard Papa's voice.

At fifteen, Lottie was conscripted into the BdM, *Bund deutscher Mädel,* the girls' equivalent to the Hitler Youth for boys. Because of her musical abilities, Lottie was allowed to stay in Berlin and continue her studies, while other Aryan girls were dispersed around the country to serve as nannies, farm helpers, tutors, and office workers. Lottie entered into two years of handicrafts, folk songs, and political rallies. She wore white flowing robes and waved flags while *Wehrmacht* soldiers and brown-shirted storm troopers goose-stepped down the Unter den Linden. She played patriotic and martial music on her cello at public shows while wearing the BdM uniform of black skirt, white blouse, and leather scarf holder. Mutti never spoke for or against the BdM to her daughter, but never once did she accompany Lottie to any of their events. Lottie didn't mind, she saw it all as a sign of her increasing freedom of mind and body. Lottie was careful to make no judgments about the National Socialists or the war, or that Jews and other non-Aryans were excluded from not just the BdM but almost all of Berlin life. She was a musician, and music inhabited a higher plane than Hitler's politics, shopkeepers' busted windows, or ugly rumors. She only knew her Papa had been in the army. She liked being around the boys in uniform, they looked like him.

When she turned eighteen, Lottie was accepted to Humboldt in Berlin to study music. She rebelled against Mutti, saying she wanted to move out and have her own flat. Freya agreed. For four years, living only eight U-bahn stops apart, the two did not see much of each other. Weeks, even a month or two, could pass without contact. Mutti arrived early for every concert at the university hall and sent flowers backstage for her daughter. Sometimes Lottie gave them away to other students. She knew her mother was in the dark seats of the theater. But she played—bowing with passion and a skill her teachers cherished—for Papa Frederick.

At university, Lottie fell in love with a boy two years older than she. He was an economics student, and a secret admirer of the writings of Marx and Engels, two old alumni of Humboldt. He spoke of compassion for the masses, the redistribution of wealth across the broadest of human spectrums. He believed Hitler was doing this, that soon Germany would need *Lebensraum,* room for its people to grow, just the way the Führer said, and that the Reich should grow to the east, into the Balkans and Russia. There Germany would correct the mistakes made by the Bolsheviks in Marx and Engels' names. He and Lottie became intimate, only for the final month before his graduation. When he left university, he was conscripted into the *Wehrmacht.* He wrote Lottie three times. She answered, then his letters stopped. Lottie told herself he was killed in battle, in Spain or later in Poland perhaps. She did not try further to find out what had happened to him. She pressed his letters in a Bible. He is the only man Lottie has ever lain with. She sometimes thinks of him, imagining Papa and him in heaven together. She believes she is loyal.

Just before Lottie's graduation, the war broke out. At first, Berlin was jubilant. Hitler had eliminated unemployment with his *Autobahn* projects and rearmament industries. Military successes came fast on every front and with little German blood, in Poland, Denmark, Norway, Holland, Belgium, France, Romania, North Africa, Greece. Music was played everywhere in Berlin, at the extravagant Adlon Hotel near Hitler's Chancellery, at Hörchner's, fat Hermann Göring's favorite restaurant, in the public parks, and at private functions thrown by Berlin society and the celebrant Nazis. Lottie tutored some students. Soon she was invited to join a well-known local string quartet—formed from members of the Berlin Philharmonic Orchestra—after they lost their elderly cellist to a heart attack. Through their intervention, Lottie was granted subcontractor status with the all-male Philharmonic. She was allowed to play only until another suitable male cellist could be found. But with the war on, and Jews excluded from the BPO, Lottie has remained in her fourth chair. During Philharmonic concerts, at the request of the renowned conductor Wilhelm Furtwängler, she wears a man's tuxedo and puts her hair up under a black net.

No one has complained, not even the strident young concertmaster Gerhard Taschner, for Lottie is a transcendent cellist. She has perfect pitch, honed as a child tuning her mother's piano. She has broad hands, strong shoulders, and preternaturally long pinkies. She is a tall girl, so she can play a big cello, her Joseph and Antonio Galiano, made in Naples in 1750. The heavy Galiano cries out in dark tones; a lesser cellist might harness its somber voice but could not wring from it the brio and brightness Lottie's fingers can. Her vibrato is wide and dizzying, ideal for the Romantic solos of Schumann, Haydn, and Schubert. The two violinists and the violist in her quartet marvel at her range, she sees it in their faces when they are at rest and she is soaring. The men of the BPO, all of them older, some ancient, accept her with nods. She will never be given a solo with the Philharmonic, but she has a chair with one of the world's finest orchestras, and that is enough.

Now the Adlon Hotel is a bombed-out shell. Hörchner's is in ruins. The trees of the Tiergarten where Mutti and Papa played as children, where Mozart and Brahms flowed from bandstands only two years ago, is a scorched and bare scar on the belly of Berlin. To help Berliners keep faith and to normalize life as much as possible in a crumbling, dangerous city, Hitler has insisted that the Philharmonic continue its seasons, playing three or four times per week, always late in the afternoons to dodge the threat of the Americans' morning bombings and the night raids of the RAF. The Allies' planes have made the orchestra something of a wanderer around Berlin, from the Beethoven Hall to the Admirals Palace to the Titania Palace, switching venues to rehearse or perform while repairs are made to whichever was bombed last.

Lottie has kept a few students, though her building on Regensburger Strasse has been hit twice, blowing in all her windows. She has had them reglazed. Her four-room flat is still sound, though others in the building have had great chunks bitten out of their apartments. There have been deaths on her block. But both she and Mutti have been fortunate. Neither has been displaced—Mutti's large stone row house near the Savigny Platz is intact—nor have they been required to take in any of the host of homeless Berliners.

Lottie raises her head from her reverie. Her mother's eyes are still fixed on the ragged stranger on the bench across from them. The man looks down, pulling dark eyes away from her stare, embarrassed at her attention, and at the effort the others in the shelter make to ignore him. But Lottie catches his eyes lifting, stealing a glimpse of Freya's interest in him. Again he casts his gaze down. Lottie shares his obvious wish, that he could be somewhere else.

Outside, the all-clear siren sounds. No one in the shelter, not even the children, moves until the stranger has risen. He is stiff. The dirt shelter is cool and the benches hard. He does not look around or utter anything. He climbs the steps with heavy treads. The thick wooden door is shoved open and he goes out into the church alley.

When the door closes overhead, someone sighs. Some others laugh, there is much weary head shaking. Three hours of tension are ended. The broken and angry world outside for a moment becomes a relief. The crowd rises to shuffle up to the remnants of this night, to the tattered beginnings of the new year in Berlin, where, one hopes, the stranger and all strangers have disappeared. Tonight was a long alert. A gentleman offers to help Lottie with her cello. She refuses and wrangles it up the steps herself. Freya is behind her on the steps and out to the street.

The air is flecked with snow. Lottie turns a full circle, so does Freya. Wilmersdorf was not bombed tonight. The all-clear sirens quit. No other klaxons fall with the snow from the reaches of the city. It appears tonight was a false alarm. The English bombers as they often do may have crossed over Berlin on their way somewhere else, then flew back over the city returning to the Channel. Or they got here to find unexpected cloud cover and circled high waiting for a break. But the people of Berlin are kept underground until the bombers have all gone.

The people from the shelter filter into the darkness. Down the block the sound of grumbling Berliners dodges through the flakes; other shelters and basements empty. The rubbled city is in complete blackout. Lottie does not need much light to know that half of the buildings here on Pariser Strasse have no roof. The cratered street might have been the sandbox of a demonic giant child with a toy shovel, who enjoys digging holes and knocking over his little castles. Freya bends to pick up a brick at her feet. Out of habit, she knocks the dried mortar from it and sets it down to rebuild Berlin later. A bit of life rumbles by: a U-bahn train on an elevated track with its windows papered over. Even though it's after two in the morning, because of the alert the trains have restarted and will run for another hour. Lottie can walk to her flat from the church. Freya will ride back to Charlottenburg.

Lottie thinks of what she has seen after some raids: the rank bodies, smoke and fire. For this snowy night of calm, she thanks someone—God, Papa, her soldier, she isn't sure—thanks that tonight there are no flames and the carnage is cool. Thanks that she has her Galiano with her safe. Freya cleans another brick and sets it beside the other.

"Mutti, why do you do that? It's stupid." Lottie does not desire the edge in her voice, but she is young and ardent and she plays what she feels.

Freya shrugs. She appears to pick out one snowflake and watch it tumble. "What else can one do?"

Lottie makes a sound with her lips, like one of the horn players limbering. There is no one else out in the snow. It is late and cold and many tables still have schnapps on them, a nightcap tipped to New Year's Eve and another night of survival. Lottie wants to go home, but something bothersome holds her in gravity to Mutti.

"Why did you talk to him?"

Freya brings her look down to her daughter.

"Because no one else would."

"No one should. You don't know who he is. He could have been Gestapo."

"Lottie, *Liebchen*." Freya laughs. "How can you have such marvelous ears and such poor eyes? Sometimes I think you're just like that cello. You make the most wonderful noise, but I believe you're made of wood."

Lottie is not prepared for Mutti to be annoyed with her. She intended to chide her mother for the breach of common sense, of security. Mutti will get herself sent to Ravensbrück if she talks to unfamiliar people once too often. She'll get Lottie taken off too.

Lottie hugs her cello case to her.

"Don't scold me, Mutti. I'm a grown woman."

Freya's hand rises to the back of Lottie's neck and combs through the golden hair.

"Yes. I know you are, *Liebchen*."

On the ground the snow builds a quick, flimsy dressing of white for Berlin's wounds. Lottie asks, "Who do you think he was, then?"

Freya shoves her hands into her coat pockets. She looks like she will ignore the question and walk away. Lottie takes up the handle of her cello case.

Freya digs a heel into the snow. Lottie stops. She waits. Mutti seems about to answer. Lottie doesn't care enough to spend much more time in this conversation, who the man was or wasn't. She wants only to haul her cello home and go to sleep.

Big flakes strike Lottie's eyelashes. Her mother still considers speaking.

Lottie smacks her lips. She will tarry no longer, this hesitation of her mother's is almost farcical.

"Mutti, goodnight." She hefts the cello. "Happy New Year."

But Freya pivots first in the snow slickness and with no words is gone.

TWO

THE PRESIDENT'S HANDS SHAKE.

To calm them, give his hands something to do, he uses them to uncross his legs. He lifts the right leg at the knee and aligns it beside the other. They make a pair. He straightens the pressed seam of his trousers on both legs. He keeps his legs neat, pampers them, for they are separate, more like possessions than his own flesh. Beside the sofa in an ashtray a cigarette smolders. He takes it up and inhales. Releasing the smoke from his lungs, he lifts his chin the way he does when there are cameras about. He watches the red ash jiggle, can't hold it still. He takes another jolt from the cigarette.

The President hears applause. Where's it coming from? He's alone in his office, not on the back of the caboose, not stumping the countryside. That's done months ago. His fourth inauguration is in two weeks. Where's the crowd?

It's in his head. His pulse roars in his temples. Not applause. He lowers the cigarette. Releasing smoke from his lungs, he lifts his glass and finishes the dregs of Scotch. Straight, no ice. Standard stuff. Who just left the office? Maloney? No, he's next. Frank O'Mahoney, senator, Wyoming, he was just here. Old friend, ally. Nice chat. Maloney is next. Connecticut.

He stubs out the cigarette, then lays his hands palms down on his legs. He looks at the backs of his big hands, they're thick and still powerful, though sixty-two years old, sixty-three in a few weeks. Why do they quake? They're messing up the trouser pleats he just made neat.

The President sits composed, balanced on the sofa. His eyes focus only a few feet beyond his long nose, at nothing. The Oval Office fuzzes, some of the colors swirl into others, and this is pleasant and soft. He'll stay here, like a cat in a basket of yarn, for a few minutes and rest.

The door opens. Through the haze of cigarette smoke and rushing blood a heavyset man walks in. A jocular voice says, "Mr. President. Good afternoon."

The man sits in a high-back chair, without receiving a greeting in return, helps himself to a cigarette from the pack on the table. The man lights up, more smoke billows into the room. The President stares into it.

Frank Maloney, that's who. Connecticut. Maloney says something, more smoke.

Silence. The President's head lowers to where his starched collar cups his chin. He wants to curl up but he is perched on his useless legs like a lamp on a table; he stays upright.

He wants to talk with the man in the chair beside the sofa, who is it again? Connecticut something. His hands are on his rumpled legs. The eclipse in his legs, how they will not listen to him, has climbed up his quivering wrists, his arms like ladders, to muddle the rest of him.

The man in the chair rises. "Mr. President?"

The man crosses himself, head to chest to shoulders. Fog. Thunderous clapping now.

The man turns and heads for the door, calling out, "Someone! Mrs. Tully, his lips are blue! Someone get in here!"

The office is empty. Roosevelt bites his lower lip hard for the splash of pain. He struggles to lift his hands to his face. He hides his eyes behind his fingers, feels their tips in his sockets, he presses his lips, which must be blue to the warm palms. Some circuit is connected when he does this, and the shaking eases. He opens his eyes behind the bars of his fingers. The colors of the room have mostly returned to their proper roosts.

There is no more applause. A dull ache is there behind his eyeballs where the blood tide has ebbed. The room is quiet. He makes fists to test the resolve of his hands to cooperate. After a few moments, the fists become solid again, the old hammers, souvenirs of his youth.

Roosevelt takes a few deep breaths. He restraightens his trousers. The legs must always look like any other man's legs. He allows himself to be viewed in public only two ways: standing behind a lectern with his leg braces locked, or seated in an open car. The nation cannot be allowed to see a hint of feebleness, not in this time when strength is what the entire world demands of America. When his pants are tidy he lifts the right leg and layers it back over the left. He strikes a match to a fresh cigarette and takes a long draw. His head clears with the cloud he sucks in. He lifts his chin, waiting for Maloney of Connecticut to return. Grace Tully, one of the White House secretaries, will send him back in. She'll tell him not to worry, everything's fine, it'll pass. He's just tired, working too much, something. She'll get him back in here.

In a minute, the rotund senator does peek around the doorjamb, sheepish. Expecting what? A dead president? A weakling?

"Come in, Frank, for Christ's sake, come in! Close the door. Pour yourself a Scotch, you know where it is. Freshen me up while you're at it."

Maloney approaches and asks how the President is feeling. Roosevelt fires back a salvo the senator will remember better than whatever it was he saw when he came in before. As good as any other man, Roosevelt thinks, legs and all, goddammit. Never better, Frank! Beat, what with this damn war, the election, plans for the inaugural, carrying Churchill on my back! Eleanor's out trying to save America from itself, that's where I ought to be but I'm stuck here with real work to do. Haw!

He gives Maloney a jaunty half hour. He swaps stories, chuckles, listens to a special political request, and agrees in his own fashion, which is to nod and make pleasant noises to the man's face, disagreeing later if he has a mind to after Maloney's gone and the subject comes up in formal fashion through committee. He has an aversion to argument and hurt feelings. He prefers to please whomever he talks to, relishes the feel of winning them over, being liked by individuals and especially crowds. He can't fire anyone, never could. He delegates that ugly chore. Eleanor once told Churchill that when the President is saying "Yes, yes," it doesn't mean he's agreeing, it means he's listening.

Maloney leaves. The President is certain he packed him off happy and unconcerned. Grace Tully slips in behind the senator's ample wake.

"Well, Mr. President, you are a charmer."

"Always have been," he says, lifting his chin, cigarette clenched in his teeth. He works his jaw and the cigarette wags.

Mrs. Tully hands him a short stack of papers. "I've pushed back your massage till four o'clock."

"Good," he says. "Join me."

Mrs. Tully laughs. "Some other time." She hands him the red top-secret folder.

"Another love letter." She smiles and makes to leave.

"Grace. For happy hour today, I want Harry, Rosenman, and Anna." The secretary waves over her shoulder on the move, she'll take care of it.

Happy hour is Roosevelt's most precious ritual. It was born in his gubernatorial days in Albany and has continued without break for three terms, soon to be four, in Roosevelt's favorite room, the second-floor study of the White House. The study is jammed full of maritime pictures, ship models, reams of paper, and worn, homey furniture. At cocktail hour, no more is said about politics beyond gossip, amusing tales, and recollections. Roosevelt uses this time to unwind, practice his self-pleasing craft of pleasing others, and experiment with strange drink concoctions of gin, vermouth, rum, and fruit juices. The participants are chosen with care. They must be abiding Roosevelt connections, the better to appreciate his stories, even the threadbare ones which the President retells but always with a new flair or mimicry to keep his audience amused. Eleanor does not attend often; the drinking offends her sensibilities, the residue of growing up under an alcoholic father. Harry Hopkins, Roosevelt's top adviser, is a willing laugher and a raconteur of ability, despite his ill health and ghastly thin frame. Sam Rosenman, known as "Judge" for having once served on the New York State Supreme Court, is a long-standing administration aide and speechwriter. Judge can hold his liquor and knows all the D.C. rumors. And Roosevelt's lovely daughter Anna, his first child, who in February of '44 moved into the White House into Harry's old digs in the Lincoln Suite, lives two doors away from Roosevelt's rooms. Anna serves as de facto White House hostess. Eleanor is too occupied with her own agenda. Sometimes after cocktails are done and his audience disperses, Roosevelt sits for hours with Anna, working on his stamp collection, playing cards, reading with the comfort of having his adoring daughter nearby, or plotting with her.

He fingers the red folder. Another cable from Winston. He undoes the string bow and slides his reading glasses from his shirt pocket.

Churchill wants another private meeting, this time on the island of Malta, a British territory in the Mediterranean. It's on the way to the upcoming conference with Uncle Joe at Yalta in the Crimea. Roosevelt reads:

IF YOU DO NOT WANT TO SPEND MORE THAN ONE DAY AT MALTA, IT COULD SURELY BE ARRANGED THAT BOTH OUR CHIEFS OF STAFFS SHOULD ARRIVE THERE SAY A COUPLE OF DAYS BEFORE US AND HAVE THEIR PRELIMINARY DISCUSSIONS. WE COULD THEN PROCEED BY AIR. . . .

Roosevelt doesn't want to convene with Churchill before sitting down with him and Stalin at Yalta. Uncle Joe is always suspicious, he'll take the notion that, with the end of the war in sight, Roosevelt is showing his true colors, that he prefers the British to the Russians. Roosevelt doesn't. This is something the President has tried to make crystal clear to Stalin from the beginning of the war: the postwar stage will be American and Russian. The British will have good seats.

"Grace," he calls out, "get Harry here."

Roosevelt hears her answer. He adds, "And call the Marine."

In seconds, a large corporal in full dress uniform enters the Oval Office, pushing the President's wheelchair. The soldier is neat, pleated and tucked. The President rises on the man's arm. His legs without the metal muscle of the ten-pound braces burn even from this little effort of standing from the sofa to fall back into the wheelchair. If they're going to be this damned useless, he thinks, they could at least be numb. The braces hurt too when he wears them, can't they make them so they don't cut into your legs? But no, pain comes with the humiliation and disappointment. The pain never lets you forget, you never get used to it. That's good, he thinks. Never want to get used to it.

Being helped from the sofa by the soldier, Roosevelt is conscious of his own heft. He thinks he has got to lose even more weight. He is one hundred seventy pounds, down from the one ninety his "ticker" doctor didn't like at all. He enjoys his new thinness, brags to daughter Anna of his "flat tummy." All his body weight is in his abdomen and shoulders; his legs and hips atrophied years ago.

When he is moved to his wheelchair and maneuvered to his desk, the soldier leaves, never speaking. Roosevelt says, "Thank you," and the soldier snaps to at the words and salutes. Roosevelt jiggles the cigarette still clamped in his mouth, waves the starched Marine out the door with it.

In minutes Harry Hopkins ambles in. He slides into the

room, being of almost too slight a build to make much impression with his steps on the floor. Hopkins is the President's closest adviser, has been since the thirties with the WPA and as secretary of commerce. One night in the spring of 1940, Harry sat down for dinner at the White House and stayed for three and a half years, moving into the family quarters with his young daughter, moving out in December of '43 only at the insistence of his new wife. Harry is the President's alter ego, envoy, and his most trusted sounding board. He knows when to talk around Roosevelt, when to tell a joke, and when to clam up. Now that a wife has come between him and the President, their relationship has changed, as it must. But no one has the sensitivity to Roosevelt's moods like Hopkins, and no one else, not even Eleanor, has such authority to speak for the President.

Harry's health has been poor for several years, he's been in and out of hospitals. His body cannot absorb fats and proteins. Roosevelt watches Harry arrange himself in a chair, thinks of a bag of coat hangers. Look at Harry. He's given up on his appearance. Baggy suit, fingers nicotined from chain smoking. His damn eye sockets are like coal mines, for God's sake. In 1939 Harry was told he had four weeks to live. Roosevelt took control of the situation personally, flying in a team of medical experts, who gave Harry an experimental plasma transfusion. The procedure staved off the man's decline. Still . . .

"Harry, you look like shit."

"Thank you, Mr. President." Harry cracks a grin, an old friend. "I'd forgotten."

Roosevelt spins the red top-secret folder through the air to Hopkins.

"Winston again."

Harry scans the thin telegraph sheet. He says, "Still on this Malta business."

"He keeps telling me he wants to meet before the Big Three."

Hopkins thins his lips, disapproving of Churchill's

nagging. "Remember what he said last week? 'I do not see any other way of realizing our hopes about world organization in five or six days. Even the Almighty took seven.'"

Roosevelt nods agreement. He knows Winston's insistence too well.

Harry shakes his head. "And what was that bullshit he wrote you on New Year's Day?"

Roosevelt lifts a finger to claim the right: Let me do this one.

"'No more let us falter! From Malta to Yalta! Let nobody alter!'"

"Good grief." Harry chuckles. "Jesus Christ, that guy."

Roosevelt enjoys the laughter with Hopkins. He says, "Look, Harry, I don't want it. I'll have dinner in Malta, a few drinks, whatever, but no powwow. The Chiefs of Staff can meet, military is fine but nothing political. And not me and Winston, not officially. Uncle Joe won't like it. Handle this for me."

"I'll write the response."

"Good."

Hopkins takes a cigarette pack from his coat pocket. He shakes one straight into his mouth. Matches are already in his hand.

"He doesn't get it, Harry." Roosevelt feels the urge to push himself back from the desk, stand and pace, it never goes away, wanting that freedom. Instead he claps a hand on the desk, settles for this. "It's not the seventeenth century anymore. England is done with that. Europe is done with that. Two world wars have been fought, in consecutive generations. Everything's changed. The whole world."

Hopkins says, "Winston's just an old-style imperialist. He's even said so. What was it? 'I have not become the King's Prime Minister to preside over the liquidation of the British Empire.'"

Roosevelt slaps the table again. "Tell me one thing, Harry. Name one thing British imperialism has done in four hundred years for their colonial peoples."

"Not damned much."

"I won't have it, Harry. We fought World War I to make the world safe for democracy and all we did was make it safe for imperialism. That is not going to be the new world order after this war. That's not what the United Nations is all about. You know, if England wants us to help them stay a first-class power, they're going to have to stop this oppressive imperialism. England's going to have to reckon with us, Harry. That's not something they're used to yet. But they will be, soon as we finish this war for them."

Hopkins scribbles notes on a pad. Without looking up he elevates his free hand, lifts the thumb. That's right.

Roosevelt says into the room, "Don't get me wrong, I love Winston. He's one of the greatest men of this century, no doubt about it. But he wants to continue old-fashioned balance-of-power politics. I've got news for him, balance-of-power is why we're in this war in the first place. All it does is hang on to the same tensions and alliances that made peace impossible after World War I. And we get sucked into two foreign wars this century. Those politics are ancient. What can you do?"

Harry's cigarette goes to his mouth. Still writing, the cigarette dangling on the dampness of his lips, he says, "England's ancient, Mr. President. What can you do?"

Roosevelt nods. "The United Nations. America. Britain. China and Russia. Got to have Russia in or it won't work."

Hopkins finishes and raises his head. He looks like a starved, neglected pooch.

"Your boy Stalin. That's a bastard."

"Oh, Joe's all right, Harry. He's get-at-able."

"He's a totalitarian."

"And he's killed eight out of ten Germans in this war. Damn it, when this is over they've got a right to be at the head table more than we do, certainly more than England or France."

"He's tricky, Mr. President."

"He knows what he wants, that's all. He's political to a fault. Ever since Stalingrad he's gotten the idea he can kick the Germans' ass without us if he has to. The key to Joe is to let him know you like him, you like Russia, and you want to work with them. They'll go turtle in a minute if you let them, but we're going to keep them in this alliance after the war, Harry. I don't care if Winston screams bloody murder all the way to Moscow and back, we're keeping the United Nations alive and the Reds are in it. That's my dream, Harry. That's my legacy. A lasting peace in the world after two world wars. No power politics. No bullies."

Roosevelt nods at his own words. He wants Harry to leave now, he's tuckered. Hopkins spots this and rises.

"I'll have the cable for you in half an hour."

"Great. Happy hour?"

"Grace has already cleared my schedule."

Hopkins departs. The Oval Office alone with Roosevelt now reverberates with the notions and actions of presidents before him who made the weightiest decisions here. Stalin, a bastard. A totalitarian. Roosevelt knows this. Ambassador Harriman and others never let him forget it. But what all the official naysayers don't reckon on is America's influence. With a powerful America as a partner and counterbalance, we can show the Red leadership how to make their country prosperous and modern without brutalizing their own people along the way. Russia can be tamed. Roosevelt's mentor Wilson, who was President during the Russian Revolution, knew this. Like Wilson, Roosevelt admires the will of the Russian people, their ability to sacrifice, suffer, and survive. They boggle the imagination.

Roosevelt regrets that Stalin is a tyrant. But communism is essentially an egalitarian form of government, isn't it? Communism wants to share resources, empower all its classes from the bottom up, build a classless society. Not too different, Roosevelt thinks, from his own New Deal. History will see the similarities if some of the currently living don't. Without the repressive tactics, you could view Stalin as another progressive liberal. A socialist. America's full of socialists. Push the analogy a little further and you get Churchill the Republican, pledged to status quo, business as usual.

So what if Uncle Joe wants to expand his reach into eastern Europe? Russia's got a right to protect its borders, how many times have invaders waltzed in through Poland? It's unfortunate but eastern Europe may be the meal the rest of us serve the Russian bear after the war. Small price, Roosevelt thinks, for a world at peace. The United Nations will just have to work hard to contain Russian expansionism the same way we'll unravel British imperialism.

There's going to be a power vacuum in western Europe after the war. Germany and France are shot to hell. England's on the ropes. If Russia fills the gap, it won't be such a bad thing. If we can make Soviet-American cooperation a reality, we might together do a far better job running European and world affairs than the old Great Powers have done.

Something big will come out of this war. A new heaven, a new earth.

But Churchill just aggravates Stalin. In March of '42, just three months after the U.S. entered the war, Roosevelt had to write Churchill:

I KNOW YOU WILL NOT MIND MY BEING BRUTALLY FRANK WHEN I TELL YOU THAT I THINK I CAN PERSONALLY HANDLE STALIN BETTER THAN EITHER YOUR FOREIGN OFFICE OR MY STATE DEPARTMENT. STALIN HATES THE GUTS OF ALL YOUR TOP PEOPLE. HE THINKS HE LIKES ME BETTER, AND I HOPE HE WILL CONTINUE TO.

Roosevelt met Stalin for the first time in November of '43 at Teheran. That was the farthest from Moscow Stalin was willing to travel. It was the only airplane trip the Marshal had ever taken, and he assured Roosevelt it was his last. Roosevelt ignored Churchill's plea to stay with the Prime Minister at the British Embassy. Instead, the President accepted Uncle Joe's invitation to take quarters at the Russian compound in Teheran.

At the Teheran meeting, Roosevelt did everything he could to establish warm relations with Stalin on this, their first face-to-face encounter. Initially, the little Marshal in his unadorned mustard-colored uniform with great shoulder boards like shelves was detached and stiff, exposing little humanity where Roosevelt could attach his charm. Three times the President met with Stalin, all the while refusing Churchill's requests for just one private lunch. The full plenary sessions were argumentative but little more than rubber stamps for what the President and Stalin had discussed in Churchill's absence. The nightly state dinners were tense affairs, with Stalin and Churchill exchanging barbed blandishments. Stalin was not going to forget how twenty-four years earlier Churchill railed in Parliament against the Red Revolution, supporting the intervention of British troops and money on the side of the czar against Lenin's forces. Roosevelt enjoyed the bald enmity between the two, hoping it would reinforce Stalin's preference for America. But he could not chip the grimace from Stalin's face until he turned on Churchill himself.

Roosevelt planned the ploy in advance. Assembling for one of the official meetings, he leaned over to Stalin to indicate the Prime Minister, who'd developed a head cold. In a stage whisper audible to all, Roosevelt said, "Winston's cranky this morning, he got up on the wrong side of the bed." When the translation was complete, the President noted a vague smile crease Stalin's mouth. He pressed on, teasing Churchill for his Britishness and his John Bull resemblance. Churchill was offended and scowled, turning ever redder, until Stalin broke into a belly laugh. For the first time in three days of meetings, Roosevelt felt an intimacy open between him and Stalin. At that moment, for the first time, he called the Marshal "Uncle Joe." It was a miscalculation. Stalin's mirth dissolved. He made to leave the table. Only when Roosevelt made the reference into a compliment, comparing him to the cherished American "Uncle Sam," was the Marshal mollified.

At another session regarding the postwar fate of Germany, on Churchill's sixty-ninth birthday, Stalin joked that at the end of the war fifty thousand German officers should be selected for execution. Churchill found this in bad taste. For comedy Roosevelt played the role of peacemaker, chiming in that Stalin's figure was too high, a compromise should be reached. They should only shoot forty-nine thousand. Churchill left the room in disgust, and was brought back by a cajoling Stalin. Then Roosevelt's eldest son, Elliott, a captain in the Army Air Corps, turned antic, exclaiming, "Hell, why not shoot a hundred thousand!" Stalin went over and wrapped his arm around the young man's shoulders.

Major decisions were made at Teheran. Uncle Joe was satisfied. Churchill was corralled. Roosevelt viewed the conference as a great success.

Now that the war's end is in sight, he sees no reason to change that formula. Let no one alter. Or falter.

Harry Hopkins returns with the proposed cable to Churchill. The President scans it. He changes the date of his arrival in Malta from February first to the second, the same day the presidential party is expected in Yalta. This way there'll be no time for an official meeting with Winston. Maybe dinner.

He tells Harry, "Send this to Uncle Joe too. That'll lock down the schedule and we shouldn't hear any more about it."

"Done."

Harry turns to go. The man's shoulder blades protrude beneath his suit coat.

Roosevelt takes up a cigarette. He thinks of Winston and his cigars. Big ostentatious ones, which the Prime Minister has trouble closing his lips over. He talks without taking them out, making his scratchy, constant voice even more strident. Roosevelt likes Winston Churchill, admires his flights of Victorian rhetoric. He's sorry he has to make one of the most extraordinary men of history, leader of one of the world's great and courageous nations, look so small.

The President spreads both hands over his legs, squeezes powerful fingers over the deadened thighs. He looks at Harry's wraith wrists swinging while the man walks away, the flesh pasty on the back of his friend's neck. Harry, who's been trying to die for years now.

Roosevelt thinks about the spell that came over him an hour ago in front of Maloney. Exhaustion. Confusion. God-dammit.

Roosevelt swallows a bilious tang, a fear. He lights his cigarette to chase the taste. After one puff he snuffs the cigarette.

Harry and me, Winston and Joe. America. England. This whole planet of men and nations. Our peace will be costly. But it's coming. We'll all birth it together.

He sits back and lowers his eyelids. One thing about the White House, it does not disappear when you close your eyes. He feels the Oval Office nudge him, history like Iago in his ear whispers, "Open your eyes, Franklin."

He complies. The old dead presidents of the room tell him. They speak with dozens of voices.

Don't ever be sorry. For anything you do as President.

We know what we're talking about, son.

History is not made by men who are sorry.

January 11, 1945, 1330 hours
SHAEF headquarters
Reims, France

IF YOU TAKE THE FACE OF EVERY MAN, WOMAN, AND child of Kansas and you blend them all together, you will get the face of General Dwight D. Eisenhower.

Bandy has snapped a hundred photos of the General for *Life*. In every one, Bandy captures the chin of a stolid farm lad, the eyes of a veteran plainsman, the soft cheeks and skin of the dairymaid, the crinkles of a girl, the doll hair of a tyke. Somehow, when Bandy releases the shutter, Ike never has his eyes closed, his mouth askew, or his hat cockeyed. He is composed when he's angry, balanced when hurried, firm when sweet. He is the erect American everyman from Abilene.

Bandy stands near the door and waits. He's in a large octagonal room that used to be a banquet hall in this former technical school for boys. The crystal chandelier dangling overhead must weigh a ton. War maps festoon every inch of wall and table. Wax pencil arrows in black, red, blue, and green crosshatch them all, a crazy quilt of troops and machines on the move, eyeing each other across Europe, antagonistic colors.

Female staffers operate banks of telephone connections, plugging and unplugging. Young men in crisp olive drab uniforms stride left and right shuttling sheaves of paper to someplace or another, where Bandy supposes they drop one and pick up a replacement. Other bright young men lean over the maps, drawing, erasing, measuring life and death in crayon. Every sound in the big room and the other rooms down the hall makes the same amount of noise, no one endeavor in here stands out. SHAEF, the Supreme Headquarters Allied Expeditionary Force, hums. Bandy watches Eisenhower in the center of it all, chain-smoking Camels. The General points, pats young men on backs, talks into phones, ponders over spread-out charts, all the while emitting smoke.

Bandy left home three days after New Year's. *Life* magazine sent a car up from Memphis to ferry him to an air base for a flight to Norfolk, where he boarded a Navy supply ship to London, then a quick flight to Paris, a car to Reims. The trip took six days. He wrote no letters to Victoria on the voyage, they didn't part the best of friends. She'll be all right, Bandy thinks. She always has been. This time is no different.

She doesn't understand, is the problem. Bandy taps his foot on the worn oriental carpet. Twenty feet away Ike taps his foot on the same carpet, impatient with some progress report he takes over the phone. Bandy's camera bag loops over his shoulder. Inside it are a new 35mm Leica and his old battle-ax Speed Graphic. They weigh much more than merely their poundage. They're not just Bandy's tools, they're his purpose. Take the cameras away and he's only a tobacco farmer, a man, flesh and blood, not exceptional at all. But with them he can stand so close to the flames of

history he can toast a marshmallow. What he sees, the whole
United States sees. But him first.

Eisenhower hasn't noticed Bandy yet, the General's focus
is tightened to where it doesn't extend past his corona of tobacco fumes. Others walk in and out of his clouds.
Eisenhower embraces what importance they bear for whatever time it takes, then moves like a little bit of Kansas
weather over someone or something else to do with the war.
Bandy wonders if Eisenhower isn't breathing some good old
Tennessee leaf in those Camels.

Eisenhower jabs a cigarette out in an ashtray on the huge
map table. He digs into his shirt pocket for the pack, finds it
empty. Scowling, he crumples it into a ball. Bandy tosses a
fresh pack through the air, spinning it to land and skid across
the map right in front of Ike. The General looks up. His
head tilts for a moment at who would toss things at the
Supreme Allied Commander.

"Charley?"

"General."

Eisenhower unwraps the pack, considering Bandy.

"You went home, I heard."

"I came back, sir."

"I take that as a failure on my part, son. I apologize. Your
wife ticked?"

"Plenty, sir."

"You'll give her my apologies. Come over here."

Bandy advances to the table, opposite Ike, who lights up,
then runs a palm over his hair, thin and pale as Midwestern
corn silk.

Eisenhower has long appreciated the value of good relations with the press. He knows America cannot wage a prolonged, costly war without popular support back home, and
only the press can create that. Ike has always treated those
men and women armed only with cameras or notepads as
valuable members of the Allied team. He has promised them
to be honest and open, and Bandy considers that for the
most part the General has kept his word. Ike knows many of
the journalists by name. Back in Washington, before taking

command of the Allied European Force, Ike became an admirer of Bandy's battle photography in *Life*. While others are ducking, Charles Bandy is standing. When others are holding their ground, Charles Bandy is creeping forward, to get shots of the soldiers from the front when they advance too. Eisenhower values courage. He rewards Bandy for his gumption as well as his contribution to the war effort with access to the Supreme Commander that other photogs and reporters are denied. The General and Bandy first met three weeks before D-Day. Bandy saw a man who spoke in plain terms, who knew his job and was loyal in how he went about doing it. A man who appreciated a good tobacco farmer.

"Take a look, Charley."

The General waves a hand clutching a Camel over the map. The glowing tip is like a meteor streaking over embattled Europe. Bandy hasn't an idea how to decipher the marks, arrows, and labels, but the shooting star he knows is a good omen.

A staffer approaches bearing paper. Eisenhower fends the soldier off. This is to make Bandy feel special and to curry favor, and Bandy is willing to let this work in him, flattered.

"Here's what we've got," Ike says. "We've won back most of what Hitler took here in the Bulge." The cigarette circles between Luxembourg and the Netherlands, swirling a hazy ring. "We're on the German border all the way from Switzerland to Holland." Ike's arm must make a broad sweep, for the map is enormous. Then he points, too far to reach. "In the east, the Reds are massing on the Polish border along the Vistula River. They're supposed to jump off any time now. That'll take even more pressure off us."

The General looks up to Bandy. He winces behind a puff. Bandy sees the chiseled face go grim, like staring out of Abilene at a twister coming. "I've got almost four million American, British, Canadian, and French soldiers. Hitler's got one million facing me, tired, cold, and beat to hell. I'm ten-to-one in tanks. Three-to-one in planes. Three-to-one in artillery. We can't lose to the Germans."

Bandy studies Eisenhower a beat.

"General. You don't mind my saying so, you don't look too happy about it."

"I am most days, Charley. Right now, I'm not."

"Can I ask why, sir?"

"Because we still might lose to the British."

"Monty."

Eisenhower lets Bandy say the name. The General nods.

Field Marshal Bernard Law Montgomery. The English hero of El Alamein, the most popular general with the British people since Wellington and the least liked of all the Anglo officers among the Americans.

In the American press corps, the enmity between Montgomery and Eisenhower—including Ike's general officers, mainly Patton and Bradley—is well known, even if it goes unreported. Monty is viewed by the American brass as something far less than the Great Captain the British press makes him out to be. The Americans remember past battles: Sicily, Falaise, and particularly the debacle of Market-Garden, Monty's brainchild, where he was thwarted in a spectacular land-air effort to clear a path through Holland into northern Germany. That collapse was costly and embarrassing. Given the responsibility of opening the Dutch port of Antwerp, Monty captured the city but failed to open the port approaches in the Scheldt estuary, leaving them in German hands. Because of this all Allied forces are suffering logistical shortages. Field Marshal Montgomery is thought by the Americans to be too considered and cautious in his conduct of battle. He is a master of the "set piece" strategy, where every item of combat is subjected to a timetable and prescribed course of action. Patton, the old warhorse who gallops at every opportunity, has called Monty a "tired old fart," a general who always wants more and accomplishes less than any other officer in the Allied forces. The American style in battle is to probe and exploit. Monty tends to be inflexible and tidy. But Montgomery is Prime Minister Churchill's favorite, and he does possess a record of valor from the years before the Americans joined the war effort.

Monty has lobbied Churchill to be named the single commander of all land forces in western Europe, the role he filled with success during the Normandy campaign. But once the Americans were fully in the war and supplying the lion's share of men and materiel, it was deemed inappropriate in Washington and Paris for their troops to be commanded by an Englishman. In September Monty was forced to hand land forces command over to Eisenhower and accept relegation to army group command, on an equal level with General Bradley. Ike, the Supreme Commander in Europe, has kept the role of ground forces C-in-C for himself and will not surrender it to Monty. Or Churchill. He won't have it.

The greatest difference between Monty and Ike, besides their personalities, is Monty's desire to press toward Berlin in a concerted strike through northern Germany. His mighty Twenty-first Army Group is assembled north of Aachen. That force includes the American First and Ninth Armies; these were assigned to Monty under duress when they were caught north of the German bulge in December. Churchill, Montgomery, and the British Chiefs of Staff together harangue Eisenhower, General Marshall, and Roosevelt to assign the northern route a priority of men and materiel. They want a quick end to the war, surely, and they want the British to be the ones to bring it about, by a charge into Berlin with Montgomery at the head. They argue that one "full-blooded"—Monty's words—strike through the northern edge of the West Wall, the fortified Siegfried Line, on a direct salient to Berlin, is the best way to gain a decisive victory. They will skirt the industrial Ruhr pocket, to surround it later in a linkup with southern forces. Along the way, the Twenty-first Army will liberate all of Holland and put a clamp on the Nazi V-1 and V-2 rocket bombs, which continue from there to curse London. Monty met twice last year with Eisenhower. During one of the meetings, on board Ike's plane, Monty launched into such a tirade over Berlin that Ike had to lay his hand on the Field Marshal's leg and remind him, "Steady, Monty. You can't talk to me like this. I'm your boss." Montgomery backed down to Eisenhower, but not over Berlin. He wrote Ike a letter on November thirtieth. In unsparing language, he insisted again on a change in the American direction of the battle for western Europe. In December, Churchill himself arranged a conference with Eisenhower to lobby for the northern route and Montgomery's command of the operation.

Again, Ike wouldn't have it.

Eisenhower is caught between two charismatic, adulated, demanding generals: Monty in the north, Patton in the south. Both men want priority for their missions, extol the virtues of their plans, and claim they can steamroll Germany and finish off Hitler. Eisenhower has more responsibility than fighting battles; he must keep together the Anglo-American military alliance. He tries to appease. He has the flaw of many Americans, the desire to be liked, to keep everyone—even subordinates—happy. In doing so, Ike has allowed his generals a great deal of leeway, even in choosing their own objectives. Monty has chosen Berlin. Patton sometimes sounds like he's set his sights on Moscow.

Bandy has spent time with both generals. He knows they possess egos that can't be appeased. And news stories of their victories make them happiest. That's why they, like Eisenhower, talk to Charley Bandy, *Life* magazine's top shooter.

The plan for Monty's "full-blooded" thrust calls for an assault through Hitler's West Wall, a vast concrete phalanx of tank barriers and pillboxes running the length of the German border with France, Belgium, Luxembourg, and part of Holland. Monty's Twenty-first will cross the Rhine and press on to the Elbe River, then to Berlin. Eisenhower agrees that a northern thrust would be deadly to Hitler. But he is concerned that such an attack, if mounted too early or independent of southern support from Bradley, will expose Montgomery's long right flank to counterattacks from the Ruhr plain. If those attacks were strong enough, they could sever Monty's supply lines and perhaps destroy the leading armies, a risk Ike will not take this late in the war. At present, with the failure to open the Belgian port of Antwerp, all materiel for the troops continues to flow from the Normandy beaches. Every mile beyond the Rhine is a mile added to that problem.

Instead, Ike insists on a broad-front strategy, with the support of Marshall and Roosevelt. As Supreme Commander, it's his judgment that the most prudent endgame is to engage the Germans on a vast front, closing to the Rhine River all the way from the Swiss border to Arnhem in Holland, reasoning that every German soldier they take care of on the west side of the Rhine is one they won't face on the other side. By engaging the enemy on so vast a front, something, somewhere, is bound to give. When it does, Ike will respond to the opportunity and commit in force. It might be Monty and his northern front, it could be Bradley up the middle, perhaps Patton breaking through in the south. If Berlin becomes a realistic and necessary military goal through any of these portals into Germany, and if the Reds don't take the city first, Eisenhower has said he will pursue it.

The war is won. The sole question left is who will claim the kill and hold up the head for history. Bandy doesn't blame Eisenhower for wanting it to be a Yank any more than he condemns Monty for wanting it to be a Tommy or Joe Stalin for laying the whip to his Red Army to keep them in the race.

Of course, Bandy wants it to be an American force that takes Berlin. He imagines the jeep ride into the enemy's capital. The pictures he'll take of the Stars and Stripes flying over the Reichstag. He sees one more cover of *Life* framed for his study in Tennessee.

"Monty," Bandy repeats, rolling the name on his tongue. It feels cool there, like a lozenge. A good nickname never hurts. "What'd he do this time?"

Eisenhower grins. Bandy can tell this is a mask face. Ike is plenty irked at something.

"Don't you read the papers, Charley?"

"I've been on a boat, General."

"When'd you get in?"

"London yesterday. Here this morning."

"What've you been doing, son?"

"Sleeping. Sir."

Eisenhower draws on his Camel. His grin stays there even while he exhales, hung like a curved wedge of moon over a dastardly act. Uh-oh, Bandy thinks. He is pissed.

"The Bulge." The name comes out with the smoke; Bandy pictures that the word itself is fuming in Eisenhower's mouth.

Ike stabs two fingers of his right hand at the map, at the Schnee Eiffel forests, near the German-Luxembourg border.

"The Germans attacked to the west here. They split Bradley's group, with the First and Ninth caught north. So I gave them to Monty. Temporarily. Patton ate me out for it, but that's George. I did it because it was the only way I could be sure Monty would commit his reserves. George and Brad felt that the German flank was exposed, and an attack by George's Third Army northward toward Houffalize and St-Vith could relieve Bastogne and cut the Germans in half."

Eisenhower's two fingers dice the air above the map. Bandy does not look at the chart, he studies the everyman face. He wishes he could photograph the General right now, this is one of the more commanding moments he has seen with Ike.

"Monty didn't think George could launch an offensive from the south, didn't believe the German flank was vulnerable. And he thought that Hodges' First would take weeks to organize a counteroffensive out of the north."

Ike's pointing hand, clutching the Camel, returns to his mouth. Ike seems to prefer speaking of Montgomery accompanied by smoke.

"He was wrong."

Eisenhower opens his hand now, palm flat, polishing the map in quick strokes.

"Monty told Hodges to disengage and pull back. Instead, on December twenty-ninth, Hodges launched a counteroffensive out of the north. Bradley and George took the bottom of the pincer, came roaring hell out of the south all the way to Bastogne, and the whole time Brad is yelling at me on the phone to make Monty launch a full and immediate counterattack out of the north. But what's Monty do?"

Bandy says nothing. Eisenhower doesn't want an answer, the General doesn't look up from his map, swelling with anger at the recollection.

"Nothing. He does nothing but submit a plan to wait until January third, more than a week after Hodges' first counteroffensive in the north. Oh, and let me tell you his plan was neat. Crackerjack. Very clean little battle plan, phase by phase."

Eisenhower fills his lungs again with the Camel. "Monty." He says the Field Marshal's name the way a dragon would say it. Ike is fully angry now.

"Charley, this is off the record?"

"General, I don't write anything down. I just take pictures."

"All right. Follow me."

Eisenhower leads Bandy away from the map table through a maze of rooms filled with desks, all of them occupied. Everyone looks up when the Supreme Commander strides by in his trademark waistcoat and pleats. Passing, Ike glances down at each desk until he finds what he is hunting for. That morning's London *Times*. He scoops it from the desktop of a female officer, who tries to smile. Ike grins back. "Thank you," he tells her.

Ike slaps Bandy in the gut with the folded paper, to make the point that this is how it hit him.

Bandy sits in a chair opposite the pretty officer behind the desk. He opens the paper to the front page. Ike furls his arms and waits. The General stands over Bandy, in the center of a hive of desks and junior officers, typists, clerks, messengers. Activity in the room is suppressed, people go on tiptoe or bear down into their desk work.

The lead article in the *Times* hails Montgomery as the savior of the Battle of the Bulge.

Bandy reads. General Bradley held a press conference yesterday to state that the First and Ninth Armies were

assigned to Montgomery on a strictly temporary basis, and
that these American forces were pivotal in the fighting in the
Ardennes. The British press responded with an attack on
Bradley and other U.S. generals, claiming that there is afoot a
concerted effort in the American camp to deflect credit
from Montgomery. The thrust of the articles was all Monty.
Monty again to the rescue. Monty must be named ground
commander of all Allied forces in western Europe. Monty
was brilliant, bold at the Bulge. Monty.

Eisenhower taps Bandy on the shoulder. "Come with
me. Not in front of the help."

The Supreme Commander walks back to the large map
room. He takes up his station, hovering in the skies above
Europe where he moves millions of men, creates clouds.

"Charley."

"Yes, General."

"The son of a bitch."

"Yes, sir."

"He called a press conference. Three days ago in Brussels. Brad heard it on the radio and almost had a conniption,
called me and then I heard it. Know what Monty said?"

"No, sir."

"Well, I'm gonna tell you. He said he won the damn battle. Said he directed it. Said, and I'm quoting the son of a
bitch here, the battle was one of the most interesting and
tricky he has ever handled. *He* has ever handled. Said the situation looked like it might become awkward. That he took
certain steps to make sure the Germans were contained, that
he was thinking ahead the whole time. Charley."

"Yes, General."

"You know what the kicker is?"

"No, sir."

Eisenhower laughs now, sardonic, disbelieving.

"As of two days ago, the Germans started pulling back.
They're going to wind up losing about a hundred thousand
men. American casualties are going to be somewhere
around seventy or eighty thousand. You know what the

British are gonna lose? About two thousand men. Two thousand. And Monty."

Eisenhower must take another drag; this finishes the cigarette, burnt like a fuse to an explosive. He tosses the butt on the floor and grinds it.

"Monty," the General breathes, "and I'm quoting here, said he had employed the whole available power of the British group of armies. That he had British troops fighting on both sides of the Americans, who he admitted suffered a hard blow."

Bandy watches Ike scratch his chin. "A hard blow. Eighty thousand American boys. Monty loses two thousand. What fighting he does do is with two of Brad's armies. And he calls a press conference to tell the world he was the savior of the Americans. He doesn't say a thing about Courtney Hodges or the Hundred and first Airborne surrounded at Bastogne. He doesn't mention Brad or George, who both tell me they'll resign if I make Monty ground C-in-C. He doesn't let the cat out of the bag that for every single British soldier fighting at the Bulge we had forty."

Ike sucks in his cheeks like he wants to spit. "Savior."

The General takes the newspaper from Bandy's grasp. He wads it and rattles it over the giant map, as though to shake the black words off the thin new sheets, separate them and sprinkle them like raindrops over western Europe and the American troops bunched there in the blue crayon arrows; let the American soldier defeat those words like they beat the Germans, let truth win by their hands. Bandy sees one more photograph for the ages slide by, untaken.

Eisenhower retracts the newspaper. He folds the pages, then drops the lump on the table.

Ike's storm has passed. "Field Marshal Montgomery and I," he says with theatrical quiet, "will discuss this at a later date."

The General smiles again. He sees Bandy in front of him, not Monty.

"I'm sorry, Charley, did you come to see me about something, or was this a social call?"

"I do have a favor I'd like to ask of you, General."

"Fire away."

"Well, sir, if I'm right, there doesn't seem to be much of the war left."

"I hope you're right."

"Then, I was hoping you might give me a tip as to where the action's going to be."

"Action."

"I've got a job to do, General. Pictures of the officers' mess don't pay the bills."

"You haven't seen enough action, son?"

"My wife call you?"

Eisenhower chuckles. Bandy knows how to play the brave bumpkin.

He presses. "General, there's going to be lots of newsies here in these last few months. Guys who haven't even got their feet wet. Me, I figure I've earned a leg up by this point. It's what I came back for. The end. I want to be there. Not chasing off somewhere else far from it, looking at someone else's photos and kicking myself. That's for the others."

"I see." Eisenhower winces, considering. "The end."

"Yes, sir. Can you point me? Where should I head to have the best shot? Whose army?"

"You want me to guess."

"Who better, General?"

Bandy holds still while Eisenhower mulls this request over. Without more words from either, the General's gaze goes to the big table map. Ike calculates for moments. His hand wanders over the chart, sensing contours, troops, possibilities, personalities, enemies.

"Action, son?"

"Yes, sir."

Ike's fingers wriggle in the low firmament over an area south of Montgomery's force, north of Patton. He studies the American front line at the middle, facing the Ruhr region, site of seventy-five percent of Germany's remaining industry, seventy percent of their coal.

Eisenhower lifts his eyes to meet Bandy's. The General's

look is sympathetic, paternal, as though at this last second he wants the younger man with the wife and tobacco farm at home, who has already lived in harm's way more than most soldiers, to reconsider his entreaty for action. The look asks: Son, are you one of those unlucky men who is at his most alive in the presence of death? Bandy makes a forgiving smile.

Like a crashing spear, one of the General's fingers lands and sticks. Bandy leans over to read.

Ike has spiked a spot on the northern reaches of the Siegfried Line.

Beneath his nail is the lethal Hürtgen Forest.

"Right here, Charley."

January 14, 1945, 0700 hours
Magnuszew bridgehead
West bank of the Vistula River
Poland

THERE HAVE BEEN NO ORDERS ISSUED FOR THE ATTACK. But the canny foot soldier learns to read the signs of his army the way a timber wolf reads his forest. Ilya smells food. When the cooks move their kitchens up, that means only one thing. You are going forward.

The offensive will erupt this morning.

The jingle-jangle of pot-laden mess wagons splits the thick mist. Last night was starry, but at midnight a heavy fog rolled in. Ilya cannot imagine ordering an attack this morning, with visibility down to four or five meters. There can be no air cover in this chilly haze. But there it is, the unmistakable aroma of eggs and frying potatoes salting the air.

Ilya sits up in the trench. He shrugs his great shoulders. They ache, sopped with dew and cold from the riverbank night. His blanket is wet. He runs a hand over his shaved pate and slides off his woolen cap, uses it to wipe his eyes. Misha next to him has spilled from under his blanket in the night and curled into a little ball, a filthy puppy. Ilya covers Misha with both blankets now and rises. Misha mumbles and will not wake.

Ilya tracks the smell and sound of the carts. Loudspeakers blare Russian folk music across no-man's-land at the German lines to hide the clatter of preparations, another sure sign that the hour is near. Last night, sappers will have crawled out to clear mines from in front of the Russian trenches, and even dared go as far as they could to do the same in front of the German positions. The mist helped with that much of the operation, but this morning the attack will be more difficult without the Red Air Force Stormoviks spreading a carpet of bombs and bullets in advance. Oh, well, Ilya thinks. The artillery doesn't need to see what they're doing. All their targets are presighted. And in the infantry, you shoot anything facing you. Simple.

Two dawns ago, Koniev's First Ukrainian Front jumped off from their Sandomierz bridgehead on the Vistula a hundred kilometers to the south. They'll slash northwest, while Ilya's force—the First Byelorussian Front—will battle straight westward. They'll all line up on the border to Germany, the river Oder, eighty kilometers from Berlin.

Ilya reaches the A Company mess wagon. Without asking for it, he is handed a double portion. Misha will get the same when he rallies and comes for breakfast. The cooks, everyone in the company, know who stole the First Guards Tank Army banner. Others shamble forward, accept steaming tin plates, and squat to eat. On each of their coats is sewn a black-and-orange patch from First Tank. This is Misha's doing. When the tank army's flag was discovered fluttering on the pole outside Chuikov's Eighth Guards HQ, a note was found pinned to it identifying the penal battalion, A Company. For days afterward the men of the company bragged and strutted, many of them holding their chins high for the first time in a long while, though they did not know who among them had pulled off the prank. The commander and commissar of A Company held a meeting, demanding to know who was responsible. Misha stepped forward. The soldiers held their breath, figuring the little coward was going to rat on their unknown hero. Misha insisted he would tell, but only if First Guards Tank Army surrendered one hundred fifty patches for the entire company to wear as trophies. "Victory must have a prize," he intoned. The commissar gave his word. Misha thumped his own chest. "Me."

Misha spent three days in the stockade. When he came out, Ilya hugged him, then sewed on his friend's First Tank patch. Over the next week, Misha told each member of the company, swearing them one by one to secrecy, that Ilya was the leader of their escapade and they could never tell because Ilya was as ferocious as he looked. Misha figured the news would filter upward to the company and battalion officers, and there would be no further negative repercussions.

The little man's voice grumbles through the fog behind Ilya.

"It's today."

"No question."

Misha collects his rations, pushes half of it onto Ilya's plate, and sits.

"You know who's out there, Ilyushka?"

"The Germans."

"The Ninth Army. One of the best armies in the whole *Wehrmacht*. General von Lüttwitz commanding. He's the latest in a long line of great generals with the Ninth. Model and von Bock both made Field Marshal out of there. Lüttwitz is good, and he fights."

Ilya shakes his head, polishes off the extra eggs. "How do you know this?"

"I ask questions. That's what I do. Intelligence. Besides, I spent three days at HQ in the stockade. When I can't ask, I listen."

Ilya sets down his plate. He pushes his gaze through the mist, past Misha, at the others gathering for their last hot meal before the assault. They're a ragged bunch, careless with their demeanor. Their pride in the successful pilferage two weeks ago has been worn off by hard labor, cold ground, and the wait. These soldiers are resigned to being on the crest of the coming attack, where the penal company stays. And if they don't get killed in today's assault, then the next one. Most of them are country boys, simpletons who broke one rule too many or mouthed off to a superior. There are a few black-sheep officers, like Misha and Ilya, but those men keep to themselves. There is little camaraderie in the company; the faces change. Men are killed, go AWOL, wind up in the brig, or get a bullet in the back of the head for more serious infractions. The battalion commissar tries hard to meld them together with communist fervor. But these slumping men are just broken spirits slogging out what will likely prove to be their last days in earthly form.

Misha says the Ninth Army is one of the best. They had better be, Ilya thinks, because they have not fought Russians before like the ones they'll fight today. The Red soldiers and officers of the main ranks will battle hard, true enough. They're well trained and have the finest mass of weapons ever assembled. By this point in the war, the Reds are toughened and wise to the man. And Ilya doesn't worry about the fighting mettle of his penal company. They'll go all out too, either to die with some final honor attached to their names or to win their way back to their regular units, like Ilya and Misha. The German Ninth knows how well the Soviet army fights; for two years they've been backpedaling in front of them across western Russia and the Ukraine, starting at Stalingrad. The ruthlessness of the German retreat from their occupied territories is seared into the mind's eye of every Ivan soldier on the front: scorched villages, brutalized women, senseless butchery. The Germans must know they will face a determined enemy today.

But the men of the second echelon, the mop-up wave behind the Red frontline troops. These are men the Ninth Army has not yet seen. These are animals.

In the past twenty months, the advancing army has liberated hundreds of thousands of Soviet soldiers from German prison camps. These men have been tortured, starved, and humiliated by their captors. They've been slaves on their own soil, and those of their comrades who escaped did so as corpses. Now the survivors have been set free to seek their vengeance, with a fanatical hatred.

Comrade Stalin has ordered that all freed POWs fit for service be fed, clothed, issued arms, and sent back into battle. But the *vozhd* does not trust these men entirely; they have been in the presence of the enemy. So, they are segregated into the second tier of soldiers, behind the main attack forces. Once the enemy's front lines have been broken, the Red Army regulars will continue to press the attack, battling their way forward, while the second echelon follows along in ever-swelling numbers.

Ilya has seen their crazed "mopping-up" work: German soldiers bound face-to-face with wire, a grenade stuck between their chests and the pin pulled. Piles of burning corpses smoldering an hour after they dropped their weapons alive. Mutilated bodies of men left naked in subzero weather, their testicles cut off. Machine gun cross fire over open fields, blood and bullet holes desecrating white flags of surrender. More, Ilya has seen.

Some say, "If Stalin knew, he would stop it." Ilya is certain, Stalin knows.

He wonders what these wild men will do once they are across the Oder, on German ground. They are not being reined in by their officers. They're being stoked to a rage by the bellows of communist rhetoric, Kill, Kill, Kill! The revenge-taking will get worse.

By 0730, rumbling activity is everywhere in the Magnuszew bridgehead. Ilya and Misha return to their trench dodging rolling tanks, wagon after wagon of artillery ammunition, and columns of trucks collecting bedrolls and blankets to be redistributed later. The fog makes the bustle dicey, the two hear a shrouded collision between vehicles.

Climbing down into their trench, Misha checks everything. He counts his rounds, attaches his four-sided bayonet to his rifle, tightens his bootlaces. His small white hands flutter about like nervous, lost chicks.

"Misha."

Misha does not look up from his busyness. Ilya layers a great hand over his friend's shoulder. Misha stops fidgeting.

"What?"

"You stay with me. All day. All night. Tomorrow, Misha. Stay three steps behind me."

"I'm not a coward, Ilya."

"All right." Ilya grants a broad smile. "Four steps."

Their laughter is buried beneath a sudden rise in the volume of the folk music blaring from the loudspeakers, there are tambourines and fiddles played by titans in the woods.

Ilya checks his watch. 0810 hours.

Eyes locked together, their faces turn grim. They both nod, and that is the seal.

At 0825, a metallic din rends the fog. This is the sound of artillery pieces of all sizes—mammoth 280mm's down to mortars, stacked wheel to wheel—loading shells. Ilya and Misha stuff cigarette butts in their ears.

The fog begins to swirl over the westward Vistula valley. The earth of Poland seems to inhale, sucking in its breath, girding itself. The sun stays locked out behind dense low clouds. Ilya's and Misha's elbows touch where they watch over the top of the trench. Two million other men of varying nations, of different tongues and intent, also stare into the mist, from both sides of it.

The first salvos rollick the ground. There is no time for echoes, the damp air is whipped, becomes frothy with reports from long barrels and turrets. The racket increases, seeming against logic not to be hundreds or even the actual tens of thousands of detonations but one gargantuan explosion that throbs but never wanes. The blast issues from the rear; Ilya turns around, the forest is full of fire-belching mouths, the fog is shredded then regroups, to be sundered again and again by orange tongues from endless death's-heads. The shells blister past over their helmets. Misha grips his pot with both hands and pulls down. Ilya returns his gaze to the west. He sees in the mist great deeds, destruction and redemption.

The smoke from the barrage adds its sheath to the fog until visibility is almost nil. The sulfurous powder stench waters Ilya's eyes. He has hunkered beneath bombardments before; at Stalingrad in August of '42 the Germans razed the city with a two-day artillery and airborne assault. Buildings there crumbled into brick hills and twists of metal, flames scoured every inch. Ilya, like every infantryman, has sat out several artillery attacks. But neither he nor any Soviet soldier has ever found himself beneath the sort of concentration of shells the Germans endure right now.

If you're not killed outright or sliced by shrapnel or whizzing debris, you're dazed. If you can see at all, your vision is blurred. Perhaps your ears and nose bleed from pressure bursts. Without question you have lost men in your company; officers in targeted bunkers lie in clusters, their orders silenced. Confusion courses through the lines. With what vision and hearing you retain, you will soon see and hear the charging screams and raking gunfire of an attacking Russian horde. With what nerve you can summon, you must rise and defend your life.

The pounding of the guns and the explosions of shells plague the ground. Waiting for the break in the bombardment and the signal to charge, Ilya replays in his head his knowledge of General Zhukov's strategies. The massive barrage will range up to seven kilometers deep into the enemy lines. Swaths of earth one hundred fifty meters wide are being left untrammeled by the artillery; these are lanes the infantry and their close support tanks will rush down in the initial attack to the Germans' first line of defense. Once the infantry has engaged, they will punch holes in the enemy fortifications. Then the full tank armies will uncoil to drive through these breaches, fanning out into the German rear, disrupting communications and support and disorganizing reserves. If the Soviets move forward with enough speed, they'll bar the paths by which the enemy's forward forces might retire. With luck and momentum, they might also beat the Germans to their own prepared retreat bastions and prevent organized stands. The tank armies will continue to press ahead. The infantry will do its best to catch up, leaving the fearsome second echelon behind to solidify gains and silence further resistance.

The initial wave will not be the whole gathered force of the Soviet infantry but rather swarms of forward battalions in attack teams. Their job will be to overwhelm the outermost German defenses and reconnoiter. Engineers will clear mines. German strong points that survived the opening salvos will be sighted for more artillery. The fighting will be at close quarters.

The penal battalion of the Eighth Guards Army is in this vanguard.

At 0855 the guns rest. The barrage lasted for twenty-five minutes. It was shorter than Ilya expected. It's the mist, he thinks. Why waste shells when you can't see what you're doing? Time to send in the men and rifles. Have them deliver their intimate brand of firepower.

Ilya's legs and feet tense. The river valley in front of him seems choked, too packed for him to spring out of this trench and run into. The land is already welling with the thickest mist and smoke, echoes of the hot-barreled weapons behind him rumble like summer thunder. The fog bristles with hatred. There is blood to be spilled in there.

Needles prick Ilya's skin. His stomach has something alive in it. It is always this way before the attack.

He stares ahead, does not look over to Misha. He will protect Misha, but he will not crawl into the man's grave for him.

Life, Ilya thinks. Thank you, you are beautiful. I cherish you. Now, help me embrace you, and take you from others.

From somewhere, it doesn't matter, an order is given. Charge.

Ilya fleers back his lips, baring his teeth. Now he turns to Misha. The little man startles at Ilya's face only for a moment, then takes its tone for his own. He opens his mouth, scrunching his eyes and cheeks. Together they scream, "Ur-rahh!!"

Around them ten thousand soldiers shrill their courage.

Ilya erupts from the trench in a bound, Misha seems to levitate beside him, and they gallop into the fog. Ilya carries a PPSh submachine gun, with a rate of fire of nine hundred rounds per minute. He is loaded like a mule with extra clips, grenades, a trenching tool, knives, binoculars, but he does not feel any of his burden. Across his back is strapped a Moisin-Nagant rifle, the same model rifle Misha points and fires at nothing. Ilya fires a burst too, just to feel the machine gun, to run behind the bullets, to be drawn into the vacuum of their plunge.

Ilya and Misha funnel with the rest of the battalion into one of the lanes left by the artillery. The ground to their left has been plowed and gouged, smoke billows up as though from hell. Tanks growl at their heels, urging them to hurry. Small arms fire erupts ahead; the lead troops have already found the enemy.

Ilya diverts off the smooth path, Misha in his steps. Two dozen or more others follow, to flank the German trenches ahead. Nothing but black water and earth is in the bottom of the craters they sidestep, but on the edges and mounds lie hundreds of shredded humans and bits of them. Some of the enemy crawl and moan, but none reach for their guns, so Ilya keeps running among them. The sounds of fighting mount ahead. Ilya leads the impromptu squad, circling to his right. He glimpses on several shoulders the black-and-orange patch of the First Guards Tank Army, won for them by Misha.

A bullet rips into one of the soldiers behind Ilya. The man goes down hard on his back, his heels flail in the dirt. Several men drop at the fire, another tends to the wounded man. Ilya is not these men's officer. He cannot issue orders. He presses ahead, they will follow or not. Misha is solid behind him.

"Spread out, Mishushka. In this fog we're easier to see if we lump up."

Ilya strides ahead warily. The mist and battle haze halt his vision at no more than ten meters. He can tell from clashing sounds that just fifty meters ahead there is combat. He reaches to his belt to unsheathe a knife. He clenches it in his teeth. It is frigid, he lays his tongue with care beneath the blade, for he has whetted the steel to a keen edge. He growls around the dagger.

Ilya breaks into a zigzagging jog. His PPSh is leveled, searching. A shape darker than the fog moves against the ground. Ilya hardens his grip on the machine gun to keep it from rearing, and yanks the trigger. He runs at the figure, pouring bullets at it from the hip. The fog closes where the German was. Then another pops up, and another, three more. Ilya keeps running forward, the weapon in his hands roaring, growing hot. Two of the men twist under Ilya's spray, the third ducks. Ilya is too close now to hit the ground and wait. The German will lob a grenade in another second. He hears nothing around him but the *unh-unh-unh* of his breathing, and his boots bring him to the brow of the trench the moment the German's arm flings a potato masher grenade. The thing strikes Ilya in the chest and bounces back into the trench. Ilya looks down into the man's flabbergasted face. Ilya takes two large steps back. The grenade interrupts the German's howl.

Ilya drops into the trench, hunkering low. Three mangled bodies lie at his feet but he wastes no time and pushes forward. He drools from the knife in his teeth, he cannot close his mouth over it, but he imagines a vision of himself with the blade there, weapons barbing every inch of him stepping with purpose along the enemy trench, through smoke, saliva on his chin; it is fierce and he likes it. The skin prickles are gone now.

January 18, 1945, 2:00 P.M.
The House of Commons
London

CHURCHILL TATTOOS HIS CANE ON THE GROUND TO GIVE a meter to his thoughts. He doesn't like it when ideas duck him. The man sitting across the wide, decorative hall, Anthony Eden, his Foreign Secretary, watches in a composed fashion, with legs crossed at the ankles. Handsome devil, Churchill thinks. Lucky. Tall, lean, full moustache. Young. I was young once. But never the rest.

"What do the Americans call it, Anthony?" the Prime Minister asks, shifting in his chair to put both heels on the floor. "In these situations."

Eden cocks his head. "I don't follow."

"Eating something. They call it eating something. It eludes me at the moment."

"Yes. Yes, I've heard that. What is it?"

"I can't recall, Anthony. That's why I'm asking you."

"I see." Eden mirrors Churchill's erect posture in his seat.

The men glance together into the lofty and dark ceiling of the waiting chamber to the House. Churchill taps his cane more on the linoleum between his shiny black boots. Eden drums his fingers.

Eden speaks first. "Is it 'crow,' Winston? I believe it is."

Churchill considers this response. "Eating crow. Yes. I believe you've got it. That's it. Sounds unsavory. Thank you."

The Prime Minister stops the light pounding of his cane. He layers both hands atop the gold knob and leans forward to prop his chin there, like a head on a pike. He is hungry and aggravated, the corner of his mouth wants a cigar to chomp. In the vast Parliament hall he can hear the MPs and his Cabinet members filing to their places on the benches.

Without lifting his head from his hands, he asks Eden, "Why crow?"

"Beg pardon?"

"Crow. It's a raven. Why is eating it an act of humility? Feathers, do you think? Like being a chicken?"

"I'm sure I don't know, Winston." Eden shrugs, head held high, legs crossed again, fingers knitted in his lap, like a poster for suits. "The Americans."

Churchill grinds his ample chin into the backs of his hands. "Yes, the Americans."

He feels sweaty. Not nerves, he thinks; a fever, a cold coming. Some cool champagne after this session, a hot bath, and to bed. That'll do the trick. Can't get sick. Must KBO. Keep Buggering On.

He says, "Not as good as our humble pie, is it."

Eden screws up his face. Churchill won't get off it.

The Prime Minister continues. "Humble pie. That says it, right? Not crow at all, Anthony. Plain and simple, English humble pie. That's what I'm eating."

"Yes, Winston."

"Hmpf," huffs Churchill, slumping his shoulders even rounder, down toward the cane and the floor tiles, like a body that has indeed lost its head.

"The Americans. Crow. Nonsense."

In the House a gavel sounds. Churchill sits up. He adjusts the thick leather folder in his lap. He doesn't need these papers. He totes everything in his head, heart, and in his gut. In another few minutes he'll move it all to where it does England the most good, to his mouth.

Churchill sees in his mind's eye the magnificent House of Commons. Parliament, the Zeus of history. So much grandeur; nation upon nation around the world for centuries have awaited word from this august body like children seeking permission from pater. Britannia. Empire.

Humble pie.

"We're broke, Anthony."

"Yes, I suppose we are. Damn."

"We've bled ourselves white in this war. We're in hock up to our ears to the Americans. And do you know what the irony is?"

"It is we who have won the war."

"Yes!" Churchill stamps down with his cane and a boot. "It was England rose first against the Germans. For two years. Two years, alone in Europe, alone in Africa. But, ho! The Battle of Britain, Anthony. The Battle of Britain."

"'Our finest hour.'" Eden quotes Churchill.

The Prime Minister nods while the projector in his head replays scenes of cat scratch smoke trails above London, bursts of airplanes and lives, crashes and prayers, history dictated by British pluck.

He raises a fist to Eden. Whenever Churchill speaks of his fighting Tommies, he inflates with pride. "We did lay a nice welt under the Hun's eye, didn't we?"

Eden smiles. "Yes, we bloody well did, Prime Minister."

"We damn well held them off."

This statement by Churchill, intended to be an accolade for Britain, tolls some unseen bell, and the mood of the two men lifts. The bell rings of truth. Both men, all of England, know it.

We did hold the Germans off, until the Americans and Russians could rearm. Until those two giant powers could step in and save England.

Churchill grunts at the notion. America and Russia. Franklin and Uncle Joe.

Save England.

Britain is in decline, he thinks, yes. But we have spent ourselves in the name of freedom. And rather than give us a hand up to reward England for her courage and sacrifice, Franklin Roosevelt wants us to crawl beside America into bed with the Bolsheviks.

No. Britain will kiss Stalin on two cheeks, but never on all four.

"Anthony."

"Yes, Winston."

"I can suffer any humiliation, you know. Carry any burden."

"As can we all."

"But I cannot stand by and let England fade. We have been too great."

Ah, Churchill sighs. Perhaps too great, for too long?

Roosevelt will not meet him in Malta before the conference in Yalta. Afraid of offending Uncle Joe, though there is much to talk about with the end of the war nearing. Only as a concession, Roosevelt agreed last week to let his Secretary of State Stettinius attend the conference at Malta, for one day. One paltry day. Churchill will have to settle for half a loaf. Politics will wait for Yalta, but meanwhile they'll hold a military session with the Combined Chiefs of Staff.

Churchill says, "Stalin I understand. He's a rotter. Fair enough. But what do we do with Roosevelt?"

Eden shrugs. "We endure. England always endures. Stiff upper lip, cheerio, all that. You're a historian. Who knows better?"

Churchill considers England's endurance. Wars, pestilence, conquerors, perfidy, but never such indignities as have been meted out in this war. Never.

"No lover," he says, "ever studied every whim of his mistress as I have those of President Roosevelt."

"Feeling jilted, Prime Minister?"

Churchill ignores the titter from Eden. "Why," he asks, "is Roosevelt so dead set against an English empire? It's our tradition. We maintain colonies around the world instead of trade pacts in Europe. We like our independence here on our little island nation. How many wars have we fought to safeguard it? Why is he so convinced that his vision of a world order is better than ours?"

Eden replies, "When you consider that the United States, a former British colony herself, hasn't done so badly."

"Exactly! And tell me, Anthony, what if after all their adventurism in Europe and their lofty goals for Euro-Russian cooperation, the Yanks pull another disappearing act? What if their renowned isolationism rears its head after this war and we're left alone again, this time with a charred continent and a hungry Russian bear licking its chops? What if America's efforts to civilize the Soviets fail? Uncle Sam might well slip out of Europe like he did after World War I. And who's left behind? You and me and Uncle Joe."

"No worries. The United Nations will see that everything goes smooth as a baby's bum."

Churchill harrumphs. "Yes. Well, if the Russians can't be convinced to treat the Poles with any more decency than I've seen, I daresay we can't attach too much value to Roosevelt's fancy."

Churchill feels too tired to continue in this vein. Like

Adam charged with naming the Garden's animals, he surveys a horizon of slights both to England and himself, large and small, public and private, too many to line up for labels. Stop, he bids. America is in fact England's greatest friend. And the truth. They and Russia did save you. What they do now they do only to become stronger themselves. England knows about this sort of smiling treachery, surely.

One last creature, an ebony bird, hops up to Churchill and begs for a name. Churchill smiles to himself at his wit, and names it "crow." Come here, he thinks, you bastard.

"What," Churchill asks Eden, "are we to do with Montgomery?"

The Field Marshal is England's only hope for any final glory in this war. His Twenty-first Army Group is best positioned of all the Anglo-American forces to take Berlin. We might still fly the Union Jack from the Brandenburg Gate, if Monty will just keep his cool. And the West must take Berlin, if we're to have any bargaining power over Stalin at war's end. Red forces will be standing on the throats of all of eastern Europe, and with Stalin's voracious appetite for territory, plus his short memory regarding signed agreements, they'll stay there unless we have something Stalin wants.

Eden shakes his head. "It'll be a cold day in hell before Eisenhower names Monty Ground Commander."

"Ground Commander! Ha! Eisenhower wanted to fire him, for God's sake! It's not bad enough that we've got less than one tenth of the men in combat in Europe. It's not sufficiently embarrassing that Stalin chides Roosevelt about me like a schoolboy nipping a mate for an ugly date at a party. Or that the sun is setting on the British Empire, on my watch! Our own Field Marshal Montgomery almost got himself sacked by Eisenhower!"

"The man can't keep his ego in check."

"Hmm. He should spend a day in my bloody shoes for a lesson in that."

"He disguises his contempt for the American generals so badly."

One more tap of the cane. Relations between the

English and American armed forces have never been this low, all over this silly episode of hubris.

"Putting it mildly, Anthony?"

Eden chuckles. "A bit."

Churchill surveys the problem. Montgomery thinks the Americans lack organization. The American way doesn't rest well with the Field Marshal. From his standpoint, the U.S. Army relies too much on subordinates, expecting lower-level commanders to make decisions on the run, to take the initiative even in the absence of orders. This is a large part of the American psyche, go, go, go. But we British are more reserved, cautious. The long-held practice of our military is to rely on a battle plan, conservation of resources, superiority in numbers. It may seem stodgy to some, but England has carved an empire armed with this mind-set. Even so, we did take a drubbing in the American Colonial War, striding to fifes and drums through the forest in echelons, wearing red coats, while the outgunned Yanks wore deerskin and ducked behind trees. We cannot change what we are. No matter our common language and heritage, we remain separate nations. Perhaps never more so than today.

Thank goodness, Monty's chief of staff saw a cable Eisenhower was about to send to Washington, saying it was either Monty or him, one had to push off. Montgomery was shocked, sending Ike a conciliatory message, eating his own portion of crow.

Eden lifts an empty palm.

"He's bent his knee to Eisenhower. Why isn't that enough? Why do you have to go this extra portion?"

"Because there can be nothing left to chance, Anthony. There is a world at stake. And the Americans, as they like to say, hold the cards."

Besides, Monty's retraction didn't end the bickering in the British papers. Bradley's subsequent press conference fanned the flames more than doused them. The calls to promote Montgomery have intensified. Something extraordinary needs to be done to heal this rift. Worse, it comes only weeks before the Big Three meeting in the Crimea, and days after the Reds have launched their assault across Poland toward Berlin.

What is almost farcical about this sad incident is that the Germans have a hand in it. Enemy propagandists edited an exaggerated version of Montgomery's words and beamed the broadcast toward the American lines. It was this version that gave many Yanks their initial news of Monty's press conference. It was this broadcast that Bradley first heard and exploded over.

It is time. Churchill pushes on his cane to stand. Eden follows.

Together they march into the House of Commons. The Prime Minister takes his seat at the well, Eden slips into the row behind him. The MPs in the great hall applaud and cheer Churchill's entry. They will stay noisy, he knows; there is not the hushed reverence in Parliament that Churchill found in the U.S. Congress when he spoke there. Here, in merry England, the MPs will shout "Oyez" and "Nay" and even "Sit down!" when they are moved to do so. Churchill waits for a trough in the clamor, then takes three steps to the center and sets the leather folder on the old, worn lectern. He looks up and around at the mumbling faces arranged on risers.

Well, he thinks, if the Prime Minister must swallow a slice of humble pie, he'll bloody well swill it down with some good, old-fashioned Westminster podium thumping.

Churchill fills his lungs. His arms hang loose beside his big belly. He raises his head but only some of his chin lifts out of his collar. He knows he looks puffy and dilapidated, but what do they expect of him, he's seventy years old.

Churchill feels the English air in his chest is ready. The scent in his nose is of human history. No matter what they expect, he will, as always, give them more.

He is vibrant in his words, emphatic in tone. Make no mistake. Almost all the fighting in the Ardennes was done by the Americans. The number of U.S. soldiers engaged with the enemy, and the weight of U.S. casualties, dwarf the contribution and losses by English forces. The Americans suffered losses "equal to both sides of the battle of Gettysburg."

Churchill addresses the clamor in the British papers for Montgomery's ascension to Ground Forces Commander, and the criticisms of Eisenhower and the U.S. generals. The Americans are true freedom fighters, they are on foreign soil for the second time in this century doing combat with tyranny in Europe. The British must celebrate them even as we bleed and weep beside them. England is indebted to America to the greatest depths of honor and humility.

In a direct slap at Montgomery and his supporters, speaking to the ears of the frontline Yank troops, plus the President and his generals, Churchill advises the British people not to "lend themselves to the shouting of mischief makers."

Churchill pauses. The chamber is grave, jolted, he's struck his targets. Monty, the English press, the grousing Opposition. Certainly the Americans heard this. England has apologized.

So be it; it was called for. But we are still proud, and that too is called for.

Enough pie, he thinks. Let's have us some meat.

"Unconditional surrender," he bellows. "Some have said this is too severe a penalty to inflict on Germany. Some have said that unconditional surrender makes the enemy fight harder, to avoid this stain of total defeat. That is because the German people know they have filled the ledgers of inhuman horror and indignity during this conflict. They know they will be handed the bill when this is over and it will be a mighty, mighty charge. But I say our foes need not fear that Britain in victory will mimic their brutality in war. I say to our foes that you know full well how strict are the moral limits within which *our* action is confined. We are no extirpators of nations, or butchers of peoples. We make no bargain with you. We accord you nothing as right. Abandon your resistance unconditionally."

Churchill removes his glasses. He lays them beside the

folder. He senses the current he has shot into the risers of the House. Old men like him, and young, feisty bounders and lords alike, Irish, Scot, Welsh, all under one flag and destiny, all under his voice and gaze. Every shoulder is back, every head held high, they are like flowers to the sun after so many days of cloud.

"Britain," he calls out, and nods in every direction.

Then, like an orangutan, Churchill strikes his own breast.

"We will remain bound by our customs."

Again he rocks his fist against himself. He draws out the last words of his message.

"And our nature."

Britain will behave with dignity. Even to defeated tyrants. Even to our Allies when we disagree. Or we are not a Britain worth defending.

Churchill takes up his glasses and the folder. He turns and walks from the hall under a hail of applause and shouts of "Oyez!"

The exhilaration of his oration fades once he has trod off the Parliament floor and into the private hall. None of his Cabinet ministers have followed; they've stayed behind to lead the cheers. He is alone with the cost of the exertion, blank and sweaty. He wants only to eat something, wash away this day with a tumbler or two of spirits, and get into his bath with a cigar.

He wishes he could go to his home at Chartwell in Kent for the weekend. Walk with his geese, paint, lay some bricks. But he has done none of these, his favorite things, since the war began. No time.

He wants to sleep, for years. Not travel to Malta and Yalta and haggle over the fates of millions with Roosevelt and Stalin.

He wants England to be not merely safe when the war is done, but strong.

He steadies himself with a hand against the wall.

Winston Churchill wants history to fall in line with the way he knows it ought to.

January 22, 1945, 11:50 A.M.
On the Kurfürstendamm
Berlin

A YOUNG GIRL SEATED BEHIND LOTTIE IN THE DARK mozartsaal cinema whispers to her companion, "I'll kill myself first."

Her friend, also a girl, perhaps they are both fourteen, shushes her. But the first one continues. "I will. I won't let one of those awful Russians touch me. I'll take poison."

The second voice hisses, irritated, she must have been poked by her friend. "Stop it."

Lottie whirls around. "Yes. Please stop it, or I'll call the manager."

The two children wilt into their seats. "Yes, ma'am."

Lottie returns her eyes to the beginning newsreel. One of the girls giggles and whispers, "Oh, they'll like her."

Lottie grips the arms of her seat to rise and complain if they say one more word, but they do not. She eases her hands and folds them in her lap. There are only a few dozen people in the cinema this morning to see the film version of *Carmen*. Lottie will move away from the girls if they start up again.

Rousing military music issues from the screen over the image of a German eagle clutching a swastika and the title of the newsreel: *Red Devils Sweep Across Poland!*

A fresh newsreel is released every Saturday for viewing before the main feature. Lottie has watched these propaganda releases change through the war years, from patriotic, happy pictures of soldiers marching through Paris and other cities of Europe to grim battle scenes of enemy dead and wounded. Lately, the reels have become graphic and brutal. Goebbels, the Information Minister, is making certain the citizens of Berlin know what awaits them if the city falls to the Russians.

On the screen, the camera pans over a primitive steppe

village of grass huts and squatting peasants. The announcer proclaims that this is the apex of Russian civilization, they are a subhuman species, the "Asiatic Bolshevik beast." The grainy black-and-white film next shows a troop of German soldiers running herky-jerky in an attack on a Russian column. Smoke pops from fired guns, geysers of earth erupt, men fall. The camera zooms on writhing faces of wounded German soldiers while the announcer extols their courage in keeping at bay the Russian scourge, which is now halfway across Poland and rushing to the West. Lottie thinks of her long-ago soldier, she imposes his face on the screen, sees it in agony, and closes her eyes just long enough to chase the image away. Now the camera dotes on dead enemy soldiers, blood spattered over their faces, eyes wide open in dismal finality, they are filmed in such a way as to look like bodies that never had souls in them. Over the music, the announcer bays that behind the hideous Russian herds there are "Jewish liquidation commandos," and behind them loom "terror, the ghost of famine, and complete European anarchy." The film cuts to a smoldering pile of bodies. The choice is clear: defend Berlin to the last breath, with every man, woman, and child, every weapon, shovel, dinner knife and fork. Or fall prey to a terrible fate at the hands of the Communists and the vanishing of everything German forever.

Lottie has seen frank newsreels before, but never one like this almost extravagantly harsh film. The two girls behind her have vanished; she heard one of them start to sob, and the two bustled away up the aisle.

The newsreel concludes with a musical flourish and again the eagle and swastika. There follows a moment of blackness while the projectionist switches to *Carmen*. In the dark and silent theater, Lottie catches herself wringing her hands. She stops and lays them in her lap, fingers curled. In a few seconds the projector in the wall behind her begins to grind, the silver screen shimmers. Lottie looks down to her lap in the strobing dim light. Her hands seem not her own but detached, gray, flickering, deathly claws. They look like the hands of someone who died clutching something, and that something was taken away. She shakes her shoulders to whisk out of her the cold shock of the thought. These are my hands, she thinks, alive and strong. They play the cello, they will not die and grasp at nothing.

She recalls five minutes before, the scared and mouthy little girls, one who swore to take poison, then left the theater in tears. I will have some protection, Lottie thinks. Somehow. I must.

Like Furtwängler. The conductor of the Berlin Philharmonic. This afternoon will be his final concert until the war is over. He's relocating to Switzerland for the duration, at the urging of Albert Speer, the Reichsminister for Armaments and Hitler's chief architect. Speer is at present the Philharmonic's most powerful patron. Wilhelm Furtwängler is a conductor of international renown. He has stayed in Germany from the beginning of the hard times, and has opposed the regime in his way, struggling to halt the bans on musicians and music, refusing to allow his orchestra to become a political plaything. Despite his resistance, Furtwängler failed to keep the Nazis' hands off the BPO, watching the list of *verboten* music grow every year, beginning in 1935 with Mahler, Milhaud, Stravinsky, and Weill, then expanding to damn Ravel, Debussy, Chopin, Bizet, Tchaikovsky. Wagner has remained the zenith of Nazi musical taste. Wilhelm Furtwängler is protected because of who he is. Fine for him, thinks Lottie. He's at least waited to the last minute to run away. The rest of us must stay and face the Russians. She wishes she could go to Switzerland too.

During the movie, Lottie rests her hands in her lap for the coming concert. She wants to play her best today, it may be her last chance to impress the maestro. When Furtwängler returns, she hopes he will suspend the prohibition against women in the orchestra, because she will be too brilliant to replace. Perhaps too—and even more likely—the BPO will all lie dead, she with them, a Wagnerian end. These two futures swing in her mind, a pendulum of fates. Lottie watches the film, trying to concentrate through the ticktocking of anxiety.

When *Carmen* is over, Lottie files out of the Mozartsaal. Though the movie palace has been bombed several times, the owners continue to repair it. It's a marvel they've been allowed to do so, in light of Goebbels' Total War edict of two years ago, after the Russian victory at Stalingrad. Hitler's little clubfooted Information Minister has done everything he can to spur fear of the Russians, to eke out of Berliners every last desperate bit of production and obedience. In 1943 he shut down every luxury restaurant. The cabarets and theaters were closed in August of last year, but many were already bombed out, the Kadeko, the Scala, the Wintergarden. Were it not for the powerful favor of Albert Speer, Lottie suspects the BPO and Berlin Opera would also have fallen beneath Goebbels' scythe. All surviving bars and clubs have been shuttered, except for two that are allowed to stay open only to entertain soldiers while in transit through Berlin. Dancing is off-limits. Berlin's famous prostitutes have been shipped to the Eastern Front to comfort the soldiers. Food rations have been reduced again. The Berlin joke runs that the bombs may end your life, but Goebbels will keep you from living. Lottie is grateful that through some oversight or political connection the Mozartsaal has stayed in operation. It's one of a diminishing few diversions anywhere in the city.

The day is a bright one; standing on the sidewalk, Lottie blinks in the confusion of darkness to sudden light. The temporary idyll of the silver screen is wrested from her by stark sunshine on the rubble. Lottie looks around. She wants to go back inside to see another film.

The time is just before noon. The BPO concert begins at four o'clock. Lottie pushes east on the Ku'damm toward the U-bahn station at the Zoological Gardens.

On all sides of her is destruction. The Kaiser Wilhelm Church, one of the grandest in all Europe, has been reduced by British bombs to a single stone tower protruding from a gargantuan heap of debris. Buildings everywhere are impossibly cleft; how can they be missing entire walls and still stand, what pride do they have to refuse to fall down? Lottie wants to know, should she need such knowledge herself. Walking, she glances up into the living rooms and bedrooms of flats three and four stories above the street carved down their middle, chairs, brocaded sofas, dressing tables, teetering beds, framed pictures still on nails, a thousand flats exposed like dollhouses held in by magic, invisible walls. Amazingly, people come and go into these rooms. Along the street, scrawled on many walls are messages in chalk: "Beloved Frau Bittner, where are you? We look for you everywhere." "Everyone in this cellar has been saved." "My little angel, where are you? I worry greatly. Your Fritz." Many of the messages have chalk answers scribbled beneath them, whereabouts and aftermaths.

Berlin, in the way of a great animal, has broad veins running through it. The city's avenues, even most side streets, are wide enough that they've been tough to choke by the collapsed buildings and craters. Here in the west end, where the bombs have been at their worst, bus and auto traffic continues. Swastikas fly from the fenders of most cars; Nazi administrators are the real industry of Berlin.

Passing among the debris, Lottie halts to watch the foreign workers crawl and stumble in the vast piles. They clean bricks the way Mutti does, stacking them. They push flat-bladed snow shovels and wheelbarrows along the sidewalks to remove hunks of stone and mortar, they sweep like automatons, lift and lower pickaxes to burrow down to broken water mains, they raise clouds of dust with their forced labor. They are guarded by uncomfortable-looking old men who stand with hands on guns. The guards are all in street clothes, wearing black armbands. These are members of the *Volkssturm,* the Home Guard.

The alien laborers get the worst of it, thinks Lottie. There are almost a million of them in Berlin, brought in from conquered countries to replace the German men gone to the front. The western European workers, the Dutch, French, Belgians, get better treatment than the rest. They at least get German food ration cards and are allowed into the shelters during raids. But not the eastern prisoners, the Slavs and Poles. They must wear humiliating insignia on their prison garb, the Poles a yellow-and-violet *"P,"* Ukrainians a blue-and-white *"Ost."* They're fed meagerly, and must endure the bombings exposed in their flimsy barracks. The most malicious treatment is reserved for the Russian prisoners of war. These wretches are given the most difficult, filthy, and dangerous toil. All contact between them and German citizens is prohibited. When they die, they're dumped into unmarked graves. The Nazis make certain that every captured Red soldier is starved and worked to death in the streets and wreckage of Berlin, where all can see. To the Nazi mind, this is good for morale.

Lottie reaches the U-bahn station and boards a train. The aboveground tracks carry her to Wilmersdorf through a moonscape of desolation. She looks out to the passing tableaus of hungry, degraded men tramping through the alleys guarded by codgers or boys; wounded soldiers in slings, with canes or stumps, swathed heads, patched and empty eye sockets; wandering refugees who have retreated to Berlin from the path of the Russian advance, villagers and city dwellers towing trunks, arms laden with children, telling terrible stories to anyone who will listen and feed them; once-fashionable women now bundled in tattered coats, wearing shoes woven of straw. Through these cold scenes outside the train window Lottie rides to her flat to pick up her cello, don her tuxedo, and perform Mozart and Brahms for an appreciative audience. The seeking, haunted, even missing, eyes of the soldiers and citizens in the streets watch her speed past. They say, The Russians are coming. The city is dying. But Lottie replies from the hurtling train, I play the cello. I must, I will, have protection, somehow.

At her flat, Lottie changes into her concert uniform and nets her hair. Being the only woman in the BPO, and a temporary one at that, she must dress at home, while the men prepare themselves in their private locker room. Unless there is a performance, she does not put on makeup. It's viewed as indulgent and unpatriotic. But today she is allowed, and people who see her carrying her big cello case will smile, knowing she's a musician and special in lipstick and a touch of rouge. She lingers in the mirror, enjoying herself in a tux. The look is vintage Berlin hermaphrodilia, recalling those prewar days of cabarets and sexual libertinism Berliners are renowned for around the world. Lottie knows she would never engage in such permissiveness herself, but she smiles at her image in the mirror nonetheless for she is proud that she is beautiful and that today there is a BPO concert.

Lugging her cello onto two more trains, by two-thirty she reaches the Admirals Palace near the Friedrichstrasse railway station. On stage, Lottie takes her chair, fourth cello. She settles the instrument against her shoulder and nods around to the men, who acknowledge her arrival. She warms her fingers and her bow hand, she tunes the strings, which have gone out from the temperature changes of her travel here. Everyone on stage, one hundred and five of them, does the same in his way with his own instrument. The collective sound is haphazard and disjointed, it is also the welcoming womb of performance to any classical musician. Lottie feels warm and connected. The despair of Berlin outside, the world's hateful spasm, is chased away by the flying fingers and pursed lips making these awful, wonderful, vintage sounds.

Dr. Gerhart von Westermann, the orchestra manager, walks on stage. The musicians rest their preparations. Von Westermann steps up on the conductor's rostrum, he wants to speak. The players seem startled. Lottie has never heard the man say one word, he does his job with brilliance, but in the background of the orchestra.

Von Westermann welcomes them all and wishes them a fine concert on behalf of Furtwängler's final appearance. The rotund man clears his throat, then swallows.

"There is a concern," he says.

He adds nothing for several seconds, until one of the trumpeters prods, "Yes, Gerhart?"

"There is a, um, problem."

Several musicians now say, "Yes, Gerhart?"

"The, ah, the entire Philharmonic may be called into the *Volkssturm.*"

The men of the orchestra are unbalanced by this sudden news. Brass horns bump music stands, tubas are put down, many men stand in anger, the violinists grip their instruments like chickens by the neck.

"No! Unheard of! Impossible! We were promised! Exempt, we're exempt!"

"Gentlemen, gentlemen, please. Gentlemen."

The musicians do not return to their chairs or soften their voices until von Westermann steps off the rostrum in frustration to leave the stage. At this they quiet as if by a conductor's baton. The orchestra manager reascends the riser.

"There is nothing definite at present. But you must be made aware that Herr Goebbels has made statements to the effect that no one, absolutely no one, will be exempt from service now that the Russian advance is picking up speed across Poland. He is revoking all exemptions. The Red Army may be in Berlin at any time."

Someone calls, "What about the Americans, the English?"

"I know as much about the intentions of the Americans and the British as you do, which I will suppose is nothing. Right now it seems that anyone who claims to know anything is worried about the Russians."

A tympany drummer with a maid's voice unlike his instrument, high and quavering, calls out the question Lottie is sure is on every man's mind.

"Well, what are you going to do?"

"Do? Me? What can I do?"

Voices raise again. "Something! Talk to Goebbels! We're the BPO, for God's sake! Goebbels has always been behind us, go talk to him! Talk to Speer!"

Lottie sits in the heart of this pandemonium, afraid for her own purposes. Certainly as a woman she will not be called into the *Volkssturm* like these hapless men of the Philharmonic. But her membership among them has provided her with status and connections. How can Goebbels do this? The orchestra provides the only citywide distraction and pride left for the miserable citizenry of Berlin, for the great and small alike, Nazis, frightened soldiers, grieving mothers. Every Monday the Philharmonic's performances are broadcast to all of Berlin and the fighting troops. Through Lottie's quartet, she has made precious money, been paid in barter food, eaten hot meals. If the BPO and with it her quartet are disbanded, if these tuxedoed men are given guns and marched off to meet the Russians, her world will fall with theirs.

The only chance is if the Americans and British reach Berlin first.

The men continue to haggle with von Westermann for some course of action, but it's clear at present there is none. Hopelessness abides in their scattershot voices. In the acoustics of the Admirals Palace, their pleas sound orchestral, as random and unmusical as was earlier the tuning of their instruments.

FEBRUARY

———

*L*et every one,
Kill a hun.

WINSTON CHURCHILL

*S*oldiers of the Red Army!
Kill the Germans!
Kill all Germans! Kill! Kill! Kill!

*From a leaflet dropped to advancing
Red troops, composed by the Russian
propagandist Ilya Ehrenburg,
signed by Stalin*

THREE

THE PRESIDENT SQUEEZES HIS DAUGHTER'S HAND.

"Look at Winston," he says. "That cigar he's smoking is so big, I can see it from here. It's like he's got a dog's leg in his mouth."

Anna laughs. "Oh my God, you're right!" Three hundred yards off, aboard the British cruiser HMS *Orion,* the Prime Minister has shouldered his way between the white sleeves of two seamen in the long, perfect queue of swabbies gathered at the ship's port rail. Churchill and his cheroot are spotted with ease, he is the only dark, animated blot in the line of British seamen, all arranged at motionless attention. He waves to the *Quincy* steaming alongside, at the President and Anna seated on the bridge.

Roosevelt sweeps back his blue cape, doffs his old cloth cap, and raises the hat in salute to the Prime Minister. Churchill seems to bounce on his heels in excitement. The man loves a show, thinks Roosevelt. Anna keeps laughing, her bright blue eyes like opals rolling in a palm, jumping from Churchill's animation to her father's face. She's a handsome woman, Roosevelt thinks, a beautiful gal. Her voice is a song of excitement: "Isn't this fun? Isn't this splendid?"

The *Quincy* makes toward its berth in Valletta harbor,

slipping broadside to the *Orion*. When the two are abreast, a flight of five RAF Spitfires in V-formation roars overhead, flying low enough for Roosevelt to see the pilots salute in their cockpits. Before the echoes of the plane engines have drained from the surrounding Malta hills, brass bands aboard both naval ships strike up "The Star-Spangled Banner." Every sailor in sight, and there are hundreds on both vessels, snaps taut to salute the American flag steaming into harbor.

The President leaves his hat in his lap and leans back his head to play the sun across his cheeks. The morning is warming and clear. His daughter's hand held in his squeezes his fingers and pulls out. Anna says, "Oh, Daddy, there's Sarah. I'm going to wave. I'll be right back." She goes to the rail to greet Churchill's daughter. He watches her step away, two sailors break attention to make room for her, she's as tall as the seamen. She goes up on tiptoe. Roosevelt guesses that all the stiff sailors around her want to look down at her legs.

The feel of the ship is good, old, and familiar. He grew up sailing on the lakes around Hyde Park in upstate New York. For seven years he was assistant secretary of the Navy. He feels himself stronger today than when he was in wintry Washington. The rest and relaxation of the Atlantic and now the sunny Mediterranean have restored him.

At the White House he's treated like a prisoner of his health. Everywhere he turns, there it is; in the news, the Republicans keep bringing it up, in his daily routine. The topic taints everything. His "ticker" doctor, heart specialist Bruenn, takes his blood pressure every afternoon and sets him out pills. His chief physician, Admiral McIntire, comes into his bedroom each morning and watches him eat breakfast in his pajamas and read his papers, gleaning God knows what medical evidence. He's restricted to less than four hours of concentrated work per day, including only one hour of meetings and interviews. He takes naps. Massages. Medication. Doctors creep in the folds of the White House like mice, multiplying every time there's some setback, a stomachache, a fever, a nasal congestion. But on this voyage, the gentle roll of the ship has helped him sleep late every day, until ten or eleven. At noon, he lunched with Anna and some of his cronies. Afternoons, the President lounged on the deck, sorting stamps or reading official documents. At five came happy hour, followed by dinner and a movie.

On the seventh day at sea, January thirtieth, Roosevelt celebrated his sixty-third birthday. Anna threw him a party with five cakes. Three were the same size, representing the first three terms in office. The fourth cake was huge, for the current term, and the last was a little cake with a question mark of frosting in the center, for a possible fifth term. Roosevelt laughed for the sake of the crowd around him, and won all the money at poker that evening. But he worried into the night over the question mark, whether or not it was on the wrong cake. His doctors don't tell him much. They don't talk to anyone but each other. Roosevelt could insist they level with him, but he doesn't ask. They have their jobs. He has his.

Anna returns to the deck chair beside him. "Daddy, now you listen. You are not to stay up until all hours with Winston this time. I'm watching you."

He nods. She is a stunning woman, the strong cut of her jaw in profile. Eleanor has given him five beautiful children, the one girl and four boys. But very early (it seems a lifetime ago now), she stopped giving to him, or he stopped asking her for, the gifts of a wife.

Anna asks, as though reading his thoughts, "Daddy, just once. Couldn't you let Mother come?"

Roosevelt imagines Eleanor here instead of Anna. She'd asked, as she always does, to come along. His wife is not sympathetic to his health. She believes in willpower as the path to cure yourself. With her constitution, that's easy for her. She's too strict, judgmental, she clashes with Winston's alcohol, his late working hours, Winston who believes women should be silent partners. With Anna's gaze on him the President shakes his head, no. He lays his cap back on his scalp and pulls down his cape, enfolding himself against the weather, his cool thoughts. Eleanor would cause too much of a ruckus with her presence. He doesn't need it or want it.

Anna says only, "Daddy." She purses her lips and wags her head.

Roosevelt looks into his daughter's sad eyes, thinking a face, like the thickest tomes, can carry so much history.

On his birthday he received no wishes from Eleanor. He was instead handed a testy cable from her describing an imbroglio that had broken out in Congress over his nomination for secretary of commerce. Eleanor's message was direct and critical of his decision.

Roosevelt takes in and releases a deep breath. He looks away from Anna to free the words into the air. "Your mother and I. We're quite a pair."

Anna pats his hand. In her own time, she says, "Yes, you are."

He wants to soften this melancholy for his daughter. She better than anyone knows how little comfort he takes in his marriage, the other places he turns for that comfort. There's no need to talk about it to her, she lives it.

"I couldn't get along without her, you know. She's irreplaceable. She's my eyes and ears. Hell, she's my legs."

Anna lowers her chin and her eyelids in an elegiac, understanding expression. She drops her head to his shoulder, smoothing the front of his old heavy cape with a strong, veined hand. Her touch on his chest is all he senses; the naval bands, the ships' engines, the rustle of men and sea all step back behind the closeness of his nestled daughter on this warship in a foreign port. So much history in a touch.

Roosevelt sits with Anna while the ceremony surges and concludes. Father and daughter do not move or disconnect. Nearing the quay, the *Quincy* slides beyond the *Orion,* Churchill and his sailors are out of sight. The British brass band fades. The Spitfires bank and return to their base. Roosevelt feels his daughter trying to give to him through her body, her strength and love, her life hooked to his, though he's aware it does no good; he bites his lip. It's too late for so many things. Too late.

But perhaps not for everything.

The legacy.

Is there still time and energy left? Or is there only the bitter question mark on the sweet cake?

"Well," he says. This is a preamble to movement, to get on with events. But Anna does not release him. Roosevelt relents. He stays in her embrace, her head on his shoulder like an angel there. They sit a long while, until the big boat is in dock, until Winston Churchill comes chugging up the gangway. Before he has both feet on the deck, the Prime Minister calls forth.

"Mr. President. My excellent friend. Ha! Ha! You made it in grand fashion, sir. Grand! Anna! My God, Franklin, you do travel with the most beautiful women. Look who's here, Anna. Sarah!"

Behind Churchill, his daughter Sarah hurries forward. Anna makes to stand to face this barrage of guests and British spunk. But it is Roosevelt who pulls on her hand, just for another moment to keep her in the nest the two of them made for a few perfect minutes. He's not ready for her to flap out, or to fly off himself. If only there were more time, for everything. Father and daughter fix eyes, and in this shared glance—miraculously somehow—all the good and awful and hidden and feared in his heart is said to her. This is more than he expected, this sudden communication. Here, of all places, now, this goodbye. He can, he must, let her go. Winston barges forth. Roosevelt presses his child's fingers for one more selfish second; let Winston wait.

As though releasing a dove, he opens his hands and off she flies, white and strong and gone.

In her place, round and blocking the sight of her, stand the gold buttons, cream braid, and blue naval jacket of Churchill. The man adores playing dress-up, especially uniforms. He wears an admiral's cap.

Roosevelt opens his hands to the Prime Minister.

"Winston, you are, as always . . ."

"Hungry, Mr. President." Churchill plops into Anna's deck chair. "Hungry. When is lunch, sir?"

Roosevelt can't help but be buoyed by the spirit of the man's arrival.

"Lunch always awaits you, Winston. Now that you're here, let's put on the feedbag."

"The feedbag." Churchill mulches this word, taps his cane. "I do love the American way with the tongue. The feedbag. Marvelous."

The two leaders share quick laughter. Their eyes meet, and the mirth is doused. Their two looks are identical, appraising and secretive. Roosevelt wonders if his own appearance is as worn as Churchill's. The Prime Minister seems frail, the weight in his face and shoulders has a soft and soggy sag. His cheeks, always ruddy, are pale today, his high forehead seems chalky. During the war Churchill has traveled hundreds of thousands of miles, to the front, to Moscow and Washington several times, to constant conferences with Eisenhower and Montgomery at their headquarters. He's all over the place, he strolls London and the cities after every bombing, thumbs up, V for Victory, "KBO." He's the oldest of the three Allied leaders, seventy. He's got to be tired. But right now Winston Churchill speaks of lunch as though it will be a coronation, of the President's arrival in Malta as a great and propitious event. Roosevelt thinks, This is real courage, this man. My God.

Lunch is filled with chatter between the two families and key staffs. No mention is made of the Montgomery gaffe or Churchill's humble and marvelous speech in the House of Commons. Roosevelt thinks it best to let those sleeping dogs lie. He relishes the ninety-minute meal, flush with charm and gossip, and draws from those at the table their own wits and best habits. Roosevelt wants to be held by this company as a brave man, no less than his admired friend Winston.

Churchill drinks champagne as though he is putting out a fire in his gut. Food goes in, words fly out, he's a locomotive, shoveling in fuel, producing speed. Roosevelt marvels but holds court despite the Prime Minister's blanketing charm.

"That's enough," says Anna, standing at her place. She

claps her hands once. "Everyone go home. Father and Winston need their rest. Big days ahead, everyone, big days. Let's conserve ourselves, shall we?"

Churchill rises, his party of a dozen follows his lead. He leans over to Roosevelt, and behind a raised hand says, "Six o'clock all right? I'll come to your cabin. We can talk an hour before dinner."

Roosevelt tips a lit cigarette in agreement. Churchill turns and raises his hands like a man being taken prisoner to Anna's dictate, saying, "I shall go quietly, madam."

When all are gone, Anna herself wheels Roosevelt to his cabin. "Nap," she says on the way. "Whew, I think I'll take one myself. Hurricane Winston."

At six o'clock sharp, the Prime Minister raps on Roosevelt's cabin door.

"Come in, Winston."

Churchill enters with a different energy from how he came aboard that afternoon. This is the private Winston, not the roaring electric personality but a calm presence, almost graceful. Roosevelt sees the intellect palpable in the man's eyes. His words at these times are not chosen for display but for reason and clarity.

"Since we only have an hour before your lovely daughter comes to drum in my head, let me jump right in, Franklin, about the meeting of the Joint Chiefs of Staff."

Roosevelt lights a cigarette, places it in his holder, and folds his hands in his lap.

"Proceed, Mr. Prime Minister."

In succinct terms, Churchill describes the results of the military conference held over the past several days here in Malta between the military staffs of General Marshall and his British counterpart General Brooke.

The American and British forces are to put their major efforts into two converging thrusts toward the Rhine, in the hopes of trapping a large number of German troops west of the river. The main drive across the river, deep into Germany, will be made by Montgomery's Twenty-first Army,

across the Lower Rhine, skirting north of the industrial
Ruhr region. Churchill calls this route "the shortest road to
Berlin." In the south, American forces are to cross the Rhine
and head toward Frankfurt, to draw off as many enemy
troops as possible from Monty's advance. This line of attack
could become the focus if Montgomery falters in the north.
Marshall and Brooke concurred that Montgomery's army
will be reinforced for this assault, with top priority in men,
air support, supplies, and equipment. The Field Marshal will
have under his command a million soldiers, including the
U.S. Ninth Army.

In the telling, Churchill appears pepped, pleased. He's at
least temporarily salvaged his dream of sending British
troops to the forefront of the war's endgame. The quest for
Berlin is alive and Monty is at the crest of the race. While
Churchill explains, Roosevelt nods, "Yes, yes." Listening,
he's surprised that the Prime Minister has won these conces-
sions for Montgomery, after hearing all the brouhaha in the
past few weeks over the Field Marshal's stupid press conference. But if General Marshall figures it's okay, then Ike must
be okay with it. Churchill's speech in Parliament must have
saved the day. Looks like everyone's kissed and made up.

Berlin and Montgomery. This is what happens when
Winston attends a meeting without the President or Stalin
around. He gets everything he wants.

Still, the military men know their stuff. Berlin would be
a prize, no question.

Joe would shit, no question either.

We'll have to see.

Churchill concludes, "Berlin is open, Franklin. Not just
militarily, but politically. To my knowledge there've been no
discussions between you, me, or Stalin about it. We can
move on the city. We're poised to. We have to. We can't sit
back and let the Russians occupy every bit of ground between Moscow and Brussels."

"No, I suppose not."

"No. Definitely not."

"Whoever gets there first, then."

"That's correct. I'm convinced we have to shake hands with the Communists as far to the east as possible."

"Yes, yes."

"We must take Berlin. Stalin only respects strength. Not agreements or morality. I assure you, there's no other way to pry him out of the rest of eastern Europe. Strength, sir."

"Yes."

The Prime Minister pauses, ready to say more, always it seems he is ready for that. But he eases back, he's made his case for now. Like Anna and Hopkins and Roosevelt's closest staff members, Churchill has developed the sense to know when the President has heard enough.

Churchill draws a cigar from his breast pocket, the thing is the size and color of a gun barrel. He asks, "Franklin, tell me honestly. How are you feeling?"

"Honestly?"

"Always."

"Every new day is an adventure. Everyone around me worries. I don't keep them around if they don't worry. Mostly I haven't got the time to do it for myself."

Churchill nibbles off the end of the cigar. Beside his chair is a lighted candle, put there by Roosevelt for the Prime Minister's purpose. Roosevelt watches his friend, his fellow world leader, work the flame around the orb of the cigar's tip. When it is glowing and aromatic, Churchill breathes in the tobacco. He licks his lips and holds in the smoke. Roosevelt studies this man, a portrait in powerful contradictions. Of British humor, style, and backbone. Crass and brilliant.

Churchill speaks in smoke. "We have profound work ahead of us, Franklin."

"Yes, we do."

"It can be done without us, of course."

The cloud released by the Prime Minister hovers over his head, shifting its coils in the breezeless stateroom. Under the haze, Churchill, pedestaled on his belly and short legs, looks to Roosevelt like a Buddha, some fortune-teller come with a grim message. He's talking about dying. Roosevelt answers from a page out of Eleanor's book, willpower.

"I'd rather it not be, Winston. I'm not going anywhere anytime soon."

Churchill does not make the obligatory reply that Roosevelt expects, the quick assurance that of course all will be well. Churchill sits under his smoke, puffs another billow into it. Roosevelt wants him to speak; damn it, man, say something. The Prime Minister nods, as though he heard this thought. But the cigar glows and smolders in his grasp, and that is all he says. Roosevelt realizes, as he did this tender morning with his daughter; as he did the night of his birthday party on the Atlantic, alone in his rocking bed with the question mark like Damocles' sword over his head; as he has guessed from the postures of his doctors, a suspicion that seeps out of their closed meetings the way a smell creeps out of a sickroom. Churchill tonight is saying goodbye.

Roosevelt looks at the fortunate man across from him, who will be here to witness and guide the end, and most important, the new beginning.

"Franklin."

"Yes, Winston?"

Churchill rolls the cigar over on his lips. He takes a puff, then removes it; the cigar is so fat, his fingers are spread wide in an inadvertent V for Victory. He pokes out his lower lip and cocks his head. Churchill resembles a very thoughtful bulldog.

"Yes, Winston?"

The Prime Minister jumps to his feet. Roosevelt envies this too.

"I'm famished."

February 2, 1945, 10:10 A.M.
Regensburger Strasse
Wilmersdorf, Berlin

THE TICKING STOPS.

"Oh, for God's sake," Lottie says aloud in her flat to no one, "leave us alone."

She crosses the room slump-shouldered and folds into the chair beside the radio. The box is large, of polished brown wood, with black plastic knobs and a gold lamé mouth. The *Drahtfunk,* the constant, steady ticking on a special frequency that tells Berliners there are no enemy bombers over Germany, has stopped.

Lottie pulls her knees up on the chair, she wraps her arms around them and buries her face.

Where are the Americans headed this time? It's been several weeks since there was a raid on Berlin. Lottie recalls what she has seen, what every German has seen by now.

It's awful, she thinks. Too awful. She makes herself hum something in the little cave of her knees and wrists.

After seconds of silence, the radio emits a pinging sound, foretelling an imminent air raid.

Lottie's forehead goes limp on her knees.

Leave us alone.

An announcer comes on the radio. The woman is calm, official in her tone. Air defense reports that a large formation of Allied bombers has crossed the frontier this morning and is headed in an easterly direction. The target is as yet unknown. Stay tuned.

"Ahhhh!" Lottie stands from the chair. She casts her eyes around her flat, her walls, an identity that has lasted this long. Here she is singular, not a refugee, not one of the unfortunates. In these rooms is where she maintains her hold on the young woman Lottie. In a war-ravaged city, with lunacy roaming the streets, sanity is the greatest challenge, after survival.

Her swinging gaze is growing edgy, jumping from thing to place like a bird frightened by the pinging radio. She puts out her hands as though to fend off a collision. She falls back into the chair, her balance stolen for the moment.

Her only companion, the radio, is rankling, pinging while the officials observe and calculate the American bombers' course. Lottie's breath speeds in her breast. Saliva cloys in her mouth. The walls, her guardians, seem to advance on her, bringing to her seat by the radio her framed pictures, her memories, the absorbed sounds of her solitary tears. The Galiano cello standing in its case, like Charlie Chaplin wide at the bottom, narrow to the top, waddles from its corner.

Lottie stands again. The walls and cello halt their march, they skitter back in place while she stares at them. She runs a hand through her hair.

"That's enough," she says. "Quite enough."

She goes into the small kitchen and opens a cabinet. She takes out a tiny bundle wrapped in paper.

This is the last of it.

Lottie unties the string and pours the final grains of real ground coffee bean onto a filter.

This is the last filter too.

From a bucket on the counter she dips two cups of water. This morning, like every morning, she and her neighbors lugged their buckets up the stairs after filling them from a broken water main in a crater behind their building.

She tosses the emptied package into the wastebasket. She was given the coffee months ago, before a private performance of her string quartet at a big house out in Potsdam. The host, a Nazi colonel, presented her the parcel with a pinch on the cheek. Lottie saw the man surrounded by his family, lacy daughters and fat wife, his friends and fellow black-shirted officers. She did not wonder what the man's hand squeezing her flesh might have done in the war. Lottie knows what little good choosing sides has done anyone. She took the impertinence and the coffee, and she played.

When the kettle is prepared, she lights her spirit lamp.

The many little flames jet out in curves under the pot. The smell of the fuel flowers the entire room, it is the last of her eau de cologne.

Lottie sits by the lamp, cup in hand. She has no cream or sugar. She doesn't even want a cup of coffee very much. What she does desire, and will have in another minute, is one tiny scene of normalcy. A hot drink in her flat. Why save the coffee, or the perfume? she asks. Save it all for when, tomorrow? Tomorrow—if there is one—she will only ask again, Why save it? For tomorrow?

The coffee boils beneath her gaze. She pours it steaming into the cup, then folds her palms around it. She breathes in the coffee smell, redolent of luxury, a proper place and time.

The radio pinging continues. Lottie snaps it off.

Enough.

She spreads her knees to straddle the burning lamp. She does not douse the lamp, but lets the flames live a while longer, lets them waste themselves into the cold air, sets them loose. Between her legs, between her palms, the warmth is fine.

Outside, sudden sirens surge across the city. Lottie takes a sip. Only a taste; she gasps behind the swallow, it is lovely.

Beyond her door in the hallway, frantic footsteps begin to scramble down the stairs. Lottie listens, seated, sipping. One of her neighbor women pauses long enough to bang on her door. "Are you in? Hello?"

Lottie makes no answer. The knocking goes one more round, then stops. The neighbor joins the noisy traffic to the cellar. Lottie hears suitcases bumping on the treads, babies handed ahead, children urged from behind to keep moving, let's go, *schnell*!

Another knock on the door. Lottie takes another sip. The coffee cools fast. The spirit lamp coughs in its hiss, the perfume is almost gone.

"Lottie!"

She recognizes the voice at the door, the landlady, old Mrs. Preutzmann from the first floor.

"Lottie! You must come, *Liebling*! I saw you go in, I know you're home! Come on!"

Lottie rubs the ceramic mug against her cheek, flushing from it the last throb of warmth.

She says to the door, "I'm having coffee."

The landlady shouts, "Lottie, the cellar!"

Lottie holds the cup to her heart.

"Lottie! The radio says it's *Luftgefahr* fifteen. Fifteen!"

This is the highest degree of danger. It means the radio has announced that Berlin is the target.

"Liebling!"

Lottie sets the mug on her lap. The lamp stutters.

She says in a voice sure to be heard in the hall, "Leave me alone."

"Are you coming? Lottie?"

"I'm having coffee."

"*Ach!* What? That's ridiculous. Get to the cellar."

Lottie stands too fast. Some of the coffee spills on her shin.

She screeches, *"I'm having coffee!"*

Lottie sinks back into the chair. The quiet radio gawks at her, golden open mouth.

Mrs. Preutzmann backs away from the door. Down the stairwell, Lottie hears her shout, "Hans! Hans! Come up here, bring the keys! Yes, up here now!"

Out in the city the air raid sirens caterwaul. Mrs. Preutzmann yelps for her old husband to fetch the keys to pry Lottie out of her flat. The radio wants to join in but Lottie has shut it up. The walls want to start their inch forward again but Lottie glares them rigid. Her cello says, Whatever you think best, Lottie.

"Oh, let's go down to the damn cellar."

She tows the big cello case to the door just as Mr. Preutzmann, jingling like a nervous Santa Claus, turns the lock and steps into the flat. His wife stands in the emptied hall, determined, fists on hips.

Lottie issues the old woman a wan smile. To the husband, she nods. "Thank you. I was sound asleep."

"Let me help you with that," he says, but Lottie handles the cello on her own down the steps to the cellar.

Mr. and Mrs. Preutzmann and Lottie are the last in the basement. The old landlord slams shut the wooden door behind him, then clomps down the oaken steps. He's a burly man with an ample, chubby midsection. His hands and shoulders are thick from years spent maintaining this building and the one next door. The Nazis will come for him soon enough, thinks Lottie. He'll be yanked into the *Volkssturm* and pissy little Mrs. Preutzmann will be left to the Russians.

Thirteen people fill the cellar; all but the landlord are women. Hungry war. The main course is men. Women are dessert. Children, a candy.

One naked electric bulb hangs cockeyed from the ceiling. The cellar's roof is the bottom of the first-floor flat, heavy wooden beams and the rough undersides of floorboards. Mr. Preutzmann has brought down water buckets and a halved fifty-gallon drum for a privy. The walls are stacked with sandbags. He has shored up the beams with scrap metal scavenged from the rubble everywhere in the city. Beneath the bench where he and the landlady sit are a pickax and a shovel. All the women have wet towels tucked around their necks. In case of smoke or a gas explosion, they will pull them up over their noses like bandannas. Several of the women hold hands. Mr. Preutzmann crosses his arms over his meaty chest.

Precautions, Lottie thinks, chaff in the wind. Good luck charms are all they've gathered around themselves down here, not security.

"I didn't hear the radio," a second-floor woman says. "Are we sure it was fifteen?"

"I heard the radio," Mrs. Preutzmann snipes. "It's fifteen. It's Berlin."

Together they sit, tense and waiting, staring down at the floor as though a bomb were right there fizzling in the middle of their circle. Lottie's cello case lies at her feet, the size of a small, extra person, someone who has fainted. They do their duty, these good Prussians, the duty Hitler has chosen for them. They sit beneath the Allies' bombs.

Lottie is certain that each one in the cellar dwells on the same thought. Run away. But run where? It's a lottery out there in the shattering morn. You might run toward death just as surely as away from it. Who knows? Best to sit still. This building has been hit twice before, it's still standing, lightning never strikes thrice, yes? Take your chances here.

They picture particular deaths, the ones that can reach them down here in the flimsy cocoon of their basement, the types of death they've all witnessed in Berlin. The ghastly end from a direct hit on the cellar by a burrowing bomb, the shell that crashes right through the building's roof and continues until it hits bottom. Death by a time-release bomb, exploding hours after you've ignored it as a dud. Death by phosphorus bombs, the white-hot spray that melts flesh to the bone. One dot will drill a hole into you inches deep and torch the building above your head. Death by crushing or suffocation when your building collapses over your cellar. By gas, when a bomb only partially explodes and instead of shrapnel releases a toxic, invisible seepage (these are the saddest-looking corpses, they are pristine, smothered, shocked to be dead). Or by concussion, where the pressure from a blast bursts every sac in your body, your ears, lungs, organs.

Thirteen people breathe and huddle. In Berlin, like a gavel announcing court, rumbles the first explosion.

Now the sounds of battle begin to unfurl. Antiaircraft gunnery chatters from the concrete flak towers around the city. Faraway thumps of bombs come in quick clusters, *foom foom foom foom*! A worse sign: Lottie hears the massed buzzing of American B-17 bombers. The *Amis* are dense over the city. This is a major raid.

The floorboards shudder. A shower of dust lands on their heads. The lightbulb flicks off. The women take sharp breaths. The bulb comes back. The women tuck their towels tighter. Mr. Preutzmann spits and does not uncross his arms. He mutters, *"Schweine."*

Behind Lottie the wall shakes, nudging her. She reaches down to her cello case. She lifts it and wraps it in her arms.

More explosions sound deep in the earth, closer on all

sides of them. The sense is of being underwater, of being hunted by some sea monster that swims in the dark waters unseen, bearing down, tasting the ocean for you.

Foom, foom, foom, FOOM! The last report comes from somewhere scarily near. Lottie jerks, rattling the handle on her cello case. Dust sifts out of the floorboards with every shiver of the ground. Eyes are pinched shut in the cellar. Hands in hands are veined with the effort of squeezing. Mr. Preutzmann uncrosses his arms now and finds the hand of his wife.

A moment of silence descends. Lottie in her mind enters the sky with the bomber pilots. The first wave of planes has passed the target. They've dropped their loads, taken their hits from the guns below, and banked for home. The second flight of planes follows close on their heels.

The bombardiers zero in on the fires already started beneath them in Wilmersdorf.

It's easy.

In the cellar, Lottie wraps her legs and arms around the Galiano. She cannot protect it, she is not hard enough, only a soft human.

Another explosion somewhere in the depths. The monster closes.

Another. *Foom!*

Another.

The lightbulb flashes and leaves them.

Mr. Preutzmann curses again.

Lottie licks her lips. There is the savor of real coffee there.

She thinks, That was the last of it.

She closes her eyes. The cello case is against her cheek, cool and dear.

The last of it.

FUH-WOOOM!!

Lottie's eardrums are rammed inward. Her mouth flies open in a reflex of pain.

The world comes uprooted. The cellar jumps, spilling everyone onto the floor. The air is clotted with dust and smoke, splinters hail from the floorboards. Some sandbags have burst, grains bleed out.

Lottie lies deafened under a jumble of arms and legs and luggage. Her cello is still in her arms, she has saved it. There is dirt on her lips; the coffee is gone. The people in the ruck scramble as best they can to arrange themselves. In the confusion she notices there is light again. Did the bulb come back?

She looks up when a knee is taken from her head. No, there is no lightbulb anymore. There is a hole in the ceiling. Through the opening, the flat above is awash in flames.

Lottie's heart sinks. Her building, her home, on fire.

She cannot rise from the floor, one person is still heavy across her back. She waits a second for whoever it is to gather herself and rise. When she does not move, Lottie kicks.

"No, no!" Lottie's ears are stunned, the voice seems far off. It is Mr. Preutzmann, coated in white dust like a baker, blurting. The man scoops his beefy hands under the armpits of the woman on top, then lifts Lottie to her feet, and bends again for the cello. The woman who had splayed across Lottie's back is on the floor, face up, but without a whole face. Beside her lies one of the floor joists, swooped from its place, bloody and guilty. The woman is not one known well to the rest in the cellar, she was a displaced person assigned last week to their building. Lottie cannot hear all the syllables when someone says the woman's name, Frau Something.

Lottie wants to shudder at the sight of this stranger's death, the proximity of it, but she can't out of relief that it was not her own fate. She doesn't reproach herself for this; she sees the thin gruel of horror and gladness in the others' faces too, even the neighbor who knew the lady's name.

The floorboards crackle. Lottie wants to see how bad the fire is. Maybe it hasn't spread upstairs yet, maybe her flat is all right. She moves with Mr. Preutzmann beneath the hole and glances up. The entire first floor is being consumed. A wind whips through the rooms, the flames inhale through busted windows. The blaze splashes here and there as though on the tip of a painter's brush. Upholstery ignites, carpets and white curtains drink flame like wicks. The Preutzmanns' flat is volcanic; the conflagration takes only seconds to consume everything while Lottie and the owner watch. Sparks rain into the basement. Lottie stares in disbelief. Her flat. Her sanctuary.

Mr. Preutzmann pulls her away. The hole is the mouth of a furnace.

The building's residents cluster around Mr. Preutzmann, the only man among them. The same expression sits on all their flickering faces. They are homeless. Shocked. The war has come knocking, hard. The woman's body with the staved head reminds them that death—war's mate—is here too.

Mr. Preutzmann looks at them, stymied. His building above is burning, it's going to crash down on them. Or it will first consume all their oxygen. The wooden steps to the cellar are already on fire. Even if they weren't, who would climb them into that?

Lottie says, "Mr. Preutzmann, we've got to get out of here. Now."

The landlord stands mum, ghostly in his coating of white dust. He runs his hands over his face. His sweating palms wipe clean swaths, now he looks striped.

Another woman prods, "Mr. Preutzmann? What are we going to do?"

When he makes no reply, panic sends out shoots. The women bunch closer around the big landlord. The man backs away from them, until he is against a wall.

"Do something," they insist. "We're going to die down here. You see? Do something!" Lottie does not take her hands from her Galiano. She drags it with her toward Mr. Preutzmann. It too must get out.

She crowds the landlord with the other ladies. She resents them their presence in the basement, where they will die along with Lottie. Her life will end down here and people will say, "What a shame, thirteen people were killed in that building." Instead, she wants them to cry out, "Oh!

Lottie the cellist died there!" She's afraid to be subsumed in their number, divided to one-thirteenth. Her life mustn't be robbed of its singularity.

Mrs. Preutzmann shouts over the pressing women. "Hans!"

Lottie turns her attention when Mr. Preutzmann does. His wife stands at the far wall, behind the corpse. Mrs. Preutzmann holds the pickax.

She shouts to her husband, to all of them. "Next door! The building next door! It has a basement just like this. Right behind this wall!"

A bolt goes through Mr. Preutzmann. He stands firmer. The women step away to make room for him. "We can dig to it!" he calls to his wife, advancing. "We can get out that way!" He says this as though the idea is his. The landlady nods, yes, yes, yes! and waves him to come faster.

Several of the women hurry to the far wall with him, patting him on the back, uttering encouragement. They slide the dead woman out of his way, then stand aside while he takes the first whack with the pickax. Brick bits skitter across the floor. The dent Mr. Preutzmann made in the wall is no more than a chink.

Upstairs something heavy falls, a chandelier perhaps. A howl skates across the fiery opening, a splitting sound.

Mr. Preutzmann spits in his hands. He takes a full swing. The pick sticks in the wall. When he levers it out, several bricks tumble broken at his feet.

In one minute of intense labor the landlord has broken through a fist-sized aperture into the next cellar. The wall between basements is three layers thick. The pick droops in Mr. Preutzmann's mitts. He is exhausted.

Lottie looks over her shoulder. The first five treads of the wooden staircase have caught fire. It's as though the flames are walking down the steps to get to them. Lottie leans her cello case into the hands of the woman beside her. She strides forward and reaches for the pick from the landlord. He shakes his head, no, just give me a moment. Lottie takes the tool from him. She is a cellist, with athletic shoulders and long, strong hands. She is more than merely one of thirteen.

The pick is heavier than she imagined. But she is sturdier, less clumsy than she thought she would be with her first clout against the wall. Bricks spew under her onslaught. She attacks the wall ten, fifteen swings. Lottie descends into a mindless fury, banging, banging, twenty swings. She grunts. Mr. Preutzmann and the others watch. Then someone cheers. Lottie senses performance. Through the heat and smoke, the clang of the blade and bricks, this emboldens her. She's the youngest one in the cellar, the most beautiful and talented. They will all live because they are with her. Lottie rescues them. That's what they'll say.

She reaches her limit. Her shoulders and back ache. She pauses to take a breather before she continues. In that still moment, the pain in her hands scales up her arms and overwhelms her. The pickax slips from her numb fingers. The handle is slick and red. Her knees are rubbery; Mrs. Preutzmann steps up and supports her. Blisters have burst in both of Lottie's palms. She is disappointed to be so frail. A pick handle is not a cello, it seems. A rescue is not so simple a thing.

Behind them, the entire staircase smashes down, charred from its mooring. Everyone jerks and cringes. Now the fire, like death, lies close at their feet.

In desperation, the women as one assault the wall. They claw at it like trapped rats, with the shovel and pick, with blackened shards of the disintegrating building that drop through the hole at their backs, even ripping their own nails and hands. Beneath the hole a pyre of burning debris forms on the floor. Smoke begins to sour in Lottie's lungs. A woman takes the damp towel from around her throat and swabs Lottie's hands.

Mr. Preutzmann holds the cello case while the women tear at the wall. Within minutes the hole is made the size of a rain barrel. One woman crawls through, landing roughly on the floor in the adjacent basement. She rises, almost laughing. She reaches back for the next in line. Together the eleven remaining women help each other to safety. Lottie is last.

Once through, she unravels her hands from the towel and reaches back for her Galiano. Mr. Preutzmann is not there with it. Lottie cries out for him.

In a moment he fills the hole. It is not her cello the landlord pushes through the opening but the body of the poor woman. Mrs. Preutzmann muscles Lottie aside, screaming through the wall, "Hans! What are you doing? Come through! Put her down! Hans!"

"Take her!" the landlord demands. "Take her. We can't leave her in here!"

Some of the women have already scurried up the stairs to flee this cellar for the street. Three of them who have stayed behind push past Mrs. Preutzmann. They reach their arms into the opening. With effort, they pull the limp form through, bumping her on the sharp edges of the bricks. The corpse is shunted up the steps by the last of the women. All have gone now except Lottie, the landlady, and her husband. No one knows how long it will be until this building too is ablaze. Lottie thinks it's on fire right now. The basement was empty when they broke through; that's not a good sign. They must get out, all of them, immediately.

The wife shouts again, "Hans! Come!"

Lottie shoves her head into the cavity.

"My cello! Please! Mr. Preutzmann!"

The landlord whirls for the hard shell case. He rams it into the hole. But the bottom of the case is too broad. It jams and will not come through.

Lottie gasps.

The landlady points at her husband. "Leave the damn thing! Hans!"

Lottie watches through the hole. The basement behind the landlord fills with dripping fire. Flaming floorboards break and dangle, they loll like burning tongues. The inferno on the fallen staircase is in full bloom. The big man sets the Galiano on the floor. He takes up the pick, yelling, "Get back!"

Mr. Preutzmann winds up and takes a swing. His strength has returned. More bits of brick ricochet and scatter. The hole needs only to be enlarged a few inches.

After a half-dozen blows, the landlord drops the tool. Lottie rushes forward while he wriggles her cello case through the cavity. She leaves crimson prints on its length, her hands flare gripping her cello as though the flames are in her flesh.

She looks through the hole. Mr. Preutzmann stands erect. His face is flushed. He's satisfied, he's done his job as landlord, and a man. He puffs his cheeks, as though to snuff out a candle.

His wife sticks her head in beside Lottie.

"Hans."

Lottie senses a rumble in the wall and floor. Her dread rises fast. She opens her lips to yell to Mr. Preutzmann but her mouth is stopped by a gigantic and invisible hand swatting her and the landlady backward from the hole. Their feet lift from the shaking floor, a gale of furious, scalding wind flings them backward across the room, unleashed by the collapsing building. Lottie clings to the cello in the dusty air on the cusp of the blast.

Blinking, Lottie sits up. Her eyes are baked dry in their sockets. The back of her head will have a lump. Her cello is beside her. Mrs. Preutzmann has been blown to the other side of the room and sprawls moaning in a thicket of debris, a new widow. Wood and twisted metal fill the hole, sticking out of it like broken bones.

Lottie is stunned. Every part of her sears. She has cuts on her legs and arms. She wobbles to her feet. She lifts her cello. The ground looks very far off; she seems to stand on top of some tall mound, a pyramid of events molded out of the last several terrible seconds, stacked so high under her she is dizzied. She does not shake her head to clear her mind. She wants to stay muddled right now, swaddled in the bafflement. There's too much.

Lottie is blank.

One notion only.

Get out.

She hesitates to take a step, afraid she will tumble from the peak. She might not get up if that happens. She stumbles to Mrs. Preutzmann.

Must get out.

Teetering over the prone landlady, Lottie does not know what to do to wake the woman. She appears to be a long way down. In these seconds another single thought bubbles up through the miasma. It floats beside her, outside her. She doesn't want the thought, doesn't want to be sensate. But she cannot chase it away, she can't hide from it on the blurred mountain of events. Lottie closes her eyes. She feels herself swaying. The thought enters her.

That was the last of it.

The last of it.

February 5, 1945, 1:30 P.M.
The Hürtgen Forest, near the Belgian border
Germany

THE DRIVER ASKS, "SIR?"

Bandy looks at the corporal behind the wheel of the jeep. He's been bumping along with this assigned courier for fifteen minutes out of Aachen and the lad hasn't said a word until now. Bandy likes this. It's a country way. You don't always have to be flapping off about something.

"You don't have to call me 'sir.'"

The boy, rawboned and freckled, speaks without taking his eyes from the rutted mud road. The steering wheel jumps a lot in his thin hands. His knuckles are pink. His knees are up almost to his chest, he's tall.

"They told me you was a captain."

"I am and I'm not. All civilian war photographers get that rank. But it doesn't mean anything. Just unless we're captured. Then all of a sudden we're officers."

Bandy sees in profile the boy smiling. "That sounds dumb, don't it?"

Bandy agrees. "FUBAR."

The jeep tires cut hard to the left in the muck. The soldier, maybe nineteen, fights the wheel, straightens the car. Bandy resists the urge to drive, but the boy is serious, he's doing his best.

"Are you *the* Charles Bandy?"

Bandy grins. He has no advantage with a camera over other photographers. If there's action in front of you, you snap it. You send the film through the censors to the photo pool, then it goes home. You hope it gets in print. All of them out here in Europe and in the Pacific have the same crapshoot. Bandy has just one edge on the competition. His name. And the title behind it, LIFE SPECIAL CORRESPONDENT. He's famous.

"Yes, I reckon I am. And you are?"

The boy hesitates. He steals a quick glimpse at his passenger.

"You interviewing me?"

"I just take pictures, son. No, I'm not interviewing you."

The soldier nods. "Stewie." The boy waits until he reaches a smooth enough plot in the road to handle the steering wheel with one mitt. He flashes the free hand to Bandy for a quick shake. "Stewie Stewart. Pleased."

"Same, Stewie. Where you from?"

"California. Outside Stockton."

"Cattle?"

"Horses. Quarter horses."

"You play ball? You look like you did."

"Yeah. You can tell, huh? In high school. You?"

"Naw."

Most of the snow has melted along this ridge, leaving the trail soupy. The road approaches a sharp turn along the lip of a gorge. The tendons in Stewie's wrists work like guy wires behind his fingers. The conversation drops. In the heavy woods below Bandy's shoulder in the open jeep, an abandoned tank and a few trucks are spilled on their sides. They did not negotiate these slippery curves. Bandy pulls his camera bag into his lap, in the event that Stewie doesn't either and he has to jump.

Bandy says nothing. He could reanimate the talk, share what he knows about horses and basketball, which isn't much. He could be famous for tall, skinny, far-from-home Stewie Stewart, give him something to write his folks about. The corporal seems like a nice kid. But Bandy decides to leave it. Stewie's a soldier, yes, but not a combatant. Bandy doesn't want to hear about Stockton.

All around him is the dreaded Hürtgen, scene of some of the bloodiest fighting of the entire war. It's good that Stewie has taken the cue and stayed quiet again, for Bandy plays God in his head and brings the battle alive. He watches ghost soldiers run and dive, hears trees explode, aims his mind's camera into the recent past. From September to December of last year, Hodges' First Army tried to penetrate the Hürtgen Forest to reach the Roer River running down its eastern edge. This is the thickest wood Bandy can imagine. Not in Tennessee or the North Carolina Smokies is there a forest like this. The fir trees are dense with low branches. A man couldn't walk upright among them. Even on a bright day like today, the sun never touches the forest floor, so it stays dark and damp, with no covering underbrush. It's a forest out of a scary fairy tale. And through the heart of it, like a black knight, runs the stolid Siegfried Line. The Hürtgen is the worst place Bandy has ever seen for a man to go if someone is waiting in there to kill him.

Why did the generals want to take on the Germans in here?

The Roer River. It's the last natural barrier before the Rhine. First Army had the task of capturing the dams on the Roer, to stop the Germans from blowing them and flooding the Ruhr valley. With the dams safe, the river could be crossed quickly. But if the Germans kept the dams, they'd be able to flood the valley and the Allied advance would be halted until the waters receded. That would give the enemy more time to prepare for the final onslaught, and cost more Allied lives.

The journalists have all heard the grumblings. In September, First Army could have assaulted the Roer dams from the south. The Hürtgen could have been bypassed. The forest without the dams is useless. The dams without the forest should have been the goal. But the generals wanted the Hürtgen cleared of enemy before they headed for the Roer. The forest would be in the rear of Montgomery's precious northern thrust to Berlin. So they went in.

And the Hürtgen chewed up men. First Army crept in there and came limping out, gut shot. In ninety days of fighting the casualty rate was extraordinary, almost twenty-five thousand battle losses. Whole divisions were decimated. The Americans got a bad and bloody reversal.

Now, two months later, the Germans have retreated out of the Hürtgen. They still hold the dams. The current plan is for First Army to advance again through the forest, as well as through a corridor in the southeast. They'll breach the Siegfried Line and attack the dams. Once they've been captured, Ninth Army and Montgomery's British and Canadian forces can cross the Roer and close to the Rhine, protecting each other's flanks. Beyond the Rhine there's nothing but flatland and villages all the way to the Elbe River and on to Berlin. The race for the German capital gets back on track.

Stewie wrestles the jeep down the slope. He avoids the precarious ledge. More overturned vehicles litter the woods below. Tanks, tank destroyers, trucks, not all of them slipped off the road. Some have gaping holes in their sides, some have charred battle scars. Near the bottom of the canyon, many of the conifers have been snapped in half, as though lightning struck. Many more trees have their tops missing. Artillery blasts in these woods would have turned standing timber into a zipping hail of razor blades. A man could get cut to ribbons by flying wood.

How do you fight in there? No visibility through the crowds of firs. Tangled dark terrain. You're facing an enemy on his own turf, who's had ten years to dig in.

Stewie guides the jeep around the foot of the hill. In a glen ahead, Bandy gets his first look at the Siegfried Line. He tells Stewie to pull over. He scrambles in his pack for his 35mm Leica to take some shots of the dragon's teeth.

The Germans have withdrawn from this section of the Line. Even empty, it's forbidding. The dragon's teeth protrude from a concrete mat thirty yards wide. The teeth are pyramids of reinforced concrete three feet high in the front, rising to twice that height toward the rear. They're staggered in such a way that a tank couldn't drive through them without getting stuck or tipping. Bandy can tell from busted spots that the mat itself is up to six feet thick. Concertina wire runs across all the gaps. An American sign has been posted in front of the barriers warning of trip wires and antitank mines. Placed as bookends are two massive concrete pillboxes, located to give the Germans interlocking fields of fire. Both are darkened to blend with the forest. Spread everywhere are gun pits, foxholes, bunkers, redoubts for artillery pieces. Seventy-five meters back through the trees, Bandy views another line of teeth, pillboxes, and fortifications just as forbidding.

He raises his Leica, meters the light, and squeezes off several shots. He hears the quiet clack of his shutter and thinks how tinny and puny a sound it is next to the missing cacophony of this place. Again, unbidden, he hears and sees the phantom roar of artillery, smashing trees, galloping desperate men. War. The Hürtgen is soaked with war.

Bandy marvels at the labor that must have gone into creating this complex of strongholds. The Siegfried Line runs for hundreds of miles, the length of the German border with Belgium and France. Bandy considers the Egyptian pyramids and the incredible toil that went into building them. He will send a caption with these photos mentioning Egypt. He wonders how many died just building the damned things there, and here in Germany.

Stewie leaves the jeep to walk up beside Bandy. The boy whistles.

"Big."

Bandy nods behind his camera. He doesn't want to talk. Stewie's whistle was out of place. This isn't a foldout in a girlie mag. It's a battlefield, a reverent spot. Bandy knows what happens to soldiers in these places, has recorded it, shared it.

"Where'd they all get to?"

Bandy shoots his last two frames. He lets the Leica hang by its strap.

He points into the Hürtgen. "Backing up."

Stewie puts his hands in his pockets. "Well, I reckon they're gonna keep backin' up all the way to Berlin."

No, Bandy thinks. Not true. The Germans are going to turn and fight. We're in their homeland now. They're going to put the Rhine to their backs and bare their teeth. The Nazis, the German soldiers, even the people know full well what they've done in this war. They know about the Jews, the treatment of prisoners, the wretchedness they've spread over Europe and Russia. They'll fight back because it's their only hope to escape their guilt. There are more battlefields in the making, more undug graves and shrines unnamed. But Bandy doesn't bother to answer the boy's bravado this way. Stewie will not be among the ones facing the Germans when they make their stand here and in the east against the Reds. He's a nice kid. A good driver. Probably a decent ballplayer. Bandy and his camera will press forward, will be there.

"Let's go."

After another half hour slogging in the jeep without chat, they're stopped by a guard posted on the road.

"Got to leave the vehicle here, sir," the soldier says. Bandy notes he's a paratrooper with the Eighty-second Airborne.

Bandy smiles. Where the Eighty-second is, there's action. Italy. Normandy. Holland. The Bulge.

The soldier adds, "The road stops here, sir. We haven't cleared the rest of the mines yet."

Bandy hands the guard his press credentials. The soldier looks the plastic card over and returns it. "We're bivouacked about a mile ahead, in Vossenach. Just stay off the road, keep to the left. That's cleared."

"All right. Thanks."

To the right, behind the soldier, a well-trod path heads into the trees.

Bandy asks, "What's down there?"

The paratrooper shakes his head. "The Kall River, sir. But the trail is off limits."

Bandy's instincts tingle. The Leica around his neck tugs like a divining rod in the direction of the path.

"Why's it off limits?"

"Orders from my lieutenant."

"And where did he get his orders?"

"I don't know, sir."

"Sergeant. You know who I am."

"Yes, sir, Mr. Bandy. You're the *Life* photographer."

"You saw my press credentials. I'm cleared for classified areas."

"Yes, sir."

"You understand I'm a captain."

The trooper wags his head and starts to speak but stops himself. This is bull and he knows it but can't prevent it.

"So I understand, sir."

Bandy climbs out of the jeep and shoulders his packs. He raps Stewie on the shoulder.

"Thanks, pal," he says to the driver. "I'll take it from here."

Before Bandy can step away from the jeep, the para-trooper intercepts him.

"Sir."

Bandy softens. "Son, look. I'm not gonna get you into any trouble. I'll make sure if anyone asks they know I pulled a rotten trick on you."

"It's not that, sir. I just gotta ask you something."

"Okay."

"I gotta ask you to be respectful. Down there."

The soldier's face, young and strong, has gone solemn, an ancient plea in his eyes. Bandy's gut quivers. Something bad, ancient as death, has happened in the valley below.

"Always, sergeant."

The paratrooper nods, believing. Bandy walks away.

Stewie throws the jeep into gear and does a quick half circle. He cuts the engine and uncoils from the seat. He jogs ungainly to Bandy.

"Mind if I tag along?"

"Yes, Stewie."

The boy considers this for a moment. His voice is polite.

"Mr. Bandy. You said you really wasn't an officer or nothing. You can't order me not to come."

"But I can have that fella back there stop you. Sounds to me like he'd do it."

"But he'll let me if I'm with you. I'd like to come, Mr. Bandy. Just partway."

Bandy cocks his head.

"Like you said. I'm no officer."

The trail winds through the trees, down into another canyon. Receding patches of snow on the branches and earth cling in the dark forest like vanishing innocence. Bandy strides ahead of the young driver. He does not turn to look back but figures the boy is walking bent double to get under the limbs. Bandy imagines having to fight like that. On all sides of the path is strewn jetsam of battle: brass bullet casings, trash from med kits, tree trunks scalded bare by glancing rounds. Stewie walks without noise. He falls behind. Stewie is stopping to look. Maybe, Bandy thinks, now he sees the ghosts.

But in another minute there are not ghosts but bodies. On all sides of the trail corpses, dozens of dead men, lie in the freeze frame of death, where they fell and how they fell. They've been refrigerated by winter, not touched by the living in months. The men look freshly killed, the chill has kept them from bloating and rotting. Their skin looks almost supple. Snow melt has washed the blood from the ground, but darkness stains the soldiers' uniforms and clings in the crevices of hands and wounds.

In shock, Bandy stops walking.

How can this be? The dead left on the ground like this, uncollected in such numbers? He scrambles in his head for an answer.

There is no smell, the sap in the pines is thick with the cold. The valley is silent, no birds, no wind, not a voice. But there are hands and feet and eyes and guns everywhere. Three months ago there was too much noise and smell, hand-to-hand fighting, hot horror. Now it's frozen, as though Nature took her own photograph of the war this way.

Stewie comes behind him. The boy's face, a full head above Bandy's eyes, is stamped in terror. This is the great dread for a soldier, for every man in uniform in every capacity of arms, that he will die and be abandoned on the ground. His sacrifice unknown, eaten into the earth. To give your life and in return be forgotten.

Stewie doubles over and tries to retch. Bandy walks on.

He could say something to the boy but chooses not to. He's not responsible for Stewie, who pivots on the trail and flees. Bandy answers to America; his camera answers to history. And here both lie.

Bandy is alone now with the bodies. Americans and Germans rest side by side. Bandy sees ultimate stories in their positions and final gestures, hieroglyphs of how grisly the fighting must have been here in the Hürtgen. Men have their hands on rifle stocks ramming bayonets into the enemy, to be killed from behind by another man who himself was felled somehow by one of the attackers or defenders. Kindled tanks and trucks rest farther off the trail where they were destroyed, some have charred men hanging from them, their attempts to escape their blasted vehicles thwarted. Strange, Bandy thinks, when there's only a fortress or a field of quiet weapons before him, the air bristles full in his mind with battle sounds. But here, with the dead flung on the ground, his brain stays mum.

Bandy kneels on the trail. He takes from the pack his Speed Graphic and stows the Leica. The Speed Graphic is a big camera, bulky once it's folded out of its case. It is the more difficult camera to use but it produces a four-by-five-inch negative, providing unchallenged clarity. Bandy has entered the valley of death, it is an honor to be here. He'll be respectful, as requested. He slides the expanding leather bellows into place with a snap. The metal click flits off among the corpses, a petty and alive sound. Bandy shoulders his pack and walks farther down into the canyon almost on tiptoe.

Between every photo, Bandy has to slide out from the camera's rear a thin, two-shot film pack, reverse it or get out a new pack and slip it in. His hands and eyes are absorbed. His heart stays nimble, dodging out of the way, negotiating the scene as carefully as do his feet. He does not feel ghoulish or inappropriate busy among the dead. He's exhilarated. The job, the opportunity, courses through his veins. The clink of the shutter is the armor around his life, the flipping mirror is his shield; the camera's quiet clatter keeps emotion at bay. So long as he looks through the camera lens, he sees this scene the way a reader of *Life* will later see the images on the page, from a distance. Bandy is moved, yes, but also removed. There's no other way, if he or any war photographer is to do this work.

And it is vital work. Images of war must be on coffee tables and in breakfast nooks back home. Mom and Pop and Sissy must behold war. Bandy can't make them smell it or hear or touch it from their sofas and church pews but he can help them see it. The costs must be made true, real and horrible for everyone, so nations will be cautious before choosing conflict. History repeats when the lessons go unchronicled.

Bandy is careful not to take pictures showing the faces of American dead. He frames them to avoid name patches or divisional insignia. No mother at home will see a Charles Bandy photo and recognize her fallen son. With German bodies, he is not so cautious.

The men wear the "Bloody Bucket," the red keystone emblem of the Twenty-eighth Infantry Division. They must have fought through this canyon toward the Kall River valley in the late fall before the first snow. The combat was savage. But afterward, how could these bodies not have been retrieved and buried? How could Army Headquarters not have been aware of the disaster down here?

Bandy imagines the canyon filled with snow soon after the battle. The steep trail from the west would have become impassable with the first storm. The Germans withdrew east from this part of the Hürtgen, perhaps planning on coming back but never making it. So the dead, hundreds of comrades from both armies, were left winterbound and neglected. In the thaw of the past week the bodies resurfaced. The Americans have only now returned to the Hürtgen and found them.

Bandy tucks in his lips, boggled. How to explain this? War, he thinks. It's just war, the catastrophic made commonplace. No one will take responsibility for this. The Kall River canyon, so hideous right now, will be tidied up by administrators, washed white not with snow, but more permanently, with paper and some lies.

The trail leads a half mile to the bottom of the canyon. There, Bandy finds a mountain stream swollen with run-off. The water makes a peaceful riffle. He follows the stream around a wooded bend. Emerging into a clearing Bandy sees an abandoned American aid station. The pretty water surges past two large canvas tents. There is a jeep marked with a red cross. Litter cases, more than two dozen of them, are arranged in a neat line beside the stream, like railroad ties. The eerie silence of the Hürtgen is not chased by the moving water, the almost antiseptic air hovers sharp and empty. The forest seems asleep.

Bandy steps toward the tents. A cold suspicion rises in him that the bundles on the stretchers are not empty blankets. His approach soon reveals they are dead U.S. soldiers.

On reflex he halts far enough away to encompass the whole scene through the viewfinder of his Speed Graphic.

Once the aid station is inside the metal square, he prepares to release the shutter.

These men too have been preserved by the cold. But unlike their fellows felled in the calamity among the trees, nothing comes through Bandy's lens to suggest that these soldiers are dead. They made it this far, they had a chance. The corpses are in repose, hands crossed over their pulled-up blankets, chests and heads still wrapped in bloody gauze gone black. The fighting must have overtaken them here, in what should have been sanctuary. In the melee the aid station was abandoned. The men could not be moved. They died on their stretchers, alone with each other and the anointing specter.

The canyon rises around him in shambled trees, cluttered with cadavers. The stream burbles poisonously. He feels like he's in the cupped palms of Death itself. The camera wavers in his own hands. Does history need to see this?

On the stretchers mouths are open. What would they say?

Bandy promised. He is respectful. Always.

He drops to a knee. He opens his camera bag and fills his pockets with film.

———

February 6, 1945, 11:35 A.M.
Livadia Palace
Yalta, Soviet Union

STALIN NEVER TIRES OF HAVING MEN SALUTE HIM. HE walks through the preposterous foyer of the palace with strides as broad as his short legs will allow. He swings his arms, too long for his torso. He carries no folders or papers to his meeting. He remembers everything; why carry papers? When he passes, Americans snap straight as though electric currents have run up their legs.

Stalin walks alone. His heels click on the marble floor, little socialist hammer shots against the walls and statuary of Czar Nicholas II. Every echoed step expands to fill the vast cavity of the dead czar's entrance hall above the Black Sea. Every footfall makes these foreigners watching him rigid. Stalin does not acknowledge the attention he generates. This is as it should be.

They have come to me, he thinks. The two most powerful figures in world politics have done Stalin's bidding. The President of the United States and the Prime Minister of Great Britain have made highly inconvenient journeys, both of them ailing, bringing caravans of three hundred and fifty aides apiece. They traveled to Yalta for no reason other than that is how Stalin wanted it.

The Red Army under Stalin is about to secure the greatest victory in Russian history, grander than the one over Napoleon. Those old Bolsheviks, the few left alive, they remember Lenin. They have never accepted Stalin as Lenin's equal, regardless of their varnished praise. But now. Roosevelt and Churchill! America and the British Empire! Both come to the Crimea. To curry favor with Stalin. To accept Stalin and the Soviet Union as equals. Lenin never had that.

Stalin rounds a corner, headed for the left wing of the palace, the czar's former bedroom, where Roosevelt is installed. More Americans whizzing about the halls freeze in their tracks. The President's pretty daughter, Anna, even bows. That is something.

Smiling, the Marshal raps on the ornate door to Roosevelt's room. And why should Stalin not smile? So far he's gotten almost everything he wants at Yalta. No direct interference from the West in Poland. Territory in the Far East in exchange for a mere promise that Russia will enter the Pacific war. Extra seats allotted at Roosevelt's pet project, the United Nations. The lowly French want an occupation zone; Stalin is opposed, Churchill is in favor, Roosevelt waffles. All typical. War reparations, the dismemberment of German industry, these need more talks. But they're topics that will be handled later.

Best of all, in the past three weeks two million Soviet soldiers have swamped Poland. They're massing right now on the Oder River, fifty miles from Berlin. Finally, the Red Army is anchored across all of eastern Europe.

Whoever occupies a territory imposes on it his own social system. That is the political reality of tomorrow, no matter what is decided here at Yalta. Stalin may sit beside Churchill and Roosevelt at the conference table. But today, on the battlefield, in the liberated territories, Stalin towers over them.

The President's door opens. Chip Bohlen, Roosevelt's interpreter, greets Stalin in fluent Russian and steps aside. Entering the lavish room, Stalin swells in his approach to the seated President. He prefers these private meetings with Roosevelt, away from the fiery mouth of Churchill. Roosevelt said in advance he wants to discuss France. Fine, Stalin thinks, we'll settle the French. Privately, he wants also to divine what Roosevelt and his generals intend for Berlin.

Stalin says, "Mr. President. You are looking well."

Bohlen the interpreter speaks. He follows Stalin to the President. The two leaders shake hands with much muscle, using all four hands in their clasp. Stalin eases into a chair placed across from Roosevelt's sofa, continuing his morning pleasantries. Bohlen sits in a chair between them, muttering in alternating English and Russian. One of Roosevelt's women secretaries stands far to the side, she will scribble notes after the real talk begins. When they are all seated, Stalin goes quiet. He glances first to Bohlen's face, then down at the feet of the man's chair and the carpet. The interpreter sits as close to Stalin as does the President. Stalin cocks his head. Bohlen slides his seat one pace back. This is proper. Roosevelt should have taken care of it. Logs crackle in the fireplace. There are brandy and treats on a silver server between them.

Roosevelt preens. He enjoys Stalin's flexing. He envies Stalin's power. Little wonder. Though his nation is the most powerful on earth, the man himself is an invalid, he cannot even stand when Stalin enters the room.

Roosevelt natters about his accommodations, marvelous, magnificent. The view of the Black Sea from his porch is spectacular. On and on. Those czars really knew how to live it up. Yes, Stalin thinks, they did, and that is why the last of them was shot in the back of the head along with his family. Stalin makes agreeable noises, mentions that someday he would like to see the White House in Washington, D.C., he is certain that their poor Russian palaces pale by comparison. Roosevelt guffaws at this, waves his cigarette holder about like an ingenue.

Unlike Roosevelt, Stalin is ill at ease in the Livadia. He is equally uncomfortable in the splendor of Churchill's mock Scottish castle at the Vorontzov villa and in his own accommodations at the Koreiz Palace, former home of Prince Yusupov, supposedly the assassin of Rasputin. Stalin listens to Roosevelt extol the virtues of a comfortable bed, the President believing that by doing so he is playing the grateful guest. Roosevelt does not know that this is the crux of why their two nations can never be friends. The Soviet Union is pledged by Marxism and Leninism to destroy capitalism. To burn the West's plush beds so long as Soviet peoples sleep on straw. Roosevelt speaks always of peace. Doesn't he know that the Communists are committed to war, either of men or ideology, against the West? Too much of the world's power has been held in their sway for too long. Too much of the world's wealth stuffs their mattresses to make them cozy. But those unfortunate arrangements have already begun to change.

Stalin is the one who is grateful to Roosevelt, for this dying man's generosity. After the President is gone, and from the looks of him it will be soon, his successor will surely be of a different mold. Stalin takes what he can, while he can. This is plunder.

He laughs in the middle of one of Roosevelt's sentences, before the translation. Stalin can't help himself, he is in a grand mood.

This is politics.

Bohlen tells him the President has said, "I'm glad I could give you a good laugh, Joe."

Stalin inclines his head. This nonsense again with his

name. But he is too merry to grimace at this vulgarity. No one dares call him "Joe" or "Iosif." He goes years without hearing any address but "Comrade" and "Marshal." Stalin, man of steel, is not "Joe." Now twice the President of the United States has done it. But Roosevelt is tickled that this informality is finally allowed. A small thing for what Stalin receives in return. He leaves it alone.

Stalin's chuckle goes on while Roosevelt waits. Stalin recalls his quick meeting that morning with Churchill in the Prime Minister's mobile map room, where he invited Churchill to transfer a portion of his British troops now stationed in Italy up to Yugoslavia and Hungary, to link with Soviet forces already there and go after the Germans in Austria. This was a subtle slap in Churchill's face and, clever fellow, he caught it. The Red Army has advanced so far that those nations will be under Soviet dominion in a few more days. There is no time for the English to get involved! Insulted, red-faced, all Churchill could say was, "The Red Army may not give us time to complete this operation." Stalin enjoyed that immensely. Ah, even Churchill is good for a laugh on occasion.

The jocularity settles inside him. Stalin knits his fingers. Enough.

"Tell me what you are thinking about France, Mr. President."

"Well." Roosevelt shifts on the sofa cushions as best he can. Stalin sees how stranded the man is atop his legs. He guesses that Roosevelt has changed his mind on the French. Churchill has gotten to him. The President hesitates always before telling Stalin he disagrees with anything Stalin wants.

"Winston has made some good points to me lately about France."

Stalin waits. He twiddles his thumbs to express displeasure.

Roosevelt explains that he still agrees with Stalin that the French do not deserve much in the way of generosity after the war. After all, they did collaborate with the Germans. But France is Germany's largest neighbor. And Churchill makes a good case that a weakened France will be less of a deterrent to future German aggression than a strong France.

Stalin shakes his head. "It is not postwar Germany which Mr. Churchill worries about. It is me."

"Joe, no." Roosevelt swats this assertion aside. "Winston, you, and me, we're all on the same team. England knows what a strong ally they have in the Soviet Union. Sure there are differences. But none so strong that our joint commitment to world peace isn't stronger. Am I right?"

Stalin cannot always believe that the President speaks candidly when he says these things. You do not go from a world of international rivalries suddenly to a world of international cooperation.

"Yes, Mr. President. Of course."

Roosevelt turns to Bohlen and says something that goes untranslated. The secretary does not record it. Stalin suspects it was nothing more than a "There, see?"

Stalin holds out a palm. "So you are saying that you wish for the French to be allowed an occupation zone."

"Yes. Winston and I both feel it's important for French prestige."

That is an odd phrase, Stalin thinks, to ascribe prestige to a people who threw up their hands rather than see their Eiffel Tower in ruins. Russia could build an Eiffel Tower from the bones of Stalingrad alone.

"Then I must agree. But the French zone has to come from the American and British zones. We will cede no territory."

Roosevelt anticipated this and says it poses no problem.

"This is to include a zone in Berlin?"

"Yes."

Stalin has set the city's name out for discussion like a new piece at an auction. Roosevelt speeds past it to another topic, how much money Germany should have to pay in reparations after the war.

Stalin waits for Berlin to come around again. He addresses Roosevelt's choice of topic; he wants to set a reparations figure now, of twenty billion dollars. Roosevelt agrees that this sum can be the basis for future discussions. This means the President is not ready to take a position.

After another half hour, Roosevelt appears finished. The French question is the only one put to rest. Let Churchill win that one, thinks Stalin. No matter. The Western Allies will withdraw from their zones in a few years. The Soviet Union has no intention of doing so.

Roosevelt claps his hands. They make a large sound, they are big mitts. Stalin considers, he must have been a beautiful man before his illness, graceful and patrician. The President leans forward, extending a hand to Stalin. The Marshal stands to shake it, signaling that he will go.

"Thank you, Joe, thank you. I'm sure these little sessions of ours do a great deal to keep the big meetings on track. I'll let Winston know what we've discussed. He'll be pleased. And again, I just want to tell you how much I and my staff are enjoying your hospitality."

"It is our pleasure and duty, Mr. President."

"You know," says Roosevelt. The President seems not to want the conversation to conclude. This is a ritual habit that Stalin has noticed. After proper discussions, Roosevelt enjoys a drink and some chat, almost as a reward for work. He likes a joke or a story, he relaxes as though under a sun when there is idle banter. Stalin pauses while Roosevelt tips the brandy decanter for himself and Bohlen. He lifts his eyebrows at Stalin. Stalin waves the suggestion off.

"You know," Roosevelt says after his first sip, "on the way over here on the *Quincy*, I made a bet with some of the sailors."

"Yes?"

"I bet them that your troops would be in Berlin before ours get into Manila."

This is an incredible thing to say. Stalin cannot believe what he hears. Is the President of the United States handing him Berlin?

What of the American and British armies assembling

north of the Ruhr? The million soldiers preparing to breach the Rhine? Are they going to stop shy of the Reich's capital? No, inconceivable! Berlin is the prize!

Danger signals nick in Stalin's stomach. This must be a trick. Has smiling Roosevelt turned cunning?

"You believe this, Mr. President? There is very hard fighting going on right now on the Oder line. The Germans are very determined to keep us out."

Roosevelt nods. "The Japanese are pretty determined to hang on to Manila as well."

"No." Stalin smooths down his moustache, trying to mask his surprise, his glee at the prospect that this is really happening. His patience has been rewarded. "No, I am certain you will be in Manila first. Berlin will be very tough."

"Well, we'll see, Joe. I know your army is tough too. I've got faith in my bet."

Stalin decides to sit and accept an offering of brandy. The President pours. Why would Stalin consider leaving the room when Roosevelt wants to talk like this? This is no time to be a teetotaler.

To be the first to reach Hitler's bunker? To haul him and his whore out in the street, to try them and their Nazi cohorts in a Soviet court before the world? This would be the crowning and most historic victory in Europe.

Stalin sips an unspoken toast. To Berlin.

Roosevelt eases one arm across the back of the sofa. "Another thing I wanted to ask you about."

"Yes."

"Our armies are getting pretty close to each other. I think it's time you and I authorize them to have direct contact. It'll help prevent any mistakes or unfortunate incidents. Those things can happen in the absence of clear lines of communication."

Stalin cannot think of any reason to resist. It would be very bad if an altercation erupted, even accidentally, between U.S. and Red forces. At least not now, before the Soviet Union is ready.

"Mistakes must be minimized, yes. I agree."

"Fine, fine. Also, I'd like your permission for General Eisenhower to speak directly with your Soviet staff instead of having to go through the Chiefs of Staff in London and Washington, like he's been doing."

"I think that is very important. It is an excellent suggestion, Mr. President."

"Good, good."

"I will have our two staffs work out the details."

Stalin lifts his brandy in tribute.

"Na zdrovya." In the Russian manner, he drains the glass. He is not a drinker of the quality of Churchill and Roosevelt. But he can perform as well as them when needed, in anything.

"Mr. President, I will take my leave. Thank you for a very fruitful session. I will see you at the plenary meeting this afternoon."

Stalin lets himself out. Perhaps he has left too precipitously but he had to be alone. In the hall, where other Americans can still see him, he cannot contain it. Walking fast, he balls his fists and holds them before his face as though he has grabbed someone by the lapels and pulled him close. Marshal Stalin mutters, triumphant, *"Da. Da!"*

He hurries to his waiting car outside the Livadia Palace. The drive to the Koreiz takes ten minutes. In the rear seat, he beats a soft rhythm on his lap with open hands to bleed off some of his excitement.

If Roosevelt is telling the truth, then the race for Berlin is off. This is a marvel, a blessing of timing. Even though Stalin's leading forces are only fifty miles from Berlin, they're in disarray. Koniev and Zhukov have outpaced their supply lines. Determined German bastions remain in their rear, sapping the steam from the advance and blocking supply routes. The Red flanks are too exposed in the north, the front there has lagged almost a hundred miles behind. Some divisions have been ravaged down to four thousand men, less than a quarter their normal size. The weather is atrocious.

Even with all these factors at hand, the current plan is to keep pushing, to follow momentum all the way through

Poland, across the Oder, and ram into the German capital. Stalin's generals are plotting the final dash to Hitler's doorstep, set to jump off next week. Zhukov in particular insists on pressing the reeling German forces, he believes it is the only way to beat the Western Allies to Berlin. The strategy is known to be premature, costly, even risky. Now it is obsolete. Stalin can wait until he assembles an armed strength that will be unstoppable.

Stalin will not only win Berlin. Roosevelt has granted him the time—which equates to permission—to gather enough force to take and hold Central Europe.

What if Roosevelt's jest turns out to be a feint? What if, instead of speaking behind Churchill's back, the President spoke at the Prime Minister's behest, to lull the Red forces into a lapse so they can make their own move? If Montgomery gets across the Roer River in the next week, what's to stop him from charging the Rhine and then on to Berlin? Nothing.

Soviet forces can still be mustered quickly enough to outstrip any move Montgomery or Eisenhower makes on Berlin. It would be a bloodbath for the Soviet army. But not the first.

Arriving at the Koreiz villa, Stalin hurries to his office. He tells his secretary to find Zhukov and get him on the line.

Stalin paces the minutes away until his line rings.

"Where are you?" he demands of his top general.

"I'm at Kolpakchi's headquarters, and all the army commanders of the front are here too."

"What are you doing?"

"We're planning the Berlin operation."

"No, no, you're wasting your time. We must consolidate on the Oder, then send all the forces you can to Rokossovsky to bring him up on your northern flank."

Zhukov hesitates.

"What about Berlin?"

"It is postponed."

"Comrade?"

Stalin puts down the phone.

He looks up over the mantel, to the portrait of Lenin that travels with him. Lenin is depicted in three-quarters profile, gazing ahead like a captain on the prow of a ship in turbulent waters.

"Vladimir Ilyich," he says to the stern painted face. "They came to see *me*."

February 17, 1945, 2120 hours
Posen, Poland

SOMEONE TOSSES ANOTHER LOG ON THE BONFIRE. SPARKS flee. There's enough firelight to see. Ilya casts his eyes over the circle of seventy gathered faces. He recognizes only a dozen, and Misha beside him. These familiar men maintain numb visages; they've learned to save their fury for battle. The rest fidget. They look scared or angry.

The political commissar Pushkov stands at the center. Flames crackle around his voice. He welcomes the new men into the penal company. They are replacements; over eighty percent of the company has been cut away since Ilya arrived four weeks ago. The Germans have fought with desperation while backing out of Poland, battling to keep the Russians out of their homeland.

While the commissar speaks, Ilya whispers to Misha.

"Would you look at what they're giving us to fight with."

Misha nods. "Peasants."

"Idiots."

"Mostly liberated prisoners."

"Crazy men."

Misha elbows Ilya. "No crazier than you."

Ilya digs his own elbow at Misha in playful retaliation, too hard. The little soldier staggers forward into the circle.

The commissar turns.

The politico is tall and hollow cheeked, missing a front tooth. Approaching Misha, who stands caught in the firelight, the commissar directs an open hand at him, as though indicating a curiosity. Ilya swears under his breath at Misha for attracting the commissar's attention.

"Comrade Misha Bakov," the commissar announces. The gap in the man's teeth hisses. He shifts the hand over to Ilya. "Ah, and of course, right behind you, Comrade Ilya Shokhin."

Pushkov feigns puzzlement. "Isn't Shokhin normally in front?"

Misha shows no sign of the insult. He snaps to attention and declares, "Yes, Comrade Commissar!"

Pushkov glances to Ilya. Ilya smiles, showing his teeth. I have all of mine, he thinks, you shit.

The commissar walks to within three feet of Misha. Ilya could toss him onto the fire.

Pushkov makes no secret of his disdain for the two of them. He does not like it that any of the penal men, even men as aggressive as Ilya and clever as Misha, leads during battle. They are not officers any longer and Pushkov has reminded them of that. Ilya doesn't try to collect others around him when the bullets fly, the men simply appear and follow. And Misha just seems to always know more about the battle and objectives than any commissar or officer present. Pushkov doesn't mind if the two friends survive, but he doesn't want them to be a distraction to his authority. For Pushkov, the penal company is not the place to show initiative and intelligence. It is only the venue to kill, die if you must, and atone.

Facing the commissar, Misha speaks in a formal tone.

"Please allow me to state for our new comrades that under your excellent tutelage, Comrade Commissar, our penal unit has made great socialist strides."

The commissar slats his eyes.

"Yes. Thank you, Comrade Bakov." The commissar says no more. He waits, expecting Misha to retire into the ring of faces. Misha sets one foot behind the other as if to retreat. The commissar walks on, satisfied, putting Ilya and Misha at his back. He strides beside the fire, feet kicking out the hem of his long greatcoat.

Ilya despises this sort of language, the slavish mouthings of an automaton. But this is how one must pretend around the Communists. The commissars have such capricious power. They can actually shoot you on the spot if they think you're shirking, or reluctant to fight. Best to behave like a proper machine. The words sounded funny coming from crafty little Misha, like a shirt that's too big for him.

Ilya suppresses a giggle. If a mongrel dog like Pushkov has noticed him, then others, more important ones, have too. Pushkov is not the last word, far from it. Ilya has survived worse than this skinny *apparatchik*.

Misha does not leave the circle. He stands fast. Ilya growls at him, "Come here. Misha, come here."

"You know," Misha proclaims to the group with a wave of his arms, "Comrade Shokhin was at Stalingrad."

The crowd murmurs. Ilya's head sinks.

Pushkov halts his stroll. He pivots and glares. He does not invite Misha to continue. The little soldier doesn't wait.

"He's an expert in house-to-house, close-in fighting. He knows everything about going after the Germans in fortresses. Just like the one here in Posen. You'll see tomorrow."

Misha grabs Ilya's coat to pull him into the circle alongside him. He might as well tug on a tree trunk, Ilya doesn't move.

"Anyway, if you have any questions, Ilya is very willing to talk to you. Anyone. Just feel free. Okay. Thank you."

Misha steps back beside Ilya. He looks up into Ilya's face.

"Stop it," the little man says, grinning, "you're seething."

On the far side of the bonfire, Pushkov rubs his forehead, then resumes his political screed. Ilya yanks Misha away from the circle so fast, Misha's legs tangle.

He demands, "What was that?"

"Calm down, Ilya." Misha straightens his coat and tunic, all untucked by the force of Ilya's pull.

"Misha."

"I don't like Pushkov. If I was his officer I'd stick him in the front line armed with a toothpick."

"You're not his officer. You're not anyone's officer."

"No. But you watch. Tomorrow morning, when we take on the citadel, you and I will have our own platoon. Just wait and see."

Misha is right. The only way to get back their positions of command is to lead these men, to constantly demonstrate that their value is far greater than just serving as cannon fodder. They must lead, even without the authority or blessing of their superiors.

"From now on, let's try to do it without tweaking Pushkov."

"Don't worry about him, Ilyushka. He'll catch his bullet long before he can do anything to us. You and me, we're charmed."

Misha smacks his big friend square on the back and steps off into the night. Ilya watches the gait of bluster in the little soldier and wonders what bantam he has set loose.

The two men walk from the bonfire to the trench where they'll wait out the morning offensive. Since January 26, Chuikov's Eighth Guards have held the city of Posen under siege. The city straddles a critical rail and highway junction in central Poland, including the main avenues from the East to Berlin. Posen cannot just be bypassed, surrounded, and throttled slowly; it has to be taken, the German garrison of over sixty thousand men eliminated, so that the Red troops moving to the east can be adequately supplied. Only half of Chuikov's forces are here for the fight; four other divisions have pressed ahead to join the armies massing on the Oder. Posen lies a hundred miles in the rear, a dangerous canker, a vital crossroads.

The city has been determined by Hitler to be one of his "fortresses." And a fortress it is. Posen, formerly a city of over a hundred thousand Poles, stippled with high cathedral towers, a college, green squares and parks, museums, fashionable shops, and artists' alleys, has been girded by the Third Reich into a genuine stronghold. The outskirts of

Posen are defended by a ring of eight massive forts, nineteenth-century relics from the days of Prussian occupation. At the center of the rings is the citadel.

The huge, pentagonal citadel sits on an elevation crowning the city. Its several forts and ramparts are reinforced by three-meter-thick bulwarks of earth. The approaches to the forts are protected by a deep and wide depression—a brick-lined moat without the water—every part of which can be put under intense fire from embrasures in the walls, dirt ramparts, and machine-gun nests concealed within. The citadel is manned by a corps of twelve thousand Germans who have been ordered by Hitler to delay the Russian advance, to defend their posts to the last man.

Over the past two weeks, Posen has been transformed again, this time by the Red Army, into a burning husk. With great effort Chuikov stormed the outer forts and defense rings, razing every obstacle with artillery and street fighting. Rows of public buildings and homes have been blown to the ground by tank fire, blackened by flamethrowers, riddled by sweeping machine guns. Hitler's fortress Posen is now occupied by Eighth Guards, except for the citadel in the center. Now all weapons are turned toward the soldiers inside.

Into the night, huddled in their trench, Ilya and Misha talk. During the combat of February they've made each other pupils. Misha teaches Ilya broad strategy, not from the ground level where Ilya is a proven master, but operational tactics, military theory. Until his fall from grace, Misha claims he was being groomed for high command. Ilya, accustomed to killing a single man at a time, with bullet or thrust, listens in admiration. Misha's expertise is apparent, his knowledge of military history the clear result of years of study and fascination. He visits not only Soviet strategies but classic generals, campaigns, and mistakes, Wellington, Patton, Thermopylae, Little Big Horn. Misha has even developed an acceptable facility with the German language.

In return, Ilya spins tales of his own battles. His recollections are vivid, imprinted in his memory by the most indelible inks, black fear and crimson scrawls. The stories are individual scenes and killings. He describes the setting, a basement, a hallway, a field, a street. He tells Misha what weapons he used, or how he did it with his bare hands. What he was feeling, how dry his mouth and skittish his nerves. How he approached, running, creeping, crawling, how he escaped. Misha listens and pulls his knees into an embrace, balling up and sometimes jerking at the crescendos of some of Ilya's tales. Ilya doesn't relate lessons. He lets clever Misha glean what he will.

During February, Ilya has watched Misha's courage grow. The little man is no war hero, yet neither is he a coward. Misha is cautious, where Ilya is brazen, wanting to prove and reprove his mettle. Together, their instincts counterbalance. Ilya and Misha stay alive. Together, they refuse to die.

In the night around them, preparations are made for the final assault on the citadel. Ammo carts squeak when unloaded. Bundles of sticks—fascines—are tied with string and flung onto gigantic piles. These will be tossed into the moat so that men might run across to the inner ramparts. Assault ladders and walk bridges are lashed together from logs and leather. Flamethrowers are topped off with incendiary oil. Misha says if you took away the modern rifles and big cannons, you'd have an old-fashioned attack on a medieval castle.

They sleep against each other for warmth. Misha curls inside Ilya's frame like a piglet, but neither feels embarrassment, men do what they must in war. There will be time to laugh about it and shrug, years later, if alive.

Two hours before dawn their company is assembled and fed. When the first tincture of morning lifts the citadel out of darkness, Ilya and Misha have crawled with their company to within one hundred meters of the edge of the moat. The three other companies of their battalion line up to their right, three hundred men total. The remainder of the infantry division waits in reserve. Behind the four companies inching forward are sapper squads, carrying explosive satchels and assault ladders.

Rising ahead is the long southwestern face of the citadel. All five sides of the fortress are besieged every day to keep the German garrison inside split and occupied. Ilya's battalion is ordered to charge the moat at this spot, enter it, cross and climb the inner rampart on the far side, and establish a foothold on top. When they are secure there, the rest of the division will advance and an attempt will be made to insert the first Red troops inside.

Once down in the moat, Ilya's company will face fire from slits in the moat walls and rampart, bunkered machine guns in the moat, and enfilading fire from both flanks out of redoubts at the corners of the citadel. Ilya does not say it to Misha, but he likens this dawn mission to sprinting into a hailstorm. The bullets will be so thick, you might run on them like stepping stones.

The first salvos from the heavy artillery two hundred meters to the rear rocket low over their heads. The men bury their chins in the dirt. The big guns don't have their turrets elevated; they're so close, they fire trajectories level with the ground. Ilya recognizes the reports, there's an array of firepower pouring in: T-34 tanks, captured German 88s, even the big 203mm cannons. A five-minute barrage batters the inner walls of the moat and dirt rampart in a concentrated area. The earth under Ilya's belly shivers like a cold woman. There's nothing he can do to comfort her.

When the explosions abate, the smoke thins. Ilya's spirit sinks seeing that the shelling did little but plow up the thick sheath of dirt above the rampart. Chunks have been chewed out of the citadel walls but the bastion stands marred only, not breached. Ilya spits. He wants to curse, but now is not the time to try one's luck.

The battalion lies still. No orders have come forward to charge the moat. Ilya looks up to see it will be a clear day, a rarity in February over Poland.

Another roar issues from behind. More artillery screeches past, exploding into the rampart. Again the earth shivers. This time the bursts are even more narrowed against the wall. The big Russian guns hammer at some bull's-eye on the rampart. The barrage sounds so low-flying, Ilya thinks if he stood he would have his head taken off.

For another five minutes, shells whomp into the citadel. The rising sun and the battered building, Misha beside him and the rest of the men, all of the morning, disappear from Ilya's sight behind a shower of brick chips, vapor, and concussion. He closes his eyes and rests his face in the crook of his elbow.

He lifts his head when the bombardment halts. Echoes and smoke hold the morn, then depart.

A "hurrah!" issues from up and down the battalion line. Misha points. "There's a hole! In the rampart!"

Ilya sees it. The gap is no wider than two meters, but it is a black wound punched in the side of the citadel. Now there's a goal to aim for in their dash through the moat.

Ilya readies to rise to his feet and charge. At that moment, on the parapet above the rampart in front of the company, a white flag emerges.

First, several cautious heads, then chests and arms, appear around the flag. More white flags step forward. At least forty German soldiers shout, *"Nicht schiessen!"* Don't shoot.

Every man in Ilya's company lifts his gun but no triggers are pulled. The Germans walk to the edge of the rampart, dropping their weapons as they come. With hands held high, the first soldier slides down its face.

He is the only man to reach the moat floor alive.

From behind, a machine gun chatters. The men are gunned down. They jerk as if kicked in the back, then roll like lost toys into the moat. The last standing soldiers twist to face the guns, to die with bullets not in the back. In moments, they too have crumpled to the bottom, an avalanche of murder.

Ilya is stunned. Some diehard Nazi inside the walls refuses to let these men choose life. When the final soldier is down, the citadel grows quiet. Along the line the fighting has stopped. All have turned their eyes to this terrible spectacle.

At the near crest of the moat, a white cloth rears. Even at a hundred meters Ilya sees it is blood-spattered. The surrender flag rises; beneath it is a scared and shaken man, the lone soldier who stood at the bottom of the moat, with the betrayed bodies of his comrades a high tide around his feet. He has no choice but to walk forward to the Russians, all eyes on him. He reaches the lip of the moat wall. He strides toward Ilya's company. Ilya and the men shout to him, "Come on! Come on!" Behind the soldier a shot barks. The man stops. He turns to face the citadel, pitifully small, appealing his fate. Two more shots finish him and his banner.

Ilya growls, he hears it from his tongue before he knows what the sound is. He is the first to his feet.

He charges. The growl becomes a bellow. Like a beast the citadel howls its defiance. Taking a running leap forward, Ilya senses bullets thud into flesh behind him. The men who are slow to rise and run with him are the bodies who stay behind forever; once the guns see you they choose the best targets, the hesitant ones. Misha is on his feet too. He is smaller and quicker. He shouts at Ilya's heels, "Go, go, go, go!"

Ilya lifts his PPSh. He releases a burst at a muzzle flash coming from a narrow slit in the rampart wall. He can't hit anything running at this distance but the closer he gets he might make them blink. The galloping men on all sides of him fire as well, and from three hundred joggling weapons they emit an effective covering fire.

The company hustles to within ten meters of the edge of the moat. A handful in Ilya's company are wounded in the surge and lie on the short plain the rest have crossed. The dead German soldier lies on his back just steps from where Ilya drops. The company sets up a firing line. Quickly the sappers crawl forward dragging assault ladders. Ilya and the line open up with every rifle to cover the sappers. The ladders are hauled a pace at a time to the edge of the moat. Once they're in place, the company will stream down them and break across the floor to the opposite bank. Two of the sappers jump up and hurl smoke canisters into the moat, then are shot down to tumble out of sight behind their billowing bombs.

Next a pair of men wearing portable flamethrowers

hurry forward. Ilya and the rest of the men keep up their firing. The rampart wall grows cottony behind pink puffs of busting brick. The flamethrowers spew streams of fire twenty-five meters across the moat. The flames splash over the embrasures, trying to silence them. Ilya rotates his submachine gun to accompany the flames. Bullets and eruptions strain every muscle, smoke and fire fill every dart of his eyes. Hundreds of weapons are in full voice around him. Men scream when they're hit, those still firing bray for revenge and fire more, madder. Even in Stalingrad, where Ilya took part in battles this pitched and dangerous, never was a fight so chaotic.

The flamethrowers exhaust themselves. The two men pull back. This section of the citadel pauses to collect itself. The company stops firing. Elsewhere down the line, men continue to engage the brick monster.

Ilya knows they cannot hold this position. They've thrown everything at the walls and can't approach any closer to the moat. After the blunted charge, eight more men in his company lie dead or wounded. Without concern for who is supposed to give the orders, Ilya readies himself to shout "Fall back."

He glances over his shoulder to see how the men are arranged, how best to retreat. He shifts to sit up higher, to holler and motion the company a hundred meters back.

A tug comes at his pants leg. Misha lies beside him.

"Maybe you shouldn't do that, Ilyushka."

Blood stains Misha's front and collar, trickling down the side of his neck. A gash streaks his cheek. His right earlobe has been shot away.

Misha looks to the rear. With his head turned, Ilya sees the little man will bleed for a while but the dribble will stop. He'll need stitches. He'll have a battle scar.

Ilya tells him, "We're going to get killed up here."

The little man pinches his shoulders together. "They'll just send us up again. That hole in the wall is the only way in."

Ilya eases to his elbows to listen. "All right," he says, "Captain Misha. You have some grand strategy?"

Misha points at the battered walls. "I figure it this way. The citadel's a fortress, right? They're surrounded. They've got no supply lines. All the ammo they have is all they're going to get. If I was in command in there, you know what I'd do? I'd tell my men to fire only to repulse attacks. Save your rounds, you won't be getting any more."

"Why not just pick us off right here?"

"Because, Ilya, this is a delaying action. They've got absolutely no intention of winning, or getting out of there. You saw what happened when those men tried to surrender. Some dyed-in-the-wool Nazi officer dick made an example out of them. No one gets out alive, that's their order. Just like Hitler told Sixth Army at Stalingrad."

Ilya recalls the starving wraiths that were German and Italian soldiers, left by Hitler to hold "Fortress Stalingrad," one million men left to rot.

Misha continues. "In the last two weeks, Posen has already tied up four of Chuikov's divisions. That's seventy thousand men along with tanks and artillery. If the Germans can hold out in the citadel for another two weeks, down to the last man, they've won as far as Hitler's concerned."

Misha draws a tender finger down his cheek. He winces crossing the bullet gash. He examines his blood on the fingertip, then sucks it off with a scrunched face.

"Besides, if we retreat it just means we'll be back attacking again in another hour. We're pretty dispensable, you know." Misha takes in the crop of bodies around them. "But running up, running back, running up again, I don't like it. And I don't think the officers will either. We're here now, let's see what we can do. I think it's our best chance."

"All right. You have a plan?"

"Almost."

Ilya reaches to Misha's mangled ear. "Does that hurt?"

"Fucking *yes* that hurts! Ow!" Misha slaps the big hand down.

"You're going to look stupid when that heals."

"It's a worry I want very much to have someday. Now let me think."

Misha sticks his tongue behind his lower lip. Ilya taps the dirt with his fingertips. A burst from one of the company is answered by a tower, stitching the ground two meters from Ilya's boots. He shinnies out of the way. The company answers. The tower shuts up, broods, waits.

"Now would be a good time, Misha."

Misha nods.

Without a word he crawls away, to the sappers behind. A minute later he returns with two satchel explosives and four sappers hauling a ladder.

"Ilya." He juts his thin chin at the citadel walls. "I'll bet it's awful loud in there."

"Probably."

"Brick walls. Low ceilings. Tiny windows."

"Yes, I'm sure it's less than ideal lodgings. Your point."

"Let's try something."

Misha hands over one of the satchels. He sets the ten-second timer on his pack and slithers toward the lip of the moat. Shocked at the little man's eagerness, Ilya hesitates, but recovers and joins him. Five meters from the lip, the citadel opens up on them, answered by the company. Bullets sizzle in both directions.

Misha hurls his satchel, landing it directly beneath a firing embrasure in the rampart. Ilya tosses his next to it, a lucky fling, but he doesn't stop to admire his work. The two scramble away from the moat and bury their noses in the dirt.

The twin explosions rock the ground, clods of dirt rattle down on their helmets. Misha rises and fires at the left tower. Ilya sees the plan and joins in. The rest of the company turn their weapons on both towers left and right, keeping them under fire, gnawing at them. The embrasures are obscured behind wasps of bullets at their sills. The sappers hurry forward and lower their ladder over the edge of the moat. They scurry back behind the company. When the shooting stops, the ladder is in place.

Ilya is impressed. Misha's tactic is simple. The Germans have three defense points covering every meter of the moat:

from straight ahead, and with flanking fire from the tower redoubts. The company can't storm the rampart head-on, they'll be cut to ribbons from front and sides before they even drop the ladders in place, much less get down them. They can't just sit back and bombard the citadel, it's too solid; the defenders are barricaded under brick and mounds. And with the infantry this close to the citadel, the artillery can't operate. But if the gunners inside the walls can't be eradicated with artillery or reached by bullets, they can be stunned with big enough explosions. If the flanks are kept busy with suppressing fire, the company can surge down the ladders and attack the rampart before they regain their senses.

How to make big enough explosions?

Misha answers the question before Ilya can ask it.

"Oil drums."

Ilya hoists his eyebrows.

"Big empty oil drums. We pack them with explosives. Light the fuses and roll them down the slope, right under the firing points. Boom. We stun them cross-eyed. We cover the towers, rush down the ladders, and head for the hole. And we get someone up on top of the rampart to drop satchel charges down the ventilation ducts."

Ilya pokes out his bottom lip and nods. "I haven't got anything better."

"Let's go tell Pushkov."

"He'll be thrilled to see us."

"He'll have to give us credit, Ilya. It'll work."

Ilya lowers to his stomach to scrabble back to Pushkov's position, behind the sappers. Misha is beside him.

Before moving, he asks, "And what's your plan after we're inside? Pushkov will want to know that too."

"Simple."

Misha sticks a finger in Ilya's breast, the spot where Ilya used to wear his medals.

"You take over."

FOUR

———

L OTTIE STARES AT THE YELLOW DOOR.
She tightens her sweater around her, expressing
huffiness, but her mother pays no heed. Freya busies
herself making sandwiches and a big pot of potato soup,
humming over the stove in a pretty, warbly voice. There is
electricity this morning and she wants to cook as much as
she can during these random hours of civilization. For
months Freya has hoarded a salami, hiding it wrapped in
waxed paper under a loose floorboard. This morning she
carves from it precious slices.

Lottie leans against the wall in the short hall between the
dining room and the kitchen. She could stick out her foot
and kick the door leading to the basement. That would get
some attention.

The basement door is painted a meringue yellow. A gross
color, it looks like pus. Behind the door she imagines hell. A
demon waits behind that door, her personal devil, come into
her life to ruin her.

She might have survived. Her chances were good. But
now there is a devil.

Invited into her life. By her own mother.

A Jew.

In the basement, Freya keeps a Jew.

He sits at the top of the steps—Freya says that's what he does—listening to them, to Freya hum, Lottie grumble. He hears everything, he never moves from the step. It's always dark in the basement, he lives on what little light creeps under the door, what little sound he can snatch through it. Lottie thinks of him as a gargoyle, folded wings, cleft pupils in his eyes.

Lottie will not speak to the Jew behind the door. For two weeks, since she came to stay with Freya when her building was destroyed, she has refused. Lottie leaves the room whenever Freya talks to him, she does not want to hear the Jew. She goes from the house whenever Freya opens the door to take him food. She does not want to be there if they're caught. She reasons that if she's ever questioned, she can claim no knowledge of the Jew; her mother said he was there but Lottie never heard or saw him. This is her only slim hope to survive him.

She wants to throw him out. Kick open the door, bruise him on his stoop for the outrage of his presence, and order him to leave. But this is not her home, it's her mother's. She suspects Freya would sooner order Lottie banished than the Jew.

Lottie shifts her gaze from the basement door to the kitchen. Freya pares potatoes over a skillet. The peels she will fry in lard and seasonings. She has a lovely voice. Her dress hem seems a bit higher lately, her shoes shine. She swore to save the salami for the most dire times. Now she makes sandwiches. It's the Jew's fault, Lottie believes, that she thinks these evil thoughts about her mother.

The morning her building was bombed Lottie collapsed in the street. Rescue workers carried Mrs. Preutzmann up from the blazing neighbor building before it too fell in on itself. The landlady awoke screaming for her husband. A fireman covered Lottie with a blanket, then she was left alone. She curled beside her cello, locking out behind closed eyes the crashes, sirens, shouts. A wailing crowd milled in Regensburger Strasse. Volunteers handed out hot drinks and bland buns. In the afternoon, with the sun cloaked in smoke, Lottie rose. Her body carried an ache that seemed to outweigh the cello case; she dragged it and herself to Char-lottenburg. All the trains were stopped, there was so much wreckage across the tracks. The whole city was ignited. One train had barreled on fire into the Anhalter Station, slam-ming into the station like a flaming arrow. In backyards, winter piles of coal burned, giant anthills of angry red. They will smolder for weeks. The air was polluted with the cre-mation of buildings and escaping gas. Lottie's progress through the city was held up by uprooted trees, broken tele-graph poles, torn wires, craters, and mounds of smoking rubble. The fire-borne wind hurled roof tiles, gutters, and glass shards into the streets. She staggered through it all to Mutti.

When Freya opened her door, she wept to see her daughter. She took Lottie upstairs to bed and tended to the many scratches and cuts on her face and arms. She soaked her daughter's blistered hands in Epsom salts. The two did not talk much. For three days Lottie lay in Freya's bedroom, wrapped in quilts. Her mother slept on the sofa in the room or in a guest bed. She shuttled in hot tea and soups. Freya sat on the edge of the mattress resting her hand on Lottie's foot or her forehead. Lottie fixed on the ceiling or shut her eyes. The Galiano stood in the corner like a patient friend, wait-ing for her to rouse and play.

On the fourth morning, Lottie left the house with the cello. She was weak and downhearted, but there was a re-hearsal for the Philharmonic. She could not miss it, even with swollen hands, her place with the BPO as tenuous as it is. Freya walked with her to the U-bahn station, carrying the cello. The two kissed cheeks. Despite her worries, Lottie felt her spirits stir. A glimmer inside her hoped everything might be all right. Her mother could make it so. Lottie had not lost everything; not her cello, and not Mutti.

At dusk when she returned, Freya sat her down in the den. She took her daughter's hands. Her eyes slid sideways to the basement door several times. Then Freya took a deep breath and spoke.

"You're feeling better."

"Yes."

"Good. I can tell you now."

Lottie blinked.

"I've taken in a Jew."

Lottie shook her head, balking at understanding what she'd just heard.

Freya repeated. "I've taken in a Jew."

Lottie jerked back her hands as though from the maws of mad dogs.

"You've done what?"

"He's in the basement."

Lottie rattled her head. "No, no, no."

"Lottie, listen to me. He has nowhere else to go. He's been hiding from the Nazis for two years. If we turn him out he's dead."

Comprehension crashed into Lottie's brain like the burning train at the station.

"He's dead? *He's* dead? What about us? We're dead if he stays here."

"No."

"Yes! He's got to go. Right now!"

"No. He's already been here for a month. He's going to stay. To the end."

"A month! You've . . ."

Lottie leaped from the sofa. She ran down the hall to the basement door, envisioning for the first time the demon behind it. She spoke to the door, an exorcism.

"Listen. You hear me? You've got to leave. We can't have you here. Get out!"

The door was silent. Lottie feared the doorknob, what she might see if she turned it, moist and white, the Jew in the darkness, the Jew eclipsing her life.

She put her hand on the knob.

Freya laid her hand over Lottie's. Her mother's grip was shocking, hard.

Her tone was calm, not just a mother's words but a protector's, firm and righteous.

"Get away from this door, Lottie."

As strong as Lottie's hands were, Freya pried her fingers from the door.

She took Lottie by the elbow and towed her back to the sofa. With a yank the two women sat.

"Mutti."

"No."

"Do you understand the danger you've put us in?"

"Yes."

Lottie needed to explain it anyway to her mother, who couldn't possibly understand, or else she wouldn't have done this. "If we're caught, we'll be shot. Right outside in the street, in front of your house. The SS will *shoot* us, Mutti."

"And what will they do to him if he's caught?"

"I don't know."

Freya was stricken. She wagged her head, solemn, almost a shudder.

"That's the worst of all possible answers."

Lottie stood. She wanted to look down on her mother, that was her mood.

"Mutti. We're not heroes."

Freya also stood.

"We're not monsters. Today, in Berlin and everywhere in Germany, that's all there is. It's a choice and every German makes it. Do nothing, know nothing. Or act. Monster or hero. That's all there is for the whole world until this is over."

Freya put her hands to her hips. She spread her legs.

"Lottie, *Liebchen,* I only put myself in this danger. I had no idea you'd be coming to live with me. You're here now and you're welcome, of course. But I've made my choice in this matter. You've got to make yours."

The arguments lasted for days. Lottie demanded to know how they could feed a third mouth when they could barely scrape by themselves? Their ration cards are already growing more and more useless, government stores are drying up. The few remaining shops are being burned out from the bombings. They have not enough money for black-market food.

Who else knows about the Jew? Will Mutti keep her mouth shut and not tell her friends, not want to show off how good she's being, how heroic? Who among her acquaintances will trade in Mutti's and Lottie's lives for an extra portion of horsemeat?

How can the Jew be trusted? How does she know he's not a spy, just waiting to grab her and some ring of imagined conspirators?

Who's to say how long he'll keep his word and stay put? That he won't go crazy in the dank basement and go out for a stroll? It'll all be over then.

What happens if the house is bombed and he's found in the basement, moaning, "Get me out, get me out." After they rescue him, they shoot him. And then Lottie and Mutti. He's a Jew in their basement.

Why give a stranger such control over them?

Freya held her ground. Lottie caved in. She had no choice. She has nowhere else to go. Like the Jew. They are trapped in Mutti's house together. But trapped or not, Lottie will not acknowledge him.

She finds it creepy that he sits there on the top step, listening, waiting for someone to walk by, capture a word or two outside his barrier. He perches there probably even when the house is empty. What kind of human being is it who can tolerate such darkness, silence, hatred, danger, suspicion, fear? The Jew scares her for his power, not only over her life, but what it must take to withstand his own.

At night Lottie awakes from nightmares and stares in the cold gloom at the door to her room. He's down there, crouched on the top step behind the door. The nightmares must come from him. She's afraid he'll sneak out and touch her while she sleeps, that she'll wake up and find him over her.

Mutti says he's a wonderful man. A teacher of history, he knows all sorts of tales. His own is a horrible story. If Lottie would only let him tell it to her, she would see there's no choice but to help him. He's alone. His people, all his people, terrible, terrible.

For the two weeks she has been in Mutti's household, the Jew has respected Lottie's wish not to be seen or heard by her. She has never said it directly to him; she has not spoken one word to him since she demanded that he leave; but he has heard her say it to Mutti. Lottie thinks he might not even be real. He might be nothing more than an empty wish by Mutti, a fantasy that she could be so brave as to help a Jew.

When Lottie is out of the house, she doesn't know what he does. Does he come out and sip tea with Mutti? Do they chat on the sofa? No, he must stay hidden. If a neighbor happened by, if a curtain were left opened to the street . . . no, the consequences of the smallest slipup will be awful.

Lottie watches her mother move the soup kettle to the burner. The skillet begins to spit grease. The Jew behind the door can smell food coming, he rises like a goldfish to it. Lottie cannot stand the house, the malaise and tension, another moment. How can the Jew sit day after day, weeks without light, with such silence? How can a human being live like a rat? She wants to rap the door hard with her toe, make him jump, tumble down the steps.

Lottie whirls away from the kitchen, arms bound around her. She stomps the long walk to the front parlor. She goes to the sofa and folds with a bounce. It's quiet in the parlor, the kitchen is a long way back. The rooms in Mutti's house are narrow, and there are a lot of them. The building is a two-story row house, with a face of fat gray stone. The Gothic facade has been marred by shrapnel and some windows have been shattered, but Freya has been lucky with the bombings. And fortunate with the authorities; there's room here for three more families.

She goes to her cello case. She takes out the Galiano, it is shiny and ancient. Placing a chair in the center of the room, she arranges the instrument between her knees. She hugs the cello, lays her head on its cool wooden shoulder. The Galiano is innocent, she thinks, perfect and good. In its big chest is nothing but the songs of maestros. Lottie knows how to caress it to bring them out, the music in the cello's breath. She strokes its waist. Why are we here now, she wonders, you and me in this awful time and place? She's ashamed that the Galiano—two hundred years old, it has cried and laughed on stages in Vienna, Rome, Paris, London, seen centuries of opulence and honor—must find itself today in Berlin.

Lottie lifts her head. Her cheek wears the flat kiss of the cello.

She flicks her glance at the kitchen, to her cooking, courageous mother. Then to the basement door, behind which an unknown manner of man suffers for deliverance.

Fine for the two of you, Lottie thinks.

Now, listen. This is what I can do.

She inclines her head, her eyes half closed. Lottie descends to the place inside her where the music waits with its arms out, always, like a child to be lifted. She draws the bow across the strings, slowly, the opening strain to the first solo of Schumann's Concerto for Cello in A minor, Opus 129. This is Lottie's dream piece. She's practiced it a hundred times. One day she will play the solo in front of the Berlin Philharmonic and adoring thousands. In her mind they're in their seats in the theater now.

Her playing builds with the work. This is not her private, rehearsal tone but full concert pitch. Her vibrato and bow stroke would fill the Beethoven Hall to the rafters were she there. Lottie lifts her chin, her head undulates left and right with the sound, the cello charms her as though out of a basket. Under lowered lids, Lottie sees her mother in the doorway.

The music broods for many measures, exploring the lower registers of the cello, the sounds of a father weeping. Then the music becomes the keen of a mother, high-pitched, sweeping into a quicker lament, the beating of fists. Lottie surrenders to the pain and the selfishness of her genius. She is strapped to the passages and cascades with them. She is oblivious to all else but the cello and her cause, to play as powerfully as the Jew, to play as loftily as anything Mutti might behold of herself.

Lottie listens. She knows her performance is compelling.

The cello is a treasure box she sweeps clean, the Schumann piece is her broom; she leaves nothing inside the instrument, bringing out every bauble and secret of it for her mother and the Jew to marvel at.

When she is done, her eyes are fully closed. She lowers the bow gracefully, with flourish. By instinct of her imagination, she stands to the applause of the concert hall. She lifts her head and there is Freya clapping, a dish towel over her shoulder. Mutti's eyes are red-rimmed.

Freya says, "Bravo, child. Bravo." She pulls the towel off her shoulder to dry her eyes.

The clapping continues.

It carries from far down the hall. From the basement.

Freya beams at her daughter, but only for a moment. She turns away, walking a few steps into the dining room. She calls, "I told you she plays beautifully. Doesn't she?"

The single clapping continues, softened by distance and walls. Lottie wants it to stop. This is wrong, a violation of the rules. He should not become real. It was the bargain they all made. He's clapping. He's there. The Jew behind the door speaks to Lottie.

Freya returns fully to the parlor. She has been moved.

"Liebchen, that was magnificent. Was that for me?"

Lottie fumbles with the bow and the cello, putting them in the case. The clapping does not die out. He's there. A Jew in their house.

"No."

"Well." Freya folds the kitchen towel. "It was practice, then. Wonderful."

Make him stop, Lottie thinks. It's ridiculous.

Freya cocks her head backward, to the basement. "Listen to him."

"I have to get ready. There's a concert at four."

"I didn't know. Will you be playing the Schumann?"

Stupid question. Stupid mother.

"No."

The clapping stops.

Freya stays in the room while Lottie stows the Galiano. Lottie replaces the chair and makes for the stairs. Freya speaks to stop her.

"*Liebchen.*"

"Yes."

"Thank you. You can see what that meant to him."

Lottie imagines the history teacher on his dark stoop. He probably cried too.

Making no reply, she climbs the steps, aggravated. She did a self-centered thing. An awful thing. She played with all her might to humble them both, show them who was extraordinary among the three. Plenty of people suffer, everyone in Berlin. Millions are brave. But who possesses Lottie's gift? A handful in the world.

Mutti chose to see Lottie's vanity as noble. Mutti warped her daughter's egotism into generosity. The Jew clapped a full minute after the music stopped. He's ludicrously appreciative. The two of them stole the music from Lottie. They wept and molded it into their own images, for their purposes, further proof that they're the most special and good of anyone.

Lottie changes into the tuxedo and puts up her hair. Twenty minutes later she lands in the foyer. The cello is by the door, beside a paper sack of salami sandwiches. Lottie dons her overcoat, and without saying goodbye takes both packages into the chill city afternoon.

By two o'clock she has arrived at the Beethoven Hall. Today's concert is Mozart and Schubert. There's plenty of cello in the Schubert, even for fourth chair. Outside the theater, people stand in line. The afternoon concerts are free, but there are limited seats available for the public. Large sections are blocked off for Nazi officials and servicemen. When the lights go up after performances, Lottie and the musicians look out over a lake of black uniforms, whitecaps of bandages. Sometimes there are no lights; ushers use lanterns to lead the audience out.

Backstage, there is animated chatter. Whenever the musicians of the BPO gather, the first thing they do is weigh their fates. Lottie doesn't take part in the discussions; she's a woman, only a provisional member of the orchestra.

The men lump into clatches of five to ten, often by instrument. What will happen to them? Will they be conscripted into the *Volkssturm*? Will Speer act to save them? Is Goebbels just going to throw them to the wolves after all they've done for Berlin? Lottie sits alone, her back to a wall, casting her attention left and right like a fishing lure. An oboist found some black-market bread, here's the address. A French-horn player saw a Belgian worker crushed to death by a falling beam. Another string player was bombed out of his house; oddly, along with Lottie, the string section has been hit hardest. Someone in the percussion section has been listening to Allied broadcasts. This can get him executed so he whispers, though he is among men he can trust. They all have the same interest: survival, for themselves and the BPO. He says the Americans and British are ready to cross the Roer River, headed for the Rhine. They're aiming at Berlin. He believes the German troops will lay down their arms and escort the *Amis* in. Then they'll all band together and take care of the dirty Reds.

The French-horn player hears this. He shakes his nose at his grouping of brass players. The Russians will be here first, he says. They're only fifty miles away. He's a sad, spongy old man, dripping of ugly tales and depressing news. Lottie avoids him and his clique.

The Russians are brutes, he says. The things he's heard, *tsk*. You don't want to know. You may even have heard worse. And they're getting angrier and more out of control with every step closer to Berlin.

Pity the city, says a trumpeter.

The French-horn player answers. Oh, Berlin can take it. We just have to keep our heads down and lie low. But pity the women.

When several heads in the group tilt toward Lottie, they seem surprised to see her glaring back. Chagrined, they lean again into their circle, their voices ratcheted down. Lottie hears another *tsk*.

The day's performance is lackadaisical. The image of a Russian plague massing on the Polish border is a pall over the performers. Furtwängler is gone; the director until he returns is Robert Heger. He appears perplexed waving his baton, a jockey on a distracted horse. Heger beats the BPO but they respond with reluctant speed. The Mozart is mangled; Lottie cannot even muster much gusto for the Schubert. But the house erupts in applause when they are finished. Heger drops his arms and turns for his bow, he is snappy, badly hiding his anger. The orchestra stands and bows. To Lottie they look like an orchestra stretching their necks to a guillotine.

The house lights come up. The musicians shuffle off the stage. Lottie hears low-slung curses from the men. Chairs skid out of the way, sheets of music flutter to the stage floor. Lottie holds her spot, focusing her eyes on the back of the auditorium, at the top of the aisles where Berliners queue to exit. The line on the right is slow, a few soldiers on crutches hobble as best they can. Berliners are patient behind them.

The line on the left is also slow. Something unusual is going on. Two men in uniform are at the head of each aisle, handing out items from baskets. Lottie eases the Galiano to its side on the floor. She steps into the wings, then down the stairs to the house floor.

At the tail of the right-hand line in the emptying house, Lottie accepts a few kind statements from an elderly couple. She bites her tongue and says thank you. They congratulate her for being a woman in the orchestra and admit surprise; from the audience they could not spot her for the tuxedo. Lottie explains it's only until the war is over; they nod. Approaching the top of the aisle, Lottie discerns that the men in uniform are boys, Hitler Youth. From thirty feet away, she sees the blue of their eyes, like welders' torches. Their paramilitary outfits are hard things, dark shells of leather and spiny creases, they look so wrong for boys of fourteen or fifteen.

Lottie follows the slow gait to the boys. Ahead, some people dig into the baskets, then hurry away. Others halt and gaze down at what the two youths offer, seeming to fall into a spell until someone prods them and they either dig in or walk on, dazed. No one speaks. The two Nazi youths say nothing. They look everyone in the face. They are stony, sober children.

When the old couple in front of Lottie gain the top of the aisle, the two peer down into the basket. Their eyes stay in there for several moments, netted in what they see. Their glances rebound up together, and in the look they share Lottie reads the lives these two have spent by each other's side. Fifty years or more, husband and wife. On their twin faces are love, children, tragedy, loyalty. Still as twins, they nod just slightly, never unlocking their eyes. The man reaches into the basket for both of them and takes two.

Lottie steps up. The basket is held out.

Inside are capsules, wrapped and labeled in tiny plastic packets.

Cyanide.

Lottie catches her breath. Her gut plummets.

Dear God.

This is all the protection Hitler can summon at the end for his German people against the Russians. Baskets of poison, government-sanctioned suicide. A Home Guard made up of old men and frightened musicians. Cities of ruins. And dead-faced boys, whose hands holding out these baskets are smaller-boned than Lottie's.

She's disgusted. Neither of the Hitler Youth twitches, they could be mannequins.

Her disgust twists in her gut like a dirk, twists into nausea.

The Jew in the basement is real. The Russians are real. The cyanide is real.

Doom.

Lottie loses her balance. Neither ebon boy moves to aid her. One knee buckles; she grabs hold of the gilded door frame. The theater spins. She wants to vomit.

One of the boys speaks. "*Fräulein*. We cannot protect you."

Lottie lifts her chin above the tide of her rising insides.

Looking into their faces, she does not know which of the boys talked. She dips a hand into the basket. The packets beneath her fingertips are white, soft, little kisses in the basket. She fingers a pill. So small, so enormous. She'll put the thing in the Jew's food. That'll take care of one problem.

Her hand digs deeper. The tablets play around her knuckles. They seem gentle, competent. The pills make a vow to her: we'll keep our promise. Trust us, but nothing else. We're the only things in your world that will do what we say. Take me. Me! No, pick me!

She hovers over the basket.

She won't poison the Jew. He may live like a rat in the basement but she won't kill him like one.

Lottie's head clears. Her hand is still plunged in the pills. They nibble at the backs of her fingers like minnows.

She chooses. You. Little friend, you are for me.

She plucks another. And you. You can come also.

For Mutti.

The Gestapo or the Russians—one or the other, when they come—will be coming for Mutti too.

Everything is real.

February 22, 1945, 11:10 P.M.
With the Ninth Army on the west bank
of the Roer River, near Jülich
Germany

BANDY NEVER LIKES NIGHT OPERATIONS. HE CAN'T TAKE photos in the dark.

He pulls a lantern closer to his lap, not for the light but the heat. The air is river-damp and chilly, even in his tent. He takes a quick look around at his setup: cot, desk and chair, blankets, magazines. He's been living high on the hog the last ten days, staying in one place. By afternoon this'll all be torn down, moved across the river and given to someone else. Bandy doesn't want to spend any more nights in tents. He, along with the whole U.S. Ninth Army, wants to get going again, to Berlin. He wants to sleep in the front seat of a rolling truck on the *Autobahn*. In the last week he hasn't sent one photo back to New York. Photos of what—waiting? Even so, his instincts tell him he's in the right place.

Along Ike's broad front, both Bradley in the middle and Patton in the south are facing a lot of opposition getting to the Rhine. Even after they're across, they'll be staring at the bulk of the German forces in the West. Plus, there's a rumor that Hitler's preparing a southern route out of Berlin for his escape to the alpine regions of Bavaria, Austria, and Italy. The story goes the Führer's going to retreat there to a prepared redoubt, his Eagle's Nest, set up a microphone and radio transmitter and keep the fight alive with a Nazi resistance force of maniacs in the mountains. If Hitler does get in there, it'll take another million men to pry him out. Look at the killing in the Hürtgen; triple it. So Ike has to worry about intercepting enemy troops possibly heading south. But up here on the northern track, Monty's free from having to cut off any breakout. He's got Berlin in his bonnet and a straight shot once he's across the Rhine. The Ninth Army is still under him, Eisenhower let the Field Marshal keep it. Bandy gambles that these U.S. forces will be the ones to break through, with Montgomery and Churchill spurring them on.

Jump-off this morning is at 0245. Bandy figures he'd better get in a letter to Victoria. Who knows when he'll have another chance to write. Like all servicemen around the world at war, Bandy has his final letter written out and sealed in his breast pocket. It's been there for three years now. In his career he's written five of them, goodbyes to Victoria.

Her recent letter was another plaint. She's getting more annoyed every time she writes. When are you coming home? I'm so mad at you, if the Krauts don't kill you I might, and so on. She never acted like this before when he was gone. What's different now?

On the cot he touches the pen to the pad. What can he say? Dear Vic, I'm not sorry I'm here. I'm not sorry I'm the man I am and drawn where and when I am. I'm not sorry that I'm risking making you a widow so I can take pictures of other men doing it worse to their own gals. How does Bandy tell her this?

He lowers his forehead into his palm and thinks, You just plain don't tell her. The pen stands at attention, waiting for orders.

Bandy writes:

Dearest Victoria,

Hi, doll. I'm here in the middle of nowhere again. Next to the Roer River with a division of the Ninth Army, about ten thousand men. We're going across tonight. Well, they are. I'll wait for morning.

That was some spread Life *gave me on the Hürtgen, wasn't it? It was pretty awful being there. Not as bad as being one of the soldiers. Of course.*

After I got through the forest with the First Army, I came up here north with the Ninth for the Roer crossing. But the Germans blew the river dams two weeks ago and we've been held up here ever since, waiting for the water to recede. Dammit (ha-ha). In the downtime the men have practiced the crossing a bunch of times, and we've had some big brass visit, wearing ties. Even some correspondents came up to take a few notes, watch a couple artillery shells fired, then scoot back to the rear to file their reports "from the front." Papa Hemingway was one. Everybody made a fuss over him. Me, I'm here all the time. Anyway. A prophet is not without honor. . . .

With luck, by next week I should be able to write from the east bank of the Rhine. Then it's on to Berlin. I'm going to keep trying to find out what

outfit has the best shot of getting there first and join
up. That'll be the best, Vic. Won't it? Charles
Bandy, IN BERLIN. Can you see it?
I know this is hard on you, but it's almost over.
We're on our way, every man here feels it!

In his head Bandy hears the responses from his wife. He
doesn't want to argue with her. He writes something conciliatory.

Look, I swear. When this is over I'll stay home
permanent. Just you and me, tobacco, babies, and
some domestic assignments just to keep my hand in.

This is mostly a lie, everything but the part about the babies. He wants to scratch it all out but that would mar the
letter, make her suspicious that he'd written something even
worse. There's worse he could have written. A kind lie's not
so bad. If he was face-to-face with her he'd say it, whatever,
to make her feel better about things, to get through this.

But Bandy won't quit *Life* magazine. Not so long as history gets made in the world, and that's every dang day. After
this war there's going to be another conflict somewhere, big
or small. Mankind only knows one way to exist with each
other and that's with some measure of mayhem. Victoria
teaches schoolkids about things that Bandy has pho-
tographed, and will photograph. How can he give this up?
How can she not understand? It's always been bigger than
one man and one woman, or it wouldn't be history.

Lies are like punches, they come best in combinations.

The brass here figure weeks, Vic, maybe a month
more. The Germans are hightailing it. This'll all be
over real soon and you can give me up the country in
person. That sound good?

A whopper. Hitler's not rolling over for the West, no
way. Though he ought to be. No one can figure out why

the little shit is fighting so hard against the Americans and British. The guns are all on German soil now. These are German towns and cities going up in flames. The country's being destroyed, while the soldiers and people and even teenage boys fight back fanatically. It doesn't make sense— for what? They're beat. Bandy's heard only three possible explanations: first, the National Redoubt in the Alps, Hitler's buying time to get it ready. Second, the Führer thinks if he can give the Western Allies one more bloody nose like he did at the Bulge, we'll make a separate peace with him and join with the Nazis against the Reds, which won't happen. Nobody wants that fight, from Roosevelt on down. The last explanation is that the German people are scared to death of paying the piper for what they've done here in Europe. If they put up a good enough fight, the Allies might consider accepting something less than unconditional surrender from Germany, just to get the war over with. That's not going to happen either. Not from everything Bandy's heard about what went on in Russia and Poland, and what he's seen with his own eyes, his precious history. The piper is owed far too much.

Outside the tent a convoy growls past. Bandy's tent rattles. He shoves aside the flap. Trucks carrying the four-hundred-pound, eight-man assault boats make for the river's edge.

> *I got to go now. With luck I'll write you next from the east bank of the Rhine.*
> *I love you. Always. Everywhere.*
>
> *Charley*

Bandy sticks the letter in an envelope. He gathers his camera bags, stuffs an extra blanket into his pack, and leaves the tent. He hooks a ride with a truck in the convoy and heads to the riverbank, leaving the letter with the GI driver to mail.

Along the bank, valves have been opened on giant steel canisters mounted on flatbed trucks. Clouds of oil smoke roil out, spilling across the water to obscure those engineers hoisting the assault boats to the lip of the water. The receding Roer has turned the approach to the river into a two-hundred-yard swath of marshy, muddy goop. Bandy watches the engineers go and return. He wishes for daylight to shoot them, the men are covered chin-down in muck, they steam stepping out of the fog, like swamp creatures. All around, the might of the Ninth Army slips and clutches for purchase against the river and earth. Giant trucks haul forward girders and pontoons to erect bridges once a beachhead is secured on the east bank. Dozens of assault companies, each a hundred fifty men strong, hunker in clearings, waiting; they clatter like cicadas in the dark, fidgeting with their rifles, rations, helmets, packs, fears, smokes, chatter, prayers. Their breaths, lit by passing headlamps, make false mists over the glens. Bandy knows he sees only a fraction of the activity along the twenty-mile Roer front; this gargantuan bustle is going on in dozens of other places out there in the night. Ten thousand men will attempt the crossing before daybreak; over the next few days four hundred thousand will follow.

What waits for them? First, natural barriers. The river is up to ten feet deep, with strong currents and icy temperature. After the troops make landfall there's no cover for three hundred yards, just bald mud and backwash. Even more menacing are the man-made obstacles, almost comparable to what the Allies faced on Normandy's beaches. The river and bank are mined, there's concertina wire in the water, fortified trenches, minefields deep into enemy territory, presighted guns, a dug-in and determined enemy. Their objective is Jülich, a town of ten thousand on a low rise above the river. From there, east to the Rhine.

For two hours Bandy roams alone. He strides among trucks grinding gears, bleating men, silent huddled groups, cold equipment in high stacks. All this weight—millions of tons and dollars, millions of hopes for life and freedom, history!—resting on the shoulders of one man at a time, one soldier with a gun and running legs and a pumping heart.

Bandy breathes in their glory and their coming horrors. He walks through them, wanting to touch each one, record every face and story so they will not pass unnoted. But it's night and there is no role for him. He thinks something is unfair. He feels the way he does sometimes on the farm, like he's just a man and the world does not know him, the way the world does not know each soldier.

At 0230, the preparations stutter to a stop. All the trucks cut their lights. The men are with the boats beside the Roer, officers stop calling orders. The engineers head for dry clothes. Bandy climbs up on the warm hood of a still truck. He stares across the gloomy swatch that is the unseen river.

Right on time, at 0245, an artillery barrage all along the front splits the night into splinters. The dark flashes on and off as though some prankster has his hand on the light switch. Bandy, warming his butt, watches the far bank of the river mushroom behind the oil smoke and gun smoke into circlets of orange flame. The sound rushes back across the wide water and thumps his chest.

For forty-five minutes the big guns rage at the Germans, killing them, stunning them, forcing them out of their holes. In both directions, up and down the river to the distant bends, the opposite bank and a mile inland are drenched in a rain of explosives. Bandy reaches into his memory and cannot recall a bombardment to equal it. The shelling at night is particularly fearsome, every explosion in its moment ignites the blackness, trembling through the fog like lightning in storm clouds.

At 0330, the shelling halts. Bandy gazes into restored dark and quiet. Neon spots ghost his vision from the shells. That was some pummeling. Right now the opposite bank must look like the moon. The first assault companies slip into the water. Engineers on thirty-two inflated boats will ferry the initial wave over, then they'll come back for another load.

Bandy can't see much from his truck hood. But the night is full with unseen men motoring across the misted water, clutching fear and resolve as tight as rifles. For which ones will the Roer be their river Styx? For whom will there be no return? The river is wide, the current strong. The enemy waiting. Bandy senses his own heartbeat pulse behind his breast pocket, nudging at the plastic-sealed final note to Victoria, the one letter that he and all men in war hope their women and folks never get.

In minutes the first cracks of small arms fire speed across the water, returning harbingers to report the battle is on. Muffled thumps like beaten laundry tell of detonated mines. Bandy builds for himself visions and photographs from the sounds, mosaics of imagination. Men slog through the mud into German lines, weapons bark, men fall, men run, trenches smoke, ruins and craters pock the ground.

There's nothing he can do until sunup but sit on this truck, or walk about some more. For now, Bandy is useless. He climbs down, pulls out his blanket, and crawls into the truck cab. He curls on the seat. The upholstery stinks of cigarettes.

Bandy's last thought, the one he recalls when he wakes four hours later, is of tobacco. He opens his eyes. He feels as if he has dreamed, though he can't remember a dream. But it was sad, long ago, and in another country. He thinks of Victoria. He sits up to war.

Stiff, Bandy steps down from the truck cab. He shoulders his packs and makes for the river's edge. In the night, engineers have erected two footbridges and a cable ferry secured on the opposite bank. The artillery and the assault must have taken solid hold, dislodging the Germans. Men and materiel pour single file across the Roer. Pontoons and large beams are piled by the river to begin construction of a treadway bridge to move tanks and trucks. The engineers are like ants, crawling over everything, seeming to lift many times their own weight.

Hungry and cold, shuffling in the line to cross, Bandy bums a K ration. At 0740, he moves out over the river. The footbridge sways in the current under his feet, half the boards are underwater. He moves hand over hand along the lone cable. His balance is faulty from just waking up, his boots slosh and the oil smoke burns his eyes and nostrils.

It takes him ten minutes to get halfway over the river, fearing all the while that his hands or feet will slip and he'll fall in. If his Speed Graphic and Leica get wet, Bandy becomes a civilian without a mission. He'd have to fall back to resupply. By the time he finagles his way back up here, Berlin might have already fallen. He moves with caution. Soldiers behind him bunch up, some call out at him to get going. Screw 'em, Bandy thinks, I'm the oldest guy out here by fifteen years. He hears a splash through the smoke ahead, a man cusses, the voice floats downstream. Bandy grits his teeth. This is miserable.

To add to his ordeal, artillery shells begin to fall on all sides of the footbridge. Apparently the Germans have regrouped on some high ground over there near the town and are trying to stem the flow of Americans crossing the Roer. Pillars of water fountain left and right, soaking every soldier on the river. In an instant Bandy is dripping. The frigid water seeps down to his underwear, his skin puckers. The cameras in his pack are wrapped in oilskins, they're safe so long as he isn't submerged. The barrage is random, the Germans can't draw a bead through the smoke. But the crossing is made that much more dangerous. Bandy thinks how just minutes ago he was asleep.

It takes him only six more minutes to cover the second half of the footbridge. Hitting the bank, he steps into sludge that sucks his boots and legs up to the calves. As unhappy as he is, Bandy's relieved to see so few American bodies. The attack went well, clearly. But the dead lie in such an awful, apocalyptic place, under a greasy haze, half dissolved into the mud. The charge on Berlin is on, the Allies are coursing forward with power and pace. It's a tragedy to die at all, but a pity to die now with the end in sight. Bandy wants to take pictures. He's reminded of scenes of World War I, smoke and filth, rushing men. But his hands are too slimy, there's no dry or clean place on him or anywhere around him. He leaves the cameras in their protection, nods to the dead, and hurries forward with the others who cannot stop, to Jülich.

Bandy struggles in the deep steps of soldiers making their way ahead of him. No one stops to shoot at anything, the Germans have left the bank and fallen back to the town. Through the winter-bare trees appear streets, a steeple, red slate roofs. The drier the ground gets under Bandy's boots, the clearer are the sounds of battle; near the river all he could hear was the *swoook, swoook* of muddy treads. Behind a clump of bushes, he drops to his knees and takes from his camera bag the 35mm Leica. He loads a roll, slaps the case shut, and sticks three more rolls in his coat pocket. The Leica is Bandy's action camera, compact and quick to focus, and he can handle it with one hand. The negatives are less crisp than those of the big Speed Graphic, but that's not a concern this morning. He won't be photographing faces. The subject will be smoking, crumbling buildings.

On the edge of town Bandy joins a squad of fifteen men. Their assignment is to move up and take a block in the southwestern corner of Jülich. The troops who came over the Roer by boat in the dark didn't bother to take the town; their task was to keep moving, deeper and deeper, to expand the bridgehead. The second, larger echelon will consolidate the gains.

The American soldiers have reaped the methods of street fighting from France, Belgium, Holland, and Luxembourg. Now they know what to do, and because they're in Germany they take a particular pleasure in doing it.

Bandy squats with the squad in a mound of rubble. About fifty feet away is the first of a row of brick buildings along a wide street. The structures are all two-story, attached. They appear to be businesses mingled with private homes. A sign has been painted in white letters on the wall facing them: WELCOME UNCLE SAM. SEE GERMANY AND DIE! Without looking behind him the squad sergeant wags a finger over his shoulder. The two-man bazooka crew skittles forward.

The sergeant says, "My guess is right on that big ol' G in Germany."

The two bazooka handlers, grizzled and sable-toothed from tobacco chaws, purse their lips and spit together. Bandy snaps their picture, spittle in midflight. Not publishable, he thinks, but a great shot for his private archive. The twin soldiers arrange themselves, one knee each on the ground. The rest of the squad clear the areas in front and rear. The bigger of the two hefts the bazooka pipe to his shoulder and lays his eye to the sight. The second soldier—a face bearded and squinty; Bandy sees how a shower, a shave, and a weekend in Bermuda would turn him into a handsome man—pats his comrade on the back. He gets a quick helmeted nod and slides in a shell the size of a bread loaf. He ducks, the bazooka recoils with a belch of flame out its tail, the firing man rocks, but the bazooka is firm in his grasp. Across the clearing the building explodes in the same moment. The bazooka stays in place, the crew is ready to fire again if necessary. The rest of the squad get set to rush forward. Smoke swirls out of the way, and the sign reads only WELCOME UNCLE SAM.

Someone pulls the pin on a smoke grenade and rolls it into the open. It spews a small cloud bank. Four men scurry out, making slits in the mist, which quickly heals itself. Bandy waits for gunfire. The unit that has dashed inside is rushing from room to room looking for enemy soldiers. They're kicking in closed doors, going leapfrog down halls, with hand signals and tense trigger fingers.

Around the town, from other blocks, Bandy hears sporadic bursts of gunplay. More thumps of bazooka fire. More Americans pour into the town, Jülich is being swarmed. By afternoon when the heavy bridges are built over the Roer, there'll be tanks and artillery growling around whatever's left of the place. Any German soldiers will be dead, captured, or somewhere else. Waiting in the rubble, Bandy takes a photo of the blasted brick wall showing through breezy fissures in the haze. He can read the funny remainder of the message;

great story, this shot might get in *Life*. By nightfall there'll be a command post set up in the best remaining building in town. The brass will move in. Bandy will have a press liaison officer to hand his film to for the flight to London, where the military censors get first crack, then the photo pool, then New York. In the middle of this thought a whistle comes through the smoke. The sergeant leaps first, his Thompson machine gun is leveled and ready. Bandy waits until last and runs through the greasy coils. He rushes with one hand over the Leica strapped around his neck to keep it from flying up and busting him in the nose.

The building is secure. Stepping into the wrecked first floor, Bandy sees it was a home. Everything is smashed. Furniture is splintered, white cushion foam is splattered around like a hundred dead doves. Over the hearth there's a framed photograph of Adolf Hitler, the glass oddly unbroken by the blast. Below the picture on the mantel are several decorative beer steins with metal caps, the only other things that survived unharmed. A few of the men grab the steins and put them in their rucksacks, then kick through the debris looking for other mementos. A corporal takes down the Führer's picture. This soldier is mud-caked like the rest of them. He moves not like an invader on foreign land but like a man in his neighborhood bar, slowly and easily. He's a veteran. He's got a beer gut, Bandy can't figure how he maintains that protuberance over here with the exertion and frayed nerves of war. But it makes him look cheery. The corporal throws his belly into his laugh.

"Hey, Pendleton!"

One of the bazooka men answers, the handsome one. "Yeah?"

The corporal hangs Hitler on the intact inner wall that divides the building from the one attached to it.

"I think right on the fucker's kisser would be nice."

This is how the platoon works its way to the end of the street, as do all the other Americans who are taking Jülich. They stay off the streets, moving through the cover of buildings, blowing holes in shared walls or across narrow alleys to scoot unseen through the block. At the end of each brick row, when they need to cross a street, they start over: knock an opening in the initial wall, smoke grenade first, then go! The ten thousands of men who died in the streets of the months before are not on their minds right now. But the lessons those men made them learn are.

The squad is done scavenging. They move to the opposite wall, crouching behind upturned chairs, tables, and a sofa. The bazooka crew takes a position as distant from the wall as they can get. Hitler's image hangs in the center of the target, a determined, thoughtful bull's-eye, showing the way to his country's destruction one wall at a time. The man in the rear handles the shell. He pats his partner on the shoulder, gets a nod.

The men of the platoon all shout at the tops of their lungs. They've done this before.

"Heil Hitler!"

February 23, 1945, 1430 hours
Six kilometers east of Posen
Poland

ILYA WATCHES THE BOOTS OF THE FIVE DOZEN GERMANS in front of him.

Their heels shamble on the road through the forest. Livestock walk with more bearing, Ilya thinks. A defeated man loses his honor so fast; even a cow on the way to the abattoir walks with its head up. A rooster squawks with your hand around its throat until you cut it. But a man heading to his fate has imagination. He sees the unseen territory. These men see Siberia. So they shuffle, they stink, they dissolve into captivity. Ilya prefers death to becoming one of these scarecrows.

Yesterday the Germans surrendered. The commander of the Posen garrison laid a Nazi battle flag on the floor in his office inside the citadel and shot himself in the head. What kind of officer does that? It's desertion in the face of battle. Is that some Prussian notion of honor? Ilya doesn't fathom these Germans, who fight so ferociously then become unmanned when they lose. A soldier doesn't have to be victorious to remain a soldier. Duty defines him; do it or don't do it. Simple. Victory is for politicians and historians.

One of the Germans stumbles. He's awkward, exhausted, freighted with shame. And well he ought to be, considers Ilya, recalling what he's seen not on battlefields but in unforgivable places: mass executions in Polish villages, the Majdanek concentration camp, bodies lining the roadways of the German retreat, unmarked mass graves, naked death heaps. One of the men in Ilya's company kicks the prisoner in the ribs to prod him off the ground and moving again. This German is slow, he's been battered once before on this march already. He looks starving, like the rest. He gets another kick until a sheepish comrade helps him upright and he continues. Ilya says nothing.

He takes off his stocking cap. His big palm feels bristles over his pate. Time to shave it again. With the battle of the citadel lasting almost a month, there was no time.

Today is Red Army Day, the twenty-seventh anniversary of the Soviet force. General Chuikov announced this morning that in Moscow they've celebrated the taking of Posen with twenty salvos from over two hundred guns. Ilya rubs his head harder, he is aggravated. He was an officer in the Red Army. Even yesterday, he was a soldier. This afternoon, he's a shepherd.

The line of captives is becoming too ragged. Ilya wants it straight, for no good reason other than he can't bring himself to kick the Germans but he can make them march properly. If he's going to be a damn shepherd.

"Misha. Tell them to firm up."

A few meters away Misha calls out some command in German. The order has little effect.

"Tell them again."

Misha strides over to walk beside Ilya. A bandage covers

his right cheek and ear. A local Polish doctor helping to treat the Russian wounded stitched him up. Beneath the bandage, Misha has a black row across his cheek like barbed wire.

"It doesn't matter, Ilyushka. Leave it alone. They're moving."

"I want them to march in an orderly fashion."

"Why?"

"Because I said so."

"Who are you giving orders to?"

Ilya draws out the word.

"You."

Misha walks, nodding. "I see. And what am I supposed to do, Private? Follow them?"

Ilya crushes his cloth cap in a fist.

Misha asks, "Why're you in such a foul mood? You've been like this since we left Posen."

Little Misha with his pirate scar forming doesn't put any distance between him and Ilya, he's not afraid to stand close beside his gargantuan comrade and question him, even disobey him. Ilya eyes the sixty captives. Walking in a loose cordon outside them are six others from the punishment company, assigned with Ilya and Misha to escort the prisoners on foot twenty kilometers to the rear, to process the Germans for transport to detention. No one else speaks, just bare trees, dragging soles, dust, and eight guns.

"This is shit, Misha."

"This is an honor, you lunkhead. We took these men prisoner! We stormed their citadel! Marching them to the rear and handing them over is recognition. Pushkov is actually rewarding us with this."

Everyone else in Zhukov's force is heading west to the Oder, massing for the attack on Berlin. Ilya's walking the wrong way. How's that an honor?

"I've taken ten thousand prisoners. I've never once been told to leave the front line to nursemaid them."

"You were an officer. This is an acknowledgment for foot soldiers. And that's what we are, Ilya. Foot soldiers.

Lucky-to-be-alive foot soldiers, at that. So stop giving me orders."

Ilya takes a cold breath. "Is that an order?"

"No. It's a request. From a friend."

Ilya puts on his green watch cap. They did storm the citadel. And they did it in more ways than Ilya has ever seen in battle. With Misha's rolling exploding drums. With bundles of sticks filling the moat for bridges. With heaps of chairs and crates thrown into the crevasse to obscure the vision of enemy gunners at the bottom. With burning barrels of oil to smoke them out. With lashed-together logs for trestles and ladders. With cudgels and bayonets and flamethrowers and bullets and man after man after man.

For the final week Ilya, Misha, and two dozen men who followed them into the citadel fought in close quarters with the Germans. It was like Stalingrad all over again, and Ilya was ready. He taught the men with him by example and stern whispers how to survive and kill in the bowels of a building. Creep. Stay low. Stay apart. Stay alert. Storm a room or a stronghold from many angles. Roll grenades ahead of you to clear paths. Work at night and in the morning, around the clock, wear the enemy down, no rest for them or you until they're finished. Use feints, false attacks, dummy positions, fool them, be everywhere and nowhere. No mercy, no grief, swallow your fear. Ilya and Misha survived the citadel with the six men who are with them right now. Ilya does not know any of their names. He saw no need inside the citadel to become familiar. He commanded them first with his own actions, and when he needed them to move he pointed and said, "You, you, and you!" In the citadel fighting, Misha stayed near Ilya. He's not a terrific fighter but is a gifted tactician. Misha has the rear officer's tolerance for sending men to their deaths.

Ilya casts his eyes over the line of haggard prisoners tramping in *ersatz*-wool greatcoats. Another loses his footing, trips over himself, two others stumble over him. In confusion the line bunches to a halt. Two of the guards make angry noises and approach. Why did they fight like that, Ilya wonders? Why did the Germans have to kill and be killed, sixty thousand defenders in Posen ground down to twelve thousand. Defending what? How many young Russian men are dead, hurt, ruined, how many more to come? How much needless destruction is there in Posen, all of Poland, Russia, and now in Germany because of them?

Duty. The lone answer to every soldierly question. There is nothing beyond it.

But what about all the havoc that's gone beyond duty? Again, Ilya smells Majdanek. The mounds. The ditches. Ashes. Cruelty.

That is not the work of soldiers. It's the spawn of madmen. Rabidness. Hitler's not here. Who answers for it?

Do these men in line?

Is revenge part of Ilya's duty?

He hates these Germans. He doesn't detest them in constellation but individually, each sunken face and skittish eyeball, each defeated brute, one at a time, the way he's killed them.

The march has stopped. Ilya holds his ground at the rear of the pack. Misha strides forward. In German he tells the fallen soldiers to get up, *schnell*! Two of them climb to their feet, the third lifts no farther than his knees before he collapses again to the earth. Misha reaches down and clasps the collar of the prisoner's coat. He yanks, but the man like a downed mule will not rise.

Misha sends a swift kick into the prisoner's midsection. In Russian he shouts, "Get up, you piece of shit! Get up!"

Ilya sees his own hatred taking form around the Germans, like blood clotting. The other guards and Misha take steps away from the fallen man. The prisoners close ranks around their comrade, who can barely sit up on the ground. The air thickens into a paste of anger and tension.

Misha puts his little fists to his hips. He says in Russian, so it is intended not for the prisoners but the armed guards around him, "I said get up, you German piece of shit."

The German knows what Misha wants. The man looks ill. His cheeks work as though to keep down vomit. He does not—probably cannot—stand.

With a flourishing hand Misha draws a pistol, a captured Luger. The six other guards see this. One by one they follow suit, leveling their rifles behind Misha into a firing line. The Germans' eyes go wide, their knees stiffen before the guns.

One of the guards spits on the ground. In a snarling voice he says, "Smolensk."

Another Red soldier spits. He says, "Leningrad."

A third. "Moscow."

These are Russian cities that withstood sieges of terrible carnage. These are curses the Russians put in the ears of the Germans.

A fourth. "Minsk."

"Chelmno."

"Kursk."

Misha looks over to Ilya, who has not moved. In the surrounding woods a crow caws, a bad sound.

The guards hurl more names at the Germans. Names of prison camps, Rovno, Ternopol, Zitomir; names of occupied villages, Braslav, Balvi, Vigala; names of death camps, Auschwitz, Sobibor, Treblinka; names of dead comrades, Kazora, Vozny, Smirnov, Zubkov, Mastavenko; names of fathers and mothers, brothers, women. The Red soldiers vent themselves on the Germans, who cower under the onslaught of condemnation. The names are stones. Russian throats strain, neck tendons bulge, faces go red with the effort of throwing them.

Ilya stands watching Misha.

They're on a country road, far from any town, hidden in Poland. What they do here no one else will see. What happens here, no one will care. The eight of them can report back to their company in Posen claiming the prisoners made a break into the trees. Shrugs will answer that tale. Perhaps it's even expected of them. They will have been poor shepherds, that's all. They can join the rest of their battalion on the river Oder, aimed at Berlin, to unleash more anger.

Misha holds still under Ilya's inquiring gaze.

The guards continue their barrage of names and vitriol. Each man in his turn leans in to skirl another word, like snapping dogs. Ilya can only imagine the vengeful millstones these men must carry on their souls. They're simple peasants. Freed prisoners of war. The dreaded men of the second echelon. These are the Red soldiers who've endured the worst of all the battles. They get no leave, rarely get paid. They've been bombarded by inflaming rhetoric from the Communists, prodded forward by threats from NKVD commissars. Right now they're on their own with the enemy in their hands, and they've had enough. They're stupid with rage and vendetta. Their eyes are glassy like corpses'. Hate like that kills the man and leaves the body. Ilya knows many of the places they shout, and the ones he does not recognize he understands what they represent. But Ilya has been fortunate, he's been able to fight the Germans, to exact his toll and soothe his demons on the battlefields. These barking men have been corralled, beaten, starved, tortured by the Germans. They have debts to collect.

All but Misha. He appears very calm, almost entertained.

The bandaged little man breaks his eyes from Ilya. He spits the way the others did. He shouts over the guards. "That's enough!"

They listen to him. Ilya leads them in battle. Misha takes the fore now in terror.

Steam issues from all the mouths on the road. The Russian screamers catch their breaths, the Germans fear these are their last breaths. Again, a crow caws from the cold bare woods.

Misha calls out, "There's one left. For you, Ilyushka."

Misha cocks his Luger. He says to the Germans, "Stalingrad."

One of the Germans mutters in Russian, "Bastards."

All of these men hate. Back and forth, volleys of loathing.

Two of the Germans reach to the ground to lift their comrade. They put the man on his feet and release him with care. He stays erect, shaking. The rest of the prisoners move by instinct closer, penned animals do the same. They do not take their eyes from the guns facing them, but every man of them backs until he can feel the shoulder of another.

One of the Russians raises his rifle to his cheek, ridiculous, as though he needs to aim this close to his targets. Ilya's mouth is bone dry. He could speak. They listened to him in the frenzy of the citadel. He could make them listen now. He would say, what?

Another crow dispatches his voice from the trees.

Ilya turns his back.

MARCH

---

*W*orld history occupies a higher ground than that on which morality has properly its position, which is personal character and the conscience of individuals. . . . Moral claims which are irrelevant must not be brought into collision with world-historical deeds and their accomplishment. The litany of private virtues—modesty, humility, philanthropy, and forbearance—must not be raised against them.

So mighty a form must trample down many an innocent flower—crush to pieces many an object in its path.

G.W.F. HEGEL
Lectures on the
Philosophy of History

F I V E

March 1, 1945, 11:50 A.M.
An anteroom in the House of Representatives
Washington, D.C.

PEOPLE BUSTLE ON ALL SIDES, CHECKING LAST-minute arrangements. The President in his wheelchair looks at them from hip level. Hands in pockets, pocket watches, belted skirts, fat bellies parade past his eyes.

The President thinks about sledding.

This is his favorite dream. He is a child at Hyde Park in winter. He stands on top of a hill, pushes his sled off the peak. He picks up speed, negotiates turns, dodges trees, and outruns dogs. He is gliding, fleet and free.

More members of his staff slide by his seat. He sleds through them like they are tree trunks, turns the rudders sharply, heads out into the open fields, keeps going.

Anna walks past, brushing long fingers along his shoulder, saying nothing. Roosevelt wants her to stop and speak, to chase away his daydreaming. But she is off, arranging something for his speech in a few minutes to a joint session of Congress. His mind—the way tired minds will—wanders further, plays leapfrog to another thought. Anna did not tarry with him. His daughter, who has the widest entry of anyone into him, did not come in, she left him alone. This sends him to think on his greatest fear. The President is afraid of being alone in a burning building. He will not be able to escape on his useless legs. When he first became a paraplegic, he used to practice for hours rolling from his bed and crawling to the door to escape, in case he was alone. Sometimes he confuses his fears. Fire, or alone, which is greatest for him?

Fire. Alone. His thoughts pick up pace. Next dot. Death. Pa Watson died on the voyage back from Yalta. Cerebral hemorrhage. Had an argument with Harry, so sick himself he couldn't leave his stateroom. Pa went back to his cabin and just stopped breathing. Major General Edwin "Pa" Watson, one of the best storytellers, poker players, and friends Roosevelt ever knew. Gone. The great alone. Harry left the *Quincy* in Algiers to fly home to the Mayo Clinic. He's still there. Roosevelt spent the last part of the Atlantic trip alone, either in his cabin or on the admiral's deck, somber in his blue cloak and gray floppy hat, watching the blue and gray sea for portents.

A new dot. Backward to Yalta. Where Pa was last alive. Where Roosevelt was with Joe and Winston, his greatest company of men, every breath and word and meal was historic. How remarkable and exhilarating! Roosevelt is going to report to Congress in another few minutes. Forward dot. He's in his chair. His staff mills around him.

Report on Yalta to Congress. Tell them Yalta was a success, at least for America. Russia agreed to engage in the war against Japan. Russia will also join the United Nations; yes, with two extra voting seats, but that'll be of no consequence in the long run, not when every nation on earth will be a member, what's two more votes for the Soviets? The occupation zones were ratified. Russia gets the eastern half of Germany, the flat agricultural part, plus the eastern half of Berlin. Britain, France, and the U.S. will occupy the west of Germany, home of the country's industry, waterways, and minerals, the better part by far. Poland—what can be done for Poland? Stalin has millions of men there. Millions more spread all over eastern Europe. Churchill wants them out. Americans don't care. This nation's place as the world's greatest superpower is assured after the war, no matter what happens over there. America's not willing to go to war with the Soviets to make them abide by their agreements in Europe. In a way, it serves the Europeans right for fighting so damned much. At least Stalin is strong enough to keep the peace. And peace is not something to be sneezed at, at any rate not by war-weary Americans who've been dragged against their will into European conflicts twice in consecutive generations. Anyway, Stalin is determined. The totalitarian, he'll have his way. What can be done?

Take Berlin. That's what Winston says. Get it first and hold it as a bargaining chip. We'll have to back out of half the city eventually. But we can do it after some horse trading. If Stalin points at our agreement to leave part of Berlin, we can point at his agreement to leave a half-dozen other places.

The Allied attacks across the Roer have gone well. British and American troops are closing fast to the Rhine.

Winston might be right. Taking Berlin could be the way to make Stalin sit up and notice.

General Marshall says Berlin will cost an extra hundred thousand lives. It might also jeopardize Russia's participation in the Pacific and the United Nations. And Eisenhower's worried that Hitler might set up a resistance force in the southern mountains, which would make Berlin moot. It's a sled ride, fast with lots of trees to miss, turns to handle.

Roosevelt smiles at the image, the roundness of his thinking.

We'll see what develops. There's still time.

"Time," says Anna.

She has appeared right in front of him, he didn't see her. He was on the sled the whole way, skirting through issues and memories. He rubs his forehead with a strong squeeze of his hand. The dots he connected didn't draw anything, just a straight line away, off alone.

"Daddy," Anna says again, "time."

"Yes, yes, sweetheart." Roosevelt takes his fingers from his face and reaches to his daughter. Her touch is electric, veins and muscles marble her forearm. Roosevelt gave this woman life. It was such a good thing to do. Anna and the boys; the President can't conceive of any other accomplishment in his life so true as bringing them into the world. You'll hear that truth is an absolute. It's not. Truth is a gem cut with facets—the way it appears depends on where you stand to look at it. His children, more than his presidency, are his most honest legacy. They do not rely on perspective, historians, or witnesses. Anna's broad toothy smile is Eleanor's, her strength is his, her charm is his. Her hand in his palm is the one absolute truth.

Today, there will be another.

For twelve years, every time Roosevelt has appeared before the nation, he has done so standing with ten-pound leg braces locked. Or seated in an open motorcar. On every occasion he has addressed Congress, he has walked down the aisle on the arm of one of his staff or relying on crutches.

Not today. As Anna said, it's time.

Inside the chamber, the doorkeeper announces first the Justices of the Supreme Court, then the members of the Cabinet.

"The President of the United States."

The massive doors part. Roosevelt looks into the chamber, the giant room is filled to the rafters. Rows upon rows of standing people gape back at him. Not a voice stirs.

Then there is applause, a thunderous clap. Shouts and whistles issue from the heads and hearts attending. For the first time, the President of the United States appears publicly in his wheelchair.

Through three terms and now his fourth, this has been the grand deception. The American people have not been trusted with the knowledge that their President is a crippled and vulnerable man, who cannot stand but for minutes at a time with grunting effort. The country has not been allowed to know that Secret Service men have to lift him like a doll and transfer him from chair to bed. The national press corps do not publish reports or photos of Roosevelt in his wheelchair or of his handicap. America has been permitted to believe only in a myth of a President. It is feared they would think less of him and his leadership during a Depression, then a world war. But Americans have proven their mettle. They've won for themselves a truth.

Anna's hands are on his shoulders again. The applause increases.

Roosevelt pushes off the peak of the aisle. This is his dream. He glides forward.

———

March 3, 1945, 10:30 A.M.
Outside Ninth Army headquarters
Jülich, Germany

CHURCHILL BENDS TO PICK UP A BRICK. MORTAR CLUMPS cling to it, the violence of the blasts that shook it loose reside in the clay. He imagines the explosion, he tells himself he can sense the blow of shell against wall. He feels a moment of guilt; there could have been more he might have done against the events that felled this brick from its peaceful place and spun it into the street, in his path with uncountable others.

He carries the brick with him along the street. He wonders what manner of man Hitler must be, in his private moments, not the screeching demagogue. Is he insane to keep fighting? He's surrounded, retreating. He's being pounded day and night by American, British, and now Russian bombers. The noose closes on him east and west. Doesn't Hitler ever pick up a fallen brick and consider, "I put this here"? Doesn't the little corporal think, "I can stop this"? Churchill has held in his hands a thousand bricks of London, Brighton, Devonshire, Bath, but none has made him sadder than this one in Germany. The others were orphans of war. This brick smacks of waste and madness.

Churchill has not been across the German border since 1932. The devastation he sees in this river town of Jülich dismays him, though he will not show it. For the officers and men of the American Ninth strolling alongside him, the ones who wrecked this town, he smiles and congratulates them. He is chatty and upbeat. But Churchill has not viewed a single building here left untouched. Walls have been bored through as though by giant brick-eating moles. Every spire, cupola, and steeple of what must have been a lovely little town has been sheared off, no elevated havens left for snipers. Rafters and beams show under the broken skin of roofs; every house, business, and public building is skeletal. The Prime Minister sees no bodies in the rubble, they will have been removed before his visit. He sees no local residents, they will have been cordoned off. He glimpses no prisoners. But he observes what is being done to Germany, and the power of the Americans doing it.

Around him touring the conquered town are five members of his own staff, plus General William Simpson, head of the U.S. Ninth Army, two dozen neatly wrapped officers belonging to the general, and a dozen American photographers. Their street parade passes troops who take little notice, men who keep about their own business. Churchill thinks they seem marvelously comfortable in the presence of the British Prime Minister and their own officers. The Yanks seem to slouch and slink through the debris, sitting, smoking, digging out rations with bayonets, hauling ammo boxes here and there. Some wave, some fire off sloppy salutes, some call out, "Howdy, Winston." Simpson beams at them with a paternal grin. The photographers chuckle. Churchill likes a neatly shaved face, a tucked shirttail, a proper mien, but these Americans—tired as they are—come and destroy and go home better than any soldiers in history. He lets the casualness of the fighting men go by unremarked.

Churchill leads the group around him, he does not follow, the way Simpson seems to indicate he ought. The brick has grown heavy. Churchill hands it off to an aide, telling the young man to hang on to it, he will after the war lay it in a wall at his house at Chartwell.

He meanders the group to the riverside. The buildings here are outrageously shattered. The degree of ruin from every caliber of weapon in the American arsenal is almost humorous. Structures are in heaps, brought down by bullet holes and shrapnel rents. Chasms loom where barns and warehouses were days before. Churchill clamps his cigar between his teeth. What was it like to be here facing the Americans? Such firepower. Such will to use it.

This is the tragedy of involving the Americans in Europe, Churchill thinks. They cannot be made to care what they leave behind.

He gazes over the river. Twisted beams like licorice sticks in the Roer are all that is left of the town's lone suspension bridge, dynamited by the evacuating Germans. Empty assault boats sway on the bank a hundred meters away, beyond them is a plain of muck. The attackers had to claw through that, under a withering enemy fire. Heroes, martyrs; yes, Churchill nods, saviors. He removes the cigar from his mouth so he can swallow. Soldiers and machines now trundle across a dozen man-made bridges in an uninterrupted course, the Allied force heaves farther into the Reich. Soon the sword will be up to the hilt. Is Hitler out of his mind?

Churchill turns to Simpson. This general's army is still attached to Montgomery's Twenty-first. Eisenhower is making good on his word to keep Monty's force strong and supported for his thrust. Churchill wants to hear what Simpson intends.

"General, sir. What is next on your agenda?"

Photographers slip around the two for good angles, putting the littered river in the background. Simpson is tall and handsome, with a weathered face and stern jaw. He has been chiseled out of soldier stock.

"Find a bridge, Mr. Prime Minister. Get over the Rhine."

"And?"

Cameras click.

"And, sir, by your leave, kick some butt all the way to Berlin."

Churchill points his cigar, a merry gesture.

"General, you pander to me. You know full well I want to hear that."

"Yes, sir. And I wanted to say it. Ike assures me up here

in the north we're on the best route, straight into Berlin. The Roer crossing went right on schedule. Far as I know, we've got the green light to go all the way. Soon as we can find us a bridge, we're off like a shot."

"What about the Russians? They're only fifty miles from Berlin."

Simpson smiles. For seconds his eyes flick to his domain, his part of Germany where he has massed three hundred thousand soldiers, trainloads of supplies, tanks, and artillery. To apply a favorite Americanism, Churchill thinks Simpson has men and weapons "coming out of his ears." This American general is in the right place at the right time. He can do it. And if he does it, Montgomery does it.

Simpson has toted up his strength. It is indeed mammoth, equal to the job.

"Mr. Prime Minister, I say good luck to 'em."

Churchill pats the general on the back. He has to reach up to hit the man between the shoulder blades.

On the way back to Ninth Army headquarters, billeted in the remains of the town hall, Simpson tells Churchill about his two recent attempts to take a bridge.

After the Roer crossing, the main force of Ninth Army met only token resistance. The Germans were scattered and making for the Rhine themselves. Just last night, March second, a group of Simpson's tanks sped into the small town of Neuss, across the Rhine from the industrial city of Düsseldorf. To the tankers' shock, one major bridge was left intact over the river. Without waiting for orders, they rushed to get across, figuring they could hold it long enough to call for reinforcements and establish a bridgehead. Three of the tanks were on the span when German engineers blew it.

Later the same night, the commander of Simpson's 330th Infantry put into effect an idea he had. It was the same trick that Americans executed German prisoners for trying in reverse during the Battle of the Bulge. The 330th painted out the white stars on their tanks and applied German crosses and camouflage. They put German-speaking GIs in the turrets in *Wehrmacht* uniforms and headed off for the Rhine bridge at Oberkassel. At the approach to the bridge a sentry challenged the column. The tanks roared past and fought their way right to the foot of the bridge. An alarm sounded and the span was exploded with the American tanks growling at the edge of the river.

Simpson assures Churchill, "We'll get one."

Returning to Ninth Army HQ, Churchill forges a different path through the town. The desolation he sees throughout Jülich is complete. The dozen photographers take their shots, jogging ahead and alongside like hunting dogs. Churchill flashes his famous V several times. It's important to be seen at the front. To let the free world witness him here, one of the Big Three with the troops. Stalin stays behind the Byzantine domes and minarets of his Kremlin walls, not even his own people catch sight of him. And Roosevelt cannot possibly make this sort of tour. Churchill displays his famous cigar. The cameras click. Today he wears a green campaign waistcoat with epaulets, riding breeches, high leather boots, and a general's billed cap. Last night while the American tanks were prowling the Rhine for a bridge, the Prime Minister had dinner with Montgomery. This morning he visits Ninth Army, then it's off to see the vaunted Siegfried Line. He'll spend the night on Eisenhower's train at Geldrop in Holland. Tomorrow he'll review the First Canadian Army. Sleep the night on Ike's train, awake in Reims for a chat with the good Supreme Commander. Keep the fires stoked for the march on Berlin. Show the colors; flash the V; Advance, Britannia! and all that.

Once the party is near Ninth Army HQ, the photographers drift away. Churchill sends them off with a "Cheerio!" He crosses the street with Simpson to enter the shattered town hall. On the steps to the building sits a gaunt man with a battered khaki sack in his lap. The fellow's uniform bears no insignia, but beside him on the steps is the worn leather case of a Speed Graphic camera.

This one is not part of the pack, Churchill thinks, stopping in the street. This one hunts alone.

The man is narrow-shouldered and long of bone. He

stands with a laconic grace, leaving the sack on the steps. The bulky camera hangs from his mitt. He looks more dog-tired than most of the soldiers.

"General Simpson." The photographer approaches, greeting the general. "May I ask a favor of your esteemed guest?"

Simpson holds up a halting hand.

"Charley, the Prime Minister here has done all the photo ops he's gonna do for today. You had your chance to join in with the rest."

"Yes, sir." The photographer smiles at Churchill. The green tape above his pocket reads: BANDY.

"You are Charles Bandy."

"Yessir, Mr. Prime Minister."

The man's voice is that wonderful Yank twang, honey in tea, mint.

"That would be *Life* magazine Bandy?"

"Yessir."

Churchill chomps his cigar. This is one he has heard of. A tobacco farmer in his other life. Churchill honors anyone and anything to do with that splendid leaf. And his magazine is at the top. *Life* gives this man's work full spreads. He's a favorite of the American soldiers, like that marvelous writer Ernie Pyle. Bandy shares their load, their danger. Their exhaustion. He's done a lot for the war effort.

"What do you propose, Mr. Bandy?"

"If you'd step over here, sir. I'll show you."

The photographer leads the whole entourage around to the rear of the town hall. He walks slumped, the camera dangling from his hand like a burden. Behind the hall a square opens, where once market stalls may have stood. In every direction is the same utter devastation Churchill has observed throughout Jülich. But this he did not see. A sign.

Churchill walks up to it alone. He beams broadly; yes, he wants to have his picture taken before it. Clever man, this Bandy. One picture he will take, not dozens like the others. And this one will be the cream, telltale of irony and wit. *Life* will love it. The British papers will likely grab this as well.

The sign has been posted by some clever bilingual GI. It reads: *GEBT MIR FUNF JAHRE UND IHR WERDET DEUTSCHLAND NICHT WIEDER ERKENNEN.*

Beneath these words are the English translation:

GIVE ME FIVE YEARS AND YOU WILL NOT RECOGNIZE GERMANY AGAIN.

Signed, ADOLF HITLER.

Churchill gives Bandy the V. The photographer shakes his head, no. Hmm, Churchill thinks. Cheeky as well.

"Just say cheese, Mr. Prime Minister."

The boxy Speed Graphic creaks and it is done. Bandy approaches with his hand out in thanks.

Churchill shakes the hand. The man's fingers are long, slender, artistic digits. His eyes are old and crinkled by too much squinting, probably not under sun but under too many whizzing bullets.

"Mr. Bandy, sir. May I offer you some advice in return?"

"Please."

"Go home."

General Simpson hears this and seems to snigger, as though this is a ridiculous thing to suggest.

The photographer snaps the Speed Graphic into its worn case, like a turtle.

"Why does everybody tell me that?"

"I suppose because it's rather disturbing to see a man who doesn't have to be here . . . well, be here."

The photographer shuffles in the dirt for a moment. He looks up at the sign and speaks.

"Don't misunderstand me, sir, but *you* don't have to be here."

"Well, no." Churchill doffs his general's cap. He runs his hand through the wisps of his once-red hair, now gray and desolate.

Churchill continues. "But you realize that while many men are called forth by their draft board, some of us are summoned by . . . other, greater forces. Those unlucky few of us who are singled out must be present no less than the rest."

Charles Bandy actually lays his hand on the Prime Minister's shoulder. It is an act of uncommon familiarity, even for a Yank. But there's a wonderful comradeliness about the gesture, a draw in the pressure of his hand, and a sadness about the lines in his face, a tale or two there. Churchill wishes he could linger to read them.

The man says, "Me too, sir. Just the same."

Churchill layers his hand over Bandy's resting at his shoulder. The two men clasp that way.

He nods, pats Bandy's wrist once, and takes his leave.

Joining General Simpson, Churchill looks past his shoulder to watch Bandy saunter away. With acute sadness, the Prime Minister thinks, Damn. There is another brick. Blasted out of its peaceful, rightful place by war.

March 5, 1945, 11:50 P.M.
Savigny Platz bomb shelter
Charlottenburg, Berlin

THE POISON GOES EVERYWHERE WITH LOTTIE.

She keeps the caplets in her pocket. In idle moments she slips her hand in and plays with them, juggling them between her fingers like coins. At night they rest under her pillow. During concerts they're in her tuxedo. She has even put one, plastic packet and all, in her mouth for a second, daring herself, sucking it, then taking it out lest the cyanide seep through the wrapper. The pill on her tongue scared her; it had no weight at all. It was nothing; at the same time it was everything.

Tonight in the shelter beneath a dry goods store on the Kant Strasse, Lottie fondles the pills, the secrets of power in her pocket. Every one of the women down here is known to the others. The talk is frank. One woman, a dressmaker, drones tirelessly about the horrors she has heard related by refugees from the East. Lottie has no reason to disbelieve the woman; they match tales she herself has heard. In Poland

and in German border towns, husbands, fathers, sons, and brothers have been made to hold lanterns while their women are raped by entire squads of Soviet soldiers. Those local men who resist are shot or castrated. Women who put up too much of a fight are knifed, even gutted. Soviet machine guns have borne down on refugee caravans, slaughtering fleeing innocents, horses, and livestock. Babies are found with heads bashed in. Children are forced to clear mines. Old militiamen are doused in gasoline and torched. Lottie, Freya, and the ten other ladies endure the woman's stories, told as though she were speaking to tykes, working her hands and tone, foolish, as if these atrocities need added dramatics. Some of the women in the bunker offer their own versions but the dressmaker always trumps them with another, greater, inhumanity.

The pills have become for Lottie an armor. The stories do not pierce her skin the way they might have two weeks ago. She does not see herself captive and spoiled like the terrorized people in the refugee accounts. The pills give her the capacity to escape such fates, and to free Mutti as well. She no longer feels any fear. Lottie already has put the cyanide once in her mouth. She can do it again. All she has to do is first tear away the plastic, and bite down. A simple act. Nothing, really. And everything.

"There are two and a half million people in Berlin right now," the woman goes on. She points a shaking finger upward like a preacher, not to heaven but through the earth to the wretched dark city above. "Two million of those are women. The rest are doddering old men who haven't held more than a garden rake in forty years and now they're being handed rifles. And boys." The woman shoots out a hand like a scythe, cutting the air only feet from the plank floor. "Boys, on bicycles, with *Panzerfausts* against tanks! These are the ones expected to defend us! Berlin!"

In her pocket Lottie rolls a pill between finger and thumb. Like a button, but one you push with your teeth. Then it's over. You're protected.

Tonight Berlin is not the *Amis*' target. After three hours

in the bunker, the all-clear sirens wail. Lottie moves first. She lugs her cello case up the steps; she can't help it, she begins to hate the instrument just a little. It is so big and unwieldy, demanding, unlike the little pills, her new favorite possessions. Pulling the case up the steps, the hard shell bumps on the treads. Freya offers to carry the cello but Lottie shakes her mother off. Lottie is not tired, no. That isn't the reason she is careless. The Galiano is her biggest anchor to this life, and she begrudges it.

Out in the street, there is a choice of two scenes always played out in Berlin following an alert. One is after an actual raid, and there is a firestorm and dust, bodies, stench, and loss, frantic running, intense noise, wailing, and heroism. The other option is the quiet plodding back to whatever Berliners have left to them as a life and a home, hefting back whatever loads they bring into the shelters with them time after time: luggage, briefcases of papers and probably jewels, paintings, sleeping infants slung over shoulders. When the all-clear klaxon quits, the night murmurs with dragging feet and skidding steamer trunks. People head home gray and slumped, like ghouls making for their graves before sunup. The cyanide in her pocket cannot free Lottie from this drudgery, things aren't yet bad enough to warrant taking a pill. She almost longs for the coming time when life will become too terrible to live, when the decision makes itself.

On the way back to Goethe Strasse, Lottie and Freya do not talk. There has been less and less to say between them in the past weeks. Freya spends a great deal of time out of the house trying to obtain food. The rations she can get with their two cards have been cut twice more this month. The third mouth in the basement keeps them all on starvation's cusp. Lottie's string quartet hasn't played in two weeks. The BPO hasn't met payroll in three weeks. There is little household money, and what there is gets devoured by Freya's scant purchases of black-market food. Lottie spends her days lying in bed, or playing the cello. She has run out of makeup, shoe polish, toothpaste, a hundred little thorns prick her life every day.

She plays her cello, but she does not play for Mutti or the

Jew. She doesn't admit that she plays for anyone or any reason, it simply feels automatic to take the Galiano between her legs and spend her day. In her heart she expects to die, and there is so much music still in her that she gives in to a deep urgency to get it out before she is gone. She is discharging a responsibility. For hours she sits on the parlor sofa and plays. To her own ear she has never performed better, though she plays with disdain.

The BPO continues its schedule, three and four concerts per week, right through the end of April when the season will officially end. The men of the orchestra are restive, not knowing their fate. Rumor has it that the young violinist, concertmaster Taschner, went to Minister Albert Speer for help. Speer has promised to do something; already it's whispered that he's dispatched an officer on his staff to the draft board to secretly extract and destroy all the musicians' papers. But this ploy won't stop Reichschancellor Goebbels for long. If the little clubfoot sets his sights on an epic end for Berlin, he'll see to it that all share in the fall.

Reaching Freya's house, Lottie leaves the cello in the front hall. She hauls herself up the steps to her room. It's after one in the morning. The house is chilly. Freya goes to the parlor to stir the fireplace ashes. Lottie hears her mother clanking the iron tools and shoveling on coal. Upstairs she takes off only her shoes and climbs under the covers.

Downstairs the front door opens. It closes with a quiet pressure. Footsteps trickle along the hallway. Freya says something to someone. Lottie springs up on the edge of the mattress.

The Jew.

He was outside! During the air raid alert!

Lottie rips away the blanket. She tears down the steps, swinging on the newel post at the bottom.

She flies past Freya.

The basement door closes.

"You!" She points at the yellow door as though the Jew could see the accusing finger. "You left the house!"

Freya drops the fireplace tool. She comes down the hall.

"Lottie."

"No, no! This is unbearable."

Lottie turns again to the basement door. These wooden panels, flat and wide and flimsy, have become the Jew's face and body for her, they are all she sees of him.

Not looking away from the yellow boards, she addresses Mutti. "He went outside the house. That's against the law. What if he's caught? What if he's seen? The Gestapo will follow him back here! Then what happens to us, Mutti, tell me that."

Freya moves to stand close to her daughter. Lottie pulls away but her mother's hands on her shoulders hold her in place.

She whispers, "Nothing happens to us, *Liebchen*. He went for a walk. He's careful, he promises he's careful, always. He doesn't go far. Just outside, to sit in a dark spot and see the stars. He stays out of sight. No one can stay in that basement without ever breathing some fresh air. It's asking too much. Too much."

Lottie's mouth goes slack. The notion shocks her.

"I'm asking too much of him?"

She speaks her first words in a month, since she demanded he go away, to the Jew behind the door.

"I'm asking too much of *you*?"

Lottie brushes her mother's fingers from her shoulders.

He's right there, on the top stair, just behind the yellow door, listening. He says nothing to explain or defend himself. He makes no sound, not even a creak.

During every air raid, he strolls in the night. He ducks the police and SS. He hurries to get back before Lottie returns. Does he understand the danger his walks could bring to the good women who hide him? If he did, he wouldn't risk the stupid indulgence of stars and fresh air.

When the police or the SS spot him—and they will—he'll lead them here.

This is unbearable.

Lottie grabs her mother's forearm. She tows Freya away to the parlor, shutting the door to the hall.

"Mutti."

"Yes?"

"Listen to me, and believe this. We are going to be caught. And when we are, we will be tortured. We'll be humiliated. And then we are going to be killed."

Her mother is sanguine, kind. "Lottie, darling. Don't let those old ladies' scare stories in the bunker tonight make you so upset. He's told me he's careful. He doesn't take unnecessary risks."

"Unnecessary for who? For him? I risk my life so he can stretch his legs? Don't you get it? If he gets caught, we get caught. When he takes a risk, we take risks, unnecessary or not!"

Freya reaches for one of Lottie's hands. Lottie leaves her mother's overture dangling in the air. Freya retracts her arm, folding it with the other across her breast.

"We've lived this long through the war, *Liebchen*. It's been almost six years. We'll see it to the end."

"It's the end that scares me. The Jew is going to bring the Nazis down on us or the Russians will get us. One or the other will happen. I know it. I don't care which. I don't want to be here for either."

"The *Amis* will come first. Everything will be all right."

"No."

"I'm not sending him away, Lottie. You know I won't do that."

"I know."

"What do you mean you don't want to be here? Where can you go?"

"I have a way . . ."

Lottie puts her hand in her pocket.

". . . we can go together."

She holds out to her mother the cyanide pills.

Freya's face and body lock. Lottie is prepared to snatch the pills away should Mutti react to seize them. But Freya stands rock-still.

"Where did you get those?"

"After a concert. The Nazis hand them out."

"And people take them."

Lottie lofts her eyebrows at her mother, so blind to reality. "Yes."

"And you expect that I, we, should take them?"

It's a simple question, not unexpected. But with it finally in the air, left unanswered the way Lottie left Mutti's offered hand untouched, the two pills become something for Lottie they have not been. They have been until now a fantasy, romantic and weightless as gossamer riding around in her pocket. With wishes, Lottie could make them into anything, a gleaming shield, a funeral bier, whatever she needed to fit her mood or circumstance. The pills have given her the means to reject the pitiful lot set aside for her, to be the master, not the beggar, to fate. If she so chooses she will swoon and die like Brunhild, her soul conducted away by Valkyries. She will put on her best dress and lie on the sofa, her Galiano in her arms. It could be beautiful. But now, the Jew has ruined everything. Now Lottie has to take the pill because he's going to be caught sneaking around and if she doesn't take the pill she'll have her hair sheared, be paraded through Berlin on the back of a cart, they'll throw garbage at her and she will be hung on a meat hook. The Jew chose this path, not Lottie. The Jew did it. He stole hope from her, all for a selfish walk under the stars. Now she has to take the pill and just die.

Freya lifts a hand, careful not to spook Lottie into clamping her fist shut around the pills.

"May I?"

Lottie holds out the poison.

Freya takes one with ginger fingertips.

She drops it to the floor. She grinds it under a heel, fixing her gaze on Lottie, no emotion in her eyes. When Freya removes her foot, she looks down. The clear plastic packet shows the pill's powdered gore.

"You keep the other one, *Liebchen*. If you don't have the strength, then take it."

Lottie's jaw works as though she's suffered a blow there.

Freya's words are so cold. A mother tells her daughter to die alone. Lottie wasn't going to do that to her; Lottie had secured escape for them both.

Freya says, "Come with me."

She pushes open the hallway door, holding it back for her daughter. Lottie balls her hand around the remaining pill.

"Come on."

Lottie wants to make a show of defiance. Her pill is still with her, she maintains her path out of all this. Tear it open, bite down, and be finished.

In the silence of the parlor, Mutti stares hard at her daughter. Lottie hears a sigh in her mother's throat. The sound is gentle, not steely like the look in her mother's eyes. There are years stored inside Lottie, she can't do anything about them. Stowed away in those years is an old place. Lottie thought she'd forgotten how to find it, when she stopped hearing Papa's voice. But her mother's glare sends her there. Papa is not in there the way he used to be, young and fetching. Only Mutti is in there now, with soup smells and giggles and songs sung beside a crib and a bed. The finger of a small girl taps inside Lottie's rib cage. The voice of a child urges, "Go with her now. She is Mutti. She makes things all right."

The cyanide is in Lottie's hand. She is powerless in this world except for it. It's her only weapon. She feels vengeful. She wants to throw the capsule into the night and poison Berlin, make it be the one to swallow and die and finish instead. She will live and laugh, and the Russians and Nazis can all go to hell. But no pill will halt the city's fate. Berlin is to be butchered. And Lottie is to be . . . what?

Freya waits, holding the hall door back like an usher.

Lottie puts the lone pill back in her pocket and follows Mutti to the basement door.

In the hall Freya takes Lottie's hand. She puts her back against the wall and sinks slowly to the floor. She tugs Lottie down beside her. Freya lays her daughter's hand in her lap and cradles it.

Shoulders touching, the two sit opposite the yellow door. Freya says nothing, Lottie mirrors her mother's silence. Minutes pass like this. Lottie watches her mother's face; Mutti's sternness has ebbed. She is reverent here at the door, prayerful, as though the Jew behind it is some slumped oracle. She has brought Lottie here to ask something.

Freya speaks. "Julius?"

No answer.

So this is the Jew's name. Like a puzzle, piece by piece, he emerges. Now the Jew is named Julius.

"Julius. Tell Lottie."

Lottie wants to say no. She wants to go upstairs and go to sleep, it's late and she is drained. She can't carry anyone else's tale of woe inside her. Lottie's own is all the burden she can manage. But Freya strokes her hand, anticipating her, calming her like a horse. Freya mutters, "Sshhh."

The Jew—Julius—still does not speak.

Lottie thinks this is silly, staring at a shut door in their own home, trying to talk to a man through it. She asks Mutti, "Why doesn't he just open the door?"

"Because," replies the door, "I've already been out tonight."

Freya's hands tighten over Lottie's. The oracle answers.

He says, "I'm sorry if I've scared you."

Yes, he scared her, and Lottie's impatient with him for that, and for this ritualistic sitting at his door like a supplicant. He's a Jew, he's on the run. He can wander outside only when everyone else is underground. Why must Lottie sit on the cold floor and converse with him? She preferred it when she could pretend he didn't exist, when she didn't know his name.

His voice is low-pitched, quiet, with cracks in it. This is natural, he has only Freya to speak with rarely. He doesn't sound young; mature, maybe Freya's age. He squats in the dark on a step behind a door when he could sit with them in a civilized way and talk.

"So just come out again."

Freya shifts her eyes between her daughter and the door. She does nothing to interfere.

He says, "That would be asking too much of me."

This again, Lottie thinks.

"Why?"

"Because I don't want to get used to it."

Freya raises a hand from her lap to daub at her eye.

He asks, "Lottie?"

She can tell where his head is, near the doorjamb, opposite the knob.

"Yes?"

"We're all frightened. You're not alone in that."

A minute passes without words. Now that he cannot be a gargoyle, Lottie is unable to build an image of Julius behind the door. She knows little about Jews, other than what she's been told over a dozen years by the Nazi machinery. She's seen them on the street and in their shops, and admitted privately that they did bear a resemblance to the overblown swarthy caricatures drawn in the papers and on posters. The stories of Jews selling their own children, of hatching a secret plot in Zion to rule the world, Jews as demons, these are bogeyman slanders no one can take seriously. But she has never had a Jewish friend. They've been excluded from all the circles she's moved in, mostly musicians. Jewish music has been banned for half her life. Jews are different. They confuse her, so she has not thought about them. She was a child when the Jews' troubles began. And they were not her troubles.

"Do you know what it's like outside during the raids?"

An odd question. He's nervous speaking to Lottie, like a young suitor calling for the first time.

"No."

"First comes the lead plane. It flies faster and lower than the others. It drops four flares in a quadrangle, to mark the bombing zone for the night. The first wave is right behind him. They always drop incendiary bombs to start fires, so the next squadron can spot the targets better. The sky lights up and the ground shakes. You can see the bombs falling, like black eggs. Searchlights swing back and forth until they find a plane. The flak towers open up with tracers. It looks like a battle between gods, between light and dark. Do you know what I do?"

"No."

"I cheer under my breath with every bomb that lands on Berlin." He pauses. "I know that sounds awful."

It does. But Freya answers him, "No, Julius, it doesn't."

"Lottie?"

"Yes."

"Do you know how long Jews have been in Berlin?"

Another strange question. Leaping from topic to topic. Lottie thinks, he doesn't get to talk much, with months spent in the silence of the cellar. And how many other cellars and years before that?

"No. How long?"

"The oldest Jewish grave in Berlin is in Spandau. The headstone says 1244."

"Have you seen it?"

"Yes. When I was a boy."

Another puzzle piece. Now Julius has a childhood. Lottie sees a boy in kneesocks and a cap, in a weedy old cemetery, some wizened hat-wearing elder holding his hand, a grandfather, telling him of the Jews' long history in Berlin.

As though he can read this vision in her head, the Jew says, "When the war started, there were over a hundred and fifty thousand Jews here. By 1943 there were less than twenty-five thousand."

He does not have to say it, the terrible math speaks for itself. He may be the last one left.

Lottie glances to Mutti's profile. Her mother's eyes are fixed on the flat yellow door. Lottie turns to see if she can read the images there, what Freya sees, what the Jew seems to cast like a film projector with his baritone voice, his halting, sad rambles.

Lottie's memory surprises her with how it awaits her. Broken glass, crystals on the sidewalks, remains of windows from shops, synagogues, homes. Little Lottie walks through the glass shards, scared of the sharp anger in them, that she might cut her feet even through her shoes and the anger infect her. The glass crunches and she feels like a monster walking on bones, she runs through a patch of it home and stays inside for days, she pretends to be sick, not telling Mutti that she is afraid. Signs. Hateful slogans, cheap white paper and black paint, yellow cloth stars sewed on overcoats. Stories whispered about *Hausjuden,* the house Jews, the good ones; everyone seemed to know one or two Jewish families who didn't deserve such and such. Laws. Race laws. Shopping laws. Work laws. Art laws. Trucks. Rumbling trucks in the early morning hours through damp streets. Lottie looks out through her curtains. Men, women, and children are crowded like cows in the open beds. They wear as many clothes as they can put on, even in summer, hats, overcoats, scarves, and gloves. Trains. From Anhalter station, boxcars rolling through the city headed east, jam-packed, pale fingers sticking out of holes in the sides. Names. Theresienstadt, Ravensbrück, Sachsenhausen.

Lottie knew all this. Of course. Every Berliner knew these things. Every Berliner had a butcher, a milliner, a doctor, a teacher, a bookkeeper, and had to find another one when they went missing. When their families were taken. When their houses were occupied by Nazi officials, or some displaced Aryan family. For the dozen years since the hatred was unleashed, Lottie has done what even the best Berliners have done: avoid adding to the Jews' misery. Just leave it alone. It is a tradition here. Seven hundred years old.

Julius the Jew is speaking. He's telling his story, apparently for Lottie's benefit. Freya has asked him to do this. It's a fearful story, certainly. Married to a Gentile woman. She was his protection. She dies in a bombing raid. He loses his shield. Loses his job in an armaments factory. He hides day and night, becomes a "U-boat," a submarine, a skulker. He fights treachery, hunger, fear, failing hope. Goebbels looks for the last Jews, with a powerful will to make Berlin, the capital of the Reich, a *Judenfrei* city. Lottie listens with half an ear. Julius's story is remarkable and tragic, almost beyond comprehension for her. She doesn't know this kind of passion for life, to live in such pain just to live. The closest she has ever been to that flame is in the music of the masters. Julius's voice is soaring Beethoven, heart-pounding Wagner, breathtaking Mozart. Julius's tale of catastrophe and endurance is operatic, musical. And though it is a music Lottie can hear, she cannot play it, so the travails of Julius the Jew begin to lose their hold on her. She slides back on his voice into old, comfortable German thinking. For an entire people to suffer so, they must have deserved it somehow, *nicht wahr*?

What is he asking of Lottie with his tale? That she change? That by hearing of his misfortune she will metamorphose into someone better? That she will from this point on think only of his safety and not her own? That she will become good like Mutti, brave and feral like him?

No. Lottie knew of all these things he has endured before she was ever aware of Julius the Jew. She has averted her eyes; yes, all right, that much is true, she has been callous to the plight of the Jews. But being reminded of it in her own home doesn't mean that suddenly she will learn some lesson. If that was going to happen, it would have already happened.

Lottie just wants to survive. That is the only thing she's learned about herself slouching here at Julius's yellow door. She shares that much with him. But only that. She's not willing to be so damned honorable and peaceful and strong about it. Lottie is a brilliant cellist; her life does not lack for higher purpose or value. The Jew stays in the basement because he doesn't want to get used to the open. Such discipline. So admirable. Ugh. Lottie winces as if she has bitten into a candy that strikes a raw tooth.

She reaches into her pocket for the remaining cyanide pill. She pulls her other hand free of Freya's sweaty palms, the backs of her mother's fingers wet with her constant drying of tears.

Lottie puts the poison packet into Mutti's hand.

"Here," she says, standing to go off to bed. "Give this to Julius in case his life gets too much for even *him* to live it."

———————

March 9, 1945, 9:15 A.M.
With the Ninth U.S. Army
Krefeld, Germany

BANDY DROPS TO HIS BEDROLL, FOLDING AT THE KNEES, collapsing in stages like a camel. The flimsy mat barely eases the hard bakery shop floor to his shinbones, he aches and rolls to his fanny. He spreads his legs wide for balance and dips into his dozen pockets. He dumps film canisters and packets on the mat like a tired little boy emptying his pockets to survey hard-won prizes.

He arrived—hitchhiking—in Krefeld yesterday, one day behind a vanguard battalion of the Ninth. He found shelter in the basement of a ruined bakery in the outskirts of the town. The street outside is ruined to the same degree as the rest of the town; Bandy has noticed how destruction leavens itself over the German villages and cities, spreading evenly in the manner of heat through a skillet.

Krefeld, four miles west of the Rhine, like every other place the eastward-pushing Allies have entered in the past two weeks, put up a skirmish, emptying itself of bullets and willpower, until there came a sudden capitulation. There's almost a tragicomic regularity to it. The local SS men shove into the fray crazy believing boys with *Panzerfausts* and old Home Guardsmen with antiquated carbines. Together they fight with a bewildering fervor. The Americans make Swiss cheese out of every building that issues even a puff of smoke. Tankers have been known to level any structure that displays a Nazi banner over a railing, and equally to try to preserve any buildings hanging out white flags. The soldiers stay back and let the artillery do as much of the work as it can. When the infantry moves in, they do their best to avoid the teenagers they see riding bikes from hot spot to hot spot, antitank weapons strapped across the handlebars, and armed old men in gardening gloves; but always after the battles the body count goes far past German military uniforms. At some point, long after the fight has become clearly futile, hands go up, weapons go down, and voices call, *"Nicht schiessen, nicht schiessen! Halten Sie, bitte!"* The women of the villages and towns, the inevitable survivors, start sweeping up under the boots of the Americans. They thank the *Amis* for coming before the Russians. They kiss goodbye their living sons and husbands and fathers even before the men can lower their hands to be marched to the rear. The women cover the bodies with the white sheets of surrender.

Bandy takes photos of beautiful blond lads and grizzled World War I vets, lying dead shoulder to shoulder with Hitler's finest. He snaps shots of prisoners, their frightened wrinkled cheeks and wet fuzzy cheeks, old and young with the same relieved and cowed eyes. He wonders with the U.S. soldiers taking them away: Are these the faces that an hour before were set behind triggers? What were the looks on them then? Bandy wants to hate the Germans for this waste of their only remaining resource, their people, but he can't find hate in himself. He's too frazzled. Some days he looks inside and finds only an unplanted field in his gut, nothing seeded, not hatred, not anger, not even sorrow, he can find nothing but black-and-white images of these sensations on other people's faces.

In those times when the warfare is loud and trying to kill him and the men he is with, he is moved by a medley of dread and exhilaration. But when it's quiet, like this morning, Bandy views the carnage around him through a strange intellectual filter; he has fallen into the habit of seeing the war as if it were already in the past, already history. The photographs he takes are not of smashed beings and crumbling things present and immediate but rather objects reduced by his lenses to monochromatic visions, reproduced flat on some future page in a book or newspaper, and he is not here looking now, but there looking back.

History is always. Bandy senses that he is becoming always too.

He's been told by Victoria that a man cannot be that. He must live in his own life and time, he must be only now. She says history will kidnap you.

He is too worn out at the moment to put any more thought into history or his wife. They live on the same shelf in his head, bookends around the war. He pushes the film off the bedroll and lays back his head. He draws a deep breath. The wooden racks lining the walls in the bakery basement exhale their scent of bread they've held for perhaps a century. Bandy is glad that something good has taken hold so firmly that it cannot be uprooted even by war. The smells of flour, rye, pumpernickel, yeast, the tinkle of coins spread on the broken tables upstairs, dusty white aprons still hung on hooks, lay quilted across his chest.

This morning he caught a ride twenty miles south of Krefeld to the blasted city of Cologne, once the proudest German metropolis west of the Rhine. Bandy wanted to catch the blackened ruins in the slanting light of sunup. Cologne has been the target of incessant Allied bombings until the only recognizable trace left is the famous cathedral, a marvel of medieval construction or one lucky damn building.

Bandy was tempted to stay down there with the entering First Army. He's still looking for the right horse to bet on in the race to Berlin. But the First is under Bradley, and Bandy has not forgotten that Ike advised him to stay up here on the northern track with Monty's Twenty-first.

Like a good handicapper, Bandy has studied the odds, on maps, through chats with officers, and drawing on his own journalistic experience. South of Cologne, there are only a few good points to cross the Rhine. Beyond the river heading east from there, the land is heavily wooded, broken up by narrow valleys and corrugated hills, and sparsely laid with serviceable roads. Not good for offensive battle. The farther south you move, the longer becomes the salient to Berlin, and the less likely any army south of Cologne will make for the capital of the Reich.

In the north, Montgomery enjoys plenty of excellent lo-
cations for a river crossing, suitable terrain for mechanized
warfare, and a north German plain and *Autobahns* that lead
straight into Berlin. In his path are several major Allied objectives, especially the factory-rich Ruhr valley and the V-1
and V-2 missile sites in Holland. Most important, Montgomery has Eisenhower's promise of support and the weight
of agreed-upon Allied strategy, that his route is the route to
Berlin.

At dawn this morning Bandy was in Cologne. He was
impressed with the apocalyptic annihilation, the appalling
might of Allied bombers seen from ground level. The
bridges over the Rhine there have all been sunk by the retreating Germans. With the sun lifting its head, women of
every age began to scratch the streets with brooms made of
bound straw. The children cleaned and stacked bricks, shopkeepers cleared room in the rubble for stalls. Bandy is sure
he caught life—real and elusive life—sending out green
shoots through the ashes. He snapped American soldiers
standing bewildered with hands on hips, watching what to
them must seem like hapless labor. When he was done he
came back to Krefeld and his bread-smelling bunker.

Footfalls descend the bakery steps. Bandy sits up. His
watch says it's after noon. His back is in knots, his neck is
kinked. He prefers sleeping on dirt to concrete, but he likes
a real roof and walls better than a tent.

A young PRO—Public Relations Officer—steps into the
basement. He's tall and lean. The man's gait down the steps is
angular, all knees and elbows, like a bag of coat hangers.

"Mr. Bandy? Sir, how are you?"

Bandy stands, again in sore phases. He's getting old for
this work.

"Good, good." He sees the silver bar. "Lieutenant . . ."

"Rubin, sir."

"Rubin." They shake hands. "What can I do for you,
Lieutenant?"

"Just checking in, sir. I'm kind of new on board. I've
heard a lot about you and wanted to meet face-to-face. See

if there was anything I could do for you. We all think you're
doing a bang-up job for the Ninth, sir. We're sort of stuck
up here with Montgomery's Twenty-first. Most of the
American press is down south running along behind Patton
and Bradley. So I just wanted to tell you we're glad you're
with us. Anything I can do, you let me know."

"Just keep me posted," Bandy says. His tone is tired. He
makes an effort to smile. "I hate to be the last to know something."

Rubin nods, a brisk tilt to his helmet. Bandy bets he does
everything like that, sharp. The frontline boys lose that crisp
edge the first time a round whizzes past their ears. The vet-
erans are all rounded off, like old gravestones. Rubin's okay,
but he's a press boy, not a GI Joe, not exhausted and running
on fumes of pride and fear like the fighting men. Some of
the guys haven't been out of action since D-Day. Some of
them are hoping for a "million-dollar wound," the one that
doesn't kill them, just plugs them enough to get a Red Cross
ticket Stateside. Bandy will hand nice young Lieutenant Rubin his exposed film to be sent to the censors, he'll read Rubin's releases, listen to his briefings, catch a ride with Rubin
when he needs one. And that's it for the tall skinny clean
PRO. Bandy doesn't feel bad about this prejudice. Bandy
reads war in faces the way generals read it on maps. There's
brotherhood conferred on the men in Bandy's photographs,
dead and alive.

The kid waits for more conversation; that's how he fights
his war. Bandy gives him a weary look. Rubin begins his retreat.

Bandy is on one knee on the bedroll, scattered rolls of
film around him, when Rubin says, "Oh, Mr. Bandy. In
keeping with making sure you stay informed, I don't know
if you heard. We got a bridge."

Bandy straightens as though he has bounced on a diving
board.

"What?"

"We got a bridge. Over the Rhine."

"Where? When did we get it?"

"Well"—the young officer makes a sort of apologetic wringing of his hands—"it's down in Remagen."

Remagen. South of Cologne by another thirty miles. It's smack in the middle of Courtney Hodges' First Army sector, a nothing little Rhine town between Bonn and Koblenz.

"So it wasn't really *we* who got it, to be exact. But . . ."

Bandy holds up a flat palm. Be quiet. Rubin is about to happily explain that it's still "we," technically, the Americans, who got the first bridge.

"When?"

"Two days ago, the seventh. The Krauts tried to blow it up, but it just fired off the pilings and settled right back down. Amazing. Big railroad bridge too, called Ludendorff. Ninth Armored Division was doing some recon and they just came up on this big Rhine bridge. You believe that? I'll tell you, it's some breakthrough. I hear First Army already has two whole divisions across the river. I bet the brass is throwing a party."

Rubin's telling is too chirpy for Bandy, this is rotten news. In fact, Charles Bandy may be the only American in Europe for whom this is rotten news. The images of party favors and confetti are stillborn in Bandy's head.

He whirls for his helmet and his camera bag. He scoops up film canisters from the floor and stuffs them in pockets. Rubin steps back to give him room to rotate.

Bandy says nothing. When he has enough supplies on him to last a few days, he flashes past the tall kid and takes the bakery steps in a few bounds. He scoots through the wreckage of the bakery shop and finds himself in the ruined street, under a gray and dank sky, before he stops.

Trucks rumble past, towing artillery pieces. Soldiers lug crates and weapons. Bandy stands in the middle of a war noon in Krefeld, on the wrong bank of the Rhine.

He sits on the brick curb. His knees come up high, his pack settles between his ankles.

"Where am I going?" he asks some part of him he hopes might have an answer.

Rubin catches up.

"Mr. Bandy, where're you going?"

Two weeks. That's how big a jump First Army has gotten on Montgomery with their miracle bridge down in nowheresville Remagen. Monty's D-day to jump across the Rhine isn't until March twenty-fourth. *Two more weeks.*

Bandy is frozen between alternatives. His horse looked good early, leading out of the gate. But it's been overtaken on the first stinking turn by a goddamned fifty-to-one dark horse. Remagen. The Germans blew the bridge up. Why didn't it fall into the river?

Remagen is right in the heart of Bradley country. General Omar Bradley, commander of Twelfth Army Group, which includes the First. He is Ike's most favored officer, a classmate at West Point.

Oh, Ike is having himself a laugh over this. A real knee-slapping hoot.

Bandy recalls the disdain with which Eisenhower described his struggles with Montgomery. Every correspondent in the European theater knows how Ike and Monty feel about each other. It's been an open tug-of-war since the beaches of Normandy, no secret about it. And now that the breakthrough has finally happened, Eisenhower can commit his reserves and surge ahead. Ike's got a rabbit's foot, Bandy thinks, Remagen is some kind of wish granted. Bridges are down along every foot of the Rhine, four hundred miles from Holland to Switzerland. And Omar Bradley gets one.

This could shift the weight of the campaign to Bradley's middle sector, away from the British in the north. If Ike wants to—and Bandy believes he well might—he's been given the chance to snub Monty, not politically or personally, for which he would justly take a lot of heat, but the right way, for military reasons. The Supreme Commander will be simply exploiting an amazing stroke of good fortune, the result of a farsighted, flexible battle plan.

Should Bandy head for Remagen and hook up with First Army?

Or should he stay put, and figure that Monty still has the inside track?

Bradley will have a big lead. In two weeks, who knows

how far he can get? But he has a tougher course ahead of him. And his forces are spread out all over the middle and southern sectors. Berlin was never in Twelfth Army's sights. Will Bradley and Ike adjust their plans and strike to the northeast?

Montgomery is deliberate, a plodder in this race. But he has the best route, and has the bit in his teeth for nothing short of glory in Berlin.

Soon it will be too late for Bandy to make this choice. Once the two armies light out over the German countryside, after their advances take on the shape of spear thrusts, it'll be impossible to move from one leading point to another.

Who is going to Berlin? Twelfth Army or Twenty-first Army?

What will Eisenhower do?

Behind him on the sidewalk, Rubin asks again.

"Mr. Bandy, sir. Where are you going?"

March 10, 1945, 0640 hours
Ten kilometers east of the Oder River
Stonsk, Poland

THE SOUND OF GUNFIRE NEVER SEEMS TO QUIT IN HIS head.

It's not his imagination. He hears the guns, whether they're in the rumble of a passing truck, a stream tumbling down rocks, or the actual report of a weapon somewhere. He wonders often if gunfire isn't truly the sound of the world and he, in the manner of a doctor with a stethoscope to a patient's chest, hears the unheard, deep sound, the real clamor of life that is the din of death.

Ilya sleeps the soldier's sleep. He doesn't dream, but stays on guard at the outpost to consciousness. He knows he is cold. He knows he is curled on his side in a foxhole he dug a week ago. He knows he is filthy. There it is, the pop of rifles, the chatter like freezing teeth of machine guns. Ilya doesn't bother to decipher if these are real weapons he hears or the ghosts of gunfire hiding inside something innocent. He is half asleep and they are at least half guns, and that is enough.

A weight like drunkenness lies over his shoulder. He's not tired anymore, he ought to wake up. The weight doesn't keep him warm or comfortable but holds him to the ground anyway, making him reluctant to rise. In this straddling state, with eyes and ears in twilight, everything coming from outside him is baffled. He can grapple with his own thoughts.

It's a cliché to keep seeing the German prisoners in the road. Ilya has been at war since 1942. More than any other object in a man's world, more than toothbrushes or hammers or ink pens, he has held a gun. He's seen the blood of almost as many men as he has seen their faces. He would expect to read in a novel about this sort of thing, a soldier haunted by a deed such as the massacre of the German prisoners. Ilya feels pestered because there they are, alive again on the road. Greatcoats and cloth caps. They stumble. They clot in fear under the hurled abuse. He turns his back once more and there it is, the gunfire. This time he's sure that's what the sound is.

Ilya wants to be done with whatever this is, guilt or grief, he has no idea; he can't get a clear look at it, not as clear as the vision of the prisoners alive in their last minutes. But he figures that if he can muster up a healthy dollop of remorse, the scene will go away inside him, or at least join the other images of war as a memory and not a recurrent burr. Maybe when the German prisoners leave they'll take the constant gunfire with them.

He opens his eyes. He sits up with griping shoulders and hips. Overhead, a glowering sky is packed low, as though the gods are creeping closer under cover to watch what the Red Army does in the days before storming the gates of their enemy.

There is no remorse in the measly daylight. Not a shred of regret. For too long Ilya has chased these emotions from his door, kicked at them whenever they came around, and now when they might help he cannot summon them. He brings his eyes down from the clouds and stares straight into the dirt wall of his foxhole, the dank earth, the receptacle for all he has done.

Judge me, he thinks. Curse me.

Nothing.

The rattle of guns flies from the little town.

Again, Ilya feels nagged.

Out of his breast pocket he pulls a crudely made cigarette. Ilya's not very good at rolling his own yet, his hands are very big for the delicate task and his fingers are almost always swollen. The cigarette unravels and spills some tobacco. He relicks the paper and sticks it shut. He lights it. The cigarette makes him cough. He doesn't even know how to smoke the thing, but he stays with it through another hack. Lousy, he thinks, this is lousy.

He stands in the foxhole. The field around him is pitted with foxholes. He shoulders his submachine gun and clambers out of his hole. He stretches his back, rubs his bare pate, then walks. The field is empty, the whole company is in the town shooting. Ilya was left to sleep past dawn. Or Misha tried to wake him and caught an unconscious cuff for it, it's happened before.

Ilya takes another puff and tosses the cigarette to the ground where it smolders pitifully, abandoned with still more life in it. He steps on it on his way into Stonsk.

In town he halts outside the remains of a hardware store. He perches on top of a barrel. It's a tall wooden cask, his feet come off the ground. He wonders what was kept in the barrel at one time, he does not read Polish. Maybe nails, definitely something heavy. Ilya brings his knees up on top and bends them to his chest.

From his seat he watches a four-story building in the center of this small town being eaten away by bullets. The rounds are like locusts at wheat stalks, they chew mortar and bricks into dust, the building seems to steam. He lights another ragged cigarette. This first puff stays in his lungs and does not trouble his throat so badly. Behind his back, the wall of the shop is shell-pocked. He shifts to find a smoother place for his spine.

The firing at the building down the street is all wrong. The soldiers aim at the lower rows of windows. The bullets come from only one direction.

Ilya spits. He unlocks his legs and stands, the keg rocks behind him. He leaves his submachine gun leaning against the wall, he'll be right back. He strides down the center of the street. Ilya advances almost into the firing line, to where he hears the bullets whisk the air. He waves his arms and the shooting stops. He cups his hands around his mouth.

"Misha!"

From a building up the street, the little man's voice rises.

"What? Get back!"

"Come out here!"

No answer. Ilya sees the bristles of Russian guns sticking out of a dozen busted and blackened windows.

"Misha!"

"Yes, yes, all right!" Misha's voice is irked. Ilya waits in the street, the filthy tang of cigarette smoke is on his tongue. He blames Misha for getting him started. In the lull, the building at Ilya's back continues to crumble in chips, as though it knows its job and faithfully keeps at it even without bullets gnawing its skin.

Misha comes out of a doorway backward. He is issuing some orders before leaving. He is a platoon sergeant now, Ilya is too. They share command over fifty men. They were both promoted by Pushkov after the battle for the citadel, rewarded for Misha's cleverness and Ilya's fighting prowess. For their leadership. The battalion absorbed terrible losses at Posen. New men have been added to bolster the numbers back to full strength, sentenced to their company. But the men are raw. Some have been prisoners under the Germans for years, some are plain ignorant, almost all are angry and just want to rampage over the Oder River into Berlin and maul everything in their path. And so they will, but as an army. Misha and Ilya have been charged with helping train their company in this evacuated, ruined Polish border town.

The failure to deliver the German prisoners to the rear has never been mentioned. Not from the moment the guns stopped squalling on that lonesome crow-flown road, not from the second the last German head tipped over and stilled. Ilya turned around to watch them being mowed down. He hadn't wanted to, but not watching seemed to take too much effort. It was easy to see. It is too easy to re-call.

The gun smoke drifted away and the executioners said nothing, as though the smoke were the last evidence of those sixty German lives, and when it was cleansed by the wind the episode was cleansed too. The Red soldiers all shoul-dered their hot rifles and turned to the west, to return the way they'd come. The bodies were left in the road unburied. Ilya hung back, looking at the gray heap, sixty, a massive jumble. He tried to sense the life that had been spilled, the stories that would never happen, children unfathered, and that was the first moment the war became nothing. They were bodies and he had seen bodies. The good news was they were German bodies. That was all Ilya felt, the good news and nothing. A kilometer down the country road, Misha halted the men until Ilya caught up. Walking in si-lence, one of the men began to roll cigarettes, handing them out. Misha, who did not smoke either, reached for one. Ilya did too. Two weeks later, Misha smokes easily now.

Pushkov greeted them like new men. He called a meet-ing. He made a speech in front of the entire company, then promoted Ilya and Misha.

Ilya looks for signs of the sixty in the world. But there are none. He seems to carry the only bits of them left, those vi-sions of them alive and the sound of gunfire he hears in everything.

The bandage is gone from Misha's face. The stitches have been removed. A virulent red ridge runs across his cheek, below his ear to his neck. His left earlobe is gone. He looks like he has been in a fight with claws and teeth.

"Ilya, what," the little man asks, approaching with quick and short steps, "what?"

"You're doing it wrong."

Up close, Ilya smells tobacco on the little man. He's taking this smoking thing a bit far, Ilya thinks.

Misha makes an exasperated grunt. "I'm following the street-fighting manual."

"The manual wasn't at Stalingrad. I'm the manual, Misha."

"Fine, yes. Then you take over. Fine."

"I don't want to. You're a sergeant. You brought them out here this morning without me. I understand. I even approve. You train them."

"But you want to embarrass me in front of the men."

"No. I want you to train them properly so they won't get either of us killed."

Misha crosses his arms.

"Yes, Ilya. So tell me."

"Concentrate your fire first at the top floor. That's where the command staff will be set up. That's where the artillery spotters are too. Snipers will be up high. These are the targets you have to prioritize before you storm a building."

"All right. Even though the bulk of the defenders are on the ground floor."

"Even though."

"Yes. What else?"

"After that, concentrate on the middle floors. That's where heavy machine guns will be bunkered. You don't take them out before you rush, you'll never make it."

Misha's eyes cast over Ilya's head. He sees the attack in his head, adds in Ilya's dictates and nods, seeing the wisdom.

Ilya continues: "Split up. Position your forces at three or four different angles to your target. If their mortars get your range you'll lose your whole platoon."

"All right."

"When you storm the building, do it in waves with squads. Don't commit everyone at once. Keep the defenders under pressure."

Misha presses his lips and nods.

"That's it. I'll stay over here out of the way and watch. We can talk about it this afternoon when you're done."

"All right. Ilya?"

"What."

"In front of the men. Please, don't call me Misha. Sergeant Bakov. And I'll call you Sergeant Shokhin. It's better for discipline."

"Fine."

Misha smiles up at him. The budding scar appears to produce its own red grin.

"Ilyushka. We're sergeants now. We're on our way back. What do you think?"

Ilya takes this in. He glances beyond the little, newly minted sergeant to the building at the far corner, which Misha's fifty men will destroy this morning with guns and mortars, explosives and handheld rockets, the captured *Panzerfausts*. That building will fall and the Russians will turn their backs and march away and the stories that might have come from the building will never occur. This will be repeated a hundred thousand times or a million times until it is done to Berlin and the war ends. Ilya and Misha will stop a million histories from happening.

"Yes," Ilya replies. He leaves Misha in the street to return to his barrel outside the hardware store.

"We're on our way back!" Misha cheers.

Ilya lowers his eyes to his scuffling boots.

There is no way back, sergeants or not. That road is blocked by a pile of sixty corpses.

And the way ahead leads to nothing.

————

NO BERLINER WANTS TO BE NOTICED.

Nothing good comes from it. There is evil in the land, a multieyed spider that crouches at the center of a city-sized web. It notes any vibration in the strands and runs to it. Every Berliner stands as still as he can, hides when he must, trusts only in betrayal.

There is nothing threatening about Gerhart von Westermann. He is a quiet, roly-poly presence, like a sleeping child. But the BPO manager has summoned Lottie to his office this afternoon before the day's performance, so she fears everything in the world right now; the attention, the heavy chair under her, the carpet, the big desk between her and the manager, the wavering candle flames that let them see each other with the thick blast curtains drawn. It's just an office without electricity on a chilly day, but it feels to Lottie like a lair. Bleached bones on the floor could not make her more apprehensive.

What could von Westermann want? She's been in this chair for ten seconds already and he hasn't spoken. The man has knit his fingers over his rounded vest, his face rests on platters of chins, surveying her. Lottie wants words in the room, every ticking second seems a sentence to a worsening fate, but she will not speak first, it's not her place. She perches on the edge of the chair and sits perfectly motionless. Perhaps he won't say anything at all if she stays inert. Maybe he's waiting for motion, to pounce. Lottie is very afraid.

The orchestra manager draws a deep breath, as though awakening.

"Charlotta, is it?"

"Yes, Herr von Westermann."

"How are you? How are you faring?"

"Well enough, sir."

"Things are tough, yes?"

"For everyone, sir. I get by."

"You wear a tuxedo in the orchestra."

"Yes, sir."

"Very good. I shall require its return."

Lottie is strangled, the spiderweb circles her throat. She wants to protest but there is no air. She hears herself make grunting sounds, the starts of words that die the moment they peak on her lips. In their place, her heart heaves up tears.

"Charlotta."

She closes her eyes. She waves a long-fingered hand, begging from the manager a moment of peace to accept her dismissal from the BPO. The first moment she is able, she will beg, "Why?"

"Charlotta. I only want the tuxedo. You are still in the orchestra."

Lottie sniffs instantly. Her tears seem impossibly to reverse flow up her cheek.

"Oh, oh, Herr von Westermann, I . . . sir . . ."

"My apologies. I did not anticipate you might react that way. It was awkward of me."

Lottie swallows. She has no kerchief. Von Westermann has nothing to give her to dry her cheeks. Her elbow lifts from the chair arm and hesitates; the manager nods and gestures that it is fine for her to wipe her face with her sleeve.

She composes herself, smoothing back her hair, believing her moment of panic has disheveled her. When she is done, with a graceful movement she layers her hands in her lap, placated and calmer.

"There," says the BPO manager.

Lottie clears her throat.

"May I ask, please, sir, why you need the tuxedo?"

Lottie is aware of von Westermann's discomfiture with people. He is known in the orchestra as a man of paper, of notes and scores and charts. He is the BPO's scheduler and organizer. He is one of the larger deities of the Philharmonic, the one who operates invisibly but indelibly. She has never heard any report that he is kind or otherwise. He is revered simply for being competent and silent.

"You see, Charlotta. It's really Lottie, isn't it?"

"Yes, sir."

"May I?"

"Yes, please."

"Lottie, then. You know that Gauleiter Goebbels considers himself to be the government's greatest patron of the Berlin Philharmonic."

"Yes. He makes quite a show of it."

Von Westermann chuckles to himself over some irony.

"Yes. He does. The good minister believes it is he who has raised our orchestra to its current professional level. But in the past few months he has been . . . let me say, less than generous in his views of the Philharmonic. He has mentioned several times that the orchestra may well wind up on the barricades defending the city. That would be a shame and a waste."

"Very much so."

"You have seen Minister Speer in the theaters?"

"Yes. He always sits in the middle of the front row."

"Correct. He rarely misses a performance. To be frank with you, Minister Speer is the real force in the government behind the BPO."

Lottie knows nothing about this arena of the music world; who takes credit and who makes decisions. She doesn't even care about the orchestra itself as much more than a vehicle for her own talent. Her love is her instrument, the beauty of her part. The mechanics and glory of the whole are not her concern.

"You know," says von Westermann, "the Russians are eighty kilometers from Berlin. They're on the Oder River. In the millions."

These statements all seem out of sequence. What do Speer and the Russians have to do with his need for her tuxedo?

Lottie says, "Yes."

"You have heard . . . well. You understand what this forebodes. The Russians, I mean."

"I have heard stories, Herr von Westermann."

"As have we all, child. If they reach Berlin before the Western Allies"—his hands rise and fall, hopeless and empty—"imagination fails."

Lottie's does not. But von Westermann is not a woman.

"This is a dangerous question. But we are colleagues here. We trust each other, yes?"

"Yes."

"Fine. Good. So."

"Yes, sir?"

The manager hesitates.

"Does your family have a car?"

"No, sir."

"Do you have papers? Any way to leave Berlin?"

"No."

"Hmm. No, of course not."

These are things only the wealthy and the Nazis have. Lottie sees them every day loading their autos with boxes and luggage and children, all the while exhorting Berliners to stand and fight to the last man. We are very close already, she thinks, to the last man.

The manager sinks again into his chins and rotund hush. His fingertips tap without noise on the desk. He doesn't want to say what comes next. He senses the spider.

"Lottie, I have something to tell you. It must be held in the utmost secrecy. Do you understand?"

"Yes, sir. Of course."

"Nothing of course about it, girl. Many people will die senseless deaths if you cannot be trusted with what I am going to say."

"I understand, Herr von Westermann. I do."

"All right."

The manager lays his hands flat on his desk. He looks over both his shoulders, the *Berliner Blick,* even in his own office. He lowers his voice.

"Minister Speer has a plan to save the orchestra."

Lottie gasps. The manager hoists a thick finger to shush her, make her conscious of her reaction, remind her of the web.

"I tell you this because you are indeed a gifted musician. Even though you are only a provisional member of the orchestra. But more important, you are a woman. I do not need to explain."

The Russians.

"No, sir."

"Only a selected number in the orchestra have been made aware that anything is under way. The others we will tell in due time. You will not discuss this with anyone. Your family, the other musicians, your boyfriend, no one. Absolutely."

Lottie wants to run down the Unter den Linden and announce, "I am to be saved! I am to be saved!" They will look at her, all of them, and approve, that Lottie is the one to be protected.

"I understand."

"I will rely on that with my life, Lottie."

"Yes, sir."

"After tomorrow's performance, you will leave your tuxedo with the stage manager. We will announce to the orchestra that they are to be stored for the duration of the war. In addition, you will notice in the coming weeks that several of our finer instruments will be missing. Some pianos, the better tubas and harps. We will also be relocating as much of our library of scores as possible. Everything is to be loaded onto vans and shipped west, directly into the path of the *Amis'* advance, where they will be surrendered."

The coming weeks?

"Herr von Westermann, sir. Why not just go now? Tonight, tomorrow. Why stall, the Russians could come any time." Lottie has trouble staying in her seat, she wants to rise and float away from Berlin on this wonderful news.

"We are the Berlin Philharmonic Orchestra. We will finish as much of our season as we can. Then we will go."

Lottie bites her tongue. If she lets it wag any looser, she will lecture this aloof man. Only days ago she'd made up her mind to take cyanide. Now, with this marvelous plot, Lottie desires more than ever to survive, and she wants to take no risks, especially not for things as illusory as principle or patriotism.

The manager watches the flashes on her face, her struggle with disappointment. It's hypocritical, Lottie thinks, for the BPO to abandon the city, to use its high connections to flee the fate that will surely fall on others just as deserving of deliverance, and to imagine that this can be done with honor. Lottie has no problem with the hypocrisy, just the wait.

She licks her lips. "Yes, sir. Of course."

"Minister Speer has arranged for transportation for all one hundred and five musicians. There will be vans and buses to take you and your instruments plus selected staff members west to the American lines. Herr Speer will send along his personal adjutant to negotiate the surrender. We will not allow the Philharmonic to fall to the Red Army. It is a great orchestra. An internationally renowned institution. It must be preserved."

The manager speaks as though he has to convince Lottie that scheming, treason, and desertion are warranted. He does not.

She asks, "Will we be allowed to bring anyone along with us?"

The manager shakes his head, a deliberate and elegiac gesture.

"No. This pains me but the danger is too great. Only a few can know. And only a few can escape. It is one of many unpleasant realities of the war."

Mutti and her Jew. They will have to be brave all the way to the end now. Just as well; it is their intention.

"Yes, sir."

"I must remind you again that this is all strictly confidential."

Lottie assents with a grave nod.

"Good. We must wait until the *Amis* are close enough in the west. We will not make it through our own lines if we have to drive too far, we'll be sent back. That would have its own unpleasant repercussions."

This is the Berliner's dilemma. Whose petard to be hoisted on, the Nazis' or the Reds'?

Von Westermann continues. "There will be a signal. It will not come until the entire orchestra is assembled on stage."

What kind of signal could be given to the whole orchestra while it is sitting in the public eye?

Von Westermann flinches in one more *Berliner Blick*. He leans forward, his manner has succumbed completely to the conspiratorial.

"When the time is right, you will all find on your music stands a selection that will not have been announced for that performance. It will be familiar to the orchestra, you will need no rehearsal. You will play it as part of the program, without surprise or comment. You will draw no attention to it other than playing it well. When you are finished for the afternoon, stand and accept your applause. Then file quietly to the rear stage entrance. In the alley out back will be the transportation. Take your instrument only, no luggage, and get on one of the vehicles."

Lottie doesn't savor all this intrigue. To her the need is simple: get out. The answer is equally direct: go. Now.

"May I ask what the signal will be?"

"You will play the finale from *Die Götterdämmerung*."

Lottie thinks: Fitting.

Wagner's depiction of the destruction of Valhalla. The death of the gods. The end of the world.

SIX

————————

"Y AKOV."
"Yes, Father."
"You are a traitor."
"Yes, Father."
"This is what happens. Look at you."

The young man's body is strewn against a barbed-wire fence, hanging like a spineless scarecrow, one arm reaching high, the other dangling loose, legs at impossible angles.

Stalin thinks he has seen very little actual death. He never attends the executions he orders with a flick of a blue pencil on the lists of enemies. He never ventures to the front, only once since the war began and that was so the history books will have a record of him mingling with the fighting men. He does not visit factories or villages where people work and live and die. What death he does see comes from the newsreels he watches often at the Kremlin. But they are so sanitized and colorless. Yakov here is quite real and well described. Years ago Stalin saw Lenin's body lying in state, his hands folded for a long nap with flowers. Lenin was in a much better predicament than Yakov.

"What is this place? A prison camp?"
"Yes, Father."
"I remember. Sachsenhausen. You died at Sachsen-

hausen. April 1943. You threw yourself against the barbed wire."

"Yes, Father."

"So they would shoot you."

"Yes, Father."

Stalin sits on the ground beside the suspended body of his son. The boy wears a Red Army uniform. His tunic is torn by the metal quills and by some bullets. A pipe appears in Stalin's hand.

"You surrendered, Yasha. You were surrounded and you gave up your post. Do you know what that signified? The son of Stalin would rather save his own skin than die for the *Rodina*. The Germans made a lot of hay with that. Did you know? They circulated a photograph showing you in prison. It was quite a propaganda coup for them."

Stalin takes a puff on the pipe, then points the stem at his son.

"What if they had made you talk? What if after torture and drugs, they had pried open the mouth of Stalin's eldest son? That would have been disastrous."

"Yes, Father."

"Did you know the lousy Germans came to me with a deal, to negotiate with them for your release? I told them no! As if Stalin would trade with the Nazis. 'No! War is war,' I said."

"Yes, Father."

"I ask millions to die every day, Yasha. Every day they do it, for Russia, for the Party, for me. But you. I never liked you."

"Yes, Father."

"And your mother. Yekaterina. My first wife. I'll tell you a secret, Yasha."

"Yes, Father."

"I loved her. She was a Georgian, like me. We were young together. When she died, I wept. Wept, like Stalin was a baby. But I did my weeping in private. That's where a man suffers. Not like you, in photographs, in public. I'm sad to say it, but do you know what else? Nothing good ever came from your mother."

Beside the body of Yakov Dzhugashvili, other figures appear, not stark as the boy, flimsy but visible to Stalin. Women and men, they wear dresses and three-piece suits with fobs. They too are embedded and tangled on the wire, hung like twisted laundry. Stalin knows by looking that they are ghosts and not really there, so he continues talking only to his son.

"Yekaterina's brother, your uncle Alexander. Once he was a good friend to me, but he had to be shot as a spy. And Alexander's wife and his son, both became enemies of the people, both sent to Siberia. She died there, I've heard."

Yes. Stalin sees them. There they are, spiked in their finery.

"Some family I've been given. Do you hear me? My second wife, Nadezhda, the fucking suicide. Her sister Anna is a spy. Anna's husband was shot ten years ago, an enemy of the people. His brother, another spy. Your brother, a drunkard. Your sister, a shrew. My family, a nest of spies and traitors and loudmouths."

The lineup on the barbed wire is long now. Every one of them is flung against the fence like Yakov, torn and limp.

"Go away."

All but Yakov disappear at his whim. Stalin drags on the pipe. It calms him. He watches the smoke curl. It does not drift away, but dances for him as long as he wants it to. He looks through the gray swirls to take in what he imagines of the prison camp.

"Sachsenhausen, eh?"

"Yes, Father."

The boy is dead. He robbed the bastards of their prize Russian.

"Well, you did this to yourself, then. You knew you were weak. You knew you would break. So you ended it like a man, at least. Good for you."

Stalin nods. The boy's body makes its only motion and nods also.

"I'll tell you what I'll do, Yasha. Sachsenhausen is right outside Berlin, I believe. I'm going to take that damned city, I don't give a shit what the little Americans and British think they have up their sleeves. After I do, I'll string up a few

Nazis for you right in their own camp. We'll take over Sachsenhausen and turn it on its masters. Would you like that?"

"Yes, Father."

"There then, it's settled. Good for you, boy. You had me worried, but you did the right thing. I like you better now."

Stalin decides to end the dream. It is within his power, certainly.

"Go away."

Yakov and the Nazi camp and the web of barbed wire do not fade at Stalin's wish. Yakov's head continues to nod and hold his father's gaze.

"I said go away."

Blood burbles from Yakov's lips. Stalin is taken aback. A wet warmth dribbles over Stalin's lips, down his chin, mirroring his son.

"Go away!"

The blood builds from Stalin's mouth and he is soaked in it. He thrashes his arms as if he can wipe it off him, but the blood is tacky and comes alive, it swarms on him like wasps in treacle. He is stung over and over.

Yakov is gone. It is Stalin who hangs on the wire.

Stalin snaps as though hit by a bullet. He hears a crackle, like very small bones breaking.

A *Pravda* newspaper is across his lap and belly. Stalin's fists have crumpled the sheets like an accordion. Relaxing his arms, he spreads the paper out. Stalin blinks many times to clear his eyes, to bring his focus into this world.

Stalin's house is small. A puny clock two rooms away is its heartbeat, a brittle sound.

One of the wrinkled newspaper pages bears a photograph of Winston Churchill standing before a sign somewhere on the Western Front in Germany. The town behind him is a wreck. At the bottom of the page is a wet spot where Stalin has drooled. His shirt is damp too. He wipes a palm across his chin and moustache, and curses.

He sits under a lamp. The shade is translucent, yellow. In the struggling light everything in the room bears a sallow tint, even the backs of Stalin's hands.

Stalin closes the newspaper sloppily and releases it to the floor. Let the housekeeper get it.

He reaches for his pipe. This makes him recall the dream pipe. In a moment, he calls up the entire dream. Yakov and the others, strung up, dead dolls.

Then it was him meshed in the fence, captured. Dead.

Stalin feels scoured inside, as though the vision were a pipe cleaner run through his guts. Nothing happens by accident. Why did he dream of Yakov and the others?

He doesn't know, and doesn't care to discover at this hour of the morning. He is Stalin, the *vozhd,* and whatever he decides the dream means, it means.

This is the interpretation, then. It's easy. If others do not throw themselves—or are not thrown—on the barbed wire, then it will be Stalin who will be lost. They must sacrifice, all of them. The blood in his mouth is theirs, it flows through Stalin.

The meaning of the dream: Stalin *is* the *Rodina.*

It's a good feeling to be decisive about things that might otherwise torment one. The dream was a rough one, it took a nasty turn there at the end. It's left Stalin achy. But this is the kind of ache that makes a man not forget, that makes a man take action.

He likes Yakov better now.

Yes. Sachsenhausen.

Stalin made the boy a promise. Stalin remembers. He doesn't care what the Allies have up their sleeves.

Yakov died outside Berlin.

Again, there it is.

Always Berlin.

March 18, 1945, 9:20 A.M.
Goethe Strasse
Charlottenburg, Berlin

FOR THE FIRST TIME IN FOUR YEARS, LOTTIE DOES NOT GO underground to a shelter.

The air raids over Berlin have become daily occurrences; in the last eleven weeks there have been eighty-five attacks. Freya insists that both she and Lottie always go to the public bunkers for every raid. This way, they'll be seen and no one will suspect the two have a cellar below their house and come banging to use it in an emergency.

For some reason, this morning Lottie wants to stay aboveground and watch. She doesn't know why she holds still when the flurry starts in the streets. But in a chamber of her heart she does know. The Jew watches the bombers. Lottie thinks she ought to see them too. He's just a school-teacher. Lottie is an artist, and this is just the sort of thing that drives art and passion. To stand close to the human flame, to take part in spectacle. Lottie will remember what she sees in the Berlin skies this morning, its brand will come out someday and somehow through her cello. All Berliners see the aftermath of the attacks when they climb out of their dungeons; Lottie will be one of the few who stood under the black rain.

She remains in her room on the second floor. She thinks to be cautious and pull the mattress from her bed to wrap it around the hard Galiano case. The cello is two centuries old, Lottie must not let it die while she owns it. But she leaves it standing in its corner. The instrument is safe, she knows. She slides open the window and arranges herself in the sill. It's against the law to be up here during a raid but Lottie isn't concerned. After the conversation with von Westermann last week, she understands she is to be preserved. Minister Speer's plan to save her and the BPO has taken the place of the cyanide pill as the blueprint of Lottie's future. Though she senses she ought to be very careful this close to the end, she is, without logic, pervaded by a sense of invulnerability. Lottie has always believed in fate; she believes hers—in the matter of rescue—has been settled.

So she lets the Galiano alone and sits in the window. Her mother was not home thirty minutes ago when the radio ticked and the sirens sounded. Mutti's days are spent harvesting food and water from wherever she can scrape them. She's in a shelter somewhere on the Ku'damm now, maybe in the giant flak bunker at the Zoo. The Jew will fend for himself, he always does. Up on the second floor Lottie hopes not to bump into him or even see him. Her sense is that during the daylight hours he remains a subterranean creature.

It is a lovely Sunday morning. The Americans have a gorgeous clear day to do their work. From her second-story window she sees the B-17s flocking high over the city center. The bombs tumbling from the planes' midsections look like railroad tracks, they look like stitches. Lottie sits transfixed, her head bent back, her eyes skyward and squinty in the clarity of the light. There are a thousand American bombers, more than a thousand. Slicing above and around them are many hundreds of fighter planes, protecting the mission. It's an evil sight, buzzing locusts, something god-sent and vengeful in their numbers. A plague.

Four distinct sounds yammer at Lottie's window. At the bottom, like the bass voice in a quartet, is the hum of the planes, a pleasant sound really, a deep purr that seems to come from everywhere at once. Next up is the beat of explosions going off in the city. The bombs fall in the north and northeast sectors of Berlin, in Reinickendorf, Wedding, and Pankow, on the factories there, and in the city center, around the Brandenburg Tor and Hitler's Chancellery, only two miles from where Lottie sits. Higher pitched than the detonations is the tattoo of German flak guns situated on top of four massive concrete towers, spread across the city. The flak breaks the manicured vision of the bombers high overhead with black cottony puffs in their path. The last voice is the bombs themselves, they whistle and squeal on their way down like excited schoolchildren hurrying to play.

Lottie does not hear the four voices in cacophony but separately, as instruments and scripted parts in the music of the killing of Berlin.

For twenty minutes she stares across the cityscape and into the cloud-free sky. She watches the bombs go to earth and hears the eruptions without horror, she imagines buildings staggering and tumbling just two miles away from her window in Charlottenburg. Lottie is not afraid; she feels she has already been taken away from here, she is on the bus and safe, and all that she sees today and tomorrow and until she is safe is nothing but the overture. The fact that the bombs fall close to her but miss is a nice bit of proof.

How will the *Amis* receive her and the BPO? Lottie imagines the nightfall bus ride, all the men in suits clutching their instruments, their passports to life. There will be challenges at roadblocks, but the trucks and buses will be waved through when the German guards learn who the passengers are. Every minute will be another mile away from Berlin. Finally, an English voice will bark in the dark. Halt! The convoy will stop and the musicians will climb off and kiss the ground. We are world-class musicians, not combatants, we'll be honored by the *Amis*. Perhaps we'll assemble right there and play for them.

But these are the Americans right now in the sky, lashing Berlin. Maybe to them, all Germans are bad. No Germans are to be honored.

How will the people of Berlin react when they learn we have escaped? What happens to the BPO's proud name? Cowards?

A particularly loud report makes Lottie jump on her windowsill seat. She is shaken from her reverie. Her eyes return to the skies.

Something different is taking place overhead. The American bombers have not broken their close ranks, but there is a new presence in their midst, a new handwriting in the vapor trails behind them. Some of the lines are curved, like chalk in a fainted hand; these planes are shot down, falling out of the crowd. What could do this, with so many fighters to protect them?

Lottie hears a new sound join the morning war chorus, not the thump of explosions or the drone of propellers but a rocket ship's *whoosh*. She catches a glimpse of things up there moving faster than the bombers and their escorts. They are airplanes, but flashing silver, diving and cutting new crazy, fast patterns.

Jets! *Luftwaffe* jets! For months Goebbels has been promising to unveil them, a secret weapon in the skies over Germany to make the cities safe from Allied bombers. Lottie, like the rest of Berlin's civilians, began to believe the rumors were just bold hype, wishful thinking by the Nazi propagandists. But here the jet planes are. Lottie watches their debut.

This is awry from her fate. This is dreadful. The German superplanes, the jet fighters, are taking a toll. Another American bomber skews out of line. It falls seeping fire and white billows. It will crash. No!

Lottie's stomach knots. Is it possible that she's watching the moment of a German turnaround in the fortunes of the war? A dozen parachutes drift over the city, American airmen out of dead planes. The jets slash, the American fighters counter. Lottie balls her fists. The sky, already concentrated with plunging bombs and black-winged flecks, thickens now with even more tumult, a swarming smoking dogfight. There seem to be only two dozen jets against vastly superior enemy numbers. Lottie wants nothing to interfere with her fate. These German fighters risk altering the outcome.

Without moving or speaking, she cheers for the German pilots. This is against common sense. But if the jets can swipe a few bombers out of the sky, maybe the attacks will come less often. Maybe the Americans will learn a little more respect. But nothing more will come of this day. Lottie's sense of her deliverance has reasserted itself. The end of the war cannot be stopped. It will come when the Russians bring it. Lottie will be long gone. Everything is on track.

And nothing will stop the bombs. Lottie watches the impact of the jets. They shoot down fifteen American bombers, the flak claims another seven. She sees two of the bombers fall into the Tiergarten only a mile away. Dozens of parachutes descend, white wisps of failure. But twenty-two bombers out of a thousand is a drop in the ocean. The American might is overwhelming. Goebbels' secret weapons withdraw. The bombers' formations spread out. For another hour Berlin continues to be rocked, it teeters and crumbles. Lottie in her window surprises herself; she begins to despise the *Amis*. Berlin is defenseless. The bombs are like pummeling a man after he's down. Those four sounds she heard so distinctly at the beginning of the raid now blend into a single shriek. Lottie leaves her sill and closes the window. She throws herself on her bed, covering her ears with her pillow.

When the all-clear sirens sound, Lottie rises. She walks to her window and looks again at the sky. It's not there. She looks at a black mist, like an iron pot clamped over Berlin. Fires belch an eclipse of greasy clouds into the air. Fallen structures leave whorls of brick and mortar dust as ghostly markers where they stood minutes before. Steam breaks into the wind from fire departments trying to stem blazes with their little efforts. Lottie has seen all this before. But this morning, because she will soon be leaving Berlin, because she will not share the city's doom, she's outraged at its treatment at the hands of the Americans. Tonight, the British Mosquito bombers will come and add to the agony. In her heart Lottie has left Berlin. She looks at her home now with the protective and chauvinistic eyes of the expatriate.

She hurries down the stairs and darts for the front door. She moves quickly to avoid encountering the Jew, should he be returning to his basement lair. She slams the door behind her. Out in the street, Lottie heads in the direction of the city center and the destruction.

The air in her lungs is acrid. The people of her mother's

neighborhood return to their homes. They all glance into the smoke wafting low overhead. Many women bring their hands to their breasts in relief that it is not their house on fire or lying in shards. Lottie scoots through the trudging crowds. The closer she gets to the Charlottenburger Chausée, which travels through the heart of the Tiergarten, the more the atmosphere thickens to an almost velvet shroud.

Inside the park, the trunks of trees are aflame. The trees themselves have long ago been hewn by shrapnel down to mangled staffs. Far off, across a sward of stripped earth where there once were grass and shrubs, parasols and artists, the sheared wing of an American bomber lies, the propellers on the huge engine are bent back like dry and dying petals. Lottie finds herself running.

She speeds through the park. Berliners wander on all sides hefting bundles and babes, in bowler hats and scarves, some wear gas masks, they all seem nomadic in their own city. Lottie jogs farther. She dodges a crater, then a fallen tree. An elderly couple sitting idly on the cold ground watch her fly past, there is nothing on their faces, they seem stunned like the park.

She runs for five, then ten minutes. At Hermann Göring Strasse, along the eastern boundary of the park, she slows to a walk. The Brandenburg Tor, the triumphal arched gateway to the park, is chewed badly and smirched with soot, but intact. On top, the winged goddess of victory in her two-wheeled Prussian chariot is still pulled by her four horses, but her journey looks to have been through hell.

Lottie comes to a stop at the foot of the gate. Her lungs are seared from her haste and the soiled air. A charred bicycle rests on its side in the street. Mixed up with the frame of the bike are leg bones; above the melted seat a rib cage nests in cloth tatters, a skull is in an air raid sentry's helmet. The remains will have to be collected with a shovel and a broom, like street litter. This was an old man, a brave old man, riding his bicycle to warn Berliners off the streets, the Americans are coming. The Americans rewarded him, proved him correct, by dropping a firebomb on him.

Lottie is rooted beside the skeleton, under the loom of the scorched Brandenburg Tor, beneath a sky rippling past in black sheaths. In the streets around her, rescue squads begin to pump air into basements to trapped survivors. The newly homeless sit because there is nowhere to walk. Already women and more old men appear with shovels to clear avenues through the rubble. Food stations are being set up on card tables to hand out soup and bread.

Tonight, the British will come with more bombs. Tomorrow, perhaps, the Americans again.

Lottie sits on the curb near the air raid warden. He has no smell.

She hates the *Amis*. She tries to fight it because they will be her salvation. But they have left the old man on the bicycle nothing, not even his flesh.

March 24, 1945, 1020 hours
In a C-46, 600 feet over Holland, with the
U.S. Seventeenth Airborne Division
Nearing Wesel, Germany

THE CRIMSON GET-READY LIGHT FLASHES ON.

Bandy stands. He's steady on the flooring, even loaded down as he is. The morning air is clean; the fat transport plane's flight has been slow and smooth all the way, nobody puked. There are two lines, Bandy's at the rear of the right-hand one. Fifty paratroopers ahead of him check their gear and weapons. The twin doors are open on both sides of the plane and all Bandy can hear is the roar of the wind and engines. Some soldiers pound hard on the helmets and shoulders of the men around them, jacking each other up for the jump and the fight.

Bandy reaches down to his legs to make sure that his

cameras are strapped on securely. He doesn't trust them in his backpack or across his chest, in case his landing is rough. He's only had one other jump before this, into Spain six years ago, and that didn't go too badly, he only separated his shoulder. He thinks, you can't get injured *every* time you jump. This one ought to go easy.

The first burst of flak shakes the plane. They must be nearing the Drop Zone. Men shuffle toward the doors, the two queues tighten. Bandy at the tail end pats his breast pocket. A metal flask of Tennessee whiskey answers his knock. His last letter to Victoria, the one in the plastic wrap he keeps with him always, hides behind the liquor.

In another few minutes he'll be leaping out over the east bank of the Rhine. He'll land just north of the town of Wesel, about fifty miles north of Jülich. To get on this plane, Bandy had to hitchhike last week all the way from Jülich back to northern France, to the staging town of Arras, where he pulled a few "famous-photographer" strings and got permission to join the Seventeenth Airborne for this jump. Yesterday the entire division shaved their heads in Mohawk fashion, leaving just a thin pelt from their napes to their foreheads. Bandy turned down the offer of a similar coif. But he is reassured to know that he is jumping into battle with the best kind of soldiers, berserkers.

The Seventeenth's mission is to land behind enemy lines and push westward, the direction they come from, to stop the Germans from retreating in the face of Montgomery's infantry assault across the river, under way right now. The paratroopers will take all the wooded high ground they can find in the Dierforderwald, overlooking river crossings and paved routes in and out of Wesel. As soon as they can, they'll link up with Monty's charging infantry and turn east together.

The airborne operation is code-named Varsity; the land operation, Plunder. Together they are the twin prongs of Montgomery's gigantic push for Berlin. The land offensive started last night. This is the biggest assault on enemy forces since D-Day, aimed through the north rim of the Ruhr valley, then set to roll across the north German plains to the Elbe River, stopping only once they get to Hitler's front yard. Monty sent the troops off with a final preattack message: ". . . The enemy has in fact been driven into a corner, and he cannot escape. Over the Rhine, then, let us go. And good hunting to you on the other side."

At 0100 hours this morning, a solid sixty minutes of artillery barrage plastered the east bank of the Rhine. Thirty-five hundred field guns plus two thousand antitank guns and rocket launchers poured more than a thousand shells per minute over the German positions. Fourteen hundred B-17s bombarded the DZ until daybreak. Throughout the night and into the morning, Plunder shoved eighty thousand American, British, and Canadian troops across the Rhine in eight-man assault boats at ten crossings along a twenty-mile front. Right now, on all sides of Bandy in the air over the Dutch-German border, Varsity wings east with seventeen hundred transport planes and six hundred and fifty tug planes towing two infantry-bearing gliders apiece. Over the DZ and Landing Zones, two thousand fighter planes patrol for enemy activity.

In Bandy's plane, the jump master raises a balled fist, the hand signal to hook up static lines to the wires overhead. Bandy clips in. He gives his lanyard a good testing tug. The soldier in front of him turns to give a big, American cornfield grin and a thumbs-up. The kid has freckles and a little caterpillar moustache.

Bandy pats the boy on the shoulder.

In the din, the soldier mouths the words, "You take my picture when we get down. Okay?"

Bandy hoists his own thumb in answer.

The flak worsens. Black smoke sweeps in the doors from a blast off the starboard wing. The plane jumps. Bandy hears a rattle like hail on the fuselage. Another thump sounds close by. The paratroopers in line clench fists around their static lines, they bunch toward the doors, they want to get the hell out of the plane.

A few other photographers will be on the ground with

Montgomery's infantry, dozens more are in a B-17 at this moment circling the DZ. Hundreds of civilian and military journalists are spread out across Eisenhower's broad front facing the enemy all along the Rhine. But Bandy has made up his mind that the northern route with Monty is still the best bet to get to Berlin. Two weeks ago, the breakthrough at Remagen in the middle sector had been dramatic, but Bradley's bridgehead on the east bank has been bottled up by a remarkably fast German response. In the south, Patton is going great guns; his Third U.S. Army crossed the Rhine two days ago, scooping Montgomery's bigger operation. When Patton himself walked across the river on a pontoon bridge, he unzipped his fly and pissed in the Rhine, calling it the "pause that refreshes." But Patton's not a realistic threat to reach Berlin from down there. Too much territory to cover and occupy. Besides, Ike will probably send him south to make sure the Nazis aren't gearing up their rumored National Redoubt in the Bavarian Alps. In a few minutes Bandy is going to parachute in with the men and machines of the Seventeenth Airborne at the farthest point east of any Allied army. Again, Charles Bandy will be at the vanguard of the war.

The C-46 comes in low and slow, altitude six hundred feet at one-twenty knots. The gush of air coming in the open doorways is fresh against Bandy's face, the black flak stink has cleared out. Spring invades Germany.

The jump master yanks his balled fist up and down, a pistoning motion that says, Get ready! He kneels by the door and raises his index finger. The first soldier moves to the opening, the rest shuffle and tighten up behind him. Stepping forward, Bandy looks down; it's required paratrooper style to tuck their pants legs into their jump boots. Bandy has too.

Bandy thinks Vic would brain him if she knew where he was and what he was about to do. She'd tell him in no uncertain terms he should be on a tractor tilling soil for seed, not falling out of a plane at six hundred feet into gunfire and artillery. He should be home, in green hills and the first budding azaleas. Cool nights on the porch swing. Warm wifely arms and crisp bedsheets. The cameras wrapped to his thighs jiggle with the flak-dancing airplane, snatching his attention away from home, hugging at his legs like children from a second and competing family, telling him, No, stay here with us! This'll be great!

The red ready light goes out and the green light under it flashes on. The jump master drops his arm like a checkered flag and aims his finger now at the ground. The first soldier without hesitation skips out of the door. The jump master's pointing hand goes up, pauses, then down, a metronome marking the two-second pause between leaping men. Bandy can't hear him, but he sees the man's mouth go round, his neck tendons bulge, shouting, "Go!"

The flak thickens over the DZ. The plane bucks, the men stagger and hold on to the static line. Bandy allows some space between him and the young soldier ahead. The lashing of shrapnel against the fuselage intensifies. Sabers of light dice like a magician's swords through the cabin ahead of Bandy where hot metal has pierced the plane's skin. Bandy tells himself he wants to get the hell out of here too, but the rest of him isn't quite as certain as that voice in his head.

He doesn't let himself think. His turn to jump is only four men away, eight seconds. The voice warns, this is no time to start reviewing your life. No regrets to Victoria or promises to the Almighty. Just step forward, pause, step again, pause, step.

Bandy's toes are inches from wide-open destiny. Everyone else is gone except the jump master, who lifts his gateway hand, smiles up behind his goggles to Bandy, salutes, then points down. This time Bandy hears him through the wind and heartbeat and fear, clear as a bell: "Go!"

What is extraordinary to Bandy is the emerald of the world. Below him are trees and fields peacefully verdant and endless in all directions. Above him and all around in the sky are olive drab airplanes almost wing to wing everywhere he looks, an unbelievable armada sent from free, green nations.

Companies of men in battle fatigues float down under white chutes, like pearls set around the emerald.

Bandy thinks of spring pollen and tobacco blossoms. Mountains. Rain-dappled moss. And Victoria.

"Go!"

Bandy's yell, "Aaaaaaaah!" disappears in the boom of the engine wash and the rush of nothing catching him.

The static line yanks the chute out of his pack. The canopy unfolds with a wonderful swish above his head. His crotch and armpits jolt. His teeth clack when his fall is broken and the blue sky goes blank and he's under the shade of a white firmament. For a few seconds he sways in his harness, then he only dangles and drifts. Everything worked. Bandy is glad.

Now the morning takes on a different tone. The day roars. Plane engines of every kind storm above. Small arms fire spits out of the ground and Bandy feels as though he is falling into a crackling blaze. German 88mm guns and tracers scream at the sky. Above it all, Bandy hears his own breathing.

Then silence, so quickly. Nothing exists but the coming grass. Fast. Is it supposed to come up so fast? Bandy doesn't remember his other jump, was it like this? No time . . .

His helmet hits the back of his shoulders, his neck smarts from the snap. His knees buckle, his ankles roll on their own, and he collapses facedown, barely able to get his hands out in front. He opens his eyes and the ground is a lot closer now, inches.

He has bit his lip. His right knee feels jammed, his hips ache. The turf under his nose could be Tennessee on a cloudy day. It's just grass and dirt, it has the odor of fecundity. He relaxes for a moment and lays his bare cheek to the earth.

But the clouds are his parachute lapped over him prone. The sounds are gunplay and running and war shouts. The earth under him is behind enemy lines.

Bandy rolls over to check that his cameras made it down safely. This tangles him in the chute and cords. He bats the silk away and after seconds of struggle sits up, feeling stupid for lying here as he did.

Men and guns scramble everywhere. Sergeants and lieutenants shout and wave their arms for their platoons to form up. A shadow crosses Bandy's place. There is no attendant engine blare, it's an eerie sensation like a winged doom crossing your path, then one of the canvas-and-wood gliders comes to ground just missing Bandy with an ugly but effective landing. The plane is shredded with bullet holes though Bandy sees the young pilot alive and gripping the stick. While the thing settles ungainly and tilts on busted landing struts, Bandy is up and running. Even with legs pumping, he reaches to loose the straps holding his Speed Graphic and the 35mm Leica.

He finds cover in a hedgerow boundary of the field where he landed. The shrubs won't stop a bullet but they will conceal him until he gets his bearings. He squats among the branches to discover the bushes have stickers, so he lies under them instead.

His lower body feels like it wants to swell up on him, but of his two jumps this was by far the most successful—if, he thinks, he manages to survive what he has jumped into.

Bandy unleashes his cameras. He stows the bulky Speed Graphic in his pack and begins sweeping the Leica over the battle scene before him. He looks through the lens now, his vision and all his senses becoming more acute. The camera is his third eye and it makes him keener, the way three men are stronger than two. Through the Leica the combat is no longer helter-skelter but reveals to Bandy its linear nature, lines against light, force measured by tempo, arithmetic where men are the integers; the historic scale of war exposes its constituent, single human moments as though Bandy's camera lens were a microscope and he views the nucleus and electrons that make up a complex atom.

Another thousand soldiers arrive under parachutes or in gliders, all hushed until they touch the ground, then they scrabble for cover, drawing fire from the surrounding hedgerows and farm buildings, and returning it. Some of the chutes have gotten tangled in tall tree limbs, their riders have to cut their way out of the harness with a knife to drop precarious distances. The white silk splayed in the trees looks oddly decorative. One of the paratroopers is dead in these trees, shot while strung up and helpless. The soldier hangs and sags like a waiting puppet.

Bandy uses up the first roll of film and loads another. He moves with practiced velocity, eagerly wanting the camera back in front of his face. He snaps pictures of men running in crouches, their carbines ready at the hip. He records those masses overhead still falling from planes, he composes a poetic caption: "Black dots transforming into silken flowers." Men on the ground clamber out of shriveled chutes and mangled gliders, thankfulness in their eyes, then sudden ducking fright hits them when the first bullet whizzes by. Alarm becomes purpose. All of this enters Bandy's lens.

It's time to move out of the hedge.

Fifty yards off is the south edge of the field and a rim of trees. There the platoon Bandy jumped alongside has clotted around their lieutenant and sergeants. Bandy rises on complaining knees and ankles. Bent low, he jogs the open distance to the men. At these times, exposed and under enemy fire, Bandy inhabits not just the hands and eyes of his body like he does when taking photos; now he is in every inch of his own skin and bone and gut, his brain has sent out nervous sentries into all parts of him. He feels his toes in the hurrying boots, his brow under the bouncing helmet, the muscles in his abdomen that keep him in a running hunch. He has waited through six years of combat photography for the meeting with his first bullet. He waits now. Several rounds come to greet him in this field east of the Rhine; a few whisper "Welcome" flying past, others plow a path for his feet in the dirt, but none yet embraces him.

Bandy slides like a baseball player into the middle of the platoon. One wag says, "Safe."

The lieutenant smiles. "Mr. Bandy, sir. Will you be joinin' us this mornin'?"

Bandy works to catch his breath. "If you don't mind."

"Not at all. You just stay toward the rear. Keep your head down and follow. That okay?"

Bandy sees his young, caterpillar-moustached paratrooper. The boy's freckles glow when he gives Bandy another thumbs-up.

The officer doesn't wait for a reply. He pulls his rifle from his shoulder.

"Fan out. Move up."

The platoon absorbs itself into the trees and heads west, away from the sporadic firefight in the Drop Zone. They are part of a large moving force tramping with care through the rising countryside. A gentle slope begins. The trees here are not thick, there's plenty of room between them, and their branches bear only the first blooms, so Bandy can see well in all directions, and be seen.

From this wooded hill Bandy hears the fight for Wesel, two miles to his right. At this height, through the trees he makes out the red roofs and steeple of the nestled town. Sporadic gunfire comes from all directions while the Americans encounter German defenders in isolated homes, barns, and cowsheds. The area is riven with streambeds, ditches, hillocks, and clay roads. Bandy knows this kind of land, was sired and raised on it. It seems a great shame to him to see blood spilled on it.

After ten minutes, the platoon enters an apple orchard. Within ten steps of the boundary they encounter fire from a big farmhouse seventy yards away. The platoon splits instantly into three squads which seemingly by instinct head left, right, and charge the center. Bandy freezes for a moment, left without the training to go one way or the other. He dives to the ground and finds himself alone and in the open.

Out of the farmhouse a bank of rifles opens up. Bullets spray everywhere, not well aimed. From one second-floor window a streak of smoke issues and misses trees until it crashes into a big trunk twenty yards ahead of where Bandy lies. The Germans have *Panzerfaust* antitank grenades. The tree cracks in the middle and teeters, flame in its branches.

The platoon moves up in grand fashion, answering the fire from the farmhouse, getting in position to take the building from all sides.

The lieutenant pauses in his rush forward. He drops a knee and turns back to Bandy. He shouts.

"Mr. Bandy, you'd best run *some*where!"

The farmhouse looks like a storage place for fireworks that have gone off; *Panzerfaust* smoke trails erupt out of several windows, muzzle flashes from automatic weapons and carbines jitter in every aperture. Whoever's inside is squeezing whatever triggers they can get their hands on. Some of them are intended for Bandy.

He jumps to his feet, girding himself for another open run. His objective is a pile of cordwood thirty yards ahead, just beyond the burning tree. He takes off. The Leica waves in his left hand, the Speed Graphic bounces in his backpack against his spine like a worrisome and ignored old friend tapping him, Hey, let me out, use me some!

Bandy fixes his eyes on the pile of wood. Once behind it, he'll sit tight until this farmhouse is taken. The people inside the house are nuts. They're firing at everything. Bullets tear into the branches twenty feet over Bandy's head.

Only a few more running strides to cover. Bandy thinks he'll make it. He always makes it.

His right thigh trips him. An electric pain rips into his leg and splashes like barbed shock over his whole body. The Leica flies from his hand and skids to the woodpile. Bandy falls forward, pitching in the air—somehow deftly, instinctively—onto his left side to avoid landing on the bullet wound. The ground receives him hard, jamming his bad shoulder, the one he'd hurt on his Spanish jump six years ago. Bandy skids and even before he loses momentum from the running fall he crawls.

The right leg will not move. It will, but just one try to incorporate it into his fast slither toward cover is enough to tell him it's best to rely only on the good leg, so he drags it. His left shoulder feels like a giant is pinching him. Damn, he thinks. He tries for better language than a garden variety curse, he wants some inspiration or thought of note to mark his first battle wound, but all that arrives in his head is *damn*. Shit. This hurts.

Finally leaning his back against the woodpile, Bandy takes stock. The inside of his right pants leg is torn in the meat of his thigh. Another few inches higher. Damn. Christ. With careful fingers he pulls back the bloody cloth flaps and peers in. He sucks through clamped teeth, the electricity in the wound is still on.

Lucky. He's got a nasty gash, a perfect C the size of an 8mm bullet carved out of his flesh. The wound is dumping blood pretty fast, dribbling a rivulet that pools under his knee. Bandy's fingers are red, tacky from probing.

The cut smarts like it's embedded with thorns. He has no bandage and the medic is with the platoon assaulting the farmhouse. Bandy doesn't bother to listen to the battle going on beyond the woodpile. He unbuttons his coat. He slides out of it with grinding discomfort, his left shoulder is deeply wrenched and swelling fast. He slides one sleeve of the jacket under his hemorrhaging leg and knots it tight with the other sleeve around the wound. He's sweating by the time he is done. A minute ago he was running for cover, Charles Bandy, *Life* photographer on the scene east of the Rhine. Now he's beat to hell with one good leg and one good arm.

He waits like this for another five minutes. His pulse beats so strong out of the wrapped leg, he feels like a clock. The noises of combat flow around the stacked wood. Men's voices ricochet among the trees. Over there! Move, move, move! Leaves rustle, sticks break under galloping boots. Rifles bay. Bullets strike glass, dirt, bark, the siding of the farmhouse. The orchard husbands all these sounds to itself. Bandy, blinded by cover, his eyes shut in pain, hears every developing detail and for once does not concern himself with what it looks like.

Finally the fighting wanes with the easing clop–clop of a reined–in horse. When the orchard is still, voices emanate from the farmhouse.

"Nicht schiessen! Wir kommen aus!"

Boys' voices. High, choirboy voices.

Bandy can't believe it. No. Not true.

He's been shot by children.

He wants to stand, to roll over, he wants to see for himself who shot him. To see if it wasn't even a man, a real enemy soldier, who got him. After all these years in combat he deserved at least that much. But Bandy hears no mature voices emerging from the farmhouse. The paratroopers rush forward, shouting, to take the surrender.

"Hände hoch!" The GI lieutenant speaks some German. He orders the prisoners to put their hands up. Then he adds, *"Schnell, Kinder."*

Quickly, kiddies.

Bandy puts his hand to his forehead, slurring blood there. He mutters to himself, "Oh, I don't fucking believe this."

He can't stand it. He rolls over to his left, bad shoulder protesting, and once clear of the wood sees a dozen teenagers, some of them perhaps even younger, all thin and fair-skinned. Each one wears a black SS clone uniform, with silver braided piping and eagle patches. Their hands are high and empty. None wears a helmet, they have caps or are bareheaded. Only two or three have boots, the rest shuffle in street shoes. The paratroopers surround them, guns aimed. Bandy hears sniffles from the boys. One openly bawls with a cardinal face.

These children were allowed by the Nazis to play dress-up. They were given an arsenal and told to use it on the Americans. And they did. When they ran out of ammo or they suffered enough casualties, they threw up their hands and came out cringing. How much of Germany's youth is Hitler willing to sacrifice to defend his lost lousy cause? If he can do this, he's desperate and capable of anything. He's a bigger bastard and even more dangerous than Bandy imagined. What else will we find, he wonders, the closer we get to Berlin?

Bandy doesn't see the medic. He's embarrassed to do it, but he calls out.

"Hey. Medic!"

One of the sergeants comes over.

"Hey, pal. You okay?"

"Sort of. No."

"Hang on. Doc's busy."

The sergeant squats to inspect Bandy's wound and makeshift dressing.

"You're gonna be all right."

"I reckon."

The soldier stands to go back to corralling the Hitler boys.

Bandy says, "Hey."

"Yeah?"

"How many were there? In the farmhouse. Any regular soldiers?"

"No. Just these. We killed five before they came out."

Bandy nods.

The soldier says, "I hate this. I goddam hate this."

The man is not curious for Bandy's reaction. Though Bandy has been hit, this soldier has killed children. His wound will never heal. The sergeant mulls over his own words for a moment and decides no more are needed. He spits and starts to walk off.

Bandy grabs his Leica off the ground.

"Sarge."

The soldier stops.

"Gimme a hand up, will ya?"

"You want to take pictures, Mr. Bandy?"

Yes, he does.

"No. No, I just . . . I just want to see them."

The paratrooper wraps a strong arm around Bandy's back and lifts. Bandy pushes one-legged and rises with a choked groan. The knotted coat flaps and drags the ground behind him. The sergeant grips Bandy's shoulder. This sets off a howl. The soldier sets him back on the ground.

"Separated," Bandy huffs. "It's separated. Jesus. Gimme a minute."

The sergeant looms over Bandy rocking on his butt. Without ceremony he reaches down and grips Bandy's left arm. Bandy can't stop him.

"No! Wait!"

The sergeant anchors himself against Bandy's good shoulder and yanks. The left joint pops in his heavy grip. Bandy feels torn apart, then just as suddenly the pain ebbs.

"Ahhh. Ahhh, for Christ's sake, Sarge. Jesus."

"Better?"

"Yeah, but Jesus."

The soldier lifts him with the same strength he held Bandy down a moment ago. Together they walk to the farmhouse, Bandy hobbled and leaning on the paratrooper's arm. Cooled blood trickles down Bandy's calf into his sock and boot. The leg pain is no more acute walking than it was when he was sitting still. He'll have the memento of a mean scar, that should be the extent of the injury. His shoulder grabs most of his attention. It's fixed, yes, but banging at him.

Twenty yards ahead stand fourteen German boys in a cluster. Their hands are on their heads and they are surrounded by stone-faced paratroopers and leveled rifles. More than one of the children has broken into tears. The oldest boy can't be more than sixteen.

Their eyes move to Bandy and his obvious bleeding. On a few captured faces he catches proud sneers. On most there is only relief. He wishes he could take these pictures, of fanatical delusion and weepy release, of childhood gone off the tracks.

The sergeant lugs him past the boys, around to the side of the farmhouse. There, on the edge of the orchard, a crowd of troopers stands about a man spread on the ground and the kneeling medic.

When the men see Bandy approach limping on the sergeant's arm, they part to let him into their circle. The medic does not look up from the young caterpillar-moustached soldier lying beside him.

The boy has been shot in the neck. The medic has

wrapped gauze around the wounds; blood blotches the white bandage on both sides of the soldier's throat. The bullet tore all the way through. The medic is busy with crimson hands unwrapping a plasma pack. Another soldier holds ready a morphine spike.

The flush that was in the young soldier's freckles on the transport plane has faded. His face is ashen, the freckles have receded as though they too are being bled white.

His eyes are focused straight up. But he sees Bandy and rolls his head. The medic rips open the plastic plasma packet, stabs a needle into the soldier's arm, and plugs him in.

Somehow, in the midst of the boy's own unfolding and dire fate, he smiles at Bandy. Weakly, he lifts a fist just off the ground to give one more thumbs-up.

Bandy returns the gesture. He shakes his own balled hand as if to rattle out some strength and good luck to the downed boy. To pour a little more sand into his hourglass.

The boy's gaze slides down to the Leica in Bandy's hand. His blanched face changes, winces not in pain but refusal.

As he did just twenty minutes ago in the commotion of the plane, the young soldier mouths silent words to Bandy:

Don't take my photograph. Okay?

March 25, 1945, 2:30 P.M.
On the west bank of the Rhine
Büderich, Germany

"NO."

One of Winston Churchill's greatest abilities remains his tolerance for hearing that word. In his long public career, he's learned to be patient, become an alchemist, with it.

"Quite right, General. As you say."

Eisenhower doesn't appear convinced Churchill has taken him seriously. Something about the quick capitulation followed by a long draw on the cigar.

Eisenhower looks to the other generals in the room with him, Bradley, Simpson, and Montgomery. He wants numbers to gang up on Churchill.

"I mean it, Prime Minister. I'm the Supreme Commander and I refuse to let you go across. You might be killed."

"Yes," Churchill says, lowering his eyes; he read once this is how one defers to a silverback gorilla. "Yes indeed, I might. Quite correct."

Simpson and Bradley strike appropriate poses, shaking their heads at Churchill. Bradley even wags a marmish finger. But there remain amused twinkles in the generals' eyes. Montgomery openly grins at his round leader.

Churchill spreads wide his arms to display himself. "But I am dressed for it, you know."

The Prime Minister wears the uniform of his old cavalry regiment, the Fourth Hussars. Over the years he's had it tailored more than a few times. But it seemed a wonderful choice for this particular visit to the front, for the moment Churchill's been waiting for since September 1939: the final charge across the Rhine, Operation Varsity into the heart of Germany and then on to Berlin, led by an Englishman.

Bradley and Montgomery do not contain their chuckles. Simpson looks away. Eisenhower exhales a puff from his ever-present cigarette. Churchill matches Eisenhower's cloudlet with a bigger one from his stogie.

"Mr. Prime Minister. When was the last time you rode with the cavalry?"

"Not in this century, I'm afraid."

"That's why it's still no."

"I understand, General. Of course."

Churchill does not seem able to agree in a way that will convince Eisenhower.

"What about yesterday?" the General insists. "Jock."

He refers to Jock Colville, Churchill's secretary. Yesterday morning, without permission, Colville slipped across the river on an assault boat, returning covered in blood after a driver standing next to him on the far shore was hit by shrapnel.

Now Eisenhower enlists Montgomery. "Monty, what did you say yesterday when you saw Jock?"

Montgomery lifts his voice in dramatic rendition: "I said, 'Good God, man!'"

"And what did the Prime Minister say?"

Montgomery claps, a mimic of Churchill: "'Good show, man!'"

"No!" Eisenhower says as though the word is the punch line to the tale. He holds up a flat palm, a white stop sign. "I forbid it. And that's it, all right?"

Eisenhower is in a foul temper this afternoon. At lunch two hours ago the four generals and Churchill discussed the latest row with the Russians. The men ate on an elevated veranda of the riverbank castle Eisenhower has commandeered for his headquarters. The table was set with silvery gleams, ample savories, and quaffs, the way Churchill likes his lunches. The men were arrayed around a broad white tablecloth, tobacco smoke wafting about them, and Churchill thought there was something Olympian about their gathering. In full view below them, assault boats ferried to and fro across the river bearing soldiers to rout the enemy. Overhead, thousands of Allied planes lofted paratroops behind enemy lines. The end of the war stampeded eastward past them and Churchill watched enthralled. Lunch was intended to be celebratory. But Eisenhower was in a fit. After the meal their party was driven to this mansion in Büderich beside the river for an even closer look at the operation. It's a lovely spring day. But the Supreme Commander has not cheered up.

The Reds have overreacted to a very simple situation. In late February, General Karl Wolff, the ranking SS officer in Italy, expressed through an Italian businessman a desire to contact the Allies. His intention was to explore terms to surrender all German forces in North Italy. In March, Wolff was met in Zurich by OSS Chief Allen Dulles. The SS officer was told the Allies have interest only in the unconditional surrender of his forces. Wolff still had to return to Italy and convince General Kesselring, the German Commander in Chief there, of the need for surrender. A second meeting was arranged for Bern, Switzerland. The parameters were very clearly stated: this was to be a surrender on a military basis only and have nothing to do with politics. The Russian government was notified of the second impending session with Wolff. Soviet Foreign Minister Molotov agreed that the meeting should take place, but insisted that the Soviet Union be represented. Because the Bern meeting was nothing more than a preliminary to surrender, Molotov's request was turned down by the British and Americans. It was felt that Russian attendance might scare off the Germans, and that Soviet participation would not speed the process; what might take an hour could be drawn out by Red input to weeks, and more soldiers would die accordingly. Besides, there are no Soviet troops fighting in Italy. It's inconceivable that Stalin would invite U.S. and British observers to any surrender of German forces in the East. Molotov was informed that, at such time as there is a formal surrender of Italian forces, the USSR will be fully represented.

But Molotov and Stalin are incensed. They smell a rat, as though the Western Allies might be plotting with the Germans a separate peace. They worry that Hitler will be allowed to transfer his defeated Italian forces or equipment to the Russian front. Or worse, that the West will agree to join hands with Germany and all turn against Mother Russia. More likely, Churchill thinks, the Bolsheviks are simply defending their prestige on the world stage, so that the first major surrender of German forces not be a purely Anglo victory. The Bern meetings are as advertised, purely military in nature, without any political consequences to the Soviet Union. Stalin is simply judging every act by his own standards of paranoia.

In any event, Molotov and his master have sent a series of increasingly contemptuous and cutting cables to Churchill and Roosevelt. Another one arrived last night in Churchill's red leather–covered ministerial box. Molotov's language, in diplomatic terms, is venomous. The West's refusal to allow Soviet attendance at the initial meetings is called *"utterly un-*

expected and incomprehensible from the point of view of Allied relations between our countries." Both the U.S. and British governments have officially denied the charges Molotov levels, explaining that at no stage has anything been concealed from the Soviets. Dulles acted on his own, and all talks to date have been informal and unbinding. But the vitriol has not abated.

Churchill showed Molotov's letter to the generals at lunch. The Soviet Foreign Secretary writes:

IN BERN FOR TWO WEEKS, BEHIND THE BACKS OF THE SOVIET UNION, WHICH IS BEARING THE BRUNT OF THE WAR AGAINST GERMANY, NEGOTIATIONS HAVE BEEN GOING ON BETWEEN THE REPRESENTATIVES OF THE GERMAN MILITARY COMMAND ON THE ONE HAND AND REPRESENTATIVES OF THE ENGLISH AND AMERICAN COMMANDS ON THE OTHER.

This language— *"behind the backs"*—is a blatant accusation that the American and British governments are liars. To Western protests that this affair is nothing more than a misunderstanding, Molotov responds:

IN THIS INSTANCE, THE SOVIET GOVERNMENT SEES NOT A MISUNDERSTANDING BUT SOMETHING WORSE.

Eisenhower was so angered, he did not eat his lunch, which Churchill saw as a shame. The Supreme Commander thundered at the table: the Russian accusations of bad faith are unjust and unfounded. As military commander, he will accept the unconditional surrender of any body of enemy troops on his front, from a company to the entire damn German army, and this is a purely military matter for which he needs no political permission. Churchill and the others kept their counsel while Eisenhower fumed.

After his fury was spent, Eisenhower sat sullenly exhausting a cigarette. Only Montgomery spoke.

"Ike, this is why we have to take Berlin first. The Reds don't respect anything else. Just strength."

The Supreme Commander made no response to that, he just eyed the British Field Marshal with the same smolders in his pupils that glowed in the Chesterfield between his fingers.

For his part, Churchill is not surprised at Stalin and Molotov. He—sometimes alone—has sounded the alarm against the Communists for thirty years. Though he admits to himself he has sometimes been swayed by the charm and authority of Stalin—he has made more than a few embarrassingly effusive toasts to Stalin's and the Soviet Union's good fortune, health, and friendship—Churchill has never been blinded to what the Reds are and what they must have. Not the way Roosevelt has, with the averted eyes of a campaigning and forgiving lover.

The truth is out now, like a snake dropped from a branch. Yalta is in shreds. In complete derogation of the Declaration on Liberated Europe and the earlier Atlantic Charter, Stalin has imposed communist regimes on every country he's occupied: Poland, Romania, Bulgaria, Hungary, and Yugoslavia. He would have done Greece too, had it not been for Churchill's horse trading. In every Soviet-occupied land, Stalin's communist henchmen are systematically putting in place programs of terror, execution, and imprisonment. Churchill's fear is that if Stalin can tear up his agreements over these nations, refusing to allow them the right to choose the forms of government they wish to live under, refusing to allow even whispers of dissent, then he might well do the same over the chief prizes, Germany and Berlin. If Stalin's tanks sweep far across Germany, can he be trusted to withdraw to the agreed-upon boundaries? If the Reds enter Berlin first, will they dutifully hand over two-thirds of the city to the Western Allies, especially since they believe they have borne the greater share of the fighting for it?

And what of Roosevelt? If the worst comes to pass—and nothing but the worst has been happening in this arena—will the United States stand firm against Marxist imperialism? Will the U.S. take the Red threat seriously at last, now that Stalin and Molotov have bitten the hand that's fed them throughout the war? Or will Uncle Sam continue to be trusting and generous with Uncle Joe, instead of putting them on a regimen of punishments and rewards, the only thing the Soviets respond to? Will the United States send up their hands in frustration, at the same time gleeful that the Soviet Union sits in a few chairs at President Roosevelt's precious United Nations? Churchill wonders, will Roosevelt even see the mockery when Poland and Romania vote as Soviet satellites at his UN?

The United Nations. Roosevelt's dream palace to world peace.

Purchased at what cost to human freedom in Europe?

There's one last place to make a stand.

Churchill knows. Berlin.

General Eisenhower glares at Churchill.

The Prime Minister stands in the midst of these generals, war gods all. He's done his best to infiltrate them, even draping himself for this visit in his old cavalry uniform. But these men preside over a separate realm from his. They are military commanders, he—even in his vintage khaki pleats and jackboots—is a political creature. By agreement and convention these officers serve at the sufferance of the political, but this is not wholly the case in war. Churchill and all world leaders know this, that's why Stalin purged the ranks of his Red Army of every independent-thinking officer. This sort of man commands not through documents and parliaments but with millions of armed soldiers who march where and when they point. Their combat is decided not by votes but blood. Their deeds determine not budgets but nations. They halt tyranny. They fill graveyards.

These men. Eisenhower. Simpson. Bradley. Montgomery. Throw in the absent Patton for good measure. There are jealousies and loyalties between them, spoils of fame to be shared or hoarded. Churchill observes, history will be shaped as much by these generals' wisdom as by their pettiness. This can't be helped, it's always the way.

Right now, Churchill must yield to Eisenhower's decree, even while gazing longingly at the Rhine and all the transports going back and forth.

"I've got to go," Eisenhower says.

Churchill pulls his eyes from the river. He mounts an instant beaming face.

"Travel safely, General. We'll speak anon."

"All right." Eisenhower's tone remains taut. He wants to go brood over Molotov's insulting letter, maybe write a response.

Churchill reads the Supreme Commander's mind. In parting, he gentles, "Let it go, General. There's no surprise in this. None whatsoever. The best response for now is silence."

Eisenhower nods. "Maybe. I still don't like it."

"No. Of course not."

Eisenhower pats Bradley on the arm, who falls in behind him to depart. Eisenhower tosses a quick look at Simpson and Montgomery and turns to leave. Montgomery calls at his back, "Berlin, Ike. It's ours for the taking."

Monty, Churchill thinks, needs to learn to stuff it.

Eisenhower stalks off, trailing cigarette smoke like a plane with an engine out. Bradley follows in tow.

Churchill and Montgomery are alone with General Simpson, commander of the Ninth U.S. Army, assigned to Montgomery. It's Simpson's front here.

"Well," says Churchill obligingly.

"Well," answers Field Marshal Montgomery.

Churchill puffs and says, "Looks like two Englishmen and one Yank. Field Marshal, this may be the only time left in the war when we have superior numbers."

Simpson waves one slender finger in the air. "No, no, no, gentlemen. You heard Ike."

Churchill sidles beside the tall, gray general. He laps an arm as well as he can around Simpson's shoulders, reaching far up.

"Yes. I recall him ordering me not to go. But he's not here right now. And if my memory of military protocol does not fail me, it would seem that you, being the front commander, are in charge, General."

Simpson does not take this seriously. He laughs. "I see what you're getting at."

"And?"

"And no, Mr. Prime Minister."

"Ah." Churchill removes his awkward embrace. He walks beside Montgomery. "I do quite dislike doing this to you, General. But, I must appeal now to an even higher authority. Field Marshal?"

"Yes, Prime Minister?"

"The Ninth Army is still under your Twenty-first Group, is it not?"

"It is indeed, Prime Minister."

Outside, a small U.S. Navy motor launch churns nearby to the mansion's dock.

"Why don't we go across and have a look at the other side?"

Montgomery is a jaunty character in his beret and red cravat. He enjoys this bit of rebellion. Churchill considers they should both be more careful about gigging Eisenhower. But crossing the Rhine as part of this great and final invasion of the German heartland, after so much loss and agony, is not something to be missed if there is any way possible.

Montgomery grins. "Why not?"

Churchill catches only a quick glimpse of General Simpson's gesture of appeal. He races Montgomery for the door to get outside and reach the shore to flag down the motorboat.

On the way through the yard Churchill passes Field Marshal Alan Brooke, his military Chief of Staff.

"Alan, come on! We're going across!"

Montgomery gains the bank first and gets the attention of the launch's skipper. Churchill and Brooke arrive while the boat eases to the quay. Simpson arrives seconds behind with four other officers, all bearing sidearms.

He says, "Ike will kill me for letting you go. But he'll kill me slow if I don't at least keep an eye on you."

The skipper of the motor launch and his one-man crew are agog at their passengers clambering over the gunwales.

"Captain," Churchill addresses the sailor, who is not a captain and can barely close his mouth, "be so kind as to take us to the far shore."

The boat moves onto the Rhine under a cloudless sky. Churchill chomps on a fresh cigar like a man in a winner's circle. This is magnificent, he thinks, exhilarating. Surrounded by fighting men, on the forefront of the action, right here at the nib of history's pen where you can hear the scritching of ink to the page just as history is written. Not obsessing over who attends what meeting, who insulted whom, no ping-ponging back and forth over politics and mongering for votes. No, by God, this day is real. The vibrating deck beneath his feet, the danger, the company! Churchill thinks of the two others who with him make up the Grand Alliance, one confined not only to a wheelchair but by privilege and naiveté, the other imprisoned behind walls of dogma and delusion. Alas, if the President and the Marshal could only be here alongside him, the glare of the sun and of great events would surely open their minds beyond their current limits.

When the war is over, Churchill thinks, those two may indeed have the power. But this, *this* is the glory.

The ride across is smooth and unchallenged by enemy attention. Upon landing, Churchill strides in front of Simpson, who tries with his armed cadre to be the first ashore. The Prime Minister steps on the quay on nimble legs. The rap of artillery and small arms fire bowls out of the hilly plain beyond the small town. Churchill does not hesitate, he heads for it, the cavalryman without a horse. Simpson catches up and stakes a position to block him.

"No, sir."

"General, why come this far if not to see some of the action?"

"We'll just have to be satisfied with being close enough to hear it, Prime Minister."

"Oh, pishposh."

"We'll walk around the riverbank as long as you want, but no farther inland."

"General."

"Prime Minister, as you say, this is my front."

Churchill pauses to take this in, but there is no question he will obey. After a moment of good-natured obstinacy, he pops his cigar into his mouth like a dart. He says in a voice warped by the dark tobacco tube, "Right! Quite right!"

He calls to the others, Field Marshals Montgomery and Brooke, "There we are, men. Let's take a stroll about the riverbank, shall we? Marvelous!"

For half an hour the coterie tramps about, with Churchill in the lead, narrating: "Hah! Yesterday there were Nazis here! Masters of Europe, my hat! Where are they now, what? Blighters!"

On the return voyage, Churchill remains luminous with enthusiasm. In the middle of the Rhine he appeals to be taken downriver to Wesel, the town at the center of the offensive. Simpson shrugs in reply, he's only along on guard duty. Montgomery stands and points the way for the still-awed sailors running the launch. He seems proud of his Prime Minister's urging and pugnacity. The boat turns with the current. In minutes a chain across the river stops them from reaching the town.

Churchill chomps his cigar in disappointment until Montgomery slips close and says, "Don't worry, PM. We'll go have a look at Wesel in my car. What do you think?"

Returning to Büderich, the party climbs into three cars, Churchill with Montgomery. They take off for Wesel. After a ten-minute ride Montgomery pulls up to the remains of a railway bridge at the outskirts of town. Churchill steps from the car and climbs into the piles of twisted girders and masonry. He marvels at the force of the Allied bombs which fell here just this morning, pretends to feel the heat of them emanating from the rubble. He plays alone in the wreckage and does not mind.

A mile away, an artillery shell lands in the river and explodes on contact with the bottom. Churchill stops his meandering and goes wooden like a hunting dog, his nose and cigar pointing at the report. In seconds two more rounds break the river into fountains of spray, the impacts come closer to the bridge.

Churchill stands his ground, though he senses Simpson shoving through the morass of material to fetch him. More shells whoosh in, one flies directly over their heads to detonate within a hundred yards of their parked cars. The blasts send a thrill into Churchill's abdomen. He catches sight of Montgomery and Brooke. The two soldiers are in crouches, looking like their next move will be to the ground and their bellies. Simpson reaches Churchill in the ruins.

"Prime Minister. There are snipers in front of you. They are shelling both sides of the bridge. And now they've started shelling the road behind you. I can't accept responsibility for your being here and must ask you to come away."

Churchill wraps his arms around a protruding steel beam. He lets go only when General Simpson makes it clear that he will pry the Prime Minister from it.

———

March 28, 1945, 2245 hours
Küstrin, Poland

IN HIS LIFE ILYA HAS NEVER THOUGHT MUCH ON GOD.

He was raised in a military family with those traditions, of honor and country. God hovered over everything, but thinly, like the glow from candles.

From a hilltop on the east bank of the Warta River, Ilya watches the aerial bombardment of another citadel. Invisible Red Air Force planes ruffle the night sky, moving between him and the stars to make the pinpoints of light wink. Bombs whistle unseen in their fall, until they strike the fortress to erupt flashes and sailing sparks which are embers of burning logs and hot concrete into the air. The explosions weave a vaguely religious fabric in Ilya's head. The ancient citadel of Küstrin stands on an island formed by the confluence of the Warta and Oder Rivers. The blasts and flaming debris reflect in the water, making the scene appear even larger. Ilya recalls that hell stands across a river. Hell burns, there is darkness even beside the fire, there is pain and struggle without end.

It's a surprise that God tries to come to him like this, unbidden, in blotted-out stars and a detonating enemy fortress. He's had plenty of other moments to enter Ilya, quieter moments, why pick now with this magnified cacophony going on?

Ilya remembers what little he was taught as a child of God. God rules heaven and all the angels. God created the earth. He gives and takes life.

This last bit troubles Ilya.

Stalingrad first made him doubt; the citadels have made Ilya certain. God only gives life. He has delegated to man the task of taking it.

Ilya takes a swig of vodka from a cool bottle. Always on the nights before attacks, jiggling, ringing cartons of vodka are laid out in plenty for the men. Ilya has never been a drinker, not on the scale of most Soviet soldiers. But tonight he is thoughtful, and the bottle seems a willing and quiet partner. He will not get drunk, the bottle serves just to fill his hands. He can't tolerate much smoking. He thinks he'll quit and leave that vice to Misha.

Beside him Misha gazes through binoculars at the besieged citadel. The little man's lips move beneath the goggles the whole time the bombs fall, his voice drones with the propellers of the fighters and bombers flying low and uncontested.

". . . are bombing the main fortress, see? This way, the Germans will head out into the field fortifications. Then, tomorrow morning, we'll bomb the center again, I bet. The Germans will think they're smart, but what we're really doing is flushing them out from behind the walls where we can get at them with infantry and artillery. Oh, man! Look at that one go up!"

Ilya listens with half an ear to Misha's intelligence and projections of strategy. Misha is another reason Ilya is convinced

God does not kill. God could not be so enthusiastic about it, reduce it to such science, as man.

Misha will be right. He's always right in these matters. In the morning the war will happen just as the little man says. Ilya thinks sometimes the scar has given Misha another, almost occult, power to know what will happen. Sometimes the scar seems to do the talking.

More hours into the night pass like this. The fortress stays under assault from above. Misha narrates as though Ilya cannot see the citadel for himself. Ilya contemplates against this backdrop. They share a white blanket over their shoulders. Ilya is so much larger than Misha that the two appear to be a mother swan with a wing draped about her gosling.

Men die inside the citadel. Each bomb takes another and another. Ilya imagines the sparks are souls liberated and aloft. He marvels, in three years at war he has never once considered any man's soul. He does not feel remorse at the enemy deaths, or the thousands on both sides that will follow in the morning when the infantry attacks. He doesn't fear for his own life. No life concerns him.

But thoughts of God nag him. It's the sixty again. It's them. "What about us?" they ask Ilya in the explosions. Shut up, he answers. You were bound for death, either in the camps of Siberia or on the journey to your prisons. "No, it's the way we were taken. Like animals." And what of animals, Ilya retorts. What in your conduct lifted you above animals? Was it your torture of civilians, your rapes and pillaging, your death factories? "We were men, simple soldiers like you, Ilya Borisovich. Duty defined us, that's all, not the acts of others you've heard about." Shut up. You paid for those acts, whether you did them or not. "Who made you the collector of that debt, Ilya? Was it God?" Shut up about God. He watched you be butchered. He didn't care. "Ilya, *you* watched us butchered. *You* didn't care." Shut up!

"Ilyushka? Am I bothering you?"

Ilya starts at the voice. Misha lowers his binoculars.

"Ilya?"

"Misha. I . . . sorry."

"You told me to shut up."

"I didn't mean to say that."

"You sounded like you meant it."

Ilya says nothing. The citadel on the river continues to suffer.

"Ilya?"

"What?" His tone is annoyed.

"You're shaking."

Ilya flings an arm outside the blanket and stands. A breeze chills the back of his neck. He is sweating.

Behind him and Misha the rest of their platoon has gathered on the hillside. They are all wrapped under woolen blankets too, some on their sides trying to sleep, most watching the fireworks on the river. Ilya strides off among them.

"Tomorrow, Sergeant," they say, "we'll get them, right? German bastards. We'll kill every one we get our hands on. We'll give it to them. Tomorrow, Sergeant." Ilya hears reverence in their voices, they worship what they've heard about Ilya Shokhin, his remarkable ability to take life.

He stomps past the tongues and huddled shapes. He walks until he finds a place under a tree where he cannot see the river. He sits on a jumble of roots and looks up through bare branches. In this moment the last bomb strikes the citadel, no more whines come from the sky. The throb of airplanes recedes to the east. The night seems to collapse like a boxer into its corner, gasping for breath, hurting for this quiet. No more, it says, no more. But Ilya knows the sun will bring more, the sun like the boxing bell will ring another round, and many more days' suns will do the same. Don't feel your body or your mind or you can't go the distance. Just fight. Fight.

Ilya sits in this spot until morning. When the sun climbs he has a conclusion. He's talked with the sixty, dozed some, and talked with them again. They have helped him come to a resolution.

God must take back the responsibility. He can't trust man anymore to do it for him. God has to do the killing.

At first Ilya didn't know what course to take. How to

make God do anything? You can't, after all. But Ilya has a talent. God gave it to him. So he's going to use it to influence God. He's going to steep himself in so much killing that God will have no choice but to admit that it's madness. God will have to stop Ilya. And all the madness. If He chooses to let it continue, there will be no one left.

The breakfast wagons clatter over the hills before Ilya rises. In his gut is a driving appetite, his hunger is another surprise to him. For the first time in weeks he's eager for the taste of greasy ham and wheat paste, mopped up with black bread, chased with steaming tea. Ilya stretches, his muscles are taut from the brisk night but he feels fine. He walks to the top of the hill; the citadel below waits in a bath of perfect orange light. A long shadow floats on the river behind the fortress, like a compass needle pointing west, in the direction of Berlin.

Ilya approaches a wagon and helps himself to an extra portion. The cook says nothing. Ilya sits where he can look over the citadel. Something of the prescience he attributes to Misha's wound comes over him. Perhaps this is a bonus God throws into the bargain when you make some arrangement with Him, the way Misha has with darkness. Ilya can see the coming attack. Without knowing a reason, even chewing, he smiles.

For months the island citadel of Küstrin has been the anchor of a German corridor stretching eighty kilometers all the way from the Oder River to Berlin. Counterattacks out of the fortress have prevented Red forces from linking their bridgeheads on the west bank of the Oder. That corridor was closed three days ago, and the river citadel is now surrounded. Two days ago, on the twenty-seventh, German reinforcements tried to break into Küstrin from the south. Four divisions and supporting tanks made it as far as the outskirts, until Chuikov's dug-in artillery slaughtered them in the open mucky ground along the riverbank. The German offensive was a fiasco and they withdrew, leaving a thousand bodies in the mud.

Sitting next to Misha's nervous mouth last night, Ilya

learned that the fortress dates to the sixteenth century. The citadel itself is a complex of works; a reinforced fortress sits in the middle of a web of outlying redoubts, pillboxes, and bunkers. The only links to the island are four dikes fanning out from the center, each of which is so narrow a single tank would fill the approach. The Germans have stacked defenses along these paths, piling on tiers of pillboxes, trenches, barbed wire, and minefields. Red units have gotten so close to these fortifications that exchanges of *Panzerfausts* and hand grenades go on day and night.

Misha told him that back in February, a regiment of the Fifth Shock Army actually penetrated the citadel's outer defenses. The official news agency *Sovinform* reported that Küstrin had fallen, and the mistaken victory was greeted with cannon salvos in Moscow. Word has it that General Zhukov was mightily embarrassed. He has instructed Chuikov's Eighth Guards that the error must be corrected this morning.

On his hillside, Ilya finishes breakfast. The gusto with which he greeted the dawn and the food have seeped out of him with the eating and the rising sun. The citadel on the glistening waters beckons him. The day's battle rages inside him already, before the first shot is fired. This is not fear. He feels a grip much colder than fear. It's knowledge that he shouldn't possess: that he will not die today, that God is not going to be so easily moved.

Ilya walks down to rejoin his platoon. Every step in their direction stiffens him as though he walks through ice, until he is ice. Misha greets him with irritation and a glowing scar.

"Where have you been?"

Ilya doesn't want to speak. Language is human. On the cusp of combat and until it is done, he wills himself to be, to accept, something else.

"Handle the men," he says. "Follow me, Sergeant."

Misha cocks his head at Ilya's flat tone. Ilya looks over the platoon, fifty craven men and snivelers, he thinks. No loss if they die too.

Misha steps back and holds out a hand to Ilya, pointing at him like an exhibit.

"Men," the little one says, "here is the best fighter in the whole Red Army. I know. I've fought beside him. Now you heard what he said. Follow Sergeant Shokhin, right down the Germans' goddam throats. What do you think?"

The platoon shouts, "Urrah!"

Ilya puts the sun to his back and walks to the staging area. The platoon and Misha mingle their long shadows with his, but he is, he thinks, alone.

Their punishment company has drawn the assignment of leading the charge across the easternmost dike to storm the fortress. Ilya and Misha's platoon will form the company vanguard. There won't be enough room for more than three men abreast to run the two hundred meters along the top of the dike. The rest of the division will attack from boats across the river.

Ilya checks his watch: 0825 hours. The staging area for their company is a big crater in the riverbank road. Thirty meters away stands the concrete foot of their assigned dike. One hundred and fifty soldiers and officers gather in and behind the depression. Cigarettes are passed to and fro, a few vodka bottles that survived the night chart their own course through the men. Ilya stares across the water at the fortress. The enemy garrison in there waits for him.

Why are the Germans still here? Why haven't they slipped out in one of the nights and run back to their lines? They stay in Küstrin for a single reason: to hold back the Ivans, the Asiatic barbarians. Brave men, these soldiers of the citadel, sacrificing themselves to stall the Reds and give more time for refugees to throng into Berlin. Just as well, Ilya thinks. Corral them all. Today we take these Germans on their island. Later, in their capital, we'll see the rest.

Minutes pass around the crater. Attempts to talk with Ilya only anger him. He snarls at the first few who try to touch him, the rest he ignores. He decides he hates everything. Not just man and machines but the river, the trees and hills, the sky, the stones of the fortress, they're all accomplices, aren't they? Brave men. Fah! What is brave? To take ground and kill, or stand your ground and be killed. Stupidity. He

wants to change his course from what he decided last night
and this dawn, he wants to drop his weapons and walk away,
to be the first real brave man.

But he'll convince no one like that. The armies around
him and God alike will think he's simply lost his nerve. Gone
weak.

No. He must become the thing he despises. To defy God
you must be a god. Ilya will reap so many lives, undo so
much of His work, that He will have to pay attention. Only
then, Ilya will rest.

At 0845 the air force returns and bombs the heart of the
citadel just as Misha predicted. For an hour the fortress is
slammed, continuing to drive the enemy garrison outward
into their field defenses. Again Misha chooses the spot beside
Ilya to watch the bombardment; again he issues a running
commentary. Ilya has learned that Misha calms himself with
the sound of his own voice. Ilya makes no response. He can
barely hear the little motoring mouth. Inside him, the sixty
hold out their arms, they accept a great deal and hold it in
trust for Ilya. He takes them things: the *whomp*ing bombs,
Misha's yak, crawling time, his own fading humanity. The
sixty enfold whatever Ilya brings them, he bears gifts to
them from life. They nod slowly, waver like seaweed, and
Ilya moves on lighter.

At 1000 hours, the last bomb falls, the planes wane from
the sky. A minute of heavy silence settles in the crater around
Ilya. The men tense at his back.

Misha tells them, "Not yet. Stay loose."

He is right. The banks on both sides of the Oder vent a
sudden and powerful noise. Three huge artillery pieces,
203mm howitzers with shells as big as butter churns, have
been fanned out and positioned at point-blank range, no
more than four hundred meters from the citadel's fortifications. The rounds from these guns strike their targets almost
the moment they're out of the barrels. Concrete dugouts and
pillboxes are ripped apart in deafening explosions, reduced to
rubble and steel bars. Stones the size of men are flung up and
into the river, Ilya thinks some of them are men.

At 1030 hours two divisions and one full regiment, almost twenty thousand men, began to creep from all sides into the river in assault boats. At 1040 a yellow alert flare scorches across the morning.

Ilya rises. The platoon crowds at his back.

Misha appears at Ilya's elbow. His brows are just below Ilya's great shoulder.

"Sergeant Shokhin?"

"Yes?"

"I'll be right here. Today, I mean. Right here. All right?"

Talking is an effort for Ilya, as it would be for a corpse. He looks away from the little man when he says, "All right. Stay next to me."

"Thank you, Ilya."

The red flare of attack sears a high, arcing scratch over the morning.

Ilya bounds out of the crater. The company shouts, "Urrah! Urrah!"

In ten steps Ilya leaps onto the top of the dike. Running one stride back, but at his side, is little Misha. Behind them, the fifty-man platoon screams their revenge, obviously terrified.

Ilya moves fast to distance himself from the clumping men at his back. Bullets reduce their number in the first twenty meters. He hears the sough of rounds, catches the soft clap of bullets hitting bone behind him. He leaps off the parapet into the wreckage of the first pillbox. Misha lands beside him, wild-eyed.

The stunned Germans manning the machine gun cannot swivel as fast as Ilya moves in from their left. He rises into the air as though winged. He ricochets off the busted masonry to crash down behind them and rip them with his own submachine gun. Misha stupidly runs right in front of their muzzle but they are dead before a finger can jerk. Ilya glares at him, then flashes into the debris.

He emerges again on the strip of dike leading to the citadel walls. The platoon has already taken cover in the rubble. Ilya alone, without hesitation, without yelling orders, turns and runs forward, headlong at the fortress. Misha shouts at the ducking platoon, "Go, go, go! With Ilya, dammit! Go!"

Ilya's feet pound under him, his heart pounds throughout him, boots scrape and run behind. Voices and rifles and bullets are in full throat. Enemy blood, enemy metal and concrete, everything is mad and dashing about, running out of place, blood belongs inside men, bricks belong in neat walls, water should be flat and not coughed up in pillars. But the sky is a lovely gentle blue, the light is tempered and even, as though God maintains His home nicely, no matter what chaos of man rails below.

Ilya levels his submachine gun and fires bursts from the hip. He runs in a serpentine path over the dike, never letting enemy gunners draw a bead. He tosses grenades ahead, he swivels his own gun barrel left and right and straight, firing like three men, running behind his weapons like a hunter riding behind his hounds. He leaps down into craters and emerges at full tilt, his long footfalls land wherever there is heavy debris on the concrete surface, these are the spots where Ilya knows there are no unexploded mines. He pauses behind cover only enough to let the lagging platoon that advances in his footsteps close the gap, or to let Misha gather himself. There is no strategy in his head. Misha with a heaving chest continues to suggest, "You go round that way, I'll take five men and go this way." Ilya answers him with another wordless charge into the enemy guns. All Misha can do is mutter, "Shit," and run behind.

In combat Ilya has always been quick and agile, even with his size and strength. He's often battled calmly, other times—at Stalingrad—enraged. But he's never fought with this kind of physical prowess. He leaps barbed obstacles, dodges bullets which seem to bend around him like light through a prism, he feels nothing of the wounds mounting on his legs and arms. His own gun silences every German who challenges him. His flung grenades fly through the smallest apertures in those remaining concrete casements. No fatigue mounts his back. No falter slows his legs.

There's a way a man moves in open warfare, even the boldest man. When an enemy gunner sights along his barrel for this target, he sees a figure, a familiar sight, he's shot at running men before. But when one comes who is totally without fear—not merely courageous but a man devoid of dread—he comes differently, oddly, with a rare force. This one is hard to predict, hardest of all to survive.

In his advance Ilya is not cruel, in the same manner he is not heroic. He kills those of the enemy who have been placed in front of him to kill. This is what he set out to do. He seems to run beside himself, outside his body. All effort and will are gone, he acts without need of them.

Eight minutes after the attack signal, Ilya reaches the thick fortress wall. He moves along it to spot where the wall has been shattered by the artillery. This gap is dead ground, where flanking fire cannot find him for the moment. Misha is behind him the whole way. He arrives looking flayed, his scar vibrant.

"Ah," Misha huffs, his hands on his knees. "Ilya, what . . . ? Ah, shit."

Ilya can hear Misha no better than a man standing near a dynamo could hear him.

Within a minute the platoon catches up. There are only two dozen left. The rest lie out on the dike or float in the Oder. The survivors grit their teeth in exhaustion and pain. Ilya sees several bullet-riddled uniforms, almost every one of them has his own blood on his hands. The men are on their feet leaning against the bricks and looking at him with strange faces.

Awe.

Ilya picks out two soldiers who answer his eyes with a quaver. Then some alchemy strikes them under Ilya's gaze and they become firm before him, resolute to go where he goes.

"Ready?" he asks.

The two nod.

"Everyone reload."

All the soldiers put new clips into their rifles. Many

hands tremble. Ilya shoves a new magazine into his PPSh. Spent clips fall to the ground.

When they are done, Ilya says, "Misha, follow with the rest. You understand?"

The little soldier spits once to clear his mouth. His eyes plead with Ilya for something small, some accommodation in this hell. He insists he be called, even now, "Sergeant Bakov."

Ilya answers. "Then follow, Sergeant Bakov."

The two chosen move close behind him. Ilya presses close to the wall. He raises his barrel beside his cheek. The metal has cooled to a fleshly warmth.

He nods his helmet, one, two . . .

Together the three leap around the jutting bricks and into the gap.

Bullets peel the two men away from Ilya. They die in a second, in grunts, their alchemy completed. The Germans in the fortress yard have presighted a machine gun at the gap. Ilya feints right and dives left. A vein of bullets pulses inches from his waist. There's nowhere to hide. He runs right at the enemy machine gun, no dodge, no confusion. He lowers his submachine gun and fires to empty his weapon, to empty himself through it. He screams to hasten the draining of himself into the battle.

Ahead, the machine gun is silenced. Ilya doesn't slow to wonder at it. He slides to his belly and lifts his gun to cover the gap. He takes shots at scurrying Germans, knocks down two. Behind him comes Misha's shout, "Urrah, Ilyushka! Urrah!" The platoon courses through, firing and bellowing his name. On top of the parapets, Red soldiers from the assault boats have climbed the walls with ropes and grappling hooks and now pour into the courtyard. Someone up there brandishes a crimson Soviet banner.

In minutes, the courtyard swarms with hand-to-hand fighting. *Panzerfausts* and grenades blow at close range, bullets knit back and forth across the yard. Ilya stays at the heart of the battle, dropping his gun to pick up another and another when each is spent. The combat quickly becomes savage. The point is soon passed where surrender is not an option; defenders and attackers alike fight in the passages, staircases, and courtyard not for country or leaders but for the unadorned human lust to kill an enemy. For an hour, every man in the ancient Prussian fortress is unleashed to further Ilya's cause, to kill.

By noon the German garrison is overwhelmed. The trickery of the air bombardment last night and this morning worked; most of the enemy were caught outside the fortress when the Red infantry attacked over the dikes and across the river.

Ilya sits alone crumpled against a pillar when Misha finds him. The little man doesn't have much of a body over which to spread such weariness and fright.

His voice is listless when he slides down another column to sit opposite Ilya.

"Well. We need a new platoon again."

Ilya says nothing. There are no words after this kind of fighting. Smoke is not a word, blood is not, and they are the only responses.

The two sit facing each other for a long while. Soldiers and officers walk about, marching off prisoners, collecting weapons and bodies, doing the aftermath of the struggle for the Küstrin citadel.

Ilya closes his eyes but opens them when he finds too much there. He leaves them open, preferring the world outside him, it's less unsettling, even this world. He watches Misha and feels himself go blank.

After a time Misha looses a low chuckle. The sound is damaged, like a broken music box. Slowly he slides over from his post.

"Now, Ilyushka, don't bite me."

The little man skids close to look at Ilya's wounds, all snips, nothing deep. Ilya doesn't move under the scrutiny. Misha himself bears several bullet marks. When he's satisfied that Ilya isn't going to bleed to death propped against his pillar, he moves away.

Another crooked snicker escapes Misha.

"Well, I guess we'll be lieutenants next."

SEVEN

BESIDE THE TRAIN TRACKS CITIZENS STAND WAVING hankies and flags and pink palms. A warm Good Friday afternoon puts them in shirtsleeves. These are farmers and small-town folk, the best believers in democracy, the givers of sons and daughters to the war, the poor and honest for whom Roosevelt has crusaded in all his four terms.

He is so tired, he must be careful not to let his forehead rest against the windowpane watching them flow past. Behind the people, fields of alfalfa and corn are still mostly crested dirt, little green tufts show where America's wealth will grow under this sun. Peach trees blossom. Evergreens and oaks freshen their color. Nature keeps most of her promises. Roosevelt likes that thought.

He wants to be done. He wants to shake the constraints of office after thirteen years and keep some promises to himself, see how he could bloom as a natural man outside the presidency. His vigor will come back, he's sure of it. He's said this before, privately to his aides, that he'll resign once the United Nations is operating. Let Truman take over, let power pass from the Hudson to the Missouri. But he's never before spoken seriously of quitting; always he does it in jest or to cheer up Eleanor, or address his doctors' concerns, every time he's said he'll toss in the towel he's done it just to put a temporary stop to some irksome discussion of worry over his health. But now he thinks he might mean it. He just might want this over with.

The overnight ride down from Washington was restless. Roosevelt slept in fits on the train. He'd spent the previous four days in Hyde Park trying to restore himself. It didn't work, he still feels weary. He stayed in the White House just for yesterday afternoon, enough to sign some cables to Churchill drafted by his staff and hold some luncheon meetings. Now he intends to rejuvenate with two weeks beside the ravine at the Little White House in Warm Springs. He's got his stamp collection with him. He'll take long country drives, he'll watch the sun set over the mountain. He'll hold a book in his lap so no one will bother him, and nap. Anna couldn't come this time, her six-year-old boy got a last-minute gland infection. He asked Eleanor not to come, said he didn't want to take her away from her important agendas—she's never liked Georgia anyway, all the poverty and segregation, honeyed accents and Spanish moss. Instead, he has his two favorite female cousins along for company, so he'll be pampered by women.

A mile outside the Warm Springs station the momentum of the train breaks. It's the moment of anticipation in all journeys, when the trip slows to arrival. Roosevelt does not feel the accustomed tinge of pleasure. He wants the train to accelerate and keep going, not stop, not creep at this creaky, tippy speed. The ride was better, life was more of an even thing when it was lived faster. He doesn't want to be in Warm Springs to heal. He wants to be a movie cowboy and climb out on the roof of the train cars, fight a villain, duck a coming tunnel. Roosevelt misses pace. He misses the coal shoveled into his belly, the resultant fire. He wants the train to charge on forever.

He pulls his face from the glowing window. He wants no more Georgia strangers looking in at him. He eases his head against the seat back. His secretary Grace Tully moves down the aisle to him. She braces herself with each step against the rocking floor.

"Mr. President. We're almost at the station. Let me take these papers and put them away."

"Toss 'em out the window." Roosevelt would like to smile when he makes this joke but he doesn't.

"Sit down, Grace."

"Yes, sir."

Roosevelt takes a hand from his lap and lays it on the tabletop. Under his fingertips are thin paper sheets and folders. Strong veins run ridges into his big hand. He still has the wrists of a boxer and a hero.

"You looking forward to the vacation?"

"Yes, Mr. President. You could use some real rest and quiet."

He meant to ask about her feelings, but if she wants to turn it back to him, that's fine.

He taps a finger on one of the sheets.

"You know what this one says?"

Grace Tully doesn't take her eyes from his. Roosevelt observes her face reflect everything on his own. He crinkles his eyes before he speaks, she does the same, she catches the identical expression of disappointment he tries to mount. She's like all the women around him, sympathetic, Harry is that way too, all but Eleanor.

"It says I'm a liar."

She shakes her head. "It's not true."

"Says so right here. Stalin calls me a liar. Not in so many words, of course. He says the talks with that Nazi in Switzerland are just a smoke screen. That while we're negotiating with the Germans, Hitler's moved three more divisions out of Italy to the Russian front. Right here, Grace, listen: *This circumstance is irritating to the Soviet Command and is grounds for distrust.*"

Grace Tully repeats the last word. "Distrust. Oh for heaven's sake!" This time she leads the way, her scrunching face sends Roosevelt the cue and he follows.

"I know, I know. I can't be trusted by the Russians, that's what Joe's saying."

"After all you've done for him."

Roosevelt enjoys that he doesn't have to say this for himself.

He taps another sheet, as though to wake it, to have it tell out loud what perfidy resides on it.

"This one here. Know what it says? It's from Ambassador Harriman. He's furious at the way the Reds are treating American POWs rescued from German camps. Says they're being beaten and held against their will as spies. The Reds aren't returning them to us. Harriman wants me to climb on Joe's back about it, take some retaliatory steps. Know what I'm going to do, Grace?"

"No, sir."

"Nothing."

Grace Tully's face waits for its cue. Roosevelt watches her to gauge but she reveals no clue what she thinks until he asks, "Want to know why?"

Another tap, this one with the middle finger, a crisp knock on the table.

"Because of this one. Right here. Molotov's not coming to the first meeting of the United Nations in San Francisco next month. Stalin's sending Gromyko. Gromyko. When every participating nation is sending their top foreign minister, the Reds are giving us Gromyko, an ambassador. What the hell kind of signal does that send to the world about how much importance the Reds put on this first meeting? This is a slap, Grace. A slap in the face of the countries who supported Stalin during the whole war. A slap at me, personally. Call me a liar. All right, I've been called worse. Stalin wants to bully some American soldiers. Well, for now we can swallow that, I'm sure those boys have seen worse too. But the United Nations. Grace, it's the only single answer. All these other issues are nothing compared to it. The UN is the place everything'll get sorted out. Stalin wants to forget every agreement we made at Teheran and Yalta. Fine. But you just let me get him to the table at the UN, with the world at my back. Then we'll see."

Roosevelt chews on his lower lip. He wags his head.

"But this Stalin is something else. He's . . . I'll tell you,

Grace. I'm not so sure Winston hasn't been right all this time. About us not being able to do business with the Soviets. With Joe, in particular."

Grace Tully's face falls.

"No," the President says, "I'm not sure anymore at all."

She sees something on his face. Her expression becomes vivid and broken-hearted.

"Yes, Grace," says Roosevelt. She is his mirror, his heartbreak. "That's right. That's all too damn right."

With both hands he sweeps the papers together into a ball of litter. He hands them like trash to Grace Tully.

"Take 'em."

The secretary is jolted, she stands to accept the pages. Several folders and sheets slip from her grasp. Roosevelt watches her struggle to make order from what he has handed her, he does nothing to help. The train shudders coming into the station. Grace Tully stumbles forward and has to put a hand to the tabletop to catch herself. A few more pages scatter.

The train is at the station now. The secretary sits across from the President and takes a deep breath for composure. She begins to match each page with its mates and proper folder. Roosevelt looks away from her patient labor. More little American flags flutter, and hats are in the air outside the window. A bad brass band made up of Warm Springs locals plays "Hail to the Chief."

Yes, he thinks, after all he's done for Stalin. After all he's given. Money, materiel, armaments, planes, ships. Political concession after concession. He's taken pieces out of Churchill and England and tossed them to the Russian bear. He's ignored his own advisers. He's backed down over Poland, gone deaf and dumb over the rest of eastern Europe. He'll end up giving Stalin Berlin. Christ, what does it take to satisfy that man's appetite?

The President makes a fist and brings it down. The sound on the table he creates is poor, barely a dropping thud. He can't even get Grace Tully to look up at him in surprise.

One bit of temper is all Roosevelt can muster. Now he

admires Grace's calm assembly of his papers. Piece it all back
together. Haven't got the energy like Churchill to be
shocked and dismayed so often, to fight every battle. Got to
fight the big ones, win them. The United Nations. The
Grand Alliance. Peace in the world. Replace war with prosperity. Replace old rivalries with trust. He's got to save his
powers for these. Who cares if Stalin says he's a shit-heel?

There's still time to set it right.

Then he can quit.

Outside on the platform, the faulty strains of the presidential song stop.

For now, take a firm tone, certainly. Tell Stalin this is un-
acceptable. Work with Winston, get the words perfect, put
forth a united Anglo-American position.

Careful, though. Don't rock the boat. Too close to the
finish line. This is natural, just like the train: draw close to
the station, slow down, and the ride gets fidgety. Don't over-
react. Winston's going to want a blunt and forceful response.
Got to stay measured. Tolerant.

But good God.

What devil did we make a deal with?

"Grace, leave it." He waves an impatient hand. "Go get
Mike. Tell him I'm ready."

The secretary smiles and stands, clutching to her what
papers she has arranged. She pauses in front of Roosevelt,
looks down on him. He wants to make some conciliation for
his tone but he doesn't, he shuts his eyes and hears her tread
away.

His legs are dead to him, from the waist down he is a
cemetery. Nothing resides in them but memory and melancholy. This is where the sadness rises, like mist, from his
silent legs.

He expects to see her first. Eleanor lives here in the sadness—in the manner of some plant that prefers shade. She
steps forward. This time she wears her wedding gown. She
waves at him. Next, each of his children, born fresh and
squalling, appears and wafts to him. The mist swirls; he
knows it's blood throbbing in his head but outside his closed

eyes he lifts a real hand to stroke their cheeks. What is this, a podium? Yes, he stands solidly even on braces, for his inauguration as Governor of New York, then as President of the United States, his mother always beside him.

Roosevelt opens his eyes to the coziness of his train car office. He squeezes the padded arms on his wheelchair.

Stalin can't have those things, he thinks. Not his children or his wife or mother. Stalin can't take away the millions of votes, the conventions and cheers. These are Roosevelt's life, damn it, his life. They're past Stalin's reach.

But Roosevelt's dream. His legacy for the world. Stalin has the power to hold it hostage, torture it and kill it.

Murder a man's dream, and what was his life for?

A knock comes at the door. Roosevelt thinks his dream may be gone, there may not be time after all. He folds his hands in his lap. The throb remains in his head, though the greater pain is in his heart.

Mike Reilly, a burly Secret Service agent, pushes open the door with caution.

"Mr. President? Grace says you're ready to go, sir."

Roosevelt looks at the strong man without envy, without even the sense of competition he always has, that he'll show these young bucks he's still got some moxie left.

"Mike" is all he says.

Reilly pulls the wheelchair back from the desk and pushes the President forward to the door. In the past, Roosevelt would wrap his arms around the agent's shoulders and pull himself into the man's arms to be carried down the steps and put into the waiting limousine. Now he is vague and limp. Reilly grunts lifting him.

"Sorry, Mike," Roosevelt says.

The agent grins big, negotiating the train steps. He whispers, "It's okay, boss."

On the platform behind a satin cord and more Secret Service men, a small crowd of well-wishers waits. They greet Roosevelt with a cheer and more undulating flags and signs. A few boys are in uniform, one of them is on crutches. The limo door is open.

Sagging in Mike Reilly's arms, Roosevelt lifts his face to the gathered.

The crowd goes hushed.

———————

CHURCHILL SITS IN A BANK OF SMOKE AND VAPOR. HE rages above the roiled water like a great storm cloud. He is naked, white, and puffy.

"Jock!" he shouts with the space left to his mouth around the cigar. "For the love of God, man! Jock!"

The secretary's voice approaches outside the door. "Here, here, here, Prime Minister. Here."

The bathroom door opens, some steam escapes into the cooler hall. Jock Colville enters balancing a silver tray and a tall glass of Caucasian champagne.

Soothingly, he says, "Here, Prime Minister."

Churchill grabs for the glass. He yanks the stogie from his mouth, gripping it between two fingers, the champagne glass is tipped in its place. Then he pops the cigar back in.

Jock Colville receives the empty glass. He turns to leave. Churchill stops him.

"This!" The Prime Minister brandishes a sheet of paper from the special oak tabletop stretched across his tub. The papers littering it are held down by Churchill's fat pocket watch, nicknamed by his daughter "the Turnip."

"This is what did it, Jock. One word too many from that damned Montgomery! He couldn't let it alone, couldn't just go about his business. No!"

He wants Colville to stay and heed. The secretary sees this. Churchill waits while Colville sets the tray aside and folds to the wooden bench placed in the bathroom for secretaries. Colville is familiar with the telegram Churchill wields, as he is with all the documents curling in the damp above the bathwater. But certain things by their nature deserve to be shouted about. Churchill has served this function publicly in England for fifty years.

"The man's a braggart and a fool. How he never got himself shot as such is something I do not understand!"

Churchill waves a dripping arm. "He's got his orders from Eisenhower. Mop up the Ruhr pocket before any attempt to head east. Right! Clear enough. Then his army starts making progress. Good! Bully! The Hun is collapsing. Marvelous! But what does Monty do? Does the good Field Marshal just go about his job and keep his head down? Does he keep his eyes on the prize and his lips tight?"

Colville shakes his head. "No."

Churchill pulls up short and scowls. His secretary should know better than to assist in the Prime Minister's storytelling.

"No." Churchill draws the word out, like a lesson. He pauses, takes another deep drag on the cigar. As punishment, he might not continue the tale.

Too much momentum and aggravation push him past the point of petty silence.

"No! By God, he sends Ike this. This!" Churchill rattles the page once, then shoves it away from his eyes to read without glasses:

I HAVE ORDERED NINTH AND SECOND ARMIES ARMORED AND MOBILE FORCES FORWARD AT ONCE TO GET THROUGH TO THE ELBE WITH UTMOST SPEED AND DRIVE. THE SITUATION LOOKS GOOD AND EVENTS SHOULD BEGIN TO MOVE RAPIDLY IN A FEW DAYS.

MY TACTICAL HEADQUARTERS MOVE TO NORTHWEST OF BONNINGHARDT ON THURSDAY, MARCH 29. THEREAFTER . . . MY HQ WILL MOVE TO WESEMÜNSTER–WIDENBRUCK–HERFORD–HANNOVER, THENCE BY AUTOBAHN TO BERLIN, I HOPE.

Churchill swings his cheroot about as though fighting off a wasp.

"Thence to Berlin. For God's sake, why not just wave a red flag in front of a bull?"

Colville says, "Eisenhower doesn't want an Englishman in Berlin."

"No!" Churchill jerks with the word, water spills over the lip of the tub. Colville stands to avoid getting his pants wet.

"He and Roosevelt want a damn Russian in Berlin, and if this keeps up that's what we're all going to get!"

"Quite." Colville picks up the tray and drained glass. "Excuse me, Prime Minister." The secretary retreats and closes the door behind him. Churchill champs on the cigar. He leans back against the warm porcelain of the tub. Colville, he thinks; the man keeps his nerve when someone gets blown up next to him but won't stay in the bathroom with a little temper. Hell with it.

Churchill sets Montgomery's telegram on the table with the other papers. He sighs and glances down at his bare chest. His skin is blushed from the hot water and his anger. The pocket watch ticks, the water stills and steams.

Monty and Eisenhower.

Things have gotten so rotten between the two, they don't even talk anymore, just exchange curt cables. Monty completely misjudged the situation with this last little note. Eisenhower paid him back in spades.

Churchill fingers the sheets before him. His head is too low, sunk against the back of the tub, to see which one is which. He shoves his legs under him to push higher. There it is. Not much as turning points go, just a thin sheet. But history's not always written in the blood of rolling heads. Paper is the equal to steel as the stuff of momentous events.

There. Supreme Commander Allied Forces telegram number 252.

SCAF 252. Sent directly from General Eisenhower to Marshal Stalin.

"How dare he," mutters Churchill, sliding back into the water with a reptilian malice. "How bloody dare he."

A direct communication between a military leader and a foreign head of state. Outside the bounds. Beyond the General's authority. Damned awkward. Even worse, Eisenhower deliberately circumvented all proper channels, neglecting to first contact anyone on the Combined Chiefs of Staff or even a single soul in the U.S. or British governments. London only found out about it secondhand, through copies distributed "for information." Eisenhower didn't even consult his own British chief deputy, Air Chief Marshal Sir Tedder. He just charged ahead and reached out to Joe Stalin.

Churchill chews the nub of his cigar, mulling over the words on Ike's cable:

MY IMMEDIATE OPERATIONS ARE DESIGNED TO EN-
CIRCLE AND DESTROY THE ENEMY DEFENDING THE
RUHR. I ESTIMATE THIS PHASE WILL END LATE IN
APRIL OR EVEN EARLIER, AND MY NEXT TASK WILL
BE TO DIVIDE THE ENEMY FORCES BY JOINING
HANDS WITH YOUR FORCES. THE BEST AXIS ON
WHICH TO EFFECT THIS JUNCTION WOULD BE
ERFURT–LEIPZIG–DRESDEN. I BELIEVE THIS IS THE
AREA TO WHICH MAIN GERMAN GOVERNMENT DE-
PARTMENTS ARE BEING MOVED. IT IS ALONG THIS
AXIS THAT I PROPOSE TO MAKE MY MAIN EFFORT.

Erfurt-Leipzig-Dresden?
For what?
To head off the mythical Southern Redoubt? Nazis in the Alps? Foolishness, backed by scraps of evidence. These are German government workers on the move, not armed combatants. It's a wild-goose chase if ever there was one.

Without advising anyone, without a by-your-leave, Eisenhower has changed longstanding, mutually agreed-upon plans. Instead of making for Berlin across Germany's northern plains with Montgomery's Twenty-first Army, which has been specially reinforced for the task, Eisenhower has shifted the thrust of the offensive to Bradley through the middle, one hundred miles south of Berlin!

This is a dangerous incursion into global and political policy, domains that are strictly cordoned off for Roosevelt, Stalin, and Churchill. Off-limits to Eisenhower, a military leader.

By gad, there's going to be dancing in Moscow.

How can the Americans be so muddleheaded? If Berlin is left to the Russians, there'll be absolutely no dealing with them after the war. The Soviets are poised to enter Vienna next and overrun Austria. Stalin is already beginning to feel the Red Army has done everything to win the war, that the Western Allies have accomplished little but divert some German divisions away from the Eastern Front. With Eisenhower's telegram, a difficult postwar situation in Europe has become almost untenable. At this late juncture the choice of military targets may well determine the political future of European democracy. Why can't Roosevelt see this? Is he so taken by his desire to be gentle with the Reds that he's forgone any possibility of ever being firm with them?

There's no document to prove it, but Churchill does not question that Eisenhower's cable to Stalin is just one more expression of Roosevelt's appeasement of Stalin. More of Uncle Sam's unsightly and dangerous courtship of Uncle Joe. Of course Eisenhower knows Roosevelt's political agenda as well as anyone. George Marshall, Roosevelt, Ike. They're all on the same bloody page. And that page says, Go ahead, Stalin. Take Berlin. Take whatever you like.

Churchill sinks lower into the water until his chin is just above it. He blows smoke across the surface, watching it shove the steam out of the way.

This couldn't come at a worse time. In the nastiest sort of language Stalin is accusing the West of negotiating behind his back with the Germans in Switzerland. Molotov is being withheld from the UN's first assembly in San Francisco. Poland is being dismembered right before our eyes, the rest of eastern Europe is being suffocated. Never before in the history of mankind have two strong nations needed more to present a concerted and solid front to a third.

And Eisenhower picks this critical time—when the war is in its final stages, when historic opportunity and chaos are at their peak—to cause the deepest rupture between England and the U.S. since the American Revolution.

Despite the warmth lapping at him, Churchill feels a chill at the magnitude of Eisenhower's misstep. The General is wrong. Berlin remains of the utmost military and political importance to the West.

Another telegram on the table—this one from Eisenhower to Montgomery—is the last straw. It strips the Ninth U.S. Army from Monty's control. Ike is returning General Simpson's powerful force to Bradley in the center, the new site of Ike's *main effort*. Whatever happened to the agreement at Malta, when that main effort was clearly stated as Berlin?

How perfect, thinks Churchill. Everything falls in place for Eisenhower. Keep the glory for the Yanks. Exploit the breakthrough at Remagen in the center, give fair-haired-boy Bradley the priority. Claim to be cutting the Nazis off from a retreat to the mountains. Stick it to Montgomery. And the whole time, Ike's telling the world he's making purely military decisions. Poppycock! The political molly-coddling and personal one-upmanship behind this decision to abandon Berlin are so thick they foam.

With SCAF 252 Eisenhower has preempted every possibility, cut off any decision but his own. Monty's been hamstrung to the point where he can't take Berlin even if it becomes available. He's stuck in the north, "mopping up."

Churchill lifts a hand out of the water. He makes a small, useless splash against the tub wall.

The Grand Alliance—so hopeful and interwoven in the beginning, so laden with possibilities—is in bitter decline.

March 30, 1945, 5:40 P.M.
Stalin's office,
the Kremlin
Moscow

BEFORE THE MEETING STALIN HAS HIS DESK CLEARED OF
all documents and maps. This is not to protect state secrets;
his purpose is to impress upon the coming American and
British officials that he has no need of papers, he remembers
everything. Stalin rules not with edicts but with a word.

He waits with his pipe lit, pacing through haze along the
bank of high windows. The shades are pulled, always. Stalin
is not one to gaze onto dusky courtyards for inspiration or
rest. In his life he has done his work in prison cells and fugitive caves. Darkness and close quarters have kept him alive
more than a few times.

When his aide knocks, Stalin moves to the chair behind
his desk. He leans back.

"Yes."

The door opens, the pipsqueak secretary announces the
delegation.

"Show them in."

Stalin changes his mind. He will stand when the visitors
enter.

The first through the door is Major General John Deane,
Chief of the U.S. Military Mission in Moscow. At Deane's
elbow is his British counterpart Admiral Ernest Archer. Behind them are the two ambassadors of Stalin's allies, Averell
Harriman and Sir Archibald Clark-Kerr. The ambassadors
are in the rear, Stalin notes.

"Gentlemen." Stalin says this in English and rises while
they cross to him. There is no carpet in his office, little comfort, the chairs he offers the Western dignitaries are like his
own, plain and hard-backed. The true Soviet citizen is a
Spartan.

All the men take their seats. Stalin's interpreter enters and moves behind Stalin with little noise, padding like a geisha, bent and humble. Harriman speaks passable Russian, but Stalin wants to know after the meeting what these men say among themselves in English.

Stalin begins.

"You have a telegram from General Eisenhower for me."

General Deane holds across his lap a red leather pouch. He does not react to Stalin's invocation, doesn't scramble to open the pouch and hand the cable over. He seems to want something.

Stalin sets his pipe aside. "I'm told it was warm today. Is that so?"

Deane makes a sound, a little burst through his nose. This is a tiny laugh.

"Quite nice, Marshal."

"Spring is coming. May I offer you gentlemen something to drink?"

"No, thank you, Marshal Stalin." Ambassador Harriman speaks. "We won't take too much of your time. Yes, we do have a personal message from General Eisenhower for you. General Deane?"

Deane unbuckles the pouch. A single typed sheet is passed over. The cable is labeled Supreme Commander Allied Forces number 252. Stalin takes it and hands it behind him without looking to the interpreter. The spectacled little man reads aloud. Stalin resumes smoking.

Eisenhower's immediate operation is to encircle the Ruhr and destroy all enemy forces defending it. This mission lies principally in General Bradley's theater of operations. The offensive should be completed by late April if not sooner.

The Allies' next effort will be to divide enemy forces by linking with the Soviet armies.

The best junction to effect this linkup is an advance east to Erfurt-Leipzig-Dresden, this being the area into which many German government departments have been reported moving.

As soon as practicable, a second, supporting advance will

go into action to join Soviet forces in the south, toward Austria, to prevent the consolidation of German resistance in the anticipated redoubt in southern Germany.

Eisenhower requests immediate information about Soviet plans as to direction and timing, in order that Allied operations be planned in accordance. The Supreme Commander regards it as essential that the two forces coordinate their actions and perfect the liaison between them.

While the interpreter reads, Stalin smooths his moustache. He looks over the heads of the Americans and the Englishmen where the smoke from his pipe hovers in gray twisting shapes.

So, the *soyuzniki*—the little allies—are worried about the Southern Redoubt. Stalin can't fathom this. His information tells him not to worry, it's only clerks and bureaucrats fleeing, not a one of whom would know which end of a rifle to point. Why does Eisenhower say he is making major military decisions based on such a thin rumor?

Eisenhower claims he's heading for Leipzig-Dresden. Bradley in the middle is the point of the Allies' lance now. And what of Montgomery's huge army on the north German plain? Will that juggernaut go unused for the very specific purpose for which it was built and positioned? Stalin imagines the mewling of Winston Churchill over this. He smiles to himself at an image of the angry English bulldog gnawing on one of Eisenhower's trouser legs. No, this seems unlikely: the letter claims Montgomery has been remaindered to clear the northern seaports and mop up while Bradley takes the fore into the German heartland. Bradley the conquering hero, not Montgomery? No, Churchill wouldn't stand for it.

The interpreter finishes. Stalin reaches back for the page. He weighs the sheet in his hands. He has not made eye contact with any of the men in the room since they entered.

Odd. The letter comes direct and personal from Eisenhower, not through the proper channels of the American and British Joint Staffs. Is this what Roosevelt was referring to in Yalta when he asked that Eisenhower be permitted to communicate directly with the Soviet General Staff? After all, Stalin is the chief of the Red military. Was Roosevelt setting this move up so far in advance?

Odder still, in effect the letter says: We give you Berlin.

Stalin cups his pipe in one fist. He brings his hands together under his chin and closes his eyes. He rubs together the tips of his thumbs.

He calculates.

The Americans and British are three hundred kilometers west of Berlin. The Red Army is only eighty to the east. But the Allies have no real resistance facing them. The toughest German divisions are all on the Eastern Front. Montgomery's forces have made spectacular progress beyond the Rhine. Bradley and Patton and Simpson move at the top speed of their tanks. Why would Eisenhower pull in the reins? Why would he call off the race for Berlin? It makes no sense.

Roosevelt. The President has to know the importance of Berlin. Churchill surely has told him if he doesn't. Why would he give Berlin to Stalin when he can take it? That thing Roosevelt said at Yalta, the bet that the Red Army would be in Berlin before the Americans were in Manila, that was a joke, yes? Of course.

No, the man cannot be that naive. But is the President too sick finally to stop some play by Eisenhower and his generals? Is Eisenhower a coward, afraid to spill a little more blood to secure the biggest prize of the war? Perhaps the rift in the West has grown so deep that Churchill and Montgomery no longer have a voice? Or is Eisenhower simply exercising a vendetta, pulling the rug out from under Montgomery in the final moments of the war and handing the torch to his fellow American, Bradley?

Someone in the room clears his throat. Perhaps this is a request that Stalin open his eyes and speak. He ignores the interruption.

Stalin asks of the seer in his head, the one true voice that has always warned him of danger and enemies. What of this letter from Eisenhower? Can it be trusted? Can any of the apparent reasons behind it be true?

No. Don't be absurd.

Eisenhower is no coward. Churchill is no defanged lion. Montgomery is not to be shoved aside so easily.

Berlin is too clearly of political importance for Roosevelt to drop it into Stalin's lap. Stalin's intentions have been barely masked throughout eastern Europe, there are no secrets. Roosevelt may be ill but he would have to be dead not to see this. He knows what will happen if Stalin takes Berlin. The little allies will have nothing, nothing at all to bargain with.

"Marshal Stalin?"

Stalin lifts his head and opens his eyes. He has the sensation of surfacing. The audience waits on him.

"Yes, General Deane?"

"What do you think?"

"I think"—Stalin will play along—"the letter meets with my approval. I agree with General Eisenhower that the Nazis' last stand will probably be in the south, in Bavaria or western Czechoslovakia. Very good idea to cut them off as soon as possible."

Stalin notes how the Americans nod in concurrence with this lie. The two Britishers have said almost nothing, they barely move; damn the English. Are they being typically remote or are they the harder to fool?

Stalin asks Deane, "Tell me, where will be the starting point for this supporting offensive into Austria? Will you be using your Italian forces now that the Nazis are all surrendering there?"

This is meant as a gig but none of the Westerners twitches.

"No, Marshal. The assault will come from the forces we currently have east of the Rhine."

Stalin thinks, good, leave the Allied army bottled in Italy where it is. Stalin doesn't want the Western powers poking around south of the Balkans.

Harriman asks, "How about your troops on the Oder? Can you tell us anything about the delays you're facing there?"

"Yes, of course. Things are improving remarkably. The spring floods are receding and the roads are drying out. I think we'll be ready to go soon, but I'll have to consult with my staff on that."

"When can General Eisenhower expect a reply?"

"Very soon. Within twenty-four hours. Now, gentlemen."

Stalin rises to dismiss them. The men all take the cue, and with handshakes the room is emptied. Stalin dismisses the interpreter; the visitors said little among themselves. The meeting was brief. Stalin returns to his desk. He lays the Eisenhower cable 252 in front of him. He stares at the English phrases on the white paper, interrogating them, they are alone with Stalin now.

He tamps and relights his Dunhill pipe. He runs the pipe stem lightly over his lips, pondering the cable. A puff of smoke strikes the sheet in the face and spreads out in blue rolling waves. The clock tower in the Kremlin gate strikes six tolls for the hour.

When the public clock is done, Stalin pushes the paper away. He nods to it. It did not make sense before; now it does.

He picks up the phone and instructs his secretary to locate both Marshals Zhukov and Koniev.

In a minute, Zhukov is on the line. Stalin instructs him to drop what he is doing and fly to Moscow tonight for a conference tomorrow. Zhukov is over a thousand miles away on the Oder Front. No matter. Tomorrow. Immediately after, Koniev is reached and receives the same order.

Stalin hangs up the phone and stands from his desk. He turns his back on Eisenhower's letter, as though the page is a comrade who has told the truth under pressure. Stalin knows everything now. He knows what to do.

He glances up at the jutting chin of Lenin's portrait. Always when addressing Lenin, Stalin holds himself still, as though standing before the real man, the titan. Tonight Stalin waves a dismissive hand and walks past.

He thinks, You were the leader to begin the Revolution, Vladimir Ilyich. You will always be honored for that.

But Stalin is the man to continue it. This is why, because of treachery. You were too trusting, too good. Look at this letter.

"A trick," Stalin says into the room so Lenin can hear and follow events.

"The *soyuzniki* pull a trick on Stalin."

Eisenhower is going to take Berlin.

APRIL

———

Only the dead have seen the end
of war.

PLATO

EIGHT

THE FAT BURGOMASTER'S EYELIDS FLUTTER. HE
brings up two thick hands while he takes a step backward. He's an ostentatious man; he's dressed himself
in a dark suit with bow tie and a velvet and silk sash across
his chest. Bandy thinks of the Tennessee State Fair and the
livestock judges.

On the wall behind the man's desk Bandy sees a place
where the paint looks warmer, fresher. A picture has been
taken down. Hitler, no doubt.

The burgomaster has a .45 Colt pistol pointed at his nose,
behind which stands an American infantry captain.

The captain speaks in fluent German. The pistol has a
universal voice.

The burgomaster backs until his desk rides up against his
fanny. With no room to retreat, the man's eyes go big as
Bing cherries. The American captain smiles while he talks.
Except for the gun and the raised hands and the glisten of
scared sweat, everything is pleasant. The burgomaster seems
very agreeable.

Bandy limps to a chair and sits. Twenty-two stitches
went into closing the gash in his leg. Only yesterday did he
take his left arm out of the sling. His left leg aches for having
to take up the slack for his bandaged right, his right shoulder

throbs from doing everything for his hurt left. He's sore
from head to toe. This makes Bandy happy. He's been shot
and busted up. He has achieved the sense with his gimp and
bad wing that he belongs among the fighting men now more
than he ever has. Charley Bandy has plunked his body down
on the table, he's anted up.

Though the language is German, Bandy knows what's
being said by both parties here in the burgomaster's large office. This is the third town in the last two days where the
Eighty-third Infantry has done this. Something like:

—You might want to pick up that phone, sir, and call
ahead to the next town.

—*Ja, ja, ja.*

—Tell them to do just what your nice little town did. If
the burgomaster there wants the place to still be standing
when we leave, he needs to get everybody to hang out
white sheets from their windows.

—*Ja.*

—If there's any German soldiers around, or any of those
crazy bastard kids, tell 'em to get out of town or lay their
guns down.

—*Ja, ja.*

—Tell him we mean business.

—*Ja.*

The captain lowers the gun. The burgomaster, who has
by now bent himself backward over his desk, straightens up.
He adjusts his sash and collar, clears his throat, some rituals
of dignity before he acts in his official capacity as traitor.
Bandy had to agree not to take any pictures of these scenes
before the captain would let him watch. Too bad, he thinks,
there's precious little comedy in war.

The burgomaster dials and reaches his counterpart in the
next town, Bevern. According to the Eighty-third's maps,
Bevern's just a little village five miles to the east on the two-
lane road.

But it's a German village.

None of the American soldiers wants to die or get

wounded this close to the end of the war. To have made it this far through all they've endured and then be gunned down by some fanatical teenager waiting around a bend. Or blown up in your jeep by a kid hiding in a grove of trees who found an unused *Panzerfaust*. That would be too much, too wasteful, with the war decided. But Hitler has raised a whole generation of children to do just this, to be his "were-wolves," boys and girls who will bleed into a cup for the Führer. There's not a single fifteen- or sixteen-year-old in Germany who's ever known any leader but Adolf Hitler. They can't imagine a world without him.

No. Today is not the day to take chances. Especially not on Easter Sunday.

The burgomaster looks at the floor while he talks to the next burgomaster. The man is animated, waving his free hand in the air telling the next burgomaster how gigantic the American force is. Hundreds of tanks! Thousands of artillery guns. Thousands and thousands of men! The fat official glances up at the captain, currying favor with his eyes and quick, furtive nods, then back down to concentrate on his fairy tale.

Bandy rises, pushing off on his left leg, careful to protect his left arm. The burgomaster gives the okay sign to the American captain, who returns the sign and holsters the Colt. A GI will be left with this burgomaster for a little while just to make sure a trap hasn't been laid in the village up the road.

Bandy moves outside to the town hall steps. Holzminden looks like a nice small burg. Main street. Shops. Red-tile-roofed houses, gardens. A square with a fountain and statue. A pretty church with a steeple you can see from most of the town. It's good that Holzminden didn't have to be blasted and looted. That's the rule here in the waning days of the war, the days of fast-rolling men and machines, thirty-five-mile-a-day progress, unprecedented advances into enemy territory. If the GIs have to fight for a town, they treat it roughly. Artillery, bazookas, tanks, any firepower it takes to reduce the threat, even if it reduces the town to ruins. These skirmishes are rarely with regular German army units; the *Wehrmacht* sees the writing on the wall and is surrendering in droves. A half million of them have laid down their weapons in the surrounded Ruhr pocket. Instead, the Americans' confrontations are almost always with Waffen SS stragglers, zealous *Volkssturm,* or Hitler Youth caravanned down from Berlin.

Regardless of who's shooting back, when the fighting is over, the GIs feel obliged to loot. They walk past whatever corpses they've made with callous disregard, the proper disdain for fools, they think. Never do the GIs take more than they can fit in a backpack—jewelry, wine, silver. The favorite booty is Nazi memorabilia. Eyes are always peeled for Lugers, swords, pins, flags. The surviving citizens are well advised to stand aside and shut their mouths, especially if the Americans have taken casualties. But if the town surrenders quietly, the populace is handled with much better care. Often the German civilians are glad to see the Yanks, hosting them to meals and drinks, inviting them to sleep in their beds, packing the soldiers off with gifts. You are welcome here, they say, because you are not the Russians.

The German citizens impress many of the soldiers, Bandy too. Villagers and townsfolk seem educated and hardworking, cleaning bricks and sweeping streets, selling items and food from carts when their stores are destroyed. They stand beside the roads and dirt tracks, jaws dropped at the displays of Allied might and mobility. They lift up their children to see over the crowds. The kids wave, loving trucks and noise and unconcerned with friend or foe. Bandy snaps photos with the 35mm Leica. The big Speed Graphic takes two hands to operate fast enough to catch the breakneck pace of the Allied advance. His left shoulder isn't up to it just yet.

Inside the burgomaster's office the negotiations have been concluded. The captain comes out on the steps beside Bandy. The day is bright. No one has died here this morning.

Easter bells ring in the church steeple.

"Mr. Bandy?" the captain asks. "You a believer?"

Soldiers and citizens alike gather in the street to enter the church doors. Services will begin in a few minutes at 1000 hours.

Bandy does not wrestle with the soldiers' paradox of God. He does not ponder how God can save you from doom via prayer when that same deity allows so many cruelties to exist. Why would God save you from Himself? Bandy is satisfied that his role is to take pictures of God's design. Bandy spreads news of God's Word, because in Bandy's life so much of His Word has been War. Bandy suffers no moral dilemma. In his logic, God rewards him for his faithfulness by giving him Victoria and Tennessee and the Leica.

He smiles at the captain. "You go ahead."

The officer chuckles and walks down the steps. The man says over his shoulder, "Lot of other fellas might become believers after a bullet misses their nuts by two inches."

Bandy watches the mingle of soldiers and citizens at the church entrance. He raises the Leica with one hand and fires a few frames. As always, he's drawn through the lens to the story behind the picture. He decides to go inside the church. Hell, he thinks, it's Easter.

He picks his way down the town hall steps and enters the street. He winds up limping to the church beside an old man with a cane. The man offers Bandy his cane. Bandy declines, using some of his smattered German, *"Danke, nein, danke schön."* The man insists and hangs it by the loop over Bandy's wrist. The old German stands there gesticulating like a man shooing goats out of the road, wanting Bandy to use the cane, impatient that the American resists. Then he turns away and outwalks Bandy to the church.

Inside, the church is full with a few hundred worshipers. The pipe organ plays an entry tune. Soldiers and citizens sit in pews shoulder to shoulder. Rifles are laid rattling on the floor at the soldiers' feet. Children fidget and giggle when GIs smile and make faces at them. Candy bars are broken in pieces and handed out. An American pastor stands at the

altar beside a German counterpart in a white robe. Bandy
finds a place in the last pew near the door. He's glad of the
cane when he folds to sit.

The service takes place in both tongues. Throughout the
service some silent signal tells the gathering to kneel and
then return to their seats. Bandy can't do it and stays in the
pew. When the times come to stand, he finds the cane a life-
saver. He can't take pictures in here. He grows bored.

The private next to him seems particularly hard-praying.
During a German part of the service when the boy is taking
a break, Bandy taps him on the leg and whispers.

"Son?"

"Yes, sir?"

"Mind if I ask you what you're praying so hard for?"

The soldier is not troubled by the query. Bandy sees gen-
tleness on his young face. He wonders what other expressions have rent these smooth features, what rage and
killing-passion, shattering panic, doubt?

"No, sir," the soldier whispers in return. "I don't mind."

Bandy waits. The boy looks into his own lap, as though
to repeat his prayer out loud requires the same bowed head.

"I was askin' God for two things."

"Uh-huh."

"First, I want Him to let me git home all in one piece. I
figure everybody's askin' for that one."

Bandy nods at this and senses the bandage around his
right leg. He concurs, a good request.

"And two, I wish for God to bring this country down to
its knees so bad they never try to make war again."

The boy seems ashamed to have asked this. He does not
lift his eyes to Bandy's. But Bandy understands. From the
mouth of this young soldier has come the wish that's been
shared by every fighting man across history, in the aeons before history: May the war he is fighting be the last one. May
the sacrifices of his comrades be for a purpose, and the destruction be enough to make men turn away forever from
warfare.

The soldier is ashamed because he doesn't pray for peace,

for everyone to join hands and forgive and fashion a new day. That would be a better, more Christian and charitable prayer. But this American boy has seen too much and realizes too much to believe that even beseeching God for peace will make it happen in this world of men. So he asks instead for the right thing, the brave thing, the prayer that will most likely work: that God be sufficiently vengeful and desolating to make us stop ourselves.

This soldier, Bandy thinks, knows the truth. What he doesn't know is history. There's never been a final war.

Bandy thanks the GI with one more finger's touch on his leg. The soldier returns to his private dialogue with heaven. Bandy takes up the cane and leaves the church.

In the street in front of the church, the Eighty-third Infantry of the Ninth Army readies itself to surge forward. Bandy was moved by the boy's sad and sage prayer, but now he lets out a fresh laugh at the Eighty-third.

A vast collection of vehicles stretches from the central square out past the town limits. Though the Eighty-third is an infantry division, they've gone mobile through another clever tactic. In every German town, whether surrendered or fought for, the division commandeers a quota of vehicles. The Eighty-third's Major General Macon has given the order: "Anything that moves, no questions asked." The men dress up the vehicles with a fast coat of olive drab paint and slap on a white U.S. Army star. Then the ten thousand–plus soldiers climb on board and off they go in a startling convoy of captured *Wehrmacht* jeeps and Mark V or Tiger tanks, civilian and staff cars, motorbikes, buses, and two fire trucks. One of the fire trucks leads the motley parade, displaying behind it a large banner reading: NEXT STOP: BERLIN.

Bandy has cast his lot with this inventive, hell-bent-for-leather bunch. Formerly it was called the "Thunderbolt" Division; American correspondents have renamed it the "Rag-Tag Circus."

Like the Eighty-third, the weight of the Ninth Army has set its sights on the final prize of the war, the German capital. The Ninth's commanding officer, General Simpson, has

issued instructions that he wants an armored division and an
infantry division set up on the *Autobahn* above Magdeburg
on the Elbe River as fast as possible. From there, he wants to
move on Potsdam, "where we'll be ready to close in on
Berlin." Every division in the Ninth that isn't involved in reducing the surrounded German force in the Ruhr pocket
has laid its plans for heading to Berlin. The Second "Hell on
Wheels" Armored Division is moving pace for pace on the
Rag-Tag Circus's left flank. The Second is so ponderous a
force that reporters say it takes half a day to move past a
given point at two miles per hour.

Elsewhere along the Ninth Army's fifty-mile-wide front,
just slightly behind the Second and Eighty-third, course the
legions and weapons of the Fifth Armored "Victory" Division, plus the Thirtieth, Eighty-fourth, and Hundred and
second Infantry Divisions. Taken together they form an in-
exorable thrust plunging east across the German interior.

Bandy looks over his chosen Eighty-third. He's saddled
them up and races them to Berlin against all the others, a
jockey on a crowded track. Right now the Rag-Tag Circus
is in a tight heat, a close second to the Hell on Wheels boys.

Holzminden has offered up two tractors with attached
hay wagons, two more buses, a motorcycle with sidecar, and
a dump truck. Out in front the fire truck sounds its siren. To
Bandy the thing looks hilarious painted green, it still bristles
with ladders and hoses. At the loud blast the last soldiers file
out of the church and surrounding buildings. For the ninety
minutes they've been in Holzminden making sure the town
is secure and gathering up all weapons, the Eighty-third has
about doubled the town's population. Bandy waits for the
captain to come out, and waves to him. He asks the officer if
he might have the space in the motorcycle sidecar. It will
give him 360 degrees of open air to shoot his photos. And
no one will jostle his tender shoulder or leg. The captain
cheerfully agrees and finds a driver for the bike. Bandy
climbs into the sidecar with delicate motions. The driver, a
corporal, locates two pairs of goggles in the sidecar's luggage

boot. He and Bandy slip them on over their helmets. The young man enjoys revving the bike's engine. He grins and shouts to Bandy that he's in ecstasy. He says he's from Jersey.

When all the GIs are mounted, the fire truck begins the parade. The hundreds of trucks, cars, motorbikes, and tractors of the Rag-Tag Circus lurch out of Holzminden issuing every kind of mechanized sound, spits and backfires, a clanging bell, diesel coughs, and the hums of many Mercedes engines. Bandy and his Jersey driver wait for several minutes before they begin to pull forward. Citizens line the road and stand on balconies. Their send-off is divided about in thirds, Bandy observes. Some folks smile and wave goodbye, some grimace, some are stunned.

Bevern is only five miles off. By the time the lead vehicles of the Eighty-third reach the village outskirts, the last soldiers will have just rolled out of Holzminden. Bandy and his driver are in the second half of the convoy, about three miles behind the wind-rippling sign on the tail of the lead fire truck. The road is a tarmac and gravel two-lane strip through easy hills and untilled farmland. Wooded patches worry Bandy, especially near bends in the road. Bandy won't even hear gunfire over the roar of the motorbike. But the Eighty-third's fleet takes up both sides of the road and fills the horizon fore and aft. An ambush would be suicide. That doesn't mean it won't happen. It has happened. The size of the division simply placates Bandy's worry; there are many other targets besides him.

The plan for the day—so long as the connect-the-burgomaster game keeps working—is to follow this road through three more villages and bivouac for the night in the town of Alfeld. Tomorrow the objective is to enter the city of Braunschweig. At this rate, without any serious scrapes with the enemy, the Eighty-third should have a good shot at being the first division to reach Magdeburg on the Elbe, the staging ground for the final push to Berlin. There, the Rag-Tag Circus will leave the back roads and hit the highway, Hitler's *Autobahn*.

Bandy loads a fresh roll into the Leica, no small feat with one good hand and a rattling lap. His instincts tell him to stay ready, everything has gone too nicely the past few days.

The moment he snaps closed the camera back, his Jersey bike driver dodges in a quick shift to the left, rocking Bandy in the sidecar. Bandy grits his teeth at the shear of pain from his stitches, right through his groin, it hurts so much he has to hold his bladder. He curses the driver, knowing the kid won't hear him. The soldier pivots in his bike seat and waves forward a long black Mercedes. The car pulls alongside, scooting fast between Bandy's bike and a farm truck loaded with GIs beside them in the other lane. The Mercedes is a German staff car, flying twin swastika banners from the front bumpers. Bandy thinks the car must have been requisitioned at the last moment in Holzminden and there was no time to paint it green and yank off those flags. But the man driving the big car wears a chauffeur's cap, black gloves, and a fretful look. In the rear seat, a well-dressed civilian careens from window to window gawping at the American column on both sides of him.

The chauffeur leans on the horn and weaves through traffic. Each vehicle in turn pulls aside and lets the Mercedes through, each American soldier stares in amazement at the lost German staff car. Bandy shakes his head; apparently the Eighty-third has captured so many German vehicles that this misbegotten staff car mistook the Rag-Tag Circus for a *Wehrmacht* column. Bandy starts taking pictures. There is too little real comedy in war.

A burst of machine gun fire brings the Mercedes to a halt. The convoy slows around it. A jeep escorts the car to the shoulder of the road. Passing, Bandy recognizes the German-speaking captain, pointing his pistol again, smiling again. The Mercedes will be painted green in about five minutes, and those Nazi flags will be tucked in some soldier's backpack.

The procession moves east at less than ten miles per hour. The Jersey driver keeps heaving the rpm's on the motorbike, wanting to peel out of the pack and go touring with Bandy locked at his hip. Bandy doesn't know the driver's name, and takes his picture as an anonymous Italian boy fighting overseas. He's got a great face, Bandy thinks, swarthy and all lit up, American as apple pie because he looks so European.

The road ahead is straight and unobstructed, and green vehicles packed with soldiers fill every inch of it. Riding in the open sidecar like this, Bandy senses the power of the Allied advance. Beyond the fields and heights on all sides of him there are other American and British divisions on the offensive, knifing into central Germany, every minute taking more miles of enemy land under occupation. Bandy wonders, Why do the Germans resist? Why do they make us wreck their towns, why do they blow their own bridges, why do they sacrifice themselves? Bandy wants to ride the Rag-Tag Circus all the way into Berlin and nab that sick fuck Hitler, get the Kraut-speaking captain and his .45 Colt and ask these and a few other questions.

The column proceeds unimpeded. This is a good sign. If Bevern had plans to resist, the shooting would start around now, with the green fire truck in the lead nearing the village outskirts. Another burgomaster has seen the common sense of surrender.

So have a small group of *Wehrmacht* regulars standing beside the road. Ten German soldiers in a line on the left-hand shoulder have their hands in the air and rifles at their feet. Every olive drab truck, tractor, car, tank, motorbike—Bandy snaps the men's picture in his turn—bus and jeep sliding past thumbs them to the rear, telling these quitted enemies to keep walking west and give up back there, we've got no time to stop, read the sign, pal, BERLIN.

After twenty minutes on the two-lane road, the first cluster of dwellings appears. These are small farmhouses with roofs of red clay tile or thatch. Those barns left standing appear ancient, weathered to a lovely woody gray, pleasing to Bandy's farmer's eye. Other outbuildings are scorched to the ground, just ridges of charcoal in the dirt like the spines of long-dead giant beasts. The Jersey boy slows the motorbike. A canopy of bare branches over the road marks the outer boundary of the village.

The convoy comes to a stop a quarter mile out. The driver rolls the throttle under his hand in impatience. He looks down at Bandy. He gets a nod.

The motorbike leaps out of formation and takes the shoulder of the road. Horns honk at them bouncing past. Bandy hears the objections through his own low grunts as the sidecar jars his sutures.

The Jersey driver twists the bike however he must through the parked vehicles to get Bandy into the village. In a minute they are in the center.

The motorbike is shut down. The Circus's green fire truck has stopped in the square, behind it a hundred vehicles bunch up. No soldier has dismounted. No citizens are out to greet the Americans. The idling of the many motors sounds like an ill wind.

All around the square, white sheets hang over the banisters of verandas, out of second-story windows, they are draped across electric lines. The laundry and the iced silence give the hamlet a cool, snowy guise.

Bandy steps out of the sidecar. The Italian boy lifts his goggles but does not follow.

On both sides of the main street, outside a bakery, a lawyer's office, a sweets shop, a leather tanner, are strung up bodies. There are twelve of them. They've been hung from lampposts and high iron railings. Five elderly men and five women. Two boys.

Around their necks, lapped over the nooses, are signs scrawled in a thick black hand: *VATERLANDVERRÄTOR.*

Traitor to the Fatherland.

Bandy stands in the middle of the empty street. Since he has walked forward, he hears at his back several coming bootsteps of soldiers and officers. The Americans will cut down these civilians, lay them out, and step back to let the townspeople cover them.

This is the work of retreating SS men. They will not allow surrender.

With the street filling now, the citizens of Bevern materialize in their doorways and on stoops. Bandy leans on his cane and walks forward through these decorations of the occasion of war, among the dangling bodies, among the sheets of surrender, and now the running women who drop and wail below the swinging feet of innocent loved ones.

The last body at the end of the street hangs from a flagpole. Bandy guesses the building behind the pole is the town hall. The corpse is dressed in a suit and shiny black shoes. A velvet sash stripes the chest. This was the burgomaster.

While Bandy stares, an old woman shuffles past him. She does not touch the rope that has killed the old man. She stands for a moment looking up at his heels as she might were he a flag. The woman contemplates something, what? That he was an old fool? That he should have stayed hidden and quiet like the rest of them who survived in Bevern?

She lowers her head. Below the bright black shoes, she folds to the ground. The woman lifts her open palms to her face like washing from a stream, and sobs into them.

Bandy takes her picture, the body hovering over her head. He thinks of a prayer he heard that Easter morning and composes a caption:

"Germany, brought to its knees."

April 1, 1945, 7:20 P.M.
Grolman Strasse
Charlottenburg, Berlin

LOTTIE GRIPS THE LONG KNIFE CAREFULLY. SHE HAS IT BY the hilt, backward, laying the blade along the meat of her forearm.

She hurries behind her mother. Freya skitters close to the charred facades of the buildings, donning their darkness.

Both she and Lottie are cloaked head to toe in black dresses
with black shawls over their heads and shoulders. Freya's
wrap flutters around her striding form, she is a raven, like
Lottie, ebon with the night and the sagging wreckage.

The knives stay hidden beneath the shawls. Freya spent
an hour running the blades against a kitchen steel to bring
out their sharpest edge. Once the foot of night was fully
down over Berlin, she led her daughter out of the house.

Lottie has to walk fast to keep up. She is afraid of the cool
blade in her hand, scared too of being out after dark against
the law. Goebbels has issued another proclamation, to keep
night looters from wandering the city. So far mother and
daughter move unseen; no cars or trucks navigate the road,
there's no more gasoline in Berlin. What fuel there is gets reserved by the Party bosses and their families, funneled into
their cushy cars and headed south out of Berlin to the
mountains, or secretly west to throw up their hands in front
of the *Amis*.

Mutti is obsessed, Lottie thinks. To be doing this, with
knives and breaking the law and dragging me along to help.
But the Jew must eat.

So must Lottie. Her hunger of late has shed pounds off
her already slim frame. In the mirror her eyes have taken on
the scooped look of birds' nests. Her golden hair has gone
brittle and her stamina, especially on the cello, is shriveling.
There would be just enough food for mother and daughter
without the Jew. But they are not without him. So Lottie
has learned the trick of heading to bombed areas as soon as
the all-clear sirens quit to snatch up emergency ration cards
and a bowl of soup. Freya has become a marvel at securing
black-market victuals, even without money or anything to
barter. Lottie no longer leaves the house when Mutti takes
the meager meals down the basement steps to Julius. She
stays in the living room or in her bed. She has stopped playing the Galiano in the house. She saves her strength for the
BPO concerts, which have gone unabated, three and four
days a week. There's been no talk among the musicians of
the plot to escape, not even a rumor. Lottie is concerned

that the plan may not have blossomed to a reality. But if there is a plot, it can't be spoken of. She will have to wait and see and worry.

At home there is no thought of making the Jew leave. There is no more talk of suicide. Those issues are long settled. Sometime in the next few weeks, Lottie will go from Berlin with the orchestra. Until then she has resolved herself to helping Mutti find food because if she does not, she fears her mother will feed the Jew and her daughter and let herself starve.

Freya halts at the corner of Savigny Platz. Lottie moves beside her, still hugging the wall of the last building. In peacetime this little park is a green and pastel gem, brimming with umbrellas, tables, and vendors. All that is gone. Tonight there's nothing in the plaza but a dead horse and children playing.

Three days ago the skies changed over Berlin. In the mornings, the Americans continue to arrive on time with their B-17s. At night—perhaps even tonight in another hour or so—the British and their Mosquito bombers return. The afternoons have always been calm, at least in those parts of town not on fire. But three days ago the Russians claimed the high sun as their own. They punish Berlin not with whistling bombs but with screaming, low-flying fighters, blasting wing-mounted machine guns onto streets and squares. There are no warnings before the Soviets whiz overhead, they come so fast and low, and from such a short distance away, that radar doesn't catch them soon enough in advance. Berlin's antiaircraft batteries must fire almost level with the ground to reach the fighters, spraying almost as many bullets on the city as the Reds. Lottie has seen the pilots in their cockpits, red stars painted on tails and wings, the ground ripping beneath them. After four years of bombings, this new and sudden plague rising from the east is hardest for Berliners to bear. These are the first armed Russians in the city.

This Easter afternoon the Soviets attacked Charlottenburg. They seemed to home in on Savigny Platz, just two blocks from Freya's house. Again and again Red fighters dove to strafe this open common. Lottie can figure no military reason for their selection of target. It was wanton. They just wanted to ruin a nice spot in Berlin.

One of the businesses surrounding the Savigny Platz was a carnival shop. Its windows and front have been demolished in the raid, an uncountable number of pockmarks spoil the walls. Tonight a pack of children have ransacked the busted shelves. These are Goebbels' littlest looters gallivanting in the plaza. They dance, trailing colored paper streamers, they wear spangly hats and wave yellow and blue lanterns in their play. Some children slide down a fallen girder, just the right size for their tiny rumps.

The horse is what brings Freya here. With the dearth of gasoline in the city, all ammunition is shuttled to the flak towers by horse-drawn carts. The animals are gaunt from too much work and not enough feed. This one was caught out and gunned down in the Soviet raid. Freya has come to butcher it.

Freya hands Lottie her knife.

"Stay here."

"What? Why? Where are you going?"

"I don't want the children to watch us."

Lottie thinks these children see plenty in Berlin, they gambol in and out of the windows of a busted shop, they prance around a dead horse. They've certainly seen human bodies. *Ach,* she thinks, Mutti.

Freya puts both hands under her shawl. She cowls her face beneath the inky lace. She creeps into the plaza, ducking behind shattered tables and benches until she's close to the kids. They do not see her until she raises her black-wrapped arms over her head and moans like a terrible ghost. Freya runs into the middle of their game keening and waving, and chases each of the children out of the square. The children squeal, some laugh, but none of them drop their stolen baubles and treasures running away home.

Freya stands over the fallen horse. Lottie approaches and hands over the knife. Freya smiles, breathing hard from her effort. She has been the children's protector, herding them off even though Lottie thinks it was silly and needless to do that. Lottie just wants to do what they came for and go.

Freya catches the disapproval on her daughter's face, for she says, "*Ach,* Lottie." Her grin falters. She bends to the dead animal.

Not until she kneels too does Lottie see how miserable the horse is. The thing was starved, its frame evident everywhere. It is a dark animal, a cordovan color. Its rib cage strains to contain a bloated abdomen, bulging stupendously. Several bullet wounds are easy to see in the dark, marked by white gobs of maggots. Mature flies buzz in nuggets over these holes and the horse's cloudy eyes and lolling, thick tongue. The smell is rotten but after a wince Lottie bears it. Freya runs a gentle hand over the carcass. Lottie touches a fingertip to the brown flank. The hide is cool and stiff like a rug. The two women kneel on a coating of black, crumbly blood.

On the ground Freya lays her knife and a cloth sack she has folded under her belt.

Lottie feels disgust cramping in her throat.

"Mutti, how can we eat this thing? It's been dead since this afternoon. It's covered in flies. I won't touch it."

Freya ignores this. She takes up the knife and moves to hunker behind the horse's neck at the shoulder and backbone.

"I was told the best meat is along the spine. Lottie, we'll just have to cook it until it's fine to eat. Now help me. Please."

Lottie draws a deep breath of reluctance and shuffles beside her mother. Freya makes several tries at gripping the knife's haft until she is comfortable that she can handle it with strength. Lottie thinks her mother has no idea what she's doing.

The blade goes in between the horse's shoulders. Freya pulls it to her, the hide makes a rasping noise like cutting burlap. Lottie expects blood but there is none. The beast's heart has long stopped, his blood has all dried or bled out.

Freya's incision is only a half inch deep, barely parting the flesh. Her hand shudders a little on the first pass. When she draws the knife again along the trough, this time deeper, her grip is firmer. Mutti digs her free hand into the incision and tugs. A flap of skin and meat peels outward. Lottie watches her mother grow bolder.

Now that the insides of the horse are exposed, the hidden smell rises. It is a putrid, pinching stink. Lottie leans away from the carcass but she will have to wash this odor away later. A cloud of flies is disturbed. They do a fast circlet above a wound in the leg where bone bits protrude. None of the flies land on Lottie nor do they switch to another gory hole, they seem to have their bounds on the horse and retake their spots.

"The rump." Freya does not look up from her work. "Do it just like this. Cut and pull."

The slab Mutti tugs from the horse is two inches thick. It is red and pliable, like steak. If it proves to be edible, they'll have a gorging meal.

But if the SS or Gestapo happen by, the two will eat a few meals in prison, if they're lucky. Carving up a horse on a public square under the sheath of night will be considered looting. At best it'll be judged a display of poor morale. An admission that they are hungry and desperate. That they are defeated. Lottie worries also, what happens if they're caught, stuffed in a cell for a week, and the BPO chooses that time to flee Berlin?

It's clear Freya will not come away until she has enough meat. The faster they finish, the sooner they'll return home. Lottie slides to the rear where a few pitiful cubes of manure were the horse's last act.

There is no life in this horse, she thinks, only meat. Only food. Cut.

Lottie tips the blade into the flank near the hipbone. She pushes hard on the handle to puncture the hide. Her nose curls at a fresh waft of putrefaction. A fly investigates the new gash but swirls away to nibble elsewhere. The knife scribes a reddening line, tracing the hump of muscle in the horse's rear. With her left-hand fingers Lottie claws into the cut and yanks, drawing the knife along the lifting meat. She has to go in again with the knife to fillet the flesh away from the white bone and network of clinging fibers.

In minutes Lottie has carved from the horse a round chunk of burgundy muscle, thick, cool, and heavy. The meat itself is not so awful, just a huge steak with a brown leather backing. The gaping hole in the horse's flank is a wrenching sight. The animal's hip joint and femur are laid bare; the strings and levers of all bodies are supposed to be hidden and they seem horribly wrong when exposed. Now the flies have discovered the ease of feeding in such a capacious crater. Lottie leaves the hunk on the horse's bloated belly and stands to ease her knees from the pavement. She steps back. Freya is a black place, a congealed piece of night, bent and hacking at the spine. The white of ligaments and bones—growing with each pass of the blade and Mutti's tugs—and of squirming larvae seem to usher the poor dead horse out of the night and away from this dark world. Lottie and Mutti wear black and bear knives and hunger. The horse, she thinks, is disappearing. The horse may be better off.

Lottie lapses into impatience now that she has cut the flank as instructed. Let's go, she thinks. How much meat does Mutti need to take back, the whole horse? The stuff won't last the night without refrigeration, and there's neither ice nor dependable electricity. Mutti will be up all night cooking the flesh until all the bacteria is out and it's palatable. She'll put the meat into stews, sausage and dried jerky, patties and paste, she'll feed the rest of the block if she can and we'll be famished again in three days. Every second they stay in the plaza is another tick on the clock of danger, of being nabbed by the authorities.

"Mutti," she hisses, "are you done?"

"Is there enough for us?"

This is not Freya's voice. It seeps from the dark, from another unstaked shadow, moving across the plaza.

Freya looks up from her trenching knife. Four shadows step forward, more women clad all in black. They too have come for the horse.

"Yes," Freya says, "of course."

With no more words, shawls are swept back from arms and long knives appear. It's too dark to recognize any of the women, Lottie does not know the voice. The women gather on their knees about the animal and now there are five slashing at it. A pair attack the front shoulder. Lottie observes no finesse or attempt to slice away just the meat, these two will drag away the entire leg. The third goes to the head. She nips off the tongue with one strong flick and drops it onto waxed paper. This woman twirls the knife edge beneath the eye to dig out the cheek muscle. The fourth woman takes Lottie's place at the rump and proceeds to find the meat that is left.

Lottie stays back. The kneeling black five strip the rotten horse.

The women work competently. The front leg is severed and dragged away from the carcass. The rump is worked for whatever meat clings around Lottie's pit. The horse's face is ruined where one black woman digs for delicacies. Freya lifts long fillets from the spine and drops them into her cloth bag.

Lottie can do no more. She stands aside. She is repelled by the smell and the insects and the hacking knives and the wet sounds of plopping horsemeat, the risk of arrest, but mostly by the sheer degradation.

Within minutes of the arrival of the new butchers, the women must roll the horse over to get at the other side. Lottie stays back and does not help. Rolling over a stiff, dead, diced-up, three-legged horse is too wretched. No.

The five women arrange themselves by instinct around the carcass. Freya and two others each take a leg, the remaining two women lay their hands beneath the distended belly to push it over when the horse tips and rolls. The sac of the gut founders around in their arms like a water bag. The women shove all at once, the horse begins to revolve. The thing's remaining legs are like iron bars, straight and frozen in rigor mortis. The belly does not roll with the horse but lies behind, cumbersome and reluctant, flopping out of their hands. One of the women stands away from it, considering what to do. Out of breath, she counts for the others. "One, two, three . . ."

She lunges with straight arms to force the bag to roll along with the rigid legs and torso. She puts her hands in the middle of the bubble. The sac pops with a damp yawn.

What emerges is the most horrifying reek Lottie has ever smelled, beyond anything she could imagine. The air is fetid with stench. The horse's intestines have spilled out and the pushing woman trips into them when the other women let go and run. Lottie's knees buckle. She stops herself from collapsing and stumbles backward, both hands rushing the shawl over her mouth and nose. Lottie doesn't stop until she has left the edge of the plaza. There, she dares to lower the cloth to take a testing breath. She gulps clean air as though she's emerged from a deep pool of filth. The other women are scattered. Lottie cannot see where they retreated. Where is Mutti?

With a shouted whisper, she calls across the plaza, "Mutti? Mutti?"

Around the square, Lottie hears voices and coughs, strangers in their flats who've caught wind of the erupted, rancid gas. "*Gott im Himmel!* What is that stink? It's that horse! *Sheiss!*"

Lottie moves into the ring of fetor. There's no breeze and the odor hovers. She takes quick, small steps and hunches to stay low. She feels like a buzzard hopping toward the carcass.

She hisses, "Mutti?"

Near the horse the smell threatens to overpower her again. She swallows a retch.

"Mutti, we've got to get out of here."

From one of the windows above the plaza Lottie hears a querulous old biddy say to someone in her flat, "Call the police. Right now! Do something!"

Out of the darkness three of the women hurry forward. They do not speak but grab the severed leg and the bits on waxed paper and stalk off. The fourth woman, the one with guts on her, stays away.

Lottie creeps closer. The horse has rocked back to its original position, it is split open and even more horrible. Mutti lies face up where she has fainted, the knife still in her hand. Lottie's eyes water. She breathes through a knot of cloth pressed against her mouth.

Lottie jumps beside her mother to shake her shoulder with her free hand. Freya does not rouse. Lottie must use both hands to drag Mutti away where she can awake. She fills her lungs through the cloth, clamps her lips tight, and hooks her fingers under Freya's armpits. She hauls backward, the knife dribbles from Mutti's fist.

Lottie tugs her mother to the rim of the plaza, whispering madly at her, "Mutti, wake up! The police are coming! Mutti!"

Freya remains out. Lottie stops and catches her breath. She knows they can't sit here in the open like this, even in the dark, if the authorities show up. They'll be stumbled over in a minute. The police will see the dropped knives and cloth bag of meat strips, and they'll be arrested as looters.

With all the strength she has left, Lottie tugs her mother farther from Savigny Platz along the sidewalk of Grolman Strasse. Only twenty meters from the plaza she runs out of steam. With her last effort, she tows Mutti behind a large metal garbage bin. She removes her mother's shawl, folding it into a pillow for her mother's head. With Mutti safe in the shadows, she runs back to the plaza. She does not think to be quiet, just quick.

In seconds she returns with both knives and the cloth bag of meat. She slides down the wall and lifts her muttering mother's head to cradle it in her lap. "Shhhh, Mutti," she whispers, stroking the chilly forehead. "Shhhh."

Police do come. Lottie hears boots, then echoing voices discuss the stench and what to do with the damn horse.

Neighbors around the plaza shout down suggestions. Lottie hears the biddy again call out, "Do something!"

Mutti sputters. She will sit up in a moment. Lottie will keep her quiet.

Lottie pushes away from her the bag of spoiled meat. The smell of the garbage is better.

———

April 1, 1945, 7:30 P.M.
Conference room adjacent to the office
of Marshal Stalin,
the Kremlin
Moscow

HE FEELS WEIGHTLESS. HIS BOOT HEELS RISE OFF THE POL-
ished floor, he has to clamp them down, cling to gravity.

But the sense of power rises under him and up come his heels. He clasps his hands behind his back, as though to fold wings, and strides from his office door to his seat at the head of the long, narrow conference table. Stalin is on tiptoes, giddy.

At the head of the gathering he lays his hands over the back of his chair. His teeth grip the stem of his favorite British Dunhill. For this most important of meetings Stalin has dressed in a plain mustard uniform, red stripes down the trouser seams, one decoration on his chest—the red ribbon and gold star of a Hero of the Soviet Union.

The men around the table, men who dare look nowhere but at him until he speaks and sits, are the most important men in the Soviet Union. The most feared. Beria, the NKVD's chief bastard. Malenkov, Communist Party Secretary. Foreign Minister Molotov. Marshal Bulganin. Ministers Kaganovich, Voznesensky, and Mikoyan. From the army staff, Generals Antonov and Shtemenko. They form the GKO, the seven members of the State Defense Committee.

At the far end of the table, impassive but surely impressed, sit Stalin's two warriors on the Oder River, rival Nazi-killers. They are the reason for this meeting. They are Marshals Zhukov and Koniev.

Stalin sweeps his gaze over them. Stalin resides on top of them all. The combined power in this room is nothing more than a pedestal for his own. He can make them tear out each other's throats with a single command. He has to keep Beria from doing it anyway.

Stalin nods to his creations. They return the inclination and mumble greetings. He takes his seat.

Pulling the pipe from his mouth, he points the wet end at Zhukov.

"How are things with the First Byelorussian Front?"

Zhukov reports that preparations in his army are proceeding apace. The roads and earth are drying nicely. The men are eager and ready. Everything is in order.

Stalin asks Koniev how fares his First Ukrainian Front and receives an equally enthusiastic response.

"Good." Stalin parcels this out in equal portions to both marshals. "Very good."

Stalin adopts a chatty tone, intending to snatch it away soon enough.

"I have received information that the Allies' plans are less than . . . allied."

This garners a satisfied chuckle from the room. Beria at Stalin's left hand has a wet laugh, a chesty snicker.

Stalin continues. "The *soyuzniki* intend to get to Berlin ahead of the Red Army."

Stalin does not mention Eisenhower's message of the previous evening. He indicates General Shtemenko. "Read the telegram."

The general rises. Stalin thinks the man's legs must tire from lifting all that honor pinned to his chest. Shtemenko adjusts his spectacles and reads.

The paper in his hand is a report from the Soviet mission to Eisenhower's headquarters. Shtemenko intones that the mission has learned the details of the Western Allies' intentions. First, British and American forces that have surrounded the Ruhr pocket will destroy all enemy positions inside. After this is accomplished, the Allies will advance southeast to Leipzig and Dresden.

The general lowers his eyeglasses to the bridge of his nose. He looks up from the report, galvanizing to him the men at the table. "But on the way," he says, "they intend to take Berlin."

Stalin grunts, an indignant rumble. Everyone turns to him but he keeps his own eyes on Shtemenko. "Continue."

The general pushes up his glasses. The report goes on to say that, under the guise of "helping the Red Army," Western troops commanded by Montgomery will attack north of the Ruhr and drive via the shortest route directly for Berlin.

"According to all the data and information, this plan—to take Berlin before the Soviet army—is regarded at the Anglo-American headquarters as fully realistic. Preparation for its fulfillment is well advanced."

Shtemenko lowers the paper, removing his glasses. Stalin gives him a sideways nod, the general sits.

The Soviet mission has done a wonderful job, Stalin thinks. They have gotten hold of Montgomery's telegram to Eisenhower. *Thence by autobahn to Berlin, I hope.*

Stalin lays his hands on the tabletop. He is so short, he barely has to lean over to do this. He looks past the men on either side, the idlers, the bureaucrats and bootlicks. He nails his eyes on the two warriors, Zhukov and Koniev.

Zhukov. Began his career in the Czar's Imperial Dragoons. In 1917 he switched sides to join the Revolution, fought for the Red cause with a fury. He's always been more Army than Party, very little politics for Zhukov. That's how he's survived the purges of all the Czarist chaff in the Red Army. Loyal, imaginative, bold, brutal. He's risen through the ranks to become the hero of Moscow and Stalingrad. He wants finally to be the conqueror of Berlin.

Koniev, taller and more brusque than Zhukov, stands in his way. They've been promoted at the same pace. In many ways their careers have been parallel; Koniev also changed allegiances from the Czar to the revolutionaries, but unlike

Zhukov, who joined the Red Army as a private, Koniev became a political commissar. Although he switched to military command twenty years ago, Koniev bears the taint of the former *apparatchik,* viewed by Zhukov and the soldierly brethren as something less than career military, someone to be wary of.

Stalin has handpicked these two from the kennel of young generals to be his attack hounds. Zhukov and Koniev share many traits: brilliance, Party soundness, an unforgiving hatred of the Nazis. Openly, mercilessly, Stalin pits one against the other. The men have developed, to Stalin's pleasure, a mutual dislike.

Both marshals sit bolt upright under the stare of the *vozhd.*

"Well now," he says, "who is going to take Berlin? We or the little allies?"

Koniev rises first to the bait.

"We will," the big man claims, "and before the Allies."

Stalin licks his moustache. He leans even more onto his hands flat on the table.

"So, that's the sort of fellow you are."

Koniev has spoken very quickly, Stalin thinks. How will his force capture Berlin from the south? We'll see just how eager he is. Then we'll get from Zhukov what we can.

Stalin asks, "How will you be able to organize a proper strike group for it? Your main forces are on your southern flank. Wouldn't you have to do a lot of regrouping?"

Koniev does not falter in the face of Stalin's doubt.

"My front will carry out all the necessary measures, Comrade Stalin. We will regroup in time to take Berlin."

"May I speak?"

It is Zhukov. His tone drips with condescension.

Stalin turns from Koniev. Zhukov does not wait for permission.

"With due respect," he says, inclining his head to Koniev, "the men of the First Byelorussian Front need no regrouping. They are ready now. We are aimed directly at Berlin. We are the shortest distance from Berlin."

Zhukov pauses for effect. One hand on the table curls into a fist. He shakes it.

"We will take Berlin."

Stalin eases his palms from the tabletop. He settles back into his chair. He has gotten what he wants, a declaration of competition from the two vast Red armies on the brink of Germany. He has gotten his race for Berlin.

"Very well. You will both stay in Moscow and prepare your plans with the general staff. I expect them ready within forty-eight hours. Then you can return to the front with everything approved."

Stalin observes the shock staggering across the brows of both his marshals. He knows the problem he's handed them. The assault on Berlin was until this meeting planned for early May. Now that Stalin is convinced that Eisenhower is a liar and Montgomery is charging for Berlin, he has decided to move the final offensive up by two weeks.

Koniev faces an immense logistical challenge. His force is spread out all over the south. He's short of men and supplies and must rush everything he's got to the Oder. He'll have a transportation nightmare meeting Stalin's demand.

Zhukov too is far from ready. His front is badly depleted from the fighting for the citadels, with many divisions at less than half strength. He'll have to find replacements fast. Those men will be raw. Just as well, Stalin thinks, let them catch the bullets first to protect the better soldiers.

Stalin stands. The meeting is adjourned. The others rise in congregation. Zhukov and Koniev have fallen jaws, they still reel from the command Stalin has laid on them. Forty-eight hours to prepare the impossible.

Stalin is not done turning the screw.

"Marshals Zhukov and Koniev?"

"Yes, Comrade Stalin?"

"I must tell you that we will pay special attention to the starting dates for your operations."

The two men lower their eyes in acquiescence, then flick glances at each other as though crossing swords. Stalin lays the pipe stem on his tongue and sucks once. The Dunhill is warm in his mitt, it is a fine pipe. He turns on his heels. Again they feel so light.

He steps across the polished floor to his office. The men at his back file out of the conference room without conversation. That's the way, Stalin thinks. All of you, at each others' throat.

At his desk he composes the first draft of his response to General Eisenhower. In an hour it is wired to the Allied Supreme Commander.

He informs Eisenhower that the Allied plan to cut the German forces in half by joining with Soviet armies "entirely coincides with the plan of the Soviet High Command." He agrees the linkup should indeed be in the Leipzig-Dresden area, and the main blow of the Soviet offensive will be in that direction. The date for the Red Army's launch into Germany from the Oder River is to be "approximately the second half of May."

In the third paragraph, Stalin sets the hook. Echoing the sentiment of Eisenhower's message, believing he is simply volleying lie for lie, Stalin writes: *The Soviet High Command plans to allot secondary forces in the direction of Berlin.*

Berlin has lost its former strategic importance.

April 5, 1945, 1:15 A.M.
Six kilometers west of Küstrin
Seelow Plain, Germany

"TELL HIM I'LL KILL HIM."

Misha brings his lips close. He whispers in German.

Ilya holds his face only inches from the enemy. The words he speaks to Misha are pronounced around the shaft of a knife bitten between his teeth. His chest is pressed flat against the enemy's uniform, nailing the man backward into the dirt wall of the trench. Ilya holds the soldier's arms spread wide, a violent dance partner. He squeezes his right fist around the man's wrist until he feels something in the

mechanics of the soldier's arm give way. The enemy fingers
go limp, the Luger drops to the ground. Ilya smells cabbage
on the man's breath, thinks he sees fright in the wide-open
pupils. Everything is sallow under the light of flares and
search beacons.

"Tell him if he makes any sound I'll kill him."

Misha brings his lips closer to the trembling ear. The little sergeant's teeth are nicotine yellow around his hiss.

In Ilya's arms the soldier's body loses tension, Ilya almost
has to support him. Crumpled at their feet is a dead German,
this man's companion. Farther up the trench is another.
Their throats are slit, done by the knife in Ilya's mouth. The
blood from the killings is on his lips. Ilya watches the man's
eyes flutter down to his comrade. The corpse's fingers are
curled, as though in the last moment they reached for something and missed. The living soldier locks his eyes again on
Ilya. He draws a laden breath and nods.

Ilya lowers his hands and backs off a step. He puts the
knife in his fist, wipes his mouth on his sleeve. The German
soldier leaves his arms plastered against the dirt, staying
spread-eagled. Misha produces a length of cord. Ilya mimics
what he wants the man to do, bring his hands together to be
tied. Obeying, the character of the soldier's breathing swells,
becomes a pant.

Misha steps in front of Ilya to bind the prisoner.

Misha recoils, bumping into Ilya.

"Ah, fuck. He's pissed himself. Look."

The front of the German's pants is spotted, and there is
sodden soil at his boots. Ilya smells the urine.

Now the soldier thrusts out his hands, blinking, afraid to
speak and apologize but eager to be tied by his captors and
led away, alive. Misha retreats, keeping his voice low.

"No, no, Ilya. I don't want to cross no-man's-land with
this."

"We came out here to take a prisoner. We've got one.
Tie him up, Misha."

"No. He'll stink. Kill him. We'll get another."

Ilya looks at the frightened, shamed soldier whose fists

are balled tight and held out as though already tethered in Misha's rope. He nods, Yes, yes, take me, I won't do anything more wrong.

"Tell him to take off his pants."

"What?"

"Do it, Sergeant."

By saying this, Ilya makes it an order. After the siege of the Küstrin citadel he was given a field promotion to lieutenant. Misha was not.

"Tell him. And you take the trousers off the dead one."

Ilya sheaths his knife, the blade slides away with a menacing sibilance. Misha does not move to obey. Ilya flexes his hands open and closed once in warning. Misha spits.

"Fuck, Ilya. Fuck."

Misha mutters to the German. The soldier is thin and young, no more than twenty or so. He reacts to Misha's words with stifled, frenzied happiness. He suppresses a laugh.

Ilya watches the effort of stripping and dressing. Misha is careless with the corpse, whipping the boots and pants off it and leaving the body in disarray. The head lies still while the body is twisted about, Ilya's gash at the throat was deep.

When the soldier is in clean trousers, Misha wraps his wrists with the cord. After this is done, the soldier catches Ilya's eye. He smiles in gratitude and nods.

Ilya flashes out a hand, gripping the German's throat—his hand is so large, the white neck is almost encircled—and pins the soldier backward against the trench wall.

Ilya says nothing. He glares into the popping eyes. Ilya doesn't hate this man. He hates everything.

He finds he is squeezing. The soldier's tongue is out. He hears Misha whisper, "Go ahead."

Ilya releases the soldier. The young man reaches his tethered hands up to his neck. He coughs, then looks up, begging to be forgiven for the cough. The soldier straightens and struggles to swallow. He does not look up again, but locks his eyes on his boots.

Ilya stares at Misha. He licks his teeth.

"Let's go."

Misha hazards only one glance at Ilya, a puzzled flicker. The look says, You've left us, Ilyushka.

The three make their way to the far end of the forward observation trench. There lies the first German body, the dead soldier still holding a canteen. Misha clambers out onto level ground. He will lead them, retracing their path across no-man's-land, avoiding mines. Misha has an uncanny ability to read a map once and recall its every contour. Plus, his German has improved steadily. These are the reasons Ilya brought him on this mission. Ilya needs no other help.

In single file they hurry from cover to cover, tree trunk to boulder to ditch. When flares burst overhead, they drop and freeze, facedown. The German captive moves cooperatively, he steps stride for stride in Misha's track. He too knows there are mines all around.

They have five kilometers to return to the Soviet bridgehead that stretches across the river Oder. At their backs, ten kilometers to the west, is the Seelow Heights. The German town of Seelow resides on a seventy-meter-high ridge forming one boundary of a flat alluvial plain. The valley between the Heights and the river—the Germans call this the "Oderbruch"—is fissured with creekbeds and spring-fed water holes. For centuries the land has been tilled by the Poles and Prussians, depending on which regime in history ruled this cold quarter. There are few trees and scant roads. The ground oozes from runoff and flooded streams, the *Rasputitsa,* spring thaw. It is over this arduous tract that Marshal Zhukov's First Byelorussian Front—with Chuikov's Eighth Guards Army in the van—will attack with a million men and ten thousand tanks. They will strike due west, aimed only at Berlin.

From their heavily armed, high plateau in Seelow, the German defenders keep vigil over this flat and highly visible patch of earth. During daylight the two sides watch each other with ease. The trees in the plain have not yet broken out in leaf. Digging in has become an impossibility in the soaking soil; every shoveled hole fills with water in minutes. At night, German spotter planes drop flares to light up the

Oderbruch, and soldiers in the forward trenches record what they see of Red activity. In addition to the aircraft, giant searchlights in Seelow beam down on Soviet positions in the Küstrin bridgehead, observing the shifting of troops, artillery, and tanks into assault positions. Zhukov has ordered Soviet artillery not to fire on these beacons, hoping to avoid betraying the guns' location and density. The result is the Germans know every move the Reds make. The Soviets are aware that every approach to the Heights has been pre-sighted by hundreds of enemy guns. To counter this, Zhukov has ordered the taking of German prisoners for interrogation.

With Misha in the lead and the German sandwiched in the middle, the three move quickly beyond the German network of trenches. In twenty minutes they reach the dead zone, where there will be no one else out tonight except other Red patrols returning from forays. A fresh flare sparkles above the valley. They've come far enough now that there's no need to drop and hide. Ilya presses them onward.

Twenty more minutes of silent plodding follow. Their boots cake with mud. The sucking clod-step of heels is the only noise, save for the fizzling of flares above. The young German hangs his head, his slender shoulders are rounded. Ilya walks the entire time poised to kill the man if he bolts left or right.

Under the flare Misha pivots to tread backward and face the German. The scar across his cheek glows pustulant in the nervous ocher light.

Without lowering his voice, Misha asks the prisoner, *"Wie heisst du?"*

The soldier makes no reply. He glances over his shoulder at Ilya, who warned him earlier that to make any sound would be to die. The eyes seek: What do I do? I've been asked a question. Ilya doesn't care now, they're out of danger. He can see the silhouettes of cannons and tanks lined up a few hundred meters farther off in the burgeoning bridgehead.

Ilya shrugs.

The German turns his eyes back to Misha, who injects a little frolic in his backward skip over the Seelow plain. Misha repeats, *"Wie heisst du?"*

"Ho . . ." The soldier's voice fails him. He hasn't been able to clear or rub his throat where Ilya choked him. He's been petrified with fear for forty-five minutes. He tries again.

"Horst."

Misha grins, still prancing backward.

"Well, Horst." The little sergeant looks over to Ilya to see if he'll get away with whatever it is he wants to do next. Ilya just walks.

Misha grabs himself in the crotch. He brings his hand up to his nose and apes disgust at the smell. *"Ach, Horst, du bist ein Baby. Phew!"*

Misha laughs and skips higher. Horst's helmeted head drops to his chest. His feet drag.

Misha makes a squeal like a piglet. He brings up his hands to his chest, folding his fingers in weak little fists. He knocks his thumbs together, implying some stupid animal motion.

"Horst! Horst! Du bist ein Ferkel."

The soldier marches head down, hands bound.

"Hey, Ilya. Ilya! I told him he was a little pig. A little scared pig who pisses on himself. Fucking German. Huh? They're going to kill him anyway after they interrogate him."

Misha speaks to the soldier again. By the inflection in Misha's voice Ilya guesses the little backward sergeant has told this to the soldier as well. You're going to die anyway, Horst.

Ilya stops walking.

"Horst."

The German halts his bowed gait. Misha comes to a stop but continues to weave from foot to foot, reluctant to quit his fun.

Ilya draws his knife. The blade whispers.

"Horst."

The prisoner turns, putting his back to Misha. Now his head is up.

Ilya sees the soldier well. Several days' growth of sparse black beard mar his cheeks and chin. His eyes are blue, sockets smooth. His fettered wrists bulge with bone, dirty nails are black crescents at his fingertips. Ilya steps forward.

Misha bounces. "Gut the piggy, Ilyushka."

Ilya takes the young soldier's trussed hands and yanks him close, as close as they were in the trench. The soldier's bottom lip trembles, but nothing else flinches.

"Genug," the soldier says into Ilya's face.

Ilya leans nearer. He speaks past the man.

"Misha? What is *genug*?"

"It means 'enough.'"

Ilya tells the soldier, "Yes, Horst. *Genug.*"

With the knife, Ilya slashes.

The soldier's hands are free. The cut rope falls like a dead snake to his ankles.

Ilya makes a very small jig with his head, in the direction of Misha.

The soldier wheels and leaps at Misha. The little sergeant's rifle is strapped over his shoulder and he cannot grab it. The soldier smashes his fist into Misha's scar, smacking Misha back several paces. The rifle falls to the soupy ground. Horst advances and delivers one more full blow into Misha's mouth, punching the smaller man down. Misha scrambles on his backside, coating himself in mud.

The soldier grabs for the fallen rifle. He rises with it in his hands, pointed at Misha.

Before he can pull the trigger, Ilya shoots him dead.

Misha stops backpedaling in the muck.

"Ilya!" he sputters. "What . . . fuck!"

Ilya hoists his submachine gun and straps it over his shoulder. There are echoes; the report from the blast takes longer to die out here in the Seelow plain than did the soldier Horst.

Ilya lifts Misha's rifle out of the untied hands. He holds it for Misha to stand and reclaim.

Ilya looks down on the young German. There are five leaking holes ripped in his narrow back.

He died with a gun in his hands. He died fighting. So he counts.

But Horst was wrong.

There has not yet been enough.

April 5, 1945, 8:05 P.M.
Prime Minister's residence at Chequers
Buckinghamshire, England

CHURCHILL SIPS A DRAM OF CHAMPAGNE. HE SETS THE TALL flute carefully in its spot, forward and to the right. The glass sweats, he wipes dewy fingertips against his vest. The bubbles cast up white hats like happy sailors.

Closer on his right a brass ashtray supports a smoldering fat cigar. Gray fog wreathes his head, manufacturing his favorite kind of air, redolent of back rooms, politics, men. By his left elbow there's a warm platter of lamb and chutney, garnished with pickles and rice. Behind that, crackers and black Russian caviar. At the head of this meal, holding the top of the circle, stands a photograph of his wife, Clementine, and daughter Sarah.

Directly in front of him lies a short pile of cables and messages. The sheets are white and starchy, inedible, undrinkable, unenjoyable. He's surrounded the papers with a ring of his favorite things, allies of succor for these private, trying moments.

Outside the circle waits a pen and a ream of crisp PM's stationery. Farther outside the ring lies the open, ticking Turnip.

The telegrams are arranged in order of arrival, by time and date. The greatest adventure of the twentieth century began with trust and cooperation, with hope for a better world, but it has all been poisoned, and the sheets in front of him are the white pills that did the deed. Jealousy, ideology, suspicion, glory; these have overwhelmed hope like jackals sicced on a pup. Churchill lifts the first flimsy page. Through pince-nez glasses, he reads it again.

General Eisenhower's telegram to Stalin. SCAF 252.

After first seeing this cable a week ago on March 29, Churchill immediately called the General on the scrambler telephone, near midnight. He didn't mention SCAF 252, just asked for clarification of the Supreme Commander's intentions. Churchill stressed to Eisenhower the continuing importance of Berlin as a target, arguing for Montgomery to be allowed to continue his northern assault with the Ninth U.S. Army in his quiver. Churchill restated his strong view that it was vital for the Western Allies to capture Berlin before the Reds. Eisenhower listened and replied, "Berlin is no longer a military objective."

Churchill puts this cable aside. History, he thinks, will not set it down so lightly.

The next page carries the date 30 Mar. 45. *General Eisenhower to Prime Minister.* In this letter Eisenhower put the content of his telephone conversation into print for Churchill. The Elbe River will be his goal, south of Berlin, to cut off enemy forces heading that direction and divide the German army in half. The main thrust *lies in Bradley's zone, and he will have the Third, First, and Ninth Armies to carry it out.*

Eisenhower's letter relegates the entire English force to protecting Bradley's left flank. Monty loses the Ninth, enfeebling his Twenty-first Army Group. Later in the offensive, Eisenhower explains, *once the success of main thrust is assured,* Montgomery will get to mop up the northern seaports.

Jolly, Churchill thinks. Mopping-up duty. The English maid.

Churchill scoops some caviar onto a cracker. He washes it down with champagne. Those old Russians who first married caviar with bubbly certainly knew what was what.

Eisenhower is still on a wild-goose chase. He continues to be obsessed with the specter of German resistance burrowing into some mountain fortress in the south. Weeks ago British intelligence judged this to be a rumor. Why, Churchill puzzles not for the first time, can't the Americans take their teeth out of it? How can they allow something so unsubstantiated to dictate such major strategy decisions?

The champagne tangs his tongue. He reaches for the cigar and sucks deeply, meshing the several flavors, making them squabble in his mouth, that's the way to relish.

Churchill is not getting upset surveying these cables. He told himself even before he instructed Jock Colville to assemble them on his desk, and again before he embarked through them with his dinner, that he would not. This is merely a review parade. A farewell.

By contrast, he's heard in the wind that Eisenhower, short-tempered in the best of times, is furious at being challenged by the English. A flurry of telegrams to Marshall, Montgomery, the Joint Chiefs, Bradley, everyone involved, displays his anger at being questioned. Churchill likes Eisenhower the man, but is committed that the General's decision in this historic instance—handing over Berlin to the Reds—is quite dead wrong.

But what can one do? Churchill sighs and makes the only move available to him, like a chess king in check. He sets the cigar in the ashtray, licks his lips, and flips to the next page.

On March 30, the British Chiefs of Staff sent a lengthy complaint to their opposite numbers in Washington, D.C. This was done without first having it pass muster with Churchill. The English generals were miffed primarily that Eisenhower circumvented proper channels when he made direct contact with Stalin. This seems to Churchill a sideshow to the real topic, Eisenhower's unilateral dismissal of Berlin as an objective.

Next page. The Americans' riposte of the same date. They firmly state that Eisenhower's communication with Stalin was appropriate and an operational necessity. They give their support to aiming the main offensive thrust to the southeast, saying it's in line with approved strategy and exploits military opportunities.

> THE BATTLE OF GERMANY IS NOW AT THE POINT WHERE THE COMMANDER IN THE FIELD IS THE BEST JUDGE OF THE MEASURES WHICH OFFER THE EARLIEST PROSPECTS OF DESTROYING THE GERMAN ARMIES OR THEIR POWER TO RESIST. . . . THE SINGLE OBJECTIVE SHOULD BE QUICK AND COMPLETE VICTORY.

Blah blah, thinks Churchill. Single objective. There *is* no single objective in war. That's what soldiers never can see. It's not over when a man lays down his gun. The question remains as to which fellow will pick up the weapon next. That's politics.

Churchill catches a wisp of testiness in his thinking. No, no, he calms himself. You are looking for an end, not another chapter. Drink. Smoke. Chew. Better, that's better.

He rubs his nose where the glasses ride. He settles deeper into the leather desk chair. Next page.

Eisenhower's cable of March 31 to Montgomery. Antagonism coats every word like scum. Eisenhower gives vent to his distaste both for the debate over his decrees as Allied Supreme Commander and for the British Field Marshal:

> I MUST ADHERE TO MY DECISION ABOUT NINTH ARMY PASSING TO BRADLEY'S COMMAND. . . . YOU WILL NOTE THAT IN NONE OF THIS DO I MENTION BERLIN. THAT PLACE HAS BECOME, AS FAR AS I AM CONCERNED, NOTHING BUT A GEOGRAPHICAL LOCATION, AND I HAVE NEVER BEEN INTERESTED IN THESE.

Montgomery could make no response to his military commander's very direct orders. He was slapped down good and hard. If there are operations beyond the Elbe for

Monty's Twenty-first, they will be simply to clear the northern seaports, nothing else. Definitely not Berlin. But Churchill could talk back, and did. On the same day, he cabled Eisenhower again, refuting every point.

Churchill lays the cable from Eisenhower on the growing, sloppy sheaf with the others he's reviewed. He picks up his reply, written in language as tart as what Ike pointed at Montgomery:

PRIME MINISTER TO   31 MAR. 45
GENERAL EISENHOWER

VERY MANY THANKS. IT SEEMS TO ME PERSONALLY
THAT IF THE ENEMY'S RESISTANCE DOES NOT COL-
LAPSE, THE SHIFTING OF THE MAIN AXIS OF AD-
VANCE SO MUCH FURTHER TO THE SOUTHWARD AND
THE WITHDRAWAL OF THE NINTH U.S. ARMY FROM
THE TWENTY-FIRST ARMY GROUP MAY STRETCH
MONTGOMERY'S FRONT SO WIDELY THAT THE OF-
FENSIVE ROLE WHICH WAS ASSIGNED TO HIM MAY
PETER OUT. I DO NOT KNOW WHY IT WOULD BE AN
ADVANTAGE NOT TO CROSS THE ELBE. IF THE EN-
EMY'S RESISTANCE SHOULD WEAKEN, AS YOU EVI-
DENTLY EXPECT AND WHICH MAY WELL BE
FULFILLED, WHY SHOULD WE NOT CROSS THE ELBE
AND ADVANCE AS FAR EASTWARD AS POSSIBLE? THIS
HAS AN IMPORTANT POLITICAL BEARING, AS THE
RUSSIAN ARMIES OF THE SOUTH SEEM CERTAIN TO
ENTER VIENNA AND OVERRUN AUSTRIA. IF WE DE-
LIBERATELY LEAVE BERLIN TO THEM, EVEN IF IT
SHOULD BE IN OUR GRASP, THE DOUBLE EVENT MAY
STRENGTHEN THEIR CONVICTION, ALREADY APPAR-
ENT, THAT THEY HAVE DONE EVERYTHING.

2. FURTHER, I DO NOT CONSIDER MYSELF THAT
BERLIN HAS YET LOST ITS MILITARY AND CERTAINLY
NOT ITS POLITICAL SIGNIFICANCE. THE FALL OF
BERLIN WOULD HAVE A PROFOUND PSYCHOLOGICAL
EFFECT ON GERMAN RESISTANCE IN EVERY PART OF

THE REICH. WHILE BERLIN HOLDS OUT, GREAT
MASSES OF GERMANS WILL FEEL IT THEIR DUTY TO
GO DOWN FIGHTING. THE IDEA THAT THE CAPTURE
OF DRESDEN AND JUNCTION WITH THE RUSSIANS
THERE WOULD BE A SUPERIOR GAIN DOES NOT COM-
MEND ITSELF TO ME. THE PARTS OF THE GERMAN
GOVERNMENT DEPARTMENTS WHICH HAVE MOVED
SOUTH CAN VERY QUICKLY MOVE SOUTHWARD
AGAIN. BUT WHILE BERLIN REMAINS UNDER THE
GERMAN FLAG IT CANNOT, IN MY OPINION, FAIL TO
BE THE MOST DECISIVE POINT IN GERMANY.

3. THEREFORE I SHOULD GREATLY PREFER PERSIS-
TENCE IN THE PLAN ON WHICH WE CROSSED THE
RHINE, NAMELY THAT THE NINTH U.S. ARMY SHOULD
MARCH WITH THE TWENTY-FIRST ARMY GROUP ON
TO THE ELBE AND BEYOND BERLIN. THIS WOULD
NOT BE IN ANY WAY INCONSISTENT WITH THE
GREAT CENTRAL THRUST WHICH YOU ARE NOW SO
RIGHTLY DEVELOPING AS THE RESULT OF THE BRIL-
LIANT OPERATIONS OF YOUR ARMIES SOUTH OF THE
RUHR. IT ONLY SHIFTS THE WEIGHT OF ONE ARMY
TO THE NORTHERN FLANK.

Churchill leaves this page flat before him for several seconds. It was a fine effort, he thinks. He freshens his champagne glass and toasts himself. History will not accuse him of
slacking, he thinks, history will not say Winston Churchill
stood idle while the bear gobbled Berlin off an American silver platter.

The next two pages he turns over quickly, just perusing
them. He has a dislike for this cable, a lengthy and kissy mis-
sive to President Roosevelt. It was Churchill's first mentioning of the SCAF controversy to Roosevelt. In it he repeats
for the President point for point the rebuttal he sent to
Eisenhower, but the message this time is couched in careful,
courtly terms.

Everyone in His Majesty's Government admires *the great*

and shining qualities of character and personality of Eisenhower.
The good Supreme Commander is to receive *heartfelt congratulations on the glorious victories and advances by all the armies
of the United States Centre in the recent battles on the Rhine and
over it.*

Before Churchill even ventured to mention to the President his difficulties with Eisenhower's conduct and judgment, he'd written a full page of homage to America and
begging excuse for England. After so much stroking, finally
brooking the troubles, he did so like a burglar cracking a
windowsill, entering with stealth and a light tread:

HAVING DEALT WITH AND I TRUST HAVING DIS-
POSED OF THESE MISUNDERSTANDINGS BETWEEN
THE TRUEST FRIENDS AND COMRADES THAT EVER
FOUGHT SIDE-BY-SIDE AS ALLIES, I VENTURE TO
PUT TO YOU A FEW CONSIDERATIONS UPON THE
MERITS OF THE CHANGES IN OUR ORIGINAL PLAN
NOW DESIRED BY GENERAL EISENHOWER. IT SEEMS
TO ME THE DIFFERENCES ARE SMALL, AND, AS
USUAL, NOT OF PRINCIPLE BUT OF EMPHASIS.

Churchill gently reminds the President of the agreements
made at Malta. In those preparatory meetings to Yalta held
by the Joint Chiefs of Staff, the capture of Berlin was singled
out as a priority, and Montgomery's northern track to Berlin
was approved by all.

Churchill forks a bit of lamb, slides it through the slurry
of chutney and lays it on his tongue. He sets the emptied
fork down on the plate, ringing the china. The food in his
mouth is the last he'll eat tonight, his appetite is gone. Appropriate, he thinks, it was the lamb that finished him off.

The following page is Eisenhower's response to the
Prime Minister, dated April 1. The General insists that he
has not changed any plans at all. At all times since Normandy, he claims his intention has been to cross the Rhine
and disrupt, destroy, or surround the defending German

forces. This is as far as any strategic projections from him have gone. Eisenhower maintains that he has done nothing more than what he always said he would do, exploit opportunities and enemy weaknesses as they appear.

Eisenhower explains again to the Prime Minister that he must first concentrate in the center with Bradley. To shift forces north to Montgomery now would be to allow himself *to be dispersed by attempting to do all these projects at once,* and that he cannot allow. But if the German resistance should crumble, *if at any moment collapse should suddenly come about everywhere along the front, we would rush forward, and Lübeck and Berlin would be included in our important targets.*

Transparent, thinks Churchill, a clear attempt to mollify the Prime Minister and shut him up on the topic of Berlin. Eisenhower as much as said it: if there is *collapse everywhere along the front,* we'll go after Berlin. Shy of that miracle—which will not come to pass so long as Hitler is alive, and Hitler will stay alive so long as Berlin is unconquered by someone!—don't bother asking again.

There are three pages left.

The first is Stalin's response to SCAF 252, received in London April 2. Stalin informs Eisenhower that Berlin has also lost its status as a critical target for the Soviets. Churchill guffawed when he read this the first time. Stalin give up Berlin? He'd sooner abandon Moscow!

Churchill peels this page away with a shake of his head. Who could believe this nonsense? Only those who want to. The Americans.

The Turnip ticks with impatient taps on the desk. Churchill pours himself one more tall glass of champagne. He will not drink it, he's had enough, he simply enjoys the cheer it sends up from the flute.

But Churchill is not buoyed by the fizz, the pink, the moist odor hovering over the last two pages lying before him. He knows the unsatisfying place this story leads.

After Stalin's reply Churchill tried one last time to convince Eisenhower to move on Berlin. His logic was, if Eisenhower wants to behave as though he is conducting a candid and truthful correspondence with Stalin, then the General ought to be encouraged to rely on Stalin accordingly:

PRIME MINISTER TO   2 APR. 45
GENERAL EISENHOWER

THANK YOU AGAIN FOR YOUR MOST KIND TELEGRAM. . . . I AM HOWEVER ALL THE MORE IMPRESSED WITH THE IMPORTANCE OF ENTERING BERLIN, WHICH MAY WELL BE OPEN TO US, BY THE REPLY FROM MOSCOW TO YOU, WHICH IN PARAGRAPH 3 SAYS, "BERLIN HAS LOST ITS FORMER STRATEGIC IMPORTANCE." THIS SHOULD BE READ IN LIGHT OF WHAT I MENTIONED OF THE POLITICAL ASPECTS. I DEEM IT HIGHLY IMPORTANT THAT WE SHOULD SHAKE HANDS WITH THE RUSSIANS AS FAR TO THE EAST AS POSSIBLE. . . .

AGAIN MY CONGRATULATIONS ON THE GREAT DEVELOPMENTS. MUCH MAY HAPPEN IN THE WEST BEFORE THE DATE OF STALIN'S MAIN OFFENSIVE.

Much may happen in the West before Stalin's attack. Yes, indeed. Much *has* happened. The German defense in the west is thin and disjointed. The Allied armies in the north— especially Simpson's Ninth U.S. Army, now operating under Bradley—have made spectacular leaps, dashing eastward almost unimpeded. They grow nearer to the Elbe every day. Before the week is out, at this pace, they'll be within striking distance of Berlin with only shaky resistance before them. But will Eisenhower unleash them to cross the Elbe and rush for the German capital, as he promised in his letter? Will the Allies beat the Reds to the punch?

The definitive answer came on April 4. *Top Secret and Personal from the President to the Prime Minister.* It was clear to Churchill that Roosevelt's hand was not in this message. The language had the unmistakable terseness of General Marshall, lacking at the end even the informal, friendly closing the President always adds in his messages to the PM.

AS TO THE "FAR REACHING CHANGES DESIRED BY GENERAL EISENHOWER IN THE PLANS THAT HAD BEEN CONCERTED BY THE COMMAND CHIEFS OF STAFF AT MALTA AND HAD RECEIVED YOUR AND MY JOINT APPROVAL," I DO NOT GET THE POINT. FOR EXAMPLE, THE STRENGTH AND ALL THE RESOURCES AGREED UPON FOR THE NORTHERN GROUP OF ARMIES WERE MADE AVAILABLE TO MONTGOMERY. FOLLOWING THE UNEXPECTED REMAGEN BRIDGE-HEAD AND THE DESTRUCTION OF THE GERMAN ARMIES IN THE SAAR BASIN THERE DEVELOPED SO GREAT A WEAKNESS ON THOSE FRONTS THAT THE SECONDARY EFFORTS REALIZED AN OUTSTANDING SUCCESS. THIS FACT MUST HAVE A VERY IMPORTANT RELATION TO THE FURTHER CONDUCT OF THE BAT-TLE. HOWEVER, GENERAL EISENHOWER'S DIRECTIVE OF APRIL 2, IT SEEMS TO ME, DOES ALL AND POSSI-BLY A LITTLE MORE TO THE NORTH THAN WAS AN-TICIPATED AT MALTA. LEIPZIG IS NOT FAR REMOVED FROM BERLIN, WHICH IS WELL WITHIN THE CENTER OF THE COMBINED EFFORT. AT THE SAME TIME THE BRITISH ARMY IS GIVEN WHAT SEEMS TO ME VERY LOGICAL OBJECTIVES ON THE NORTHERN FLANK. . . .

I APPRECIATE YOUR GENEROUS EXPRESSIONS OF CONFIDENCE IN EISENHOWER AND I HAVE ALWAYS BEEN DEEPLY APPRECIATIVE OF THE BACKING YOU HAVE GIVEN HIM AND THE FACT THAT YOU YOUR-SELF PROPOSED HIM FOR THIS COMMAND. I REGRET THAT THE PHRASING OF A FORMAL DISCUSSION SHOULD HAVE SO DISTURBED YOU BUT I REGRET EVEN MORE THAT AT THE MOMENT OF A GREAT VIC-TORY BY OUR COMBINED FORCES WE SHOULD BECOME INVOLVED IN SUCH UNFORTUNATE REAC-TIONS.

So that's it, Churchill thinks. When words like *regret* and *unfortunate reactions* and *I do not get the point* crop up in correspondence; when it was agreed at Malta between all parties that Berlin was a principal target and now to read that such was never the case; when Montgomery's mission—along with British prestige, sentenced to second-class status—has been relegated to what is called *logical objectives;* these are clear and present signs that this particular affair has gone too far. Churchill has wheedled and scolded, made arguments of logic and emotion, and been rebuffed each time, at every level. Time, as the Americans say, to "take the hint."

The Americans have done a masterful job of hiding political and personal agendas behind sound military strategy. Without ever saying it, they do their master's bidding, as they should. Their master is the President. For his own well-known purposes, over Churchill's well-documented objections, Roosevelt wants Stalin to have Berlin.

So Stalin shall.

Churchill lays the final page of this sad series to the side. He pulls to him a sheet of stationery and his pen. The blank paper beckons a fight for one more round, it is full of possibility with its whiteness. The tick-tocking Turnip says there's time left, still time to pick up the cudgels again.

But this game is lost, Churchill thinks. There will be others, many others, to follow.

He writes an end, feeling mealymouthed.

PRIME MINISTER TO PRESIDENT   5 APR. 45
ROOSEVELT. PERSONAL AND TOP SECRET

I STILL THINK IT WAS A PITY THAT EISENHOWER'S TELEGRAM WAS SENT TO STALIN WITHOUT ANYTHING BEING SAID TO OUR CHIEFS OF STAFF OR TO OUR DEPUTY, AIR CHIEF MARSHAL TEDDER, OR TO OUR COMMANDER-IN-CHIEF MARSHAL MONTGOMERY. THE CHANGES IN THE MAIN PLAN HAVE NOW TURNED OUT TO BE VERY MUCH LESS THAN WE AT FIRST SUPPOSED. MY PERSONAL RELATIONS WITH GENERAL EISENHOWER ARE OF THE MOST FRIENDLY CHARACTER. I REGARD THE MATTER AS CLOSED AND TO PROVE MY SINCERITY I WILL USE

ONE OF MY VERY FEW LATIN QUOTATIONS, "AMAN-
TIUM IRAE AMORIS INTEGRATIO EST."

"Lovers' quarrels always go with true love."

Churchill changes his mind about the champagne. He
reaches for the tall glass and drains it in one hoist.

England has quit the race for Berlin. It's over.

He rings for Jock to come clear his desk of plates and
apostasy.

Churchill grinds the cigar between his incisors, waiting
for the secretary. Capitulation makes him want to do something, take some action. All he can do in this case is chew
the cigar.

There's one chance left.

Not Montgomery. The British are ruled out.

But all this chicanery is taking place behind the scenes,
through top-secret cables and letters. Maybe some plucky
American commander in the field, who doesn't know he's
not supposed to, will take the bit in his teeth and go, go so
fast past buckling German resistance that he's in Berlin before Eisenhower and Roosevelt can stop him.

That would change everything.

Whoever you are, Churchill thinks, *if* you are: God-
speed.

———

April 12, 1945, 1:00 P.M.
The Little White House
Warm Springs, Georgia

"PLEASE, MR. PRESIDENT," THE ARTIST SAYS. "TRY TO SIT
quietly. Just a while longer."

Roosevelt clears his throat and attempts again to be still.

"You look very handsome today." The woman painter
daubs the canvas at her easel. Roosevelt has noted the tinge
on her bristles right now is sanguine. His face must be showing good color.

"Better than yesterday?"

"Yes, Mr. President. Better than yesterday."

He expected her to backtrack, to be mindful of his ego, but the artist eyes her portrait's details and says no more for the moment.

Roosevelt composes his head and shoulders, then risks lowering his gaze to the newspaper on the desk in front of him. A copy of the *Atlanta Constitution* displays the headline: "9th—57 Miles from Berlin."

The Second Armored Division of the Ninth U.S. Army has reached the Elbe and is preparing to establish a bridgehead south of Magdeburg. The Ninth's Eighty-third Division is only a day behind and should reach the river in stride.

No reports have come in yet that the Soviets have jumped out of the gate from their positions on the Oder. The impossible has happened. American troops are as close to Berlin as the Reds. Remarkable, when they were two hundred miles out just a week ago. The U.S. forces in place are strong enough to have a go at the city.

Is some crazy commander in the Ninth going to make a grab for Berlin without orders? Roosevelt imagines tomorrow's headline: "Berlin Falls to U.S. Army."

If that happens, if that even looks like it might happen, Stalin will erupt. Churchill will fan the flames. Hitler will head for the hills. Everything will tilt way out of balance.

Roosevelt lifts his eyes from the news page to the painter. He's glad to find he's not concerned. Like this artist staring at her canvas, confident, touching texture and tint to the whole one jot at a time, Roosevelt has crafted the situation in Europe carefully, a dab here, a stroke there, years of vision and coddling. Politics and the military, blended on his palette. Everything will sit still and the final portrait will be captured just the way he's envisioned it. Nothing is going to change that. Not the Ninth U.S. Army, that's for certain.

He looks to the faces of the women in the room with him. He loves this rustic cottage, the Little White House. He can sit in any spot and demand privacy just by closing his eyes, receive attention just by opening his mouth. The women adore him. He's even charmed this painter, a Russian lady, Shoumatoff, into a chatty intimacy. Today is a fine, warm day, and the warmth seems to permeate him, it's there in the looks of the women, in the clement colors the painter puts in his face.

What to do with Stalin? This nasty business about the secret meeting in Bern. Uncle Joe has certainly shown himself to be a sharp-tongued jerk along with being a dictator. In an April 4 message, Stalin as much as called Roosevelt a liar. Or an old fool, take your pick. He claimed that the President of the United States has *not been fully informed* about events in Switzerland. Stalin insists that something rotten is being done by his allies behind his back, no matter how strongly worded the denials have come from the British and Americans. Roosevelt spat back, deciding it was time to give Stalin as good as he gave for once. He opened his response with: *I have received in astonishment your message. . . .* The note finished on an equally stern footing: *Frankly, I cannot avoid a feeling of bitter resentment toward your informers, whoever they are, for such vile misrepresentations of my actions or those of my trusted subordinates.*

It's always tempting for Roosevelt to fall in line with Churchill about the Soviets, and Stalin in particular. He even sent Churchill a quick cable, agreeing that a "tougher" stance with the Soviets might be appropriate now in light of their own armies' lightning progress on the Western Front.

Stalin did not apologize for his accusations, but he did relent. In a cable dated April 7, Joe refuted that he had any intention of "blackening" anyone's integrity. He even sounded a little wounded:

MY MESSAGES ARE PERSONAL AND STRICTLY CONFIDENTIAL. THIS MAKES IT POSSIBLE TO SPEAK ONE'S MIND CLEARLY AND FRANKLY. THIS IS THE ADVANTAGE OF CONFIDENTIAL COMMUNICATIONS.

IF, HOWEVER, YOU ARE GOING TO REGARD EVERY FRANK STATEMENT OF MINE AS OFFENSIVE, IT WILL MAKE THIS KIND OF COMMUNICATION VERY DIFFI-

CULT. I CAN ASSURE YOU THAT I HAD AND HAVE NO
INTENTION OF OFFENDING ANYONE.

That telegram confirmed Roosevelt's initial beliefs about
Stalin, Churchill, the war, politics, and people. It's a matter
of style. Just minimize the problems, procrastinate if you
have to in order to buy some time, take as few hard stands as
you can manage, and obstacles will most often resolve themselves. Dissolve, more like it, just run out of juice and fade
away. This one has. This morning Roosevelt dictated to
Stalin one of the few telegrams he's written himself during
this stay at Warm Springs, telling the Marshal that vital message word for word:

THANK YOU FOR YOUR FRANK EXPLANATION OF THE
SOVIET POINT OF VIEW OF THE BERN INCIDENT,
WHICH NOW APPEARS TO HAVE FADED INTO THE
PAST WITHOUT HAVING ACCOMPLISHED ANY USEFUL
PURPOSE.
    THERE MUST NOT, IN ANY EVENT, BE MUTUAL
MISTRUST, AND MINOR MISUNDERSTANDINGS OF
THIS CHARACTER SHOULD NOT ARISE IN THE FU-
TURE.

Ambassador Harriman asked to take out the word *minor*
before presenting the cable to Stalin. He was concerned it
might be misinterpreted in Moscow; the incident was, in
Harriman's opinion, a major one. Roosevelt insisted on
leaving the message as written, wanting the episode depreci-
ated. After drafting the Stalin message, Roosevelt sent a copy
to Churchill, repeating his advice of conciliation: . . . *these
problems, in one form or another, seem to arise every day, and most
of them straighten out, as in the case of the Bern meeting.*
The incident is over and done because Roosevelt kept a
muzzle on Churchill and a firm but friendly face toward
Stalin. He didn't give in to Churchill's rashness and exhorta-
tions to stiff-arm the Soviets, and he's not going to now. The
journey into the postwar period is about to begin. Roosevelt

is committed to embark on that journey—in order to continue—peacefully.

The butler enters the room. He begins to set the table for lunch.

Roosevelt wants to end this posing session. He doesn't like being so stationary. Too much of his life already has been robbed of motion, he doesn't flourish with discipline and silence. Not when it's so warm and pleasant. He wants to eat lunch, take a ride in the open car in the sunshine with his women, and have a nap.

It is very warm. He can't sit like this much longer. He looks at his watch.

"We've got just fifteen minutes more."

It's not warm, it's hot. A prickle runs up the back of his neck, it feels like a scuttling centipede with scorching legs. He wants to stop now but he promised fifteen more minutes.

He must be sweating. He lifts his right hand to mop his brow.

The hand will not move smoothly. It seems to flick in and out of his control. It jerks across his brow once, he tries again, another twitchy gesture.

His breath snags in his chest.

He lowers his head, to look down at his legs. You, he thinks. You. And with speeding shock he realizes, This isn't you.

A woman's voice. Close to his face.

He doesn't catch what she says, doesn't see. A fog has sprung in his head, between his eyes and his understanding. But he lifts his head. The fog is burning hot, steam.

Says, "I have a terrific pain. In the back of my head."

Lifts his left hand to show the voice, kind concerned voice, where it hurts.

It hurts everywhere. Explosive hurt.

Opens his mouth to speak more, more, get it out, fast. Time! Memory! But the fog becomes blackness, faster than words or regret or hope.

It is horrible; then it is beautiful because everything completed is.

N I N E

B ANDY SQUATS TO DIG INTO HIS PACK AND GETS A
kick in the rear.

"Get moving, soldier!"

Bandy whirls to find an officer behind him with hands on
hips. A .45 pistol rides just below one of the balled mitts.
The man is short and red-faced.

"Whatever it is you're doing, son, you can do it on the
other side of the river!"

Bandy says nothing to the colonel. Without standing he
taps a finger to his armband, the one that identifies him as a
civilian in the press corps. He finishes reaching into his pack
for the Leica and holds it up to the officer.

"That's great, son. Now get your ass across the river and
take some goddam pictures over there!"

The colonel strides on, shouting and boot-prodding anyone he deems sluggardly. The Rag-Tag Circus is on the
Elbe. They have a shot at being the first division in the U.S.
Army to cross the river. This officer makes sure every man
in earshot knows it. "Get going!" he hollers at another
bunch of laggards. "Don't wait to get organized, for Pete's
sake! Get in a boat, get over the river! Come on! You're on
your way to Berlin!"

Four hours ago the Eighty-third's convoy roared into this

town of Barby on the riverbank. The central pavilion was quiet and draped in the required white sheets of surrender. Civilians stayed in their houses. There was no celebration, just as there was no resistance. All the enemy troops and Nazis had withdrawn. Once they'd retreated across the Elbe, they blew the bridge. There's nothing left but a reef of wooden and metal rubble beneath the green water and a dozen stone stanchions standing over it all without their burden.

Bandy rode into Barby in the lead on the outrageous green fire truck. The Rag-Tag Circus likes publicity and it doesn't get any better than Charles Bandy, LIFE SPECIAL CORRESPONDENT. For the past two weeks he's chronicled the Circus's race eastward, neck-and-neck with their stiffest competition in the U.S. Ninth, the Hell on Wheels division, the Second Armored. The folks back in New York at *Life* are giving the race big play. Bandy's photos are getting picked up by the news syndicates as well, everyone at home is on the trail with him, even with a lag time of two or three days. The hope is that one of these divisions will hit the Elbe, find a bridge across the river, and re-create the magic of the Remagen miracle, which back in March changed Allied strategy overnight. Every American and British vehicle within a hundred miles will divert and flow across, compliments of whatever division makes the discovery. According to reports, the U.S. Army now is only ten miles farther from Berlin than the Reds. The race with the Russians has turned into a dead heat.

The lumbering Second Armored actually beat the Circus to the Elbe, arriving in Magdeburg yesterday, after traveling two hundred miles through enemy territory in fourteen days. The Circus has stayed one day behind the Hell on Wheels boys, never able to catch up. Neither division found an intact bridge waiting for them. There would be no Remagen. But officers in both divisions decided they'd force the river anyway, establish beachheads on the east bank and bring up the engineers to construct all the pontoon bridges they'd need. There's too much momentum now to be slowed down by the lack of a lousy bridge. They'll make their own.

The Second had a day's head start on the Eighty-third.

Last night, three battalions of the Second Armored's infantry were ferried across the Elbe at the town of Westerhüsen, just south of Magdeburg, without opposition. On reaching the eastern bank, the soldiers dug defensive positions in a semicircle. At dawn, everything looked good and quiet.

Engineers rushed pontoon sections forward and floated them onto the Elbe. Once the morning sun rose enough, German shells came pouring in from the east side of the river. The barrage tore up the span, wounded several men, and convinced the Second to abandon this site for the crossing. They had only seventy-five more yards to go to the other side.

This morning while the Rag-Tag Circus pulled into Barby, the Second found another crossing site, just a few miles north of here. But the Circus has all the momentum now, and with shouts and officers' boot-tips they've got the motors revved.

Already this afternoon one battalion has been put over in assault boats, another crosses right now. Artillery pieces float across on pontoons. A treadway bridge is under feverish construction and should be finished by nightfall. All over the town of Barby the Rag-Tag Circus's odd collection of green vehicles is parked haphazardly, crammed in to watch the engineers span the river, which will carry them on to the *Autobahn* and Berlin. So far, there hasn't been a peep from the other side. And with the big guns floating over to help the defenders maintain their position, this bridgehead is going to hold. Bandy hears the officer patrolling the riverbank, convincing soldiers one way or another to climb into a boat and get across. Even with his butt smarting a little from the kick in the shorts, Bandy is jazzed that his gamble of joining this weird division might soon pay off.

He loads a fresh roll of film into the Leica. His left shoulder has stopped throbbing and reduced itself to snagging his attention only when he makes a rapid move with the arm. The stitches came out of his right thigh last week; he gave the cane away. A thick gauze bandage and a lot of tape keep him aware that he's been shot. He hasn't mentioned the bullet to Victoria in any letters. He'll let her wait for that one. Judging from the look of the progress on the river in front of him, all the crazy vehicles rammed into Barby, the determination on the men's faces, the competition between divisions hitting the river, the power of those combined forces, and that sign still hanging on the Circus's fire truck claiming BERLIN as the last stop, Vic won't have to wait long.

Bandy stands. The leg feels fine and he consigns it with the shoulder to his subconscious. All healed. Good as new. He straps the ready Leica around his neck, grabs his pack, and heads to the bank to find a spot in a boat, to cross the Elbe with the Eighty-third Infantry. This sort of thing makes not a caption but a headline: "Bandy Across the Elbe."

He walks down to the bank. There he squeezes off a dozen shots of eight-man boats plying the last natural barrier between the Americans and Berlin. The water and the afternoon are churned by the motors shuttling to and fro. On the far bank, men are shoved out of the boats even before they hit the shore so the skiffs can turn and run hard to fetch another load of passengers. Two big guns are floating on pontoon platforms, being towed against the current by three straining assault boats each. Twenty or more engineers—the most inventive and resilient of soldiers, Bandy has observed—have got the footbridge a fifth of the way across. The mood of the Rag-Tag Circus is merry, actually a carnival-like atmosphere befitting their nickname, a three-ring jubilee of activity to cross the Elbe. The men really want to get to Berlin. At the moment nothing, not Germans or nature or orders, is stopping them.

Today is Friday the thirteenth. Bandy wonders what's going to go wrong.

He stows his camera, jots a few caption ideas on a notepad. He raises a hand like hailing a taxi and in seconds one of the boats has a place for him. Bandy has to get his boots wet climbing in, there's no time for the boat to come up on shore. He sloshes over the side and the skipper whirls in a tight turn even before Bandy is seated.

The ride over is smooth and quick. The day around them is pleasant, there's no trace of threat, the river wake is frothy and clean, this could be an excursion with friends were it not for the guns and helmets. Bandy crosses the Elbe and when the boat slows he steps into the shallows with the rest. The boat pivots on its engine and is gone, as though this is one big river relay race.

He walks up to the shore. Bandy takes out the Speed Graphic this time. He wants to shoot faces and hands, the thousand soldiers in the vanguard of the deepest American penetration of the war into Germany.

He unfolds the accordion bellows of the camera, clicks the lens in place, slides in a film packet, and searches for a shot. Once this bridgehead is solidified and the span across the river complete, it won't take long for a formidable force to transport across the river. The two battalions of the Eighty-third that have been ferried across so far throw dirt in the air with shovels, picks, even helmets used as trenching tools. They burrow into the German earth, knowing the enemy may come to throw them back. They will not go back easily out of these holes and revetments, not a one of them wants to return across the river without first seeing Berlin.

Bandy wanders through the men, freezing time among them with his camera, they will be here forever digging like this, heroic and cheerful and young. Some sing with their mates while they excavate. Almost every man smokes, sportily, like movie stars playing soldiers with cigarettes dangling from sweaty lips, and Bandy feels good that he is a farmer for them too.

A lieutenant with freshly wet calves from his drop-off in the Elbe approaches Bandy. He does not bear on his shoulders the enthusiasm of the rest of the men, there's something else there.

Here it comes, Bandy thinks. Friday the thirteenth. Never fails.

"Sir. Mr. Bandy, sir." The young officer doesn't seem to know how to address him.

"Yes, Lieutenant. What can I do for you?"

"Sir, I don't know if you know."

"Know what?"

"Word is that yesterday, President Roosevelt died."

Bandy narrows his eyes and grimaces. This is sad damn news, he thinks. Rotten timing for the old man. Shitty. Just when we're standing here so close. No one wants to die this near to the end. He should've gotten to see it. He should've been able to live long enough.

Well, so should a lot of people.

"How?"

"They say he just keeled over. Down in Georgia. Just up and died."

The lieutenant nods when Bandy says nothing more. The man turns to go. Bandy sits on a rock. The heavy Speed Graphic gets lowered to the ground. Bandy takes off his helmet and rubs a hand through his hair, scratching the back of his head.

FDR's gone. Bandy drops his emptied hands into his lap. He works his fingers, trying to feel the real shape of the loss, but what he feels instead is the weight of his cameras, the pictures he's taken and the dangerous places he's trod himself, the frames of the dead, and the millions of men striving to survive. He thinks about their sacrifices and risk, and his own, and compared to it all, Roosevelt's passing kind of pales. That's not right, Bandy thinks, not fair, the man was the President for thirteen years, he brought America out of the Depression, guided us through the war.

What's missing, what refuses inside Bandy to give the President's passing its proper due? Bandy uses his eyes to search for the answer. He tries hard but what he sees instead is anonymous soldiers burrowing into enemy ground, men rushing across a river in hopes of taking a hostile city. He sees men in danger in a foreign land, far away from home and loved ones. Men who have lost dearer friends than Roosevelt, who have not finished their mission. Bandy counts himself among them. There's work left to be done by these men and Bandy. They are all dispensable to that work. The answer comes: Roosevelt is too.

Bandy dons his helmet. He watches the word spread among the digging men. They stop to hear the news. Many do as Bandy did, take off their helmets and scratch their heads with dirty hands. Most go back to work after a respectful pause, a few walk over to the next group to tell them. The men are all sorry but not stymied. This isn't a crisis for them, Bandy thinks, it's a death, and that is woefully familiar.

Before dark, the treadway bridge is finished. At dusk, the large pontoon span is completed. Another thousand men cross to solidify the bridgehead. Green tanks rumble over to add their might to the defense. The Rag-Tag Circus now straddles the Elbe.

Bandy catches a ride with an assault boat back across the river, to deliver his exposed film to the liaison officer for a flight to London in the morning.

On the west bank he pulls out the Leica for one last series of shots of the fat pontoon bridge. In the gloaming the Leica will let him shoot faster than the Speed Graphic before dark falls. A truck rumbles over the slats, the pontoons bounce on the moody water in the fading day. Bandy moves to the approach of the bridge, to photograph the span in retreating perspective with the truck on it.

He includes in his frame a sign nailed in place by the men of the Eighty-third. They have named their bridge, the first and only American bridge across the Elbe, with the typical panache of the Rag-Tag Circus. In honor of the new President of the United States, the sign reads: TRUMAN BRIDGE. GATEWAY TO BERLIN. COURTESY OF THE 83RD INFANTRY DIVISION.

April 14, 1945, 2:15 P.M.
Goethe Strasse
Charlottenburg, Berlin

FREYA SITS IN THE HALL, HER BACK AGAINST THE WALL. She slumps, legs akimbo in front of her. Her dress rides above her slim knees. Mutti on the floor looks to Lottie like a woman who has been knocked there.

Lottie stands back, arms folded, leaning in the doorjamb. She sees the loss of weight in herself now showing on Mutti's arms and calves. There hasn't been much to eat since the horsemeat ran out. The stuff was easier to stomach than Lottie would have thought. Freya cooked it into jerky and sausage, soaking the meat in salted water before frying out all the bacteria and rot, then heavily seasoning it to stave off the taste of spoilage. After a week the stores were gone. Freya, as Lottie expected, brought food into the bunkers to hand out to neighbors, old folks, and children.

The yellow door talks to Freya. They discuss flight from Berlin.

"A car," the Jew's voice says. "That's the best way."

Mutti laughs. This part of her has not weakened yet.

"Do you know what a car costs now, Julius? They're impossible. A jalopy that barely runs costs over twenty thousand marks. And petrol? One liter is fifty marks."

"That's twenty cigarettes."

"Impossible, like I said. A kilo of butter, that's best. You can get twenty liters of petrol."

The Jew echoes, "Butter."

The talk pauses to taste the delicacy in their memories.

"And what if you had a car?" the Jew asks. "Where would you get the papers to leave Berlin?"

"You'd need a travel permit."

"And a military pass. I'd need a military pass."

"Yes. And a *Volkssturm* exemption card."

"All right. How much, do you think?"

"Oh, Julius, impossible. Too much money to count."
Freya turns to lift her eyes to Lottie. "*Liebchen,* you're clever.
How much do you think?"

"I don't know."

"Oh, play along. How much?"

The Jew's voice. "How much, Lottie?"

She has grown used to the disembodied voice, but not
when it speaks to her. She has passed these conversations in
the hall a hundred times, sometimes listening in like she does
now out of boredom. But Lottie cannot stop being spooked
whenever the Jew addresses her from behind the door. Why
can't he come out? This discipline of his. *Ach,* Lottie thinks,
the Jews.

"I don't know. I've heard a hundred thousand marks for
everything."

Mutti nods and smiles, thanking her daughter for not
walking off. She pats the floor next to her to say, Come, sit
with your mother.

Lottie dons a reluctant posture, then accepts the invitation. She slides her back down the wall to touch shoulders
with Mutti. Lottie kicks out her legs beside her mother's.
They are the same legs, narrow ankles, shapely at the calf.
Freya is still a beautiful woman.

Sitting like this at the foot of the yellow door, it seems a
large figure, broad-shouldered and stolid, even towering.
But when the door speaks, the voice is small, seeming to
come from somewhere around the door's shins.

Freya says, "Julius, tomorrow is Passover, isn't it?"

"Yes."

"What would you like to eat? I know the Jewish people
have to eat special foods for the holidays. What would you
like, then?"

The game continues, where they pretend to have cars
and proper papers and money.

"I would like a lamb bone. And parsley and bitter herbs.
Yes, and matzoh."

Mutti beams to hear these things. A Jew, in danger for his
life because of who he is, still wishes to worship as a Jew.

Lottie sees on Mutti's face she thinks this is wonderful, a green sign of spring in late winter.

"Lottie?" the Jew asks. "Do you know the story of Passover?"

Lottie stares at the yellow door. She has no reply, she doesn't want to make conversation. Her mother prods her in the thigh.

"No."

"It's the story of Exodus."

Without being asked to do so the yellow door describes the Jews' flight from enslavement in Egypt three thousand years ago. Moses brought down plagues from God, but Pharaoh refused to let the people go. For the final plague, God's Angel of Death flew over Egypt taking the firstborn of every Egyptian family. The Jews' houses were marked on their doors with the blood of a lamb, and the angel passed over them. Pharaoh was horrified and stricken by this final persuasion. He demanded the Jews leave. They departed Egypt so quickly, there wasn't time for their bread to rise, so they let it bake on their backs as they left. That's why Jews eat unleavened bread, the matzoh, on Passover. To remember. But Pharaoh changed his mind and hunted the Jews down in the desert. God saved His chosen people and parted the waters to let them pass from Egypt. Then God destroyed Pharaoh's army.

It's a tale of deliverance. Lottie listens, hoping she will soon have the same good luck to leave Berlin as the Jews had out of Egypt. She wonders why God would save the Jews from Pharaoh but not from the Nazis. Perhaps God doesn't save whole peoples anymore, just in ones and twos, like Lottie, and hopefully Mutti, and maybe this Jew behind the door. Lottie thinks it's good the man wants to remember his ancestors' passage to freedom. If she is saved from the war she too will recall her salvation faithfully the rest of her life.

"It's a wonderful story," Freya says when he is done.

"I pray every day it'll be our story."

"Will boiled potatoes do, Julius? Tomorrow? With some parsley?"

The Jew laughs. It's a nice laugh, ironic and honest. "Yes."

Mutti takes her daughter's hand. She pats it and bounces their bond in her lap. "We'll see this through, don't any of you worry. We're together and we'll make it our story."

The Jew says, "Right." Lottie says nothing. Her mother gives her hand another little shake, to provide the assent for her.

"Lottie?"

She answers the door this time. She will leave Egypt soon and the rest will stay behind. She decides she can be better while she is here. The BPO's season is coming to a close. Some of the musicians listen to illegal radio broadcasts. The *Amis* are on the Elbe. It won't be much longer.

"Yes, Julius?" This is the first time Lottie has said his name.

"I have something for you."

"No. Thank you."

"Please. Let me show you. This will buy food."

Lottie expects him to slide under the door a wad of bills or some precious stones. She's prepared to think of the Jew that he has been hoarding his valuables to the last minute, until they are all on the verge of starvation.

Between her feet and Mutti's slides a cloth yellow star. It is the brand of shame all German Jews were made to wear, before they were taken away.

"When the city falls, anyone with one of these ought to get decent treatment. Even from the Russians."

Lottie stares at the six-pointed star on the floor.

The Jew says, "Sell it, Lottie. It should be worth something good. It's the blood of the lamb."

"No," Freya says. "Julius, no, you have to keep that. Lottie and I are women, we'll be fine. But you're a man, you'll be suspected of being a deserter or something. You need some way to prove you weren't one of them. No."

"Lottie. Take it. For food."

The Jew is right. This will have value. This may be someone else's salvation, someone with money.

"All right."

Lottie scoops the star off the floor. She folds it into her pocket. She'll make Mutti sell it later; Lottie doesn't know how, and Mutti seems to have become an expert in the black market. But she will accept it, and they will get food. Maybe the Jew Julius can have something more than boiled potatoes tomorrow for his holiday.

Lottie says, "Thank you." She puts her hand back into her mother's lap and they twine fingers.

They sit like this without speaking for a while. Lottie closes her eyes, letting her head sag to her mother's shoulder.

The front door jolts under a sudden knock.

Freya and Lottie both start at the sound. They stand, smoothing their skirts in the same way. Lottie walks behind Mutti down the hall to the door.

"Yes?" Freya calls through the door.

"Open up please, *Fräulein*."

"Who is it?"

"Open up, please. It's the police."

The Gestapo.

Lottie shoots a panicked gape at Freya. Her mother holds up both palms and pushes them down, pantomiming calm, hold it in, daughter. Our lives depend on it.

Freya unlocks the door and pulls it open.

"Yes, gentlemen?"

There are four men on the stoop. They wear the black uniforms of the secret police, swastika armbands, hard-brimmed hats. Lots of leather gleams on their hands, feet, and at their waists. They are spick-and-span in a city of filth and destruction.

"*Fräulein*, good afternoon. May we come in?"

All four of them are short and a bit round, pale and blue-eyed, cookie-cutter demons from a white-flour dough. They do not blink. The one speaking puts almost no inflection in his voice. They wear guns on their belts. Lottie wonders which one of these hit the door so hard it rattled on its hinges.

"Yes, of course."

Freya turns aside, Lottie does too, and the four Gestapo men stride inside. Freya leaves the door open behind them. One of the policemen closes it.

The speaker inclines his head to Lottie.

"Ladies. We are searching this neighborhood for volunteers."

The Gestapo must be combing the city to put every remaining man in the *Volkssturm*.

Freya smiles. She even comes up with a laugh. Lottie is amazed at her performance.

"*Mein Herr,* I would've liked nothing better than to have some men here I could give you. It wouldn't have been so lonely for me and my daughter."

The Gestapo men chortle with Mutti, at the ribaldness of her reply. The one who speaks quits laughing first.

"Then you won't mind if we conduct a quick search through your house."

Lottie's lungs squeeze adrenaline. It's over, she thinks.

Tell them! Tell them now, before they find the Jew themselves. They'll go easier on you if you admit it! They'll save your life. Mutti won't do it, never would she tell. Lottie screams at herself, Tell them!

"Feel free, gentlemen." Mutti ushers them into the house. Behind them, Lottie's knees almost give way, she rights herself against the hallway wall.

Freya breezes, "You'll forgive me if I have no tea to offer you."

The Gestapo men wave off the suggestion.

One officer stays in the hall where he can see both front and back doors. The others travel through the house one room at a time. They do not spread out but move in a pack, in case they should happen upon someone tucked in a closet or behind a sofa. One of the policemen proceeds with his hand resting on his pistol at his hip. They first go upstairs. They look in every place a man might hide, under beds, behind doors and furniture. In her bedroom Lottie is even asked to open her cello case. Freya tells them her daughter plays with the Berlin Philharmonic. Lottie receives flirty, raised eyebrows and curt nods.

Downstairs the three search the parlor quickly, there are no good hiding places in this room. Passing along the hall, the speaking officer stops in front of the yellow basement door. He lays a black gloved hand flat on a panel, as though trying to sense what's behind it. The other two make quick work of the kitchen, glancing inside shelves, even drawers. There is nothing in the rear yard, just dead ground.

"Open this," the officer at the yellow door says. "Your basement, yes?"

Mutti moves forward. "Yes."

Now, Lottie thinks. You have one more second to spare your life. Confess! They won't shoot you if you admit! Tell them!

Lottie does not move. Too late. Mutti shows no fear while she swings in the door and precedes the Gestapo down the basement steps. Lottie takes a deep breath, she hears how shaky it is.

Lottie stays up in the hall. In the next second when they haul the Jew up from his lair she will scream that she didn't know! They will take Mutti away, they will take the Jew away. Lottie will claim she had no idea he was down there. The Jew will hear what she says, Mutti will hear too, and they will lie to protect her. No, they'll insist, Lottie did not know. We kept it a secret to protect her. Spare Lottie.

Downstairs she hears her mother slide back the blackout curtains from the lone basement window to let in light. There are no shouts of arrest and accusation. No conversation.

Lottie moves to the head of the stairs. She has not glanced in this open door for months. There is the top step, where the Jew sits. It's a board of wood, empty. She treads on it and then goes the rest of the way down to the last step, into the basement.

The room is crowded with the three Gestapo men, Mutti, and Lottie. The basement is bare, except for a foam mattress on the floor, one cane chair, and a copy of *Völkische Beobachter*, the Nazi newspaper. The paper's bold headline is the death of the American President.

"Sometimes when the air raids come so late," Mutti says, "my daughter and I walk down here instead of going off to the bunkers." Mutti points out the newspaper on the chair. "My reading."

Lottie marvels. Where is the Jew? The Gestapo agents comb through the closet, they tap on the four walls for secret hollow spaces behind them. There is no evidence that a man has lived down here almost every minute for the last twelve weeks. How can this be?

The lead officer purses his lips and casts his eyes around the basement. He picks up the shouting Nazi newspaper.

"That bastard Roosevelt is dead," he says, black-and-white like the paper in his hand.

Freya crosses her arms. "I'd rather it be one of the damned bomber pilots who's dead. I don't care who runs America, just who drops bombs on me."

Lottie thinks her mother talks too much to these vipers. They cannot be charmed.

The officer lays the paper where he found it on the chair. "Yes. Thank you, *Fräulein*. I apologize if we have inconvenienced you."

"Not at all." Mutti replaces the thick curtain, darkening the basement. Lottie pivots on the bottom step and is the first one up. She heads into the kitchen, knowing the Gestapo will go the other way to the front door to leave the house.

"You understand," the speaking officer says, "we must defend Berlin. To the last, if need be."

"Of course," Freya agrees. "Berlin is Berlin, after all."

"I wish you luck, *Fräulein,* you and your lovely daughter. *Heil Hitler*."

"Yes, of course," Mutti says, making some high wave with her hand to approximate a parting salute.

Mutti holds open the door. The four men exit the house. The moment Mutti closes the door behind them, Lottie feels a rupture of control inside her. Her body begins to quiver.

Freya comes to her quickly. She wraps Lottie in her arms, shifting her to sit in a kitchen chair. Lottie feels frozen by the fear that has been an icy torrent through her for the past five minutes. Her quaking worsens in her mother's embrace.

"Liebchen, Liebchen," Mutti soothes, "it's all right. They're gone. Shhhh. It's all right."

After a minute Lottie manages to swallow, her throat eases its constriction. She wrings her hands for warmth, finds it, and nods to her mother. Mutti takes the chair close beside her.

Lottie looks into Freya's face, expecting to find relief and some footprints of withdrawing terror. Mutti's face shines, all teeth and crinkled eyes. Lottie is assaulted again by the awful sense that she is not strong, not brave like Freya, or not magical and invisible like the Jew. She feels like she's been the butt of an appalling joke.

She slaps at her mother's arm.

"Where was he?"

Freya laughs now, that is how she breaks the spell of her fear. She laughs hard, gripping Lottie's leg, slapping playfully back at her daughter. Lottie cannot help it, she doesn't know where the Jew hid and Freya does. She was so scared with the Gestapo in the house, she almost screamed.

"Mutti, goddammit, where was he?"

Freya's mirth slinks away at the curse. She blinks now at Lottie, calmer.

"We couldn't tell you. There are secrets, *Liebchen*, that have to be kept secrets. Always."

"Tell me now."

"Julius and I have always known there would come a time like this. When he would have to hide in the basement. We clean up after every meal. We sweep every bit of dust. He lives without books and papers. I take downstairs a fresh *Völkische Beobachter* every few days, to impress whoever comes looking that we're loyal to their cause."

"Mutti. You should have warned me at least there was a

plan." Lottie does not admit, and will never admit again to herself, that she almost betrayed her mother and Julius. "Where was he?"

"Lottie. You understand."

"Yes, Mutti, yes. I understand. Now tell me. Where was he?"

Mutti leans close. She lowers her voice.

"The foam mattress. Julius and I carved out a man-shaped hole in the back. He pulled it over him and lay down."

Lottie too cannot stop a nervous giggle now. Oh, she thinks, oh dear God, what if one of those Gestapo had kicked the mattress with his foot? What if he'd sat down to ease his feet? Oh.

Lottie shakes again, this time with Mutti, laughing together.

———

April 15, 1945, 1:15 P.M.
Stalin's office
the Kremlin
Moscow

THE AMERICANS, THINKS STALIN, THEY'RE A HANDSOME bunch.

This Harriman, talking so carefully, like a man stepping on floating logs, he's typical. Angular face, not the Asian roundness of the Soviet peoples. Long hands, a cigarette in his fingers looks like an advertisement. Dapper suit cut to perfection, silk kerchief and tie. Patrician face, sweet-tongued even though it is English and Stalin catches only a few words. The Ambassador has the same softness in his vowels that Roosevelt had.

Harriman has come to assure Stalin that the new man, Truman, will carry out all policies put in place by Roosevelt regarding relations with the Soviet Union and the conduct of the war. Stalin has on his desk a batch of black-bordered

Soviet newspapers announcing the President's passing. The eulogies in these papers are authentically sad. Roosevelt was admired here. He was considered a great friend to Russia.

Stalin glances between the two American officials—Harriman and General Hurley—and his own minister Molotov. Throw in the interpreter plus Stalin himself, and the Communists in this room look like dark, squatty peasants beside these attractive and lanky Westerners. Roosevelt was a good-looking chap too. Stalin is sorry to have him dead. Stalin recalls Roosevelt's final telegram, written just hours before the man died in his country cottage. The President was compromising and patient to the end. Generous and forgiving. How did a fellow like that ever become a world leader?

Stalin interrupts Harriman's tiptoeing rhetoric. "Mr. Ambassador, I would like to make a request regarding the passing of President Roosevelt."

"Yes, Marshal, of course."

"I should insist that an autopsy be performed. To assure that this great man was not poisoned."

Harriman chokes a bit on this, he coughs into his hand.

"Marshal Stalin, I promise you the President was not poisoned. The doctors tell me he died of a massive cerebral hemorrhage."

"Yes. Even so."

"Of course. I'll see what I can do."

"Thank you, Ambassador."

For the next half hour Stalin makes the visiting Americans squirm, repeating the charges of a conspiracy going on behind his back between the West and the Nazis. What is the real purpose of those negotiations in Switzerland regarding surrender on the Italian front? Why does it seem the Germans are not fighting as hard in their battles in the West as they do in the East against Stalin's troops? How can it be that German towns in the Americans' path are giving up by telephone, of all things? Is there a larger design to these seemingly unconnected events?

Stalin asks Harriman what show of assurance the United

States needs in order to be confident that the Soviet Union continues to be a faithful ally? Stalin wants to stem the rising tide of suspicion. What can Stalin do to allay America's fears that he is growing uncooperative?

Harriman has an answer ready.

"You might consider allowing Minister Molotov to attend the opening ceremonies of the United Nations in San Francisco."

Molotov now fidgets in his seat. He doesn't want to go. Clearly, the Minister has no desire to be the lightning rod for all the objections to the Red advances in eastern Europe. There will be a burst of voices, led by the English, of course. But the San Francisco conference will be a wonderful chance to size up the new man, this Truman. So, Molotov will go.

Harriman is appreciative.

The Ambassador points to the newspapers at Stalin's elbow. Stalin puts a palm on them in sympathy.

Harriman says, "The United States is moved by your country's show of respect."

"Your President Roosevelt will be missed."

"Yes."

It's well known that Harriman disagreed with Roosevelt at almost every turn in how to deal with Stalin. The U.S. Ambassador has long advocated strength and obstinacy, just like that Churchill. But not Roosevelt, no. Stalin smiles to himself. Roosevelt picked a good time to wither, at least for the fortunes of world communism. The dying President didn't have the physical or mental reserves to be firm; it finally killed him just being pliant. Stalin wishes he'd hung on a little longer. He will miss Roosevelt for reasons perhaps unlike anyone else's in the world.

Stalin says, "Did you see where the Prime Minister adjourned Parliament?"

Harriman nods. "Unprecedented. They met for only eight minutes."

"Yes. A very high honor. Churchill was a good friend to your President."

Harriman lets a black-draped moment hang, like the ink curtains around the news headlines. Then the Ambassador worms his way roundabout to a direct question. Stalin knows where the American Ambassador is headed. He wants to know about Berlin. The last city. The man first compliments the size of the Soviet force gathered on the Oder. He appreciates the Marshal's candid communications with General Eisenhower. He dawdles and dodges. Finally, run out of diplomacy and cover, with Stalin tapping his pipe stem to his lip, Harriman steps into the open: "Marshal, we've heard German radio broadcasts warning the citizens of Berlin of a coming Red Army offensive. Can you tell me something about this?"

"Yes," Stalin says, dismissive in his tone, "there is a Soviet offensive coming. It won't be for several weeks now, of course. It might or might not be successful, who can tell with these things? There is so much to organize. Our forces are so spread out, you understand. The Nazis are well dug in. They have the advantage of the high ground across from our positions. We'll see."

"And what will be the direction of the assault, when it does come?"

Stalin has no problem telling the lie. It is, he thinks, the least of things.

"As I have informed your General Eisenhower, the axis will be southwest, toward Dresden. There is no longer any interest by the Red Army in Berlin. None, Mr. Ambassador."

Stalin stands to end the meeting.

The American Ambassador and general take their leave. The interpreter slips out without remark. Stalin excuses Molotov, who knows better than to squirm again in the presence of foreign visitors when Stalin gives him an instruction. His office empty, Stalin tosses the newspapers in the rubbish.

———————

April 16, 1945, 0240 hours
Küstrin bridgehead
Germany

IT IS TIME TO TAKE BERLIN.

This is handed to Ilya on a slip of paper. It is a short message directly from General Zhukov. Every soldier in every crater, foxhole, and bunker is given one of these.

THE ENEMY WILL BE CRUSHED ALONG THE SHORT-
EST ROUTE TO BERLIN. THE CAPITAL OF FASCIST
GERMANY WILL BE TAKEN AND THE BANNER OF
VICTORY PLANTED OVER IT.

For the last several hours, the whole of Zhukov's assembled army has been creeping forward, with surprisingly little noise, only creaks, rustles, and low rumbles. The huge strike force steps from behind natural cover and beneath camouflage nets, coming alive minute by minute and smelling the attack. With the army coiling on all sides, Ilya and his platoon hunker in a forward trench; as before, he will be one of the first to run into battle.

Yesterday during a Communist rally, Misha joined the Party, along with about half their platoon. He tried to enlist Ilya too.

"Ilyushka, put up your hand."

"No."

"It's just a stupid oath. They make you sign a card. Why not?"

"Why?"

"Because for one, it's the best way to keep moving up in rank. And two, what if we're killed in battle? The Red Army won't notify your family. The Party's the only one that does it, and only for members. Do you want to be forgotten?"

"Yes."

Misha refuses to become exasperated with Ilya. When

Ilya allowed the German prisoner to knock him down on the Seelow plain, Misha got up, took his rifle, and led the way back to their lines. He made no mention of the incident to Ilya or anyone. When Ilya does not speak for an entire day, or sleeps only one hour before sitting up to watch the stars and sunrise, the little man observes from whatever distance Ilya puts between them. When Ilya does not want to join the Party, Misha pats his large friend the way one would pat a boulder that will not be budged from your field, so you let it stay and till around it.

Ilya is never alone. Misha is always hovering for one cause or another. Ilya is one of seven hundred and fifty thousand men in Zhukov's concentrated force aimed at Berlin. There are speeches from commissars, inspections from officers, recruits to train, supplies to haul forward. Always there is someone nearby, noise and smell, rattling activity. But he is isolated. He cannot tell if the world has shrunk or the place inside him has grown. But since the murders on the road, and the citadels, the internal and external worlds feel the same size, in balance. He can wander freely in either as he chooses, and stay indefinitely. When he was a boy he went hunting with his uncle Pavel. They tracked a wolf. They found him and shot him in the morning. The wolf did not die. He did not slow, even with a bullet in the neck. The animal dodged them for two days. Pavel and young Ilya slept on the ground, one always on watch, rifle in the lap. They petitioned food from villagers, hikers, and other hunters they passed. Pavel said you did not leave a wounded wolf on the loose. You had to kill him. The wolf was too dangerous to be left alive. Ilya could not figure why until now. The wolf is in great pain. What can the world do to it that will hurt worse? It will feel nothing less. This makes the wolf more powerful than any creature has a right to be. It will not stop until the pain stops, it will try to heal the pain by hurting other things in its path. The wolf hopes in its simple flaming heart that something will kill it. On the third morning this wolf got his wish. He mauled a farmer's dogs and was blasted by a shotgun when he came for the farmer.

Beside Ilya, Misha smokes like an old frontline hand, cupping the burning end in his palm away from the weather. Ilya has quit the cigarettes. They are too harsh. He has quit vodka too.

Misha takes one long drag, then tears the cigarette in half to stuff his ears. Ilya pulls down his cloth watch cap.

"Five more minutes," Misha says. He aims the words over his shoulder to the platoon of fifty gathered at their backs. A mixture like oil and water emanates from the men, the fear and rage do not blend, each man feels one or the other, none feels both. They cancel one another out in all the platoon except in Ilya, who feels nothing, and scarred Misha, who Ilya thinks has forgotten his fear and is not man enough to feel rage.

The early-morning air is chilly with drizzle and mist. The quilts in Ilya's jacket are sodden. On all sides the lines are silent, the only sound is the snapping of banners. Zhukov ordered all Guards' colors brought forward before the attack. The final meal was thick pea soup with canned pork and hot thermos flasks of tea.

At 0300 hours, three crimson flares pop into the sky. The Seelow plain is bathed in red.

In the next second, like a man emerging from a tunnel into a dazzling day, the world becomes a blaze of light. Every artillery piece arranged behind the troops in the Küstrin bridgehead, every mortar and tank, every bank of *Katyusha* rockets, opens up. They are lined wheel to wheel, one almost every meter, three columns deep, fifteen thousand guns. The muzzle flashes are so constant, they do not flicker, the light around Ilya is that of noon. He shies from the sudden flash, blinking until he's used to it.

The ground where the Germans have their frontline positions seems to lose its gravity, rising on bursting bubbles of fire. Squinting to watch, Ilya cannot find one patch of earth the explosions let rest. Beneath his boots the earth trembles, feverish. The noise is earsplitting; the booming artillery is joined by the high thunder of Soviet bombers making for their targets.

The cannonade goes on and on. It extends deep into the German lines, what looks to Ilya like eight to ten kilometers of killing ground. Ten minutes into the barrage a hot wind whips across Ilya's face, the explosions are so dense, they've created their own atmospheric disturbance. Along the Soviet bridgehead, hundreds of Red banners flap enthusiastically in the false breeze.

After thirty minutes of solid bombardment, a searchlight beams a brilliant girder straight up into the night sky. Immediately, hundreds of multicolored flares burst overhead. This is the signal for the infantry to move out of their trenches and advance. The artillery will shift their fire to a rolling curtain ahead of the charging troops.

It turns out to be another signal as well. Across the Küstrin bridgehead, a hundred and fifty giant antiaircraft lights are switched on, aimed straight across the battlefield at the German positions. The idea is not only to illuminate the ground for the forward troops but to sow confusion and panic among the enemy. The Germans who survived the shelling will have to struggle now with being blinded as well as shocked and deafened. The beams warm the back of Ilya's neck. He steps out of the trench.

The platoon follows at his back. Misha is in his place at Ilya's elbow. Ilya can feel the little man's eyes on him. He does not return the look.

Ilya does not run ahead. He takes one muddy tread at a time, finger resting on the trigger of his submachine gun. He jangles with knifes, grenades, another rifle across his back, but there are no targets so soon. There are on all sides of him only soldiers of his army garishly lit from behind, backs and profiles all green and damp like him, every man waiting for the enemy's response. There hasn't been a shot fired from the Germans since the attack began. Shells continue to pound and pulse several kilometers ahead. The bootsteps of a hundred thousand men make wet noises in the river-fed mud. Ilya senses the surge he is in, a tiny bit of shell swept in a tidal wave. The anonymity of his own footsteps dilutes him, comforts him.

He walks into an eerie nighttime. Every soldier, every mound of debris and whittled-down tree casts multiple shadows from the searchlights. The shadows are long and all spanning ahead so that Ilya cannot tell what is still and what is moving along the ground; he could walk into a German trench and not see it until he fell in. The explosive force of the rolling bombardment continues to heave dust and smoke into the air. Trees and village huts burn on the rims of the plain, adding their smoke to the clouds from the artillery. Those giant lights to the rear strike this fog wall and turn it into a whiteout. The Germans inside the bank will have Russian soldiers silhouetted against the mist, plastered against the searchlights, throwing many shadows onto the fog; the Reds may as well be waving their arms for attention from enemy gunners.

Misha has calculated the same. He calls a young one in the platoon to him. Ilya recognizes the boy as one sent to the punishment company for cowardice.

"Go back and tell them to cut off those lights. We can't see a damn thing up here. Tell them that. Find a general."

"Yes, Sergeant." The boy gushes, clearly glad to be sent back.

Ilya looks down now to Misha and nods. Misha pats him, again, on the back. We're still a team, the touch says. On the spongy ground Misha's shadow cuts as far ahead as Ilya's.

Ilya sends out his other senses. To the rear, he hears the grumble of support tanks and self-propelled artillery. The searchlights and their generators hum with the angry crawling sound of a hive. Behind the lights, on the east shore of the Oder, the rest of Zhukov's hundreds of thousands cheer and plunge across the water.

In fifteen minutes from the start of the assault, Ilya's platoon walks one thousand meters from their trenches. There has been no response from the Germans. Ilya sees no bodies in the smoldering crater pits, his platoon enters the charred relics of bunkers and fortifications to find them empty.

"They've figured us out," Misha says. "They've pulled back to their second line of defense."

The terrible rain of shells fell on open land. The Germans wait in the cloud, looking down from the Seelow Heights, in full strength.

The searchlights switch off. An audible groan rises from the ten thousands on all sides. As one man, they come to a halt, blinded by the sudden shift.

In moments the lights flash back on. Ilya imagines the yelling going on in some general's headquarters. The lights are a bad idea, but they are the bad idea of someone powerful.

He presses ahead, the platoon trailing, Misha on his flank. For the next twenty minutes, the lights go on and off as more irate commanders in the field order them shut down and some offended general argues to keep them burning. Ilya has walked for thirty minutes and heard or seen nothing yet from the enemy. At two thousand kilometers, with the lights off at the moment and the dust cloud thickening the dark, he stumbles into a drainage ditch. He manages to break his fall before he lands on his chest, but he is soaked and mud-caked from the knees down. Behind him, Misha halts the platoon. In the night, unseen to their right, other men crash down in the slit and curse.

Ilya slogs across and scrambles up the other side of the ditch. He continues to walk without a word. Misha leads the men splashing through.

They are two kilometers from their rear lines now, and the terrain has changed. Streams and canals dice their path. The blinking searchlights have finally gone off in this sector—some officer put his foot down or took a pistol and shot out a few.

The going grinds to a slow probe forward. Support tanks which have left the roads to accompany the infantry are stymied by the many obstacles and cuts in the plain. The soldiers who charged from their positions a half hour ago now have soaked trousers and mud-laden boots. They slip and tumble into invisible moats. The Germans have not used one shell to slow the advance, for the time being letting the earth do their work.

One by one, many of the tanks that can still move begin

to desert the open field, hoping to find one of the few roads leading to Seelow. The men, walking blind into an obscured valley, slow their progress. Layer by layer, the advance bunches up.

Misha lays a hand across Ilya's shoulder.

"Let's wait till dawn, Ilyushka. We can't see what we're doing."

"No."

"Everyone else is stopping. We're losing our tank support."

"I know that."

Without more comment Ilya continues to walk into the brothy night.

Misha overtakes him.

"They'll follow you, Ilya. You know that too."

"Yes. Aren't they supposed to?"

"They'll follow you and get killed. They're not you, Ilya. I'm not you. There's nothing ahead but Germans we can't see. We'll walk behind you right into their guns. You'll keep walking and these men and maybe me will be lying dead behind you. Ilya, no. We've got to wait for sunup."

Misha touches Ilya's arm. Misha behaves lately as though Ilya will not hear him unless there is contact between them, as though words are not a strong enough bridge to where Ilya resides.

"Ilya. Can you wait?"

"All right, Misha."

"The Germans will wait for you, I promise."

Misha turns to lead him back to the platoon. He laughs over his shoulder.

"That's because they don't know you're coming."

Misha orders the men to take out their ground cloths and settle in. Dawn is two hours off.

Waiting for the sun, Ilya listens to the battle that is not taking place. All around in the dusty, pitch night, Red forces flounder in the muck and crisscrossing streams. On the leading edge where Ilya's platoon waits, almost no forward progress is made; behind them the masses of men and machines wad up into an uncoordinated morass. The assault on Seelow has come unwound before the Germans have pulled one trigger anywhere on the plain.

At dawn the weather shows it will be a bright spring morning. Ilya stands on knees creaky from the damp. Men grunt when Misha prods them with his boot.

Ilya turns a full circle, surveying the situation on the Oderbruch. Six kilometers ahead, the Heights wait. The Germans there have a commanding view of the entire Red attack. They can pick their targets. In the near distance behind and beside him, Ilya spots those targets as easily as will the enemy: tanks, self-propelled artillery, and trucks clogging the roads, jammed at intersections, stuck in mud and streambeds. Infantry by the ten thousands are bunched behind them. Three-quarters of a million men and their machinery are trying to squeeze into this marshy valley. Ilya looks into the clearing sky. He sees himself with the clarity the German gunners can see him. With a jangle of weapons, he moves forward.

"Let's go," Misha shouts behind him. "Up, up, up!"

Within minutes the Germans on the Seelow Heights unleash their guns. The Oderbruch rocks again, but this time the shells fly into the Soviet lines. Ilya's platoon forges ahead, just fifty men out of ten thousand in the van of the assault. Artillery rounds rocket past to strike at the mired bulk of the offensive behind them. The whooshing of shells overhead makes a hissing canopy, like trees rustling before a storm.

The ground here is drier, the sun is up, and the platoon makes better time. They draw some attention from the enemy, diving to the ground a dozen times from artillery potshots at them. They advance like this for another hour, walking while trying to discern from the scrubbing sounds overhead which shell is aimed at them. But the German guns are mostly occupied trading jabs with Soviet artillery and bombers. Ilya leads the men straight at Seelow.

They are stopped two kilometers from the slopes at the bank of a flooded canal.

"The Haupt Canal," Misha says, displaying his ability to

recall maps. Ilya looks up and down the length of the ditch, fifty meters wide. The swollen green water in it runs fast. Two hundred meters to the right there's a stone bridge across. Another bridge is far to the left.

Ilya takes a step in the direction of the closer bridge. Another group of soldiers is already crossing it.

"Wait," Misha says. "Ilya, no. Watch."

In that moment the bridge is engulfed in a hail of fire and concussion. The squad on the bridge is dismembered and flung off the bridge.

"The Germans are going to have every one of these crossings presighted," Misha says. "What do you think, they're going to let us walk right up to them?"

Below Ilya the canal water rushes by reddened. Bodies and bits float past as a warning to those downstream to stay off the bridge there too.

Shaking his head, Misha says, "We'll have to wait for the engineers to bring up a crossing."

Ilya looks back across the plain, and the tangle that is the Soviet offensive. The engineers will have a devil of a time getting up here through that.

Ilya sits with the platoon, facing the Oderbruch. The screech of shells going to and from the Heights is an awesome canopy overhead. The Germans try to knock out the Oder crossings where the main body of the Soviet army still masses, waiting to enter the fray. The enemy try also to create havoc in the ranks of Red troops making their way across the soggy plain or stuffing themselves onto the few roads. In return, Zhukov's bombers and big guns must eliminate resistance on the Heights so his offensive can sweep onto the road and rail junctions in the town. Once Seelow falls, Zhukov can flank the other towns arranged along the Heights. Not until the long ridge is controlled can he aim for Berlin.

Another three hours pass before the engineers make their way to the canal. For that time Ilya's platoon hugs the ground, ducking shells fired almost straight down on them from the Heights. The morning warms with the hoisting sun, the feeling on the back of Ilya's neck is the same heat that came from the useless searchlights of the predawn launch. Misha rolls and smokes twenty cigarettes. Out on the Seelow plain there must be dead by the thousands, while the living push and shove to go nowhere under the German onslaught.

Finally a call comes to the men waiting near the canal: "We have a bridge!"

Ilya breaks into a run, forcing Misha and the rest to follow. He ignores the sound of his name hollered from Misha's complaining lips. He speeds his pace.

The bridge is on pontoons, wide enough for five men at a time to cross. The engineers begin work on another span a hundred meters downstream. The German gunners have not found the range yet, shells burst wide on either side in the Haupt Canal.

Ilya and the platoon make their way across, crowding the backs of the men in front. The bridge will be down soon, he thinks, judging from the closing distance of the artillery's misses.

But now he's across. The next obstacle will be the Heights itself.

On this side there is nothing between the canal and the foot of the slopes but even ground. Ilya and the platoon run in a pack with the five thousand of their division. After several minutes they enter a field of tall winter wheat, green and silken against Ilya's pumping knuckles. Another two hundred meters ahead the ground rises in a series of low but steep hills. Behind these hills is the point of a spire, a church, the town of Seelow.

The wheat field erupts. Ilya dives, hitting the ground the second a volcano lifts the men at his right into the air and tears them apart. Misha screams to the platoon, "Down, down!"

Ilya rises even before the wet clumps of men have landed around him. He yanks the strap of his submachine gun from his shoulder to put the gun in his hands. It will do him no good, the Germans are embedded in these hills with heavy field guns, well out of range of his weapon or any weapons they have with them on this side of the canal.

Ilya charges hard over the remaining open ground. He hits the slope of the Heights first.

His chest heaves. He bares his teeth. Ilya's legs are still. There's nothing for him to do. It will take more aerial bombardment, more artillery, more men and nightfall before Ilya can move up.

He slams a fist into the hillside. He must wait, again.

<hr>

April 16, 1945, 0930 hours
With the Eighty-third Division,
Ninth U.S. Army
In the Barby bridgehead, on the east shore
of the Elbe River
Germany

BANDY WATCHES THE WORD SPREAD IN THE BRIDGE-head. He takes pictures of the men when it hits.

Mainly officers hear it off the radio. Late yesterday afternoon, Bandy shared a command bunker with three of them, all young college men, when Edward R. Murrow did a CBS broadcast. The correspondent described what he'd seen that morning at a place liberated by Patton's Third Army, a place called Buchenwald. It was a death camp, so horrible that Murrow admitted to his audience that his report strained credulity. He begged his listeners to believe him. In a shaking voice, Murrow concluded by saying he wasn't "the least bit sorry" if he offended anyone with his telling. "I was there," he said.

The two captains and three lieutenants around the radio talked while Bandy took their pictures. Their faces were aghast, lost in wonderment at the brutality and scope of the crime. Officers tend to be the sort of men who need to talk when they hear these reports. Each one of them, and others Bandy has been with, turn to him when he lowers his camera. They get quiet; Bandy is older and they seem to look to him to do some talking, some explaining. He doesn't. Then they pick it up and say, This is why we're here, you see. This is why we have to win.

Out in the field Bandy sees the foot soldiers have a different reaction. They labor over shovels and pickaxes, digging defenses in the bridgehead. They drive trucks and unload supplies. They man forward trenches peering over barrels and sights. Not from radios but fellow soldiers do they hear tales of the ovens, vast piles of civilian bodies, poison showers, they hear about Patton vomiting at Ohrdruf, the liberation of Belsen by the British, the grim walk of Eisenhower himself through the camps. When the men are told, they stop. They bury their spades in the German dirt and lean on the handles. They pull up the parking brake of their vehicles and put both arms over the wheel while their buddy leans in the window and speaks. Most of them spit, saying usually not much more than Fucking Nazis. Jesus. Some add they hope they don't liberate one of them places. Jesus. These American fighting men pause in their work, long enough. Then they get back to it.

Bandy sees that the insanity of the camps is too much for the troops to deal with right now. He records on film their eyes and set mouths while they lay this new knowledge next to the recent death of their President Roosevelt, with mental wreaths and markers they'll revisit another time, when there's less work to be done, less danger contemplated for the next few days. These men have always been resolved to win; the accounts—grim as they are—don't make them more so. But Bandy's camera catches them work a little faster, dig a bit harder. He figures it's got to be for FDR and, sure, for the victims on the radio, just like it's for their parents and sweethearts at home, for their buddies who aren't here anymore and for the ones who are.

Bandy, too, spits. He's seen war, aggregates of death, perhaps more than any one man in any army. But nothing he's witnessed in his nine years as a combat photojournalist in two dozen lands compares in scale and savagery to these reports. Everyone knows the Germans have mistreated the Jews. There have been stories of labor camps, concentration camps. But genocide? Is this modern man's idea of war?

Bandy is revolted. Worse—and this he hesitates to admit—he's deeply disappointed.

He's begun to feel the urge to fight. Today he wants to take a gun and shoot a German, shoot a bunch of them.

His compulsion has always been to observe, to record. For most of his adult life Bandy has digested violence and inhumanity, internalizing them first, then spitting them out through his pictures. How much more, he wonders, can he run through his system before he rots from the inside?

Bandy's surrounded by thousands of weapons. Across the Elbe twenty thousand more rumble his way. Someone will hand him a gun when the shooting starts. It'll be easy.

He knows he's nearing his limit.

He has to get to Berlin.

It's still about history, about taking the photos and getting the headlines. But now it's more. He wants an end, and Berlin is where the end will be.

Bandy's been given his own jeep by the Rag-Tag Circus. He spends his morning driving around the perimeter of the Barby bridgehead, shooting the men and their preparations. In the last twenty-four hours, this tenuous riverside position has become almost impregnable. The Eighty-third Division is powerful just by itself. Now, side by side with them on this shore of the Elbe are the Hell on Wheels boys of the Second Armored.

It sticks in their throats, but the Second Armored got beat to the Elbe by the Circus. Bandy turns his jeep around in the dust and heads to the riverbank, to take pictures of the massive division crossing their rivals' Truman Bridge.

There's been no shortage of gloating by the Circus. Their Barby bridgehead has held. Yesterday the Second made two manful tries to gain a foothold on this shore a few miles to the north. They were evicted by the Germans before they could get their pontoons strung together. The battalion holding the bridgehead was attacked by panzers, and without their own armor to counter were forced back across the Elbe. So far the enemy hasn't attacked this Barby bridgehead. Bandy thinks the bridgehead is already too big and well defended. It'll stand against anything the Germans bring.

The word among the troops is that as soon as the Second has reassembled on this side of the river, these two divisions of the Ninth U.S. will push shoulder to shoulder for Berlin. Overnight, a second bridge has been floated on the Elbe, and with the manpower available from other nearby divisions west of the river, the Americans can quickly assemble a strike force of fifty thousand well-supplied and heavily armed men. The mood in the expanding bridgehead is somber but electric. The sounds are diesel and determined. Bulldozers grade the river slope to flatten paths for the heavy trucks towing big field guns. Bandy's been told that an advance patrol of the Eighty-third has already reached the town of Zerbst, just forty-five miles from Berlin. Ten miles east of this patrol is a big, fat, four-laned *Autobahn* aimed smack at Potsdam and Berlin. The American force gathering along the Elbe appears confident, organized, and unstoppable.

There've been reports that the Reds have started their assault. According to Allied radio they're meeting stiff resistance all along the line, especially outside Seelow. No way, Bandy thinks, are the Germans going to lie down in front of the Russians. They'll fight tooth and nail. But if Eisenhower lets these men of the Ninth push one last time, Bandy believes he can ride a jeep right into the middle of Berlin before the Reds get any traction. The Americans can cover their own fifty miles before the Russians can take their forty. Bandy'd lay that bet with anyone. By tomorrow evening, next day at the latest, he can be filing his pictures and captions from the enemy capital. The war will be over.

He pulls the jeep up on the riverbank. He takes out the Speed Graphic and a dozen film packets. Across the Truman Bridge and its cohort span, the Second is a slow-moving giant. As a barb, the impatient men of the Circus took one of the buses they confiscated from Barby, painted it red with yellow flames at the wheel wells, and offered it to the Hell on Wheels division as a token to hurry them up. Bandy heard the rumor that the Second stuck a tank round in it.

Bandy catches images of GIs crowded onto the beds of half-tons and hanging like barnacles off of tanks. Passing his jeep at the foot of the bridge, they wave and shoot Churchill's V for Victory. A lot of the soldiers shout, "Hi, Mom!" at his camera. The men and boys crossing the Elbe buoy Bandy's spirits. The Second looks like a proper army division, without the mishmash of private vehicles the Eighty-third has pressed into service. Bandy admires the verve of the Rag-Tag Circus, but the sight of a classic armored column rumbling into Germany girded to the teeth is awesome. He finishes the last of his Speed Graphic film, then stows the camera. He sits in the jeep and waves back, watching the Hell on Wheels Division come.

After half an hour Bandy notices the gaps between the vehicles widening. Gradually the phalanx across the two bridges slows to a trickle. By his reckoning the Second Armored should take at least until midafternoon to haul itself across the river and form up in the bridgehead. What's the holdup? There's less than a third of the division on this side of the river.

Bandy gets out of the jeep and hails a covered supply truck, one of the few vehicles on the Truman Bridge.

The truck slows. Bandy climbs up on the running board.

"Hey," he asks the driver, "where's the rest of you guys?"

The driver shrugs. He yanks a dirty thumb over his shoulder.

"Back there."

"Aren't they coming? Isn't the Second supposed to get across?"

The driver shrugs again.

"Thought we were."

"What happened?"

"Somebody pulled the plug."

Bandy looks away from the driver, across the river. There's only one other truck on the way, and it's behind them, tooting his horn.

"What happened?" Bandy asks again. "What about Berlin?"

"Don't know. Somebody pulled the plug is all."

Bandy almost loses his grip on the truck's windowsill.

The driver shrugs a last time.

"Gotta go, pal. Hey, take my picture?"

Bandy steps down. "Hey," the driver shouts, pulling away, "will ya?"

Bandy waves him off.

The driver guns his engine to move ahead of the crowding truck at his bumper, the last truck on either bridge.

Bandy gets in his jeep and heads across the Truman Bridge. Twenty minutes ago, this was unthinkable, going this direction. The U.S. Army was charging the other way.

On the west bank, Bandy wants to flail the jeep around Barby to reach the town hall and the Eighty-third Division's command post. Instead, he has to pick his way between tightly packed cars, trucks, tanks, the odd transports of the Rag-Tag Circus jammed into town all waiting for orders to shove off for the *Autobahn*. They crowd the streets, sidewalks, alleys, even yards. The heavy vehicles of the Second are not standing in line before the two bridges; they're nowhere to be seen, banished outside town where there's room. Bandy's impatience for an answer mounts with every clotted avenue that forces him farther from the town center. He abandons the jeep, grabs his camera sack, and stomps. His healing thigh pounds and his shoulder aches under the weight of the shoulder strap. These things have left him alone for the past week. They hurt now.

Someone pulled the plug? Berlin's half a day away. Fifty miles! Two full divisions can be across the Elbe in a couple more hours, with another one or two divisions across by nightfall. They can be rolling up gains before dawn, positioned on the outskirts of the capital at sunup with manpower, firepower, supplies. The Russians are bogged down, the Germans are desperate to keep them away from Berlin.

Who pulled the plug?

The closer Bandy gets to his answer, the more certain he is of what he will hear.

"Ike," a major in the town hall tells him.

"Ike," Bandy repeats.

"Word came down this morning. We're to consolidate the bridgehead but not expand it."

"Why?"

The officer spits. He looks down to see that he has done this indoors, in his own office. He leaves it.

"Mr. Bandy, I'm a soldier. I don't get to ask why. If I did ask, I wouldn't get told. Pure and simple."

Posted on the wall behind the major is a map. Blue vertical lines have been drawn to mark the projected progress and checkpoints of the Ninth U.S. Army between the Elbe and Berlin. There was a plan.

"Mr. Bandy," the major says, shaking a cigarette from an almost empty pack; he offers one over. "I can't say what I think of this decision to stop at the Elbe. But I dearly would like to hear somebody else say it out loud."

Bandy accepts the match to the tip of the cigarette. He takes in the smoke, the major does the same, and they cloud the quiet space between them. Bandy fills it.

"It's the stupidest fucking thing I have ever heard in my entire life."

The major waits. He rolls the cigarette in his fingers.

"I guess the war's over for us," he says.

Bandy brings the cigarette to his lips. It's something familiar, it keeps his hands and mouth busy while his gut grows queasy.

"But I'll tell you," the major says, turning to his map.

He sticks a finger hard into the heart of the city.

"It ain't over for Berlin. The Reds are gonna tear that place to pieces."

April 16, 1945, 2:50 P.M.
Goethe Strasse
Charlottenburg, Berlin

LOTTIE HUGS HER MOTHER LIGHTLY. SHE DOESN'T WANT to betray herself with a tight embrace. Mutti will ask what is wrong.

"Goodbye, *Liebchen*," her mother whispers, her mouth close to Lottie's ear. "Play your best today."

Lottie straightens from their clasp. She wears a man's dark suit. Mutti reaches up to align her daughter's tie in the shirt collar, then smooths her hands down Lottie's shoulders and arms. In the month since the BPO's tuxedos were shipped south into the path of the *Amis,* Lottie and Mutti have struggled to learn how to knot a man's tie. Julius has tried to teach Mutti but she cannot master it.

"Ach," Mutti says, unhappy, reaching again for the knot.

"It's fine," Lottie reproves her mother, "leave it. It doesn't matter."

Freya drops her hands. Lottie notes on her mother's face a quick lecture rise, then Mutti restrains it, the one about how everything matters. Mutti steps back to signal she will accept her daughter's appearance and Lottie may leave for her concert.

"Mutti."

Lottie gazes at her comely mother.

The Russians began their attack on Berlin in the early-morning hours. Everyone knows it. People in the eastern reaches of the city woke to the distant thunder of artillery. Immediately they jammed what telephone lines still work into Berlin. The *Mundfunk,* the Berliner "mouth radio," took over and word spread. Early this afternoon, the real radio officially announced the opening of the Soviet assault from the Oder, forty miles east of Berlin. In the west, the radio trumpets, the Americans have been halted at the Elbe River.

All day Mutti and Lottie have not spoken of the dire news. This morning, on the way to fetch water, the neighbors they passed did not natter among themselves. Everyone strode to their business in steely German reserve. But people did not greet mother and daughter with the usual "Hello" or "Good morning, ladies." Now Berliners say to each other, *"Bleib übrig."* Survive.

An hour ago a note was delivered to Goethe Strasse. Lottie read it privately. She's been summoned again to Dr. von Westermann's office at the Philharmonie before today's concert. Lottie lied to her mother about the message, claiming it was to alert her that she'll be playing second chair today; the elderly second cello has taken sick. Lottie must arrive early to practice the part. Upstairs she got dressed. She packed an extra sweater and a hairbrush in the hard shell case around her cello.

Now Lottie tries to tell her mother goodbye.

"Yes?" Freya prods after waiting for Lottie to finish whatever it was she'd begun to say.

"Mutti, will you . . . will you take care?"

Freya breaks into a gentle smile. "Yes, *Liebchen.*"

"Have you sold the yellow star yet?"

"No. I'm waiting."

"Don't wait anymore. Sell it today."

"Stop worrying, Lottie. The Russians won't be here for a while." Freya presses a hand to her daughter's cheek. "There's time for us. We'll all be fine, you'll see."

"And don't do any more silly things. Like that awful horse. What if I hadn't been there to drag you away?"

"But you were."

"Well, please, don't."

"I'll try, *Liebchen.* Nothing silly the rest of the day."

Lottie swells with her departure from Berlin, from this house, from the peril that will descend on both. She wants to tell Mutti the truth: today is the last BPO concert. She will get on a bus at dusk and ride west to the Americans. She will not be here to share the danger, not be here to protect her trusting, good mother. Lottie is to be the one protected.

She swears inwardly she will come back the first moment she can. She careens her eyes around the parlor, at the furniture and walls she leaves behind, upstairs to her room. Down the hall, to the yellow door.

What can he do?

He must look out for himself. He can't safeguard Mutti.

"Lottie?"

"Yes?"

"Are you scared?"

"Yes, Mutti. I am."

Freya lays her breast against Lottie's. She takes her daughter in her arms.

"You'll play wonderfully. Second chair can't be that much harder."

"No."

"There." Freya kisses her on the nose. She steps back and takes in the sight of her daughter in a business suit. "I always feel like a little housewife sending you off like this."

Lottie smiles. Freya—the way she always does—goes further and laughs.

"Mutti."

"Yes, my husband."

"Tell the Jew—" Lottie stops. "Tell Julius goodbye for me."

Freya cocks her head. She grins, figuring this is some small victory.

"Of course, I will. Yes. He'll be very proud of you."

Lottie will stand here and continue to let dribs and drabs of farewell and concerns and clues slip from her lips. She has to go.

Lottie lifts the cello. Freya opens the front door and she steps outside. Freya stays inside the hall, one hand high on the door, ready to close it when Lottie turns to go. Mother and daughter stand separated, not moving farther apart.

The day harbingers spring. Blackbirds tweet on the roofs and in the rubble, there are no branches for them to sing from. A vast blue sky invites the birds into it. Lottie feels the tug of the day. Come away.

She turns from her mother's eyes and takes another step. Behind her the house shuts.

Lottie lugs the cello five blocks to a tram station. Along the way Berliners stand in line for what provisions or clothing are available, they gossip and grouse like always. Folks keep their heads up on the sidewalks heading to offices, shops, and mills. The trance of normalcy is only broken when twice old women smile at Lottie hauling her cello case in her man's suit. The smiles are sad and concerned. They both reach to touch Lottie passing. The women mumble to her, *"Bleib übrig."*

The tram heads for the Tiergarten and the BPO's offices. Demolished buildings make up much of the landscape outside her window. On remnants of walls appear painted slogans that were not there yesterday. "Berlin will remain German." "Victory or Slavery!" "Believe in Hitler." Painted by children, Lottie thinks, the ones holding a paintbrush in one hand, a gun in the other, and a sack lunch from their mother in their pocket.

At the Philharmonie, Lottie goes directly to Dr. von Westermann's office. She pulls her cello behind her through the doorway when he calls out to answer her knock.

The orchestra manager does not rise from his chair. His office is stacked high with sheet music. It looks to Lottie like the manager and his staff are preparing to hide it all away.

"Lottie," he says. "Sit down."

She sets the cello against the wall, then takes the chair in front of his desk.

"You got my note. Good."

"I'm ready" is all Lottie says.

"Yes. No doubt you must be. You've heard the reports."

Lottie nods.

"Lottie."

"Yes, sir?"

"There has been a change in the situation."

Her stomach jumps.

"What?"

Von Westermann opens his hands and taps the fingertips

together. He waits for Lottie to calm. He cannot have a woman raising her voice in his office about a conspiracy.

"I'm sorry," Lottie says. She makes fists and squeezes both of them between her trouser legs. "Please."

"I continue to misjudge your reactions, my dear. That is my failing, not yours. In any event, please hear me out."

Lottie swallows. "Yes, sir."

"The advertised program for today's performance is just as you rehearsed. Beethoven's Egmont Overture. The Brahms Double Concerto. And Strauss's *Tod und Verklärung*."

Von Westermann motions to the stacks of music on his office floor.

"These have been removed from the orchestra's stands. The new program for today is at the suggestion of Minister Speer. You will play his favorites, all music the orchestra is well familiar with. Beethoven's Violin Concerto and Bruckner's Romantic Symphony. But first, you will open with *Die Götterdämmerung*."

The death of the gods. The end of the world.

"The signal," she says.

Von Westermann taps his fingertips again, scrutinizing Lottie's reaction. She says no more.

"Yes. This afternoon is the last concert of the BPO until the end of the war. You have obviously guessed as much."

"Yes, sir."

"But as I mentioned, there has been a change in our plan."

Lottie licks her lips.

The manager says, "There was a vote."

"What? When?"

Von Westermann lifts one finger, not to his lips, but it is still there to shush her.

"Yesterday. Only those who've been told about the plan were called in."

"What about me?"

"You were not."

Lottie's hands wring in her lap.

"There was no reason to invite you, Lottie. It is clear how you would have voted."

"On what?"

"The orchestra will not be leaving Berlin."

Lottie is rammed into the chair. Her breath is taken away, her lungs claw for more air.

Von Westermann continues. "The vast majority have decided to stay. For family or sentiment. Many reasons. In light of the vote, I will be staying as well."

Lottie's mouth works. The shock owns a weight across her shoulders and legs. Her wrists feel strapped to the chair arms. Tears squeeze to her eyes.

The manager raises a lone finger again. This time he waggles it in the air, as though to erase something written there he did not intend.

"Lottie, dear, no, no, no. I should have said first. You may still leave."

She gasps, yanked too fast in different directions.

"I can . . . I . . ."

"Yes, dear. After the concert tonight, Minister Speer's adjutant will be waiting in a car outside the Beethoven Hall. Gerhard Taschner will be leaving in it with his wife and two children. Also the daughter of another violinist, Georg Diburtz. They will head southwest to Bayreuth, where last month we sent the instruments and tuxedos. The American army is already there. I have set out the Wagner piece just in case any of the musicians change their minds."

Von Westermann purses his lips, recalling the meeting where it was determined by the musicians to stay and face the Russians. "Though I doubt any will."

"There will be a car?"

"Yes. You and your cello may get in it when the concert is over."

Lottie wants to ask several more simple questions. We will leave Berlin? It will be tonight? The Americans are already there? She wants to be certain this awkward von Westermann has not misstated or left anything else out.

The manager opens his hands. "Well."

"They're staying."

"Yes, Lottie. The Berlin Philharmonic Orchestra is staying."

Lottie takes this thought into the hall with her cello. How can these old men do this? Speer has gotten them exemptions from the *Volkssturm*, yes. But there are no free passes from bombs and bullets and artillery shells. Or from the SS animals who'll come looking for "volunteers."

Young concertmaster Taschner knows he must escape. The others are staying, so there's room for his family. And Diburtz sends his daughter away. They are both smart men. Not cowards at all. Realists.

Lottie thinks she could run home and grab Mutti. There is room in the car to Bayreuth. And if there is not, she can leave behind the cello. But Mutti will not go. There's no point in imagining she will.

Lottie is late to the Beethoven Hall. Most of the orchestra has already assembled on stage when she enters. One hundred and five musicians handle their instruments. The tubas and basses wrangle into place, violins bow long tuning notes, French horns and trumpets warm their cold brass valves. Woodwinds play fast and flighty little solos. Lottie dances her cello through the forest of music stands, knees, and bells, careful not to knock anything over or dent the Galiano. She receives nods or nothing from the occupied, seated men.

Lottie does not know who among the orchestra is aware of the escape plot. Tuning her Galiano, she watches faces. Who complains about the change in program for today's concert? Who smiles at her in a secretive, parting way? Who sits up straighter, sets his chin, knowing he plays his last concert before the fall of the city?

At five o'clock the concert begins. The baroque red-and-gold auditorium is filled. Minister Speer sits erect in his accustomed center seat of the first row. Von Westermann watches from a box with his wife. Everyone in the audience wears overcoats; the Beethoven Hall is not heated. The vast room is lit only by the ocher candescence of candles—normally at this time of day the electricity in Berlin is cut—but the lamps on the musicians' stands glow. Speer must have worked some final magic for this concert.

Conductor Robert Heger walks on stage through applause. When he takes up his baton and mounts the riser, the house hushes. Lottie readies her bow with the other cellos. She prepares herself to play her finest, like Mutti wants.

Now, before Heger raises his hands to begin the concert, Lottie sees, almost as if they glow, who knows. Thirty, forty, almost half the orchestra, every man who voted to stay and share the fate of Berlin lifts his head, works his jaw even behind his mouthpiece, many of them sniff back tears, several let tears roll down their cheeks. Lottie breathes in the bouquet of emotion when Heger lifts the baton.

The drums begin, tragic and slow, a dirge. The tubas respond. The joined basses add their depth. With grand sweeps Heger brings the full orchestra alive to tell Wagner's tale of the gods' evildoing, the funeral of the hero Siegfried, the devotion of Brunhild who on horseback climbs her lover's burning pyre to join him in death, the demise of the gods and the destruction of all Valhalla and the world.

Lottie plays with freedom and precision. For the first time she hears not her own notes but the whole, the passion of the orchestra. For stretches Lottie closes her eyes and bows, even during some passages she did not know she'd memorized. Her place in the music, in the moment, is so deep she is carried by it, her heart knows what to play.

The BPO pounds on *Die Götterdämmerung,* almost as though the piece were an actual signal, a giant bell to be rung in a steeple, an alarm. When they are finished, the applause from the house is the greatest Lottie has ever experienced. It takes five minutes to climax. Musicians on all sides of her exchange glances, some touch hands, there is the breathlessness of a feat accomplished.

The concert proceeds quickly, lacking the majesty of the Wagner. Twenty-three-year-old Taschner plays the solo in Beethoven's Violin Concerto without his usual bravura. He seems distracted and worn. Perhaps the concertmaster's departure with his family is not viewed by the other musicians as such a noble deed. In any event, the Beethoven symphony is acquitted as a matter of rote by the orchestra.

Heger waves the final note. The audience rewards the BPO with warmth but nothing like what followed the *Twilight of the Gods*. That performance was memorial, Lottie will recall it for the rest of her life. The director points his baton at Gerhard Taschner to accept his applause as soloist. Taschner takes a long, last bow. Then, violin in hand, the concertmaster departs the stage.

Is he leaving now? Isn't Taschner staying until the end, for the Bruckner? The concertmaster is gone. Lottie looks into the front row, where Minister Speer stands clapping at the edge of the stage in a tan, belted overcoat. The Minister returns Lottie's gaze. His lips form a silent word. Go.

Lottie's eyes dart through the dim house to von Westermann's box. The fat orchestra manager halts his own applause to hold out one hand, like a man ushering her to a seat. There, the gesture says, there is the way out. Take it. Now.

Heger turns his baton to the orchestra, to lift them from their seats for a bow. All the musicians stand. To Lottie's left, a trim little cellist with magnificent veined hands, Herr Kleber, takes hold of her Galiano.

"That'll slow you down, dear. I'll watch it for you."

On her right, another voice hones in under the applause.

"Start coughing. Start crying. Do something, girl. Run offstage."

Heger keeps the orchestra standing. The applause begins to wane, he cannot leave them on their feet but for a few seconds more. Lottie must turn and exit.

Heads pivot. Faces glower at her. The director puffs out his cheeks.

Lottie looks into the hall lit in faint yellow tones. She thinks of Mutti. Did she sell the yellow star?

She takes a deep breath.

"Herr Kleber."

"Yes, dear?"

"Thank you."
Lottie reaches for her cello.
She sits.

═══════

April 16, 1945, 11:40 P.M.
Stalin's office
the Kremlin
Moscow

HE SNATCHES THE RED PHONE THE INSTANT IT RINGS.
   "Yes. This is Stalin."
   "Comrade Stalin. This is Zhukov."
   "General. Report. Have you taken Seelow yet?"
   Zhukov pauses.
   "No, Comrade. Not yet."
   Stalin taps the bowl of his Dunhill pipe on the table.
   "Why not, General?"
   Stalin has given this hero of Moscow, Kursk, and Stalingrad every opportunity, every spare man and machine. Zhukov has the straightest path into Berlin. A ten-to-one advantage over the enemy in firepower. He has everything. And he cannot take one town on a hill.
   At three this afternoon Zhukov called the Kremlin to report. His progress against the Heights is grinding. By midmorning the Red Air Force had shut up many of the guns on top of the Heights. Portions of Chuikov's Eighth Guards penetrated the first two lines of German defense at the foot of the slope. But the third line, dug into the slope itself, has proven tough to crack. Chuikov can't get tanks or self-propelled guns up the steep grade. The only way into Seelow itself is along the roads, and every meter of them is controlled by heavy fortifications plus the remaining artillery on the hill.
   At noon Zhukov lost patience. Against the agreed battle plan, he committed his two tank armies, both of which were to be kept in reserve until the Heights was taken. Zhukov set

loose almost fourteen hundred tanks and SP guns to charge ahead of Chuikov's infantry columns. Zhukov would smash his way to Seelow.

This was the last Stalin heard. He waited all day for word.

Now he hears: No. Not yet.

"Tell me why not."

"The German resistance has stiffened on the Heights. We are attacking through the night, Comrade."

"You are attacking with your two tank armies?"

Again, Zhukov hesitates to respond. Stalin fills the gap.

"I remind you, General, that was not your instructions. You should not have sent the First Tank Army into the Eighth Guards sector instead of where and when you were ordered. Those tanks were to be held until Seelow is taken, then used on the plateau to Berlin. You've ordered them in too early. And now you report they have failed."

In his mind Stalin pictures Zhukov lift his nose and swell his chest at that word, *fail*.

"Comrade Marshal, we will take Seelow tomorrow."

"Tell me how this happened today."

Zhukov explains: The emergence of the tanks from the Küstrin bridgehead snarled movement all across the Oderbruch. Chuikov's infantry and towed artillery were forced off the roads by the advancing tanks. The boggy ground and many streams slowed the momentum of the assault. There are still many uncleared minefields. Nothing moved fast. The enemy artillery on the commanding bluffs was particularly effective in this setting.

Zhukov has issued new orders to regroup and reorganize his artillery and scattered armor. In addition, at this moment eight hundred Soviet bombers hammer German positions on the Heights to deny the enemy rest and take out more of their artillery. Advance groups of Chuikov's Eighth Guards have already entered the town's outskirts and soon will take control of several houses at key road approaches.

Stalin does not hear any report from his general on casu-

alties. Zhukov assumes, correctly, that Stalin is not interested.

Zhukov says, "By midnight we should have a foothold."

Stalin looks at his watch. He is not impressed with a
foothold in Seelow. He wants Berlin. "Are you sure you will
take the Seelow Heights tomorrow?"

"You have my assurance, Comrade Stalin. Tomorrow."

"I will expect confirmation of that."

"Comrade."

Stalin adopts a weary tone.

"Yes."

"This might not be entirely a bad thing."

"What do you mean?"

"The more troops the enemy throws in to counter us in
Seelow, the quicker we'll be able to take Berlin. It will be
easier to destroy their forces here on an open battlefield than
in a fortified city."

"This is not sounding easy, General."

"No, Comrade."

Stalin thinks it is time to put away the crop and take out
the lash.

"Koniev is making very good progress."

Zhukov clears his throat.

"Excellent."

"We have been thinking of ordering Koniev to swing
both his tank armies from the south toward Berlin. Also, it
might be a good idea to have Rokossovsky speed up crossing
the Oder to strike at Berlin from the north."

Stalin hears nothing from the phone. Again in his mind
he sees proud Zhukov grimace under the stripe of the whip.
Zhukov wants Berlin, his page in military history. Stalin
doesn't care who takes the damn city, just take it.

"General."

"Comrade, I agree that Koniev's force might make such a
maneuver at this time. However, I must advise, the northern
army could not possibly mount an attack on Berlin for at
least another week."

The point is made, Stalin thinks. Do not beat the mule too much, or he won't sting enough when you do.

Whoever's standing near this mule is going to hear him bray and perhaps get a swift kick. Right now.

"General."

"Yes?"

"Da svidaniya."

Stalin hangs up.

TEN

MEN DIE BY THE LIGHT OF BURNING TANKS.
Ilya does not hear his own running boots or his
heaving breath, not the weapons bouncing on his
back and at his waist. The wrench of steel and the sizzle of
gunpowder forge a gauntlet of pandemonium on all sides.
He lowers his head and bolts through it. He waits for the rip
of shrapnel into his body, somewhere, and readies himself to
keep running even after it hits.

The surprise and stealth of night are gone, there is so
much flame around. Troops and tanks alike are blasted by
German 88mm and 155mm guns, firing over open sights at
point-blank range. Tanks reel off the road one after another.
Many explode and never move again; tanks behind have to
shove them out of the way or maneuver around them across
the slope. Men pour out of hatches to escape frying inside
their armor; lit by the flaring of their machines, many are
shot down by small arms fire and machine guns.

Ilya dodges but keeps his direction, north across the face
of this last hill. He doesn't fire his gun, doesn't even have it in
his hand. This is not his fight. These tanks have been ordered
up here where they have no business trying to wage an
infantry-style battle. Ilya's company has been sent elsewhere,

into the northern rim of Seelow. This flaming, useless battle of giants lies in their path.

The only thing human Ilya hears is Misha's voice. The little sergeant belts, "Go! Go!" at Ilya's back. Misha runs very fast when there is shooting. Ilya does not speed up, even with Misha nearing at his heels. No matter how methodically Ilya travels through the battle, Misha will not get in front.

Ilya leads his platoon to every broken, burning tank in his way, dashing from one to the next. The Germans turn their fire away from these targets to concentrate on more prominent enemies. What Ilya sees makes him glad he's always been a foot soldier; he is nimble next to these behemoths. He's a smaller mark, harder to kill. In his experience, in this kind of close-quarters fight, one man on the loose is more dangerous than any tank.

It takes eight minutes to reach the other side of the skirmish. Ilya squats behind a rock outcropping. He catches his breath and waits for Misha and the rest of the platoon to assemble. The battle sounds like a blacksmith's shop, the clouting of metal against metal—*p-tang!*—the warble of flames, woofing guns. The platoon rushes to the safety of the rock and the shadows, some arrive shaking their heads. Ilya counts. There are forty-four left of the fifty he started with this morning. Three of the men did not make it past the Haupt Canal, three more did not last through the tanks tonight. In between, the platoon spent the day lying flat against the Seelow slope, not able to move ahead and drawing little attention from the Germans. They were ordered to wait for nightfall, then enter the town.

Ahead of them are the seared remains of a small wood. The grade here is gradual. If they move with care, the platoon can blend with the charcoaled trunks. Ilya doesn't know where the rest of the company is; the other hundred men may still be mired back in the firefight alongside the tanks. They'll make their way when they can. His forty-five will push on into Seelow.

Another five hundred meters, at the crest of the road

they just ran across, stand their objectives. Three stone buildings flank the paved entry into the town. So long as these structures remain in German hands they make access into town impossible for those tanks that survive the night. By daybreak, Ilya's company must control all three buildings. His platoon must take one.

Ilya checks the men. He readies himself to move into the trees.

"Sergeant Bakov."

Misha slides closer. The scar across his cheek and the missing lobe sometimes make Misha look unpredictable, like an ill-tempered little dog, a biter.

"Yes, Ilya?"

Misha has not yet called him "Lieutenant."

"When we reach the top of the street, we divide by squads into four storm groups. We take the first house facing the slope. Leave the others."

"Got it."

"You remember the street-fighting lessons?"

"Yes."

"Top floor. Middle floors. Then ground floor."

"Yes."

"Attack from all directions possible."

"I know."

"You'll lead one of the squads."

"Me? I . . . Ilya . . . I thought you and I would . . ."

"You, Misha."

Ilya stands. Misha stays crouched.

"Give them their orders, Sergeant. Then let's move."

Misha looks off into the dark. The little man nods as if to some fate he has displeased and now must agree to serve. Ilya turns his eyes to the ruined forest. He picks a path through it, again heading for the spots of greatest devastation. This reduces the chance of trip wires and unexploded mines.

He waits for Misha to round among the men, explaining their task and giving assignments. Ilya will lead none of the squads. He'll work alone as he sees fit. One man, on the loose.

Misha returns.

"The men understand."

"Good."

"Ilya."

Ilya licks his lips at another pause for Misha.

"What."

"Pretty soon this is all going to be over, you know."

Ilya considers this. He's lost touch with that thought, of the war being over. In the past four months he's done the job at hand, killing those Germans set out before him. He's accepted promotion and leadership duties without letting those things interfere. Ilya has little faith that war will allow him to see its end, no matter how many dead pile up, no matter how faithfully he serves its purpose. After Berlin there will be more enemies. The Americans. The Poles. The Japanese. Maybe Russian against Russian. Who knows? Someone. The notion of no war eludes him.

"Before we're done," Misha says, "the day is coming, you know. When you'll follow me."

Ilya lowers his voice.

"You care, don't you. About that sort of thing. Who follows who."

"Yes. I thought you did too. You used to."

Ilya looks behind Misha to the road and fields of burning tanks, he sees a man running in flaming clothes. What difference does it make, when you go into that, who goes first?

He thinks of the sixty prisoners. Which one of them died first? Did he get somewhere faster? Who fired first? Did Misha? Is he more damned or blessed for it?

Ilya brings his eyes back to Misha.

"All sorts of days are coming," he says, hefting his machine gun. "Maybe even that one. Let's move."

Ilya steps away into the trees. The platoon rises behind him, splitting into quarters. Misha fades from his side.

The tramp up the rest of the hill is without incident. The men disappear into the dark, spreading among the stout sticks of trunks. Ilya moves ahead on his own.

One hundred meters from the crown of the road, a

white flare rockets into the air. The men know what to do: sprint forward until the first bullets fly, gain all the free ground you can. Then drop to cover and begin your attack. On all sides of him the platoon races up the hill.

Another flare follows. Ilya lags back, to watch the assault mount on the building. The first reports of German machine guns slap at the men out of the face of the building. The platoon doesn't answer yet. They're still taking ground. Good. Under the flares Ilya sees what they're up against.

The three buildings at the head of the road are arranged around a traffic circle, with a pedestal in the center that likely held a fountain or some statue until a shell found it. Each building is three stories tall. Their roofs have been sheared off by bombs. Some windowsills show soot over them like black eyebrows; they've been on fire, but weren't gutted enough to keep them from being used as fortresses. There's no way these buildings can be surrounded; the center will be a dead zone until at least one of the targets falls. Misha didn't see a map, or he certainly would have known they were arranged in a ring.

Now the platoon opens up. The stones on one face of the facade zing with bullets. Another flare goes up. Ilya spots squads hustling left and right of the building. The windows on the top two floors disappear in a mist of dust and ricochet.

Flares shoot up from the other two buildings. Windows in them flicker with muzzle flashes. The red-spark trail of a *Panzerfaust* flies out of one to blow a hole in the dirt. One of the squads has headed into a cross fire. In minutes they're forced to retreat. Without the rest of the company here to launch assaults on the other buildings, only one face of their target can be covered.

Ilya's seen this before, in Stalingrad. Unless a storm group can attack a building from at least three angles, the defenders can concentrate their force on a few portals. With Ilya's platoon this far out front, there'll be no resupply of ammunition. The four squads will crowd together and slow their assault. Then, it becomes a stalemate.

Ilya rushes forward. He finds Misha's squad firing at the building. They haven't advanced since the first wave of bullets.

"Misha."

Even now, Ilya is returned a strained look. He corrects himself. "Sergeant."

"What's wrong?" Misha is quick to think Ilya has come to reprimand him.

"I've got another job for you. We have to find the rest of the company, or the assault won't work. Tell your squad to save their bullets and hold this position. If we're not back in one hour, another team of two has to go. Tell them, then come with me."

When this is done, Ilya leads Misha back through the ruined wood to the rock outcropping. They settle, again within sight and sound of the raging tank battle.

Misha doesn't wait. He speaks first. "I knew you'd miss me."

Ilya asks, "Where do you think they are?"

Misha points at the Armageddon on the hillside.

"In there. Just stuck. Shooting at shadows. Stupid bastards."

Misha nods again as though to that unseen force that guides his luck tonight. "All right. We have to go back in there. You and me, Ilya."

Ilya lays his machine gun beside the boulder. He pulls the rifle off his back and sets it aside too. Misha follows suit.

Ilya holds Misha's eyes with his own. He puts no expression on his face, but gestures at the shootout, blazing hotter than it was twenty minutes ago when they passed through it.

"After you, Sergeant. I'll follow."

Misha scrunches his brow and waves off the suggestion. He makes no pretense about where he prefers to be in combat.

"Maybe that day isn't here just yet, Ilyushka." The little sergeant chuckles. "But it is coming. How about I run beside you? For once, eh?"

Ilya accepts.

Misha takes a deep breath. "Keep up, big one," he says.

Then, lifting his little rump in the air like a sprinter, Misha begins a comic bellow that mounts in volume, "Aaaaaaaa . . ." until he's in full cry, ". . . AAAAH!" and he takes off into the heart of the battle. Ilya lights out after him.

The next ten minutes are a miasma of heat and crashing clamor. Misha covers twice the distance Ilya does, zipping like a rabbit from rumbling tanks and torched hulks to crouching soldiers, asking every officer he crosses if the man has any idea where the rest of the punishment company is. Ilya works to keep pace. Misha has to cast one eye over his shoulder to hold him in view. It appears the tank assault is progressing, though the snarl of men and machinery causes needless slaughter against the slope. Zhukov's body count for his poor planning and impatience will be weighty. But the Heights will fall. Soviet men and tanks will charge this hill until they do; there's no shortage of either, and no lack of will in the Red Army to count the losses.

The rest of the company is found, just as Misha predicted, caught up in the advance on the hillside next to the tanks, exchanging fire with Germans they can't see or reach. The company suffered the confusion of the whole assault on the Heights. Misha speaks to the company captain, with Ilya looming behind him, and explains the situation at the northern edge of town where the platoon has been stymied, reminding him of the mission. If they don't secure the approach into Seelow, these tanks won't be able to enter even after they take this road.

The company has already lost a dozen of its men. The captain seems glad to get them back on their assigned task, to have something else to do with his troops than cling to this pitch and fire into the night, waiting to get sliced up by swirling shrapnel or exploded bits of tanks. The remainder of the company is firmed up and rushed through the battle. Ilya falls toward the rear, his stamina for the run draining. Misha lopes behind him. On the way Ilya sees at least three more of the company go down.

On the other side of the tank battle, Ilya and Misha pick

up their rifles where they left them at the rock. Heading through the scorched trees, Ilya straggles to the back of the unit. Misha fades from the pack to walk with him.

"You look beat, Ilya."

"I'll be fine."

"You're a plow horse. You're not made for all this running around."

"What are you then?"

"Me? I'm a rat. Scurry all night long."

The little man's scar does look like one long rodent's whisker.

"Ilya, I've got another idea."

"More exploding barrels?"

"Something like that. I don't think it's in the street-fighting manual. But then, you are the manual."

Misha laughs and skips aside at this, mocking that Ilya might reach to throttle him. He leaves Ilya to walk alone in the rear and jogs to the front of the company.

At the rim of the trees, the captain halts their march. The three buildings wait in night silence. The slugging between them and the platoon has stopped. Ilya senses the gun barrels trained out of every window, enemy nerves pulled taut, fingers on many triggers. The company sits in a circle around Misha, who stands on his knees to tell them his plan.

"How many flare guns do we have?"

There are six here, three more with Ilya and Misha's platoon. They count eight flares to each gun.

"That's plenty," Misha says. "Here's what we'll do."

The scheme unfolds. Ilya thinks it's excellent. The company will arrange itself in squads on all possible sides of the three targets, covering every approach except for the inner traffic circle. At a signal—one green flare fired straight up—all nine flare guns will be trained on the busted windows of the buildings. The Germans are expecting nighttime tactics from their Red attackers. Misha's intent is to blind the defenders not with darkness but blazing, smoking little comets bouncing off their walls, and even some lucky shots lying at their feet. Under cover of this barrage of hot light and haze, every gun will open up against all three stories on three sides each.

Next, two men per building will rush, hopefully unnoticed, not straight at the banks of windows but on the diagonals. When near enough, they'll toss grenades in the closest first-floor windows and dive for cover at the foot of the walls. With the explosions, one squad each will storm forward, take the ground floor of their designated building, then hold while the rest of their platoon charges behind them. Then they can clear the buildings from the inside.

The captain makes assignments. The eighty-plus soldiers disperse around the perimeter. Ilya and Misha creep back to their platoon, which they find bunched together, waiting. Misha explains the coming strategy. While he talks, the men check their store of flare guns and flares. They split again into squads, dissolving left or right into the night to take up firing positions. Misha's squad stays put around him.

Misha points at a young private, a thin boy who looks fast, a scurrier like Misha. Ilya has barely noticed him before.

Misha motions the soldier close. "Anton Danielovich. Get out two grenades."

Ilya feels a flush of shame. Misha knows the lad's name and Ilya knows no one's name in the platoon. The men come and go so fast, from such odd and different circumstances, all of them tainted. Ilya rarely speaks to them. He leads in combat from the front, they come behind or they don't. Outside of battle he keeps to himself. His only conversation for a month now has been with Misha, and that happens less and less frequently. Ilya confesses to himself he has never dropped the disdain he felt as an officer for these men of the punishment battalion, the drunkards and recalcitrants and cowards. He's held himself at a distance from them for several reasons, distracted by ghosts, but he admits now he's avoided them partially because they reflect his own hard fall from grace. Ilya, the good and elite soldier, has always held himself blameless of whatever these men are guilty of.

He couldn't accept his presence among them. He looks at young Anton Danielovich and thinks again about who follows whom in war.

First man or last. King or pawn. War and death don't care. There's only one line and everyone's in it.

And innocence? Guilt? These are suspended while bigger themes are played out. War doesn't determine who's right or wrong. Just who's left.

He pulls the strap of his submachine gun up over his shoulder, crisscrossing the rifle already there. He takes from his own belt two grenades, hefting one in each hand.

"Anton Danielovich," he says. "Which side would you prefer, left or right?"

The boy is startled. The lieutenant has never spoken to him, to anyone but Sergeant Bakov.

"Sir," the boy begins, his nerves tripping him, "I . . ."

"He'll go right." Misha puts his hands over Ilya's mitts to grab hold of the grenades. "I'll go left."

Ilya opens his hands. Misha takes the burdens.

Ilya says, "I'll bring the squad right in behind you, Sergeant."

"Do that," Misha says, "Lieutenant."

A minute later a single green flare arches into the sky.

In the following seconds the three German-held buildings are swallowed in streaks of red and yellow light. The scene is an explosion in reverse, with all the concussion and fire flowing inward instead of out. Many flares strike the stone walls of the house in front of Ilya. Most fall to the ground to emit spumes of smoke and searing, colored light. One by one, a few lucky torches sail past those defenders spot-lit in the windows, to glimmer and fume at their backs. Ilya sees heads turn in the windows, hands come up to shield eyes, and Misha and the fast-looking boy take off.

The company opens up against the building, mixing bullets with the flying flares. This is repeated around the circle of three buildings. Ilya sweeps his PPSh over the stone face in front of him, the submachine gun leaps like an engine in his hands. The rest of the squad does the same, beating chips out of the stones. Ilya doesn't aim, just moves the barrel to spray as much firepower as he can. His eyes are on Misha.

The little sergeant is quick and smart. Under the dripping sparks he runs fifty meters in a serpentine path at the corner of the building. Ilya can't tell if Misha's drawing fire, but the man doesn't slow. When he's close enough, Misha hurls one grenade through a first-floor window. The bomb detonates with an immediate burst: Misha must have set the charge while running to make sure it couldn't be thrown back out. He doesn't dive for cover but runs right through the explosion and pitches the last grenade into another opening. This time the fuse is delayed seconds and Misha hits the dirt beneath the blast.

Ilya sets his legs under him. The squad behind him tautens at his sides. The rest of the platoon left and right continue to batter the building. The last flares erupt out of the guns. Ilya surges forward.

Ahead of him is fifty meters of flat ground, a sidewalk, then a half-dozen steps rising to the back door. He turns his weapon on the door, knowing he won't hit it much with this running aim, but hoping to knock down whoever's behind it and splinter it enough to drive through with his shoulder. He bounds up the steps, continuing to fire at the door, perforating it near the frame and hinges. At the last moment he takes his finger from the trigger and turns sideways. He accelerates his last strides and plunges at the door with all his weight. The barrier gives and goes down, taking Ilya with it. Slanting to the ground, he fires into the swirling dust and glaring light, striking the shadow of a man with his hands up.

Ilya rolls fast on the fallen door to catch who might be behind him, but the dust and smoke are too great to see through. He fires another blind burst into that side of the room, then scrambles out of the way for the rest of the squad to tear in after him. Once in the building, the men split up, just as Ilya schooled Misha and Misha taught them, the lessons of the Stalingrad storm groups. They move first with grenades in hand, tossing them down halls and into rooms before rushing in. Two men guard the foot of the stairs to keep the defenders bottled up on the higher floors. Once the first level is clear, they'll regroup and go in strength against the rest of the enemy.

Ilya walks behind the squad, pleased with their execution. Outside, the rest of the platoon keeps up the drumbeat against the upper floors. More men flow across the busted transom. Ilya's collarbone aches. He works the stiff shoulder.

Dying flares illuminate a dozen German bodies on the first floor, killed by Misha's grenades. At least twenty men from Ilya's platoon are now in the building. Explosions sound farther in the interior. The first floor will be secure in a few more minutes. The rest of the Germans are trapped upstairs. Five men of the platoon point their guns up the stairs, screaming in Russian: Drop your weapons! Come down, hands up! The Germans scream back. No one understands the tongues, but everyone here knows this fight is decided. That doesn't mean no one else will die.

Outside, the squads stop firing. The yelling inside the house halts. Ilya hears the rhythm of grenades and rifle fire from the other buildings around the circle. Each one plays out a different violence.

Misha steps in through the doorway. The last fading flare bathes him in scarlet. Smoke trails off him, his scar glows redder than his face. Misha looks like a demon.

There is a big, smoldering hole in the chest of his padded coat.

He drudges up to Ilya, gritting his teeth with every step.

Ilya asks, "What happened to you?"

Misha pats his hands over the hole. Scorched bits of cloth fall away.

"I landed on a fucking flare. It hurts."

Misha puffs his cheeks, tired and sore. He treads to the foot of the stairs.

Ilya calls after him. "Anton Danielovich?"

Misha shakes his head.

He goes to stand behind the men aiming their guns up the stairs. Ilya gives a corporal an order: Bring the rest of the platoon inside. He'll arrange half of them along the rear windows facing the traffic circle to take up firing lines at the other buildings. The rest of the platoon need to be ready to rush the second floor.

Ilya moves beside Misha.

"Tell them to come down or we'll kill every one of them."

Misha shouts in German.

A hysterical voice from above answers.

"Nein! Heil Hitler!"

Misha is visibly disgusted at this. He slumps, turns to Ilya.

"What the . . . ? Did you hear that?"

He reaches up to Ilya's sore shoulder to pull down the strap of the submachine gun. Ilya lets it slide off him.

Misha points the barrel up the stairwell. He pulls the trigger, unleashing a four-second burst, sixty rounds. This shreds the wall at the head of the steps.

Into the echo and tumbling plaster, Misha hollers up, *"Idioten!"*

He stuffs the weapon back into Ilya's hands. The barrel warms.

"Go get them, Ilya."

Misha steps aside. Ilya unbelts two grenades. He draws two more from the men around him. He'll give a signal. The men will fire their guns into the ceiling, pushing the Germans away from the stairwell. Ilya will dash up the steps, heave the grenades and duck, then lead a rush into the upstairs hallway. Once established on the second floor, the platoon will move room by room like they did on the ground level, killing every one of them as was promised. If anyone is on the third floor, the same will follow.

Ilya takes a firm hold on the first grenade. The others he cradles in his left arm. He sets his foot on the first step. The tread squeaks. Twelve men raise their rifles as though to fire a salute.

Ilya climbs the second and third steps. He drops his hand to fling the first grenade. He expects every second to see a German grenade bounce the opposite direction.

He stops. Voices scream in the rooms above. The language is addressed not at the Reds below but at each other, in vicious argument.

A shot rings out. Ilya crouches by instinct. Another shot. Ilya slips his thumb through the grenade's pin, it will pull out with the fling. Men and arms rustle below him. The platoon readies to fire into the ceiling at his signal.

Upstairs, a door opens. Heavy footsteps drag over the floor to the edge of the stairwell. Ilya glares upward, ready to act, but his machine gun is not in his hands, his mitts are full with the grenades. He's a sitting duck if the Germans counterattack now.

Something crosses the banister over his head. A hand. Then an arm and a head. Ilya freezes. Footsteps shuffle above. Three men appear. Ilya locks eyes on them.

One of them leans over the railing, as though to speak to Ilya. But he leans too far. He is limp. Blood spills over his chin. His feet fly up behind him, the other two dump him over the railing onto the steps. The body lands and tumbles a few steps, bumping and jumbled to stop beside Ilya's knees. The two heads beyond the railing look down for a moment, then disappear.

The body is an SS major.

"Wir kommen," a voice calls down. *"Ja? Wir kommen unten. Nicht schiessen, bitte. Bitte."*

Ilya hooks the grenades on his belt. He takes the PPSh in hand. Over his head, metal and wood clack as weapons are dropped. Ilya stands. He gives the SS officer's corpse a nudge with his boot and lets the body cascade the rest of the trip. At the bottom, the men sling it out a window with the rest of the German dead.

Ilya mounts the steps, his gun level. Enemy soldiers crowd the hallway, hands high on their helmets. In the hall he nods to the ones in front, the two who shot the Nazi fanatic who would trade their lives for nothing, for Hitler. More than twenty soldiers surrender.

While the prisoners walk past him, Ilya looks at their boots. He doesn't want their faces in his memory beside

Anton Danielovich. He'll have these Germans bunched into a corner and guarded until they can be turned over in the morning. Then he'll have the body of the fast boy brought inside and covered.

Now that the first building has fallen, the other two will collapse. Ilya's platoon takes up positions and begins firing at them from this vulnerable angle. A few leftover flares are shot across the circle as well.

The battle churns around the ring for another hour. Misha and Ilya do nothing more. They slump side-by-side in an empty room and sleep.

Zhukov's forces barge in at dawn. The three buildings at the head of the road have been captured and form a protected bridgehead into Seelow. The company is fed and reinforced. Tanks stream past, spreading into the rest of the town, setting off melees on every block. Tank crews run into German houses and emerge carrying bedsprings; they hitch these to the noses and flanks of their tanks. Someone figured out the coils will deflect *Panzerfaust* rockets.

At midmorning, Chuikov's artillery bombards the Heights again to soften the Germans for another massed infantry charge. Out on the muddy Oderbruch and against the slopes, several thousand lie uncollected.

By early evening the defense of Seelow is teetering. Only pockets of diehard resistance remain. Unorganized Soviet troops and vehicles jam every corner of the town. Looting begins. Prisoners are herded in droves into the streets, where they collapse on the cobblestones.

The following day, the last defense buckles. The Soviet army stands across the length of the Heights. The plain below shows the marks of the battle for it.

But the road to Berlin is thrown open.

BEYOND CHURCHILL'S BEDROOM WINDOW, SUNLIGHT
spreads over British fields. Already, tillermen are at work.
Cows trundle well-worn paths to the barns. Village chimneys smoke when the night's ashes are stoked. Churchill rolls
his head on his pillow to look out over an England that
Hitler did not defeat.

Today is Hitler's birthday. Fifty-six years old. He wonders if the little corporal is buried so deep in his Berlin
bunker, he doesn't even see this morning? If he does, what
does he look on? Surely not farmers and cattle, not peace or
anything sweet. Churchill hopes Hitler gazes out over his
own ruined nation and weeps.

A tray of quails' eggs, bangers, and rye toast rests on a
cart beside the bed. Churchill does not drink fruit juice, too
acidic for his stomach. No coffee either. Chilled champagne
first thing in the morning. He pats his belly beneath the silk
pajamas, under the goose-down comforter. It's like a trained
and temperamental pet, his digestion. Spoiled rotten, perhaps, but at least he's accustomed to it.

A glass has been poured for him. Not the slender dinner-
table flute but a fat breakfast mug. He raises the champagne
to the window.

"Your health, you bastard. Drop dead in your bloody
tracks this morning."

Churchill sips. He pulls aside the comforter and drops his
feet into his monogrammed slippers waiting beside the bed.
The cart is pulled close. He tucks a napkin over his lap.

"Ah, the old gang," he says aloud, taking up the silver-
ware. "They're falling apart."

Hitler will indeed be dead soon. The Russian assault has
sealed that deal.

Mussolini is on the lam; reports say he's trying to get into

Switzerland with his mistress. Italian partisans are looking for him. He'll likely swing when they nab him.

Roosevelt is gone. Poor bugger. A young man.

Well, Churchill thinks, looks like it's just me and Joe left. There is a new member, Roosevelt's replacement.

What of this new President, Harry Truman?

Harry. That's a solid name. Not like Franklin, or Winston, Adolf or Benito. Just Harry.

Churchill dices through the membrane of a sausage and forks the piece onto his tongue. The zip of spiced pork gets his mouth going. On the wall beside him a rectangle of tangerine light is pinned to the wall. Hitler's birthday will come up clear and clement. A good bombing day. The Americans have decided to make their next-to-final visit to Berlin today, a one-thousand-plane armada to drop off some presents for the Führer. The RAF will follow with afternoon and evening raids. The Americans will finish up tomorrow morning. That will be the last of it from the West.

Berlin. What a trebly hard fate the city has suffered. To be first made the Nazi capital. Then destroyed as systematically as any city since Carthage. And finally to be handed over to the mercies of the Soviets.

Over his eggs and toast, Churchill ponders Truman. He's never met the new man. Not even spoken to him on the telephone. Churchill wanted to attend Roosevelt's funeral, had ordered an airplane, but affairs of state in England prevented him. It was clearly the place of the Prime Minister to deliver the tribute to the late President before Parliament and the world. Roosevelt's death was sudden; schedules and debates in government over pivotal wartime matters could not be altered. For the moment, Churchill satisfies himself exchanging telegrams with Truman, judging the new President's mettle through alternate eyes and ears of those who've encountered him, principally Ambassador Lord Halifax and Anthony Eden.

The first reports on Truman are good. He appears resolute and fearless, not the sort who'll be bullied. On the issue of Soviet treatment of Poland, Truman signals that

Stalin's attitude is less than hopeful, but insists the West should "have another go at him." Halifax depicts Truman as a President whose "methods will be quite different from FDR," describing a more organized and hands-on approach, relying less on personal relationships and more on responsibility and accountability. Interestingly, Truman's hobby is the history of military strategy, on which he seems widely read. Halifax was surprised one evening at the depth of Truman's knowledge on Hannibal's campaigns. Eden's latest telegram portrays Truman as *honest and friendly. He is conscious of but not overwhelmed by his new responsibilities. His references to you could not have been warmer. I believe we shall have in him a loyal collaborator, and I am much heartened by this first conversation.*

Churchill pushes the cart away. He has eaten quickly, absentmindedly. He feels disloyal to the memory of Roosevelt and all they shared, because he views the coming of Truman as a godsend. A firmer American hand has been needed for some time now. A well-read man in the White House, a fellow who understands world military history, this cannot be a bad thing at this juncture. The President is dead. Long live the President.

What concerns Churchill are the reports that Truman is starting from scratch. It has surfaced that Roosevelt treated his Vice President—the man who was one bound away from the country's highest office—as a minor official in his government. Truman has been left uninformed on the most vital domestic and international issues. He's inherited a jury-rigged government, one that bears the stamp of informality of the great personality that was at its helm for thirteen years. Truman must familiarize himself with Roosevelt's positions and policies across the board. Though he may be a man of great abilities, the new President will be hampered in bringing his best traits to the fore until he can get up to speed. All this takes place at a climactic time when the world needs an able American leader, not a promising student.

Churchill finishes the cup of champagne. He grabs the folder of overnight papers from the second shelf of the cart.

He kicks off the slippers and rolls his bare feet back under the comforter.

How could Roosevelt allow this to happen? Especially in these last few months, when the tides of war were turning, when Roosevelt's health was so obviously deteriorating? If anything happens to Churchill, Anthony Eden knows everything about England's business and could at a moment's notice take over the entire direction of affairs. But Harry Truman of Missouri has leaped from a role of little information and less power into a position of supreme authority.

Churchill had his disagreements with Roosevelt during the man's life. Now that he's gone, Churchill wants to be charitable and think well of him. But by leaving his deputy so utterly in the dark, Roosevelt has done a disservice to the war effort, and to his own precious cause of lasting world peace. Were Roosevelt's ghost to visit, Churchill would scold him for this.

Stalin has undone Yalta in Yugoslavia; he's days away from doing the same in Poland. In weeks or months, the rest of eastern Europe will become Soviet puppets as well. Tens of millions of people are to be subjugated to the communist will, against their own.

Roosevelt was willing to allow this to happen, and so it shall and cannot be stopped.

But there is one final city and nation, not yet defeated by the Bear.

Churchill considers picking up the phone and holding his first conversation with Truman over the fate of Berlin. There's still time to mobilize and take it. The Russians are facing the bulk of German defense; the U.S. Ninth is across the Elbe, with token resistance in front of them. Berlin can be captured by the West, then traded to save how many other cities from the Soviets?

General Eisenhower listened to Roosevelt. Now he'll have to listen to Truman.

But will Truman listen to Churchill? *Can* he, with all the man has to do just now?

No. It's too late.

This time, it's really too late.

But we're not done with Berlin, Churchill thinks. Not by a long shot. Stalin will take the city and Stalin will break his word, like he's done over every territory he occupies. The situation surrounding Berlin will worsen in the years to follow. Churchill can only wait to see how the new President will respond.

Churchill studies the brightening fields. He looks at his watch, open on the bedside table. The American bombers are in the air.

Today, they fly for the birthday. Tomorrow, for the last time.

———————

April 21, 1945, 10:40 A.M.
Hardenberg Strasse U-bahn station
Charlottenburg, Berlin

FOR A MINUTE, THERE HAS NOT BEEN AN EXPLOSION.

Lottie hugs her knees to her chest, waiting for the next deep rumble. She sits shoulder to shoulder in a crowd of several hundred on the floor of the underground chamber. The only light and fresh air tumble in from the passageways up to the street. The floor is tiled and cold; smells of urine and unwashed bodies creep along it.

The people are packed tight around a radio. Its owner has cut it off during the bombing to save the battery. This morning the sirens wailed promptly at 9:00; the raid began at 9:25. Lottie was heading toward the Kurfürstendamm to stand in line for rations. At the klaxons she flocked down the steps with these others. For the past hour the city has boomed overhead. The hammershot blows enter the station from both directions through the tunnel, traveling with dark breezes along the empty tracks, sounding like trains coming and going.

Two more minutes pass without a detonation. The radio's owner clicks a knob. The seated crowd leans in.

The tinny speaker declares the all-clear. The American

Flying Fortresses have left the skies over Berlin. Minor damage was done in the eastern and southern portions of the city. The radio voice speculates this raid was to assist the Russian advances from those directions.

Lottie starts to stand. Her buttocks are numbed by the hardness and chill of the floor. Others begin to straighten, then the crowd nearest the radio makes shushing noises. Lottie settles with the others, there is more news.

"What?" Lottie asks a woman in front of her. "I missed it. What did they say?"

"That was the last American attack," the woman replies. "The English finished up last night. They won't be back."

"That's it!" some old man shouts. "That's it! We outlasted them!"

The old voice is shushed down. The radio report is not done. The crowd holds very still.

The radio explains that, from now on, the bombardment of Berlin will be the responsibility of the Soviet air force.

The woman who owns the radio is the first to speak out. "Oh, to hell with the Soviet air force."

Others take up this call. It's true, Lottie thinks. The Americans and British have come with such terrible numbers and efficiency. It's been four years of living through them. Now they're leaving their duties to the Reds, who are so scattershot. Russian air raids are no match for what the *Amis* have mounted. Their bombs are much smaller, their raids less frequent. This is happy news.

Applause starts and Lottie joins in. The radio is snapped off and lifted away. The crowd rises. Hands reach down to assist the weak and the elder ones. Moving up the steps into fresh air, the talk is a reprise of the old man's boast, We outlasted them!

On the sidewalk Lottie turns again for the Ku'damm. Many of the old folks head that direction as well. A cap of gray clouds nestles over Berlin. The last of the *Amis'* air raids did nothing here in the west end of town. It was a small barrage, not like yesterday's birthday bashing. Why drop the bombs one more time? To Lottie it just seems spiteful.

Yesterday was enough, a grand finale for the raids. The Americans started at ten o'clock in the morning. For a full two hours, the sky was full of them, unhounded by any German defense. Throughout the rest of the day, the English appeared, dropped their loads, disappeared, and arrived again, maddeningly random for them. Berliners were forced to spend the entire day hiding in shelters. At night, the English came back in big numbers. By midnight, every part of the city had felt the blows.

For the first time in twelve years, Hitler's birthday passed without banners or speeches. April twentieth was also the last day of water and gas in Berlin. The toilets no longer flush. Garbage is not going to be picked up. Electricity comes on for seconds at a time. All telephones are down. Subways and trains have stopped running. Berlin is no longer a living city. It's a shell; the three million frightened occupants live in it now like crabs.

Lottie walks east, an empty canvas bag dangling from her wrist. The shops on the Ku'damm will be giving out extra allocations of food today. Whether the bonus is in celebration of Hitler's birth or a nod to the coming siege, she doesn't care. But today, on government decree, Lottie will be able to take home one pound of bacon or sausage, one-half pound of rice or oatmeal, two hundred fifty dried lentils, peas, or beans, one can of vegetables, a tin of fruit, two pounds of sugar, one ounce of coffee, three and a half ounces of the *ersatz* malt coffee, and a bag of fats. Also, it was announced that the next two weeks' supplies will be made available in advance. After today, there will be no more foodstuffs issued for the next eight days. Already the Berliners' black humor has named this extra food "Ascension Day rations." With these final morsels in their mouths, they say, they will ascend to heaven.

In his many radio tirades, Minister Goebbels calls the city a *Festung,* a fortress. He claims Berlin has been transformed into a death trap for the invaders. Walking to the streets of shops, with the Russians only a handful of miles from the city limits, Lottie sees little trace of Fortress Berlin. *Volkssturm* units in civilian garb shuffle through the ruins with old rifles over their shoulders. The last time these guns were fired they and the men were both young. Hitler boys on bicycles make a big show of their one-shot *Panzerfausts* held across their handlebars. Foreign workers are made to stack stones and bricks to build little bastions but there are no soldiers to man them. Brigades of shovel-toting women head east out of town, presumably to dig tank traps. There are no firemen or police, they've all been called into fighting units. The occasional SS and Gestapo men stomp to and fro with some purpose in mind, shining and angry. The amount of activity dedicated to the defense of Berlin is small; it pales beside the greater performance of the streets, people searching for food.

Lottie reaches the main thoroughfare. Everywhere women stand in long lines in front of the shops. Knowing this might be their last chance to secure provisions before the Russians reach the city center, thousands have come out to use their final food coupons. They've been emboldened too by the news that this morning was the last of the *Amis'* air raids. Lottie catches snippets of talk. The rumor flies that there will be peace now, that's why the West quit bombing. There'll be no Russian assault, no *Schlacht um Berlin.* The broad Ku'damm is swamped by queues, even snaking down into the craters in the boulevard where broken water pipes leak their last drops into waiting Berliners' buckets. She heads several blocks east on the avenue, toward the Tiergarten, hoping to find shorter lines nearer the park.

Lottie surveys the damage along the Ku'damm and the many side streets and alleys. The wreckage follows no pattern; some blocks have a house blasted out of the middle like a broken tooth, some streets are untouched. Other rows are shorn down to brick mounds and twisted steel bars. Rust, dust, and rubble pile up next to proud and pock-free buildings. Lottie thinks she could line up Berliners along the street just like these buildings and find their fates no different. Some have survived unscathed, many have been deeply hurt but remain standing, others are gone, vacant places where humans were.

Lottie cannot form a picture of herself as a building. Her story isn't played out yet. Nor is Berlin's. In this way, she's not like a single house but the whole city. Waiting, undetermined, in jeopardy.

In the five days since the final BPO concert, Lottie has drifted between despair and hope. The Nazis' news organs fan fear of the Red Army, with constant reports of rapes, murders, horrors upon horrors. Suicides in Berlin have multiplied. No one in the bunkers is without a tale of his own to tell: the family sitting down to their evening meal and never getting up, poisoned by the parents; the German officer who slit his wrists and walked toward the advancing Russians, blood dripping from all ten fingertips, pleading, "There, I've killed myself. Now will you leave my wife alone?"; nuns violated in their chapel. The stories are so dreadful as to be numbing, almost unbelievable. In that backward way, Lottie has lapsed into hope. These tales can't be true, she figures, they must be made up to scare us, to make Berliners fight harder. Freya says this too. The Russians are human beings, she says, but these are tales of animals. Don't believe them. Besides, Mutti adds, even if true, nothing in these stories of Russian cruelty compares to what the Nazis have done to the Jews. The real animals are among us, Mutti says. Lottie does not weigh crimes the way her mother can, this is worse than that. Lottie wants to be freed from all of it. She hopes, because her hands are not busy with music and because there is nothing else she can do. She goes to bed every night, she walks through the ruins for scraps of food, she will sit in the parlor this afternoon and stare out the window, and hope, somehow, still to be protected.

Lottie crosses to Budapester Strasse and strolls another few blocks. She stops at a shop across the avenue from the Zoo. Along with the BPO, the Zoological Gardens has been the other important public institution that remained open for the entire course of the war. Now the gate between the two giant terra-cotta elephants is padlocked. The sign says CLOSED. The shuttered Zoo is an unexpected dagger to Lottie's gut. Of course it had to close, she thinks; even so, this was the absolute last bit of light in Berlin's life, and now it too is extinguished.

She steps into line at a grocery. There are fifty or more women ahead of her. She was wrong; the lines are not shorter here, or anywhere up and down the street. But the walk helped use up a portion of the day.

Lottie waits. She takes a step forward every minute or so. She'll be in this queue for at least an hour. She doesn't care. She's got to be somewhere.

She talks to no one in the line. The older women look at her and lower their gazes, returning to whispered gossip. A few others in the line are near Lottie's age. These younger ones keep their eyes on the sidewalk. One pretty girl looks back at Lottie. She smiles. Lottie sees this girl wants some returned gesture, some piece of Lottie's hope she can take for herself. Lottie gives her none, and looks away.

After a half hour, Lottie's feet begin to tingle from standing on the hard concrete. She walks out of the line a few steps to stretch her legs. The woman behind her closes the gap fast, and argues when Lottie wants to reclaim her space. The nearer the line gets to the door and the food inside, the more tension Lottie senses among the women. She plants her feet on the sidewalk to make a statement to the woman behind her and all of them, that she is their equal, as resolute as they.

When she is less than a dozen spaces from the door, Lottie hears sharp voices inside the shop. A few women complain about the portions the shopkeeper doles out. "This can't be right!" they say. "This is too small! I need more! You're cheating!" The shopkeeper takes a barbed tone in return. "Get out," he says, "if you're not happy with what I give you. Go to another store and see what they put out for you. Go on!"

Lottie hears the shopkeeper yell, "No you don't!" In the next moment, the ten women in line in front of her push through the door, jamming themselves into the small shop. Lottie doesn't know what they've heard or seen, but it was something to make them rush forward, and she bulls in at their backs.

The shopkeeper behind his counter flails a white towel at the grabbing hands of twenty women. They fill their bags with as much as they can clutch off the counter, sweeping into their arms anything edible within reach. One woman hurries behind the counter to gain access to the shelves back there. In seconds she is followed by others, and Lottie. The shopkeeper is a fat man; no one should be fat when so many are hungry. This angers the women too. It implies that he's a hoarder. Lottie hears the women tell him to stand aside, fatty, while they denude his store.

Lottie shoves into her bag a loaf of bread and many tins of pressed meat. She digs her hand into a pile of dry beans and scoops them in, spilling too much on the floor. Another woman doing the same pauses to give Lottie a stern look, admonishing her to be more careful and waste less when looting.

The shopkeeper throws down his towel. "Damn it! All right!" he shouts. Lottie sees him cross his arms and stand aside.

Women pour in the front door, as many as can cram into the shop. The items in the window are snatched up. Lottie can't get to the place behind the counter where the coffee is kept, this is what she really wants. Her bag is full now and heavy. She got more than her rations would have allowed, but less variety. She heaves against the shoulders and bosoms on all sides of her, grabbing anything she sees, but she lacks the leverage some of these old women have.

In a minute the frenzy subsides. Lottie knifes through and makes her way out the door. There are foodstuffs left to be stolen but Lottie has enough and she wants to get out. The many women in line who did not participate in the ransacking confront the first few to emerge. Share! they demand. Thief! Lottie has no thought of letting any of these others have what she fought for. She uses her youth and runs away at the first angry voices aimed at her.

She doesn't run far, no one gives chase. She crosses to the Zoo side of the street. The sack weighs less than the cello, but she's grabbed plenty. Mutti will be pleased at her daughter's audacity.

She walks along the brick wall of the Zoo grounds. Between the big elephants, at the closed gate, she pauses to stick her chin between the bars. The ticket booth to the left is empty. The mature trees of the Zoo are mostly chewed up, but several have the buds of spring pushing out. The Zoo smell remains, vast and green, the intrigue of wild animals and exotic lands stained forever into the air here. Lottie hears a monkey hoot, something big trumpets. Lottie stands in the gateway, breathing in this sorrow of Berlin.

A noise makes her look into the sky. A bird, an impossibly large bird, must be flying past. It must have a huge wingspan, it makes a low, swooping sound like nothing Lottie has heard before.

There is no bird. Turning from the gate, her stomach seizes. The sky above whispers, then screams.

The ground sunders.

Lottie is heaved back into the grate, slamming her head to the iron. The weight of the sack drags her to the sidewalk, stunned. Her vision blurs. A detonation has gone off across the street. There were women there a moment ago, a hundred waiting in line. Lottie blinks to clear her eyes. The women in the middle of the line are gone. No, Lottie sees, they're still there, in bits. A hole smokes in the street, decorated with confetti of cloth and human beings. The survivors stagger away from the crater, blood on their dresses and overcoats. Those who can, run.

The back of Lottie's head sears. She knows she is bleeding. She can't get to her feet.

She isn't sure for a second if the sounds she hears are only inside her head. There's more hissing in the sky, more giant and impossible birds.

The Budapester Strasse erupts with explosions. There are no airplanes, no falling bombs, no air raid warning.

Lottie's confusion parts with the blasts.

Russian artillery. They've come close enough to Berlin to shoot their long guns into the city.

Havoc bursts with the shells. The thousands of people gathered on the avenues are caught out of their shelters by the attack. They thought it was safe for the moment. Now they flee in every direction, shrieking, panicked, tricked.

Lottie looks up and down the boulevard. Flames rage on all sides, even behind her in the Zoo. She can't hear the animals cry but guesses they're dying in their cages and pools, just like the people running to nowhere in the street. Some citizens drop their bags and bolt, ducking from doorway to doorway, others brave the shells to pick up the spilled goods. Shells plow the road and buildings from one end to the other, no one knows how to dodge them, bodies are cleaved. Cars get knocked over and set on fire. Roofs buckle. One building that was barely standing is finished off by a direct hit and collapses.

Lottie keeps her seat against the Zoo gate. Several people running past vault her legs sticking out on the sidewalk. The pain in her head settles to a throb and she decides she can bear it. She folds her legs under her to be less of an obstacle for the runners. Lottie wonders, They run where? There are no havens in Berlin. The Russians have announced they are coming and they will destroy everything. These shells are not aimed at shops and old women. They're not aimed at all. The Russians are just shooting from miles away, with no thought or design at all except killing Berlin. The reports are true, after all. So must be the bunker stories. There will be no mercy for Berlin or its people.

Lottie could stand and make her way back home. Her legs will work, her head wound is not blinding her any longer. But she sits, deflated, without the air of hope any longer inside her. She watches the rest of the attack, waiting for one of these Russian shells to land between her legs and blow a hole, an empty spot, where she sits.

Where there is no mercy there is also no protection. For the first time, Lottie senses she is no different from anyone in this city, not even the dead ones.

She should have gone in Speer's car when she had the chance. She was wrong to think she could be a hero, that she could stay and bear this.

Two horses gallop down the middle of Budapester Strasse. Their manes and tails are on fire. Both animals are wild, neighing in pain. Lottie knows why they run, it's all they can do.

With every explosion, she turns more inward. She heads in the only direction she can find that leads away.

April 27, 1945, 10:30 A.M.
With the Second Armored Division,
Ninth U.S. Army
Northwest of the Barby bridgehead
Leitzkau village, Germany

THE PEOPLE RUNNING OUT OF THE VILLAGE ARRIVE BY age. The first ones to reach the tanks are the young girls, followed by mothers carrying small fry. Last are the older folks making headway on canes and each other's arms. Frail ones stay back on their stoops, close to their own doors.

The captain in the lead tank speaks German and Norwegian, he's from Minneapolis. Bandy stands behind the wheel in his jeep, the Leica around his neck. He shoots the captain leaning out of his hatch to take a bunch of wildflowers from a pretty lady. A scarf wraps her brown hair, she has long white arms outside of her maiden's smock. When she goes up on tiptoe, Bandy squeezes the picture.

He steps down from the jeep and walks around the two Hell on Wheels tanks, to get a picture of three codgers in World War I medals. These men stand arm in arm, as though to block Bandy's passage, but they're just old war comrades supporting each other. They look to be seventy or eighty, but when he gets closer Bandy sees the old soldiers are not that ancient. They're just lean from hunger and illness. The other village men their age, the ones who've fared better in health, are gone, probably sucked into the Home Guard. These three glare at Bandy, the American who has not come to free them.

The Russians are coming. No amount of flowers and pretty ladies will change that. The two Second Division tanks are just patrolling the outer edge of the Barby bridgehead, with Bandy tagging along in his jeep scavenging for photos. The Red Army has already reached the Elbe across from U.S. positions. Just two days ago, at the town of Torgau, fifty miles south of Barby on the river, soldiers of the Sixty-ninth Division of Hodges' First Army linked up with a unit of Koniev's First Ukrainians. Germany's been cut in half. Berlin is surrounded. It will be a great picture, the Soviets and Americans meeting up. Someone else got it, some photographer who bet on the Sixty-ninth, who ended up in the middle of nowhere, then got the break of his life when his unit was the first to meet the Reds.

Bandy takes what shots he can in the Barby bridgehead. He has no idea how the photos are being treated at home. It's not big news, this dead end on the Elbe. He pans the Leica's lens across the village.

The whole place is sheathed in white sheets, banners of surrender hang from every window and veranda. The villagers hope the American tanks have come to accept this surrender. The captain explains to the dozens pressed around his tank that he's not here to liberate them.

"Die Russen kommen," he says.

Bandy puts on film the outstretched arms, pointing fingers, and shocked faces, which translate easily: How can this be? You Americans are here now! You are right across the river. How can you leave us to them?

Bandy is the only Yank who steps down from his vehicle. The twin tanks have their turrets aimed in different directions, their engines at an idling growl. The captain and his counterpart ride high, above the white arms and old medals.

Bandy is circled by the civilians. They plead with him. They insist. He lowers his camera. He looks into their eyes and does not even shake his head to tell them "No." Bandy stands dumb.

Someone pulls on his arm. He turns in the direction of the tug but can't tell who did it, there are so many crowding him. These are farmers' daughters and wives and parents. All their young men are missing, many won't be coming back. Bandy recalls a quote from Cicero: In peace, sons bury fathers. In war, fathers bury sons. The village livestock have vanished, taken by the retreating German soldiers. Their fields aren't planted. If the seeds don't go in soon, if the Reds don't finish this quickly and send the surviving men back to their homes, there'll be nothing from the fields come winter. The women want to start living their lives again this minute, with the Americans here. They bark at Bandy: Tell us we can go on. He wants them to know this is the way the Big Shots want it. You're the ones who pay when they draw lines on a map. But he looks at them and listens to what he understands beyond language. Another hand pokes him.

He should go home. This isn't news. This isn't war either. It's politics.

There is a letter in his pocket from Victoria. He's been in one place long enough for it to catch up to him. In Tennessee too the seeds are slow getting into the earth. Where are the young men? Where are you, Charley?

A metallic whine startles the crowd. The villagers step back from Bandy and stare up at the swinging turrets of the two tanks. The people retreat together into a clump. The German-speaking captain drops the bouquet, splashing pastels against his tank's armor plating. The treads of the second tank leap forward, tearing the dirt road while the tank pivots to stand beside its partner. Both big guns come around to face north. Bandy hears the machine guns bolt. He doesn't know what's happening but makes for his jeep.

He sees why the tankers moved to defensive postures. Out of the north, three vehicles approach the village. From a distance they look just like American jeeps; they may be

American-made. But the stars painted on the hoods are not white. They're red.

The Russians slow their advance into the village. The tanks see to that. About a hundred yards away, two of the cars stop. Only one progresses, a few miles an hour. The soldier in the passenger seat stands and waves his hands over his head.

"Hello," he shouts. "Amerikanskis, hello!"

The captain in the first tank speaks down into his hatch. "Let 'em come. Keep an eye."

The Soviets creep closer. Bandy gets out of his jeep and walks to them.

"Mr. Bandy," the captain calls, "stay where you are, sir."

The villagers recoil further from the nearing Russians. The Red soldier, noticing this, turns his greeting on them. *"Gut Morgen, gut Morgen."* The citizens make no move.

The Russians pull right up to the cowlings of the tanks, beneath the big barrels. Bandy's never seen Red soldiers before; he guesses the talking one is an officer, he wears only a sidearm. The man is young. His uniform is dirty. So is the driver's.

The officer dismounts his jeep. He strides up to Bandy and proffers his hand.

"Hello. Hello."

Bandy takes the mitt and shakes. "How are you?"

"Good. Wonderful. Very, very wonderful. You are good to ask."

The officer looks up the side of the tank to the American captain. He snaps to attention to present himself.

"I am lieutenant. First Byelorussian Army. Seventh Guards Cavalry Corps. Oleg Borisovich Antsiferov. Sir."

The tanker beams down at the Russian's formal and funny announcement of his name and rank.

"Captain Lerberg. Second Armored, U.S. Ninth Army. Pleased to meet you, Lieutenant."

"Yes!" The Russian claps his hands. "Pleased to meet you!"

The officer snaps his finger. His driver reaches to the

backseat of the vehicle for a muslin sack. Bandy hears glass bottles jostle. For the moment, the villagers are ignored by the men of the two armies. Bandy lifts his camera and records the Russian lieutenant holding high a clear bottle of vodka to toast the Americans. The lieutenant drinks, then waves the flask in the air to Lerberg. The tank captain says, "No thanks." The Russian shrugs and turns the bottle to Bandy.

"Picture taker. You can take drink?"

"Sure." Bandy swallows a slug. The Russian claps him on the back. The vodka has the flavor of potatoes and gasoline.

"Yeow." Bandy wipes his lips and returns the bottle. He looks up to the tank captain. He gasps. "Stop me next time."

Lerberg waits for Bandy to finish coughing and the Russian lieutenant's enjoyment to subside.

"Lieutenant, where's your unit?"

The soldier stoppers the bottle and tosses it to his driver. "Northeast. We are in Brandenburg."

That's just twenty miles from Berlin's city limits, the last large town west of Potsdam.

"We are sent to find you. Hello."

The captain grins. "Hello again."

The lieutenant turns. He waves to the two waiting cars, telling them to come ahead.

"Nein!" the villagers shout. *"Nein!"*

The lieutenant stops the cars. He turns to the packed people.

"Is okay," he says in English. "Is no harm."

"Nein!" they scream back. The woman who handed Lerberg the flowers rushes forward. She throws herself at the side of the tank, stabbing a finger at the Russian.

"Shoot them!" she begs. "Shoot!"

The captain answers. *"Ich kann nicht."*

Lerberg looks past her. He speaks to the Red officer.

"Tell your men to come ahead. The town's yours."

The woman pounds a fist into the turret on the emblem of the American army. She whirls on the Russian soldier, unleashing a biting torrent. Behind her the villagers stand silent.

The lieutenant cannot translate what she yells. He was sent to find the Americans because he speaks English, not German. But he understands.

"No harm," he says to the harping woman, "no harm."

Bandy snaps this photograph, the German villager shouting, the conqueror promising.

Lerberg does not intercede. He speaks only to the men at his feet, the hidden ones at the controls of his tank. The engine whirs, gears shift. The other tank follows suit.

"Lieutenant," he shouts to the beleaguered Russian, "tell your commander we're three miles south of this village. We'll keep a lookout for you."

The Russian splits his attention between the woman and the American tanker. He doesn't want to take his eyes from her, she might belt him.

Lerberg calls down, "Can you do that, Lieutenant?"

The Russian asks, "Will please you tell her to be quiet?"

Lerberg adds his voice: *"Fräulein, Fräulein!"*

She clinches her lips and listens, hands on hips, chest heaving. Lerberg talks and motions to the waiting Russian cars, his two tanks, the Ninth Army's lines just a few miles away on the river. Bandy takes this picture too. A caption forms in his head: "The explanation."

Bandy climbs into his jeep. There is hatred on the woman's face for all of them: the departing Americans, the powerful force sent from a free nation, failed and reluctant, not saviors for them at all; the Russians whom they've been taught to dread, despite this placating young officer; and her own neighbors for standing by and saying nothing.

Just pawns, Bandy thinks. This outcome was rigged long before it was played out, decided not on the battlefield but in some quiet room somewhere in Washington or Moscow, with pencils and rulers for weapons. Warlords and politicians have turned the whole world into a game board. Money and power are more prized than lives and blood. History doesn't have this brave village woman's name on it. Not like Eisenhower and Roosevelt and Stalin. No. She disappears.

Quiet follows the captain's words to the woman. The Russian brings his eyes around to Bandy.

"Mr. Picture Taker. You understand this woman?"

"No."

"No. Me neither. But I know what she say."

"Yeah. Me too."

"I tell you something." The Russian lifts his gaze to the tankers. "I tell you truth. In friendship. Is sad thing. This girl, she is right."

The woman stomps away from the chatting Americans and Soviets. Bandy watches her go to a small house. An old woman holds the door for her. The crone shakes a fist at Bandy, then closes the girl inside.

The Russian shakes his head.

"The frontline soldiers. We are discipline. We are not to harm German people. We get vengeance, yes. But not on them. On Nazis. On fighting men, yes. But on civilians, what kind of soldier does this? You understand?"

"Vengeance?" Lerberg asks from his turret. "Soldiers fight, Lieutenant. We follow orders. It's not for us to take revenge. Not on civilians. Not in combat. Never."

The Russian makes a sardonic snort. Now Bandy realizes what this dirty man represents.

"Yes, well. When the Germans come to America to fight next war, you will tell me what you see then. Yes, Captain?"

Lerberg's moralizing is halted by this notion.

The lieutenant pivots to Bandy.

"Mr. Picture Taker. Understand. Is not my men. Is the ones behind. Second wave. This girl, she should be afraid. Those men, they are crazy with fighting. What they do . . ." The officer narrows his eyes. He says no more.

"Mr. Bandy," the captain calls. His tank revs. "Let's saddle up."

Bandy does not wish to shake the Russian's hand in departure. He turns for his jeep.

"You would like to come with us?"

Bandy stops. The lieutenant points up the road, past his other waiting vehicles.

"To Brandenburg, Mr. Picture Taker? You see for yourself. What Russian troops do. What German troops do. "

Bandy looks up to Lerberg. "Captain?"

"It's up to you, Mr. Bandy."

This might be Bandy's only chance to get to Berlin. If he can latch on to a Russian unit, he can go all the way. The only American photographer witnessing the fall of the last city, the true end of the war in Europe.

The letter in his pocket asks again: Where are you, Charley?

Dear Vic. I'm in Berlin.

"All right, Lieutenant. I'll come with you."

The Russian inclines his head.

Captain Lerberg tosses Bandy a quick salute. The two tanks lurch as one and grind south out of the village, spitting exhaust. The lieutenant offers Bandy a seat in his vehicle. Bandy wants to stay with his own jeep.

The villagers watch the U.S. Army tanks lumber away. They are an accusing chorus while the one remaining American makes some arrangements to go off with the Russians. Bandy catches their eyes for a last time. They glower at him and Bandy can tell they think he's a coward.

"What about these people," he asks the Russian, "this village?"

The lieutenant asks, "What is your name?"

"Bandy."

"Bandy. You have seen war?"

"Yes, Lieutenant. Plenty."

"Then do not ask about this village. You already know."

The Russian climbs into his car. The driver wheels in a tight turn and sprays dirt and gravel. Bandy is left to follow out of the village.

The road runs north. Bandy follows the three Russian vehicles at a close distance, wanting to be sure that anyone

seeing them knows his American jeep is part of this little Soviet convoy. After ten miles they pass through the eastern
fringes of Magdeburg, a medium-sized city on the Elbe. The
road skirts an industrial district; Bandy notes widespread destruction, the result of Ninth Army's artillery duels with
German guns in the city to prevent an Allied river crossing
here. He drives past warehouses stripped to their beams,
brick buildings charred and bald. No one is out walking in
the ruins. They're hiding. The Russians are coming.

The road rolls east to Brandenburg, passing through a
dozen more villages and small towns. Nowhere is there evidence of organized German troop activity. Bandy judges that
every available man, gun, and machine has been withdrawn
east to help defend Berlin from the Reds. This entire plain
between the Elbe and Berlin has been essentially vacated.
The U.S. Army could have made it through here with mini-
mal danger. This is neither a shock nor a revelation; everyone in the Barby bridgehead has figured this out.

Bandy drives through farmland and beautiful dairy hills.
There are forests and streams, picturesque stone bridges and
straw-matted huts. There are no farm animals. The land has
been plowed only by armored treads, heavy wheels, and
falling bombs.

At the sound of cars, the people of the landscape come
close to the road. When they see the red stars on the three
Russian vehicles, they swat the air, as if to make the Reds go
away. Bandy's jeep comes fast on the heels of the Soviets, appearing to chase them out of this part of Germany. When
the white U.S. star on his hood passes, the people cheer.

A sign says Brandenburg is eight kilometers away. Bandy's
escorts halt. The lieutenant walks back to Bandy's jeep.

"We take you to show you something."

"All right."

"You have film for cameras?"

"Yes."

"This is Germans. This is what we come to stop."

"What is it?"

"You follow, Bandy. You see. Take pictures."

The four vehicles set out again. The lieutenant's car moves in behind Bandy's jeep.

He's led into a small and ancient city of encircling walls, cathedrals, and cobblestone streets. A medieval castle sits on an island in the middle of a river. A bridge sign labels the waterway the Havel, the river that runs through Berlin. All this Gothic architecture stands stolid against the incursions of the twentieth century, when Brandenburg appears to have been turned into an industrial center. The Havel is wide here and apparently deep enough for the city to serve as a maritime terminal for Berlin. Bandy's convoy drives past shipyards and cranes, a brewery—he smells the hops, they're making beer even with the Russians in town—and many manufacturing plants where high chimneys once puffed. The chimneys are stubs now, snapped by Allied air raids. But the city remains greatly intact. Apparently the Reds didn't meet much resistance taking it.

Brandenburg seems to Bandy about the size of Bristol on the Tennessee-Virginia border. Maybe forty, fifty thousand folks live here. Today, Brandenburg is swamped with people, tens of thousands more than the city can handle. Civilian carts stacked with belongings have been pulled to this place by old men or strapping women and are now at a standstill. Families hunker around their possessions and wait, haggard, sitting on suitcases and trunks. The fathers are bearded from travel and neglect, women and children droop from sleep-lessness. All of them are unkempt. They pack the city, every median and sidewalk, the fishing lanes over the bridges, church properties, the parks. Clearly these are refugees, the plain and scared Germans who flocked west and south, haul-ing their belongings as fast as they could ahead of the Soviet advance, hoping to reach the American lines. They've been thwarted. Bandy sees not liberation on the faces he passes but the weight of capture.

In a parking lot, a hundred *Wehrmacht* soldiers have been corralled. Seasoning their number are dozens of older men in street clothes and felt hats, the remnants of the local

Volkssturm. This is the city's garrison, a last-ditch effort at defense that seems to have ended quickly. Soviet nurses move through their ranks handing out water, dispensing medicine, and inspecting wounds.

Brandenburg is engulfed in Soviet hardware and men. The Reds push through the clogging citizenry, avoiding violence as well as politeness. They brook no reluctance among the Germans to move out of their way. Bandy watches a personnel carrier shove a cart aside, spilling people and baggage into the street. There seems to be a law that only Red soldiers may walk straight and fast somewhere, only the hulks of Russian machines may go unhindered. The rest must sit or stand aside.

The Russians are orderly and restrained, just as the lieutenant said they would be. Bandy spots no pillaging. The locals and refugees are bullied but mostly unaccosted. Likely, Bandy thinks, it's the same for the Soviet army as it is for the Americans. If you have to battle for a town, you treat it with anger when you take it. If the town surrenders—or, in the case of Brandenburg, if the enemy has fled out of it—then more humane rules apply.

The cars ahead of Bandy turn to the western end of the city. The road runs along the banks of the Havel. The lieutenant stays close at Bandy's bumper. In minutes, a massive fortified structure looms beside the river. The cars are stopped by Russian guards at a gate. This is not some castle outside the city limits. It's too new. One of the soldiers in the vehicles in front speaks with the guards. They are waved through. One guard salutes Bandy.

This is a prison. The design is modern and stark. A vast courtyard surrounds the central structure, a four-story rectangle with a high-pitched slate roof. The effect is foreboding. Bandy slows his jeep, ignoring the lieutenant behind him. He will go at his own pace now.

Bandy passes through a perimeter of metal girders cemented into the ground; barbed wire is strung between them. Watchtowers built into the outer walls have at their crests unmanned machine guns lodged behind sandbags.

Bandy comes to a stop. The lieutenant pulls alongside and says nothing. The other two cars drive on.

The courtyard is filled with meandering men. They all wear the same ill-fitting outfits, ragged and woolly, with wide, powder-blue vertical stripes. Many wear caps of the same material. Bandy steps out of his jeep.

The lieutenant calls after him.

"Bandy. Your camera."

Bandy ignores this. What he sees is beyond what a photograph can depict.

The men are like scattered litter. They seem to move not by walking but are blown where they go, drifting on some current unwilling to lift men who've not endured what they have. There are a thousand, two thousand of them, tracing the limits of the barbed wire. One by one they reach the fence and lift a hand to touch it, an act that might have gotten them shot down, perhaps even this morning. Bandy approaches one of them.

For the first time in his life, Bandy gazes into living eyes that do not peer out. It's like looking into a lightless doorway, the man's visage only beckons Bandy in, into the dark room across its threshold. This is not just a face starved but a mouth that has had emptiness fed into it.

Bandy wants to speak. Others waft by; the barbed wire draws them, brows creased with the defiance of laying a hand to it.

He asks the man, "Are you okay?"

The prisoner looks upward, as if Bandy's voice has come from above instead of in front. Bandy follows the slow glance to a vacant gun tower on the wall.

The marble eyes return to Bandy. They bring nothing back from their sojourn to the wall.

The man nods.

"Ja."

The invisible breeze blows and the prisoner strays beyond Bandy.

The lieutenant walks up.

"This is not worst, Bandy. Come. There is more."

He drives behind the lieutenant down the central lane. On every side prisoners wander the grounds. Bandy is shocked to see them so aimless. To his eye they look alike, ravaged men, frames bent and slender like droughted plants. In the way there is one uniform for the prisoners, there is one gait among their thousands of legs, a slow and stunned march. Every hand and wrist is veined and weak. A single set of eyes is set in every head, the dulled orbs of the one Bandy spoke to. This man is inside all of us, Bandy thinks, the last living creature at the end of the road. What a terrible journey.

The lieutenant pulls up at the front door to the prison. Bandy stops behind. He grabs his camera bag. The building is tall and sheer, a brick cliff of barred windows. They go inside past thick, studded doors. The only light intrudes from the few windows.

More inmates ramble the linoleum floor. The lieutenant tromps fast among them, not letting Bandy pause to take pictures. They speed down a long, bland hall.

The Russian waves his hand. "This is prison, yes?"

"Yes."

"We took from Nazis two hours ago. They know we come. They should run, yes? They should just go, leave prison alone. We take, set people free."

"Who are the prisoners?"

"Usual German enemies. Jews, Russians, Poles, Slavs."

"Was there a fight to take the place?"

"No. Soviet army come too fast. Nazis of this prison had other business."

With this statement the lieutenant pushes on a thick door. Bandy steps alongside him into a vast cavern of cells, three tiers high. Skylights do not ease the foggy, gray color in here. Concrete catwalks run the length of the building. Bars cross every aperture.

"There are three rows like this," the lieutenant says. "Prison must take two thousand. Nazis put five thousand in here. Come."

Bandy follows the Russian into the block. All the cell

doors have been flung open. With the first steps he smells the odors of human loss: feces, decay, disease. In addition to the multitude outside on the prison grounds, the hundreds ambling in the halls, there are a thousand more lying in these cells, three or four to a cage, men too sapped of life or too hurt to rise. The hard walls and metal will not soften their groans. Bandy walks past, looking in each open cell. He beholds again the common being in misery, the lone one who can tell five thousand terrible tales.

"These men not fed," the Russian says. "There is typhus. Tuberculosis. Nazis let them rot."

Bandy unslings his shoulder pack to take out the Leica.

"Wait," the lieutenant says. "See everything first."

The two walk to the end of the row. The Russian shoves open another armored door. In echoed strides he leads Bandy to a small room at the rear of the building. Inside stands a tall wooden contraption. In the floor at the foot of the machine is a drain.

Bandy recognizes a guillotine.

The lieutenant licks his lips.

"Two thousand prisoners put to death in this room."

Bandy does not walk up to the thing to look down the black drain or feel the wide blade. He keeps his distance, as though this is where the real contagion of the prison is.

The Russian pivots and walks on.

"Where are the Nazis?" Bandy asks, keeping up. "The ones who ran the place?"

The soldier arms open a last door. This lets out onto a courtyard. He lets the metal portal slam with an ugly clang.

"Take your pictures, Bandy."

Several dozen corpses lie piled against a high wall. They are so emaciated, the mound looks more like a discarded stack of the gray-and-blue-striped uniforms. Bullet marks dent the bricks where rounds pierced the bodies of these final victims. With the Russians bearing down, the Nazi keepers of the prison made a last, desperate effort to complete their charge. These prisoners were selected for some reason. Bandy wonders, Who were they, not to be allowed to live another hour? He takes a step closer to the heap. No answer comes from it. Whatever lumped these men together or made them different in life, they shared this end. Did there need to be a reason? What could possibly make sense?

Lined along the opposite wall are two dozen German guards. Like the prisoners, they wear a single uniform. Black and merciless in attire, they stand at rigid attention. These zealots stayed behind while the rest of the prison staff fled.

Bandy takes out his Speed Graphic and enough film packets. He unfolds the accordion of the lens and locks it in place. The Russian lieutenant steps back to let the American photographer do what he was brought here to do, record for the United States press the Nazi atrocities of Brandenburg prison.

Bandy considers the bodies. He turns instead to the line of Nazi guards.

He walks close to the first, raising the camera, focusing tight on the man's face. The Nazi is still as wax.

These are the features of evil, Bandy thinks, not the dead piled at the wall. We'll see the dead time and again in every war, every conflict. But this wicked man. This is what we have to be on watch for. This is what we must recognize and stamp out of humanity. Bandy levels the viewfinder. It's a common face, not inhuman and twisted. Not beautiful and mesmerizing. A typical, grocery store, gas station, salesclerk face in Germany, or America. Waiting for the shot, Bandy questions, how to spot them? They look like the rest of us. The Nazi smirks. Bandy thinks, There you are, you fuck, and releases the shutter.

He files down the column of Nazis, aiming his camera in every face, waiting, waiting for the profanity inside each man to surface. And it does. Bandy snares it on his film like flypaper. With every portrait, he senses the approach of his own finish line, like the poor prisoners who want only to reach the barbed wire, the outer limit of their existence at this prison. With every fresh film pack, Bandy senses a growing exhaustion.

History has been his livelihood. War—the individuals

who wage it and the ground they fight for—has been his passion and art. For nine years Bandy has served as hand-maiden to history. Now he can go no farther. Not if these are the abominations he must report.

He takes another picture, flips the film pack over, and steps in front of the next Nazi. Are these humdrum-looking men really abominations? Or is their touch of massacre, is the Russian taste for vengeance, is the American tolerance for politics and its millions of victims, just business as usual for the conduct of history? Has Charles Bandy, *Life* magazine photographer—with all his travels and pictures and his noto-riety for bringing home the truth in images—simply not seen the truth until now? Is cruelty the actual face of history, the way vileness lurks in the faces of these lined-up Nazis? Bandy has hidden behind his camera so long, he's atrophied his own eyes.

All the history he's shot around the world has been the crushing of the nameless, the conquest of the weak, the ex-alting of the victor regardless of how he became so. How could Bandy have allowed himself to see it all as tidy and glorious, rewarded with medals and honor? How could Bandy have taken half a million photos of so little truth? Why would he spend one more day in the service of such heartless masters as war and history?

He'll take fifteen, twenty more pictures, then he's fin-ished. He feels used, monumentally fooled. This will be his closing gallery. Again—and this is more evidence that he's done this chore long enough with his life—Bandy sees only one man looking back at him from the two dozen Nazi faces. One loathsome man, the conductor on the passage to hell. The historic face in front of his viewfinder is normal, a mask, abhorrent.

Bandy prepares to squeeze the shutter.

The man lifts his chin and sucks his cheeks. He spits past the camera, venom striking Bandy's brow.

Without thought Bandy lets fall the Speed Graphic. The camera cracks on the ground at his feet. Before it rolls to a stop he attacks the Nazi. He throws his hands around the man's neck to slam him against the brick wall. The German defends himself. Bandy chokes with all his might. The Nazi flings his own fingers around Bandy's throat.

Bandy feels nothing but what the Nazi feels, hatred.

They are the same now, one man.

ELEVEN

A ND NOW THE ENEMY IS CHILDREN.
Four hundred boys in black school uniforms push down the street toward Ilya's position. Each one carries against his shoulder a *Panzerfaust,* like a bat for a big game to be played.

Misha reaches for the binoculars. Ilya shrugs the little man off and keeps the field glasses. The boys can't be more than fifteen years old. They don't march in lockstep. Ilya hears no song of bravado from their ranks. They just come. Hitler sends them.

They cannot know what they're walking toward. Six more blocks, amassed in the ruins where Misha and Ilya are perched, wait five hundred artillery pieces. Seven thousand men and guns. Horse carts loaded with enough ammunition to slay these boys a thousand times each.

Ilya is one of the killers of Berlin. He will kill these boys if he has to. He takes no joy in the thought.

Since taking Seelow, Ilya has seen the German defense buckle. On the Oderbruch the enemy fought ferociously. Soviet losses in the valley were terrible. Costly too was the taking of the ridge of towns along the Heights. Once on the plateau, the assault lurched into the far eastern suburbs of

Berlin. Here there were mostly summer cottages, individual wood-frame houses set in their own yards and gardens. Plenty of open space, parkland, and fields helped the Red Army move quickly through these districts. The buildings made poor strongholds, roads were wide and plentiful. The German army reeled backward toward Berlin, without the artillery and ten thousands of men they left behind on the Heights. The Russians poured in, saturating every block and avenue.

Before entering Berlin, Chuikov's Eighth Guards whirled south, to strike the city in its underbelly. Three days ago Ilya's company rode on the backs of First Tanks into the city limits, entering the Neukölln district. Here the density of the buildings thickened. Ilya's men fought past manufacturing plants and tracts of five-story, nineteenth-century rental barracks. Eighth Guards surrounded Templehof Airport, knifed through Schöneberg District, then wheeled north into Wilmersdorf. North lies Charlottenburg. After that, the giant Tiergarten. At the eastern rim of the park stands ground zero, the symbolic center of German government, the Reichstag. The watchword for the assault is speed. Zhukov has announced, when the Soviet flag flies from the roof of the Reichstag, the battle and the war will be over.

Ilya has been surprised to find the fight for Berlin so disjointed. It was not what he, Misha, or the generals expected from the capital of Hitler's regime. Once the clash of nations came to Berlin, they were all prepared for another Stalingrad—a Hitlergrad, the last chapter to the vicious campaigns of the steppe and citadels, the river crossings and titanic tank struggles. Instead, Berlin is like a drunk in a fight; it can't organize its blows, swinging wild punches. The defenders are a mixed and ill-equipped bunch. Captured units consist of regular soldiers, old Home Guardsmen, Hitler Youth, firemen, and policemen, all fighting side by side without commanders. The war has been reduced to sporadic street combat, and street fighting is what Ilya pioneered and endured at Stalingrad. Now that he's in Berlin, he knows the outcome of every skirmish before it starts, prescient like a jungle animal returned to the jungle. But this morning he faces children in battle, and he doesn't know what will happen in the next five minutes.

Ilya hands over the binoculars to Misha. The weapons these boys carry are powerful. They can't be allowed to come much closer.

The schoolmates have taken up arms because their government can't defend them. German soldiers have begun to desert in mobs. Ilya finds uniforms discarded in the ruins. SS extremists roam from cellar to cellar looking for soldiers hiding out with civilians. Many Home Guardsmen choose to face their fates beside their families and run home to them, strewing into the streets armbands and vintage Dutch rifles. Deserters are found hung in public squares or shot in the back, with signs laced around their necks reading: WE STILL HAVE THE POWER. As a result, the defense has no predictable nature; the fights are rarely more than delaying actions, ranging from flimsy to fanatical.

The responding Soviet tactic in Berlin is straightforward and harsh. General Chuikov, the hero of Stalingrad, has decided that Berlin is not going to become a Hitlergrad. At the first hint of resistance from any building or block, artillery hammers the enemy position to rubble. *Katyusha* missiles mounted on American Ford trucks spit racks of phosphorus rockets at point-blank range, igniting firestorms. Giant 203mm cannons crank their barrels even with the sidewalks to unleash rounds as heavy as a truck. A thousand shells pour onto gardens, public squares, anyplace where defenders make themselves known. One machine-gun burst, a sniper in a single window, can bring a whole building down with no thought of the residents on the other floors or in basement shelters. The Russian officers holler at the troops, "Use your weapons!" "Fire at will!" "We've got plenty to spare!"

Once the bastions are in ruins, Red tanks move in, smashing down barricades and blowing up what they can't roll over. Obstacles put in the streets to slow the Russians down, like buses, tramcars, carts loaded with rocks, are blasted to pieces rather than driven around. The tanks fan out in search of targets, emptying their magazines at will, knowing there is plenty.

After the tanks comes the infantry. Foot soldiers flood into the demolished blocks with guns, grenades, knives, and fists. Ilya has few equals in this. Again, he leads the men by deeds, leaving the orders to Misha. He keeps his platoon off the streets, guiding them through holes in walls, connecting cellars, alleys, back gates. Ilya's instincts keep his men alive. They learn fast, and they become lethal. Once an area is secured, they move on, pressing north toward the city center. In their wake, the artillery hauls itself, forming up to demolish the next targeted Berlin street.

Misha exults at the carnage of the city. All the men do. The drunk in the fight is on his knees, not yet facedown, and the less he hits back the harder they strike him, the more abuse they lavish on him. By laughing, cursing, stealing watches from citizens—even at the old folks staggering past him, Misha shouts, *"Uri!"* and points to his own wrist; under his coat he wears German watches up to his elbows, all of them set two hours ahead to Moscow time—Misha shapes the men's attitudes with his actions the way Ilya does in combat. Ilya keeps his counsel on this. He kicks aside bricks, stays low, and surges forward.

The children come closer. They're within three blocks now. A runner hustles into the rubble behind Ilya and Misha.

"Comrade Lieutenant, Comrade Sergeant."

Misha answers. "Yes?"

"What do we do?"

"About?"

The soldier is flustered at this answer. The problem is clear.

"These boys, Comrade. There are several hundred of them."

"I know."

"They're armed, Comrade Sergeant."

"I know this too."

The soldier shuffles. The black boys come nearer every second.

Misha asks, "What do you think they'll do with their *Panzerfausts*?"

"Comrade?"

"When they see our tanks and artillery? What will they do? Do you think they'll come up and bang on our tanks with them? Like sticks?"

"They'll . . . I suppose they'll fire on us, Comrade."

"Well, then." Misha opens his hands like a sage explaining something simple. "It's a good thing we saw them first, isn't it?"

Ilya reaches to Misha's hand and takes the binoculars. He is going to override what Misha is about to say.

But Misha grins at Ilya. He tells the soldier, "Find a way to disarm them. Fire flares to tell them our position. Send a few rounds over their heads. Let's scare them out of it. They're kids in knee pants. They ought to be spanked. That's all."

The soldier is pleased with this order. He turns to rush out through the debris and spread the word before anyone can pull a trigger.

Ilya stops the soldier. "Nikolai?"

Misha makes a large, comic face. Ilya knows someone's name?

"Yes, Lieutenant?"

"If they don't scare easily. Children or not."

The soldier takes in this bitter notion. Ilya is satisfied.

"Go on."

The soldier hurries out.

Little Misha says nothing. He moves to the opposite wall and slumps against it, sticking out one leg, raising a knee; he looks rakish. He pulls out his tobacco pouch to roll another cigarette. Ilya watches Misha's hands; the man is deft, forging the cylinder tight and even. He tosses it on his lips with the cavalier flip of a seasoned smoker, some bigger man than he is. Ilya envies Misha's chameleon abilities. He's grown a scar. He smokes more than any of the men. Misha outswears them, drinks vodka swallow for swallow with the largest country boys. He affects a brave swagger, issues orders, spouts strategies in the middle of battle. The men enjoy, embrace, even follow him. He says what they want to hear, like that order to frighten the schoolboys. In five months, Misha's transformed himself from a coward to a charismatic.

In the street, the children have advanced close enough for Ilya to hear their tramping boots. They've come through the ruins looking for the Soviet front lines. Ilya wants to grasp why this is happening, how it's come that four hundred children were given weapons and sent to die. What's been put into their heads to make them come here? Who would do this to them? There isn't time to figure it all out. Ilya takes up his submachine gun. He levels it at the advancing boys. This is crazy, Ilya thinks. Insanity aiming at insanity.

Golden flares shoot into the morning sky. There's a dozen of them, spread over several blocks. The flares demark the large Russian position in the wreckage ahead of the children. Many of those in the front ranks jump when the flares rear up. Ilya thinks, Run. But all that happens is sparks and crackle and little parachutes. The boys pack tighter in the street and continue to come. *Panzerfausts* are lowered from shoulders to hands, poised and ready.

A cannon barks. The shell crashes into the side of a building behind, gouging another chunk out of it. Heads turn in the boys' thick number. Run for it, Ilya thinks. Run.

The boys do run, but not where Ilya would have them go. They break into a charge behind flashes and smoke trails of fired *Panzerfausts*. They've spotted the Russian artillery. Ten, now twenty of the children fire their loads, the rockets streak past Ilya's position. The boys who have fired slow their dash forward, having done their duty for Fatherland and survived. The others push past them, closing on the Russians they've spotted.

More *Panzerfausts* tear down the street. Ilya tenses on his trigger. Behind him, horses whinny from wounds, explosions erupt among the Russian lines. Now the boys begin to die. Bullets rip into the ones in front. Ilya bites his teeth and fires. He kills three children with the PPSh, could kill fifty, but he stops. The remaining boys falter in attack, not a one leaps over his fallen mates. The Russians stop shooting. Another flare goes up. With a golden pop, it sails, looking down on the boys. The survivors disperse, tossing their weapons, keeping their lives.

Ilya lowers his gun. He knows which three of the many bodies in the street were the boys he shot. He wonders: Is it a battlefield—even when both sides bear arms—where children lie dead?

He wants to figure this out. This, and so many other things. He harbors questions, hordes of them, one for every person he's killed. While the gun barrel is still warm, with the smoke in his nostrils, now is the time to think.

He lays his cheek against the stock of his weapon. He closes his eyes. Ilya knows the answers. They're inside him, he's sure of it. He takes a first step to them and is stopped. He feels a void, like a bridge down. He doesn't know any other way across. Ilya senses too that what he seeks is close, just out of reach. This is maddening.

He holds the questions out: Here, he calls into himself, I need these answered. But the part of him that can lead him onward is mute.

Ilya begins to feel afraid. He hasn't traveled this path since the war began; for four years he's been on another, violent course where answers were not needed, just skill and duty. Now he wants to comprehend. He's lost and at a standstill, holding out the questions into his dark and silent self with the weight of a corpse.

Ilya fears this more than any danger he's ever faced, the threat that he might never understand what he's done.

He turns away from the street. Misha has not moved from the wall. The little man exhales a cloud.

April 28, 1945, 9:40 A.M.
In a C-46 heading west
Above the Rhine River
Germany

BANDY WANTS DISTANCE. AS MUCH AS HE CAN GET, AS fast as he can get it.

He looks down through the window of the closed jump door. The benches are empty, the steel floor is level and quiet, this ride to London is loud and smooth. No flak outside, no sweaty scared soldiers inside. Just Charley Bandy alone, trying to remember nothing, and failing.

The sun glints on the river Rhine below. The plane's not high enough, Bandy can still see the rents and rips of warfare on the earth, a bridge is down in the river. Sooted tanks and craters spoil fields that ought to be green but are brown, dotted black, and fallow. Higher, Bandy thinks, fly higher. Get above some clouds. Shut this out. Bandy wants white between him and the black, brown, and red of Europe.

He moves from the window. He takes a seat on a bench. He has no camera with him, no film. He has no pack at all, just the dirty clothes on his back. This plane flies empty, shuttling to London to bring forward press, some dignitaries, maybe more soldiers and supplies. No one is heading backward just yet. Everybody wants to go the other way, where the action is, where the war ends, to say they were there. Bandy isn't sure how long it will be before he will want to say that.

When he lands in London, he'll hitch the first ride he can find to the States. He wants a shower, he wants a meal, rest, a shave. Bandy's body makes demands, and he begrudges himself those needs because they will slow him down getting to Tennessee.

That's where he'll figure it all out. He'll stand on his grandfather's dirt, which became his father's and now his. He'll breathe the mountains and clean streams, suck the sweetness of his wife and the tobacco tar on his fingers. These are the ingredients, the conditions he requires. Home will be his darkroom.

He works his sore right hand. The knuckles are raw from the Nazi's face. Bandy bashed him as many times as he could. The Russians did nothing to pull the men apart. The Nazi got in some licks but Bandy swarmed him with blows. Bandy would die killing. He did not decide this. It just happened, it lay waiting inside him like some jack-in-the-box for the right time to spring out. Bandy didn't stop himself. The Nazi knew Bandy would kill him if he could and the Reds would watch. The man rammed a knee into Bandy's groin. He had to do it twice before Bandy let go. The Nazi staggered up and ran until a Russian clubbed him down with a rifle butt. Bandy lay dazed, shock dousing him. He was confused for minutes after he got up. He pulled the Leica from his pack and flung it against the firing squad wall, silver pieces landing on the bodies. He drove out of Brandenburg, all the way through the Barby bridgehead, across the Truman Bridge, not stopping until he was far to the rear, where he found an airstrip. He spent the night, and in the morning caught this flight to London.

"Any of us," he says aloud, but the engines drone out his words. He needs to hear himself, to use his voice instead of a camera. That's why he hurries to Victoria, because she'll ask and he'll make himself answer.

For now, he completes the sentence under the roar of the propellers.

"Any one of us can kill."

It doesn't matter a damn who you are and what you think you know about yourself.

Any one of us.

He'll tell her. What he saw, what he did. What he became in the end, the hate that changed him and exiled him. The scar on his leg will get explained, the story of the jump and his close call and the German boys. He'll show her the good-bye letter he kept for the war years wrapped in his breast pocket. The race for Berlin, the disappointment of having it taken from him. He'll turn every horror he saw into tales the way he turned them into photographs. The bodies. The hangings. The prison. The broken cameras. His desire to take a man's life, even that rotten man. He'll bury the dead under tobacco and work, he'll plant his rage in her furrows, and in time they'll fertilize something better inside him.

Bandy prays. He asks God to let it come true that something better will grow.

The green inside of the plane is hard, there are no soft surfaces to cushion the engine noise and rushing winds. Bandy leaves the bench and lies flat on the floor. The vibrations under his back are more acute than they were under his boots. He closes his eyes, feeling Germany and France slide away far beneath him. He seems to hear every rivet in the plane creak.

———

April 29, 1945, 5:30 P.M.
Savigny Platz bomb shelter
Charlottenburg, Berlin

"SHHHH!"

Mutti's hand comes into Lottie's lap. Her fingers tighten over Lottie's wrist.

One of the old women of the shelter continues to jabber. Everyone is nervous, but this one will not stop talking. She's shushed again, this time by many lips.

"All right!" the woman snaps. She shuts her coat around her as though she is cold.

"Someone's coming." Several voices say this.

In the dry goods store overhead, footfalls sound. There are three, four, it's hard to tell; from below, they seem careful steps. No heels thud the floorboards, only toes, cautious treads.

There is a knock on the door leading down to the shelter. Not a knock: a kick.

Another kick. For five hours these thirty women have

listened to explosions and fighting rock the streets above. The bare beams of the shelter have shuddered at each deep report reaching them through the earth and air. The women imagined the scene, the battleground that is their homes and shops. They've jumped in their seats and huddled against trickling dust. Nothing they've heard or envisioned frightens them like this sound of a boot against their last bulwark, the shelter door.

The hinges creak. Freya's arm shoots around Lottie's shoulder. Every woman in the shelter pulls tighter some piece of her clothing, tugging on a sweater, a raincoat, a kerchief. A flashlight beam cuts down the steps, motes of dust dance in it. The light sweeps left and right, descending in a soldier's hand.

No one draws a breath. Mutti grips Lottie with both arms, pressing her daughter close.

The talkative old woman speaks.

"Drusya."

The flashlight stops in the stairwell, leaps across the faces searching for the one who spoke. The old woman says the word again, *"Drusya."*

The beam looks for her while she explains to the rest in the shelter, "I said we're friends. I learned this word. He won't hurt us if he thinks we're . . ."

The soldier aims the beam at the woman's face. This fastens her mouth.

The spotlight stays on her for a moment, examining her wrinkles and rheumy eyes. The soldier comes the rest of the way to the last step, onto the shelter's dirt floor. The light courses over every woman in the shelter. The beam is looking for men.

The shaft settles on Freya and Lottie. It lingers. The hand holding the flashlight lets the beam be his eye and fingertips, there is a stroking in the light's play over the two clutching women.

The soldier turns the light into his own face. His eyes, set over dirty cheeks, are oblique, Mongol. He wears a hat with fur earflaps tied on top. In his other hand is a huge gun with a round magazine. He lowers the barrel of this weapon away from the women.

"*Drusya*," he says. "*Da.*"

The soldier clicks off the flashlight. The room is darker in the first seconds. The Russian shouts something up the stairwell to his comrades in the shop. Their steps tell they are leaving.

The soldier puts his big gun back in his hands. He lays his boot on the lowest tread to climb out of the shelter.

He turns to the women and speaks a word in German.

"Free."

In a few loud clomps he ascends the steps, joins the others, and they are gone.

Disbelief hangs in the shelter. That was a Russian soldier standing in the middle of them, in the center of Berlin. Now he has left, was he really there? The stain of the flashlight stays on their pupils, the smell of the man is oily and piquant with battle and sweat. The women continue to stare at the place where he stood, until one by one their eyes fall, as though the weight of what they saw is too great.

No one can speak. It seems an act of courage to comment and none of the women is up to it, not even the old mouthy one. The street above is shed of gunfire. Now the world sounds ordinary, crisp with traffic and voices.

Freya stands. All the women's chins lurch up as though they are tethered to Mutti. Only Lottie continues to gaze where the Red soldier stood.

"Come on," Freya says, gripping Lottie under the arm, "come on."

Lottie lets herself be towed up the steps. The women of the shelter stay put, there are no words of farewell, no wishes for luck.

The two emerge into the dry goods store. Days ago the shop was looted for its last bits of cloth and thread. Lottie and Mutti walk fast through empty shelves and broken glass. Mutti pushes open the door to dusk falling on the Savigny Platz. She gets a solid grip on Lottie's hand.

The Soviet army is setting up camp in the plaza. Trucks

come and go delivering men and supplies. Tents go up, stakes are driven between the cobblestones. A field kitchen already does a brisk business; a line of Russian soldiers waits with metal plates, smoke from a large brazier films the whole plaza. Well-groomed horses in livery are tethered to lamp-posts. Moseying up Knesebeck Strasse into the square is a herd of sheep and lowing cattle accompanied by horse- and ox-drawn carts. The Savigny Platz becomes a Russian barn-yard.

Freya and Lottie stay close to the buildings, skirting the massing soldiers. The odors of the men and animals are tangs in Lottie's nostrils. A Russian soldier strolls past them on the sidewalk carrying a pink summer parasol. He inclines his head.

Lottie laughs.

Freya hears this. Her squeeze on Lottie's hand hardens. She quickens her pace until the two are at a trot out of the plaza. Lottie runs behind her mother, continuing to gawk at the conquerors of Berlin.

Most of the Russians don't appear to have been in a city before. They can't ride bicycles, trying and falling, jiggling the handlebars back and forth in awful balance. They complain when they get up, scraping knees like little boys. Many Reds stand with hands on hips looking at the ruins, as though the buildings are still intact and they're just tourists marveling at Berlin's architecture. One soldier stops them, rolling back his coat sleeve to display an arm mailed in watches. His whole arm ticks. He points at Mutti and Lottie, who do not have watches. The soldier shrugs, almost friendly, and waves them on. The two women are out of breath. They walk part of the way to Goethe Strasse, past soldiers defecating in alleys, shepherds of smelly goats and pigs, weapon-laden dirty men with women's shawls lapping their shoulders. When Mutti can, she drags Lottie again into a run.

The Soviets have been heavy-handed in their battle for Charlottenburg. On some blocks the destruction is as bad as the aftermaths of the *Amis'* air raids, though the Russian demolition is of a different brand. Where the Allies' bombs crushed entire structures to dust and rubble, the Reds have clawed into Charlottenburg. Buildings bear gaping holes hollowed by artillery, smaller bite marks range from several meters to the tinier mauls of bullets and shrapnel. For the first time the dead in Berlin's streets are not civilians or foreign workers but soldiers. Freya and Lottie hurry past and notice the bodies are only German; the Reds have claimed theirs and left the defenders where they fell. The corpses are of every age, smooth boys and young soldiers and the elder *Volkssturm,* all men who thought they could make a difference, and have, for they are dead.

There is no single appearance to the Soviets. They are swarthy men, blond and fair, red-haired and freckled, olive-skinned, bearded and shaggy, or trimmed and neat. Their eyes are round or slanted or almond-shaped. Their uniforms are green, gray, brown, they wear dozens of hats and colorful caps and helmets. After years of Nazi tirades about the horrible Russians, these men simply look like foreign soldiers—ethnic, deadly, even a bit barbaric and out-of-date.

Lottie knows she must fear the invaders. She sees what their guns have done. German bodies in the road display the Russian resolve and cruelty. But Lottie in her heart has left Berlin, and the fear she senses of the Russians is the same she would feel if she were sitting safe in another land reading about Berlin. She worries for her city and her Mutti but not for herself. The Reds cannot touch her because she has protected herself, she is gone.

Freya leads Lottie back to Goethe Strasse. Reaching their block, Freya halts, bringing a flat hand to her breast at the sight of her spared house. There are marks of battle everywhere. The Russians' indiscriminate shelling has left smoke rising from many buildings. Freya's home is in the center of a row of attached stone faces that has withstood the assault. She tows Lottie to her steps. Soviet soldiers are on the street, walking with guns and heads lifted, searching rooftops and high windows for snipers. Apparently the fight for this block has ended just minutes before. Brass casings litter Freya's steps. An upstairs window has been blasted out. One bullet hole is in the door.

"*Ach*," Mutti sighs, "dear God." She turns to Lottie. "We're home. I was so worried."

Lottie is curious, not angry, at the suggestion. She asks, "About Julius?"

Mutti cocks her head. Her smile is slow, reluctant. It is honest.

"Yes, *Liebchen*."

Still hand-in-hand they walk into the house.

In the parlor Mutti lets Lottie go.

"Wait here."

Freya walks down the long hall to the yellow door. Lottie cannot hear what her mother says to the Jew. But her mother speaks, then listens, so he is still there.

Freya returns to the front room carrying a straight-backed kitchen chair. In her other hand is a towel and a pair of scissors. Tucked under her arm is a broom.

She sets the chair in the middle of the room.

"Sit down."

Lottie takes the seat. The towel is wrapped around her shoulders.

Mutti stands in front of Lottie. The two say nothing, though Mutti's eyes express, I'm sorry, I have to do this. Lottie does not let her own face convey anything.

Freya walks behind Lottie. The scissors snip. A lock flutters to Lottie's lap. She brushes it away with the back of her hand.

With every rasp of the shears another soft cascade tumbles off Lottie's shoulders. Her blond curls pile on the parlor rug. Gazing down at them, she refuses the tug of metaphor. Spilled gold. Lost innocence. The hair falls with no sound or impact, it is not a momentous thing. It's just hair, she thinks. Why make up images, why see or feel more than you have to?

Freya is glum at her work, chopping her daughter's hair back to a boy's crew cut. At first there is no talk between them, just the slice of the scissors. Mutti clucks her tongue when she exposes the scab on the back of Lottie's head from the iron gates of the Zoo.

Halfway through the cut, Lottie notes the pace of the shears speed up. Mutti seems to clip with agitation, flinging bits of her daughter's hair to the floor.

Mutti says, "Lottie, when we're finished, I want you to go upstairs and put on some old work clothes. There's a pair of baggy pants and some sweaters in your dresser. I have a pair of boots for you too. You'll put them on and keep them on."

Lottie makes no answer.

Snip.

Freya continues.

"I'm going to burn a cork. We can smear it on your face and hands."

Snip.

"Then we'll hide the silver and the good picture frames. And my rings. There's a little food left, we'll put that away somewhere."

Lottie feels the weight falling from her head.

She says, "It doesn't matter."

Next to her ear the scissors make an angry cut.

Mutti's tone is taut. "Don't fight me on this, Lottie. Do as I say."

Lottie repeats, "It doesn't matter."

One more snip, and Freya stomps her foot. She marches in front, shaking the scissors in Lottie's face.

"You have got to snap out of this! Right now! You've got to stop being so selfish. I can't fight you every step of the way. I can't bear any more."

Lottie focuses on the point of the scissors. Freya lowers them. She stops herself from saying more and moves behind her daughter to finish the haircut.

The shears snip for several minutes.

Mutti speaks again, this time in a restrained voice, not to kindle an argument.

"I want you to hide. I want you to go upstairs and find a place."

"No."

Freya continues as though she did not hear.

"Go down in the basement with Julius. I'll keep them from looking for you."

Lottie hawks up a laugh.

"How do you expect to do that?"

Mutti does not answer.

Lottie shakes her head. This stops Freya from cutting.

Lottie says, "No, it doesn't matter. Hide everything in the house. They'll find what they want anyway. They'll look, they'll tear the house apart until they do."

Mutti strides again in front of Lottie.

Lottie runs fingers through her butchered hair. She makes her voice gentle for her fraying mother.

"They'll find me."

Freya takes a step forward. Her hands rise to cup Lottie's chin, the scissors come close to her face. Her mother draws a breath, it becomes a shudder. Freya shakes her head in solemn motion.

"I know, *Liebchen*. I know."

Mutti rubs a palm over Lottie's shorn head. There's little left on her scalp but bristles.

"*Ach,* your hair."

"It'll grow back."

"I'm finished," Mutti says. "I can only make it worse."

Mutti takes her daughter's hand. The two look at each other in silence. Though they're alone, the parlor feels crowded by the Jew, the Russians, the war, the future.

Freya grows teary.

"I'll cut mine too," she says. "That'll make it up to you."

"You don't have to."

Freya takes the towel from around Lottie's shoulders. She shakes it out on the floor.

"I'll sweep up."

"Mutti?"

"Yes, *Liebchen*?"

"How will you keep them away from the basement?"

"Don't worry about me. I'm an old woman."

Freya grabs the broom and begins to clean the carpet. Lottie asks again, "How?"

Freya stops. She faces her daughter.

Lottie changes her mind. She rattles her head and looks down to her lap.

"No, Mutti. Don't tell me. It doesn't matter."

Freya clings to the broom.

"Stop saying that. It does. Now more than ever, when it seems like everything hurts. This is when we matter most."

Freya leans the broom against the parlor sofa. She stands erect, preparing herself. She smooths her hands down her dress.

"The food I've been bringing home the last few months. Since Julius moved into the basement. You know the ration cards were never enough."

"I know."

"I will never let the two of you starve."

Lottie looks on.

Freya works her hands. "The black market. I traded on it."

"I know."

"Child, I traded sex."

Lottie shows no reaction. Even she is surprised at her own stillness. This declaration should have jolted her backward. Her mother is a secret whore. For months men have paid her in packets and tins. She's saved a Jew, she's fed her daughter, and become a slut. Lottie waits, poised, waiting to hate her mother.

Lottie looks back over the past months and thinks she might have guessed this. She might have wondered at things and asked. She could have seen clues. Could have been concerned. But she wasn't.

Lottie sits in the kitchen chair. Mutti stands before her, awaiting judgment. Lottie says nothing, no verdict. She feels scoured. There is no reproach in her for Mutti. There's not even indignity for Papa's memory. She sits under this bombshell from her mother the way she sat beneath the Russian shells. Lottie is resigned, curled up into a ball like a man taking a beating, she feels each blow a little less than the one before it.

Lottie gazes up at her mother. Without emotion, she thinks: This is an extraordinary time, and Mutti has clearly become extraordinary with the war. Lottie has stayed behind. Now that music has been taken from her, and the cello stays locked in its case, she's been exposed: not exceptional at all. Mutti has sacrificed and dared without boundary to help her daughter and a stranger survive. Lottie, for all her brilliance, must be such a disappointment.

Lottie rises, spilling more hair onto the floor. She brushes clinging curls from her skirt. She lifts the chair and takes the scissors from Mutti's pocket. They've barbered Lottie's hair in the front room so Julius wouldn't hear them. She knows this without being told.

Carrying the chair and scissors back to the kitchen, Lottie walks past the yellow door. A thousand times she's done this and the silent door has reached to her every chance. The life of the man behind it always trips her with its complexity. The discipline of the Jew. His peril. His woe.

Not today.

Today Lottie's sacrifice is greater than the Jew's. The woman who debased herself for them was his protector. But she is Lottie's mother.

She sets the things in the kitchen and strides past the basement door with a new sensation. At last, Lottie's life and her own danger are equal to what sits in the dark on the top step. He is a Jew in Berlin, yes, and that has been a terrible thing. But Lottie is a young woman in Berlin. The Russians are here now. They will not come looking for Jews.

She speaks to the door.

"Julius."

He is there.

"Yes."

"Did you know that Mutti was selling herself to feed you? You and me?"

"Selling herself?"

"Yes. Sex. For black-market food."

The door pauses.

"No."

"No, of course not."

Lottie steps away.

"Did you?"

She stops.

"No. She just told me."

"What would you have done? If you'd known?"

Lottie doesn't have to answer. She has the right not to answer. But he doesn't.

She asks, "What would you have done?"

"I would have stopped her."

Lottie smirks. "How?"

"I would have left."

Yes, he would have. Because that's who this Jew is.

"Lottie, she's your mother. What would you have done?"

She gazes at the broad yellow panel of the door. Come out, she thinks, and I'll slap you. I'll choke you, I'll throw you down the stairs.

But the answer inside her is not like the Jew, it lacks his discipline to stay in the darkness any longer. It does come out.

Nothing. She would have done nothing.

She sees in her mind her mother beneath a Nazi. Lottie sits beside the bed eating a biscuit with only her cello between her legs.

Lottie's knees weaken. She stumbles against the wall.

"Lottie? Lottie, are you all right?"

The Jew would emerge from the basement if he thought she was in trouble. He would try to protect her, at his own risk.

Like Mutti. She has done everything to safeguard her daughter. So much, that by her own words she can't do any more.

Lottie has done nothing.

Nothing but wish for protection. Nothing but whisk herself away in her heart, contemplate suicide, fantasize, and complain. She hasn't lifted a finger to deserve protection. And that's why now she does not have it. The Jew can't help her, no matter how brave or selfless a man. Mutti will be defenseless when the Russians come. But they try. They suffer for each other, for her, and they try.

The reality is obvious, a simple calculation, another blow. There is no protection for Lottie. She has never been worth protecting.

Not like Julius.

And Mutti.

Lottie is nothing.

She rights herself against the wall. She steadies her voice. "Julius."

"Yes."

"I want you to know. I would have done nothing."

She expects the yellow door to grow narrow, like a disapproving eye. But the voice behind it says, "Yes, you would have. Of course you would."

Lottie walks away, into the parlor. She's relieved that the Jew is wrong. She feels better knowing this, that he fools himself like anyone else.

Freya is on her knees gathering the last of Lottie's hair. Stacked on the sofa are a pair of pants and three sweaters. Beside the table stands a pair of battered boots.

"Mutti, sit down with me."

Freya moves to the sofa. Lottie joins her and sees her mother has been crying. Mutti lifts one hand to her mouth but cannot stifle herself. Lottie has nothing to hand her to sop the tears. She reaches for one of the wool sweaters and lays it over Mutti's lap.

Lottie puts a gentle hand to her mother's back.

"Mutti?"

Freya turns with red eyes.

"Mutti, does Julius still have the yellow star?"

Freya shakes her head. "I sold it for food. Like he asked."

Lottie imparts a smile. "Did you get him his holiday potatoes and parsley?"

"Yes. And more for all of us. I did."

Mutti says this to convince her daughter that some of the food they have eaten was purchased with money. Lottie eases her mother's shame with another stroke down her back.

There is a small cache of candles and matches in the table beside the sofa. Lottie slides over to fetch a taper. She strikes a match, the burning wick lights the parlor. Night has crested in Berlin.

Freya calms slowly. Lottie watches the shifting shadows in the parlor.

She says to her mother, "He'll try to defend us."

Freya's damp eyes gleam. "Yes. He will."

Outside of the cellar, without his cloth star—that emblem of despised Jewry for so many years, now an ironic passport to survival— Julius is just another German man. A soldier out of uniform. A deserter. A Nazi. To the Russians, these are the German men.

"They'll shoot him."

"Yes."

"We've got to keep them away from the basement."

Freya purses her lips. She makes to bring her hands again to her mouth—such sad worry—but drops them to her lap. One more tear slips down her cheek.

"Lottie. Please hide."

Now it is the daughter who does not heed.

"Go back to the door. Tell Julius not to come out, no matter what he hears. Tell him the Nazis plan to take back this block and he has to stay hidden. Just a few more days. Soon. Until it's over."

From the street beyond the parlor window, Russian voices intrude through the curtains. Lottie doesn't need to decipher the tongue to know the men are drunk.

"Mutti, go!"

Freya leaps from the sofa to hurry down the hall. Another flashlight beam, like the one in the bomb shelter, flashes across the window.

The voices outside gather. Lottie's breath shivers. She runs both hands over her head, through her stiff tips of hair. Her mouth goes dry waiting for Mutti to return.

There's a knock at the door.

Not a knock: a kick.

A voice. Ganged laughter. A call.

"Frau."

More laughter. Some Russian words, a short argument.

Lottie closes her eyes.

One soldier's voice is insistent. He's sure there are women inside. He's seen them go in. This is what the voice says, in every language, in ancient tone. Lottie does not jump when the next kick strikes the door.

"Frau. Komm!"

Lottie rises from the sofa. She moves into the hall, to the outer reach of the candle. She stands in the foyer. A dark eye, lit by the sallow beam of a flashlight, blinks at her through the bullet hole in the door.

"Komm!"

Freya bustles into the hall beside her. The two women stare at the eye in the door.

"Julius knows it's Russians. I told him the Nazis were chasing them. He's hiding."

"Good."

The locked doorknob is jiggled. Another kick pounds the door.

Freya grips her daughter by the shoulders.

"This is going to be hard."

"I know."

"Liebchen, forgive me. Do you . . . Dear God, I can't believe I have to ask you like this. Do you know . . . ?"

"Yes, Mutti. It's been a while. But yes."

"Just let them. Just live through it. I'm so sorry."

"Open the door, Mutti."

Freya draws herself up. She runs a hand down her daughter's arm.

Four Russians push through the opened door. The moment they step into the foyer Lottie is repelled by the smell. Their uniforms are splotched with dirt, their breath is sodden in vodka. They all bear large rifles. Three are young men with slender faces. They mount dumb, menacing expressions; their leers are theatrical, as if forced, to show these two German women whom they're dealing with. They swagger around Lottie and Freya, swathing them in Russian and odor and flashlight beams. One points his weapon at Lottie's shorn head and jeers. The fourth soldier stands aside. He is older. He's their leader, the one who kicked the door and called out for women. He looks to be the most ignorant. He is thickset and dark, his head is poorly hung on his neck from too much liquor. He says nothing now, only grunts, looks up through shaggy eyebrows.

Lottie can see these soldiers are driven by anger, with deep scores to settle. They want plunder, the victor's prize. It means stolen watches and sex, also revenge and unbridled power, dream things denied these peasant soldiers for years of war. Tonight and tomorrow and until they're stopped, they will shame every German man, every soldier of the Reich dead or alive, by taking Berlin's women, the ultimate primal victory.

The soldiers continue to circle. The sounds of breathing fill the hallway. Freya's hand squeezes in Lottie's.

Lottie realizes she can endure this. She can deny herself to them even if they will have her body. She will not fight. She'll surrender. But they'll take nothing from her, no prize, no woman, no Russian triumph, they might as well pluck an empty vase from the table.

The soldiers stop their appraisal. The four pair off. Freya's hand slips from Lottie's. Mother and daughter separate, fixing each other's eyes. Freya nods. Lottie nods in return.

Without instruction from the soldiers, Freya heads up the stairs. Her shoes are not heavy on the treads but a controlled, determined scrape. Two of the soldiers follow, both younger ones. One man pushes Freya in the back, for no reason, just to vent some violence on this woman. The other soldier shines his flashlight ahead to navigate the steps.

Lottie walks into the candle glow of the parlor. The dark one staggers behind while the other soldier moves down the hall. This one sweeps his flashlight first into the dining room, then toward the kitchen and basement door. Lottie goes after him. She lays a hand on his narrow shoulder to pull him back to the parlor. He should be suspicious of this, but Lottie has guessed right, he's drunk and he wants her more than he wants to do his job. He follows.

In the parlor, the dark one wavers and sits on the sofa beside the anxious flame. His rifle lies across his lap, on guard first. The young one sits too, setting his gun far from Lottie's reach. He cuts off the flashlight. He leans over to untie his boots. Lottie allows herself a private snort at the accommodation.

She stands in the middle of the parlor rug, looking down. The candle makes the carpet quiver. The dark man stinks.

Lottie grits her teeth. She follows the man's hands on his boot laces. She will not look in their faces anymore.

She will keep them away from the basement. She will hold them quiet, whatever it is she has to do. She will clamp her own cries shut, no matter how much everything hurts.

Mutti and she will do these things. And more. Tonight. Tomorrow. Until it stops. Until what the first Red soldier in the shelter told them comes true: They are free.

At last, Lottie understands.

This is the only victory.

They—the Nazis, the Russians—will not have Julius.

They will not have us.

In all the war; in all Lottie's life.

This matters.

April 29, 1945, 7:10 P.M.
Prime Minister's residence at Chequers
Buckinghamshire, England

IN THE STUDY THERE IS A GLOBE. IT IS ANTIQUE AND large, rising to Churchill's chest. The ball is brown, the seas are parchment colored. With a tumbler of Scotch in hand, Churchill studies the thing. He doesn't know to whom it belongs, it's just always been a part of the PM's home. The public owns it, then. He traces fingertips from the Arctic down to the equator, imagining the ice, the ocean, trade winds. He takes hold and spins the cool world. The axis creaks, the earth pirouettes, nations and seas blur.

He lets it twirl. There's something pleasing about seeing the earth like this, without its boundaries and names, just the planet in motion in his study where the lights are low and he holds a good single malt. The ball turns well on its frame. Churchill admires his power to have made this happen.

The globe revolves a long time, reluctant to quit turning; it is well balanced, which one expects from a planet. Churchill is tempted to spin it again, that was nice. Instead, he lets it come to a standstill, like a roulette wheel, he waits as though some fate will be revealed in what will finally face him.

When it is done he is presented with Africa.

Again he touches the globe. He draws one finger across the breadth of the vast continent. Africa is the battleground where England's brave Tommies first squared off against the Axis powers, in Libya, Somaliland, Ethiopia, Egypt. The northern deserts are depicted by light shades of sienna. Churchill is not put in mind to recall those great victories of 1942 and '43. He harks back farther in time, to the final year of the previous century. He wets his tongue with the Scotch and lets his finger run where his heart has gone, to South Africa.

He thinks of escape.

He was twenty-five years old, a young military correspondent with the British forces opposing the Dutch-speaking Boers. In November 1899, while traveling with a company of one hundred fifty troops reconnoitering enemy positions, his armored train was shelled. Several cars were derailed. Many soldiers were killed. Under fire, Churchill led the effort to collect the wounded and put them on the engine to be taken to safety. He stayed behind with a platoon to hold off the approaching Boers. Churchill was captured with these men and tossed into a Boer prison camp.

After a month of captivity, he laid plans with two others to escape. He jumped the latrine house wall, but the other two could not follow. He waited in the garden for hours, then set out on his own. In civilian clothes, he walked straight down the road. He could not utter a word of Dutch, but no one, not even a sentry, addressed him.

Churchill made straight for the rail yard and hopped a car full of empty coal bags. He rode east until morning, then jumped off, figuring his escape had been noticed by then and the trains would be searched.

The Boers posted a bounty on his head, twenty-five pounds, dead or alive. Later, Churchill memorized the fugitive description of him circulated across the Transvaal: *Englishman 25 years old, about 5 ft 8 inches tall, average build, walks with a slight stoop, pale appearance, red brown hair, almost invisible small moustache, speaks through the nose, cannot pronounce the letter "s," cannot speak Dutch, has last been seen in a brown suit of clothes.* They'd gotten rather personal in their portrait, what with the stoop and the speech impediment, and that gibe at his first moustache.

He rolls the Scotch glass in his hand.

Hmpf. Stooped, indeed.

Well, he thinks, it was a stooped, lisping little shit of a nasal Englishman who got away. He lucked into a small group of sympathetic English coal miners who hid him in a cave. For three days he had no one for company but rats, the little rotters even ate his candle. He got sick in the darkness. After three days of this, he was spirited aboard another train, where he lay buried for two more days in a stack of wool bales, supplied with two roast chickens, some cooked meat slices, a loaf of bread, and a revolver. The train headed for Portuguese East Africa. When he emerged, he was black as a chimney sweep from coal dust in the car. He was so elated, he crowed and sang at the top of his lungs and fired his pistol three times in the air.

Churchill has not taken his finger from the globe. South Africa is so far away on this old ball, so far too behind time and events of his life. He was unburdened in those days by any thought but survival, driven only to see his mother and homeland again. The sense of it all returns to his breast, bracing and pure. It's akin to the feeling he had moments ago spinning the globe, of standing off the world, making it go with a shove of one hand, being so huge he is beyond the measurements of responsibility and history. That is what it was like when he was young and in danger, before this whole bloody world was put in his custody. Now his stoop is far worse.

He lifts his eyes above Africa, across the Mediterranean, to his Europe. The war here is not finished, even though the fighting will end sometime in the next few days. Berlin and Hitler will not hold out under the Russian onslaught. But what will this Europe look like once the papers have been signed and the smoke clears?

Churchill takes a swallow of Scotch. The dash of alcohol down his throat breaks him out of all reverie. There's a starkness to the reality on this globe.

He slides his finger north, to Germany. He draws his nail through the middle of the country, down the Elbe River. On one side of the line there is Belgium, Holland, Luxembourg, Norway, Sweden, Denmark, France, Italy, Spain, Portugal, Switzerland, Greece, the United Kingdom. On the other, Poland, Hungary, Czechoslovakia, Yugoslavia, Bulgaria, Romania, Austria, Albania, Finland, the Ukraine, Lithuania, Latvia, Estonia, Russia.

A curtain is falling across Europe. It splits Germany in two, and profoundly divides the free world from the Communists. Tens of millions from tens of millions, separated by ideology as surely as they are by weapons.

Churchill must watch it happen. He knows how to fight it, but Britain's voice is not heard so loudly as it once was. He begs Truman in daily correspondence to allow the Allied troops to hold their positions everywhere on the battlefields. Do not take one step back, rush east with tanks and soldiers as fast and as far as possible.

But the Americans are tired of our war, Churchill thinks. His appeals to Truman are met with polite parries. The President agrees in principle, then orders no action. The Yanks will not keep men and arms in Europe for as long as it

will take to stare Stalin down. England has the stomach for
it, but alas, England is only the gut, and maybe the head; the
United States is the legs and arms. Though Truman is a new
sort, a bolder man than Roosevelt, even he bends under political truths. There is no support in the U.S. for another
fight, especially against Russia, their ally. Americans are a
friendly bunch, taken as a whole. They are reluctant to
brand villains. They just finished with Hitler, they're about
to settle Hirohito's hash, and they have no longing to iden-
tify another threat. Truman and his countrymen want to finish the war in the Pacific, then get on with the business of
making America greater.

Well, good for them.

Churchill stands before the globe in checkmate. There is
nowhere he can put his finger now. The days of power are
gone.

There's little left for him to do but accept defeat in the
jaws of victory.

He cannot demand anything from Stalin. He can only ask.
So ask he will.

Churchill moves to his desk. He freshens his Scotch glass,
takes a bolt, and writes. The telegram is long. Point by point
he sets out again his arguments for Stalin to accept the dictates of Yalta. He pleads for a sovereign, free, and democratic Poland. He sounds the warning of Tito's ambitions in
Yugoslavia. He addresses Stalin's suspicion and ill-treatment
of his allies and the people subjugated on his side of the
curtain.

Churchill writes like a man behind in a race, with desperation and his last, best efforts. He knows this is futile; he
will lose. In a few days Stalin will have Berlin, the war will
be over, and Russia will not give back anything, not one
inch, not one soul. Even so, Churchill cannot stand idle beside the real world the way he can next to the dead globe in
his study. He cannot be silent. That was never Winston
Churchill's calling.

Writing for two hours, he ends his message with
prophecy:

THERE IS NOT MUCH COMFORT IN LOOKING INTO A
FUTURE WHERE YOU AND THE COUNTRIES YOU
DOMINATE, PLUS THE COMMUNIST PARTIES IN MANY
OTHER STATES, ARE ALL DRAWN UP ON ONE SIDE,
AND THOSE WHO RALLY TO THE ENGLISH-SPEAKING
NATIONS AND THEIR ASSOCIATES OR DOMINIONS
ARE ON THE OTHER. IT IS QUITE OBVIOUS THAT
THEIR QUARREL WOULD TEAR THE WORLD TO
PIECES AND THAT ALL OF US LEADING MEN ON EI-
THER SIDE WHO HAD ANYTHING TO DO WITH THAT
WOULD BE SHAMED BEFORE HISTORY.

When he is done, he rings for his secretary to code the
pages and have them sent to Stalin. He rises on unsteady
legs, exhausted. He leaves the sheets on the table, does not
proofread them, trusting his draft. He heads for dinner.
Then, a movie, yes, *The Mikado.*

Churchill walks past the globe on his way out of the
study. He lays a palm flat against it, the globe is willing to
spin for him one more time. He considers the earth under
his hand. He's laid it right over Moscow.

He sticks his mitt in his pocket and leaves the world
alone.

———

April 30, 1945, 11:50 A.M.
Bandy farm
Big Laurel, Tennessee

SHE ALMOST KNOCKS HIM DOWN IN THE YARD. HE DROPS
his duffel bag right before she lands on him.

Her arms go around his neck, her legs wrap his waist,
and he is carrying her. He totters backward. He feels the
flush of her like a bucket of hot water thrown on him. He
laughs.

Conscious that they're not alone, Bandy stumbles under
her weight in a half circle. He waves at the army driver who

ferried him into the hills from the airport in Knoxville. The
driver salutes and pulls off. Bandy yanks his face back to
plant a kiss on her, but Victoria has her head jammed over
his shoulder, wedging it there to help squeeze him.

"Vic. I can't breathe."

"Shut up."

Her feet are way off the ground. Her hair is the cleanest
thing he believes he's ever smelled. She crushes herself into
him and he hugs back hard. He knows what she's doing, and
he tries to do the same in return, press together so hard they
stick this time.

She undoes her ankles from behind him. He tilts forward
to put her feet on the grass. She lowers her arms to his
thinned biceps. He's leaned out from months of nerves and
bad sleep. Bandy hasn't noticed how much he's dropped
overseas until now, with his wife against him, with her familiar shape and size to measure against. She kisses him with a
tender mouth, not the passionate devour he's longed for over
every inch of his three-day journey home from Europe.

She looks up the road, at the disappearing green staff car.

"You pass anybody on the road in?"

"Not that I saw."

"No one knows you're here?"

"Not yet."

"Inside."

He has to double back for his duffel bag.

"I want to hear all about it," she says, heading for the
screen door with him closing at her heels. She says this to
mean she wants to hear about his trip home and the war and
everything that was not in his letters, later. Hurrying
through the long yard lugging his bag, Bandy lets his eyes
gather in his home. The tobacco barn is empty, the sun
shines through the slats to show him the Fordson tractor's
out. His dad or an uncle is on it, he thinks he can hear it
down the hollow. The fields are prettiest this time of year,
the barley and vetch cover has been plowed under, the raw
earth is harrowed and smoothed. It's all anticipation and

preparation right now. Spring. The seedlings will go in soon, Bandy and his clan on their knees in the soil.

Victoria gets up the porch steps in front of him. Bandy follows the bare patches of her, which are familiar to him like nothing else in the world, but right now are exotic and driving. Elbows, arms, and neck, exposed outside her dress, are naked just for him. Her calves and Achilles tendons stretch and relax with every stride. She looks over her shoulder to check and grin, he feels on his lips her profiled cheek. Bandy in his mind connects these common places of his wife into a nude whole. He's come back to his land and his wife and in his excitement they blend, her back is fretted pond water, her hair is loam, the spring-minted oak trees swish in her skirt. He's home.

Bandy's house thrills him like his wife, familiar and wanting to leap into his arms. But objects can wait to welcome him. Victoria leads him up the stairs.

In the bedroom he drops his duffel. Victoria halts in front of the bed. She turns on her heels to him, arms at her sides. Bandy does not break stride. He pushes her shoulders to the mattress and tumbles on top. The bedsprings bounce and when the two are motionless enough to not knock teeth they kiss as if to drink from the other.

In the kiss the question arises if they will take each other's clothes off or if they will remove their own. Bandy tugs at Victoria's buttons, but clumsily; she answers the quandary and takes care of it herself. This sends Bandy snatching at his own pinnings. In under a minute they are flesh and did not stop the kiss to do so, with smashed lips and married giggles at the haste and mess they make of undressing.

Their lovemaking is no different from their greeting minutes before in the front yard. Victoria wraps her husband in arms and legs, she pulls him to her so hard he can't move well at all. For Bandy, he doesn't notice any strictures on him. His wife's embrace and aroma is wide open, even the pillow filling his vision is a vista of cool green. There's time and peace and a free world now. He's in his own country and this is his bed and his woman, and they're all gripping him, begging him to plunge deeper, as deep as he likes, and stay.

Bandy finishes quickly. This leaves him a little desperate and confused, but Victoria holds him her tightest. She whispers, "Oh, Charley," and acts like he has given her a great gift. Everything slows. He lies in her clasp, what more can he need?

Two days ago flying out of Germany, he knew once he got home he'd never leave again. He'd rejected it all, figured he'd done his stint for fame and history, he'd wallowed long enough in every vomitive thing war and glory could spit out. Now, barely set foot in his own house, he looks inside himself expecting to see more of the same absoluteness, anticipating the same comfort from inside that crosses his skin from his wife and the warm mussed sheets. After all, he's home, just like he wished. But it's not there. He's not so sure. Damn it! he thinks. He feels burgled. This rises out of nothing Victoria's done wrong, nothing he can point to. Everything is perfect. He wants to bang his head against the pillow but that would look stupid and he'd have to explain it so he stays limp. He looks at his wife; he is just too damned used to seeing her as someone to love and come home to, to rest beside for the upcoming journey. It's his nature, and man relies on nature. Seeds, if you plant them right, will always grow. Babies are made just like this, no other way. Christ everything's nature, even when it's something a reasonable man would do everything in his power to change. Bandy can kill. Bandy can leave this woman and this land again. His nature. But can't he take a break from this knowledge, can't he have a rest? Does it have to report to him right now, in bed, just done?

Christ, he thinks.

But the phone doesn't ring and nothing sends him out of his wife's arms. Hitler is finished. Japan can kiss his ass, he's not going, not even for the big finale. Bandy will tend his crops here in Tennessee. They can start a whole new war for all he cares. Though they probably will. He makes Vic that promise. He'll try to stay, try as hard as a man can. It's all he can do. It's not much, but he'll try to stick. The desperation in his loins fades. He feels honest for the moment.

In his head Bandy sounds confident—but it's the same voice that told him he would never leave once he got back to Tennessee and he knows not to trust it.

In a little while she's going to see the pink scar an inch below his nuts. That's when she'll ask. She'll pull the covers up, sit against the headboard, and ask.

She runs a hand down his spine. Her thighs remain strapped around his. She rocks. Bandy sways on her, as though she is his cradle. Victoria begins to hum in his ear, a lullaby.

April 30, 1945, 4:00 P.M.
Charlottenburg, Berlin

"IT'S OVER," MISHA MUTTERS.

Ilya looks above the ruined structures lining the boulevard where he and Misha walk. The sounds of battle are no longer on all sides of them, war's pulse is gone from Berlin. Now there is only a heartbeat at the center, four kilometers east, where the Reichstag is under siege.

To make sure the Red troops fight hard to the end, Chuikov has handed out nine banners to the elite regiments of his Eighth Guards. Whoever waves the Red flag from the roof of the Reichstag will be forever declared a Hero of the Soviet Union. Chuikov has not invited his punishment brigade to participate in the final assault. History will not be made by Ilya and Misha. So Misha says with cigarette smoke, at least for the two of them, it's over.

The echoes of *Katyusha*s and heavy artillery rebound through the rubble to Ilya's ears. Gray clouds ascend from flames and the wrack of speeding metal against brick and concrete. The last battleground is marked by these. Ilya is drawn in their direction, he wants to be in the thick of the fray. The SS is putting up a furious last-ditch defense. Ilya does not wonder why. It simply seems in the course of things. Momentum. Fight is what the Germans and Russians have done for the past four years. Ilya can't imagine this city, or any place, without these noises and smoke. Until he can, it's not over.

He does not recall peace, that time and place without war. He knows he's lived in it before but cannot bring up the sense of peace, like a long-dead loved one whose face you recollect but not the voice. There was once a home and parents. A garden and school. Games and hunting. Girls, good Russian girls. Rest. But all this is in a vault, locked behind more vivid, riled-up memories. He doesn't try to reach back to peace. Too much separates him from it.

The struggle for the Reichstag seethes overhead. Ilya walks beside Misha in this part of Berlin where the little man says the war is over. Ilya is given the chance to compare. Here, soldiers steal and bully. Civilians cower and hand over whatever's demanded: watches, food, alcohol, jewels, their homes, their wives and daughters. Resistance is punished. Soldiers ride bicycles, drink and stumble publicly, they drag women by the neck into the ruins or drub on doors to be let in. Ilya passes through and longs to take nothing, he's seen enough of revenge. He feels out of place walking in the open down Charlottenburg's streets. He's more comfortable with artillery than this kind of bedlam.

Misha wants to join in the final fight too, but for a different reason. The little man still wants his officer's commission back. He's been stuck a sergeant at the end of the war. He's angry that there will be no more chances to redeem himself. Misha wants to be career military and is afraid the Red Army won't return him to his old position if he finishes up no better than he has. He figures he's done his penance. It's not fair. He and Ilya could have taken one of Chuikov's battle flags right to the top of the Reichstag. They've gone through worse. He's mad at Ilya for being made a lieutenant.

On the avenue, the lawlessness intensifies every minute. Calls of *Frau, komm!* mewl from the soldiers like from feral

cats. There is no authority to curb it. Ilya and Misha, a lieutenant and sergeant, are ignored by the men. Some of those
on the prowl are higher ranking than Ilya. The battle beckons
both of them away: Ilya, to the familiarity of the only world
where he is a true denizen; and Misha, for one last grab at
glory and attention. Misha grows surly. His scar flushes when
he gets this way, like a thermometer. The power in this van-
quished street, the free rein to despoil the defeated, lures
Misha, invites his restiveness in place of the battle. So far,
Misha has only stolen more watches.

"Stop looking up," the little man says, irritated. "It's over.
They'll take the Reichstag by morning."

Ilya shrugs. "Then what?"

"Then we win."

Ilya kicks a brick aside.

"Then what?"

Misha speeds his gait to pull away. "No, no, Ilya. I don't
want to play word games. I'm tired. It's over. We win. We
go home."

Misha takes several more steps, then stops, hands on hips.
This halts Ilya. A soldier jangles past on a beat-up bicycle.

"All right," Misha says, flicking away his cigarette. "All
right, I'll play. You want to know then what?"

Ilya is surprised at the keenness of Misha's agitation. Before he can mollify the little man, Misha shouts: "This! This
is what follows!"

Misha rams a finger at the city. "Look! This is what you
fought for, Ilya. Do you approve? You'd better, because it's
yours. All fucking yours! Take a look."

Misha's finger flits and pauses, aiming at one then another
shard of evidence. An ancient city is bombed and burned to
bring down the empire of it. There. And look! Across the
street a Russian soldier tips a vodka bottle, drains it to the
last, then throws it at his feet to splinter and satisfy some
need in him to bash it. A German corpse lies uncollected in
the gutter. Some broken glass settles on the body. Misha
turns a circle, aiming his finger like a white rifle at a hundred
targets of proof. Over there! And here! Misha's finger builds

the case, he has all he needs in plain view from where he stands. The last place his finger lights is on Ilya.

"Yours, Ilya. And a thousand times this. All right? Now leave me the fuck alone. I liked you better when you never talked."

Ilya answers slowly.

"It's not mine."

"Oh!" Misha throws up his hands. "What did you think, Lieutenant? That every one of those bodies you made was going to stand up, dust himself off, and go about his business when the war was over? Did you believe all these buildings we shot up were going to be like new when we were done with them? Look at what we did, man! Look! And what about the men, Ilya? Do you think they can get to the end of a war without any damage to themselves? Just because you did?"

Misha takes a step as if to walk on and be done with his tirade. Ilya holds his ground, what he has done under every onslaught. Misha stops and turns. His voice is milder.

"Ilyushka, every man wants war to end. You're not special, you know. Everyone hates it. But you. You're the only one in millions who thought he could personally make it stop. I watched you. You never fought for Stalin. You didn't even fight against the Germans. You were in a battle with war itself. Who do you think you are? Tell me the truth. Do you really have some idea that it's up to you to figure all this out? To lead us to the end?"

The answer is yes. Ilya does not say it.

Misha spits. "You think you're so fucking special. Who knows, maybe you are."

This does not call for an answer. He's kept this little man alive. Misha should think that is special.

"Well, this is the end you led us to."

Misha approaches. He pokes his reedy finger into Ilya's chest.

"You, Ilya Shokhin. God of war. You've done everything in your power to make it worse. And you've got some weird kind of power, I've seen it. Everybody gets killed on both sides and you run right through it. You figure there's got to be some stopping point and you're the one who can take us to it."

Misha throws both flat palms at his own breast. The gesture is comic, mimicking a frantic man patting himself for bullet holes.

"And me? Following you every damn step of the way. I never could figure out why I'm not dead too. I ought to be."

Misha's finger goes to the sky. The Reichstag battle is up there in fumes and fury.

"But now I know. It's so I could be here today to tell you. That's been my job all along. The little sergeant. My friend, listen to me. If you've learned nothing else in the last four years, remember this. There is no stopping point. War doesn't end."

Misha lowers his finger to Berlin.

"It just becomes this."

Misha drops his hand with a slap to his thigh. He seems angry when he mutters again, "Who do you think you are?"

Misha walks off.

Ilya stays still. He winces.

Is that true?

Is this the conclusion to his search for answers?

That he's been that transparent? A fool? Self-styled god of war?

Mulling profound thoughts. Stargazing, weighing morals on his own scale.

Even praying like an equal to heaven, making bargains.

Killing and destroying, all the while giving them different names. Why? In order to bear them? Make them palatable, part of a greater good?

Making war to end war.

Misha says this can't be done.

Is he right?

The little man has gone a block ahead. Ilya follows.

Misha stalks down the middle of the street. From behind he doesn't seem to Ilya so small anymore. There's no battle to make Misha bend and scurry. The man walks upright through the city and people with some confidence and swinging arms.

Ilya tails him around a corner, into a smaller street where there is less wreckage. Here are undamaged homes and shops. Fewer Russian soldiers prowl this lane; the men seem to prefer the larger lanes where they can congregate and harass the Germans in numbers. Misha stops at the lip of a deep crater in the road. Ilya halts farther back. Misha stands looking down, until a woman emerges hauling a metal bucket sloshing water. Climbing out from the pit, she keeps her eyes on her feet, turning away from the Russian sergeant staring at her. The woman wears a long overcoat that is too heavy for the spring weather, men's pants, high mud boots, and a kerchief over her hair. Misha lets her get far ahead of him, then moves. Ilya stays to the rear. Passing the hole, he sees in the bottom a broken water main.

The woman leads them three blocks on. Ilya can't tell if she's aware there are two soldiers in her wake; she walks awkwardly with the bucket but seems to hurry. Misha is not furtive but casual, he strolls.

She lugs the bucket to a row of stone-faced homes. There's been fighting on this street, some of the houses bear the marks. She enters a door in the center of the block. Misha advances to the foot of her steps and pulls up. He considers the dark door.

Standing at the foot of the steps, Misha rolls up the sleeves of his coat. One by one, he peels the pilfered wristwatches from his arms. He drops them, two dozen or more, on the sidewalk.

Ilya arrives beside him.

"Go away, Ilyushka."

"No."

"I don't need your company."

He could order Misha away from this door. He is an officer. But the little man has run through as much hell as Ilya has. He won't give Misha any more orders.

Ilya says, "That's a first."

"Yes, it is."

"Perhaps I need yours."

Misha nods, turning his eyes to the door. There's a bullet hole in the center panel. The little man appears to see through the door, through the time directly ahead of them, what will happen inside that door and time, the way he can look at a map and predict how an attack will fare.

"Well then," Misha says.

He climbs the steps and knocks on the door.

Ilya expects they'll be made to wait, even to pound on the door, but the woman in the man's clothes opens it soon. She puts her head in the open doorway. The kerchief is gone. Her hair is flaxen and there are hints of gray. She is not as young as her body made her seem carrying the water bucket. Her face is creased and thin, veiled with weariness, and striking.

"*Ja?*" she asks.

Misha greets her calmly. Ilya does not know what he says but there is courtesy in Misha's voice, and there is want, like a door-to-door vendor.

"*Ja,*" she says, "*komm.*"

She pulls open the door and turns away. Before going in, Misha looks at Ilya with approval.

The house is in disarray. It has been ransacked. Drawers are emptied on the floor, the contents of closets tossed into piles. Furniture has been ripped by knives and the stuffing yanked out. Pictures are knocked from the walls.

In the hallway, a skinny teenage boy hangs a photograph back on a hook. He is listless, he doesn't turn to look at the armed Russian soldiers in his house. His blond hair is pruned close, an inmate's cut.

Misha speaks to the woman. She replies with a sardonic chortle. He answers her.

He interprets to Ilya, "I told her I was tired. She said I ought to sit down. I told her I wanted to lie down."

The woman puts a hand on the newel post and hauls

herself onto the first stair, to head to the upper floor. She says again, *"Ja, komm."* The words seem not spoken but drained like oil out of her mouth.

Misha follows two steps behind. Halfway up the stairs the woman stops. She points at Ilya and speaks.

Misha says, "She wants you too. Both of us."

Ilya shakes his head. He doesn't want to be here. But he doesn't know where else to go. There's no more battle for him. This is the world that's left, what he's led them to.

He'll stay downstairs. He's in this house, there are answers here. He doesn't need to be in the same bed as Misha and this woman. He's here. Maybe that will suffice.

The woman hurries down the stairs. A renewed vigor infuses her step. She lays a hand on Ilya's wrist. She smiles; the lines in her face are deep. She says, *"Ja, komm. Komm mit uns."*

Ilya takes back his arm. "No. *Nein*. Misha, tell her."

From the stairwell Misha speaks. The German on his tongue sounds imperious.

Misha says, "I told her to be patient. I want to be first."

The woman laughs now. She speaks.

Misha says, "She said I won't be the first. Not by a dozen. Well, Ilyushka, we take what we can find, eh? Come along, *Frau*."

The woman stays in front of Ilya. He towers over her, twice as wide, threatening and foreign in this house, but the woman seems inured to everything that he is. She glances to the boy in the hall, who now stands watching, listening. She must be his mother. She brings her gaze back to Ilya; she changes for those moments looking into his eyes, seeming to ask from him something she does not require of Misha. More than mercy, as though there is a thread of kindredness she has spotted. She wants Ilya to understand.

She says, *"Bitte. Komm."*

Ilya says nothing, frozen in front of her. This woman's face conveys to him an entirely separate war, one fought from this house. It teems on her cheeks and in her home like it does throughout Berlin. There is tragedy and suffering here to equal anything on the battlefield, all of it a different type from his, as though war is bragging to Ilya how many ways it can strike. But Ilya has no room for her war inside him, he has no desire to carry more load than is strapped to him already, the war he's fought is abundant enough.

She asks too much.

"Misha, take her. Go on."

The little sergeant comes down the steps. He lays hands on the woman and tows her onto the steps. Disappearing up the stairwell, she pulls her eyes from Ilya's. She lays them on her son.

Her daughter.

Ilya sees it now. He sees everything in this house more clearly after looking for seconds through the mother's eyes. The girl. Chopped, dressed, disguised. That's why the mother wanted both soldiers upstairs with her. To protect the girl.

Ilya walks to her in the hall. She does not back away. She turns to face him, blocking the hall and, yes, she has a girl's figure. Scrawnier than the mother, she is more beautiful, even with such stubbly hair. The beauty is her youth, and something else. The mother has courage, certainly; both women have it. Ilya knows bravery at an instant. But the mother's courage is a wrapping to contain something else. Fear, perhaps. There is something hidden. This girl is not so frightened as the mother. She doesn't ask for anything. She glares at Ilya's approach.

She stops him with an outstretched hand to his chest. He could push her over with a stride. She finishes setting the photograph on the wall. It's an old picture of a young man in uniform, from the previous German World War.

She walks by him in the hall, grabbing his big wrist. Her fingers are stronger than Ilya expects from a woman, she almost encircles his wrist. She leads him out of the hall. He notes a scab on the back of her cropped head. She guides him into the front room, a parlor. The sofa has been gutted. Some idiot soldiers came looting with knives. Ilya imagines what else these women have given at knifepoint.

In the center of the room, on a bloodred carpet, she

releases him. Without a word, her eyes downcast, she hooks one heel behind the other to slide out of her boots. Ilya watches the girl set them aside. She unbuttons her pants. They are too big for her, they collapse from her waist into a pool at her feet. She steps out of them.

She wears no undergarment, she is immediately naked there. She does not pull her sweater over her head. Her pelvis protrudes in horns out of her hips, this girl is hungry. Bruises discolor her knees and thighs and groin.

She stands splay-footed on the carpet. She is two statues welded at the middle, a comely boy on top, a sad and trammeled woman on the bottom. Her face is a cipher. She has learned to keep it empty.

The girl bends. Her motion is empty too. It gives everything, and so grants nothing to be taken. There is no conquest of this girl.

She lies on the carpet, arms at her side, legs slightly spread. Her head is back, eyes at the ceiling. Her boots and the bunch of her dropped pants are beside her, like a melted man, another symbol of absence.

Ilya has not been with a woman since before Stalingrad. Three years. She is gaunt but beautiful.

Ilya walks forward. He stands over the girl. Her eyes shift to his. Looking down at her, the sense Ilya has is staring down into a well. If the black bottom has a face, it is this face below him now. He feels a chill.

Ilya has quested for answers but has he gone far enough for them? He's seen life and death daily for four years now, in more manners than he would have once thought conceivable. But how much is there in between that he's missed? Everything. Everything.

This girl on the floor is a casualty. Ilya is the same, but still on his feet. He is drawn to her the way a man is drawn to a mirror, to get a better look at himself. This girl, her hair is almost as short as Ilya's. Her hands, for a woman, are stronger than his. Her body is marked too; Ilya lowers his eyes to her crotch, threads of her pubis are rusty with dried blood. She has battled, she and her mother, as much as any soldier. The cost of her war is not measured in other battered bodies, only her own. The battlefield is not a tract of torn-up, faraway land, but the carpet in her own parlor. And what she fights for is far more precious, more rightful, than anything Ilya has ever waged for. She fights to live. Only live.

Misha is right. War doesn't end. It turns into this. This is where it waits and incubates, in this girl. You can see it already, in her body, the bruises like purple explosions, bloodshed between her legs.

As much as Ilya has done, he cannot do this.

Misha is wrong.

Ilya is war.

War stops right now. Here.

He kicks the clump of pants over her bare legs.

"Get dressed."

Ilya whirls from the supine girl. The chill he felt moments before is a sirocco now.

He stomps out of the parlor. His boots on the steps are heavy, purposefully announcing he is coming.

Ilya finds Misha in a bedroom. The little man is on top of the mother. His trousers are bundled around his ankles, he did not take off his boots. They are on a bed. Misha does not stop humping or look around from his labor. The woman lies beneath him like a five-pointed star, spread wide and white. Ilya grabs Misha's lowered pants and yanks, pulling him by the legs backward off the woman until Misha hits the floor facedown, buttocks in the air. Misha blusters and curses for Ilya to let him go and get out. Ilya presses Misha to the floor with his boot between the man's squirming shoulder blades. The woman does not slide out of bed. She must figure the big one wants her now and is tossing the little one out. Her lower body bears the same ugly badges as her daughter's.

Ilya hoists Misha from the floor. The little sergeant is livid. Ilya does not listen to his tirade, does not give him time to pull up his pants. He makes Misha hop, dragging him out of the room. Snatching up Misha's rifle and coat,

Ilya heaves them into the hall and down the steps. Misha stumbles, grabbing at his pants. Ilya hauls him like a garbage sack.

At the bottom of the steps Ilya lets him fasten his trousers and shoves him his coat. Misha has not stopped yelling.

Ilya says nothing. The girl has risen from the parlor floor. She stands again where she was when they entered, in the hallway. Misha sputters. Ilya does not listen. He reaches back to cuff Misha across the scar on his cheek. The little man recoils and clams up. Untucked and flummoxed, Misha slings open the door. He flees into the street. Ilya walks out of the house behind him, tossing Misha's rifle to clatter in the road. Misha steps forward with care to pick it up. The watches he left outside are gone, snatched by other greedy hands.

"Ilya."

"Go away, Misha. Now. Don't come back."

"What . . . ?" Misha staggers, still confounded, only seconds ago he was buried in a woman.

"Go. I won't say it again."

Misha jams his tunic into his pants. He bounces from small foot to foot doing it. Not taking his eyes from the sergeant, Ilya leans back and closes the door.

"What are you doing?"

Ilya answers by sitting on the stoop. He brings his PPSh down from his shoulder and lays it across his knees.

Misha nods at this.

"All right."

The little man laughs.

"Good for you, Ilyushka. And good fucking luck."

Misha pivots and walks away with even more of the false stature Ilya noticed before. Misha has swollen, bigger now that the whole war is inside him. Ilya thinks: Good luck to him, as well. Ilya watches him go.

The battle for the Reichstag is still in the air. Thumps and haze denote the final front lines between the warring countries. A new front line is drawn at Ilya's feet. He will sit here on the steps of this house and anchor his end of it, to see how far it may reach.

Behind him, the door opens. Ilya doesn't look over his shoulder. He expects some soft touch, perhaps a sob. He doesn't want gratitude.

An odd man sits down on the step beside him. He is slighter than either of the women, his skin as pale as their bellies. He wears a gray civilian suit, bedraggled, the hems unravel at the wrists and ankles. A brown tie is pulled tight to a yellowed collar. Thinning dark hair lies greasy across a speckled scalp. The man mimics Ilya's resolved posture on the steps, elbows on knees, except he has no gun.

He lofts his gaze up to the sky. He seems to admire the size of it.

He turns a large nose and unblinking black eyes to Ilya. The men are face-to-face only for seconds. In that short space Ilya sees the man has questions, as many as Ilya. He has strength too, more than Ilya.

Neither man will budge from these steps.

Ilya smiles. There is an ally. The new front grows.

EPILOGUE

THE WAR IS OVER.

Stalin slams a fist on the telegram. The few items on his desk jiggle.

The general who brought him the sheet retreats as though Stalin's fist might split open the floor.

The cable is from Eisenhower. It was sent an hour ago from the Supreme Commander's headquarters in Reims, France:

THE MISSION OF THIS ALLIED FORCE WAS FULFILLED AT 0241, LOCAL TIME, MAY 7, 1945.

Stalin surveys the disarray on his desktop. His pipe has spilled tobacco. Lenin's picture has tipped on its face. A blue pencil has rolled to the carpet. Stalin knows his teeth are bared. He takes one long breath through his nose. His jaw is tight, he can barely unclamp his molars to speak.

He lifts his eyes.

"General?"

"Yes. Yes, Comrade?"

"Who is responsible for this?"

The soldier in front of Stalin's desk is clearly a man of long service. He has his code of loyalty. He is reluctant. He bends to retrieve Stalin's blue pencil. He reaches it out. Stalin does not extend his hand to accept it. The general places it on the desk.

Stalin glares.

"General. Who signed the surrender on behalf of the Soviet Union?"

"It was Susloparov."

The officer begins to fidget. The man wants to do something. What? Straighten Stalin's desk? He wants to say something more. To defend his comrade. To tell Stalin that Susloparov is innocent.

Innocent? This Susloparov flies to fucking France to accept the surrender of the German army, in Eisenhower's headquarters? France! What did the French lose? How many bottles of wine did they have smashed? And Eisenhower. How many soldiers did he expend? Two, three hundred thousand? The Red Army lost that many between the Vistula and Berlin. This war cost Russia ten million of its people.

A week ago Hitler shot himself in his bunker. His whore Eva Braun took cyanide. Goebbels and his wife poisoned their children, then killed themselves. That's because the Red Army was one block away and storming their gates. The next day the Soviet battle flag flew over the Reichstag.

The Nazi empire slipped and fell on Russian blood. Germany lies coated in it.

Who is Susloparov? He wasn't authorized to report to France like one of Eisenhower's lackeys. Who designated him to accept the German surrender? He has no right to agree to anything on behalf of the Soviet Union. Stalin was not even shown the surrender document before it was signed. In France.

"General, do me a kindness."

"Of course, Comrade."

"Somewhere in the Kremlin there is a bottle of vodka, yes?"

The general does not trust the question. It's barely dawn. And Stalin does not drink alcohol.

"It's all right," Stalin assures the man, there is no trap here. "A bottle of vodka, General. And two glasses. You will join me in a victory drink."

The officer licks his lips. There is hesitation. The man lifts his head and neck, giving the impression of a proud man at the gallows.

Stalin smiles, showing his yellow teeth again. The general comes to rigid attention. Such fuss, Stalin thinks, for a bottle and two glasses.

"Of course, Comrade Stalin. At once." The officer spins on his boots and departs.

While the officer is gone, Stalin tidies his desk. He repacks his pipe and puts it aside. When he is done, he stands from his chair to pace. The *soyuzniki*. They nibble always at Stalin's authority. Little gambits like this one. Eisenhower commanded the French, British, Americans, and Russians to come to him and sign his paper. To him, like he is some big shot. No, no, no, Stalin chuckles, you will not catch me so easily. It is you, little allies, who have been nabbed.

Stalin is ever on guard. Daily he reads Churchill's telegrams and Truman's cables of concurrence. They warn Stalin, they request, they beg. They offer nothing but friendship, threaten nothing but the withdrawal of their good graces. They bear no cudgel Stalin fears, no treasure Stalin covets. Every utterance from his allies is an attempt to sway him one way or another. Like wind.

The West is afraid. They fling charges of communist takeovers in eastern Europe. These are not takeovers. They are liberations. But the revolution can grow too fast, so Stalin must be careful.

To quell criticism, he makes certain that every postwar government in the countries occupied by his Red Army is fashioned as a coalition. Radical and peasant factions are joined with communist parties, so long as Communists hold key ministries. These include Interior, responsible for the police, Agriculture for land reform, Information, and Education. The strategy is working well in Yugoslavia, where

Tito included five non-Communists in his government. When those men resigned, protesting they were given no real power, Tito had them arrested for seeking to provoke foreign intervention. The same transition goes on in Hungary, Czechoslovakia, Romania, and Bulgaria. Even in Poland, despite the commotion kicked up by that Churchill. The world does not hear the Soviet whispers in these lands, only indigenous voices crying out for equality and prosperity, for closer ties with Russia, and for communism. This is the ultimate will of the people.

The general returns. He was not gone long. Apparently the bottle was nearer at hand than Stalin expected.

The glasses and bottle are set on the desk. The general steps back, allowing Stalin to pour. Stalin unstoppers the unlabeled bottle.

He pours only a little in both glasses, then raises one. The general lifts the second glass. Stalin faces the soldier across the ordered desk and Eisenhower's telegram.

Stalin says, "I will require the Americans, British, and French to fly back to Berlin with the Nazi leadership. I refuse to accept the surrender signed this morning as genuine."

"Comrade?"

"I did not approve the document in advance. The Soviet Union was not represented by a suitable envoy. And the ceremony took place in France."

The general is stock-still. The glass is held out like a crystal nest in a tree.

"In France." Stalin shakes his head, disbelieving. He is wasting himself on this general, this man. He will not react. Stalin finds it all humorous now. Ah, well.

"Another act of surrender will be signed by all parties at the Red Army headquarters in Karlshorst. This is where history will mark the final victory over the Nazis, not some office building in France of Eisenhower's choosing. You will see to it that Zhukov is present, a proper figure to represent the Soviet Union. Understood?"

"Yes, Comrade."

"Well, then. Let us make our toast. Would you like to say something, General?"

"I should be honored to drink to Comrade Stalin's toast."

"All right, then. Let me see."

Stalin runs thumb and fingers over his moustache. He rounds his lips in thought.

"We'll stay simple. There's still work to be done before breakfast."

"Of course, Comrade."

Stalin hoists his glass. The general follows suit.

"Today the world celebrates. Today we Russians embrace the Americans and the English. Our fighting allies. First, to Roosevelt, our missing friend."

Stalin drinks. The general tosses his down. The vodka goes right to Stalin's eyes, raising false tears.

He holds out his glass for the general to pour. The man is timid with the bottle, he barely wets the bottoms.

"Come, General. Mr. Churchill is next. He would be ashamed of us if we were to drink so little on his behalf."

The officer adds more to each glass.

Stalin lifts his and grins. "To that Churchill. His health."

Both men drain their glasses. The vodka makes Stalin blink. The general holds his liquor well.

Stalin sets his glass on the desk.

"Thank you, General."

"Comrade."

The officer collects the glasses and bottle. Stalin lets him almost reach the door.

"General."

"Yes, Comrade Stalin?"

"Have Susloparov recalled immediately."

A glass bounces on the carpet.

Stalin sits behind his desk. The officer has not moved.

Stalin doesn't care. He'll have no trouble taking this man's head as well.

He waves the soldier out of his office.

"It's war, General."

FINAL HISTORICAL NOTES

WILLY BRANDT, MAYOR OF WEST BERLIN FROM 1957 to 1966 and West German chancellor from 1969 to 1972, wrote in his memoir: "In April 1945, the Americans had stopped at the Elbe; if they had marched on they would have saved themselves a good deal of trouble and given the world a different face. But they left the triumph of marching into Hitler's capital to the Russians. One reason was that Gen. Eisenhower no longer considered Berlin an especially important objective. He failed to understand the symbolic value of the place. . . . At the end of the 1950s, when I broached the topic with Eisenhower, then President of the United States, he freely admitted that he had not foreseen the consequences of his order not to advance on Berlin."

General Omar Bradley, whose army group was directed southeast to cut off the supposed Nazi National Redoubt rather than support an assault on Berlin, expressed puzzlement in later years that he and the rest of the American leadership should have been taken in by the myth of the Redoubt.

There are no official figures for the number of Berlin women raped by occupying Soviet soldiers. Nonetheless, the amount and frequency of rape was staggering. Estimates exceed 300,000 women in the city who suffered this fate, primarily in retaliation for similar abuses reported against German soldiers while on Russian soil. With typical bravura and humor, Berliner women tried to defuse their horror with a quip: "It's better to have a Russian on the belly than an American on the head," meaning sexual assault was a preferable fate to dying beneath an Allied bomb.

When faced with complaints about the conduct of his troops, Stalin once replied: "Can't you understand it if a soldier who has crossed thousands of kilometers through blood and fire has fun with a woman or takes a trifle?"

At the end of the war, the Jewish population in Berlin had been cut down from 160,000 in 1933 to 1,500 men, women, and children, all "U-boats" hidden and abetted by courageous German citizens.

The Berlin Philharmonic Orchestra, which refused to flee the city, survived the final battle intact and played its first postwar concert at the Titania Palace on May 26, just eighteen days after the city's fall. Directed by Leo Borchard, the BPO's program included pieces by Mozart, Mendelssohn, and the Russian composer Tchaikovsky.

In August 1945, the concentration camp north of Berlin at Sachsenhausen was turned against its former keepers. Nazi functionaries were held in the camp by their Red captors, as were several thousand political undesirables. Until it was closed in 1950, Sachsenhausen became the largest of the special camps in the Soviet Zone of Occupation. At least twelve thousand of the sixty thousand Germans who suffered imprisonment there after the war died of malnutrition and disease.

Franklin Roosevelt has been evaluated by modern historians as arguably the finest American President of the twentieth century. His death was caused by a severe brain hemorrhage. No other President will again serve four terms.

Winston Churchill was turned out of office on July 26, 1945, barely eleven weeks after the war ended. In 1951 he was again named Prime Minister, serving until 1955. An able and prolific historian, he received the Nobel Prize for Literature. He was knighted in 1953. Churchill died in 1965 at the age of ninety.

Josef Stalin died of complications from a stroke in 1953. Although the nation was plunged into grief, Stalin's political successors expressed relief and moved quickly to reverse some of the cruelest features of his regime. Nikita Khrushchev denounced Stalin's methods of rule and political theories. Stalin's name was purged, allowing history to brand him one of the most brutal dictators the world has endured.

Upon his return to Moscow, General Susloparov, the Soviet general who signed the German surrender in France without Stalin's permission, was executed.

ACKNOWLEDGMENTS

The author wishes to thank the following for their help in the creation of this book:

Teresa Bjornes, for all things regarding the cello and classical music; Jane and Edgar Wallin, for their ancestral knowledge of farming tobacco; my good friend Dr. Jim Redington for sterling medical advice, as always; Gene Pendleton for building my office; the staff at the Berlin Philharmonic Orchestra for their research and patience; the staffs of the battlefield museums in Seelow, Germany, and Küstrin, Poland; and the staffs at the Sachsenhausen camp and Brandenburg prison.

Special thanks are reserved for the Magnificent Seven:

First, at Bantam, where my work and career are treated with remarkable respect and support. My great appreciation goes to Chris Artis in publicity, editor Katie Hall, her boss Nita Taublib, and everyone's boss Irwyn Applebaum. My advice to all aspiring and current authors is get clever people around you and listen to them.

Next, my faithful agent Marcy Posner and her assistant Shana Kelly of the William Morris Agency, who inspire me with their confidence and competence.

Finally, I wish to thank the wise Dan Kohler, whose advice on all matters psychological and the constancy of his attention to the manuscript as it grew were anchors for my long and buffeted season of researching and creating this novel.

BIBLIOGRAPHY

This novel has been drawn in part from these excellent histories, documentaries, biographies, and autobiographies. The author appreciates the achievement and scholarship of every author listed below and wishes to recommend their work to the interested reader.

Ambrose, Stephen E., *Band of Brothers: E Company, 506th Regiment, 101st Airborne from Normandy to Hitler's Eagle's Nest*. Simon & Schuster, 1990.

Ambrose, Stephen E., *Citizen Soldiers: The U.S. Army from the Normandy Beaches to the Bulge to the Surrender of Germany*. Simon & Schuster, 1997.

Ambrose, Stephen E., *Eisenhower and Berlin, 1945: The Decision to Halt at the Elbe*. Norton, 1967.

Bohlen, Charles E., *Witness to History*. Norton, 1973.

Bradley, Omar, *A General's Life*. Simon & Schuster, 1983.

Brandt, Willy, *My Life in Politics*. London, 1992.

Bullock, Alan, *Hitler and Stalin: Parallel Lives*. Alfred A. Knopf, 1992.

Chuikov, V. I., *The End of the Third Reich*. Progress Publishers, 1978.

Churchill, Winston S., *The Second World War: Triumph and Tragedy*. Houghton Mifflin, 1953.

Duffy, Christopher, *Red Storm on the Reich: The Soviet March on Germany, 1945*. Da Capo Press, 1993.

Eisenhower, Dwight D., *Crusade in Europe*. Doubleday, 1948.

Erickson, John, *The Road to Berlin*. Weidenfeld and Nicolson, 1983.

Feis, Herbert, *Churchill, Roosevelt, Stalin: The War They Waged and the Peace They Sought*. Princeton University Press, 1957.

Ferrell, Robert H., *The Dying President: Franklin D. Roosevelt, 1944–1945*. University of Missouri Press, 1998.

Fritz, Stephen G., *Frontsoldaten: The German Soldier in World War II*. University Press of Kentucky, 1995.

Gavin, James M., *On to Berlin: Battles of an Airborne Commander, 1943–1946*. Viking, 1978.

Gilbert, Martin, *Churchill: A Life*. Henry Holt, 1991.

Glantz, David M., and House, Jonathan, *When Titans Clashed*. University Press of Kansas, 1995.

Goodwin, Doris Kearns, *No Ordinary Time: Franklin and Eleanor Roosevelt: The Home Front in World War II*. Simon & Schuster, 1995.

Gross, Leonard, *The Last Jews in Berlin*. Simon & Schuster, 1982.

Harper, John L., and Nitze, Paul H., editors, *American Visions of Europe: Franklin D. Roosevelt, George F. Kennan, and Dean G. Acheson*. Cambridge University Press, 1994.

Harriman, W. A., and Abel, E., *Special Envoy to Churchill and Stalin: 1941–1946*. Random House, 1975.

Kimball, Warren F., editor, *Churchill and Roosevelt, The Complete Correspondence*. Princeton University Press, 1984.

Kimball, Warren F., *Forged in War: Roosevelt, Churchill and the Second World War*. William Morrow, 1997.

Kimball, Warren F., *The Juggler: Franklin Roosevelt as Wartime Statesman*. Princeton University Press, 1994.

Knappe, Siegfried, and Brusaw, Charles T., *Soldat: Reflections of a German Soldier, 1936–1949*. Dell, 1992.

Lande, Nathaniel, *Dispatches from the Front: News Accounts of American Wars, 1776–1991*. Oxford University Press, 1996.

LeTissier, Tony, *Zhukov at the Oder*. Praeger Publishers, 1996.

Loengard, John, Life *Photographers: What They Saw.*. Bullfinch, 1998.

MacDonogh, Giles, *Berlin: A Portrait of Its History, Architecture and Society*. St. Martin's Press, 1997.

Maslowski, Peter, *Armed with Cameras: The American Military Photographers of World War II*. The Free Press, 1993.

Moeller, Susan D., *Shooting War: Photography and the American Experience of Combat*. Basic Books, 1989.

Morris, John G., *Get the Picture: A Personal History of Photojournalism*. Random House, 1998.

Nadeau, Remi, *Stalin, Churchill and Roosevelt Divide Europe*. Praeger Publishers, 1990.

Nisbet, Robert, *Roosevelt and Stalin: The Failed Courtship*. Regnery Gateway, 1988.

Owings, Alison, *Frauen: German Women Recall the Third Reich*. Rutgers University Press, 1995.

Perlmutter, Amos, *FDR and Stalin: A Not So Grand Alliance, 1943–45*. University of Missouri Press, 1993.

Read, Anthony, and Fisher, David, *The Fall of Berlin*. Hutchinson, 1992.

Richie, Alexandra, *Faust's Metropolis: A History of Berlin*. Carroll & Graf, 1998.

Rose, Norman, *Churchill: The Unruly Giant*. The Free Press, 1995.

Ryan, Cornelius, *The Last Battle*. Simon & Schuster, 1966.

Rzheshevsky, Oleg A., *War and Diplomacy: The Making of the Grand Alliance*. Harwood Academic Publishers, 1996.

Sainsbury, Keith, *Churchill and Roosevelt at War*. New York University Press, 1994.

Tobin, James, *Ernie Pyle's War: America's Eyewitness to World War II*. The Free Press, 1997.

Tsouras, Peter G., editor, *Fighting in Hell: The German Ordeal on the Eastern Front*. Ivy Books, 1995.

Vance, Heidi Scriba, and Speer, Janet Barton, *Shadows over My Berlin: One Woman's Story of World War II*. Southfarm Press, 1996.

Vassiltchikov, Marie, *Berlin Diaries, 1940–1945*. Vintage Books, 1988.

Volkogonov, Dmitri, *Stalin: Triumph and Tragedy*. Grove Weidenfeld, 1991.

Whelan, Richard, *Robert Capa: A Biography*. University of Nebraska Press, 1994.

Whiting, Charles, and the Editors of Time-Life Books, *The Home Front: Germany, World War II Series*. Time-Life Books, 1982.

Zhukov, G. K. (ed. H. E. Salisbury), *Marshal Zhukov's Greatest Battles*. MacDonald, 1969.

Ziemke, Earl F., *Battle for Berlin: End of the Third Reich*. Ballantine Books, 1969.

Ziemke, Earl F., *Stalingrad to Berlin: The German Defeat in the East*. Army Historical Series, 1968.

ABOUT THE AUTHOR

David L. Robbins is the author of *War of the Rats* and *Souls to Keep*. He is a former attorney and freelance writer who lives in Richmond, Virginia.

DON'T MISS THE CHILLING MEDICAL THRILLERS OF
NEW YORK TIMES BESTSELLING AUTHOR

MICHAEL PALMER

SIDE EFFECTS
FLASHBACK
THE SISTERHOOD
EXTREME MEASURES
NATURAL CAUSES
SILENT TREATMENT
CRITICAL JUDGMENT
MIRACLE CURE
THE PATIENT

FL6 6/01

W9-BWC-745

IVORY COAST
in Pictures

Janice Hamilton

‎ᒪ

Lerner Publications Company

SOUTH HUNTINGTON
PUBLIC LIBRARY
HUNTINGTON STATION, NY 11746

Contents

Lerner Publishing Group realizes that current information and statistics quickly become out of date. To extend the usefulness of the Visual Geography Series, we developed www.vgsbooks.com, a website offering links to up-to-date information, as well as in-depth material, on a wide variety of subjects. All of the websites listed on www.vgsbooks.com have been carefully selected by researchers at Lerner Publishing Group. However, Lerner Publishing Group is not responsible for the accuracy or suitability of the material on any website other than <www.lernerbooks.com>. It is recommended that students using the Internet be supervised by a parent or teacher. Links on www.vgsbooks.com will be regularly reviewed and updated as needed.

Copyright © 2004 by Janice Hamilton

All rights reserved. International copyright secured. No part of this book may be reproduced, stored in a retrieval system, or transmitted in any form or by any means—electronic, mechanical, photocopying, recording, or otherwise—without the prior written permission of Lerner Publications Company, except for the inclusion of brief quotations in an acknowledged review.

Lerner Publications Company
A division of Lerner Publishing Group
241 First Avenue North
Minneapolis, MN 55401 U.S.A.

Website address: www.lernerbooks.com

J 916.66
qHamilton

web enhanced @ www.vgsbooks.com

Library of Congress Cataloging-in-Publication Data

Hamilton, Janice.
    Ivory coast in pictures / Janice Hamilton.
      p.   cm. – (Visual geography series)
    Summary: Discusses the geography, history and government, people, cultural life, and economy of the
Ivory Coast, West Africa's second richest nation.
    Includes bibliographical references and index.
    ISBN: 0-8225-1992-5 (lib. bdg. : alk. paper)
    1. Côte d'Ivoire. 2. Côte d'Ivoire–Pictorial works. [1. Côte d'Ivoire.] I. Title. II. Series: Visual geography
series (Minneapolis, Minn.)
DT545.22.H36 2004
966.68–dc22   2003018792

Manufactured in the United States of America
1 2 3 4 5 6 - JR - 09 08 07 06 05 04

30652001569229

INTRODUCTION

The Republic of Ivory Coast is a country in West Africa. It is located on the Gulf of Guinea, part of the Atlantic Ocean. The nation is named for the ivory trade that flourished there several hundred years ago. The ivory came from the tusks of elephants, which once lived in West Africa in great numbers.

Ivory Coast was once a French colony. It is often called by its French name, Côte d'Ivoire. Its nickname is the Elephant of Africa because, like the elephant, the nation is said to be large, strong, and steady—especially compared to neighboring countries. It has many natural resources and a diverse economy. For many years, its government was seen as a model of stability in a region plagued by civil wars.

The land of Ivory Coast rises gradually from sea level at the Gulf of Guinea to about 1,640 feet (500 meters) in the north. Mountain ranges extend along the nation's western border, and hills dot the northeast. Four parallel rivers flow south toward the gulf. Sandbars and peaceful lagoons are found along the coast, a region of lush forests and farms in

the south, and a drier savanna—an area characterized by grasslands and scattered trees—in the north.

The capital city, Yamoussoukro, is in the central part of the country, where the forest meets the savanna. Abidjan, the largest city, is one of West Africa's most sophisticated business centers. It has a variety of industries and a large port that serves much of West Africa.

Agricultural products, including cocoa, coffee, tropical fruits, and rubber, are the backbone of the nation's economy. Ivory Coast produces about 40 percent of the world's supply of cocoa, which is made into chocolate. Other resources include timber and undersea oil and gas reserves.

Ivory Coast is a rapidly growing country, with a population of about 16.8 million people in the early twenty-first century. The population includes several million immigrants from neighboring countries. Many of the immigrants work in low-paying jobs, such as farm labor.

Ivorians, as the inhabitants of Ivory Coast call themselves, are an extremely diverse people. Some rural Ivorians follow traditional

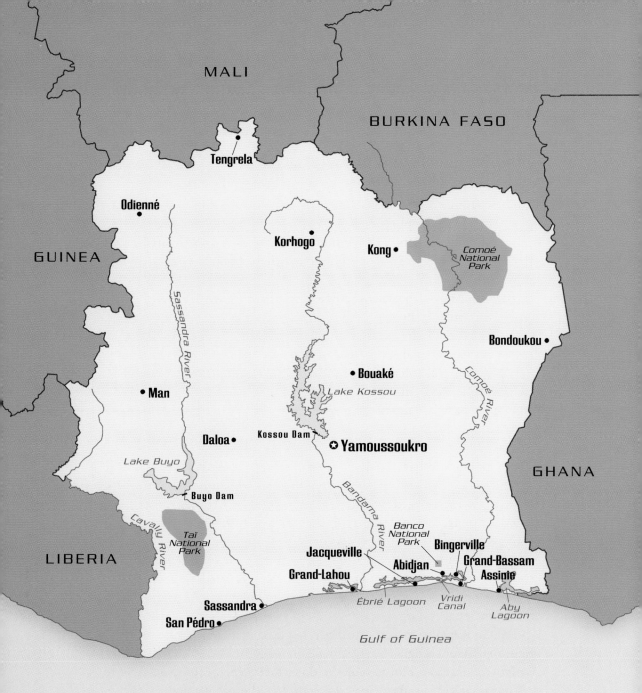

MALI

BURKINA FASO

Tengrela

Odienné

GUINEA

Korhogo

Kong

Comoé
National
Park

Bondoukou

Man

Bouaké

Lake Kossou

Sassandra River

Comoé River

Daloa

Kossou Dam

Yamoussoukro

GHANA

Lake Buyo

Buyo Dam

Bandama River

Cavally River

Taï
National
Park

LIBERIA

Banco
National
Park

Jacqueville

Bingerville

Abidjan

Grand-Bassam

Grand-Lahou

Assinie

Sassandra

Ébrié Lagoon

*Vridi
Canal*

*Aby
Lagoon*

San Pédro

Gulf of Guinea

ATLANTIC

OCEAN

Ivory Coast

	International border
✪	Capital city
•	City
–	Dam

N

| 0 | | 100 Miles |
| 0 | | 100 KM |

African religions. They believe in good and evil spirits and worship the spirits of their ancestors. Many Ivorians, especially in the north, are Muslims—people who practice the Islamic religion. There are large Christian congregations in the south.

The nation has at least sixty ethnic groups, each with its own cultural and social traditions. For example, the Baoulé people grow yams, which form the basis of their diet, and hold a yam festival every year. Many Kru people live along the coast, where Kru men work as fishers or dockworkers. The Senoufo, who live in the north, are known as peaceful farmers. They are famed for their woodcarving, weaving, and decorated cloth.

Each ethnic group speaks its own language or a variation of a local language, but French is the official language of Ivory Coast. Government documents are written in French, students read and write French at school, and radio and TV stations broadcast in French. The region became a colony of France in 1893, but some local people fought the French until 1915.

Ivory Coast became an independent country in 1960. President Félix Houphouët-Boigny governed for the next thirty-three years. He held almost complete power. Although the nation held presidential elections, no one was allowed to run against him. During much of his regime, the country enjoyed great economic growth, especially because of its strong coffee and cocoa industries. Economists referred to this growth as the Ivorian miracle. Then, in the 1980s, cocoa and coffee prices fell, and the miracle ended.

Houphouët-Boigny died in 1993. In 1999 a military general over-threw the government of his successor. Violent conflicts followed in 2000. Another serious rebellion began in late 2002, with Muslim and northern rebels charging that the government discriminated against them and kept them from powerful government positions. Political tensions are ongoing.

Ivory Coast has a lot of work to do to strengthen democracy and to restore political stability. Poverty underlies the nation's political tensions, and social and economic changes are necessary. Despite the country's wealth compared with neighboring nations, many Ivorians are poor. Life expectancy is low and access to education and health care is limited. The country will need all of the elephant's legendary strength and steadiness to solve these problems.

THE LAND

On a map, Ivory Coast is roughly square, with an area of 123,553 square miles (320,783 square kilometers), similar in size to the state of New Mexico. The nation has a 300-mile (480-km) seacoast along the Gulf of Guinea (part of the Atlantic Ocean). It borders Liberia and Guinea to the west, Mali and Burkina Faso to the north, and Ghana to the east.

The western coastline features rocky cliffs. The eastern shore, from the Ghana border to the mouth of the Sassandra River to the west, is known as the lagoon region. Here, waves and currents have created sandbars, which have blocked the mouths of rivers. Lagoons—quiet, narrow waterways that parallel the sea—have formed behind the sandbars. The low-lying sandbars are dotted with coconut palms and shrubs, while the mainland shore features farmland, towns, and a few pockets of undisturbed mangrove trees.

Beyond this coastal fringe in the southern part of the country, from Man in the west to Bondoukou near the Ghana border, is a humid region, once covered by a vast rain forest. This region is known as the

rain forest zone. Much of the original forest has been replaced by plantations, or large farms. Coffee plants and cocoa trees grow well here.

The land rises gradually from the seacoast. The eastern forest zone
is gently rolling. The country's highest points are west of the
Sassandra River, where the Toura Mountains reach heights of about
4,265 feet (1,300 m) above sea level. The highest peak, Mount Nimba,
sits near the junction of Ivory Coast, Liberia, and Guinea. It reaches
5,748 feet (1,752 m) above sea level.

The northern half of Ivory Coast is a vast savanna, a region of grass-
land with low shrubs and scattered trees. In the center of the country,
the savanna dips south in a large V shape.

Rivers and Lakes

All of Ivory Coast's major rivers flow south toward the Gulf of Guinea.
The rivers have rapids and waterfalls that prevent boats from traveling
very far inland.

MALI

BURKINA FASO

GUINEA

S A V A N N A

R A I N   F O R E S T   Z O N E

Sassandra River

Mount
Nimba

TOURA
MOUNTAINS

Lake Kossou

Comoé River

Lake Buyo

GHANA

Cavally River

Bandama River

LIBERIA

L A G O O N   R E G I O N

Ébrié Lagoon

Aby Lagoon

Gulf of Guinea

ATLANTIC

OCEAN

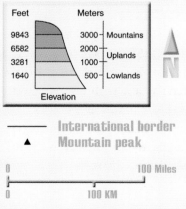

Ivory Coast

Feet	Meters	
9843	3000	Mountains
6582	2000	Uplands
3281	1000	
1640	500	Lowlands

Elevation

N

——— International border
▲ Mountain peak

0   100 Miles
0   100 KM

The main rivers from west to east are the Cavally, Sassandra, Bandama, and Comoé. Many rivers are dry except during the rainy season.

The Cavally River rises in the mountains of Guinea. It functions as a border between Ivory Coast and Liberia for much of its length. It is navigable—accessible to boat travel—for about 50 miles (80 km) inland from its mouth.

The Sassandra originates in the hills of the northwest and flows southeast. It winds across the savanna, broadens into a human-made lake behind the Buyo Dam, skirts the rain forest reserve of Taï National Park, and joins the sea near Sassandra. It is navigable for about 50 miles (80 km) inland.

The Bandama is the country's longest river. Several smaller rivers flow into the Bandama from central Ivory Coast. Human-made Lake Kossou, behind the Kossou Dam, is the country's largest inland body of water, covering more than 620 square miles (1,600 sq. km). During the rainy season, the Bandama is navigable for a short distance from its mouth near Grand-Lahou.

The Comoé River begins its course in Burkina Faso and forms the boundary between the two countries for some distance. It meanders through Comoé National Park, providing drinking water to the park's many animals, and empties into the Ébrié Lagoon near Grand-Bassam.

The Kossou Dam on the Bandama River is the country's largest dam, at 187 feet (57 m) in height and 4,920 feet (1,500 m) across. When the dam was completed in 1972 and the lake behind it was flooded (to create a hydroelectric power station), some 210,000 acres (85,000 hectares) of farmland and forestland disappeared underwater. Thousands of local people had to move, many to nearby cities. Some people feel that they were never properly paid for the loss of their land.

◉ Climate

Ivory Coast is warm year-round. Daily temperatures average between 77°F (25°C) and 86°F (30°C). The south is warmer than the north. In coastal areas, there is little difference in temperature between the seasons or between day and night. Temperatures vary more widely on the savanna.

Southern areas, being close to the ocean, are very humid. The savanna is drier, although it too is quite humid. Winds from the southwest bring warm air and rain to Ivory Coast during half of the year. Dry winds blow from the northeast the other half of the year.

In the savanna region, the dry season lasts from November to March. The harmattan, a cool, dry wind from the Sahara Desert to the north and east, blows from December to February. The rainy season occurs between June and October. Rainfall totals about 45 inches (114 centimeters) in the northeast and central regions and approximately 60 inches (152 cm) in the northwest.

Southern parts of the country receive some rain almost every month, with two main rainy seasons. Along the coastal fringe, heavy rains fall from May through July, lighter rains fall in October and November, and a dry season lasts from December to April. The western mountains have no dry season. Total annual rainfall there averages about 80 inches (203 cm).

Flora and Fauna

The coastal and southwestern forests are always green because they receive abundant rain year-round. Known as rain forests, these areas feature a thick tangle of tree branches, hanging vines, and epiphytes (plants that get their nutrients from the air and rain and usually grow on other plants). Only a few pockets of virgin, or original, rain forest remain in Ivory Coast, since so much of the forest has been logged. In the central and northern parts of the forest zone, the vegetation is less dense. Some taller trees lose their leaves for a short time during the dry season. Among the more than 225 species of trees native to Ivory Coast's forests are mahogany, African teak, ebony, and palms.

In the savanna of the north, trees are more scattered. In some

Baobab trees

places, they grow close enough together that their top branches touch. The shrubby undergrowth is sparse. Frequent bush fires during the dry season prevent shrubs from growing. Trees are protected from fire damage by their thick layers of bark. Other parts of the savanna have thick grasslands, many shrubs, and fewer trees. The baobab tree, common in the savanna, is unusual in that it stores water in its huge trunk. Stretches of trees also grow along moist riverbanks.

Ivory Coast is home to a huge variety of birds, mammals, reptiles, and insects. More than five hundred species of birds spend all or part of the year there. They include cattle egrets, hornbills, gray parrots, African white-backed vultures, and various species of swallows, bee-eaters, kingfishers, flycatchers, cuckoos, and sunbirds. Several species of small antelopes are common in both forests and open grasslands. Reptiles such as snakes and geckos are

A **termite mound** on the Ivorian grasslands. A queen termite can lay as many as 52,000 eggs per day. Learn more about the wildlife of Ivory Coast at vgsbooks.com.

plentiful. Termite mounds, reaching more than 3 feet (1 m) high on the savanna, indicate the presence of busy insects underground. About ninety species of freshwater fish are found in the Comoé River. During the dry season, most fish have to survive in what shallow pools of water remain in the rivers. One species of lungfish can survive on land, buried in the mud.

The habitats, or natural homes, of some wildlife species are disappearing, however, as humans expand towns, farms, and roads. As a result, some species are increasingly rare and endangered. They are seldom seen, except within the boundaries of the country's half-dozen national parks. Elephants roam the savanna of Comoé National Park. Other animals found in the park include waterbucks, leopards, green monkeys, aardvarks, and crocodiles. Some thirty species of snakes live in the park, as do birds such as storks, vultures, and herons.

In Taï National Park, a large area of virgin rain forest is protected from loggers, farmers, and poachers (illegal hunters). It is home to chimpanzees, diana monkeys, red colobus monkeys, and several other species of primates, as well as giant forest hogs, bushpigs, and many small forest antelopes. Predators—animals that live by eating other animals—include leopards and African golden cats. The park has one of the world's only remaining populations of pygmy hippopotamuses, so called because they are much smaller than the more familiar river

A baby **pygmy hippopotamus** and its sleeping mother. Pygmy hippos are noisy eaters. They can be heard feeding from as far away as 150 feet (50 m).

hippopotamuses. The endangered Jentink's duiker also lives in the park. This shy antelope hides in fallen or hollow tree trunks during the day, then ventures out at night to eat fruit. Although seldom seen, it has unmistakable markings: a black head and neck; a thin, whitish stripe across its back and sides; and gray legs and hindquarters.

Natural Resources

The most important resource for Ivory Coast's economy is its agricultural land. The nation's fairly flat terrain and abundant rainfall allow farmers to grow large quantities of crops such as cocoa beans, coffee beans, pineapples, and rubber. These products are called cash crops because farmers sell them, rather than eat them themselves. Cocoa and coffee plants require lots of rain, partial shade, and shelter from the wind, so they grow best in the rain forest zone. Other important agricultural products include yams, cassava (an edible root), plantains (similar to bananas), sugarcane, corn, rice, palm oil, peanuts, and cotton.

The forest's most valuable timber has already been cut, but some tropical hardwoods like mahogany, teak, and ebony remain. Trucks haul logs from deep in the forest to sawmills and ports. The biggest trees were cut long ago.

Fish are another important resource, with a catch of about 74,000 tons (67,000 metric tons) every year. Fishers sail offshore to catch large ocean species such as skipjack tuna, marlin, and shark. Shrimp and crab are found in the peaceful waters of the lagoons.

Mineral resources include deposits of diamonds, gold, nickel, manganese, and bauxite. The Mount Nimba region has iron ore deposits. Offshore oil and gas deposits, including an estimated 100 million barrels of oil, are considered key to the country's economic strength. The oil and gas provide for Ivory Coast's own energy needs, with enough left over for exports to neighboring countries. Six hydroelectric generating stations have been built on the country's rivers. These stations use the power of rushing water to produce electricity.

Environmental Issues

Logging began in Ivory Coast during the nineteenth century. Mahogany and other valuable trees were cut for their timber, which was sold around the world. Trees were also cut to make way for cocoa, coffee, and rubber plantations or for farmland to feed the nation's growing population. In the 1980s, when world market prices of cocoa and coffee fell, the country turned back to its timber resources for income, and more trees were cut.

By the 1990s, only 13.6 million acres (5.5 million hectares) of rain forest remained in Ivory Coast, down from an estimated 32 million acres (13 million hectares) in 1900. The trees that remain are the smaller, less valuable ones. Meanwhile, noisy trucks and logging roads disturb the animals that live in the forest. Farmers and villagers put additional pressure on the forests by cutting and burning trees to make charcoal for cooking fires. As the forests are cut, plants and animals have fewer places to live.

Tree stumps on a cleared hillside are an indicator of **deforestation.** Lime trees, less valuable than those that have been cut, rise in the background.

THE FANICOS OF BANCO NATIONAL PARK

Not far from Abidjan is Banco National Park, a lush rain forest preserve. Near its entrance, along the banks of the Banco River, is a well-known outdoor laundry facility, workplace of washers called *fanicos (below)*. Early each morning, hundreds of fanicos collect laundry from customers and bring it to the river, where they scrub it against rocks and piles of old tires. They use black soap, made from palm oil. They lay the clothing out to dry on the nearby grass and rocks, then deliver it back to their customers. This longstanding practice provides income but pollutes the water. Most of the washers are from Burkina Faso or Mali.

Environmental organizations and the government are trying to conserve the remaining rain forest and its animal inhabitants. For example, environmental groups encourage residents to prepare charcoal from waste wood from sawmills rather than from newly cut trees. The government has passed laws that restrict logging and hunting. But some farmers cut trees illegally to clear space for plantations, some villagers poach endangered animals for food, and some loggers ignore regulations designed to preserve what remains of the forest.

The expansion of farmland also leads to widespread use of chemical fertilizers and pesticides, applied to increase crop production. Many of these chemicals run off from the fields and eventually pollute streams and rivers. Also, large-scale production of just a few crops, as opposed to the rotation of several different types of crops, can cause soil to erode and become less fertile.

Water quality is another environmental concern throughout the country. In Abidjan, an aquifer—a natural underground water supply—is the city's only source of water for drinking and industrial use. Many experts worry that the aquifer may not be able to meet future demands. Some say the water supply is poorly managed. A large proportion of the city's poor people do not have access to running water. They must buy water at high prices from street vendors.

Sewer and plumbing services have not kept up with population growth. In the cities, one household in three has neither an indoor toilet nor its own latrine (a pit in the ground used as a toilet). In rural areas, that ratio rises to three out of five households. Without adequate sewer systems, human and industrial waste run off into rivers and lagoons. The majority of Ivorians have no garbage collection service and dispose of their household trash outside.

 For links to websites where you can find out more about the cities of Ivory Coast—including Abidjan, Yamoussoukro, Bouaké, Daloa, San Pédro, and Odienné—plus climate information and weather forecasts, go to vgsbooks.com.

Cities

ABIDJAN, population 2.5 million, is the country's largest city and its commercial capital. Built on the shores of the Ébrié Lagoon, it is a city of contrasts. The Plateau, the downtown business area, has high-rise office buildings, luxury hotels, expensive restaurants, and wide boulevards. Modern and sophisticated, it inspires the nicknames Paris of West Africa and Pearl of the Lagoon. Poorer neighborhoods such as Treichville are packed with immigrants from rural areas and neighboring African countries.

Originally, Abidjan was the site of a small fishing village. French colonists arrived there at the beginning of the twentieth century to build a railway to the interior. Abidjan became the capital of Ivory Coast in 1934. (The capital moved to Yamoussoukro in 1984.) The city's biggest growth spurt began in 1950, when the Vridi Canal was completed. The canal, connecting the lagoon to the Gulf of Guinea, made Abidjan one of West Africa's major seaports. Deepwater port facilities along the canal handle oil shipments, as well as exports such as cocoa, coffee, and pineapples. The canal also has facilities for a fishing fleet. About 60 percent of the goods imported to the region pass through Abidjan.

The Abidjan skyline is clustered around a large lagoon. Abidjan is Ivory Coast's largest and most densely populated city.

Abidjan is a transportation hub with paved highways, rail connections to Burkina Faso, and a large international airport. The city is also a cultural and educational center, with a museum dedicated to traditional Ivorian art, a national library, and the National University of Ivory Coast.

BOUAKÉ With a population of about 600,000, Bouaké is the country's second largest city. Located in the middle of the country, it is a commercial and transportation center served by highways and an airport. Originally a French military outpost, the town experienced rapid growth in the 1970s with the creation of nearby Lake Kossou. Creation of the lake, the result of damming the Bandama River, forced many rural people to move to the city because their farmland was flooded. Cotton, tobacco, rice, and textiles are processed in Bouaké. It has a busy open-air market.

DALOA, with about 160,000 inhabitants, is a transportation, administrative, and trade center in the west-central part of the country. Its original inhabitants were mostly Bété and Gur people. The city became a French military post in 1903. Capital of the cocoa industry, the region also produces coffee and timber.

YAMOUSSOUKRO Since 1984 Yamoussoukro has been the official capital of Ivory Coast, although most foreign embassies and government offices remain in the former capital, Abidjan. Yamoussoukro, often called Yamko or Yam, was the birthplace of former president Félix Houphouët-Boigny. He was responsible for moving the capital there. The city has a population of about 100,000. It has several large and beautiful buildings, including the Our Lady of Peace Basilica and a presidential palace with a lake and sacred crocodiles. There is also a technical institute—a school that trains scientists, engineers, and agricultural specialists.

SAN PÉDRO, population 70,600, is the country's second largest seaport. Located in the southwest, it was once a tiny fishing village. It exploded in size when port facilities were completed in 1970. Many of its residents live in crowded shantytowns—poor neighborhoods with crude houses. Timber is an important industry there, as well as the city's major export product. The city is also a fishing port.

ODIENNÉ, in the northwest, began as a Muslim trade center. It later provided strong support to Samory Touré, a Mandinka warrior who fought the French in the late 1800s. The city, with a population of 28,300, sits at the crossroads of highways to Guinea and Mali and to the Ivorian cities of Man and Korhogo. People from the surrounding savanna bring their yams, cassavas, cattle, and sheep to market there. Many people come to worship at the city's famous mosque (Muslim house of worship).

HISTORY AND GOVERNMENT

Archaeologists, scientists who study the remains of past cultures, have found evidence of people living in Ivorian territory in prehistoric times. But little is known about these early inhabitants. There are no written records of Ivory Coast until early Roman times (about the eighth century B.C.). From these records, we know that people in Ivory Coast did business with traders from North Africa. The North Africans carried salt from the Sahara Desert to southern and western Africa, where salt is rare. They traded the salt for gold, ivory, and kola nuts (a seed containing caffeine used in beverages and for chewing). The traders also bought and sold people as slaves.

Although few records exist, the early peoples of Ivory Coast probably lived in small villages. For food, they hunted, fished, and gathered wild plants. Local kings and chieftains provided leadership. Around A.D. 1000, new groups began to arrive in Ivory Coast from neighboring areas. The Senoufo, farming people from present-day Mali, settled peacefully in the north. Like other Africans of this era, they practiced

a traditional animist religion. That is, they worshipped their ancestors and believed in good and evil spirits. They founded a village at Kong in the twelfth century and later established other towns, including Korhogo.

From the thirteenth to the fifteenth centuries, people from the Malinké Empire, based in modern-day Mali, expanded their territory, pushing into northwestern Ivory Coast. Some settled near the site of present-day Odienné, forcing out the Senoufo people who lived there. The Malinké were Muslims—they practiced the Islamic religion. They tried to convert their new neighbors to Islam. Many people in the north did adopt Islam, but others, such as the Senoufo, refused to convert. They kept their traditional beliefs in good and evil spirits.

At the beginning of the fifteenth century, small groups of Malinké merchants, called the Dioula, settled peacefully in northeastern Ivory Coast territory. About 1600 another group of Dioula arrived in Kong, while others continued farther west to the Korhogo area. The Dioula

Dioula merchants settled in the areas surrounding modern-day Korhogo and Kong.

opened trade routes between the rain forest and savanna regions. They traded kola nuts, ivory, slaves, firearms, and gold. Each Ivorian ethnic group had its own language, but the language of the Dioula—also called Dioula—eventually became the shared language of travelers and merchants throughout the region. Because so many of its residents were Muslim, Kong became a vibrant Muslim city and study center.

Other outsiders continued to move into Ivory Coast. From the fifteenth to the seventeenth century, the Kru people moved into the southwestern forest and coastal areas. The Abron, an ethnic group who had fled fighting in neighboring Ghana (then called the Gold Coast), settled south of the town of Bondoukou in the seventeenth century. More large waves of immigrants, the Agni and the Baoulé, arrived during the eighteenth century. They established kingdoms of their own in the east-central region of Ivory Coast.

Arrival of the Europeans

Portuguese sailors, looking for gold and slaves, began to explore the coast of West Africa in the fifteenth century. They reached the Gold Coast in 1471. Portuguese traders supplied Africans with textiles, firearms, and other goods in exchange for gold, slaves, ivory, and pepper.

Southern Ivory Coast had thick forests, a rugged coastline with heavy surf, and few good harbors, so most Europeans preferred to trade elsewhere. During the seventeenth century, however, a profitable trade in elephant tusks sprang up. Elephant tusks are made of ivory,

and Europeans wanted ivory to make piano keys, knife handles, and decorative items. To get the valuable ivory, hunters killed elephants by the thousands. Traders piled so many tusks on the shore that Europeans started to call the region the Ivory Coast. By the beginning of the eighteenth century, the elephant population had declined so drastically that the ivory trade died out.

Like other European nations, France wanted to gain territory, wealth, and power in West Africa. In 1637 French missionaries—religious teachers who wanted to convert the local people to Christianity—landed at Assinie, at the mouth of the Aby Lagoon. They were quickly felled by malaria, a tropical disease, however. The French tried again to establish an outpost at Assinie, sending soldiers there in 1687 and from 1701 to 1704. In 1842 the French signed a treaty with the king of the Sanwi people, establishing a French protectorate (a region under French control) in southeastern Ivory Coast. Soon similar treaties brought the coastal area between Assinie and Sassandra under French influence. These treaties allowed the French to establish permanent, fortified trading posts at strategic spots on the Gulf of Guinea.

The posts were home to French sailors, soldiers, merchants, and government officials. The French constructed a wharf at Grand-Bassam, but because of dangerous surf, ships could not travel all the way to the shoreline. Instead, they remained anchored offshore, and people and goods were transported to and fro aboard small boats.

For several years in the 1870s, the French were forced to put aside their ambitions to establish colonies in Africa. Busy with affairs closer to home—the Franco-Prussian War, the

THE LEGEND OF QUEEN ABLA POKOU

Folklore has grown up around the exploits of the Akan people, who fled fighting in their native Ghana and crossed into Ivory Coast in the 1700s. The most famous story is about Queen Abla Pokou, who became a hero by sacrificing the life of her child. When her people arrived at the banks of the Comoé River with no way to cross to safety, she consulted her advisers. They told her to throw her baby into the water. When she did, enormous hippopotamuses lined up and formed a bridge across the river. Queen Pokou was the last across the living bridge. When she reached the shore, the people sank to their knees to thank her. All she could think about, however, was her baby. She cried out *ba ouil*, which means "the child is dead." That is how her people became known as the Baoulé.

reign of Emperor Napoleon III, civil war, and the establishment of a republic—the French turned over responsibility for their West African outposts to merchants. Arthur Verdier, a merchant from Marseille, France, took over as official caretaker of Grand-Bassam and other nearby ports in 1878.

In the 1880s, Verdier established the first coffee plantation in Ivory Coast. Other merchants began cutting the timber of the area's vast rain forests. Meanwhile, French explorers such as Marcel Treich-Laplène and Lieutenant Louis Binger traveled up the major rivers to explore the interior of Ivory Coast.

A French Colony

By 1885 several European powers, including France, Great Britain, and Germany, were vying for control of trade and territory in Africa. To resolve the "scramble for Africa," European leaders held a meeting known as the Berlin Conference. At the conference, France snapped up unclaimed sections of West African coastline. By 1889 Treich-Laplène and Binger had made treaties with nine Ivorian ethnic groups, and France had declared all of southern Ivory Coast a French protectorate. In 1893 the area became an official French colony, with its capital at Grand-Bassam and Lieutenant Binger as its first governor.

Explorer Louis Binger surveys the city of Kong. Binger explored Ivory Coast in the late 1800s and went on to become its first French governor.

Meanwhile, also in the early 1890s, Guinean-born warrior Samory Touré and his army of Mandinka warriors had created an Islamic empire in northern Ivory Coast. Touré's power worried the French, who wanted to expand into the interior themselves. In 1895 Touré's troops destroyed the city of Kong and slaughtered its citizens. The French defeated Touré in 1898, and the next year, France took control of the northern savanna of Ivory Coast.

Back on the coast, the French colonists had built a small but impressive capital on the narrow strip of sand that was Grand-Bassam. In 1899 many residents died during an outbreak of yellow fever, and the capital was moved the next year. The new capital, called Bingerville, was inland, near the Ébrié Lagoon. In 1904 Ivory Coast became part of French West Africa, a union of eight African colonies (modern-day Benin, Burkina Faso, Guinea, Ivory Coast, Mali, Mauritania, Niger, and Senegal).

Creating a colony in Ivory Coast was easier said than done. For many years, the Baoulé, Lobi, Dan, Bété, and other ethnic groups fought back against the French. In 1908 the French governor of the colony undertook a so-called pacification—or peacemaking—campaign. For the next seven years, French troops sought out and killed suspected rebels and burned their homes and crops. Thousands of Africans died. By 1915 the French controlled the territory, but many residents remained resentful.

France wanted to make the colony profitable by exporting its natural resources. Colonial officials gave land to both Europeans and Africans to run coffee plantations, logging businesses, and mines. Cocoa trees were introduced in 1912. Around this time, the government constructed a railroad to transport coffee, timber, cocoa, and other products from the interior to Abidjan.

SAMORY TOURÉ

Samory Touré was born around 1830 in the area that became modern-day Guinea. He was a member of the Mandinka ethnic group and a Muslim. He started out his career as a merchant but eventually became a warrior and leader. Through a combination of military strength and diplomatic negotiations, he built two Islamic empires. The first was centered on the Upper Niger River in the 1870s and 1880s. After the French defeated his forces there, he retreated east in 1892. He built another empire in northern Ivory Coast. The French captured him in 1898 and sent him into exile in Gabon, where he died of natural causes in 1900. Some people looked upon him as a hero who fought the French. But many followers of traditional African religions resented him because his empire forced Islam on its subjects.

Cocoa trees were introduced to Ivory Coast farmers in the early 1900s.

The French needed laborers to build the railway, roads, and other projects and to work at state-run mines and plantations. So the colony introduced a system of forced labor. Under this system, local African men had to work without pay for ten days a year on government projects, but they were often forced to stay longer. Forced labor became one of the most hated aspects of colonial rule.

The French also imposed many of their institutions and laws on the colony. French Catholic missionaries built churches and schools and converted many native people to Christianity. A small group of educated Africans, people who were loyal to the French, held government jobs that brought good salaries. They were allowed to purchase land and to send their children to French-run schools.

But the majority of Africans did not benefit from colonial rule. They were considered subjects of France, but they did not have the same rights as French people, such as the right to free speech. Those Africans who were allowed to own farms received less money for their crops than French landowners did, and they sometimes had to work on the farms of their French neighbors. Africans were also forced to serve in the French military. They were allowed to keep their own languages, religions, and social customs, however.

French officials made important decisions regarding the colony, but there was little opportunity for Ivorians to participate. The French promised that Ivorians could continue to choose their own kings and chiefs without interference. In reality, traditional leaders had very little power. Much of the traditional leadership system broke down.

Meanwhile, Ivory Coast's economy was thriving, and plantation owners and other employers complained that they could not find enough workers. The government began encouraging workers from Upper Volta (modern-day Burkina Faso) to work in Ivory Coast. Between 1932 and 1947, part of Upper Volta was annexed to (became part of) Ivory Coast.

The Seeds of Independence

World War II broke out in Europe in 1939. France soon fell to the Germans, who controlled the northern two-thirds of the country. The French created an organization called the Vichy government in southern France. This government held power only with German approval.

Many French people remained loyal to the old French government, headed in exile by General Charles de Gaulle. Operating first from England, later from North Africa, de Gaulle's Free French government was recognized by the nations fighting the Germans as the legitimate government of France. The governors of French West Africa supported the Vichy government, but many Ivorians backed the exiled Free French. Ivorians especially resented the way the Vichy regime forced them to supply labor and food to its army.

In 1944 a wealthy Baoulé planter named Félix Houphouët-Boigny organized a group of African planters into the African Agricultural Syndicate. The group protested the treatment of African plantation owners and the forced labor laws. In 1944 representatives of Charles de Gaulle's exiled government met with colonial officials at the Brazzaville Conference in the Belgian Congo (modern-day Republic of the Congo) to discuss making reforms in France's colonies.

World War II ended with the defeat of Germany in 1945, and de Gaulle became president of France. He instituted laws that gave Africans a greater say in their colonial governments. Each colony of French West Africa was allowed to elect two representatives to the French National Assembly—the French legislature. One represented the African majority, the other the European minority. Félix Houphouët-Boigny was elected as Ivory Coast's African member of the French National Assembly. He served in this position from 1946 to 1959, and for three years (1956–1959) he was also a cabinet minister in the French government.

Houphouët-Boigny became a major figure in Ivorian politics, especially after he succeeded in persuading the French National Assembly

Félix Houphouët-Boigny *(left)* shakes hands with French president Charles de Gaulle. These two politicians met during Houphouët-Boigny's service in the French National Assembly.

to ban the hated forced labor system. In 1946 he organized a new political party, the Democratic Party of Ivory Coast. He then became the leader of the Democratic African Assembly (the initials of its French name are RDA), a new political organization with participants from across French West Africa.

In the French National Assembly, RDA members pushed for reforms such as equal rights for African citizens in French West Africa. Meanwhile, France was also feeling pressure from its colonies in North Africa and Southeast Asia, where armed independence movements were gaining strength.

When, in 1948, RDA members of the French National Assembly allied themselves with the Communist Party, the French government was alarmed. People in many European and North American countries hated and feared Communism, a political and economic system in which property is owned by the state and there is no private business. French officials tried to suppress the RDA and harassed Houphouët-Boigny and other party members. Eventually, Houphouët-Boigny decided the RDA could make more progress by itself. In 1950 he broke

with the Communists and concentrated on cooperating with the French and building his party's strength.

In the 1950s, colonies around the world began to gain independence from Great Britain, France, and other powerful nations. West Africans, too, desired independence. Charles de Gaulle understood this desire, and he was willing to grant partial independence to France's West African colonies. In 1958 voters in Ivory Coast and several other colonies approved a proposal for partial self-government, with some control retained by France. But after three colonies opted for complete independence from France, all the other colonies asked for and were granted full independence. France declared Ivory Coast independent on August 7, 1960. Félix Houphouët-Boigny was elected its first president two months later.

The Houphouët-Boigny Regime

Houphouët-Boigny was a skilled politician. In part because of this leader's strength and personality, Ivory Coast did not experience the civil wars or military upheavals that plagued many other newly independent African nations. Reelected without opposition five times between 1965 and 1985, he headed a single-party "democracy," meaning that elections were held, but he was the only candidate allowed on the ballot. He ruled with unlimited power, but he gave the impression of listening to citizens' ideas by holding public forums. When rumors of a coup, or violent over-throw of his government, circulated in the early 1960s, he threw the people who disagreed with him out of the Democratic Party. Meanwhile, he built a loyal following of people who owed their power, prestige, and

Houphouët-Boigny's political savvy kept him in office for decades.

wealth to him. The country's financial success also helped maintain his popularity.

Houphouët-Boigny believed in free enterprise—allowing private businesses to operate without much government interference. He also encouraged investment in Ivory Coast, especially by French businesses. The development of factories, completion of the port of Abidjan, and the discovery of offshore oil reserves combined to boost the economy so much that people referred to the growth as the Ivorian miracle. Plantations, logging operations, and cash-crop farms thrived, and the government encouraged low-paid laborers from neighboring countries to immigrate to Ivory Coast. Many of these immigrants stayed and eventually purchased land there. Meanwhile, the government hired a number of French advisers, although some people thought the jobs should have gone to Ivorians.

In the 1980s, the situation began to unravel. Several factors hurt the economy, including severe droughts, a worldwide recession (economic downturn), and a dramatic fall in the international prices paid for coffee and cocoa beans. The government had borrowed large sums of money, and its debts started to pile up. Inflation (rising prices), wage cuts, and unemployment caused many families to feel the pinch. They began to protest.

Many Ivorians wanted a real choice at election time. Houphouët-Boigny made some minor changes to make the government more democratic. But when teachers and student groups held protests, he closed the schools and arrested the protesters. One of the leading opposition voices, Professor Laurent Gbagbo, fled to safety in Paris.

To deal with the economic crisis, in 1987 international financial organizations such as the International Monetary Fund forced the Ivorian government to cut expenses and raise taxes. People in all income groups were hurt by these measures, the poor most of all. By

Laurent Gbagbo

then Houphouët-Boigny had grown old, and many people were worried that trouble would break out if there were no clear successor in the wings when he died. Students, teachers, and other protesters also continued to push for more democracy.

In 1990 Houphouët-Boigny agreed to allow a multiparty presidential election for the first time in the country's history. Gbagbo, by then leader of a new party called the Ivorian Popular Front, ran against him. Although Gbagbo's campaign got off to a late and disorganized start and Houphouët-Boigny won the election with a big lead, more than

Beginning in 1990, Ivorians were allowed to choose from a slate of several presidential candidates at **election time.**

one Ivorian in ten voted for Gbagbo—a sizable show of support. The Ivorian Popular Front became an important political force.

Ivorité

In mid-1993, Houphouët-Boigny was diagnosed with cancer. When he died that December, Henri Konan Bédié, the president of the Ivorian National Assembly—the Ivorian legislature—succeeded him as president. Bédié ran the country in much the same manner as his predecessor, discouraging dissent and encouraging economic growth. The economy stumbled and then recovered. Financed by foreign aid, the government undertook projects to improve the country's basic services, including health care, education, and roads.

Bédié, a Baoulé from the south, pushed the notion of Ivorité, or "Ivorian-ness." He encouraged xenophobia (the fear or hatred of strangers). According to Bédié, the people of the south, who were mostly Christians, were the only true Ivorians. He scorned immigrants and northerners, who were mostly Muslims. Ivorité wasn't a difficult notion to implant, especially when the economy was doing badly. Many Ivorians were willing to blame their financial difficulties on those further down the rung—immigrants. People from Burkina Faso in particular faced discrimination. There were also deadly clashes over fishing rights between native Ivorians and immigrant fishers from Ghana. Soon northerners began to complain of police harassment and exclusion from positions of power.

Despite such problems, most Ivorians and foreign observers still considered Ivory Coast a peaceful, stable state, so they were stunned by the events of Christmas Eve 1999. On that day, army general Robert

Gueï organized a coup and took over the government. Accusing the Bédié government of corruption and mismanagement of the economy, Gueï said he wanted to "sweep the house clean." He promised to restore democracy to Ivory Coast.

The 2000 presidential elections were chaotic. The race pitted Gueï against Laurent Gbagbo, whose supporters were mainly Christians from the south. Alassane Ouattara, a Muslim based in the north, wanted to run but was barred because a court ruled he did not meet the citizenship qualifications.

After mass demonstrations, military interventions, protests from Ouattara, and about three hundred deaths, Gbagbo emerged as the winning candidate. But unrest continued. In 2001 human rights organizations accused government security forces of harassing and beating immigrants. Many frightened foreigners left the country, leaving the agricultural fields without enough workers.

The Rebellion of 2002

In September 2002, about eight hundred rebel soldiers attacked government forces in Abidjan. The rebels were northerners who charged that Gbagbo's southern-based government discriminated against them. The government quickly regained control of the city, but not before several hundred people, including Robert Gueï, were killed.

Over the next weeks, the rebels gained control over a vast area of the north, including the cities of Bouaké and Korhogo. Calling themselves the Patriotic Movement of Ivory Coast,

Ivorian rebel soldiers carrying automatic rifles make their way up a country road.

they demanded that Gbagbo step down and that new elections be held. In response, government forces in Abidjan raided and burned the homes of hundreds of immigrants and Ivorians suspected of being rebel sympathizers.

The rebellion disrupted the transportation of food, raw materials, and other goods throughout West Africa. Furthermore, thousands of immigrant workers, who had routinely sent their earnings home from Ivory Coast, left their jobs and returned to their home countries. Leaders of surrounding West African nations met to discuss the crisis. They worried that the rebellion threatened all of West Africa, since Ivory Coast was so important to the region's economic and political stability. The leaders were also concerned that the conflict would spread to neighboring countries.

A month after the crisis began, the government and rebels agreed to stop shooting. France, which had continued to maintain a small military force in Ivory Coast, sent troops to keep the two sides apart. But the unrest spread to western regions of the country, where two more armed rebel groups appeared. For more than five months, Ivory Coast was divided into government-held and rebel-held areas, and sporadic fighting continued.

FRANCE AND ITS FORMER COLONY

France has had a close relationship with its former colony, especially during the peaceful and prosperous Houphouët-Boigny regime. In 2002 some 20,000 French citizens lived and worked in Ivory Coast. The two countries had a strong trade relationship, with French business investments in Ivory Coast worth $1 billion. During the 2002–2003 rebellion, France got involved in the dispute. It sent more than 2,500 soldiers to protect French citizens and help keep rebel and government forces apart. The French government also helped work out a peace agreement. When that agreement proved unpopular, some Ivorians attacked French schools and businesses, and many French families left Ivory Coast. By the time the crisis eased in the spring of 2003, only about 3,000 Europeans (mostly French) remained in the country. The French government found itself in a difficult and strained relationship with Ivory Coast.

In January 2003, the French government organized talks in Paris between government and rebel representatives, and a peace deal was reached. Although Gbagbo signed the agreement, when he returned home, he did not promote it. Government supporters organized huge rallies against the agreement and against the French. Violence broke out again in some communities, with Christians burning mosques and Muslims destroying churches in revenge.

◉ Peace at Last?

During the conflict, an estimated 400,000 people—Ivorians and those of other nationalities—left Ivory Coast to take refuge in neighboring states. At least 800,000 people were displaced from their homes by the fighting. People who lived in rebel-held areas had no access to banks. Health care and other government services were cut off. Diseases such as cholera, yellow fever, and meningitis spread. The country's economic strength and reputation as a solid democracy took a huge beating.

Many foreign leaders pressured Gbagbo to resolve the situation. If a peace agreement could not be achieved, people feared the eruption of a full-scale civil war. Finally, in March 2003, the opposing factions agreed to form a new government. Seydou Diarra, a former Ivorian diplomat and a Muslim from the north, was named prime minister. President Gbagbo gave him broad powers to disarm the rebels, reestablish peace and governmental authority, and fix a date for the next elections. Fighting continued, however, and it remains to be

seen whether this new government will be able to keep the peace in Ivory Coast.

Visit vgsbooks.com where you can find the most up-to-date population figures, government information, current headlines, interesting facts, customs, and photographs from Ivory Coast.

Government

The president of the Republic of Ivory Coast is the head of state—the leader of the executive branch of government. The president is elected through a secret ballot for a five-year term. All citizens over age eighteen are entitled to vote. The constitution was revised in 2000 to require that anyone running for president had to be an Ivorian citizen with two Ivorian parents.

The Ivorian National Assembly, the national legislature, is composed of 225 members, elected at the same time as the president. The National Assembly passes laws, usually proposed by the president, although the assembly also can introduce laws. The president appoints a prime minister to coordinate government action.

For purposes of local government, the country is divided into sixteen administrative regions, which are further divided into departments, with fifty-eight departments in all. The court system rules on criminal and civil cases. The supreme court is the highest court in the land. Traditional kings and chiefs still exist in Ivory Coast, with some positions being hereditary. The kings and chiefs have influence in their communities, but they have no formal authority in the Ivorian government.

THE PEOPLE

The population of Ivory Coast in the early twenty-first century is an estimated 16.8 million, with an annual growth rate of 2 percent. At this rate of growth, the population could double in thirty-five years. It is projected to reach 35.7 million in 2050. Such rapid population growth hampers the country's development, since schools, health-care facilities, electricity, and other services cannot keep up. Furthermore, population growth increases the demand for farmland. Large-scale immigration only adds to the need for land and services.

The nation's population density is 135 people per square mile (52 people per sq. km). This figure is fairly low compared to nearby Nigeria, with 364 people per square mile (141 people per sq. km), and France, with 279 per square mile (108 people per sq. km). Ivory Coast's population is unevenly distributed, however, with 78 percent of the people living in the southern half of the country. The other 22 percent live in the northern half, in the savanna region. People from the north tend to migrate south, since more jobs are available there. About 46 percent of

the nation's people live in urban areas. Conditions are often crowded in urban homes because people moving to the city to study or work generally move in with relatives. They may stay for years, sleeping in corners or on sofas. This overcrowding can cause family friction and strain household budgets.

The Ivory Coast population is young, with 42 percent of the people under age 15 and only 2 percent over age 65. Life expectancy is low—only 44 years for males and 47 years for females. Many young women marry in their teens, begin to have children right away, and give birth frequently. The average number of children born to a woman during her lifetime is 5.2.

To address overpopulation, the government introduced a family-planning policy in 1997, encouraging the use of modern birth control methods. Ivory Coast has 250 family-planning clinics, but their services reach only about one-third of the population. Only about 15 percent of single women and 4.3 percent of married women use modern

birth control methods. Abortion is permitted only when the mother's life is in danger.

Ethnic Groups

Ivory Coast's population is made up of sixty different ethnic groups. Most of these sixty groups can be classified within five major groups, however. The major groups are the Akan (42 percent), the Gur (18 percent), the Northern Mandé (16 percent), the Kru (11 percent), and the Southern Mandé (10 percent). Many ethnic groups, including the Malinké, Lobi, Dan, and Agni, are related to or descended from similar groups in neighboring countries. Some ethnic groups practice animist religions, some follow Islam, and others are Christian.

The Baoulé (part of the Akan group) represent more than 15 percent of the Ivory Coast population. Most live around Yamoussoukro and Bouaké. The Baoulé are primarily farmers. They grow cash crops and yams, a staple of their diet. Every year they hold a yam harvest festival, offering the first of the season's crop to their ancestors. Baoulé society is based on matrilineal traditions, meaning that people trace their family history through their mothers to a common female ancestor. In many Baoulé villages, matrilineal relatives live in the same neighborhoods. Members of extended families, including grandparents, cousins, aunts, and uncles, share family compounds (housing complexes). Through their fathers, the Baoulé inherit membership in groups that share certain taboos (prohibitions against touching, saying, or doing something for fear of upsetting

This **Baoulé chief** lives in the village of Lolobo, outside of Yamoussoukro.

supernatural powers), ceremonies, and names. Most Baoulé are Christians.

The Senoufo (part of the Gur group) live primarily in the northern and central savanna. The region around Korhogo is dotted with Senoufo villages, which typically feature rectangular, modern houses and small yellowish grain storage buildings with cone-shaped roofs. Famous for their woodcarving and weaving skills, the Senoufo are primarily farming people. They practice a traditional animist religion, and they strive to create a balance between the spiritual world and their everyday lives. There is a strong matrilineal tradition in Senoufo society.

The Northern Mandé, living in the north and northwest, include the Malinké and Bambara peoples. The Malinké, who live near Odienné, grow crops for their own use, including millet, rice, and peanuts, with little left over to sell. They also raise

THE PORO CULT

Senoufo boys carry on a secret and ancient tradition known as the *poro* cult. In modern times, however, this tradition has been simplified and shortened. At age nine, boys join the poro cult with others of the same age. Every Senoufo community has a sacred wooded area where the boys train in practices such as the use of ceremonial masks. Training is divided into three phases, each lasting seven years, with ceremonies to mark the passage from one phase to the next. At age thirty, a Senoufo man reaches full adulthood with a big celebration and masked dancing.

poultry, goats, and cattle. The Malinké are almost exclusively Muslims, while the Bambara primarily practice traditional African religions. The Dioula, related to the Malinké, were traditionally merchants. They live in the Kong region.

The Kru people, including the Bété, live southwest of the Bandama River. Many Kru villages are inhabited by members of the same patrilineage, meaning people trace their family history to a common male ancestor. A Kru must marry someone from outside his or her own village. Polygamy—the practice of a man having more than one wife—is fairly common among the Kru. But such marriages are not legal and are frowned upon by the Christian church (to which many Kru belong). Many Kru make their living by fishing or farming.

The Southern Mandé include the Dan and the Gouru. Despite their name, the Southern Mandé have little in common with the Northern Mandé. The Dan, who live around the city of Man, are famous for the carved masks they use on ceremonial occasions.

Before the 2002–2003 political crisis forced many immigrants to leave, immigrants accounted for more than 29 percent of the total

Immigrants, like these three Lebanese women walking on the beach near Grand-Bassam, make up a large portion of the Ivorian population.

Ivory Coast population. Of the estimated 5 million non-Ivorians living in Ivory Coast, about 2.2 million were from Burkina Faso, 230,000 were from Guinea, and 800,000 were from Mali. Others were from Ghana, Nigeria, Benin, Senegal, Liberia, Mauritania, Lebanon, and France. Ivory Coast also served as home for some 110,000 refugees—people who had escaped from danger in their own countries, primarily Liberia. They lived in the west, in a special zone set aside for refugees.

Languages

Many Ivorians speak more than one language. French, the country's official language, is taught at school. Newspapers are published in French, and French is the language used by the government. Highly educated Ivorians speak French well, but people who have little education do not. Many Ivorians speak French with local accents that are difficult to understand elsewhere. Arabic, a Middle Eastern language and the language of the Quran, the Islamic holy book, is taught in Muslim schools.

Each ethnic group speaks its own language or dialect. No indigenous, or native, African language is dominant, although Dioula is most widely spoken in the north. When people need to communicate in a common language—on the streets, in comic strips, and on radio and television advertising, for instance—they use pidgin French, a simplified version of French.

A Poor Country

Although it may be better off than some of its neighbors, Ivory Coast is still a poor country. According to government statistics, almost 34 per-

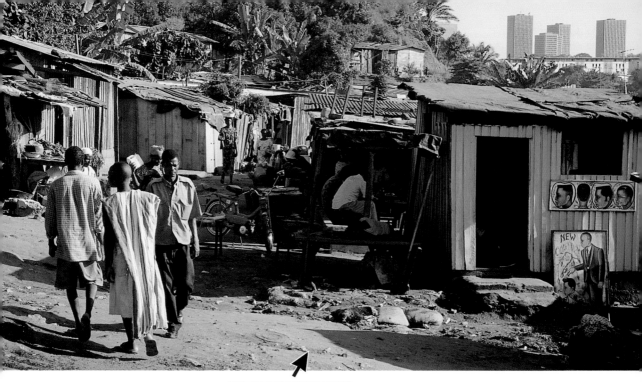

Abidjan is ringed by **slums like this one.** Many poor Ivorians make their homes in such areas.

cent of Ivorians live below the poverty line. Farmworkers, street vendors, and those who do odd jobs are among the poorest people in the country. More than 50 percent of the poor are women. More than one-quarter of children under age five are malnourished and underweight. There is also a large gap between rich and poor, and that gap is getting wider. The wealthiest 20 percent of the Ivory Coast population holds 48 percent of the total national income, while the poorest 50 percent has less than 25 percent of the total national income.

Living conditions are harsh. Access to clean drinking water is limited, although the situation is a little better in Abidjan and other large cities than in rural areas. In the villages and farms of the countryside, only about 37 percent of people have access to well water. The others must collect water from streams and lakes, which might be several miles away. Much of this water is not clean. The government undertook an ambitious program to drill five thousand new wells in rural villages in the years leading up to 2000. The program did not reach its target, however.

Nationwide, 43 percent of households have electric power. In rural areas, only 14 percent of households have electricity, compared with 87 percent in Abidjan and 77 percent in urban areas overall. In the late 1990s, the government planned to bring electricity to an additional two thousand

A girl selling freshwater

villages, but this plan also fell far short of its goal. Ivory Coast has a nationwide housing shortage, with the lack of housing particularly severe in fast-growing urban areas.

Education and Literacy

In the early 1900s, French missionaries founded numerous schools in the colony, providing an elite few with a European-style education. The country's modern educational system is still modeled after the French system, and French is the language of instruction. Most schools are run by the government, but some are run by Catholic, Protestant, and Islamic organizations. Religious-based schools follow the government-set curriculum and receive money from the government. Students attend primary school from age six through eleven. Secondary education begins at age twelve and lasts for up to seven years. At the college level, students can attend technical schools, teacher training institutions, or the National University.

The quality of public education has declined in recent years, with increasingly overcrowded classrooms. The school system has also

This **elementary school in Bouaké** is run by a Catholic organization. Religious-based schools are a small but important part of the Ivorian educational system.

been criticized for not preparing graduates for the local job market. Enrollment numbers are low. At the primary level, only 78 percent of school-age children attend school—89 percent of boys and 66 percent of girls. At the secondary level, only about 34 percent of boys and 16 percent of girls attend school. These figures are lower than those in nearby Benin, Burkina Faso, Mali, and Senegal. Among Ivorians age 15 and over, only 55 percent of men and 39 percent of women are literate—able to read. In comparison, throughout the rest of Africa, an average 70 percent of men and 52 percent of women are literate. In 2001 the government announced plans to improve the school system and provide primary education to all children.

Child Labor

School enrollment figures are low in part because many children have to work to help support their families. A workers' union claimed that in 2002, 40 percent of Ivorian children between the ages of five and fourteen held some kind of paying job. Most working children—almost 65 percent—live in the north, where families are poorest. Most child workers perform farm jobs or domestic chores. Teenage girls from poor families are sometimes hired to clean or look after young children in the homes of the wealthy.

Child labor is harmful for several reasons. Some children are assigned dangerous work, and others are beaten. Girls who work in domestic service often receive food and housing as compensation, but no wages. Since they don't attend school, most young workers do not receive the education that would allow them to escape poverty. Some are put out on the street to fend for themselves when they become old enough to talk back to their employers. Children from cocoa farms are especially at risk of being undereducated. A 2002 survey found that one-third of school-age children

CHILD BRIDES

Although it is illegal, Ivorian girls as young as twelve might be forced into arranged marriages, often with distant relatives who are considerably older than they are. The practice is especially common in predominantly Muslim parts of the country. The groom often pays a bride price—money or gifts to the girl's family. Supporters claim that this practice keeps girls from having sex outside of marriage. It also helps cement ties between families. Health experts say the high rate of Ivorian mothers and babies who die during childbirth is partly due to the fact that girls give birth so young.

(ages 6 to 17) living in cocoa-producing households had never attended school. Children of immigrant cocoa farmers are even less likely to be enrolled in school than the children of local cocoa farmers.

Health Care and HIV/AIDS

Medical facilities are operated by the government, and some health services are free. The government spends about 5.5 percent of its domestic budget on health care. Yet health services are very inadequate. According to recent figures, the nation has only nine physicians, thirty-one nurses, and fifteen midwives for every 100,000 people. And the quality of public health care declined in the 1990s as the economy sputtered. Epidemics of diseases such as cholera (caused by contaminated food and water) returned. Malaria is widespread throughout the nation.

Infant and maternal death rates are high. In the early twenty-first century, about 1,200 Ivorian women die in childbirth each year for every 100,000 live births, and 95 infants die for every 1,000 live births. This rate has decreased since 1960, when there were 195 infant deaths out of 1,000 live births. However, the rate is worse than the African average of 86 infant deaths per 1,000 live births.

Ivory Coast has one of West Africa's highest rates of HIV (human immunodeficiency virus) infection. The incidence of AIDS, the disease caused by HIV, is on the increase. According to government

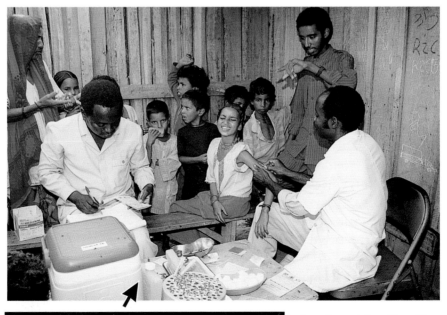

Volunteers at a medical clinic give vaccinations to immigrant families. Due to poor health care, Ivorians are at risk for some deadly diseases that have been wiped out in other parts of the world.

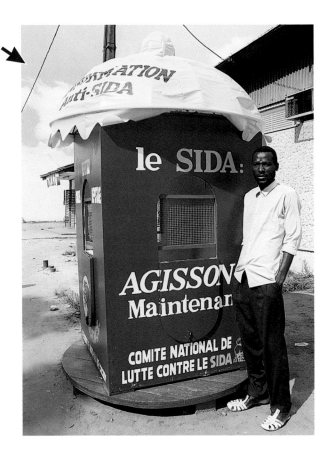

A condom vendor stands next to his **anti-AIDS kiosk** in Abidjan. Despite a government-sponsored AIDS/HIV education program, thousands of Ivorians contract HIV every year.

figures, HIV/AIDS affects between 10 and 14 percent of the population, including 14 percent of pregnant women. The United Nations estimates that some 72,000 Ivorian adults and children died of AIDS in 1999, and a total of 420,000 children had been orphaned by the disease since it first appeared in the 1980s.

The government launched an AIDS information program in 2002 to increase awareness of the disease and to encourage the use of condoms, which help prevent the spread of HIV during sex. The government also tries to keep HIV-infected blood out of the supply used for transfusions, and it trains health-care workers in treating AIDS. Hospitals in Abidjan and two other cities specialize in treating the disease. Anti-AIDS drugs have been available since 2001. Although these drugs are sold at greatly reduced prices, poor people still cannot afford them, and they are in very limited supply.

Efforts to control the spread of AIDS were badly set back by the 2002 rebellion. There was no money or system to pass out prevention information, and condoms were not available in rebel-held cities. The economic crisis forced many women into prostitution, furthering the spread of HIV through sexual contact. The mass movement of migrant workers and refugees threatened to spread HIV further throughout the region.

CULTURAL LIFE

With its many ethnic groups and customs, Ivory Coast is culturally diverse. It has a rich tradition of art, literature, and music. Language acts as a common thread, since many people speak French, Dioula, or pidgin French. At the same time, friction exists between some ethnic groups and between followers of the two main religions, Islam and Christianity.

▶ Religion

Muslims make up about 39 percent of the Ivory Coast population, Catholics account for almost 20 percent, and Protestants and people of other Christian denominations account for 11 percent. Twelve percent of Ivorians are animists, or followers of traditional African religions. Another 18 percent say they have no official religious affiliation.

Christianity arrived with French missionaries in the 1800s. In modern times, most Christians (including Catholics and Protestants) live

in the southern, central, and eastern parts of the country. Christians hold most of the important positions in the Ivory Coast government. The late president Houphouët-Boigny, a Roman Catholic, left a Catholic stamp on the country with the construction of a huge basilica—a Catholic church—in his hometown.

Islam, a religion that originated on the Arabian Peninsula in the A.D. 600s, was brought to the region by the Malinké people. Most Muslims live in the north, although many have migrated to the cities of the south. The majority of immigrants to Ivory Coast are Muslims. In cities and towns across the country, Muslims attend services at local mosques each Friday. They follow the teachings of the Quran, the Islamic holy book. Some send their children to Muslim schools.

Animist religions are the oldest religions in Ivory Coast. These traditions were practiced long before the arrival of Muslims or Christians. Although each ethnic group has its own customs and beliefs, in general people who practice animism believe that natural

Many ethnic groups in Ivory Coast, like these Senoufo dancers and musicians, continue to practice the animist religions of their ancestors.

things such as plants, rocks, the wind, and even ancestors have spirits. These spirits can be helpful or harmful. People use rituals to please the spirits—asking their help in curing diseases or avoiding misfortunes. Animist religions primarily are practiced in rural regions. Muslim and Christian missionaries, immigration to the cities, and modern education have all caused a decline in traditional religions. In 1975, 37 percent of the population practiced animism. At the beginning of the twenty-first century, that figure was down to 12 percent.

Many people who are officially Christian or Muslim also follow some animist practices as well. For example, although most Baoulé are Catholic, their traditional beliefs are far from dead. Ancestor worship is the basis of Baoulé religious practice, and each matrilineal group has a ceremonial stool that embodies the spirit of the group's ancestors.

The Senoufo have struggled to maintain their traditional beliefs despite the strong influence of Islam. According to Senoufo beliefs, one god rules the mineral, plant, and animal worlds, and evil forces are always present. People practice rituals and call on helpful spirits to keep them in contact with their distant god and to guard against harmful spirits. Senoufo myths tell how the world was created. Each Senoufo family is said to be descended from a mythical ancestor, usually identified with an animal.

Art

The arts in Ivory Coast are part of the fabric of everyday life. Clothing, religious figurines, and jewelry are all beautifully crafted objects. Many ethnic groups are famous for their striking carved wooden masks. A small museum in Abidjan is dedicated to contemporary art and another is dedicated to traditional Ivorian art.

Woman wearing pagnes

Many people wear colorful clothing, made of *pagnes*, or lengths of printed cloth in a vast array of vibrant designs. Women often wear pagnes as blouses and skirts. Men tend to wear American-style pants and shirts, but on ceremonial occasions, men often wear brightly colored robes, wrapped around the body and over one shoulder. In parts of the southeast, chiefs wear elaborate gold jewelry and other ornaments that show off their wealth and symbolize their authority.

The Baoulé people carve wooden figures that represent the spirits, with detailed hair and facial features. They also create masks used for ceremonies associated with ancestor worship. The Senoufo make statues and masks in the form of monkeys, crocodiles, birds, and mythical creatures. These masks are worn at funerals, dances, and harvest rituals. Each Dan or Wobé mask is carefully carved out of a block of wood, then polished and dyed. These masks are used to communicate with the high god through the spirits of the ancestors. They often are passed

Groups such as the Dan, Senoufo, and Baoulé create **intricate ritual masks.**

down through several generations. A mask that belonged to an important person is said to retain that person's power.

Architecture

This diverse country offers a variety of architecture, from the modern high-rises of downtown Abidjan, reflected in the lagoon, to the round grain storage buildings with cone-shaped roofs of dusty Senoufo villages. The country's architectural heritage includes imposing buildings, such as the governor's palace and courthouse in Grand-Bassam, dating from the French colonial era.

Several famous mosques are found in the savanna region. The mosque at Tengrela in the far north was built in the fifteenth century. Kong's famous mosque, with its protruding wooden beams, dates from the seventeenth century, but it was rebuilt after Samory Touré destroyed the city in 1895. There is no doubt, however, that the most impressive building in Ivory Coast is the Our Lady of Peace Basilica in Yamoussoukro. With its air-conditioned seating, stained-glass windows, and gold-topped dome, it reflects the financial excesses of its creator, the late President Félix Houphouët-Boigny.

Yamoussoukro's **Our Lady of Peace Basilica** took nearly four years to build. Behind the basilica are two identical buildings. One is home to the priest, and the other is reserved for visits by the Pope (the head of the Catholic Church).

Literature

Ivory Coast has a strong tradition of storytelling. In earlier centuries, griots—West African musician-storytellers—were treated with great respect. The griots sang and told stories and poems about family histories and important events. They even served as advisers to prominent families. In modern times, griots still play a valued role as entertainers, poets, and historians.

Ivory Coast has several well-known writers. Bernard Dadié, the best-known Ivorian author, has written poetry, plays, and novels, several of which have been translated from the original French into English. *Climbié*, his first novel, is based on his youth in colonial Africa. Some of his later works stem from his experiences in the United States and Paris. Ahmadou Kourouma is another internationally known Ivorian writer whose books have been translated from French into English. The country has also produced a number of respected authors in the fields of history, economics, philosophy, and sociology.

Ahmadou Kourouma

Music and Dance

Each ethnic group has its own musical traditions. Many dances are linked to rituals and religious practices. The Lobi people of the northeast use xylophones in their traditional music. In the lagoon region, the Appolo people make their drums do the talking during their annual *abissa* purification dance. The Baoulé brought their vocal traditions from Ghana.

Two ceremonial dances are particularly spectacular. One is performed by young Dan men. They train secretly for years to learn the dance, which they perform wearing masks and standing on tall stilts. People believe that during the dance, the dancers communicate with spirits. The other dance is famed for the acrobatic skill it requires of the dancers. During this dance, performed by Dan, Wobé, and Guéré dancers, men decorated with small, white cowrie shells juggle young girls, throwing them in the air and holding them aloft.

The National Ballet of Ivory Coast was formed in the 1970s to preserve the traditional dances of the country's ethnic groups. It gave many dancers an opportunity to learn new techniques and skills. Some of the dancers have gone on to create their own local dance troupes or to dance in other countries.

A group of dancers from the **National Ballet of Ivory Coast** perform a traditional dance.

Ivorians also enjoy contemporary music. In the 1970s, Ivorian musician Ernesto Djedje combined elements of traditional Bété music with rhythms from the Republic of the Congo, creating a style known as *ziglibithy*. In the early 1990s, a style called *zouglou* appeared. Marked by satirical lyrics, it was the theme music of a student protest movement that helped force Ivory Coast's transition to a multiparty political system. The music then became popular with young people throughout West Africa. Reggae made its way from Jamaica and the United States to Ivory Coast in the late 1900s. Ivorian-born Alpha Blondy is a world-famous reggae star. He brings messages of peace through his songs, with lyrics in Dioula, French, English, Arabic, and Hebrew. Trends such as Afro-pop have also become extremely popular in Ivory Coast. Abidjan is the heart of the music industry in West Africa, with sophisticated recording studios located there. Numerous nightclubs are found in nearby Treichville, where local musicians perform.

Theater and Film

Ivory Coast does not have an acclaimed theater, even in Abidjan. Nevertheless, the country does have a small but vibrant theatrical

tradition. Many of its best authors have also written for the stage. One of Abidjan's best-known live theater groups is the Kotéba Ensemble. Founded in 1994, it borrows a Malian tradition to blend contemporary music, dance, and drama. This group has created new works and has trained many performers over the years.

Ivory Coast's first films were produced in the early 1960s. Since then, a number of movies featuring local actors have been shot there, along with a few French films made in the savanna region. In 1998 Abidjan hosted a festival of short films.

Communications and Media

Ivory Coast has about a dozen daily newspapers and several others that publish less frequently. Most newspapers have well-known ties to one political party or another. Papers that do not sympathize with the government have been censored at times.

Radio is popular in Ivory Coast. Government statistics show that almost 40 percent of households have a radio, while only 1 percent have a television set. A state-owned station, Radiodiffusion Télévision Ivorienne, broadcasts in French and several native languages on both television and radio. People can also tune in TV and radio broadcasts from Europe and other parts of Africa. Catholic, Protestant, and Islamic radio stations broadcast as well.

Less than 1 percent of households have a home telephone line, but many Ivorians have access to cellular phones. Merchants on city street corners sell cell phone use by the minute. Few households have access to the Internet, but cyber cafés, where people can pay for a period of time online, are popular, especially in well-to-do areas of Abidjan. Some young Ivorians use the Internet to meet people—especially Europeans or Americans—interested in marriage.

MEDIA CENSORSHIP

Media outlets have always played an important role in Ivory Coast politics. The daily newspaper *Fraternité Matin*, called "his master's voice" in the days of Houphouët-Boigny, reflects official government views. During the 2002 rebellion, the government silenced many foreign media sources such as Radio France International, the British Broadcasting Corporation (BBC), and Africa No. 1. Many Ivorians felt that foreign journalists misreported events or stirred up trouble and thus were the enemies of Ivory Coast. Several newspapers that were normally critical of the government disappeared from newsstands, and their journalists were physically attacked. Other newspapers played it safe and lined up behind the government.

For links to various cultural websites where you'll find recipes, information on holidays and festivals, artwork, literature, and more, go to vgsbooks.com.

● Food

Every region has its specialties, but several staples of Ivorian cooking are found everywhere. *Foutou*, the nation's most famous dish, is made of boiled yam or plantain, formed into sticky balls and served with sauce. Fish and meat sauces, peanut sauce, eggplant sauce, and okra sauces are all popular.

Attiéké, made with grated cassava, is a common side dish. So is rice. *Kedjenou* (meat cooked with vegetables in an earthenware pot) is popular, as are grilled chicken and beef. Many Ivorians like to eat cooked agouti (bush rat). Along the coast, fish and shrimp are available, but refrigeration is a luxury in Ivory Coast, so a seafood dinner must be freshly caught.

Typical drinks include *bissap*, a sweet drink made from the hibiscus flower, and *bandji*, or palm wine, best when made from the sap of freshly tapped palm trees. Bandji is sometimes distilled to make *koutoukou*, a drink so high in alcohol content that it is officially banned.

Two marketplace vendors sell **spices and dry ingredients.** Spiced sauces are common in Ivorian cuisine.

KEDJENOU

Kedjenou is a very popular dish in Ivory Coast. Traditionally it is cooked in a tightly sealed clay jar over a wood fire or in a tightly wrapped banana leaf, but you can use a Crock-Pot™ or a large casserole dish with an airtight lid.

2- to 3-pound chicken, cut into serving-size pieces

1 eggplant, cubed and salted

2 large onions, finely chopped

1 fresh hot chili pepper, seeds removed, chopped

4 tomatoes, chopped

1 small piece fresh ginger, peeled and grated

1 bay leaf

1 teaspoon dried thyme

1 or 2 cloves of garlic, peeled and minced

½ cup water or chicken broth

2 teaspoons peanut oil or other cooking oil (enough to lightly cover the bottom of the pot)

1. Put all the ingredients in a large casserole or Crock-Pot™, put the lid on tightly, and place on top of the stove (or cook in the Crock-Pot™) at low heat. Do not remove the lid during cooking.
2. Give the pot a shake every 5 or 10 minutes to avoid burning the bottom. Cook for 90 minutes or until chicken is no longer pink inside.

Serves 6

Typical eating establishments in Ivory Coast are called *maquis*. These open-air restaurants, with tables outside under a thatched roof, are found everywhere. Restaurants called *alokodromes* specialize in *aloko*—bananas that have been sliced and fried in oil.

► Sports

Like many other Africans, Ivorians are crazy about soccer. They avidly follow the national men's team, the Elephants, especially every two years during the African Nations Cup soccer tournament. Some of the country's best soccer players play professionally for European teams.

Secondary school students enjoy playing team sports like volleyball, basketball and, of course, soccer. Handball and tennis are also popular. Exceptional young tennis players can win scholarships to study abroad. Many Ivorians enjoy a tabletop game called babyfoot, known as foosball in the United States. In this game, players manipulate figures that resemble soccer players and try to score points by getting a small ball into the other team's net. *Awale* is a popular game throughout Africa.

Awale is popular in Ivory Coast and across western Africa.

During this game, players move game pieces, such as pebbles or seeds, through a series of holes and try to capture an opponent's pieces.

Holidays

Public holidays in Ivory Coast include January 1 (New Year's Day) and May 1 (Labor Day). On August 7 (National Day), Ivorians celebrate their country's independence from France in 1960. A December 7 holiday marks the death of Félix Houphouët-Boigny. August 15 (Assumption Day, when Catholics remember the Virgin Mary going up to heaven) is another official holiday, as is All Saints' Day on November 1. Christmas is celebrated on December 25. On New Year's Eve, Christians gather in a huge stadium in Abidjan, where they hold an overnight prayer vigil. The Christian holidays of Good Friday, Easter Monday, and Whitmonday are also public holidays, although the dates are variable.

During the holy month of Ramadan, Muslim Ivorians fast during the day. At the end of the month, they pray and feast. Many also don their best clothes and head for the zoo, where they enjoy family outings, pose for photographs, and eat ice cream. Since 1994, two major Islamic holy days have been recognized as national public holidays. These holidays

A Muslim family prepares chickens for the feast of **Eid al-Fitr,** which comes at the end of the Islamic holy month of Ramadan.

are Eid al-Adha, the Feast of the Sacrifice, and Eid al-Fitr, marking the end of Ramadan. The dates of the holidays vary according to the Islamic calendar, which is based on the cycles of the moon.

The country's many ethnic groups have their own festivals at various times of the year. People in the villages around Man celebrate the Festival of Masks in February. Bouaké hosts a carnival in March. Drumming and dancing continue for a week during the Festival of Abissa in Grand-Bassam at the beginning of November. During the February yam festival, the traditional king of the Akan people, dressed in gold finery, leads a procession. It is followed by offerings of yams to the ancestors, symbolizing the unity between the living and the dead.

Baoulé dancers from the Man region celebrate the **Festival of Masks.**

THE ECONOMY

Although Ivory Coast is West Africa's second richest nation (after Nigeria), its economy faces many difficulties. For one thing, the nation relies on a small base of products that are vulnerable to conditions beyond its control. For example, in the late 1990s, decreases in world prices for cocoa, rubber, and palm oil hurt the Ivorian economy. Weather conditions, such as a lack of rainfall, can delay harvests or ruin crops. Most farmers are poor and have only simple hand tools—factors that keep agricultural production low. Other obstacles to prosperity include high prices for consumer goods; an unskilled, undereducated workforce; an unhealthy workforce affected by AIDS and other illnesses; and government corruption.

The 2002–2003 rebellion, which broke out at the beginning of the cocoa harvest season, devastated that industry. Almost one-third of the crop was lost when frightened immigrant farmworkers left the country. With no one to pick them, cocoa pods rotted on the trees. By January, when the coffee harvest began and the political situation remained unresolved, that industry encountered similar problems.

As the crisis dragged on for more than five months, many French-owned and Ivorian businesses closed. Large organizations such as the African Development Bank and the African office of the Nestlé food corporation told foreign employees to leave Abidjan. With so many high-wage earners gone, restaurants and other businesses closed. It will take hard work to rebuild Ivory Coast's shattered economy after the brush with civil war.

○ Agriculture

Agriculture, including farming, forestry, and fishing, has traditionally been the mainstay of the Ivorian economy. This sector accounts for 27 percent of the gross domestic product (GDP, or the value of all goods and services produced annually by the country's residents) and employs 50 percent of the labor force.

Ivory Coast is the world's largest producer and exporter of cocoa and one of the largest producers of coffee. Each year Ivorians produce about 1.27 million tons (1.15 million metric tons) of cocoa beans and

COFFEE

Coffee has been grown as a cash crop in Ivory Coast since French colonial days. The type of coffee tree grown in West Africa is called robusta. It produces smaller, lower-quality beans than the arabica varieties grown elsewhere, but the plants are more resistant to disease.

The trees produce berries, each of which contains two brown beans. The beans are dried and hulled, then sold to large coffee companies such as Nestlé, which has huge processing plants in Man. Between 1970 and 1990, Ivory Coast produced more coffee than any other African country.

an estimated 402,000 tons (365,000 metric tons) of coffee beans. Other important cash crops include pineapples, cotton, bananas, rubber, sugarcane, oil palms, coconuts, and peanuts.

Ivory Coast is one of Africa's most important rubber producers. A species of rubber tree native to South America was successfully introduced to plantations in southwestern Ivory Coast in the 1960s. Oil palm plantations are located in the southwest (palm oil is used in cooking and soap making). In the north, farmers grow cotton.

The main food crops grown for local consumption are corn, yams, cassava, plantains, and rice. Farmers raise chickens for meat and eggs, and some livestock—primarily goats and sheep—for meat and milk. Meat also has to be imported from neighboring countries to meet the demand for food.

Timber is an important export product. Rafts of logs waiting to be loaded onto ships float in the nation's two main ports. The most important commercial trees include teak, mahogany, and ebony. The

Cut logs stacked in a lumberyard await shipment. The lumber business has caused severe deforestation in Ivory Coast.

best timber was harvested years ago, however, and the forests have not been replanted. Logging companies have to apply to a government agency for a license to cut trees.

The fishing industry is important in the lagoon region. Abidjan is the largest tuna fishing port in West Africa. Most of the tuna is canned and exported.

Cocoa

Since cocoa was introduced as a cash crop in 1912, Ivory Coast has become the source of about 40 percent of the world's cocoa. The nation has hundreds of thousands of cocoa plantations, most of them very small. After harvesting, cocoa beans are made into chocolate.

Cocoa beans

Although consumers pay high prices for fine chocolate, it is the big chocolate manufacturers and cocoa exporters that benefit from the high prices. The West African farmers who produce the raw beans don't make much money. Each farm produces a relatively small amount of cocoa, although production has increased in recent years with the use of fertilizers and pesticides.

A great deal of hard work is involved in cocoa farming, from clearing and weeding the fields to drying the beans. Farmers have no mechanized tools, and everyone in the family must help. Many cocoa plantation workers are immigrants from very poor countries such as Burkina Faso and Mali. Working for wages so low that many Ivorians refuse to accept them, they send their earnings home to support their families.

Child Labor and the Chocolate Industry

Many West African teenagers go to Ivory Coast to work on cocoa plantations. Some youngsters come voluntarily, attracted by the country's relative prosperity. Some parents send their children to Ivory Coast with a middleman, often a trusted relative or community leader who makes sure that the child receives fair wages and an education. Other children are kidnapped and smuggled into Ivory Coast by traffickers, who then sell the children to employers, even openly in Abidjan markets. A growing number of children are at risk of falling into the hands of traffickers because their parents have died of AIDS.

While some youngsters have decent experiences on the cocoa farms, others—especially those brought in by traffickers—work hard but are never paid, have no chance to go to school, and are even locked up at night to

prevent escape. They must do a variety of dangerous tasks, such as clearing fields with machetes (large knives) and applying poisonous pesticides to crops. About 60 percent of the children working on cocoa farms are boys.

Although child labor has existed in West Africa for years, it began to receive international media attention in 2001, when child rights organizations called on consumers to boycott chocolate until something was done about the issue. In 2002 representatives of the chocolate industry, labor and human rights groups, and the government of Ivory Coast agreed to eliminate abusive child labor practices on cocoa farms. These groups hope to increase cocoa production and raise prices paid for beans, enabling farm owners to pay decent wages to adult workers, rather than exploiting children.

Industry

Ivory Coast has one of Africa's best-developed industrial bases. Industry, including manufacturing, mining, and power, represents an estimated 27 percent of the GDP, and 11.5 percent of the labor force was employed in industry in the late twentieth century. The food-processing sector, in which raw foods are dried, canned, or prepared for sale in other ways, is especially important.

The manufacturing sector grew by an average of 3.7 percent annually during the late twentieth century. It contributed 16 percent to the nation's GDP by the end of the century. Manufacturing includes agricultural processing, textile production, and petroleum (crude oil) refining. Other industrial products include rubber, fuel oil, cement, and sawn wood.

Factory workers stack processed latex. Rubber and rubber products, such as latex, are among Ivory Coast's biggest exports.

Ivory Coast's mineral resources are largely undeveloped. Some gold has been mined since the late 1980s, and small amounts of diamonds are also mined. The oil and gas industries are an increasingly important part of the economy. Offshore oil reserves were first discovered in the early 1970s, and several offshore wells began pumping oil in 1977. Oil is shuttled to the mainland by pipeline or ship. Offshore natural gas, discovered in the 1980s, is also sent to shore by pipeline. It is used to generate electricity. In the future, it may be exported to neighboring countries.

A refinery in Abidjan processes Ivorian and Nigerian crude oil into products such as gasoline, asphalt, and lubricating oils. Products from the refinery are stored in a nearby depot for shipment within Ivory Coast and to other West African countries. If expanded, the refinery might become the main supplier of petroleum products on the African Atlantic seaboard.

In the late twentieth century, almost two-thirds of the country's electricity came from natural gas. The rest came from hydroelectric power. Although Ivory Coast exports power to some of its neighbors, many of its own villages still do not have electricity.

The Service Sector

The service sector, including health and social services, banking, hotels, and restaurants, contributes about 46 percent of Ivory Coast's GDP. It employs about 37 percent of the labor force. Abidjan is an important business and financial center for the whole of West Africa, with a regional stock exchange, the headquarters of the African Development Bank, and several commercial banks, as well as communications and trade organizations.

Ivory Coast's tourism industry is struggling. The nation has excellent hotels, beaches, nature preserves, and other attractions, but political unrest and Abidjan's reputation for crime discourage visitors. Approximately 301,000 visitors come to Ivory Coast each year, including 73,000 from France. Most visitors come from other African countries.

Transportation

Ivory Coast has one of the best road systems in West Africa, with some 43,500 miles (70,000 km) of roads, 3,730 miles (6,000 km) of which are paved. A four-lane highway connects Abidjan and Yamoussoukro. Nevertheless, the roads need better maintenance, traffic accidents claim many lives, and some agricultural areas remain largely isolated, without access to roads.

A railroad links Abidjan to the border of Burkina Faso. Several times a week, freight trains rumble north and south carrying goods

Few Ivorians own cars. When Ivorians travel to another city, they generally ride large, modern buses. It takes three hours to travel by bus between Abidjan and Yammousoukro and ten hours to get from Abidjan to Korhogo. For local trips, people often take shuttle buses that carry either nine or eighteen passengers. These buses have no fixed schedule. They leave whenever all the seats are filled.

between the two countries. Within Ivory Coast, most goods are shipped by truck.

Abidjan is West Africa's most important port. Containers carrying all kinds of goods, from canned foods to television sets, are stacked in ships that travel to and from the port. Oil tankers, fishing vessels, and other ships also frequent Abidjan's port facilities. San Pédro is the country's second largest port.

The nation's main international airport is the Félix Houphouët-Boigny Airport near Abidjan. Travelers also use international airports at Bouaké and Yamoussoukro, as well as twenty-five smaller regional airports. Ivory Coast is served by several international airlines, including Air France. Air Ivoire provides service to the capitals of other nations in the region.

◉ Trade and International Relations

Ivory Coast's principal exports are cocoa beans, coffee, sawn wood, petroleum products, and canned tuna. Cocoa and coffee make up 35 and 6 percent of exports, respectively. About 14 percent of exports are destined for France, while Germany, the Netherlands, Italy, the United States, and Mali are also important customers. Imports, including medicines, electrical equipment, cereals, petroleum products, and vehicles, come primarily from France, the United States, Italy, Germany, and Nigeria.

Ivory Coast is a member of the West African Economic and Monetary Union, or WAEMU. Its eight members—Benin, Burkina Faso, Ivory Coast, Guinea-Bissau, Mali, Niger, Senegal, and Togo—all use the same currency, franc de la Communauté Financière d'Afrique (franc of the African Financial Community), or CFA franc. All eight members have access to the regional stock exchange in Abidjan. WAEMU has abolished tariffs, or taxes, on imports to member countries to encourage trade. Ivory Coast contributes some 40 percent of WAEMU's GDP. Ivory Coast is also a member of ECOWAS, the Economic Community of West African States. It has also signed onto the Cotonou Agreement, a trade agreement between the European Union (EU) and countries in Africa, the Caribbean, and the Pacific. The agreement focuses on poverty reduction, provides a new framework for economic and trade cooperation, and

includes strategies to strengthen respect for human rights, democracy, and the rule of law.

 Visit vgsbooks.com for up-to-date information about Ivory Coast's economy and a converter with the current exchange rate where you can learn how many CFA francs are in one U.S. dollar.

The Future

Ivory Coast is faced with the challenge of repairing the economic damage caused by the 2002–2003 rebellion. It must also restore confidence in its ability to deliver farm products to the international market. Even if the country's leaders successfully resolve their political differences, it may take many years until investors trust Ivory Coast as a safe place to put their money.

Even before the rebellion, poverty levels were high. Reducing poverty is key to the country's future success. The government is looking to the private sector to help increase jobs and combat poverty. It wants to encourage private businesses to grow, diversify, and increase exports. Doing business in Ivory Coast isn't easy, however. Bank loans are difficult to obtain, credit cards and checks are seldom used, and there is no well-developed insurance industry. Also, many educated Ivorians opt for the security of careers in government rather than private business. To further combat poverty, the government must improve social services such as health care and education. It must also reduce inequalities between the north and south, and between urban and rural areas.

Since 57 percent of the population is rural and many rural residents are poor, the government has focused on rural development. It needs to modernize farming techniques and equipment, improve crop yields, expand livestock and fishing industries, and improve roads so that food products can be more easily transported. The government is encouraging farmers, especially women, to increase their incomes by planting new cash crops such as vegetables. It also wants them to plant rice to decrease dependence on imported rice.

Along with reducing poverty and improving education and health care, the country needs to eliminate the xenophobia and ethnic-based political divisions that threaten to destroy national unity. Its leaders must strengthen democracy and relieve political tensions between ethnic groups, between Christians and Muslims, and between southerners and northerners. There is much work to be done. But with its many natural resources, modern industries, and rich cultural life, the Elephant of Africa has the potential for a bright and prosperous future.

Timeline

1000s The Senoufo move to Ivory Coast from present-day Mali.

1100s The Senoufo found the city of Kong.

1200s Islamic Malinké people begin to migrate into northern Ivory Coast.

1400s The Dioula people move into the Bondoukou region.

1471 Portuguese sailors explore the Gold Coast (modern Ghana).

1600s The Abron people flee Ghana and settle south of Bondoukou. A trade in elephant tusks develops but quickly disappears because of overhunting.

1637 French missionaries try and fail to set up an outpost at Assinie.

1842 The French sign a treaty with the Sanwi people, establishing a French protectorate in southeastern Ivory Coast.

1880s The French begin establishing coffee plantations and logging in the forests of Ivory Coast.

1885 European powers hold the Berlin Conference and plan to divide Africa among themselves.

1889 Southern Ivory Coast is declared a French protectorate.

1893 Ivory Coast becomes a French colony with its capital at Grand-Bassam.

1895 Samory Touré destroys Kong.

1898 French forces defeat Samory Touré.

1900 The colony's capital is moved inland from Grand-Bassam after a yellow fever epidemic.

1904 Construction begins on a railway north from Abidjan. Ivory Coast becomes part of French West Africa.

1908 The French begin a seven-year "pacification" campaign to control rebellious ethnic groups.

1912 Cocoa cultivation is introduced to Ivory Coast.

1944 Félix Houphouët-Boigny founds the African Agricultural Syndicate to protest treatment of African planters and fight for the abolition of forced labor. Delegates at the Brazzaville Conference discuss the future of the French colonies in Africa.

1946 The French National Assembly abolishes forced labor in Ivory Coast. The Democratic Party of Ivory Coast is founded.

1950 The Vridi Canal is opened, and Abidjan becomes an important deep-water port.

1956 Bernard Dadié's *Climbié* is published.

1960 Ivory Coast becomes an independent nation. Félix Houphouët-Boigny is elected president.

1983 Ivory Coast's capital is moved from Abidjan to Yamoussoukro.

1988 Laurent Gbagbo returns from France to help found the Ivorian Popular Front.

1990 The first multiparty presidential election is held, and Gbagbo takes 11 percent of the vote. The Our Lady of Peace Basilica in Yamoussoukro is consecrated.

1992 Ivory Coast's national soccer team, the Elephants, wins the African Nations Cup.

1993 Félix Houphouët-Boigny dies, and Henri Konan Bédié succeeds him as president.

1999 General Robert Gueï stages a bloodless coup and forces President Bédié out of office.

2000 The presidential elections are marred by controversy and ethnic clashes.

2002 In September a group of rebel soldiers attacks Abidjan, killing several hundred people. The rebels, known as the Patriotic Movement of Ivory Coast, attempt to force new elections. The government responds by raiding and destroying the homes of suspected rebel sympathizers. Nearly 400,000 people flee Ivory Coast during the violence.

2003 Government and rebel factions hold peace talks and agree to form a new unified government.

COUNTRY NAME Republic of Ivory Coast (Republic of Côte d'Ivoire)

AREA 123,553 square miles (320,783 sq. km)

MAIN LANDFORMS coastal lagoons, rain forest, savanna, Toura Mountains

HIGHEST POINT Mount Nimba (5,748 feet; 1,752 m)

LOWEST POINT Sea level

MAJOR RIVERS Cavally, Sassandra, Bandama, Comoé

ANIMALS elephants, pygmy hippopotamuses, chimpanzees, Nile crocodiles, green mambas, secretary birds

CAPITAL CITY Yamoussoukro

OTHER MAJOR CITIES Abidjan, Bouaké, Daloa, Odienné, San Pédro

OFFICIAL LANGUAGE French

MONETARY UNIT CFA franc

Fast Facts

Currency

IVORY COAST CURRENCY

Ivory Coast uses the CFA franc, the common currency of fourteen African countries. CFA stands for Communauté Financière Africaine (African Financial Community). Paper notes are issued in denominations of 500, 1,000, 2,000, 5,000, and 10,000 CFA francs. Coins come as 1, 5, 10, 25, 50, 100, and 250 CFA francs. The CFA franc was introduced in 1945. In 2002, 1,000 CFA francs equaled $1.64 in U.S. dollars.

The flag of Ivory Coast has three equal, vertical stripes in orange, white, and green. The orange stripe stands for the color of the earth, which is rich and generous, and for the blood shed by young people in the struggle for freedom against the French. The white stripe stands for peace and unity, and the green stripe stands for hope and faith in a better future. The flag was adopted in 1959, less than a year before Ivory Coast became independent.

The national anthem, "Song of Abidjan," sings of a land of hope and hospitality, a country of peace and dignity, thanks to the valiant efforts of those who struggled for freedom during the colonial era. The lyrics encourage citizens to be proud of being Ivorian and to work toward unity. Adopted in 1960, the anthem was a collaborative effort. The music was written by a Catholic priest, Pierre Michel Pango. The words were written by government officials Mathieu Ekra and Joachim Bony.

The anthem is sung in French. Here is an English translation of the lyrics:

"Song of Abidjan"
We salute you, O land of hope,
Country of hospitality;
Thy gallant legions
Have restored thy dignity.

Beloved Ivory Coast, thy sons,
Proud builders of thy greatness,
All mustered together for thy glory,
In joy will construct thee.

Proud citizens of the Ivory Coast, the country calls us.
If we have brought back liberty peacefully,
It will be our duty to be an example
Of the hope promised to humanity,
Forging united in new faith
The Fatherland of true brotherhood.

For a link to where you can listen to Ivory Coast's national anthem, "Song of Abidjan," go to vgsbooks.com.

IBRAHIM BAKAYOKO (b. 1976) In a country that is wild about soccer, Bakayoko is a star. Born in Séguéla (between Bouaké and Man), he has played for the Ivory Coast national team, the Elephants, and for foreign teams. He was a forward for the Everton Football (Soccer) Club in England, then joined many other African soccer professionals in France. He became one of the Marseille team's highest-paid players. He is a high scorer, but his career with Marseille was marred by injuries.

ALPHA BLONDY (b. 1953) Perhaps the nation's best-known musician, reggae singer Alpha Blondy was born in central Ivory Coast. He discovered reggae music while studying English in New York at the end of the 1970s. In the early 1980s, he released his first record. In 1984 he went to Jamaica, where he recorded the hit album *Cocody Rock*. "The African Rasta," as he bills himself, sings in Dioula, English, French, Arabic, and Hebrew. His message of love and justice is well known in many countries in Africa and South America, as well as France.

BERNARD DADIÉ (b. 1916) A poet, novelist, playwright, and administrator, Dadié is one of Africa's senior cultural figures. Born near Abidjan, he was educated in Senegal and worked there for several years, returning to Ivory Coast in 1947. He made his mark in 1956 with the appearance of *Climbié*, an autobiographical novel about colonial Ivory Coast. Over his career, he has written six books of poetry, as well as several novels, plays, and short stories. He writes in French, but his stories feature African themes and proverbs. He served as Ivory Coast's minister of culture in the 1960s.

LAURENT GBAGBO (b. 1945) A Bété born near Gagnoa, Gbagbo began his career as a history professor, but he was jailed from 1971 to 1973 for "subversive" teaching—meaning that he spoke out against the government. In the 1980s, he was active in the trade union movement and in pro-democracy protests against the Houphouët-Boigny regime. He fled to safety in Paris in 1982, returning in 1988 to help found the Ivorian Popular Front. In 1990 Gbagbo took 11 percent of the vote in Ivory Coast's first multiparty presidential election. He went to jail again in 1992 for protesting government brutality. He became president of Ivory Coast in 2000.

FÉLIX HOUPHOUËT-BOIGNY (1905–1993) As president from independence in 1960 to his death in 1993, Houphouët-Boigny has probably had more impact on Ivory Coast than anyone else. As a young man, he was a physician and a planter. He helped found an organization to protect the interests of African planters, and that work launched his political career. He was a legislator and cabinet minister in the French government, as well as leader of his party in Ivory Coast. As president, Houphouët-Boigny ran a one-party state. He set the nation's course with an agriculture-based, free-enterprise economy with close ties to France. He was born in Yamoussoukro.

AHMADOU KOUROUMA (b. 1927) This man is one of Ivory Coast's most prominent novelists, although for much of his life he worked in banking and insurance. Born in a small Malinké town, he was brought up by an uncle who was a respected traditional hunter. After high school, the French drafted Kourouma into the army and sent him to Southeast Asia. He studied in France, then returned to Ivory Coast briefly but went into exile after being jailed on false charges of taking part in an antigovernment conspiracy. He has spent much of his life in France and Cameroon. His works satirize African politics.

ROGER GNOAN M'BALA (b. 1943) Born in Grand-Bassam, M'Bala has been a director of film and television for more than thirty years. He studied filmmaking in France and Sweden and began making films in the 1970s. He has directed five full-length films, some of which have won international awards. He both directed and cowrote *Adanggaman*, his best-known film, which appeared in 2000.

ALASSANE OUATTARA (b. 1942) The leader of the Republican Assembly, a national political party, was born in Dimbokro in the northern part of Ivory Coast, but he attended college in the United States. An economist, he spent much of his career with the International Monetary Fund and West African Central Bank. He served as prime minister of Ivory Coast from 1990 to 1993. He attempted to run for president in 1995 and 2000 but was barred because he did not meet the citizenship qualifications. In 2002 he fled the dangerous political situation.

VÉRONIQUE TADJO (b. 1955) This Ivorian is well known in Africa and Europe as both an artist and a writer. Her books for children feature her own illustrations, and her paintings have been included in exhibitions from Paris to Nairobi, Kenya. She has won several international prizes for her novels and poetry. Born in Paris, she grew up and attended school and university in Abidjan, where her father worked for the government. She then obtained a Ph.D. in African American studies at the Sorbonne in Paris. She lived in a number of cities, including London, before moving to Johannesburg, South Africa.

CONSTANCE YAI (b. 1956) Born in Yamoussoukro, Constance Yai established the Association for Defense of Women's Rights, a grassroots organization that brings together rural and urban Ivorian women from all social and economic backgrounds. The group aims to improve the legal situation of women in Ivory Coast, to raise public awareness of family violence, and to set up a shelter for battered women. Yai served as minister of the family and promotion of women in the government of President Gueï.

ABIDJAN Ivory Coast's former capital and largest city is considered the country's cultural center by many. The Plateau, Abidjan's downtown business district, features American- and European-style architecture. Among the highlights are a pyramid-shaped building designed by an Italian architect and the soaring curves of the Ministry of Posts and Telecommunications Building. The Hôtel d'Ivoire, located in the exclusive Cocody area of Abidjan, is probably the most famous hotel in West Africa. Besides a conference center and casino, it has a bowling alley, seven tennis courts, colorful gardens, movie theaters, shops, a grocery store, and the only ice skating rink in West Africa.

GRAND-BASSAM This town was the first capital of the French colony in the late 1800s, until an outbreak of yellow fever drove the French to move the capital elsewhere. It is located on a narrow spit of land between the ocean and the lagoon. On weekends, vacationers from nearby Abidjan come to enjoy its beaches and restaurants. The town's colonial buildings, such as the governor's palace and courthouse, with their decorative balconies and verandas, are slowly decaying, although an effort is being made to preserve them.

MAN Located in west central Ivory Coast, this town is in one of the country's prettiest regions. It is called the city of eighteen mountains because it is nestled among green hills. Outside of the city, the peak known as La Dent de Man (Tooth of Man) is appropriately tooth shaped. To the west is an area famous for its bridges made of vines and creepers that cross the Cavally River. Each bridge is made entirely in one night, using secret techniques. Man is also well known for its Dan festivals featuring masked dancers.

OUR LADY OF PEACE BASILICA, YAMOUSSOUKRO This Catholic church is enormous. It has individually air-conditioned seats for 7,000 people and room for 11,000 standees indoors and another 180,000 in the outdoor courtyards. Including its crowning gold cross, it is the tallest church in the world. Consecrated in 1990, it was designed by an Ivorian architect of Lebanese descent, using mainly French and European materials. One of the figures portrayed in the church's stained-glass windows is that of Félix Houphouët-Boigny, shown at the feet of a blond-haired Jesus Christ.

TAÏ NATIONAL PARK Located in the southwest, this 1.1 million-acre (454,000-hectare) reserve protects the last large pocket of undisturbed rain forest in the country. Dense ebony and tall palm trees here have massive trunks and huge supporting roots. Under the canopy formed by the tree branches, hanging vines and epiphytes thrive, but the forest floor itself cannot support heavy growth because so little light reaches it. The government works with the local people, encouraging them to protect the forest, rather than cutting its trees illegally or killing the wildlife.

animist religion: a religion that involves belief in the existence of spirits, including the spirits of natural objects, natural events, and human ancestors

colony: a territory governed by a distant nation and sometimes inhabited by settlers from that nation

coup: a sudden, violent overthrow of a government by a small group

epiphyte: a plant that derives its moisture and nutrients from rain and air instead of from soil. Epiphytes usually grow on other plants.

exile: a period of forced or voluntary absence from one's home country

gross domestic product (GDP): the value of the goods and services produced by a country over a period of time, such as a year

hydroelectric power: electricity produced by the power of rushing water. People often dam rivers to create hydroelectric power stations.

indigenous: native to a particular place

Islam: the religious faith of Muslims, originating on the Arabian Peninsula in the A.D. 600s. Muslims believe in Allah as the sole god and in Muhammad as his prophet.

Ivorité: the concept of purity of Ivorian ancestry and nationality

matrilineal: tracing descent through the mother's side of the family

patrilineal: tracing descent through the father's side of the family

polygamy: the practice of having more than one wife at one time

protectorate: a territory that is controlled and protected by a more powerful nation

refugee: a person who flees his or her home to escape danger or persecution

xenophobia: fear and hatred of strangers or foreigners

Glossary

Selected Bibliography

Abidjan.com. N.d.
Website: <http://www.Abidjan.com> (September 18, 2003)
This website, updated daily, has numerous links to a current news, business, and sports articles about Ivory Coast and other African nations from a variety of sources, as well as some travel information about the country.

Else, David, et al. *West Africa.* **4th ed. Victoria, Australia: Lonely Planet Publications, 1999.**
This Lonely Planet guide tells the visitor where to go, what to see and how to get there in West Africa, including Ivory Coast. It also has sections on West African arts and culture, large ethnic groups, music, history, and bird watching.

Europa Publications. *Europa World Year Book 2002.* **London: Europa Publications, 2001.**
This annual guide includes recent political events in Ivory Coast and has a variety of economic and other statistics.

Library of Congress, Federal Research Division. *Ivory Coast: A Country Study.* **N.d.**
Website: <http://memory.loc.gov/frd/cs/citoc.html> (September 18, 2003)
This website is one in a series of country profiles. Although some of the information needs updating, the sections on Ivorian history and ethnic groups are particularly useful.

Mbendi Profile: Côte d'Ivoire. **N.d.**
Website: <http://www.mbendi.co.za/land/af/ci/p0005.htm> (September 18, 2003)
Mbendi provides economic overviews of African countries, including Ivory Coast, with background descriptions and details about sectors such as energy, mining, and oil and gas. While the site is primarily written for business, it is easy to read.

Office of the Prime Minister, Republic of Ivory Coast, Ministry of Planning and Development. *Interim Poverty Reduction Strategy Paper.*
Website: <http://poverty.worldbank.org/files/Cote_DIvoire_IPRSP.pdf> (September 18, 2003)
Published in January 2002 by the Ivory Coast government, this paper looks at poverty in Ivory Coast, its causes and conditions, and measures proposed to combat it.

Population Reference Bureau. N.d.
Website: <http://www.prb.org> (September 18, 2003)
This is a reliable site for statistics on world population trends, including those for Ivory Coast.

Republic of Ivory Coast. N.d.
Website: <http://www.pr.ci/> (September 18, 2003)
This is the homepage of the government of Ivory Coast, with background on the president, the constitution, and national symbols, but it is mainly a public relations page.

Turner, Barry, ed. *The Statesman's Yearbook: The Politics, Cultures, and Economies of the World, 2002.* **New York, Macmillan Press, 2001.**
This is a good source for statistical and background information on countries of the world, including Ivory Coast.

United Nations Integrated Regional Information Network. N.d.
Website: <http://www.irinnews.org/homepage.asp> (September 18, 2003)
This website features news items from sub-Saharan Africa and Central Asia. It is searchable by region, country, or theme, including environment, economy, children, human rights and democracy. In 2002 it prepared a special report on the crisis in Ivory Coast.

"Why the Fighting in Ivory Coast?" *BBC.* **January 31, 2003.**
Website: <http://news.bbc.co.uk/1/hi/world/africa/2308849.stm> (September 18, 2003)
This article and several others linked to this page look at the causes of the 2002 rebellion in Ivory Coast. The BBC is an excellent source of news about Africa and has a reporter based in Abidjan. Go to <http://www.bbc.co.uk>, scroll down the page and click on Africa, or search for a specific topic.

World Rainforest Information Portal. N.d.
Website: <http://www.rainforestweb.org/> (September 18, 2003)
This site from the Rainforest Action Network will tell you about the importance of rain forests throughout the world. Go to the section on Africa to learn more about the state of the rain forests of Ivory Coast.

Africa Recovery Online. **N.d.**
Website: <http://www.un.org/ecosocdev/geninfo/afrec/>
This online newsletter, published by the United Nations, focuses on issues affecting Africa, including Ivory Coast. It examines the future outlook for African children, the fight against HIV/AIDS and tuberculosis in Africa, and the dream of African union.

Africa South of the Sahara. Countries: Ivory Coast. **N.d.**
Website: <http://www-sul.stanford.edu/depts/ssrg/africa/cote.html>
This list of links relevant to Ivory Coast is extensive, including the websites of daily newspapers, political parties, and politicians, as well as business and cultural websites. You can also search the site by topic, from birds to human rights to weather.

Dadié, Bernard Binlin. ***The Black Cloth: A Collection of African Folktales.*** **Amherst: University of Massachusetts Press, 1987.**
This collection of elegantly told folktales about hunters, orphans, and animals is quite engaging. Kacou Ananzé, a trickster spider, is featured in many of these humorous stories, while several characters face challenging dilemmas. Some of the stories originate with peoples native to Ivory Coast.

Gottlieb, Alma, and Philip Graham. ***Parallel Worlds: An Anthropologist and a Writer Encounter Africa.*** **Chicago: University of Chicago Press, 1994.**
This engrossing book recounts the adventures of an American couple as they try to understand the complex web of relationships between the people and the spirits who inhabit an isolated Ivorian village. In the process, they learn something about their own cultural values.

Kourouma, Ahmadou. ***Waiting for the Vote of the Wild Animals.*** **Charlottesville: University Press of Virginia, 2001.**
This award-winning novel recounts the story of a master hunter who became the president of his country. The fictionalized account of a real African dictator (the president of Togo) sheds light on what has gone wrong with African leadership, and is full of humor, sorcery, brutality, and proverbs. Ivory Coast's former president Félix Houphouët-Boigny appears as the dictator with the crocodile totem.

Nabwire, Constance, and Bertha Vining. ***Cooking the West African Way.*** **Minneapolis: Lerner Publications Company, 2002.**
This book offers easy-to-make recipes from Ivory Coast, Nigeria, Sierra Leone, and Ghana, along with lots of interesting cultural information about these countries.

Our Lady of Peace Basilica. **N.d.**
Website: <http://basilique.free.fr/basilica/index.htm>
The homepage of Our Lady of Peace Basilica in Yamoussoukro describes the building and its construction and Catholic life in Ivory Coast. It also has background information on Ivorian ethnic groups, an excellent map of the country, and lots of pictures.

Further Reading and Websites

Sheehan, Patricia. *Côte d'Ivoire: Cultures of the World.* **New York: Marshall Cavendish, 2000.**
Written for middle-school readers, this book describes daily life in Ivory Coast.

Tadjo, Véronique. *Lord of the Dance: An African Retelling.* **London: A & C Black, 1988.**
This book tells the story of the carved wooden mask who dances the joys and sorrows of the Senoufo people of Ivory Coast. It is delightfully illustrated by the author. It may look like a book for young children, but it has a message for everyone.

vgsbooks.com. **N.d.**
Website: <http://www.vgsbooks.com>
Visit vgsbooks.com, the homepage of the Visual Geography Series®, which is updated regularly. You can get linked to all sorts of useful on-line information, including geographical, historical, demographic, cultural, and economic web-sites. The vgsbooks.com site is a great resource for late-breaking news and statistics.

World Heritage. **N.d.**
Website: <http://whc.unesco.org/nwhc/pages/home/pages/homepage.htm>
Click on the "sites" link, then on Africa to see a list of UNESCO world heritage sites in Africa. Ivory Coast has three such sites: Comoé and Taï National Parks and the Mount Nimba Strict Nature Reserve. These pages describe the climates, flora and fauna, and threats to these regions.

Captions for photos appearing on cover and chapter openers:

Cover: The village of Tiagba Pile lies near Ébrié Lagoon. Ébrié is in Ivory Coast's lagoon region on the Gulf of Guinea.

pp. 4–5 An African elephant makes its way across a savanna in northern Ivory Coast. Because of its size and relative stability, Ivory Coast has long been nicknamed the Elephant of Africa.

pp. 8–9 Ivory Coast is dotted with lush lagoons, like this one near Grand-Bassam in the southeastern part of the country.

pp. 20–21 This ancient Muslim temple is adorned with religious figures worked in dried mud.

pp. 36–37 A group of Ivorian children from Bouaké

pp. 46–47 Cloth made in the Korhogo region is woven from locally grown cotton. It is then colored with brown, black, and red vegetable dyes, in designs that range from geometric patterns to imaginary animal forms.

pp. 58–59 A worker on a coffee plantation harvests coffee beans. The Ivorian economy has relied on coffee as a major cash crop since the early 1900s.

Photo Acknowledgments
The images in this book are used with the permission of: PhotoDisc Royalty Free by Getty Images, pp. 4–5; Digital Cartographics, pp. 6, 10; © Charles O. Cecil, pp. 8–9, 13, 15, 16, 18–19, 22, 26, 38, 40, 41 (both), 45, 49 (top), 58–59, 60, 62; © Brian A. Vikander, pp. 12, 20–21, 48; © Gerard Lacz / Peter Arnold, Inc., p. 14; © Phil Porter, p. 24; Independent Picture Service, p. 28; Fraternité Matin, p. 29; © AFP/CORBIS, p. 30; AP Photo/Jean-Marc Bouju, p. 31; © Sven Torfinn/Panos Pictures, pp. 32–33; © Robert Maust/Photo Agora, pp. 36–37, 42, 54; © Giacomo Pirozzi/Panos Pictures, pp. 44, 56; © Randall Pomeroy/ International Photographic, pp. 46–47; © John Elk III, p. 49 (bottom); © TRIP/ M. Jelliffee, p. 50; © Bassouls Sophie/CORBIS SYGMA, p. 51; © TRIP/J. Highet, p. 52; AP Photo/Clement Ntaye, p. 57 (top); © Fulvio Roiter/CORBIS, p. 57 (bottom); © Wolfgang Kaehler, p. 61; Banknotes.com, p. 68.

Cover: © Yann Arthus-Bertrand/CORBIS. Back cover photo: NASA.

27·53

DEC − 2 2004

DON'T MISS ANY OF THESE BESTSELLING NOVELS BY

DEAN KOONTZ

The Master of Suspense

FALSE MEMORY
SEIZE THE NIGHT
FEAR NOTHING
SOLE SURVIVOR
TICKTOCK
INTENSITY
DARK RIVERS OF THE HEART
ICEBOUND
WINTER MOON
FROM THE CORNER OF HIS EYE

Published by Bantam Books.
Available in bookstores everywhere.